SHIELD OF SPARROWS

USA TODAY BESTSELLING AUTHOR

DEVNEY PERRY

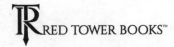
RED TOWER BOOKS™

Entangled Publishing, LLC
644 Shrewsbury Commons Ave., STE 181
Shrewsbury, PA 17361
rights@entangledpublishing.com

Red Tower Books is an imprint of Entangled Publishing, LLC.

Visit our website at www.entangledpublishing.com.

Edited by Liz Pelletier
Cover design by LJ Anderson
Edge design by Bree Archer
Case design by Elizabeth Turner Stokes
Case image by yukitama/Shutterstock
Endpaper original illustration by Juho Choi
Interior map original art by Elizabeth Turner Stokes
Interior map frame images by MassyCG/Shutterstock,
DestinaDesign/Shutterstock
Interior design by Britt Marczak

Hardcover ISBN 978-1-64937-851-4
Ebook ISBN 978-1-64937-808-8

Printed in the United States of America
First Edition May 2025

10 9 8 7 6 5 4 3 2 1

RED TOWER BOOKS™

MORE FROM DEVNEY PERRY

To the characters who came before.
To the stories that led us here.
To the chances we take. To the dreams we chase.

Trust your wings.

Shield of Sparrows is a heart-stopping romantasy set in a world of deadly monsters and even deadlier mysteries. As such, the story includes elements that might not be suitable for all readers, including combat, violence, blood, gore, death of humans and animals, injury, dismemberment, illness, hospitalization, arson, alcohol use, sexual activity, and graphic language, with mentions of poisoning and trafficking in backstory. Readers who may be sensitive to these elements, please take note. We invite you to grab a blade and prepare for a new world...

CALANDRA

NORCREST

HARROW RIVER

RIPFELL

OZARTH

GRINT MINE ROAD

OSTAN

LAINE

DEPMORE

GENESIS

CLEFTON

CORANESS

JASE

N NE E SE S SW W NW

One

What if I jumped?

Balanced on the edge of a sheer cliff, I stood at the mercy of this realm, wiggling my bare toes in the dirt beneath my feet. A strong gust of wind could tip me forward or backward. The slightest tremor in the earth, and I'd either fall.

Or fly.

What if I jumped? Would anyone care?

No. Not for me. Not for the wrong princess of Quentis.

Forty feet below, waves crashed against rock, the water's spray white as it broke against gray stone. I wanted to jump. I wanted to dive into that ocean blue. I wanted to be unshackled from everyone's expectations for just one godsforsaken moment.

Except if I jumped, I'd be late. And if I was late, I'd be in deep shit.

Margot would kick my ass if I missed this meeting with the Turan warriors Father had invited to Quentis, so there'd be no jumping. Especially not today.

I inched away from the edge. The temptation.

It wasn't like they needed me for this fiasco. Mae would charm our guests. She was the right Quentin princess.

My half sister had been groomed her entire life for this occasion. This performance. Sooner or later, she'd be the Turan queen, and today was her chance to meet some future subjects before her marriage to their crown prince later this year.

My attendance? Entirely unnecessary.

But I worked hard not to piss off my stepmother, Margot—and my father. I might not be his favorite daughter or the cherished princess, but there was a crown in my bedroom. And today was all about showing the Turans exactly how sparkly our crowns could be.

My shoulders sank as I took another step away from the cliff, then another, the soles of my feet sinking into the grass as I walked over to the charcoal slippers I'd kicked off earlier. But before I could step into a shoe, the thunder of hooves drew my attention toward the road.

The noise grew louder—no doubt a rider coming this way, likely to fetch me.

"Damn." Was I late?

Margot had prattled on and on at breakfast this morning, and I'd only half listened as she'd recited today's schedule of events before the introduction to the Turans.

The rangers had arrived late yesterday, after nightfall. The elite band of warriors had missed the window for dinner or meetings. On purpose? Probably.

I couldn't blame them. Nor could I judge them for sticking to their wing of the castle since, either resting from their journey over the Krisenth Crossing or avoiding the pomp of royal civilities. But whether I liked it or not, there would be a spectacle. A time for Mae to shine.

While the Turans were doing whatever it was that Turan warriors did when visiting foreign kingdoms, my sister was being primped.

Mae would be bathed and pampered. Mae would be massaged with scented oils and treated with the finest skin tonics on the continent. Mae would be wearing a gown her seamstress had spent a month crafting for tonight's feast.

Mae. This was all about Mae.

I doubted the men visiting would care about the embroidery or lace, but what did I know? Mae was their future queen, not me. My only obligation was to appear.

On time.

In Margot's litany of instructions over this morning's meal, it was the only time she'd mentioned my name.

Do not be late, Odessa.

I wasn't always late. Usually, but not always. Half the time, no one even noticed.

Hopping into a gray slipper, I flicked away the skirts of my matching dress and shifted to pull on the other shoe. Both were firmly covering my toes by the time a familiar rider crested the hill to the cliffside.

Banner sat proudly in the saddle, his short, light-brown hair combed, not a strand out of place. His expression was blank.

Was that a good blank? Or did it mean that I was in trouble because my fiancé had abandoned his responsibilities as general to collect me?

Banner tugged at the reins, slowing his buckskin stallion to a stop. With a fluid swing, he was off the saddle and leading his horse my way with purposeful, intimidating strides.

"Princess." His tone was serious, his brown eyes never leaving mine, but a grin tugged at the corner of his mouth.

"I was just leaving." I held up a hand. "I swear."

"Before or after you heard me riding this way?" He arched an eyebrow. "You're going to be late."

Going to be late. Meaning I wasn't late. Yet. *Phew.*

"I promise to be on time," I said. "You didn't need to come fetch me."

"Actually, I came out for a ride."

"Ah." Maybe that meant no one knew I was even outside the castle's walls. I could slip back inside unnoticed and hurry to change clothes.

Banner was already dressed for the meeting, wearing his formal uniform. The gold buttons on his teal coat were as shiny as the castle's spires in the distance. His favorite throwing knives were attached to his leather belt. Father would be wearing much the same uniform, though he preferred a sword. Mae's dress for tonight had been designed with layers of aquamarine and celeste. Margot would likely be in her signature blue.

My dress, like all of my dresses, would be gray.

Someday, when I didn't have Margot dictating my wardrobe or Father's scrutiny at every meal, I wanted to wear red. Or green. Or black. Or yellow.

Any color but gray.

"You know, you can spy on the city from your own window rather than hike all the way over here," he said.

"But this gives me a better view."

The sunlight caught the amber starbursts in Banner's eyes, the vivid color bright against the brown of his irises. That amber starburst marked all those born on Quentin soil.

His gaze drifted behind us to the castle, then shifted to the city that stretched along the coastline beside this cliff.

Roslo's white buildings practically glowed in the afternoon light. The capital city's streets teemed with people and carts. Boats crowded the harbor's docks, and the calm waters of Roslo Bay were a brilliant aquamarine beneath the sun's bright rays. Quentin flags of the same teal fluttered in the breeze from where they hung on the castle's towers, the largest of which were stitched with the royal crest—a crossbow woven with leaves and stalks of wheat.

Father considered the view from his throne room's balcony unmatched, but I much preferred my city from this spot.

That castle was my home, but this cliffside was my sanctuary. This was the one place where the air wasn't thick with judgment and guards weren't stationed at every corner, ready to report my mistakes to Margot.

From this vantage, I could smell the salt drifting off the water. The scents of food and spices carried on the wind from the markets in the square. On calm days like today, I could hear the noise from the docks and the clamor of the streets. And when I had time, I'd bring along a journal to sketch the various views.

Banner's gaze stopped on the three wooden ships docked in the bay, their forest green sails a slight contrast to the teal accents on the Quentin boats.

"Have you seen them yet?" I asked. "The Turans?"

"Not yet. But I just met with your father." His jaw clenched. "He informed me that the Guardian traveled with the rangers."

"The Guardian." My jaw dropped as my stomach twisted. "*The* Guardian. He's here? In Roslo?"

"Apparently," Banner clipped.

Oh, hell. This was bad. This was the reason my fiancé had come out for a ride.

We might not be in love, we might not even be considered friends, but there were a few things I'd learned about Banner during our engagement. He was unfailing in his loyalty to Father. He loved the status that came with his rank and betrothal to a princess. And he loathed the Guardian.

"I'm sorry." I reached for him, but he waved me off, raking a hand through his hair. "Will you be going to the meeting?"

"I'm the general of your father's legion. What do you think?"

Was it really so hard for him to just say yes?

Maybe after we were married, he'd stop treating me like a child. Though considering the fifteen-year age difference, I wasn't holding my breath.

Banner rubbed a hand over his jaw, smooth and set in an angry line. "Pray to Carine I'm able to keep my composure."

I'd pray for the Goddess of Peace to be with us all today.

"I will have my revenge," he said, more to himself than to me, and the cool, collected man who was to be my husband vanished. His frame began to vibrate with rage. His hands flexed at his sides, like he was itching to pull out a knife. "I vow it."

"Banner," I warned. "If the Guardian sailed with the Turans, he's here on Father's invitation. It's not the time. You can't go after him while—"

"Don't you think I know that?"

I flinched as he yelled into my face. It wasn't the first time a man had directed his temper my way. It wouldn't be the last. And I'd learned that it was easier to surrender than fight. "I'm sorry."

"I'm well aware that I have no choice but to stand aside and welcome these *guests* to our kingdom. That I must be in your father's throne room and meet the piece of filth who destroyed my family. I deserve to have that bastard's head on a platter, yet I can do nothing. Nothing. I know exactly what fucking time it is, Odessa."

I stayed quiet as he spat my name. "You're going to be late," he barked.

"Right." I nodded, dropping my gaze to his polished boots.

Banner exhaled, collecting himself. Then he hooked a finger under my chin, tilting my face upward until our gazes locked. The anger in his irises was fading slowly. "Sorry. I'm frustrated."

"It's understandable."

"Would you like me to take you back? I can skip the rest of my ride."

"No." I gave him a soft smile. "You go. I'll walk."

If I were wearing Banner's boots, I'd probably need to clear my head, too.

Why would my father force him to attend this meeting today? Father knew that the Guardian had killed Banner's brother. That they'd fought over a woman in Turah, and that fight had ended in death. When word of his brother's murder had reached Quentis, the news had irreparably broken Banner's mother to the point that the woman had taken her own life last year.

Apparently, Father could be as callous to his beloved general as he could be to his oldest daughter.

"I'll see you later," he said. "Don't be late, Princess."

Banner dragged a knuckle along my cheek, then retreated to his horse, swinging into the saddle and disappearing without a backward glance toward the sweeping hills and rolling fields that surrounded Roslo.

I waited until he was out of sight, then, on a sigh, I started down the trodden path that would take me to the rear entrance of the castle. From there, I could slip through a side entrance and climb the stairs to my rooms on the fourth floor.

My gray rooms.

Mae's suite was pale blue, for the virginal bride who would soon be married to a prince. Who would fulfill her role in accord with the Calandra trade treaty that kept the five kingdoms at peace.

She was the Sparrow.

But Mae was far from a sweet, delicate bird. She certainly wouldn't be a virgin on her wedding night. Funny how the guards never reported her comings and goings, not while she was screwing their captain.

I glanced over my shoulder, to the edge of the cliff and the open ocean beyond.

What was out there? Mae would find out. After the wedding, she'd set sail to Turah. "Lucky brat."

Not once in my life had I been jealous of Mae. She was Father's favored daughter. When the time had come for him to choose the Sparrow, it was no shock he'd picked Mae. And she was Margot's pride and joy. She had a mother while I had a ghost. Still, I'd never envied her, not once.

Until now.

Because soon she'd leave and discover the realm beyond Roslo's gates and Quentis's shores.

I was going to miss my half sister. From the day Margot had placed her in my arms when I was five, Mae had been mine. She fought me on everything. She pestered me relentlessly. She wasn't kind or grateful. She was a massive pain in my ass, but she was my sister.

I was going to miss her.

And I couldn't wait for her to leave.

Maybe when her shadow was gone, I'd have some freedom. Maybe not. Maybe the only moments of peace I'd find for the rest of my life were on this cliffside.

A breeze lifted my unruly hair, pushing a lock into my mouth. I spit it out, but not before the bitter tang of the brown dye Margot used each week spread across my tongue. The wild curls never stayed in their braid, no matter how hard my lady's maids tugged and yanked. The only time it cooperated was when it was wet.

The ocean beckoned. I stopped and turned.

What if I jumped? Would anyone notice?

No. Not for this princess. A smile tugged at my mouth.

I raced for the cliff. My drab, gray dress streamed behind me as I ran, faster and faster, arms pumping, legs pushing. I didn't think. I didn't falter. One moment, my feet were tethered to the earth.

The next, I was flying.

Two

Water dripped from the hem of my soaked dress, leaving a dotted trail as I tiptoed through the castle's east-wing gallery. My heart raced, the rush from the cliff dive still coursing through my veins.

I'd been sixteen years old when I made that jump for the first time. A group of servant boys had hiked that hill on a scorching summer afternoon, and I'd followed them out of curiosity. I'd watched them from a distance as, one by one, they leaped off the edge.

By the time they'd all swam to the shore and retreated to the castle, I'd worked up the courage to approach the cliff. It had taken hours of assessing the drop before I'd finally made the jump. When I'd plunged beneath the cold water, kicking furiously for the surface, I'd vowed never again. But a week later, after a berating from the weapons master about my ineptitude at archery, I'd climbed that hillside.

I'd claimed it as my own.

In the moments when I needed to feel brave, to feel free and alive, that cliff was my salvation.

Today wasn't the first or last time I'd sneak into the castle waterlogged. My slippers were gone, stolen by the sea, and my bare soles squelched on the white marble floors as I crept through the deserted gallery.

My ears stayed trained for the slightest sound as I inched past tapestries and paintings. Sneaking was probably unnecessary. No one came into this hall, especially Margot.

She didn't like the artwork in this particular gallery. It was too gruesome for her tastes.

Every piece depicted the crux from generations past. The largest mural had been crafted after their last migration, nearly thirty years ago, when the massive, eagle-like monsters had flown over Calandra and slaughtered our people.

In the painting, an auburn male crux had severed a man in two with its enormous beak. Entrails hung from its open mouth. Its talon, sharper than any blade, punctured the heart of a woman crushed beneath its weight. The male's thick, pointed horns dripped with blood and gore.

Margot wasn't wrong. This gallery *was* violent. And maybe once I lived through a migration, I wouldn't set foot in this hall again, either.

It was written that the old gods, Ama and Oda, created Calandra's animals as gifts to humans. As companions to share in this realm. The Mother and Father had been proud of their beautiful creations. They'd showered them with praise and glory.

But that pride enraged the gods' children, and in a fit of jealousy, the new gods—the Six—made animals of their own. The Six crafted predators in the image of Calandra's animals, though their variations were far more beautiful. Far more powerful. Far more deadly.

They birthed monsters to serve as a reminder to humans and animals alike that we were fragile and insignificant. And there was no monster more feared than the crux.

The first time I saw this artwork, that haunting mural, I'd gotten sick in a potted fern. But the next migration would be upon us soon, so I'd forced myself to return to this gallery, time and time again, until the scenes no longer made my stomach churn.

When I saw the crux fly for the first time, I would be prepared for the devastation our people would face.

The gods had truly outdone themselves with their creation.

There were monsters.

And then there were the crux.

According to the scholars' predictions, the next migration could come as early as next spring. Less than a year from now. I had the luxury of protection within these castle walls when so many did not.

Tearing my eyes from the mural, I rounded a corner, about to make a final dash to the stairwell, when I nearly slammed into a body, pulling back a fraction of a moment before we collided.

"I'm sorr—" The apology died on my tongue as I stared up at the Voster priest. My gasp echoed off the walls as I inched away from my father's emissary.

He stared unblinkingly from his towering frame, a head and bony shoulders above my own height. He was dressed in burgundy robes, the fabric draped around his lanky body, pooling at his ankles and feet as bare as my own. The nails on both his fingers and toes were thick and grooved with a dark-green tint. He had no hair, no eyebrows, and his skin was a chilly, pale white. His hawkish nose rested sharply above his thin, colorless lips.

My favorite lady's maid said the priest's skin gave her chills, but it was his eyes that caused a shiver to race down my spine. They were solid, endless pools without pupils, the color the same deep green as his nails.

Nightmares were born in those eyes.

I didn't care what anyone else said about the brotherhood. The Voster were terrors far worse than any monster roaming the five kingdoms.

Power radiated off his body, rocking me onto my heels. The Voster magic crackled around me like sparks. It was dizzying. Nauseating. It was like jumping off my cliff, only there was no bottom. No end to the spinning of my insides or the pit beneath my feet.

Humans weren't meant to be this close to magic.

I swallowed the urge to cry out as his power scraped and scratched along the bare skin of my arms.

The Voster cocked his head sideways, like a bird, as he took in my wet clothes. He lifted a bony hand, holding up a single finger. With a flick of his wrist, the water spun from my hair.

It swirled around my face, the droplets merging and lifting, until there was a ball of clear water spinning above my head. It stretched wider, thinning into a roped circle with a hollow center. Spikes stretched from the water, like it was being drawn toward the vaulted ceiling.

Around and around and around it spun until the priest had shaped the water into a crown that loomed over my head.

Father said the Voster brotherhood often used their fluid magic to deliver a message. That they manipulated air, water, and blood to make statements.

Well, whatever this crown of water meant, I wasn't going to ask the priest to spell it out. I bolted for the stairs, racing up the first flight, taking the steps two at a time with my soaked skirts balled in my fists. At the landing, I glanced back.

The priest's dark eyes were waiting.

Another shiver chased over my shoulders before I gripped the banister and forced myself to climb. It took until the third floor for the sensation of spiders crawling across my skin to ebb.

I wiped at the sleeves of my wet dress, like I could brush the prickling feeling away.

Why couldn't the priest have dried my dress instead of my hair? *That* would have been helpful. I could practically feel the frizz radiating through my curls.

So much for braiding it wet.

The Voster was yet another reason I didn't want to go to this meeting with the Turans.

The priests rarely visited the castle, but six days ago, without warning, Father's emissary had arrived. Every encounter with him had left me queasy.

What was he even doing here? Maybe the brotherhood had gotten word that Father had hired the Turan rangers. Or maybe he'd come because of the Guardian.

The Voster were elusive and avoided most people. At least, that's what I thought, considering the only priest I'd ever seen was Father's emissary, and on his visits, he stayed close to the castle.

I wasn't even sure how many Voster made up the brotherhood. Hundreds? Thousands? There was one and only one book in the castle's library about the Voster, and it was short. Very, very short.

Father's emissary visited for important political events, significant weddings, and royal funerals. Probably to make sure we were all behaving and following the terms of Calandra's magical treaties.

I'd asked a tutor once what it was that the Voster actually did besides wield fluid magic and craft blood oaths for kings. If the priests were humans who'd inherited magic or if they were something else entirely. He'd told me it was complicated—which meant he didn't know, either.

Father seemed on good terms with his emissary, but they certainly didn't appear to be close friends.

Well, whatever the reason the priest was here today, I was more than ready to see him go. With any luck, he'd be gone the moment the Turans left Roslo, returning to wherever it was the Voster called home. Another mystery about their people. No one knew where they lived.

Just the idea of an entire town of Voster, streets and buildings festering in their magic, made me queasy.

A niggling feeling ran down my nape like I was being watched. I twisted, expecting to find the priest, but I was alone in the stairwell.

"And clearly paranoid," I muttered as I stepped off the last stair to the fourth floor's grand hall.

"Why is your dress wet?" Margot's question caught me by surprise, my hand slapping over my breastbone. "And what happened to your hair?"

I groaned. So much for sneaking in unnoticed. *Damn.*

"Sorry, Margot."

This was the Voster's fault—the creep. Normally, I'd check the hallway to make sure it was empty before I crossed the carpet to my room. Instead, I'd been too distracted by the spiny touch of the priest's magic to pay attention.

"Odessa." There wasn't a person in Calandra who could infuse as much exasperation into my name as my stepmother.

"I'll be ready in time. I promise."

Her ocean-blue eyes with the Quentin amber starburst were as sharp as daggers as she pointed to my door. "You're already late."

"Not yet."

My stepmother's nostrils flared as I scurried past her for my rooms.

"Fine. I'm almost late."

"Hurry." She followed me inside and to my dressing room. As I pulled my hair—very dry, very curly, and very not-brown hair—over a shoulder, her fingers went to work freeing the buttons on my dress.

"You don't have to stay," I said. "Brielle or Jocelyn can help me."

She yanked so hard on the last button it popped free and went skidding across the floor. "Do you see Brielle or Jocelyn anywhere?"

"Um, no." My rooms were empty and the sleep clothes I'd shrugged off this morning still pooled on the floor beside the changing partition.

My lady's maids either had been reassigned to Mae for the day or were off spying on the Turans. My guess was the latter.

"They're busy in the southeast wing," Margot said.

Ah. Wasn't that where the Turans were staying?

"Those rangers have tracked filth into our halls."

Filth? "Haven't they been sailing on the Krisenth? Where would they get dirty?"

"Odessa." There was that irritation again.

"Right. Ask questions later."

"Please." Margot nudged me forward, sending me scampering behind the screen with the bodice of my gown clutched to my chest.

The garment landed with a plop as she thrust my new gown around the screen's edge.

The fact Margot had managed to find a shade of gray drabber than the last was actually quite astounding. My lip curled as I stepped into its skirts.

"We'll have to dye your hair. Again. And we have no time." The tap of her foot was like being repeatedly slapped on the hand. "Swimming. Fully clothed. Why are you this way? Why can't you have a normal hobby like archery or horseback riding?"

I loved to draw and paint, but did Margot appreciate my artwork? No. Instead, she'd get irked whenever my fingers were stained with charcoal or pastels.

She wanted me to be like Mae. To love swordplay and sparring. Those were acceptable hobbies for *her* daughter, *her* princess. But art and swimming, both relatively tame activities, were deemed troublesome and annoying.

Yes, I'd been swimming. Yes, it probably should have waited until tomorrow. At least Margot didn't know exactly how I'd gotten into the water. No one did.

If anyone learned I'd been diving off that cliff, there'd be hell to pay.

"I'm hurrying," I promised. "I lost track of time."

"Girl, you test the limits of my patience."

"Sorry, sorry, sorry." No matter how many times I apologized, it wouldn't make a difference, but that never stopped me from trying.

She was seething when I emerged donned in gray. "Turn."

I gave her my back so she could fasten the gown's buttons.

The fabric molded to my ribs and breasts. The neckline left my collarbones and throat exposed while the sleeves flowed to my fingertips. The skirts billowed around my hips, swishing and swaying with my movements.

In any other color, this would have been a beautiful dress.

In gray, I practically blended in with the stone floor. Maybe that was the idea.

"Hair." Margot snapped her fingers and pointed to the vanity, standing behind me as I took a seat at the bench.

I hesitated to give her the comb. In her hands, it was a weapon she wielded often. My scalp would ache for hours after she finished with the torture. "You don't need to do this. I can manage. I'm sure Mae needs you more."

"She's…occupied."

Occupied. Meaning she was with the captain of the guard for their afternoon romp.

Why was it okay for Mae to fit in a little fun before this meeting with the Turans, but I was being chastised for a tiny ocean swim?

The double standards around this castle were stifling.

Margot ripped the comb from my grasp and dragged it through my curls, pulling so hard I had to grip the bench's sides to keep from toppling to the floor. Once she'd worked through most of the snags, she snapped the fingers of her free hand. "Powder."

I stretched for the opal jar on the vanity, pulling off the lid and choking on the dye's pungent odor. The smell would fade within a few minutes, but gods, that first inhale burned my throat.

She shook the powder into my roots until my natural color was muted.

Until the orange and red and copper and caramel strands were gone. Not a single curl was missed, and when I looked into the mirror, the familiar shade of brown stared back through the glass.

I didn't mind the brown, not really. Margot said that it suited the coloring of my face. That it brought out the freckles across my nose and the gold striations in my eyes.

Mostly, I think the red reminded her too much of my mother.

I was too much of my mother.

"I have never in my life met someone who has such a penchant for finding trouble." Margot tossed the comb aside and began tugging the locks into a braid. "You could have been eaten by sharks."

"There are no sharks this close to shore."

"Oh? And I suppose there aren't any marroweels, either. Have you forgotten the reason the Turans are here in the first place?"

"No," I mumbled.

The Turans were here to kill the monsters that had wreaked havoc on Father's trade routes over the past year. What had started as sporadic attacks from the beasts had escalated, and as of this summer, only one in three ships made it to their destination. With every attack, the marroweels left no survivors.

Before this past year, before they'd started attacking our ships, they'd only been known to live in the deepest waters of the Marixmore Ocean, far from where our Quentin ships sailed. Why had they changed habitats? Had the monsters moved inland for food? Was there a new predator driving them toward Roslo's shores?

Had the gods created monsters more terrifying than even the crux?

Not only were our shipments being lost, but Quentis's best sailors were being drowned and eaten by the marroweels. It was becoming impossible — and expensive — to convince anyone to make the voyage over the Krisenth Crossing.

The trade routes had to be secured. The grain we harvested and sold to Laine, Genesis, Ozarth, and Turah had to be delivered before another king took these missing shipments as an insult. As a default on the treaty. As an invitation for war.

No one could afford a war, not when the crux migration was coming so soon.

We needed to stockpile our resources. To have weapons, food, and supplies at the ready for when the monsters came. Gods only knew the destruction they'd bring. Our ships loaded with wheat, corn, and barley couldn't go missing, especially when those crops had already been bartered for weapons and lumber.

The Quentin soldiers had tried to slay the marroweels, but the monsters were as vicious and cunning as any warrior. They moved with lightning speed, and the rigid bone that protruded from their skull could ram through a ship's frame. Our men had managed to kill some monsters, but not enough. The terrors continued to sink our ships.

So Father had hired the Turans to purge the Krisenth Crossing of the marroweels. How? I hadn't a clue.

"Do you think they'll be able to kill them?" I asked Margot.

"Well, if the six dead beasts hanging in the docks this morning are any indication, then I'd say yes."

"What? They already killed the marroweels?" I sat up straighter. "When?"

"They brought them as they arrived last night."

Had I known, I would have skipped the cliffside and headed straight for the docks. I'd never seen one of the fabled marroweels in anything but books. "How big are they? Are they blue?"

Margot scoffed. "You're more excited about six dead monsters than you are for your own wedding to Banner."

She wasn't wrong. I'd missed more planning meetings than I'd attended. I twisted around. "How do you think they killed them?"

"Odessa," she snapped, forcing my head to the mirror. "Hold. Still."

Who cared about my hair? I wasn't the woman on display today. No one cared about me. But I kept my mouth shut and let Margot keep braiding.

Before my mother's death, Margot had been her lady's maid, and since I had Mother's hair, Margot was well practiced at taming the curls.

"I saw Banner earlier." I waited until Margot's blue eyes met the gold of mine in the mirror. "He told me that the Guardian arrived with the Turans."

"Yes." A crease formed between her brows.

The Guardian.

A man rumored to be more vicious and deadly than any creature crafted by the gods.

News of the Guardian had reached Quentis's shores three years ago, and since, countless tales had been spun about his origins.

Some believed he'd crawled out of a grave in Turah. That he was more ghost than mortal being. Some said he was Izzac incarnate. That the God of Death had grown tired of his throne and disguised himself as a man to torment humankind for amusement. And others were certain he'd been gifted his powers by the old gods themselves.

He was more myth than man, and stories about him had swept across the continent like wildfire.

"What does it mean that he's here?" I asked Margot.

"It means you should not go wandering without your guards. It means we should not be late." She worked with furious fingers, pulling each lock into a thick plait. Yet today, even my hair seemed to protest this charade. When the third piece came loose around my temples, she threw up her hands.

"I don't have time for this. Finish and get to the throne room." She marched for the door, sending the skirts of her cobalt dress into a flurry.

As she passed a window, sunlight refracted through the jewels in her crown. Her silky golden hair fell in sleek panels down her shoulders and spine. She floated more than walked, her chin held high. She might not have been born royalty, but Margot Cross was every bit a queen.

Her daughter would be, too.

With my stepmother gone, I faced the mirror and slumped.

At times like this, I wished I was younger. That I was a child like Arthalayus. My half brother spent his days in the nursery, blissfully unaware of his obligations. *Good.* As heir to my father's throne, Arthy would someday sign a blood oath of fealty to Father, like most royal heirs in the five kingdoms of Calandra, and soon have more obligations than I could stomach.

Poor kid.

Despite the twenty-year age difference between us, I hoped he'd come to me if he ever needed a reprieve from Father and Margot's demands. Until then, Mae and I would bear that burden.

My hair was a mess, despite Margot's attempt at a braid, but I wrestled it into feeble submission, leaving a few errant strands to frame my face. With the end tied in a satin ribbon, I plucked the crown that had been left on the vanity, fitting it to my head.

It was heavy, the metal cool and unforgiving. Inlaid into the gleaming gold were hundreds of sparkling amber jewels.

This crown was the only thing on me that wasn't gray.

Gods, I hated gray.

I straightened my spine and assumed the posture my refinement tutors had drilled into me from the age of three. I stared into the mirror, and a princess stared back.

A princess who was late.

Three

I slipped through the side entrance of the throne room, breath held as I moved on silent feet to join Margot and Mae to the left of the royal dais.

"Welcome." Father's voice was as cold as the large, echoey space. He preferred an icy atmosphere, probably because it so often matched his mood.

Light poured through stained glass windows, casting the marble floor with different shades of blues and greens and yellows. Everyone was gathered in the center of the space, Father's golden throne empty on its dais. There were more guards than normal. Four instead of two stationed at every door.

Father's gaze didn't shift from the men standing in front of him, but without a doubt, he knew I was sneaking in late. Something I'd be berated for later.

Margot and Mae were removed from the group of men, standing side by side a few paces back, crowned and polished. Daughter as beautiful as mother. While my sister was a copy of Father in their stubborn, iron wills, Mae was a near replica of Margot in appearance, from the classic line of their noses to the tapered point of their chins.

Did I look like my mother? I wished I had a reminder of her face. She died when I was a baby, and Father had her portraits removed from the halls. The only reason I knew I'd inherited her hair was because of how often Margot cursed it. But otherwise, I had no idea if we had the same nose or chin or mouth.

As I came to a stop at Margot's side, she shot me a look of disapproval, then returned her attention to the men.

Five Turans stood shoulder to shoulder, their broad frames forming a wall. Each was a pillar of honed muscle and brute strength. Gods, they were huge.

Banner stood over six feet tall, but compared to these men, he was lean and gangly. Even Father, who was the largest man I'd ever seen, was no match for Turan stature and brawn.

No wonder they'd been able to kill the marroweels.

The Turans weren't dressed in finery, not that I'd expected tailored coats or shining boots from a band of warriors. They wore leather pants that molded to thick thighs. Their brown, tooled vests were worn over ivory cotton tunics that strained against corded biceps. Each wore leather cuffs at his wrists. Two of the men had intricate, dark tattoos covering their forearms.

Every Turan was armed with knives or swords strapped across his back. One man carried three daggers on his belt. They looked prepared for war, not a dinner with royals.

It was surprising that Father even let them into the throne room the way they were armed. Normally, guests were stripped of their weaponry before an audience with the king. Had the Turans refused? Or had the guards even bothered asking?

"Before we begin the introductions." Father's deep voice echoed through the room. "I would like to extend my gratitude for your services. My men tell me that six marroweels were brought in with your ships last night. I hadn't expected you to act so quickly. For that, you have my thanks."

The man with the daggers crossed his arms over his chest. He had a bushy bronze beard, braided beneath his chin. "We've only done what you've hired us to do."

There was something in the man's tone. A note of condescension that made Father's jaw flex as he raised a hand and snapped his fingers.

The same side door I'd snuck through moments ago flew open, and two guards carried in a chest so large I could have curled up inside and taken a nap. They set it in the center of the throne room, then unlatched the lid, flipping it back to reveal hundreds of Calandran coins.

It was more wealth than I'd ever seen. Enough gold and silver to feed all the mouths in Roslo for months.

A Turan warrior with smooth brown skin and deep-set dark eyes walked to the chest, crouching to inspect its contents. His black hair was braided in long rows, and the cords were tied at his nape. He picked up a single coin, flipping it in the air. It landed on the others with a *clink*.

Was that the Guardian?

"Should I count it, Highness?" he asked as he stood and rejoined the others.

Wait. What? Who was he calling Highness?

The warrior in the center of the line shook his head.

Except he wasn't a warrior, was he? Was that the crown prince?

I'd never seen the Turan prince before, but he must be Zavier Wolfe. The heir to the Turan throne.

Mae's soon-to-be husband.

Okay, *that* was a surprise. If Margot was shocked, too, she didn't let it show. Neither did Mae. Clearly, I'd missed something by being late.

Prince Zavier was in Roslo. The Guardian was in Roslo.

What was going on? This was supposed to be a quick meeting and a chance for Father to pay the Turan rangers he'd hired. Now it was a royal introduction? Had everyone but me known about this? That explained why the Voster priest was here.

Good thing Margot had insisted on all of that grooming for Mae earlier, if this was her first face-to-face with her betrothed.

"There is no need to count the coin." Father spoke in his cool, indifferent manner, yet the fire in his caramel eyes betrayed his appearance. "Every ounce of coin we agreed upon is there."

The warrior who'd spoken earlier, the bearded man with the daggers, gave Father an assessing look. "And what if the price we agreed upon is no longer enough?"

It was rumored that Prince Zavier didn't speak. If the gossip was true, then maybe that warrior spoke on his behalf, like an advisor. Or a general.

Father's eyes blazed hotter, the amber starbursts like twin flames. "And what, exactly, is your new price?"

Before the warrior could answer, the main doors opened, capturing everyone's attention.

The Voster priest I'd collided with earlier entered the throne room. His bare feet poked out beneath his robes, those gruesome green nails on display. But he wasn't alone this time. Two paces behind him came another member of the brotherhood in the same burgundy robes.

This priest didn't walk. Instead, he floated slightly above the ground like he was being carried on an invisible wind. Like gravity didn't weigh as heavily on his body as it did everyone else's. The nails on his hands and feet were so long they curved and curled like ribbons.

The sting of their magic was instant. The power zinged over my shoulders and down my spine. It took every bit of control not to squirm.

One Voster priest was uncomfortable. But two? It was nearly unbearable. I fought the urge to rub my arms and sprint for the door.

If Margot or Mae felt the discomfort, neither let it show.

Who was that second priest? Had he come here with the Turans? Or had he accompanied the Guardian?

The Voster couldn't shake the earth or throw balls of fire, but they could bend and twist air and water at their will. Their blood magic was used to form unbreakable bonds. But I'd never seen one levitate before. This priest's power felt stronger, sharper, than that from Father's emissary.

Both Voster looked the same, hairless with that translucent skin, but this other priest seemed older. His attention, those green-black eyes, drifted to me, lingering for just a moment, before he shifted his focus over his shoulder to the doors.

Tension coiled in the room, and as my gaze followed his, my heart climbed into my throat.

The man who entered next didn't look like a god incarnate. He didn't appear to be a ghost. He was tall and broad, like the other Turans. Muscled to the point of distraction. His chocolate-brown hair tickled the tops of his shoulders, and his chiseled jaw was covered in a short beard of the same shade.

At first glance, he was just a man. Striking. Intimidating. But still, just a man.

Yet his irises did not have the typical Turan green starburst. They were solid, molten silver. Liquid metal. Colorless, like my dress.

The Guardian.

The pounding of his boots matched the rhythm of my thundering pulse as he followed the Voster. Unlike the Turans, he wore no weapons, no sword or knives. Maybe Father had insisted he come to this meeting unarmed, yet I had a feeling he could kill us all with his bare hands.

The way he'd murdered Banner's brother. Hands tight around a throat until the windpipe was crushed.

My eyes darted to my fiancé's. There was murder in Banner's gaze. His hatred of the Guardian was as potent as the scent of my hair dye. But Goddess Carine must have heard our prayers for peace, because he kept his temper leashed, standing stoically at Father's side like the dutiful general he was.

I wasn't in love with Banner. I wasn't particularly excited about becoming the wife of a man under my father's thumb. But I didn't want to see him hanged for treason, either.

The Voster priests came to a stop, together and apart from everyone else. They were their own group in this strange ordeal, like Margot, Mae, and me.

The Guardian did not join them. Instead, the Turan line parted as he approached, making space for him beside Prince Zavier.

The room stilled and quieted. The tension was so thick it was difficult to breathe. The magic made my head ache.

One meeting. We only had to survive this one meeting of nonsense. Then Banner could excuse himself before that throbbing vein at his temple popped. And I could sneak away to my rooms, where I'd stay until the Turans and Voster left Roslo.

I leaned forward, risking another glance at my sister.

A smile toyed on her pretty lips. From the outside, it appeared modest and sweet. I knew better. There was cunning in her blue eyes, like she was in on a secret no one had bothered to share with me.

Mae loved secrets. Add in a solid dose of conflict and a dash of bloodlust, and she was happy.

Was it her nature? Or was it her upbringing?

As a child, Margot had given me dolls to celebrate my birthdays. When Mae had turned five, Father had gifted her a set of gilded blades.

She'd fit in with these Turan warriors, wouldn't she? With this prince? Mae had inherited Father's strong frame and Margot's height. Eighteen years of training had sharpened her into a weapon. The Turans wouldn't break Mae.

Perhaps Father was counting on it being the other way around.

"Where were we?" Father asked. "You had a concern about your price? How can we resolve this?"

Um...

Was he pandering to the Turans? Because that sounded like pandering. And my father did not pander.

He'd let that ranger's comment about counting the coin slide without a sharp retort. And now he was asking how he could *resolve a concern*?

Mae had learned her cunning from his instruction, so what was really happening? There was more going on here than a king hiring mercenaries.

"Introductions. Before we continue." The levitating Voster priest spoke, his voice like silk.

I'd never heard a priest speak before. I'd expected a grating noise, a tone as spiky as their power. But it was like music, soft and entrancing. The sound of a siren singing you to sleep before they swallowed you whole.

At his command, the attention of the men shifted in our direction. Five pairs of Turan eyes with green starbursts in their irises dragged over Margot and Mae while the Guardian's silver gaze locked on me instead. It was as uncomfortable as the Voster magic.

Father gave Margot a nod.

She put her hand on Mae's lower back, and together, they walked toward the Turans with me trailing a step behind.

The Turan in the center of the group wore a circlet across his forehead. The band wasn't inlaid with jewels or gems. It was a twist of metal threads, woven together to form a line of silver.

His brown hair was shorter than any of the others', the soft waves pushed away from his face, the ends curling slightly at his nape. The sides of his crown disappeared beneath the strands at his ears. A small scar cut through one of his eyebrows. His eyes were the color of moss on a stormy day. The shade nearly swallowed the green starbursts in his irises.

Prince Zavier was handsome. Stunning, really, with a robust masculinity. And he was bored. There wasn't a hint of interest at meeting his future bride.

At any moment, I expected to see him yawn.

The Guardian, however, looked amused, like this was all a joke. His eyes crinkled at the sides as he smirked.

What was funny? What was I missing?

"Prince Zavier, I present to you my daughter Mae," Father said. "In accord with the Shield of Sparrows, she is to be your bride on the autumnal equinox in three months' time."

Zavier studied Mae for a long moment, then glanced to the Guardian.

An unspoken conversation passed between them. Was that one of the Guardian's powers? Could he read minds?

Well, if he could read mine…

Go away. Please and thank you.

The Guardian gave the prince a nod, then spoke in a gravelly voice that gave me goose bumps. "Not her."

Margot blinked. "Excuse me?"

"Her." The Guardian's eyes flicked in my direction, and the whole room followed his gaze.

To me.

"Prince Zavier will marry *her*," he declared. "Tonight. As the bride prize for killing your marroweels."

Four

The silence in the throne room was as thick as billowing smoke, sucking the air from my lungs. The floor began to spin and tilt, my balance faltering.

Margot's hand wrapped around my forearm, and for a moment, I was grateful for her steadying touch. But then her fingernails bit through the fabric of my dress so hard they almost punctured my skin.

Yet even as the pain zinged from wrist to elbow, I didn't move. Couldn't move.

Her.

Me? Prince Zavier wanted to marry me?

No. Absolutely not. This wasn't happening. I was hallucinating. The ocean water had gone to my head. That, or Ferious was playing one of his tricks. This seemed like something the God of Mischief would enjoy. Maybe it was the Voster. That priest who had yet to touch the floor had planted this nightmare in my mind.

This was not real. Could not be real.

I was engaged to Banner. Mae was marrying the Turan prince. Mae. Not me. Mae.

Margot squeezed tighter, her fingertips digging into my flesh. Thankfully, I didn't bruise easily. Otherwise, there would be five round circles by morning.

But I didn't try to shake her loose. I was too busy listening to the Guardian's word screaming in my mind.

Her.

Her. Her. Her.

Me.

The silence built higher and higher and higher. The tension doubled. Tripled. The explosion was inevitable. And when the quiet finally cracked, the room erupted at once.

"There must be some mistake." Margot spoke through gritted teeth.

Every syllable was punctuated by her nails digging deeper into my arm.

"No." Father's voice was a boom, rattling the walls.

A growl, raw and ravenous, ripped from Mae's throat.

Then came Banner's declaration of the obvious. "She is *my* fiancée."

And a laugh. Gravelly. Low. Dry and humorless.

I blinked, forcing my vision into focus, homing in on that laugh.

The Guardian. He was laughing. His silver eyes flashed white like lightning, and the smirk on his mouth stretched.

Jackass.

Margot gasped.

Father's jaw clenched.

Damn. I guess I'd said that out loud. Well, he was a jackass for laughing.

I opened my mouth, not to apologize but to say it again, this time more clearly, but a slice of my father's hand through the air brought back that crushing silence.

Every man in the throne room seemed to stand taller. One of the warriors lifted his hand, just slightly, like he was readying to wield the sword on his back.

"Prince Zavier," Father said. "Mae is my daughter intended to be your bride. If you wish to forgo the planned festivities of the equinox, then we will arrange for your union tonight."

My gaze bounced around the room, hopping from Turan to Voster to Father to Banner and back around again.

The prince was still bored. The Voster seemed comatose. Banner looked lethal. Father's expression was too guarded to discern. Mae and Margot were livid. At. Me.

And the Guardian was still smirking.

I hated him instantly. Maybe I should have wished for Banner to cut his throat.

Shades, I needed to get out of this throne room. Immediately.

Father wouldn't allow this, right? He'd tell the prince exactly what he thought of a bride prize—whatever the hell that was.

Except Father stayed quiet. His mouth pursed into a thin line as he kept his steady gaze on the Turans, waiting for their reply.

Did he even care that they were asking me to be used as payment for a debt? That they were asking to trade his daughter like that coffer of coin? Or was the anger simmering in his caramel eyes simply because his orders were being questioned?

I didn't want the answer.

When I tore my eyes from Father, the Guardian's gaze was waiting.

It wasn't the same silver as it had been a moment ago. His eyes darkened, silver bleeding away to gray and brown and green. A hazel as hard as stone.

Gone was his laughter. His humor had given way to a cold, cruel malice.

My heart was beating so fast it hurt. The pulse pounding in my ears was deafening. But I didn't look away from his changing irises. From that glare. I would not wither under that murderer's stare.

Father had taught me a long time ago that only fools cowered.

I might not be his favorite daughter, but I tried not to be a fool. So I held the Guardian's stare, my will as unbendable as Ozarth iron. Mae and I shared that stubborn streak.

The corner of the Guardian's mouth turned up.

Yep, still a jackass. Glad I could be his source of amusement today. I curled my lip and shifted my attention, this time to Prince Zavier.

He was unreadable. No hint of emotion. No sign of interest or indifference. His was the most intimidating stare I'd ever seen in my life, more so than even Father's.

A shiver rolled down my spine.

If the Guardian's glare had been a test, the prince's was a promise. I was going to be his wife.

The floor beneath my slippers tilted sideways again.

"She is not yours to have." Fury crackled off Banner's frame, his body practically vibrating. "She is mine."

It might have been romantic. Except Banner wasn't mad because another man was stealing the woman he loved. No, Banner was furious to be losing his link to the royal family.

I might not be the favored princess, but I was *a* princess. A gift for his service. A symbol of his status.

The Guardian met Banner's sneer with one of his own. "She was yours. Now, she belongs to the prince. She'll satisfy both the bride prize and the treaty. She'll be our queen."

Queen.

That was laughable. I hated wearing shoes and dresses and being trapped indoors. I loathed the monotony of lessons and lectures. I wasn't meant to rule or lead. Politics were boring and regal parties overrated. I was not a queen.

The crown on my head began to itch.

"I will not stand for this," Banner announced. "You are to wed Mae."

Prince Zavier turned his chin and gave that impassive stare to my fiancé. A dare to defy royalty. A challenge to the oldest known treaty in Calandra.

Banner gulped.

Zavier dismissed him with a blink and faced Father.

"The prince will have who he desires." It was as if the Guardian were inside Zavier's mind, speaking the words the prince could not. "And he desires her."

Her. There was that word again.

Oh, gods. I was going to be sick.

"The Shield of Sparrows treaty stipulates a daughter of the king's choosing. As I am the only king in this room, the choice is mine." Father pointed to Mae. "You will wed Mae. She is the Sparrow. And you will be given the gold we have promised for your assistance with the marroweels."

These men were bartering for us like we were crops.

Mae preened, seemingly honored to be chattel. She stood taller, her shoulders pinned, as a smug smile stretched across her mouth.

My molars ground together, nearly cracking, but I managed to keep quiet. Nothing would come from my protest. No one in this room gave a damn about my opinion. My fate was not my own, and my future would be determined by these *men*.

Zavier sighed, like this argument was cutting into his afternoon nap time.

I hated him. All of them.

"King Cross is correct." Father's Voster emissary spoke with the same smooth voice as the priest. "The daughter to be offered through the Shield of Sparrows is of the king's choosing."

The air rushed from my lungs. Who would have thought a Voster would be my salvation?

"The treaty only requires a daughter be given to another kingdom each generation. Her father has the right to choose which daughter," the priest continued. "Though there is still the matter of the bride prize for the marroweels."

Father shook his head. "There is no bride prize. We will pay in gold."

"He doesn't want gold," the Guardian said.

Right. *Her.* He wanted me. Why? I was not special.

The other priest, the Voster still hovering above the floor, raised a hand, and before he spoke, I knew I'd loathe every word from his mouth. "The prince has slain seven female creatures on your behalf, per your request, King Cross. If he demands a bride prize, it must be paid. And for that, the bride is of *his* choosing."

"Six," Father corrected. "There were only six marroweels."

Six or seven. Who cared about some random number of monsters? So what if Zavier was good with a sword or crossbow or whatever he'd used to kill those beasts? Could we please get back to this bride-prize thing? Because I really wanted to know if I was or was not going to be married before dawn.

"Your informants were wrong, Majesty." The Guardian's cruel smile widened. "*Seven* female marroweels were slaughtered in the Krisenth Crossing. All by the prince himself. According to the Chain of Sevens, the prince can demand a bride prize."

The Chain of what? I glanced at Margot, and the pit in my stomach doubled as the color drained from her face.

"The Chain of Sevens is nothing more than a children's legend." Banner scoffed. "It is not enforceable. So take your gold and leave. Come back when you're ready to marry Mae and sign the Shield of Sparrows."

"The Chain of Sevens is no legend," the Guardian told Banner. "Your request to dispatch the marroweels should have been more specific."

Specific about what, exactly?

"What are you talking about?" Everyone seemed surprised that I had a voice. "The Chain of Sevens? What is it?"

"Seven lives in a chain." Father's emissary spoke gently, like he was pulling a punch. "Long ago, before the five kingdoms, the lands and seas were overrun by monsters. To regain control, the ruling lords made a decree. Any warrior who risked their life against the beasts would be granted a prize of their choosing if they returned with the heads of seven slain females from the species. As with all treaties, the Chain of Sevens was sealed with our magic."

Meaning death to any who violated its terms. If Father was indebted to the prince and refused to pay, the Voster's magic would steal his life.

Was that why the Turans had brought this other priest along? To enforce the decree? Well, if he had the power to seal the agreement, couldn't he overrule it, too?

"Why seven?" My voice wobbled. "Why is that number important?

And why females?"

"To alter the chain of life," the floating priest said. "Killing seven females will break the chain. Break it in enough places, and it holds no strength."

It wouldn't be easy to kill that many monsters and survive. So the ancient rulers had given them a boon for such feats? Those who prevailed would earn a prize.

Even a bride.

Banner was right. This sounded like a story in a children's book.

"The Chain of Sevens is not real. It is nothing but a legend." Father raised his chin. "The only bride Prince Zavier will be given is Mae to fulfill the Shield of Sparrows. I will not send Odessa in Mae's place because of an archaic myth like the Chain of Sevens."

The levitating Voster leveled Father with his stare. "What you call an archaic myth is old magic. And old magic is still magic, boy. It is quite real." On the priest's final word, an icy wind blew through the throne room. It whipped the skirts of my gown around my ankles and blew a lock of Margot's hair into my face.

Then, like it had never blown in, the wind stopped. The hems of my dress fell in a whoosh across my slippers.

Margot straightened, her grip finally loosening from my arm.

The relief was short-lived. The Voster dropped to his feet, his soles finally resting on the floor. It must have grounded his magic, intensified it in some way. The prickling of my skin penetrated deeper, sharper as his magic permeated the room.

The wind was gone, but the cold remained, plummeting lower and lower. Crystals formed on the windows. Frost coated the floor. My shallow breaths were wisps of white. My teeth chattered.

Time slowed to a crawl, minutes passed in silent agony, and still the temperature did not rise. If he kept us here, if he trapped us in this room, we'd all freeze to death.

As if the Voster hadn't made the threat clear enough, the temperature dropped again, turning so cold that the metallic tang of blood spread across my tongue. The taste of frozen lungs. My nostrils burned with every inhale.

Beside me, Margot began to tremble. Mae, for once, looked terrified. Even Father blanched.

The Turans stood as still as statues, seemingly unaffected. For a moment, I wondered if the Voster had spared them from his display, but frost was spreading over the prince's circlet. Zavier and the Guardian shared a look, not of worry but of warning.

Father had gone too far by questioning the Voster's magic.

"I sealed the Sevens with my own magic and the blood of ancient kings." The Voster's voice was as lethal as the shards of ice forming on the ceiling. "Mind what you call an archaic myth."

Father bowed his head. It was the first time in my life I'd seen him bow to another. He didn't even do that for his own Voster emissary. Granted, this priest was about to kill us all, so now was the time to show a little humility.

"I'm sorry, High Priest," Father murmured.

High Priest? *The* High Priest? I was about done with surprises for today.

My mind was running out of places to keep all of this newfound information. This meeting was only supposed to be a formality. Had I known the High Priest of the Voster would be in attendance, I would have kept swimming.

According to that one book about the brotherhood, the Voster were long-lived but not immortal. Since the High Priest hadn't been seen or heard from in decades, most believed he'd died.

No, he'd just been hiding out with the Turans. Was he Prince Zavier's ambassador? Did he live in Turah?

"She is your daughter, yes?" the High Priest asked.

"Yes." Father nodded.

"Then she will be the prince's bride for both the Shield of Sparrows and Chain of Sevens."

She. Her.

Me.

Five

The air warmed with the High Priest's declaration.

Margot exhaled, her body swaying as she breathed, her breath no longer a cloud. She hated the cold because it hurt her knees.

The ice melted as the temperature returned to normal. The plop of water droplets falling on marble echoed through the throne room.

Father's emissary raised his hand and, just like he'd done with my hair, spun his finger in a circle. Streams of water rushed for the closed front doors, escaping through its cracks.

As quickly as it had started, the show of Voster magic was finished. Other than its irritation against my skin, every trace was gone as if ice and wind had never touched this place.

Prince Zavier nodded to the Voster brothers, then turned and stalked for the exit. His rangers formed a line and followed close behind.

I guess they were done? He'd come for a bride prize—I gagged—and he'd gotten his way.

The Guardian left next, not sparing anyone a parting glance.

The High Priest lifted off the floor and floated at the Guardian's side.

Only when the doors thudded closed behind them did I risk a breath.

"Brother Dime." Father's eyes were pleading as he addressed his emissary. "There must be something we can do."

Dime. Strange that I'd never known his name.

He wasn't a regular visitor at the castle, but he'd been around on a few occasions in my lifetime. Grandfather's funeral. The feast of kings that Father had hosted five years ago. Arthalayus's presentation as heir to the Quentin crown.

I should have introduced myself before. Maybe Brother Dime would have spoken for me, stood up to the High Priest, if I'd bothered to learn his name.

"Mae is to be the Turan queen," Father said. "It cannot be Odessa. She is not capable."

Ouch. Okay, so I wasn't the chosen daughter, but was the idea of me as a queen really so inconceivable?

Not that I wanted to be queen. At. All.

"Oh, gods." I pressed my fingertips to my temples, rubbing at the ache blooming in my skull.

This wasn't happening. This wasn't real.

Brother Dime walked toward me, his nearness making the throb in my head worse.

My hands flopped at my sides as I met his fathomless gaze. "Please."

"This is your fortune, child." He reached for me, long, spindly fingers extended.

But before he could touch my face with his bony fingers, I shied away, leaning closer to Margot, hoping her body would absorb the sting of his magic.

Dime studied me for a long moment, his head tilting to the side like it had earlier. He blinked those creepy eyes once, then swept out of the throne room, disappearing to wherever he stayed when he was visiting Roslo.

Did he have a castle wing? Or did he stay in the city? Maybe I should have asked about that, too.

Without having to fight against the irritation of his magic, the last shards of strength leaked from my body. I collapsed to the floor, knees landing with a crack on the marble. My stomach churned, and the meal I'd eaten hours ago threatened to make a reappearance, but I swallowed the urge to retch.

"Gods." I signed the Eight, circling my hand around my face and around my heart. I doubted the Eight gods were listening, but if Ama, Oda, and their six children had a hint of divine intervention to spare, I'd take it.

"Odessa is to be my wife." Banner stomped a boot on the floor.

"You heard the High Priest." Father tore the crown from his head and dragged a fair hand through his golden hair. The strands at his temples appeared more ashen than they had before this debacle.

People called him the Gold King. His hair was the color of ripened wheat. His caramel eyes were flecked with the same golden shade as the coins in that chest. With the amber starbursts, Father's gaze always had a glow.

The magic rooted deep in Calandra's land tinged our irises at birth with those starbursts, linking us forever to a place. No matter where we lived, where we moved, that one color was unchanging. Every Quentin had an amber starburst.

Every Quentin except me.

My eyes were solid gold. Not a starburst in sight.

When I was a child, I used to ask Father why I was different. After he'd ignored the question countless times, I'd stopped trying to understand.

When Mae and I were girls, when the time had come for him to choose the Sparrow and he'd picked her instead of me, even though I was his eldest daughter, he hadn't explained that, either.

The Gold King owed no one an explanation.

Father's nickname was mostly due to the incredible wealth he'd brought to our kingdom since he'd been passed the crown from my grandfather.

Quentis hadn't been wealthy prior to his reign. My grandfather's passion had been women and parties and spending his people's money on extravagance. He was the reason this castle had been plated in gold.

My father had chosen to use our resources more wisely. His fortunes were locked beneath the castle, not on its walls. Yet even the Gold King couldn't pay this debt with riches.

"There must be another way," Banner said. "The Turans cannot take her from me. This cannot be—"

"Banner." Father's voice cracked off the walls. "Leave us."

"My king—"

"Leave. Us."

Banner, the ever-faithful general, left without delay, his bootheels sharp as he crossed the floor.

"Out," Father commanded to the guards. Unlike Banner, there was no argument.

With them gone, it was only us. Family.

A blade being unsheathed sounded a moment before a knife was pressed against my throat.

"What did you do?" Mae seethed.

"Get that knife away from me." On top of everything else, I didn't have the energy for my sister's antics. I was moments away from throwing myself off another cliff, and she thought *now* would be a good time to test the sharpness of her knife? Really?

I pushed at her hand, forcing the blade away from my neck. Though not before she flicked her wrist, just enough to break the skin and draw a bead of blood.

"Shit," I hissed, pressing my fingertip to the nick. "Did you really just cut me? Shades, you're a demon."

"Tell me what you did," she snapped.

"Nothing. I did nothing."

Her beautiful features contorted in rage. "Then why does Prince Zavier want you?"

"How should I know?" I wiped the blood from my neck, glaring up at her as I smeared it on the underside of my sleeve. "Maybe he doesn't like blondes."

My sister lunged, her other hand balled into a fist, ready to slam into my nose, but before she could get close, Father's hand clasped around her wrist, halting her momentum.

He ripped the knife from her grasp and flung it across the floor. It skidded to a stop at the stairs of his throne's dais.

"Mae," Margot chided. "You are not helping this situation."

"She did something, Mother. Tricked him or—"

"Enough." Father's command left no room for disobedience. He released Mae and lowered to a crouch in front of me, his caramel eyes searching mine. "Tell me honestly. Have you met Zavier before this day?"

"No." I shook my head. "Never."

"Have you crossed paths with any of the Turans since they've arrived?"

"Not once."

"Where were you today?"

Nothing good would come from the truth. Father didn't know about the cliff diving. Banner only thought I went up to the overlook to sketch, get a better view of the city, and escape the castle's walls. And Margot and Mae thought I loved to swim off the coast.

There was no chance that Father would see my beloved pastime as brave rather than reckless. "I went for a hike outside. Then I went swimming."

His eyes narrowed as if he could sense the half-truth. "And?"

"When I came inside, I bumped into Brother Dime outside a gallery."

"Which gallery?"

"The, um…crux gallery."

"Damn your curiosity with that hall," he snapped, nostrils flaring.

I winced. "I'm sorry."

He'd told me on more than one occasion it wasn't a suitable place for me to spend my time. Father didn't understand my interest in the migrations.

He also didn't realize today hadn't been about the art or monsters. That gallery was simply the easiest way for me to sneak in unnoticed.

Father sighed. "What else happened today?"

"Nothing. After I saw Brother Dime, I ran upstairs to change my gown. Margot helped with my hair." Father didn't move. He didn't speak. Suspicion filled his eyes, like he knew I hadn't given him the whole truth.

This silence was one of his favorite tactics. He liked to see who would break the quiet first.

Usually, it was me. I'd confess to hiding from my tutors or slipping table scraps to his hunting dogs. I'd admit to sneaking into the kitchen for treats or running away from my guards when I visited the docks.

But the truth about that cliffside was mine. I wouldn't give in, not with this. If by some miracle he found a way to get me out of this mess with the Turans, I wasn't going to lose that one freedom.

"Gods." Father sighed, dragging a palm over his jaw. "I'm sorry, Dess."

My entire body jolted. When was the last time he'd called me Dess? It had been years. And I'd never heard him apologize.

The gentleness in his eyes was so foreign that my heart clenched. He hadn't looked at me like that in, well...a long, long time. Since I was a child. Since I'd wake in the middle of the night, screaming from a nightmare, and Father would hold me until sunrise. "I'm sorry that you must do this."

"I can't, Father. Please don't make me."

He brushed his knuckles across my cheek. "You must."

"I don't want to marry him. There has to be a way to undo this."

He leaned back and gave me a sad smile. "The bride prize aside, we cannot afford to anger the Turans with a refusal. And we cannot break the Shield of Sparrows, not with the crux migration upon us. Mae was to go to Turah. You must take her place. You must be the Sparrow now."

It was another treaty signed in blood and sealed with magic.

If a king refused to give his daughter to another king, then the father would die. To my knowledge, no man had ever chosen his daughter over himself.

I certainly didn't expect that sort of sacrifice.

Beyond the stipulations of arranged marriages, the Shield of Sparrows was a trade treaty at its core. It kept all five kingdoms alive. Equitable-*ish*. It provided us all with the necessary resources to thrive. And when the crux migration came, survive.

We traded the resources we could reap—crops and cattle—for those we couldn't. The iron Quentis needed to forge weapons came from Ozarth. The lumber we used for buildings from Turah. Laine gave us spices and gold. And Genesis mined the oil we burned in lanterns and stoves.

From the day the Shield of Sparrows was formed, the wars that had once been commonplace across the continent had come to an abrupt halt. But our ancestors had feared that trading goods alone wouldn't be enough to keep the fragile peace, so they'd also decided to bind nations with blood.

Every generation, before every migration, a daughter would be married off to another royal family so that their children had ties to both countries.

The most recent arranged marriage had been between Laine and Ozarth.

The weddings were lavish affairs. Every kingdom was invited to celebrate, as the unions were to remind us all of the greater good. That peace must be preserved at all costs.

We could not war with ourselves and the crux. For the monsters did not care which lands they attacked. And they gave no mercy.

The crux would black out the skies for months, the sun blocked by thousands upon thousands of beating wings. Livestock would be slaughtered. Crops and harvests annihilated. Buildings razed and capitals destroyed.

Since the Shield of Sparrows, the five kingdoms had endured, surviving nine migrations.

Celebrating nine marriages.

Mae's would have been the tenth.

If not for the fucking Chain of Sevens.

"I can't believe this," I whispered. "This isn't happening."

"Listen." Father placed his hands on my shoulders and gave me a shake, the gentleness from a moment ago gone. "There is much to be done before tonight. Much you must learn."

"Isn't it a bit late to start preparing me to rule a foreign kingdom?"

"Odessa." Father shook my shoulders again. "You must find the way into Allesaria before summer's end. Then send word of how I can find and infiltrate the city."

I gaped, replaying his demand. "Wh-what?"

Did he want to send a legion to the Turan capital? There was a clause in the Shield of Sparrows forbidding invasion of one kingdom by another. Disobedience came with the same price as refusing to deliver a daughter for marriage.

A king's death.

Not only would invading the Turan capital start a war, it would cost Father his life.

He couldn't be serious. Was he?

"Your lady's maids will accompany you on the journey to Turah," he said. "Invent a reason to send one or both of them back to Quentis with whatever you learn."

"Brielle and Jocelyn?"

"Allesaria is your priority. Understand? It's crucial to my plans. We cannot delay. But you must also learn everything you can about the Guardian and his powers. Find a way to kill him."

My jaw dropped. "You want me to kill the Guardian?"

A murderer. A man who was rumored to slay the legendary monsters in Turah. Possibly the best fighter in Calandra. That Guardian?

"Yes," Father said. "You must try. At the very least, find out what he is capable of. No matter how many spies I've sent to Turah, none have been able to learn the extent of his powers or their source."

"Powers? He looks…normal." Well, mostly normal.

The rumors about the Guardian said he was as fast as a viper. That he had the strength of ten men. But his gifts weren't like the Voster's. He didn't seem to have fluid and blood magic. He certainly hadn't demonstrated any power today.

Except his eyes. He had no starburst, like me. And his eyes had changed colors—unless I'd imagined it. I wasn't sure what was real at this point. An hour ago, I hadn't known there was such a thing as the Chain of Sevens or a bride prize, but here I was, about to pay it to some bored, brooding prince.

I glanced toward Margot, hoping for a shred of compassion.

Nope. Not a bit. She was still irate.

Mae kept inching closer to her discarded knife.

And Father looked, well…peeved. Like his marionettes weren't obeying the tugs on their strings.

That's all we were. Puppets. The spinning in my head came to a sudden stop as realization dawned.

"D-did you plan this?" The marroweels and the mercenaries and whatever else he had in his head?

He frowned. "Did you really believe that Banner's legionnaires couldn't kill a handful of marroweels?"

So yes, he had planned this.

"People died. Did you send soldiers into the Krisenth, knowing they wouldn't return?" *Say no. Please say no.* I would not be able to look at him again if he'd willingly used his people as bait for some political scheme.

"The marroweels *have* been attacking along the trade route. Every life lost has been a tragedy. Once we realized it was no longer safe, we staged the disappearance of a few ships. All the soldiers aboard came home. But the Turans don't need to know that."

My frame sagged. Well, that was something. "I don't understand. Mae was to marry him in three months. Why not just wait for the equinox? Why bring them here now?"

"I can't wait three months. We've tried for years, decades, to find the way to Allesaria. From everything we can assume, the capital is deep within the Turan mountains. If so, it may be impassable for an army come winter. I wanted Mae to have enough time to find a way to breach the city and for a legion to make the journey before the snows. Otherwise, we'll have to wait until next spring. If the crux migrate earlier than the scholars predict, I will lose my chance."

"Chance at what? At conquering Turah?"

His jaw flexed. "They have something I want in that city."

"What?"

"The details are not important for you to know. But it is crucial I find a way into the city before the migration. It is our only chance at stopping the crux."

Time stilled. So did my heart.

Stopping the crux. Was it possible? Was there really a way to keep the monsters from destroying Calandra? A way to prevent the horrors shown in the castle gallery?

"How?"

"That, I cannot explain. Not yet. But for the good of our people, you must do this. You must trust me. Find me a way into Allesaria."

"But the treaties. What about—"

"Treaties can be broken, Odessa. Remember that."

The spinning in my head was back with a vengeance. "How? That would mean you'd die."

"Not necessarily."

What was he talking about? "I don't understand."

He placed his crown back on his head. "You don't need to."

It didn't matter if I comprehended the subtle details. Father would keep me in the dark unless he had no other choice. He would tell me only what I needed to know to do his bidding, apparently.

"How did you know that Prince Zavier would come when you hired them to kill the marroweels?" I asked.

He sighed, clearly annoyed with my string of questions, but answered anyway. "We've gathered from different sources that he's been traveling more frequently with his rangers. It wasn't a guarantee but worth a chance. When we learned that the Guardian and High Priest were spotted with their group, I assumed Zavier was among them, too."

"But you didn't anticipate a bride prize?"

"That was...unexpected."

I rubbed at my temples again, the ache returning as I tried to make sense of this conversation. "So you hired the Turans to kill the marroweels and brought them here so they could collect payment, knowing that Zavier would likely tag along, all in the hopes that the prince would, what? Take one look at Mae and fall desperately in love and demand they marry months earlier than planned?"

Father scoffed.

Silly me. I'd forgotten that Father didn't believe in love.

"I had hoped that he'd be open to shifting the wedding date," he said. "That if he came here, I could persuade him to marry her sooner under the guise of strengthening our trade routes. We have worked hard to build up stores in preparation for the crux. Turah has suffered two years of drought. Their production has not been enough to sustain them through the migration. I was hoping to accelerate the wedding in exchange for increased grain shipments. Then Mae would get to sail with them this summer. She'd have more time to gain knowledge of Allesaria."

"What if the prince hadn't come? What if he hadn't wanted to move the wedding?"

"Worst-case scenario, they'd take our gold as payment and she'd marry Zavier at the equinox."

Except this was the worst case. I was the worst case.

"Why would he choose me?"

A crease formed between Father's eyebrows. "I don't know."

"Does he suspect Mae was going to be a spy?"

"He'd be a fool not to. It's no secret every kingdom in Calandra is curious about Allesaria's whereabouts. But this is the only opportunity where they cannot refuse us."

An opportunity that only came with this marriage.

"I didn't think he'd dismiss Mae entirely," Father said. "A fault in my plan."

Planning, plotting, was how his mind worked. He trusted no one. He expected betrayal. And he was rarely surprised.

Mae's lip curled. "We should have left her out of this."

"You're probably right," he murmured.

But there had been no reason to exclude me today. I was a nothing princess content to blend into the walls and stand a pace behind my sister. I was Father's insignificant oldest daughter born to his dead wife. I was already engaged to his general and in no way competition to Mae's beauty or charm.

There had been no reason for anyone in my family to suspect I'd catch Prince Zavier's eye.

My hands began to shake. "I'm not a spy. I'm not a warrior. I'm sure as hell not an assassin. I can't do this." The last time I'd held a sword, the weapons master had shuffled me off to the infirmary because I'd sliced open my own palm.

"You will," Father commanded. "Repeat your orders."

I swallowed hard. "I am to find the way to Allesaria. Then I'm to learn about the Guardian's powers. And if I have the chance, you want me to kill him."

Another person.

He was asking me to take a life.

"Yes." Father's relief was palpable. "You can do this. You *must* do this. Then I will bring you home."

Impossible. When I sailed away from Quentis, I doubted I'd ever return.

Especially if—when—the Turans realized I was a spy.

Or when the Guardian killed me first.

"You must trust me," Father whispered. He brushed a kiss to my forehead, then stood and nodded to Margot. "Get her ready."

For my wedding. Tonight.

Six

Margot's growl filled my rooms. "Bring. Me. Blue."

"I'm sorry, Majesty." Brielle's cheeks were flushed, sweat beading at her temples and coating her brown hair. Above her upturned nose, her honey-colored eyes were panicked as she darted into the closet for the fifth time to trade the three gray gowns in her arms for three other gray gowns.

For the past four hours, Brielle had been racing around the castle, obeying each of my stepmother's sharp commands without fail. But finding a blue dress in my wardrobe? Impossible. We both knew that. Brielle was simply too sweet to stand up to Margot.

If Jocelyn were here, she would have told Margot from the beginning that I didn't have a stitch of blue. Except Jocelyn had been sent to the apothecary to collect contraceptive tea for us to take on the journey.

Since we'd left the throne room, Margot had done exactly as Father had instructed. With Brielle and Jocelyn's help, she'd prepared me for both a wedding and a cross-continental move.

I might not have a dress in the traditional wedding shade, but otherwise, they'd turned me into a bride.

All that pampering Mae had received this morning, they'd expedited for me this afternoon. A scalding hot bath had been drawn in my bathing chamber—I might not be able to justify my grandfather's extravagant gold plating on the castle, but I certainly enjoyed the interior plumbing. My skin was exfoliated, oiled, and scented.

Greenery was woven into my hair. Brielle had pinned it into an elaborate tangle of thick braids and twists that draped down my spine. Jocelyn had powdered my cheeks with peach rouge and stained my lips pink. There was shimmer on my lids and kohl lining my lashes. Bracelets adorned both wrists, and golden floral cuffs trailed along the shells of my ears.

In my twenty-three years, I'd never looked more beautiful. More like a princess. Yet each time I caught my reflection in the mirror, the sinking dread of what was to come would hit so hard I had to turn away again.

"You'll run out of this eventually." Margot stuffed jars of hair dye into one of three trunks stacked against the wall. "You'll need to find a market in Turah. Until then, wash your hair sparingly."

Prince Zavier had bargained for a brunette wife, so a brunette I would remain.

Margot slammed the lid of the trunk closed so hard I jerked in my seat at the vanity. With it closed and latched, she stood, surveying the room for anything she'd missed.

But all that remained was the furniture. My jewelry had been wrapped and stowed along with my soaps and creams and skin tonics. She'd sent me with three purses of gold coins. Jocelyn had packed away my sketchbook and favorite pencils. Brielle had folded my favorite dresses and stored them away with my intimates and slippers.

Was it good or bad that everything I owned fit into three trunks? One steward could move them all to a carriage in less than an hour.

There were a handful of books I would have liked to have taken, but they were in the castle's library, and when I'd asked to get them, Margot had told me there wasn't time. There were libraries in Turah, right?

Brielle rushed out of the closet with my palest gray dress. "This is the closest thing she has to a blue."

It wasn't even close to blue. Certainly not the bold, vibrant colors that most brides wore on their wedding days. The dress was almost white.

The color we clothed the dead.

The color we wore to funerals.

"Absolutely not," Margot clipped.

"It's perfect." I stood from the bench, and before Margot could take it from Brielle's hand, I snagged it and carried it behind the dressing screen.

"It's not blue," Margot said.

"It's good enough."

"We must have already packed your blue gowns."

I scoffed as I unfastened the satin robe I'd been wearing since my bath. Did she really not know I only had gray dresses? Or was she practicing the argument she'd use when Father asked why I was wearing the color of death for the ceremony?

The skirt was full and billowed from my hips to my feet. The top was made of embroidered lace, adorned with gray and white beads. A deep V in the back exposed the length of my spine.

"This dress is perfect. Mae can stab me in the back without any fabric getting in her way," I said.

"Odessa." I couldn't see her from behind the screen, but there probably was a frown on her face. "Let's not be dramatic."

A crash echoed beyond the nearest wall. It sounded like a vase being smashed against the floor.

I leaned past the screen and raised my eyebrows. "I'm dramatic?"

She was lecturing the wrong daughter.

Margot flicked her wrist. "Just get dressed."

Another crash came from next door.

While I was being primped and packed, my sister was throwing a tantrum the likes of which I hadn't seen since she was eight. Maybe when Mae finished trashing her room, she could move into mine.

It was empty now, devoid of anything *me*.

Clothed and ready, I stepped out from the screen, my gaze sweeping the space, stopping on the bed. The coverlet was wrinkled from where my belongings had been piled before being put into trunks. Would I get to sleep in this room again? Or would I be sharing Zavier's bed tonight? I shuddered.

"Brielle, leave us," Margot ordered.

"Yes, Majesty." My lady's maid curtsied and hastened to the door. She had her own packing to do if she was to accompany me to Turah.

Margot waited until the door clicked shut. "You'll need to bed him."

Shades. "Are we really having this conversation?"

I'd learned all about sex from a healer when I was thirteen. Whatever gaps she'd left in my education, the lady's maids had filled in. I did not need Margot's advice on how to sleep with my husband.

"Have you been with a man before? Banner or..."

When we'd gotten engaged, I'd wondered if Banner would want to have sex before the wedding. But Brielle had told me that he had a lover in the city. A woman he'd known for years.

Was he still sleeping with her? The idea of him with another had never bothered me. Maybe it would have after we had married, but that was no longer an issue, was it?

I'd never slept with Banner, but there'd been a boy once. When I was fifteen. A boy with freckled cheeks and an easy laugh. He'd worked in the stables.

Father must have found out that I'd been sneaking him into my rooms, because one day I'd gone to visit him at the stables and he'd left the city. How much had Father paid him to leave Roslo? Certainly not a chest of gold.

My value was going up. Good for me.

"Yes, I've been with a man before," I told Margot. "Next topic."

Did she drop it? Of course not. "Kings are powerful men. Powerful men often have…tastes."

"Margot." I cringed. "Please stop. I beg you."

I was curious by nature, but not where my father's tastes in the bedroom were concerned.

"There's a reason everyone looks the other way about Mae's escapades," Margot said.

Because Mae was practicing her seduction skills? Eww.

"You must please Zavier," she said. "The happier he is with you as his wife, the less he'll suspect ulterior motives."

Because a prince who was being fucked regularly became a fool? Possibly in Genesis or Ozarth or Laine or even Quentis. But I doubted Zavier was like other princes, not with his heritage.

Turah was nearly as much of a mystery as the Guardian.

Their rulers obeyed the Shield of Sparrows. They held up their obligations for trade and commerce, but only just. When it came to extending alliances, building relationships, and fostering unity, Turah might as well be a closed door.

Three generations ago, the crux had decimated the Turan capital city. Well, the former capital city. Before that migration, the Turan capital was Perris, a city on the coast. A mirror of Roslo across the Krisenth.

After that migration, rather than rebuilding his castle, the king had left it in ruins and moved his stronghold into the Turan mountains.

Allesaria.

To my knowledge, not a single foreign ruler had ever been invited to the Turan castle. It wasn't on Calandran maps. Its description could not be found in any book.

With every passing year, the secrecy surrounding Allesaria compounded. Was there really a way to save our people from the crux? What was hidden in the Turan capital that Father wanted so badly? Did other kings know? Or just Father?

He certainly wasn't the only king curious about Allesaria. People went in search of the city and never returned. Since no other king could force them to reveal its location, there was little to be done except let the Turans pull further and further away from diplomacy.

Until now.

Until the Sparrow.

There was a reason Mae had been trained so thoroughly since she was a child. She was to be the first foreign princess to enter Allesaria. She had the chance to tear down generations of mystery. To shine a light on a kingdom that seemed content to thrive in the dark.

And now that task had been given to me.

Zavier wasn't going to make it easy, was he? He'd watched us all too closely, too carefully, in the throne room. Did he suspect Father was up to something? There had to be more to this bride prize than Zavier wanting to marry someone other than Mae.

Maybe he'd taken one look at me and known I wouldn't be a threat.

Well, he'd be absolutely right.

Another crash echoed from Mae's room. She'd been at it for over an hour. What was left to break?

"Is there really no way out of this?" No way for Mae to take my place and disappear to a faraway land with a prince?

"You heard the Voster." Margot's expression softened, showing a hint of sympathy. "I'll tell your father you're ready."

Was I ready? Did it matter?

"Can I see Arthy before I go? I'd like to kiss him goodbye."

Margot nodded. "Of course."

"Thank you."

She smoothed the blond hair away from her face and swept out of the room.

It was too quiet with her gone, too empty. I listened for any sound, but Mae's room had gone silent, too.

If I didn't get to return here tonight, then there were a couple more things to pack. I slipped into my closet, going to the farthest corner. After a check over my shoulder to make sure I was truly alone, I crouched to the floor.

I tugged on the board closest to the wall. It popped loose, revealing a small compartment I'd stumbled upon when I was ten.

Mae and I had been playing hide-and-seek that day. She hated hiding, always preferring to be the seeker, but if my hiding place was too difficult, she'd get angry.

My sister wasn't only spoiled by Margot and Father. I'd spoiled Mae, too.

During our game that day, all those years ago, I'd tucked myself into this corner, hiding behind gray dresses as I waited for her to find me. The board had shifted beneath my foot, and I'd found this hiding spot.

I didn't know who'd had this room before my birth, but maybe another princess had used these rooms when she'd lived in this castle. Maybe a long-forgotten grandmother. I liked to think someone who shared my blood had used this compartment. That she'd been the one to pry the board loose the first time and tuck her keepsakes inside.

That the necklace I'd found thirteen years ago had been worn around her neck.

I fished out the leather journal I'd bought at the market this spring.

The first page was a sketch of Margot I'd drawn after witnessing a fight she'd had with Father. Her mouth was turned down, her face weathered and her eyes brimming with tears. It was a drawing I'd never show her. It was too real. Too raw.

Margot didn't like real or raw.

The second page was a drawing of Mae in the training center. Her mouth was stretched wide in a scream, her hands fisted at her sides. Sometimes I wondered if she screamed because there was so much piled on her shoulders.

Maybe she'd stop now that it had been loaded to mine.

Other than those couple of sketches, the pages were blank. I'd intended to fill them with drawings of Arthy or the castle or Banner or whatever else caught my eye. Instead, this book could keep my notes about Turah and the Guardian.

Beneath the book was my necklace. The delicate chain was coiled neatly. As I lifted it free, the pendant glinted in the light.

A wing of silver was inlaid in a circle of gold. Except it wasn't gold. The hue was red and orange and as bright as the harvest moon.

It was a symbol I'd never seen before. I'd scoured books in the library. I'd drawn it out and taken it to the docks to see if anyone recognized the design.

But after all these years, it remained a mystery.

I replaced the board, concealing the compartment, then stood, careful not to step on my gown's skirts. The journal was tucked into the last unopened trunk. The necklace I fitted into my dress, into the fabric that cupped my breast.

Until I reached Turah, until I felt safe enough to leave the necklace behind, it would stay with me.

The moment the pendant rested against my skin, it warmed. The metal seemed to absorb my body's heat faster than gold or silver. Or maybe it radiated that warmth on its own. It was as much an enigma as the symbol.

I was just walking out of the closet when the door to my rooms opened and Mae walked inside.

"All finished destroying your rooms?" I asked.

"So I broke a few things." She lifted a shoulder. "How would you feel if you'd spent your entire youth preparing and hoping for something only to have it ripped out of your grasp?"

"Angry."

She wasn't alone in that emotion. I was angry, too. But did I wreck my rooms?

"I want to be queen," she said.

"And I don't. But neither of us has a choice."

Mae took in my face, my dress, my hair. "You look beautiful."

"Thank you."

She sighed, her shoulders slumping. "Will you miss me? I'll miss you."

"Yes." I crossed the space between us, and even though I was the shorter, weaker sister, I hauled her into my arms.

She squirmed. My sister wasn't great at giving hugs, but I hugged her anyway. For every hug that I'd been denied, I always tried to give Mae two.

The same was true with Arthalayus. Every morning, I went to the nursery to hug my little brother.

I held Mae closer, tighter, until she finally sagged against my frame and hugged me back. She might be taller, stronger, prettier, but I was still her sister, and though it usually took coaxing, she indulged my hugs.

"You could still be a queen. Father will plan another marriage." To another prince in another kingdom.

Mae huffed a laugh. "He'll make me marry Banner."

It was possible. If there wasn't a prince available, a general was the next best match. And it would ensure Banner's loyalty to our family for years to come.

Arthy was only three. There were many years left in Father's reign, but as he got older, he needed loyal soldiers.

Margot had struggled to conceive after Mae was born. She'd had three stillborn babies in that time. But finally, before Father had found himself a new wife to give him a male heir, Margot had given birth to Arthalayus.

I wouldn't be here to watch him grow into a young man. I wouldn't know him, would I?

"You need to hug Arthy after I'm gone," I told her. "Promise me."

"I promise."

She was horrible with promises, but maybe this was one she'd keep.

We held each other for a few more heartbeats before she wiggled free. "Don't plan to return until you have the information Father wants."

Sister time was over. Back to business. "I won't."

"They will never trust you. Don't be fooled by any kindness."

"Kindness is bad. Got it."

She sighed. "You're going to make an awful spy."

"On that, we can agree." I laughed. "Any other advice?"

"Don't die." Mae touched the hair at my temple. "You must be ruthless, Dess."

Ruthless. We both knew that was her specialty, not mine. "I love you, Mae."

"I love you, too."

Before I could give her another hug, the door opened and Father strode inside, Margot trailing close behind.

Mae's demeanor shifted instantly. All softness vanished. She clasped her hands behind her back, shoulders pinned, looking more like one of the guards than a princess. Like Banner.

If Father did arrange their engagement, they might actually make a decent pair.

Father's caramel eyes assessed me from head to toe. His nostrils flared as he glanced over his shoulder to Margot. "You couldn't find her a blue dress?"

Margot's gaze dropped to the floor.

Father retrieved a glass vial and small knife from his coat pocket.

Without needing his instruction, I swallowed the bile rising in my throat and held out my hand. Gods. There was no going back, was there? Not after this.

Father took a firm hold of my fingers and dragged the knife across my skin.

Pain lanced through my palm, spreading up my arm. Tears swam in my eyes, but I blinked them away as Father tilted my hand and filled the vial with my blood, topping it with a cork. Then he wrapped a linen cloth around the wound. Three loops and a hard knot by my knuckles, like I was a soldier being bandaged on the battlefield.

I stole one last look at the view beyond my bedroom windows as the blood seeped through and speckled the cloth.

The ocean waves glittered beneath the clear blue sky. The sun cast Roslo in hues of yellow and orange as it dipped closer to the horizon.

Before it set tonight, I'd be a man's wife.

I should have stayed in the water earlier. I should have let the currents sweep me into the depths of the Marixmore and let the monsters of those ocean waters claim my flesh.

I should have kept swimming.

Seven

The castle's sanctuary was stuffy and hot. The scents of smoke and incense were so potent they singed my nostrils as Father escorted me through the carved doors.

Margot and Mae walked behind us, side by side. A stream of guards followed, the sound of their collective footfalls echoing through the dark, cramped space.

There were no windows to let in the sunlight. This sanctuary had been carved into the rocks below the castle as a place for people to worship the gods during the migration. The pews were empty tonight, but when the crux flew, the wooden benches would likely serve as both seats and beds to those who'd shelter within these walls.

I'd always planned to be with them. To spend the months of the migration in the rooms adjacent to the sanctuary that were reserved for Father and his family.

Was there a stronghold in Turah? Caverns and tunnels beneath the castle in Allesaria? Was that where they were hiding the information about the crux Father was after? Maybe there wasn't even a castle in Allesaria.

I'd find out soon enough.

The sanctuary was illuminated by hundreds of candelabras that battled against the dark shadows. When I was a girl, I'd asked a cleric how long it took them to light all of the candles each day. He'd told me that they never extinguished the flames, only replaced the candles that burned out—that way, they'd never be lost to Oda's gaze.

When I'd asked why they didn't just go outside to worship the Father, he scowled and summoned my tutor.

I'd learned two things that day. One: the sanctuary wasn't a great place to hide from my teachers. Two: the clerics weren't overly fond of the sun.

They didn't seem to venture far from their quarters in the castle, and since I avoided their two-hour vigils each evening at all costs, we rarely crossed paths.

I'd expected to see at least the Head Cleric tonight, this being a wedding ceremony and all, but the sanctuary was empty save for the two Voster priests already standing at the altar. Maybe their magic scared away the clerics.

The pinpricks on my skin were instant. Insufferable. And Quentin weddings were often three-hour affairs. I wasn't sure I could suffer through this sensation for that long.

"Where are the clerics?" I asked, my voice low enough for only Father to hear.

"There will not be a ceremony. Only the marriage decree and signing of the treaty."

"Oh." Why did I sound disappointed? At least this would be over quickly. Though that would mean I wouldn't have hours to delay joining Prince Zavier in his bedroom.

Did each Sparrow dread their wedding night this much? If I told Zavier I had a headache—not a lie—would he leave me alone? My insides roiled. Margot had told me to eat something earlier, but I'd refused. Maybe I should have scarfed down a plate of crackers and cheese. If I vomited bile on Zavier's boots at the altar, would he change his mind about this bride prize?

We stopped ten feet from the altar, and Father slipped out of my hold, leaving me with Margot and Mae as he went to speak to Brother Dime. They bent their heads together, voices too low for me to overhear.

I shifted so close to Mae that we touched, and something hard pressed against my side.

"How many knives do you have stashed in your gown?" I asked.

"A few. Why? Want to borrow one for your wedding night?" she whispered.

I pulled in my lips to hide a smile.

Father nodded to the High Priest, then turned to the guards at the sanctuary's entrance. With a wave of his hand, they opened the doors, and a heartbeat later, the Turans walked inside.

Zavier entered first, wearing the same attire he'd been in earlier. No finery or tailored coat. He looked more like one of his rangers than a prince, save for the silver circlet across his brow that glittered in the candlelight.

His four warriors trailed behind him, their expressions as solid and unreadable as their leader's. They seemed even larger than they had in the throne room. Deadlier.

"Sending you to Turah is a suicide mission," Mae murmured. There was genuine worry in her voice.

"Better me than you." I clasped her hand. Even with all her training, it would have been dangerous for Mae.

"No. Better *me* than you." She squeezed my hand once, then pulled away.

As with hugs, Mae wasn't the hand-holding type, either.

The last to enter the sanctuary was the Guardian. He ambled, his pace slower and more deliberate than the others, like he wouldn't be hurried down the aisle. His gaze was that hard, stony hazel. When it landed on me, the corner of his mouth turned up.

Smirking ass.

How much luck would I need to wipe it off his face? If I ever managed to catch him off guard, I'd sure try.

Maybe I could slip him poison. Add a few drops into a cup of wine when he wasn't watching. He seemed like the kind of man who was always watching, but still...

A girl could dream on her wedding day.

Father snapped his fingers, my cue to join him at the altar.

Mae nudged my elbow with hers as I lifted my skirts, and then I walked to Father's outstretched hand. He guided me up both steps until I was on the platform and standing beside a wooden table with a parchment scroll stretched across its smooth, glossy surface.

The Shield of Sparrows.

My stomach did another spin. This was really happening, wasn't it? There was no going back.

The treaty was simple and unadorned. Just ink on paper in a neat, clean script.

Ink. And blood.

I scanned the words on the treaty, my heart sinking deeper and deeper until it was resting beside my slippers. Zavier and I would sign this with our blood, and the Voster would seal it with their magic. Turah and Quentis would be tied together by this union. By the children I'd bear.

The document was the length of my arm, the script small but legible as it filled most of the parchment. Our ancestors had been thorough, I'd give them that. Was I supposed to read all of this?

The Turan rangers stopped beside Mae and Margot as Zavier climbed the stairs, taking his position at my side. The heat from his arm warmed mine. He smelled of soap and cedar.

It was nice. Clean and woodsy. At least he didn't stink of horses or other women.

Zavier's profile was granite, his eyes sweeping across the decree, line by line.

Okay, so we were reading this now.

I started at the top, but the sentences blended together. The words blurred. It might as well have been written in the old language that the clerics still used at times. There were too many eyes watching for me to concentrate, and that damn Voster magic was irritating my skin.

Focus, Odessa. I drew in a deep breath, closed my eyes for a long moment, then started again. If I was signing this thing in blood, I should at least have an idea of what was written.

The beginning explained the history of the treaty. The obligation of the five kingdoms to offer a king, or future king, and a Sparrow every generation.

The first bride's name had been Sparrow, hence the treaty's name and why the woman offered every generation had since been called the Sparrow. Her father, the Turan king, had given her as a bride to his sworn enemy, the Genesis king.

Would I learn about the original Sparrow in Turah? Did they praise her sacrifice for her kingdom? Was she honored with statues and paintings? Or had she been forgotten like the others from generations lost?

A Sparrow from Ozarth had been given to my great-great-grandfather. I didn't know her name or if she'd been a good queen. Did Mae know who she was? Maybe if I'd been given time to prepare for this, I could have done some research.

I sighed. If I didn't know about her, then she probably hadn't been a bad queen.

Father cleared his throat, likely sensing that my mind was wandering.

I blinked, refocusing on the page.

Trade obligations. Stipulations forbidding one kingdom from invading another. And then, the laws that bound husband to wife.

A King cannot kill his Sparrow, and a Sparrow cannot kill her King,

either directly or indirectly, without death befalling them both.

Death.

The word leaped off the parchment. Whatever magic the Voster held in their veins, when they infused it into this decree, when it mingled with our blood, I would die if I killed Zavier.

Good to know.

Beneath the declarations were five scrawled names. The signatures of the five original kings. Their blood hadn't faded over time. It looked as dark as ink, as fresh as if it had been signed moments ago, not centuries.

The kings who had followed didn't need to agree to these terms. It had been done for them by those original five. Any man who wore a crown was obligated to adhere.

Being king came with rules. The rules outlined in this treaty.

Sure, there were squabbles, especially along borders between nations. But kings were expected to maintain peace.

And the magic that radiated off the parchment enforced its intent.

There weren't lines and lines of specific dos and don'ts. Maybe that's what made the treaty so terrifying. And brilliant.

Kings had to interpret what it meant to enforce this treaty's will. They had to play nicely with their fellow rulers. Except who decided what was nice?

The vague, invisible limitations meant rulers were on their best behavior at all times. If not, they'd be dead.

Father had told me that treaties could be broken. How? This magic was too powerful. Too old. It rippled off the parchment, adding to the sting of the Voster's magic as he stood watch over the treaty. If Father truly intended to bring troops to Allesaria, the moment he acted, this ancient magic would take his life. Wouldn't it?

Father cleared his throat again. "Are you finished?"

I nodded, eyes fixed on the names etched beneath those of the five kings.

Tanis Oak
Sparrow Wolfe

The first king. The first Sparrow.

Wasn't it ironic that Genesis royals were named for a tree when they weren't known for their lumber?

Beneath Tanis and Sparrow's names were a litany of others. More Oaks. More Wolfes. Crosses, Harrows, and Kasans. Each of the royal last names was included.

It was a list three hundred years in the making.

And soon, it would include mine.

"What happens when there's no more room on this page? Will you move signatures to the back?"

Father growled. "Odessa."

"Sorry." I gave him an exaggerated frown.

He knew I asked questions when I was nervous. Honestly, he should have expected it.

I ducked my chin, feeling the heat of numerous gazes on my cheeks. When I risked a glance up, every pair of male eyes was aimed my way. Even the Voster's.

Were the priests men? We called them the brotherhood, but had anyone asked their preference?

I kept those questions inside and looked to Zavier.

Unlike the others, he was still staring straight ahead at the wall. Expressionless.

Was he this blasé about everything? Or just this marriage? Why claim a bride prize if you didn't want anything to do with said bride?

A low chuckle filled the room.

My attention whipped to the source.

The Guardian.

How was any of this funny? I gave him my fiercest glare.

He laughed again.

Poison. I was definitely poisoning that man. Was it bad to plot someone's murder while you were in a sanctuary for the gods? I mentally signed the Eight, just in case.

The Guardian, still wearing that smirk, nodded to the High Priest. Why did the jackass act like he was in charge of this disaster?

"We will begin." The High Priest's smooth voice was at odds with his prickling magic.

Zavier turned to face me, holding out his hands. For the first time, the empty expression cracked, and he gave me a tight smile.

Well, at least he wasn't laughing.

I wiped my clammy palms on my skirt before I placed them in his, one bandaged in a cloth like mine. Then I met his moss-green eyes. They were alert and assessing. He studied me as if he could read every thought racing through my mind.

Maybe he could pluck out a few of my questions and give me some hints.

"Odessa Cross." As the High Priest spoke, I stood taller, swallowing the lump in my throat. "Do you vow to uphold the Shield of Sparrows with your union to Zavier Wolfe, prince and future king of Turah?"

What would Father do if I refused? I'd endured enough of his punishments in my lifetime that I didn't want to find out.

My eyes darted to Father. He didn't so much as blink back, but the unspoken command in his gaze was unmistakable.

Vow it. Now.

Panic bubbled in my chest, my breaths short and shallow. Forget vomiting at my wedding, I might pass out.

It was too hard to hold Father's stare, so I glanced around the altar, looking first to Zavier, then the Voster priests. My gaze landed on the Guardian. On the challenge waiting in his swirling silver eyes.

Was I going to speak or not?

"I, Odessa Cross, make this vow." It came out in a rush. A whisper.

"Zavier Wolfe," the High Priest continued. "Do you vow to uphold the Shield of Sparrows with your union to Odessa Cross, princess of Quentis and future queen of Turah?"

Zavier waved a hand to the Guardian.

"Will you speak on his behalf?" the High Priest asked.

"Yes. I speak on the prince's behalf." The Guardian's baritone timbre filled the sanctuary. It was deeper than it had been in the throne room. It held an edge sharper than any of Mae's blades. "Zavier Wolfe makes this vow."

The High Priest reached into a pocket of his robe, retrieving a simple quill. He held it out with long, gnarled fingers and those curled nails.

Father took it from his grip and pulled the vial of my blood from his pocket. With a push of his thumb on the cork, it popped free. He handed me both.

A vow was one thing. A verbal promise that could be broken. This was the real choice. To sign my name. Once it was on that treaty, there was no going back.

I hesitated, staring at the names laid out before me. How many of those brides had gone unwillingly? They'd made their sacrifices for their kingdoms. For the good of Calandra. For peace.

If they could do it, then so could I.

Squaring my shoulders, I dipped the quill into my blood and pressed it to the paper, my hand steadier than it should have been as I wrote my name.

Odessa Cross

Eleven letters. And my life would never be the same.

I gave the quill to Zavier, unable to meet his gaze as he took it from my grip.

He pulled a vial of his blood from his pocket, holding it so tightly in his fist that I feared the glass would crack. It was the same fist wrapped with a cloth, similar to mine.

We'd have matching scars after this.

Without delay, he dipped the quill and signed his name with a flick of his wrist.

The air rushed from my lungs, a wave of dizziness making me unsteady.

The High Priest took the quill, tucking it into the same pocket of his robes. Then he closed his eerie eyes and placed both hands on the decree. Magic flared like invisible sparks, bombarding me from every direction, burning through my dress, sinking into my skin.

I slammed my eyes closed and gritted my teeth to keep from crying out as I rode the wave of pain until it ebbed.

"It is done."

My eyes flew open at Brother Dime's statement.

The High Priest was already rolling up the decree, stowing it in a black leather sleeve. Without another word, he and Brother Dime descended the altar and left the sanctuary.

That was it? We were done? It was over, and I was married?

There'd been no fanfare. No ceremony. No kiss.

Zavier was staring at the wall again, jaw clenched like a ten-minute wedding had been too long.

My husband.

I was his wife.

And he couldn't look at me.

Numbness crept into my limbs. Coldness settled on my skin.

"We shall honor your marriage with a feast." Father extended an arm toward the sanctuary's doors, motioning for us to go first.

He was usually the last to leave a room, save his guards, to ensure no one could stab him in the back.

Zavier tore his gaze from the wall and settled it on Father. With a quick shake of his head, he declined the feast.

Fine by me. My stomach was too twisted for food. Though the idea of wine, a lot of wine, didn't sound so bad.

Zavier stared down at me, inching closer. My heart climbed into my throat as he took my chin between his index finger and thumb, tilting it up.

An expression flashed in those green eyes. Finally, he showed some emotion. Too bad I couldn't tell what it was. Sadness, maybe? Pity? Both?

He brushed his mouth across my cheek. Then he was gone, his hand falling to his side, as he looked over his shoulder to the Guardian. Like they had in the throne room, the two men shared a silent conversation. Then Zavier nodded once and walked off the altar.

His rangers fell into step behind him, marching for the doors.

Was I supposed to go with them? Now that this was over, who did I belong with? The Quentins? Or the Turans?

Father's hands fisted at his sides. His nostrils flared as Zavier disappeared from sight.

My father was a powerful king and unaccustomed to being slighted. Since Zavier had arrived, he'd refused Father at every turn.

I had no envy for the person who'd be on the receiving end of his terrible mood. I really, *really* hoped it wouldn't be me.

Stepping forward, I was about to follow after the Turans out of the sanctuary—definitely not to follow Zavier to his wing. No, my plan was to ditch this dress and sneak out of the castle. Except before I could descend the altar, a low chuckle made me stop.

That damn laugh was getting all too familiar.

I whirled. "Yes?"

The Guardian remained by the table, arms crossed over his broad chest, that signature smirk firm on his lips. "Eager to chase Zavier to his room, my queen?"

Margot's gasp filled the sanctuary as heat flamed in my cheeks.

Now it was my turn to fist my hands at my sides. To grind my molars together so hard my jaw ached.

Poison was too good for the Guardian. Too easy. I was going to kill that man with my own two hands. Maybe a knife sliced across his throat while he was sleeping. Or an arrow shot straight through his heart while he was enjoying his midday meal.

Whatever fury he saw in my eyes only made that arrogant grin widen.

He shoved off the table, not sparing my father a glance as he passed me for the stairs. "Enjoy your last night in Quentis, Sparrow. We sail at dawn."

Eight

A yawn stretched my mouth as I stood on the docks, staring at the sun cresting the horizon. Margot would be aghast that I hadn't covered my mouth for that yawn, or the countless others since leaving the castle, but she wasn't here.

No one was here except the guards who'd ridden behind my carriage this morning.

This was the first time I'd visited the docks at dawn, before the shops and merchants were open for business. Men and women bustled about, setting up their stores and readying for the day. The scents of fish and brine were not as strong as they would be by midday. The walkways were empty and larger than I'd realized, since they weren't crowded with people.

"Pardon me, Highness." A steward with stringy blond hair and a lanky build passed by, carrying one of my three identical trunks destined for one of three identical Turan ships.

Zavier and his warriors had yet to arrive, but the ships' crews were busy preparing to set sail, loading the boxes of supplies along the docks.

Nerves churned in my stomach like the waves slapping against the piers. At least, I thought it was nerves. Maybe I was just hungry.

My wedding feast had been canceled, not that I'd been upset to miss a formal dinner. But any dinner would have been nice.

Instead, Father had taken me to his private study for spy lessons, and the meal had been forgotten entirely. So had sleep.

He'd kept me in his study all night, poring over maps and the information he'd gathered about Turah. He'd gone on and on and on about his theories of Allesaria's location until an hour ago, when Margot had come to collect me to change out of my wedding gown and into a dress suitable for travel.

Father had gone off to find breakfast.

When I'd asked for a scone or pastry or a handful of crackers, Margot had told me I could eat on the boat. That must have been her way of saying I was Zavier's problem now.

Hopefully one of the Turan crewmen was a cook. Or could point me in the direction of a snack.

The steward nodded as he passed me again, hands empty, off to fetch trunk number two.

Where was everyone? Where were Father and Margot and Mae and Arthalayus? They were coming, right? They wouldn't let me leave without a farewell, would they?

That I even had to wonder made my nose sting with the threat of tears.

It was the exhaustion. The hunger. I was on the brink of an emotional meltdown, and all I could hope for now was that I could have it alone.

My hand reached for the necklace I'd put on this morning during my carriage ride, pulling the pendant from the neckline of my plain, gray dress. I wrapped it in my hand, the metal warm against my skin, its weight a comfort.

Would I ever get to come back to Roslo? Would I see these docks again?

Would I see my family?

Maybe it was a good thing that Father hadn't left me alone last night. He hadn't given me the chance to let all of this sink in. To break down and cry.

Except I was alone now, staring at those ships, and there was no way to avoid the inevitable.

I was leaving Roslo today. I was leaving home.

The steward passed me again, this time with a quick nod, as he carted my trunk. Soon, he'd grab the third, and then it would be over. He'd drive the carriage back to the castle while I stood here alone.

I couldn't stand here alone. I couldn't stand here at all. Anxious energy made my legs and arms twitch, so I spun away from the ships and set off along the docks.

"Princess?" one of the guards called.

"I'm going for a walk," I told him.

"But—"

"Alone."

He gave me a slight bow. "Princess."

Would he follow me? Absolutely. He was assigned to me but did not take my orders. But as long as he kept his distance, I didn't care.

My slippers were quiet on the uneven boards beneath my feet, the wood creaking with my weight every few steps. The smell of cooked eggs and salted meat from a nearby building made my stomach growl.

A man toting a basket of fish did a double take as I walked by his open stall. His dark-brown eyes widened at my crown—an accessory Margot had insisted upon. He set the basket down so abruptly it tipped over as he rushed to bow. "H-Highness."

"Good morning." I walked over to help him right the basket, but as I bent for a silver fish, he waved me off.

"No, Princess. Please leave them. Your hands will smell."

A princess with fishy hands. Gods forbid.

I left him to his work and continued walking, earning more startled glances the farther I meandered along the docks.

My favorite paperman's shop was closed, the windows curtained to hide his printing press. Were there papermen in Turah? I hoped so. I loved reading the weekly periodicals.

Some papers were reserved for fictional stories. Others spun gossip from the city. And then there were those who reported on actual events, like crimes and celebrations.

There were enough papers in Roslo that a handful would arrive at the castle each day. The servants would pass them around like sweets. Margot had her own subscriptions. So did Mae. So did I.

Too bad I hadn't thought to grab some to read on the voyage.

The papermen all had actual offices and buildings, but most of the merchants at the docks operated out of open stalls. At night, they'd cover them with canvas tarps. But those tarps had been tossed over the slanted roofs this morning, pushed aside to reveal tables and baskets and displays. From fish to fruit to herbs to jewelry to tonics to cloth, there wasn't much a person couldn't buy at the docks in Roslo.

These walkways were always busy, always crowded. Except today. People openly gawked as I passed by. Others ducked out of sight. Without the normal crush of customers, it was impossible to blend in. To hide amidst the masses.

Not with this damn crown on my head.

What if I tossed it in the ocean?

I laughed to myself, imagining Margot's face. Oh, it was tempting. If it wouldn't be an incredible waste of wealth, I'd pitch it today. But the gold and gems were worth enough to feed a family for a generation.

So it stayed on my head while I kept walking. Maybe I could take it apart, piece by piece, and leave jewels sprinkled across Turah.

"Seven." A man's voice caught my ear. "Have you ever seen seven marroweels?"

"Shades no. I've never seen one." Another man laughed, both walking so quickly they didn't seem to notice me listening.

The marroweels.

Here I was wandering aimlessly when I should have been seeking out the monsters.

The notion of seeing an actual marroweel gave me a burst of energy, and I changed paths, following the men. We veered away from the market and down a long dock bordered on one side by Quentin ships bobbing in the water, their teal sails tied and stowed.

A group of men were clustered at the end of the walkway. Beside them were the tall support beams where fishermen hung the largest catches from their fleets on massive iron hooks.

But instead of sturgeon and shark, today those hooks pierced a row of dead marroweels.

Seven marroweels. For the Chain of Sevens.

Up until yesterday, I'd never loathed a number. Oh, how things had changed.

"Seven," I spat, walking closer to the monsters.

The marroweel scales were as blue as sapphires and tipped in turquoise. The fins along their backs were iridescent, like opals. The single bones that extended from their skulls were smooth and as white as snow. Their mouths were open wide in death to reveal five rows of razor-sharp teeth.

They were thicker than I'd imagined, twice the width of a man. And so long that even when they were skewered in the middle, their tails coiled on the dock's boards like thick ropes.

"Wow," I whispered.

It drew the attention of the man standing closest. He looked to me once, then again, eyes bulging as he noticed my crown. "P-Princess."

One stammered word was all it took for the others to face me. Like the man with the basket, each fumbled a bow.

"Pardon, Highness." A man wearing a weathered blue cap yanked it off his bald head as he shuffled past.

The others were soon to follow, retreating back toward the marketplace. Apparently, not even the allure of a marroweel was enough to keep them in my presence.

Was my crown really that scary? I'd never worn one to the docks before. I guess I could answer my own question this time.

Twenty feet away, attempting to blend in with the boats, my guard let out a visible exhale as the men passed by. Their leaving gave me a chance to step closer to the monsters.

Beneath their open mouths were seven pools of blood, the dried red so dark it was nearly black. It had dripped from their bodies into puddles. What blood hadn't trickled through the slats in the dock's planks, falling into the water below, was now hard and beginning to crust.

I dropped to a crouch beside the first marroweel, taking in its black eyes. Four in total, two in front, two on the sides. If there were other predators in the ocean deep, this beast would see them coming.

There was something sleek and delicate about the marroweel's face. A monster both beautiful and deadly. Yet there was something sad in those lifeless eyes. Maybe that was me simply projecting my own heartache.

This monster had died so a prince could manipulate a king. So a man could force a woman into marriage.

To hell if my hands would smell like fish. I reached for a scale, its size similar to my thumbnail, and traced along the bright-blue surface to the turquoise tip. I gasped as a jolt of pain shot through my finger and jerked my hand away to see a bead of blood.

"Those scales are as sharp as their teeth." A deep, rumbling voice came from over my shoulder.

I shot to my feet and spun. Behind me, the Guardian leaned against a wooden post. Where had he come from? How had I not heard him approach? I must have missed it while inspecting the marroweel. That, or he could disguise his footsteps when it suited him best. Maybe he could levitate like the High Priest. I made a mental note to watch out for it later—and to watch my back.

Besides the two of us, the dock was empty. He'd either dismissed my guard or chased him away.

"Morning, my queen." The corner of the Guardian's mouth turned up as I wiped the blood from my finger on the skirt of my dress.

He shoved off the post and walked closer. Too close. He towered over me, staring down with those ever-changing eyes. Today, they were a vibrant green, like emeralds. "Have you ever seen one before?"

"No."

"Aren't they beautiful?" He passed me, his strides long and unhurried as he walked from one marroweel to another to another. Down the entire line until he'd reached the last, the largest. His movements were too fluid, too graceful, to be entirely human.

He walked with the same effortlessness as the Voster.

Was he linked to the brotherhood? Was that the source of his power? Their magic?

Last night, during Father's lessons in espionage, he'd spoken about the Guardian nearly as often as he had Allesaria. His desperation to find the source of this man's powers was nearly as palpable as his need for information on the Turan capital.

The Guardian placed his hand on the monster's side and stroked its scales.

I tensed, expecting him to withdraw a bloody palm, but his hand was unmarred as he pulled away to face me with that annoying smirk.

"Nice crown."

I should have given it to that merchant with the fish.

"Thank you." I plastered on a sweet smile.

"Is that what you've put in your trunks? Crowns and jewels?"

"My belongings are none of your business." I crossed my arms over my chest, raising my chin as he walked my way, his boots a steady drum on the dock's boards.

They matched the pounding rhythm of my heart as he stopped before me with that broad frame. He was so tall that my eyes were level with his heart, and to keep his gaze, I had to tilt up my face. As I did, his eyes shifted to the brightest of greens, like a Quentis meadow after a spring rain.

Those eyes were dazzling. Terrifying. A shiver rolled down my spine. This man was a murderer. He shouldn't have such enchanting eyes.

My guard shouldn't have left me alone.

"Our ships are not known for their royal finery. How ever will you survive the crossing?" he taunted.

I shrugged. "I'm certain that if my husband can endure days without his royal finery, I'll manage just fine. No need to concern yourself with my well-being. In fact, maybe it would be best if you forgot about me completely. I'd rather not associate with a killer."

The way his eyes narrowed, that smirk faltering, he had to know I was talking about Banner's brother.

The air around us changed. Charged. There was a buzzing against my skin, but it didn't feel like Voster magic. It didn't have the same crackling bite.

The Guardian's power felt more like simmering rage. It pulsed off his frame in waves.

A smarter woman would probably have shied away. Taken that sensation as the warning it was to watch her mouth. But I was too tired and too hungry, and this man had crawled under my skin.

What was he going to do, kill his prince's bride?

He wouldn't kill me. Right?

The Guardian's gaze dragged over my face, lingering so long I fought the urge to squirm. "You look tired. Long night? I hope you weren't up late saying farewell to your fiancé."

"Also none of your business."

"Isn't it? You're married to the heir to the Turan throne. Your children will be of his line. I'd say that I have every right to be concerned with the seed you allow between your legs."

My face flamed, my jaw dropping as I stepped away like I'd been struck. "You did not say that to me."

He lifted a shoulder.

This. Asshole. "Who do you think you are?"

His answer was to lean in so close I caught his scent. It was masculine and spicy, like leather and citrus. It was an ocean breeze and fresh earth and heavy rain. It was as chaotic as his eye color.

They shifted again, his irises darkening to hazel. The green and gold and brown seemed to war with each other as they swirled, unable to settle into a single shade.

His hand snaked around my waist, spinning me so fast that I gasped. Then, with a shove against my spine, he urged me forward.

Or tried to urge me forward.

My toe caught on a deck board, and I lost my balance, staggering to the side and nearly crashing into a marroweel's corpse.

Except the Guardian gripped my arm before I could collide with those pointed scales. He grabbed the exact place where Margot had held me yesterday. There were no bruises yet, but it was tender.

A whimper escaped my throat, and he released me instantly, taking a step away. I shook off the pain in my arm and straightened, leveling him with a glare. "What is it that you want? To embarrass me? To intimidate me?"

"Perhaps."

Well, at least he was honest. I glanced over my shoulder to the marroweel. "Then I guess I'm trapped between two monsters."

"You have no idea how accurate that statement is," he muttered, stepping closer. "Your arm. Are you all right?"

"It's fine." I waved it off. "Just an injury from earlier."

He frowned, looking like he wanted the details of that injury. But instead of asking, he reached for my hair, plucking the end of a loose curl off my shoulder.

It was only half pinned up today. Margot hadn't wanted to bother with a braid.

The moment the lock was between his fingers, his nostrils flared, like he could smell the dye. With a sneer, he dropped it and wiped his fingers on his pants. He turned and walked away, snapping his fingers at me like I was a dog that needed to heel.

"Come along, Sparrow. You're late."

What if I pushed him overboard while we were at sea? Let the ocean do the killing for me.

I almost liked the idea of watching that son of a bitch drown.

Nine

Father, Margot, and Mae stood in a line dockside beside the Turan ships. Their spines were stiff, posture perfect with hands clasped and crowns gleaming in the faint rays of dawn.

They'd come to say goodbye.

The relief at seeing them was so great it knocked the wind from my lungs and drove my feet to a stop.

They came.

On the walk back from the marroweels, I'd convinced myself it didn't matter if they skipped this send-off. That I wouldn't be hurt, knowing that Father had promised to bring me home when my spying was complete. I'd been sure they wouldn't show.

But there they were, each dressed in bold teal. And they looked as miserable as I felt.

The Guardian shot me a scowl over his shoulder when he realized I was no longer trailing behind him. But he didn't snap his fingers again, didn't summon me to hurry up. He continued past my family without sparing them a glance.

It was nearly time to go. The docks were empty, the supplies loaded onto the ships along with my trunks. I searched for my two lady's maids and found Brielle boarding the middle ship alone. Jocelyn must already be on deck. The crew on the lead boat was untying the ropes wrapped around the dock cleats.

I tried to move but couldn't. Every mental command for my legs to walk was ignored.

How did I say goodbye? What if this was the end? What if I never saw my family again?

What if I failed? What if everyone I loved was killed in the migration?

Father tore his focus from a Turan ship and found me standing frozen, twenty paces away. Had he always had that much gray in his hair? Or had those sprouted sometime in the night as he'd realized I was not cut out for this task?

When Mae noticed me, her blue eyes softened, like she knew I was stuck. She stepped away from Margot's side and came to mine, looping our arms together. With a tug, she forced me to move. "You look lovely this morning."

"Thank you." Not for the compliment, but for coming to the docks. For being here so I wouldn't have to do this alone. My heart was beating so hard, and the burn in my throat warned that tears were on their way. Crying would only annoy Father, so I gulped it down.

"If you're going to cry, don't," she said, like she could read my mind. "You're ugly when you cry."

I laughed, something I didn't think would have been possible this morning. "Demon."

"Admit it. You'll miss me."

"Never." I leaned my head on her shoulder as she led me forward.

She slowed our pace, nearly dragging me backward so we wouldn't reach Father and Margot so soon. "Be careful around the Guardian."

"You think?" I deadpanned. "I hadn't considered he might be dangerous."

"I'm serious. You must always be on guard. And you must not trust them. Father needs to find Allesaria."

"Wait." I pulled her to a stop and waited until she faced me. "Do you know what he's planning?"

"Of course."

Of course. Silly me for thinking we were all in the dark. Nope, just me.

I was being taken to Turah and ordered to steal their secrets. I'd been married off to a prince and forced to sign an ancient, magical treaty in my blood. I'd done everything required of a princess in my station with barely an objection.

Yet he hadn't wanted to give me all of his truths. He hadn't given me his complete trust.

I'd learned a long time ago to live without his affection. His love. But damn it, no matter how hard I tried, I wanted his trust. His confidence.

Why would he share his intentions with Mae but not me? Was it because she had a vicious streak? Because she was bold and cunning? Because she knew how to wield a sword and win in a fight?

Regardless of the reason, he'd chosen her to be the Sparrow. He always chose her.

All I'd ever done was serve him. All I'd ever done was as he'd asked. All I'd ever done was try to make him see me.

What was it going to take?

Maybe the only way I'd earn his trust was by finding the road to Allesaria.

And by murder.

Would he trust me if I killed the Guardian? Did he care that I'd likely be the one to die instead?

"You can do this," Mae said, lowering her voice. "Get to Allesaria. Send word as soon as possible. And while you're at it, cut out the Guardian's heart."

There was the beloved sister I knew.

"You make assassination sound so simple," I muttered, facing forward.

I was met with a molten silver gaze from the man standing on the middle ship's deck.

The Guardian glared at me so intensely that a tremble rocked me on my heels. There was no way he could have overheard us from that far away, but the way he sneered, the way his jaw clenched, made me wonder if he'd heard every word.

Gods. Was that one of his powers?

Margot stepped in front of me, blocking the Guardian from sight as she put her hands on my shoulders. "Be careful."

"I will."

She pulled me into a hug, speaking into my ear. "You are strong, Odessa. Stronger than you realize."

Margot had been the only mother I'd ever known, but she wasn't a woman to deliver praise. It was as foreign as it was welcome, like a raindrop to a dying plant.

She let me go as quickly as she'd pulled me into her arms, then dabbed at the corners of her dry eyes.

Maybe it was all for show. Today, I'd take the performance, even if it was fake.

"Where's Arthy?" I glanced around, searching for my brother. Was he still in their carriage?

"Asleep." An unspoken *obviously* hung between us. "It's scarcely dawn."

"But I didn't get to say goodbye."

She'd told me she'd bring him. That I could see him, hug him, before I left. If he wasn't here, then I'd leave and there was a very real chance I'd never see him again. That burn in my throat returned with a vengeance.

"You'll see him again." She waved it off.

What if I didn't? Would he even remember me? I opened my mouth, but there was nothing to say. It was too late. I was leaving.

Father took Margot's place, standing before me with his strong hands on my shoulders. With a jerk of his chin, he sent Margot and Mae away, leaving us alone.

His caramel eyes held mine, as gentle as I'd ever seen. If it was an act, too, I refused to believe it. "You can do this."

"I'll try." I gave him a sad smile. "For you."

His large frame deflated as he wrapped me in his arms. "I've made so many mistakes as your father. I'm sorry. Your mother would be so disappointed in me."

The shock of that statement squelched the threat of tears. He never spoke of my mother. None of them did. And he'd apologized. Who was this man, and where was my cold, proud father?

"Remember all that I told you," he murmured, his voice barely a whisper.

"I will."

"Good." He loosened his hold, but before he could let me go, I held him tighter.

"Can you really save us from the crux? Will you break the Shield of Sparrows?" This was my only chance to ask. I doubted he'd tell me, but I had to try.

"I will try. But I must get into Allesaria before the migration."

"Why? What is in the city that you're looking for? If you tell me, maybe I could help find it."

"That burden is not for you to carry."

No, but he'd given it to Mae.

"How is it even possible? I read the treaty. If you invade, you'll be going against its stipulations." There weren't many noted in detail, but that had been a definite rule. "You're the king of Quentis. You'll die."

"I have no intention of dying. Not any time soon."

"But—"

"No more questions." He let me go and backed away. "I'm asking for your trust, Odessa. Do I have it?"

I gave him mine but didn't get his in return. It wasn't fair. But I spoke without hesitation. "Yes."

He closed his eyes, relief tempering his features. "Good."

Maybe I didn't have all the details. But he was my father. My king. In my lifetime, all I'd ever seen him do was what he thought best for his people. And I was still one of his people, no matter how far I sailed away.

He cupped my face with a hand, his thumb tracing along my cheek. His gaze shifted to my hair, to the crown. "I never should have allowed Margot to dye your hair. The red was your mother's."

"You told me." A long, long time ago. When I was a little girl and he hadn't forgotten Mother yet.

"Be that as it may, the brown suits you." He kissed my forehead, then shifted to the side, elbow extended to escort me to the center ship.

A wooden walkway connected the boat to the dock.

Father loosened his hold and, with his hand on the small of my back, urged me on.

Alone.

A Turan man with narrow gray eyes was waiting on the other side, his hand outstretched to help me down the single step and onto the deck. The moment both of my feet were firmly planted on board, he reached past me and hauled in the walkway.

Wood clattered against wood as he secured it against the ship's wall, then closed the door at my back, flipping its metal latch. Then he was gone, joining the others as they shouted to one another, every person on the ship ready to leave Roslo.

My knees wobbled, either from the swaying motion of the ship or the realization that this was it. Without that walkway, I was no longer tethered to Quentis. To home.

"Highness." Brielle rushed to my side, her cheeks flushed and her straight brown hair escaping the knot at her nape. After a quick bob, she motioned to the rear of the ship. "Come with me. Jocelyn is waiting. I was told we were to stay out of the way."

Meaning she was told to keep *me* out of the way.

I had no desire to mingle with the Turans, so I let her lead me up the stairs of the quarterdeck, past the captain's post, to the far railing along the stern.

As the sails were hoisted, the noise from the men faded. The water lapped at the ship's hull as we rocked side to side.

Jocelyn dipped into a curtsy as we approached. "Highness."

There were tear tracks down her cheeks, and the color had leached from her face. Her wavy blond hair was like Brielle's, knotted but in disarray.

Leaning against the wooden railing, I settled between the two. They were both taller than me with luscious curves. I'd always envied their figures. I probably looked like a girl among women with my slender frame and scrawny arms.

I wasn't like Margot or Mae. When we were children, even though Mae was younger, if there was ever a squabble with another child, I'd let her fight them for me. I'd let her be the one to push and punch.

Asking Jocelyn and Brielle to fight my battles wouldn't be right. Somehow, I'd have to find the strength to do that on my own. How? I had no idea.

"How long have you been here?" I asked Jocelyn.

"Not long," she said. "I've been belowdecks, situating our room."

"*Our* room?"

"The man who helped me aboard said we'd all be staying together."

So I wouldn't be sharing quarters with Zavier. "Fine by me."

"Last night. Was it…" Brielle looked behind us, ensuring we were alone. "Was it unpleasant?"

I hadn't seen her since she left my rooms yesterday, so it made sense that she'd think my night had been spent in Zavier's bed, not my father's study.

"He hasn't asked for me to join him in bed yet, and I have no plans to until he does."

"Oh." She opened her mouth like she was going to say something else, then closed it with a click.

Mae would probably have kept that fact to herself. She usually let her lady's maids believe whatever it was they believed, giving no answers to personal questions. She let them gossip, even when the rumors they spread were false.

But Brielle and Jocelyn would be my only allies on this journey. Eventually, we might even become friends. I didn't want to start that friendship with a lie.

"Have you seen him? The prince?" I asked.

"No, Highness," Jocelyn said.

Maybe Zavier had chosen another boat. Maybe, if Daria, the Goddess of Luck, was on my side—she rarely was—the Guardian would have slipped onto that other boat, too.

There was a crowd gathering on the docks. Besides my family and the royal guard, a group of merchants and vendors had wandered over to watch us depart. A cluster of soldiers gathered beside Margot's carriage.

Banner hadn't come. I hadn't seen him since the throne room.

It would have been nice to say goodbye, but it was probably for the best that he stayed away.

"There's my mother." Jocelyn pointed toward a woman standing apart from the others. Her hair was the same wavy blond as her daughter's. "She made me promise to return."

I hoped that in some way, I could help her keep that promise.

"Is your family here?" I asked Brielle.

She swallowed hard, shaking her head. "No, Highness. With such short notice, all I could do was send them a letter."

Her parents had a farm in Quentis. It was enough to sustain them and her brother's family, but she'd had to leave for work in the city. And their farm was too far away for word to reach them in less than a day.

Maybe I should have insisted on taking Mae's lady's maids instead. They'd known for over a year that they'd be leaving Quentis. They'd had time to prepare. In the whirlwind since the throne room, I hadn't thought to challenge Father and Margot's orders that Brielle and Jocelyn were to accompany me to Turah.

This bride prize, this godsforsaken marriage, had disrupted more lives than just my own.

"I'm sorry."

She lifted a shoulder. "It's not your fault."

"I'm still sorry."

"Thank you." Her voice wobbled as she sniffled.

We settled into a solemn quiet as we stared at Roslo.

Would I return to my beloved city? Would I ever see my golden castle again? Even if I accomplished this task, if I found the way into Allesaria, I'd never live in Quentis again, would I?

That room on the fourth floor with the narrow balcony was no longer mine. So I took in every detail, memorized every tower and spire, until the boat lurched and the men shouted and we were drifting away.

Jocelyn raised one hand in the air, waving to her mother, while the other covered her mouth and her quiet sobs. She sniffled as more tears streaked down her cheeks.

This wasn't fair. It wasn't fucking fair.

"I promise to send you home," I told her. "You'll see Quentis again."

There was a very real chance I'd break that vow. It was cruel to make a promise I wasn't sure I could keep.

I made it anyway.

Father wasn't the only person I'd fail if I didn't find the way into Allesaria. I couldn't leave Brielle and Jocelyn trapped in a foreign kingdom, separated from their families indefinitely.

The pressure of these expectations made it hard to breathe. The weight of these secrets rested heavily on my shoulders.

Could I do this?

Probably not. But I'd try anyway. From this moment forward.

I could do this.

Maybe if I told myself enough times, I'd start to believe it.

The crowd on the docks shifted as my father turned and strode toward his waiting horse. Margot and Mae retreated to their carriage.

I watched them leave, trailing along the street, protected by their guards, until they were swallowed up by the city. They'd follow the streets that wound past white buildings to the castle. They'd return to their life, while I sailed into mine.

The soldiers left next, followed by the merchants, who filtered to their stalls. To the work that would consume them until dusk and put food on their tables.

Only one person remained on the docks as we sailed out of Roslo Bay. Jocelyn's mother.

She kept waving. She never stopped. Her arms had to be tired, but she kept waving to her daughter.

I might be the woman wearing the crown, but Jocelyn was the one with the riches, wasn't she?

It was too hard to watch her mother and that wave, to see Jocelyn wave back another minute, so I looked to my cliffside.

I'd expected to find it empty, but a lone rider sat on his horse at the top. A man dressed in a teal uniform, riding a buckskin stallion.

Banner.

I lifted my arm in the air.

He did the same.

I watched him until he was only a speck on the coastline. Until the buildings blurred together in a sea of white. Until the golden castle at their backs became a glint on the horizon. I stayed at that wooden railing, watching my homeland disappear, even after Brielle and Jocelyn had excused themselves to go below.

It vanished in a blink. One moment, I could still make it out if I squinted hard. Then, it was gone, and all I could see was water.

Or maybe that was simply my tears.

I pulled the crown from my hair, blinking my eyes dry.

"You'll need other clothes." A man's deep, rumbling voice startled me with a jolt. I whirled, nearly dropping my crown as I expected to find the Guardian lurking.

But it was Zavier.

How long had he been standing there? And when the hell had he learned to talk?

"Most women in Turah dress like the men." He joined me at the rail. "They find pants to be more practical for daily living. Even in Perris courts, ladies typically only wear gowns for parties."

He wanted to talk about fashion? Absolutely not. "You can speak."

"Just because I don't talk doesn't mean I can't." He grinned. It was less of a smirk than that of the Guardian's, but it was just as arrogant and infuriating. "Welcome aboard the *Cutter*, Odessa Wolfe."

Wolfe. Not Cross.

Odessa Wolfe.

It was a gut punch. Another reminder of all that had changed in less than a day. If not for the railing, I would have been knocked on my ass.

How much of an identity could one person lose before they were hollowed into a shell?

Odessa Wolfe.

I hated it. Loathed it with every fiber of my being.

Maybe he could sense that. Maybe this was his game, to strip me of everything that was *me*.

Well, I wasn't playing. They couldn't strip me of anything if I did it myself.

"Here." I thrust my crown into his hands. "This should feed an entire family for years."

Zavier studied the gold and amber jewels, his forehead furrowing.

I didn't wait for his reply. I crossed the stern and hoped the pitiful splash I heard behind me wasn't my crown being tossed into the ocean.

Ten

The *Cutter*. The *Cannon*. The *Cleaver*.

Apparently, when naming ships, the Turans stuck to weaponry.

And they were oh-so-proud of those names.

CUTTER was inlaid into the dining table in my room. Each chair had a brass plate with the name. And it was painted in swirly, beige script on the wood above the rear windows.

Were they afraid that if it wasn't etched into the bed's headboard, someone would forget where they were sleeping?

Placards aside, at least this ship was relatively comfortable. I was still adjusting to the constant rocking motion, but I hadn't gotten sick. Unlike both Brielle and Jocelyn, who'd spent most of the night clutching bowls to their chests.

I'd been alternating between their beds, applying cool compresses to their foreheads and covering them with blankets when they got the chills. After both had finally fallen asleep a few hours ago, I'd crashed hard, planning to sleep today away. But there were no curtains over the windows that ran along the back of the ship. Nothing to block out the ocean blue reflecting the sunrise gold.

It was too bright to sleep. And this room too stuffy.

They'd crammed a lot into such a small space. A table to take meals. My trunks against the wall beside Brielle's and Jocelyn's. And three beds. Mine on one side of the room with theirs on the opposite, a narrow walkway splitting the room in half.

Jocelyn hadn't fully unpacked my trunks. She'd only taken out a few dresses to hang on the row of hooks beside the door. I'd planned to wear a simple gray dress today—like all days.

Except there was a folded pile of clothes on the floor, right inside the door.

The locked door.

At some point while I'd been asleep, someone, on my husband's errand, had broken into my room to bring me clothing. To bring me boots. To bring me pants.

I didn't wear pants. Ever.

My last name, my home, my crown, and my family were gone, but damn it, I wasn't going to lose my clothes, too. I was a woman who liked dresses, even if they were gray.

Those pants could rot.

So I went to a hook, retrieved my least wrinkled dress, and pulled it on with a pair of my most comfortable slippers. Then I snagged my necklace from beneath the pillow where I'd left it last night.

The moment I looped it over my head, resting the pendant against my heart, a warm weight settled on my frame. Not a bad weight. Not a burden. It was like something was gently securing me to the floor. Easing my shoulders away from my ears. Like I'd found a new center to keep me steady on this rocking ship.

I faced the narrow mirror hanging on the back of the door. The woman who stared back was tired. Still hungry—I'd picked at last night's dinner, afraid if I ate too much I'd get sick. But still, that woman was me.

The drab gray dress, the brown hair, the scuffed slippers, and the warm necklace. My wardrobe might be dull and boring, but it was a sliver of normalcy in this sea of uncertainty.

I tucked the pendant beneath the neckline of my gown, settling it over my sternum.

Since Zavier seemed to hold no interest in my body or consummating this marriage, it would be perfectly safe between my breasts.

I walked toward the pile of clothes and boots and swept them into a corner.

If the Turans really wanted me to wear pants, they could knock before entering my room.

Brielle and Jocelyn were both sound asleep, mouths slack and arms curled around the bowls I'd emptied out the window more than once in the night.

I smoothed the front of my dress, steeled my spine, and unlocked my door. Then I climbed the stairs that led to the ship's deck.

A blast of ocean wind lifted the ends of my hair, tangling the curls. They'd be a mess to comb later, but what else did I have to do? If tonight was anything like the last, I'd spend the hours after dinner was delivered to my room counting waves. That, and listening to Brielle and Jocelyn retch and groan.

I'd have time to brush my hair.

The deck was clean and uncluttered. The boxes and crates strewn across the space yesterday had all been stowed, our supplies secure below.

One man mopped the floorboards while others were busy with the rigging. No one looked in my direction. No one seemed to care that I'd emerged from my quarters.

I was as invisible to the Turans as I'd been at home. *Good.* That would make spying easier.

The *Cannon* and the *Cleaver* sailed beside the *Cutter*, not so close that they'd risk colliding, but not so far that a loud shout couldn't be heard from one to the next. Together, the three formed a line of wooden hulls and massive sails. A line of red cutting through a sea of blue.

I walked to the ship's portside wall, staring into the distance. There was nothing but water and sky and the puff of white clouds.

It should have been lonely. Isolating. But I'd spent too many years on my cliffside in Roslo, imagining what was beyond Quentis's shores, to feel anything but a thrill.

This was not an adventure of my choosing, but it was still an adventure.

I closed my eyes, feeling the salt water spray on my face. I tilted my head to the sky, the warmth of the sun on my cheeks, and I filled my lungs with the wind.

My adventure.

Was I happy with this situation? No. But if nothing else, maybe I could find joy in this journey.

"The crew just swabbed. Try not to hurl on the deck, my queen."

He really needed to stop calling me that.

My lip curled at that familiar deep voice. Last night, I'd mistaken Zavier's voice for the Guardian's. But they were as different as the green sails against the blue sky.

Zavier wasn't nearly as condescending.

Did the Guardian's powers include sensing moods? Had he felt that I was almost enjoying myself, so he'd come to ruin my happy moment?

"Don't you have anyone else to pester?" I asked as he came to stand at my side.

"No." And there came the smirk.

It was more arrogant than ever.

Did that arrogance come from killing? Had he deemed himself

untouchable?

He stood too close, so I inched away. It only made that smirk widen.

Gods, I wanted to slap him. Probably not a great idea, considering he was a murderer of innocent men, but the urge was overwhelming.

The men in my life didn't smirk. Father scowled. Banner would never lower himself to anything so unrefined. And the guards at the castle had been trained to keep neutral expressions.

The Guardian smirked like he'd invented the gesture. Only half of his mouth turned up into what some might consider a crooked grin, and it could have been a smile if not for the way his eyes narrowed. The man oozed scorn and superiority.

His gaze was that emerald green again and full of suspicion. He stared at me like he knew a secret. A secret he'd taunt me with mercilessly.

"Nice dress." His gaze raked over my body in slow perusal, head to toe. "Didn't want to try those clothes I left you this morning?"

"*You* came into my room?" My knuckles turned white as my grip tightened on the ship's rail. There'd be crescents in the wood from my fingernails before this conversation was finished. "The door was locked."

"Was it? My mistake."

Bastard. I tapped my nose, then leaned in, sniffing at his vest. "I thought I'd smelled something foul in the air when I woke up. Must have been you."

That smirk stretched into an actual smile with straight, white teeth. "You snore, Cross."

Cross. Not Wolfe.

He probably meant it as an insult. That I hadn't earned the Turan royal name yet. But I didn't want to be a Wolfe, so if this prick wanted to call me Cross, I wasn't going to object.

"I do not snore."

I definitely snored.

It happened whenever I was overtired, like I had been last night. There were times when I snored so loudly, I'd wake myself up.

Not that I'd ever admit it to him.

The Guardian chuckled as he turned to face the *Cleaver* sailing at our side.

What did I hate more? The smirk? Or how easily he could laugh at my expense? It was a tie.

Before I could excuse myself to go below, he planted his hands on the rail beside mine and, in one fluid swing, leaped overboard.

My jaw dropped as he plummeted into the water, disappearing beneath its waves.

I scanned the deck, expecting to find shocked faces from anyone else, but the men kept on working like this was normal. Like someone didn't need to throw him a rope before we left him behind.

The sails were full, and we were moving quickly. He couldn't swim that fast, could he?

I peered over the edge, searching the water. How long could he hold his breath? Where was he?

Yes, if he drowned that would save me a lot of trouble. And yes, I'd fantasized about tossing him overboard myself. But if he did die, it would be rather…anticlimactic. And really unsatisfying.

"There." An arm appeared in my periphery, outstretched toward the *Cleaver*. Zavier took the place where the Guardian had been standing and pointed to the other ship's hull.

To where a man who'd leaped off this boat only moments ago was already climbing up a rope and onto the other.

No mortal man could swim that fast.

"What is he?" I whispered.

Zavier dropped his arm, eyes still locked on the Guardian. He didn't answer my question. "Good morning, Odessa."

"Good morning," I said, glancing between the prince and the *Cleaver*.

Were the rangers on that ship? The Voster? As long as the High Priest or Brother Dime weren't on the *Cutter*, did it matter? I was just glad they were far enough away that I couldn't feel their magic.

Zavier held out a hand, motioning me toward the quarterdeck, up the stairs to the stern where we'd stood last night. Where we could talk alone.

"Did you rest?" he asked as we settled against the railing, eyes trained to where we'd been, not where we were going.

I shrugged. "A little."

He hummed, staring in the direction of Quentis. There was a layer of stubble on his face that contoured the hard lines of his jaw. There was a sword strapped to his back. Knives at his belt. The warrior prince.

There were dark circles under his eyes, like he'd been awake all night.

Had he stayed up in case of marroweels? Was he armed to defend us in case a monster attacked?

"Have you ever made the Krisenth Crossing?" he asked, leaning his forearms on the railing to stare out over the sea.

"I've never been on a ship."

Father had taken a trip to Ozarth once and had agreed to bring me along, but then I'd gotten sick with a cough and he'd left me behind with our healers.

"This passage is not for the weak. How's your stomach?"

"Not weak."

"Good."

"My lady's maids, on the other hand, are struggling."

"Warn them that it will only get worse. I made the crossing once with a man from Genesis. He'd never been on a ship before and spent the entire trip hurling out a window."

I doubted Brielle or Jocelyn would leave the room if that was the case. But I liked the swaying motion. It was part of why I'd slept, and snored, so soundly.

"Have you ever traveled beyond Quentis?" he asked.

"No. This is a first."

My life had been spent in Roslo with the occasional visit to other Quentin towns.

Quentis was the smallest and southernmost kingdom in Calandra. It was bordered on three sides by the Marixmore Ocean. On the fourth, our eastern border with Genesis, was a chasm. The Evon Ravine.

The ravine cut so deeply into the earth, it was almost black at the bottom. It was too wide to bridge, so travelers wound along a switchback down the cliffs, dropping lower and lower to the ravine's floor, then climbing out in the same way up the other side.

Such a treacherous route wasn't well traveled. And the monsters that lurked in the Evon's depths were more terrifying than those that swam the Marixmore.

The Krisenth Crossing might be dangerous, but it was the safest way for anyone to journey from Quentis to another kingdom. It was why our trade routes had been established by sea. Even for our neighbor, Genesis, travelers sailed along the coast. Because Turah was the largest and northernmost kingdom, the most feasible route was this crossing.

"How long will it take to reach Turah?" I asked.

"Eight to nine days, depending on the weather. We've got provisions for two weeks in case of an emergency."

"Is that why you brought three ships, not one? In case of an emergency?" I looked to the *Cleaver*, then the *Cannon*. Three ships felt unnecessary.

Unless maybe it wasn't enough. "How many ships did you leave Turah with?"

"Six."

My jaw dropped. Half hadn't made the crossing. "Marroweels?"

"And a storm," he said.

"Gods." I signed the Eight.

"Are you frightened?"

"Yes." I was too tired to deliver a decent lie.

"Good," he murmured. "You should be. So am I."

Not something I would have expected from a prince. Maybe in our honesty, we could find common ground. "It should be safer now that you killed those marroweels, right?"

"When it comes to monsters, safety is an illusion. The High Priest believes the females have chosen the Krisenth to lay their eggs. Why, no one knows. With seven dead, it should reduce their population. Make their attacks less frequent."

Maybe there really was something to the Chain of Sevens beyond the havoc it had wreaked on my life.

"So, yes," he said. "It is safer now than it was."

Well, that didn't make me feel safe in the slightest. "How did you kill them when they attacked?"

"The ships are armed with harpoons and spears."

And he'd killed all seven marroweels with those weapons to claim me as his prize.

"It's unlikely we'll be attacked," he said. "We have more to fear from a storm."

Unless the seven monsters were a fraction of the number in the Krisenth. What if there were seven more? A hundred more?

A chill snaked down my spine, making me shiver.

"We baited them, Odessa," he said. "At most, a sailor will see one marroweel in the span of ten years on this journey. Finding seven was intentional."

Right. Baited per my father's request. Baited seven so he could claim his bride prize.

"Why me?" I blurted. "Why did you want to marry me?"

If we were going to be tied together, I wanted an answer.

Except Zavier stayed quiet, leaning his elbows against the railing, his tall, strong body bent in half. His gaze affixed to the horizon.

"You're really going to ignore me, huh?"

The corners of his mouth turned up.

It wasn't even close to a full smile, but there was promise there. He was already good-looking, but he'd probably be devastating with a smile. Maybe it was safer if he didn't. The last thing I needed was to fall for my husband and let down my guard.

"I must warn you, Turah is not like Quentis," he said.

"Because the women wear pants?"

The joke earned me another handsome half smile. "Clothing choices aside, Turah is rugged and vast. We've got a long way to travel once we reach its shores."

To Allesaria.

I schooled my expression, hoping he couldn't sense the quickening of my pulse. Wouldn't it be convenient if he simply told me all about the capital city? I'd gladly stand here and listen.

"Quentis has never sent a Sparrow to Turah. Not in three hundred years. It's been the other way around, but in the past nine marriages, never this way."

The arrangements depended on the heirs each generation produced. Their ages. Their genders. Their kingdoms. Our parents didn't care much about love or preference. If a prince was in love with another, he'd still be forced to marry a princess and produce an heir. If a princess was ten years older than the prince, they'd marry as long as she could still bear a child.

As long as enough generations had passed between the mixing of bloodlines to ensure the health of future kings and Sparrows, not much else mattered.

My father came from a long line of male heirs. As far as I knew, Father had never considered me as the Sparrow. Maybe in the years before Mae was born, but as far back as I could remember, it had always been her. He had always believed she could be a queen. Why not me?

I guess it didn't matter now.

By the gods' design, this was my fate.

"The last Sparrow to come to Turah was from Laine," he said. "That was over a hundred years ago. She came and didn't stay long."

Um...what? "She left?"

We could leave? I guess there hadn't been anything in the treaty requiring me to stay. I was to produce an heir. If I was barren, well...to my knowledge, no Sparrow had ever been barren. Maybe that was part of the treaty's magic. I also wasn't allowed to kill Zavier.

But maybe, once my duties were done, I could simply leave.

"Getting ideas?" Zavier arched an eyebrow.

"Maybe," I admitted with a laugh.

He grinned—not a smile, but it had the makings of one. It was as dangerous as it was attractive.

"Yes, she left," he said. "After her daughter, my grandmother's grandmother, was born. She returned to Laine. Though not without paying a price."

Her child. She would have had to leave her child in Turah. How harsh was their kingdom that a mother would abandon her own daughter?

"Why are you telling me this?" I asked.

"To set your expectations. Turah is not Quentis."

"If you wanted the strongest wife possible, you should have chosen Mae."

He stared forward, his mossy green eyes hard and unreadable.

"Why do you pretend not to speak?"

Zavier hesitated, like he was debating whether or not to answer. "Because other leaders see it as a weakness they can exploit. It usually means they fill the silence with more than they should."

"Ah." Smart. Something to remember as I attempted to spy.

It wasn't going to be easy to learn about them, about Allesaria, was it? They'd secluded themselves from the other kingdoms for a reason. Was it simply distrust? Had they been betrayed at some point in past generations?

"Why did you trust me with your secret?" It made no sense that he'd deceive Father but reveal himself to me, especially so soon. I wasn't fool enough to believe he actually trusted his new bride.

"Turans are loyal to Turans." There was a warning in his tone.

Wait. This was a test, wasn't it?

From the moment I'd signed the Shield of Sparrows, I was considered Turan.

He'd speak in front of his own people, those loyal to his crown, but not in front of outsiders. Zavier hadn't spoken in front of Brielle or Jocelyn yesterday. I doubted he ever would. They were Quentins.

But me?

He'd drawn a line in the sand, and this secret was his way of forcing me to choose a side.

I hadn't told Brielle or Jocelyn that he'd spoken to me. Mostly because they'd been so sick last night. But there was also a part of me that liked knowing something that others did not. I was so often the last person to hear gossip. To catch rumors.

Strange how in the past few days, I'd gained more secrets than I had in the past few years combined. My father's. And now Zavier's.

It wasn't a gift of unbridled trust. I'd probably never earn that from either man. But I'd keep this secret.

For now.

"Why did you choose me?"

Like before, he didn't answer.

If he thought I'd stop asking, he was very, very wrong.

"Do you desire me?" The question slipped past my lips before I could stop it.

He cleared his throat, and I could practically see his mind racing for the gentle answer. "You're a beautiful woman."

That meant no.

"So does that mean we won't…" I couldn't even finish the question.

Which was probably good, because Zavier's response was to walk away.

"Ugh." I sagged against the railing, my entire body flaming with embarrassment. Maybe I should throw myself overboard to cool off. That, or take lessons from my husband.

And keep my damn mouth shut.

Eleven

Brielle's gasp filled our room. "Highness. What are you wearing?"

"Pants."

Caramel leather pants. A belt, the same color, was wrapped at my waist. And my top was an ecru tunic. The slit at the collar was deep, dipping to my sternum, but with a string woven through both sides, I could lace it up. The long sleeves cuffed at my wrists, and the soft fabric was embroidered with flowers at the sides.

Flowers of every color. Red, pink, blue, purple, and green. I couldn't remember the last time I'd worn anything with so much color.

I'd been staring at myself in the mirror for the last five minutes, hoping to find fault with these clothes.

But damn it.

I liked these pants.

Boredom was to blame for this. For the past four days, these clothes had lived in the corner, heaped in a pile. And for the past four days, that pile had taunted me.

Neither Brielle nor Jocelyn had overcome their seasickness, and rather than make them suffer, I'd told them to do as little as possible and rest. When they'd asked about that pile, I'd told them to ignore it. They'd had no problem overlooking the pants. Me?

I'd gotten bored, and bored meant curious.

Why did Turan women wear them? Were they uncomfortable?

I'd decided to find out. So while Brielle had gone to the kitchen to check on breakfast and Jocelyn had ducked out to bring us a fresh basin of water, I'd given in to temptation.

I'd planned to pull them on, dismiss them as inferior, then throw them out the window.

Except I couldn't seem to take them off. The fabric was smooth and supple. The leather contoured the curves of my hips and hugged my thighs. The pants had enough structure that they'd hold their shape, yet enough give to make movement easy.

My boots were black and made of a hide I'd never felt before. The texture was almost like scales. The material was thicker than the pants, sturdy, but comfortable. The soles and thick heels gave me an added inch of height. I'd never be as tall as Brielle or Jocelyn, but I'd take every bit I could get.

The tunic was slightly too large—that, or I wasn't used to a top that didn't mold to my breasts and ribs. But its flowy fit gave me a full range of motion. It didn't pinch when I raised my arms above my head.

It was strange not to be limited by clothing. It took a conscious effort not to lift my nonexistent skirts.

"They're not horrible," I told Brielle.

"But...pants are for men."

Was that her way of telling me I looked like a boy? I did, sort of. The pants coupled with the boots were slightly masculine. But I hadn't seen a single man on board the *Cutter* with flowers on his tunic.

Yes, pants were for men. In Quentis.

We were no longer in Quentis.

"I like them," I admitted. "They're comfortable. And they're not gray."

"If color is the issue here, I'm certain we can find you a gown in Turah. We don't need to resort to *this*."

I almost laughed at the horror in her expression. All I'd seen on her face for days was sadness and sickness. "Apparently, most women in Turah dress like the men."

As if that was an excuse for my attire. I was a princess of Quentis. We did not wear pants.

Sometimes my own thoughts sounded a lot like Margot's voice.

"So, you'll wear them to fit in?" she asked.

"Would that be such a bad thing? Fitting in with the Turans?"

She sighed. "Probably not. Do I have to wear them?"

"No."

Brielle wouldn't be in Turah long enough to conform to their style.

"Good." She walked to her bed, plopping down on its edge. Her face was pale and her eyes tired. The amber starbursts in her irises had dulled. "Breakfast will be ready in an hour. The galley is in disarray this morning. One of the cabinet latches broke and everything inside was tossed during last night's storm."

The Krisenth Crossing was not for the weak—Zavier's warning had proved true. For the past two days, we'd suffered through constant storms and rough seas. Brielle and Jocelyn had spent most of that time in bed.

I'd sat by the windows until it had passed, staring into the darkness until a flash of lightning would illuminate the night.

The ocean had tossed and turned for hours, until finally the winds had calmed and a deluge of rain had tempered the waves.

Looking out the window this morning, it was as if we'd sailed into a new realm. The water glittered beneath the sun and a cloudless blue sky.

"I'm going up on deck," I told Brielle. "You should come with me."

I needed to get out of this room and breathe the fresh air. It would do her some good, too.

"Are you going dressed like that?" She looked me up and down.

"Is it really that bad?"

"No."

"Liar."

She gave me a tired smile. "It's different. But you look beautiful no matter what you're wearing. And your hair looks lovely this morning. I'm sorry I haven't been much help."

"It's all right." I didn't mind braiding my own hair.

When I was a little girl, I'd had a nanny. As I'd gotten older, a lady's maid. But no matter who was supposed to be assisting me, there were always times when they'd get pulled away and I'd be left to fend for myself.

There'd be visiting guests who needed an extra attendant. A party that required all available servants to assist in preparations. Shortages in the laundry or kitchens.

That, or Mae would scare off her own lady's maid and mine would be stolen by my sister.

Brielle had been with me the longest, nearly three years. But in total, she'd probably only helped me dress or fix my hair half of that time.

Sure, I could have thrown a fit. Demanded someone braid my hair. But fits and demands were Mae's style, not mine.

"Come on." I walked to the bed and held out a hand, helping her to her feet. "Let's go up. It's stuffy in here. Jocelyn will come find us."

She opened her mouth to protest, but I dragged her toward the door, pulling her along until we reached the stairs. Then I let her go to climb to the deck.

Sunshine warmed my face, the clean, salty air filling my lungs. My head instantly cleared. Any tension in my shoulders vanished.

In another life, maybe I could have been a sailor. Before the storm hit, I'd spent most of my days on deck, leaving Brielle and Jocelyn to the room.

If I stood at the bow, staring into the ocean, I could pretend I was free. It was as close to my cliffside in Roslo as I'd ever found. The rest of the realm, the responsibilities, faded into the wind.

The crew still pretended I didn't exist. They went about their work, ignoring me wherever I stood. But this morning, as we stepped on deck, all eyes swung in our direction. A man with a mop in his hand nearly dropped it when he saw us.

Brielle was gorgeous. I couldn't blame them. They'd probably forgotten she was on board, since she'd been hiding below.

I turned, about to tell Brielle to ignore the stares, except I was alone. She was still on the stairs, one hand gripping the rail while the other hefted her skirts—taking stairs was so much faster in pants.

Which meant the men were all staring at me.

It was the pants, wasn't it?

I was not the type who craved attention. In fact, I was content to skip it altogether.

There was a gray dress in my room screaming my name. Pants be damned. I'd deal with my skirts.

I spun, about to force Brielle backward, except before I could retreat below, a towering figure appeared at the corner of my eye.

"I figured those clothes would have been tossed overboard days ago, my queen." The Guardian's voice was deeper than usual. There was a husky edge, like he'd used it too much the previous night.

In the middle of last night's storm, I'd heard men shouting. Had he been one of them? Or had he swum back to the *Cutter* after the storm had calmed?

I hadn't seen him since he leaped overboard days ago.

Forcing a tight smile, I faced him, taking in the color of his eyes. Chilling, emerald green.

"Zavier said these clothes were typical for Turan women," I said. "I thought it best I give them a try."

"You're not a Turan." He crossed his arms over his chest.

"Yes, but my husband is. He sent these to me, which you very well know, so I'll wear them at his behest."

"The dutiful wife, aren't you, Sparrow? At least in title."

He didn't bother hiding his mocking tone. He knew, didn't he? That

Zavier hadn't taken me to his bed? And rather than leave that topic alone, he threw it in my face. He made it seem that Zavier's lack of desire for his wife was my fault.

Oh, how I despised this man. More and more with each encounter.

If I ever learned how to accurately fire a crossbow, this man would be my target. Except I had horrible aim. The weapons master had tried to teach me to use a crossbow when I was eleven, and I'd nearly sent a bolt through his foot.

Crossbow lessons had started and stopped in the same day.

"Highness?" Brielle reached the top stair, her breaths labored as she gripped my arm to find her balance.

The touch snapped me out of my thoughts, breaking me from delusions of murdering the Guardian. When had I gotten so vicious? I'd never once in my life fantasized about killing someone.

Was this how Mae was wired? With bloodlust lurking beneath the surface? Maybe my sister and I weren't that different after all.

"Are you all right?" I asked her, ignoring the man watching our every move.

Didn't he have somewhere else to be? I wasn't keen on the idea of a known killer around Brielle. I was fairly certain my life was safe, but I didn't trust the Guardian with her or Jocelyn.

"A bit lightheaded," she said.

"Probably because you haven't eaten much. We'll only stay for a few—"

My sentence was cut short when Brielle crashed into my side, her arms wrapping around my body to keep from falling.

Not from a dizzy spell. Not from tripping on her skirts.

The entire ship rocked so hard that every person on deck lurched.

"What was that?" Brielle asked at the same time the Guardian bellowed, "Eel!"

Shouts filled the air as men abandoned their tasks, racing for the weapons stowed on the ship's side walls.

"To the harpoons." The Guardian's voice boomed around us, louder than any man's. Any human's. It was more like an animal's roar.

"Oh, gods." Brielle trembled. "We're going to die."

"We're not going to die." I pushed her toward the staircase. "Get below. Now."

Except before she could take the first step, the Guardian grabbed her arm and yanked her away from the stairwell.

"Do you really think the safest place to be when this ship sinks is below?" he growled. "Sit down. Hold tight. Stay the fuck out of the way."

Brielle didn't need to be told twice. She dashed across the floor, tucking herself into a corner beside the staircase that led to the quarterdeck.

"Go." The Guardian's eyes shifted from green to silver in a blink. Then he left me for the mast, climbing the ladder two steps at a time.

When he reached the platform halfway up the massive post, he stared at the water, like he could see beneath the surface to the monster lurking below.

"Cross!"

I jumped as he bellowed my name.

His back was to me. How did he know I hadn't moved?

"What about Jocelyn?" Brielle asked. "Where is she?"

Shit. "I'll get her."

Except before I could run down the stairs, a stream of men filtered from below.

The cook, his face ruddy and sheened with sweat, carried a cleaver in each hand. The others were men I'd only seen in the evenings. The night crew. Some were fastening the buttons on their pants. Others were pulling on shirts.

They blew past me, running with sure feet toward the open chests of weapons. Each man took a barbed spear and carried it to the outer railing. A man unfastened a huge harpoon. The tip was barbed, but there was no rope or chain at the end like those fishermen used on my father's ships.

That harpoon wasn't for fishing. It was for slaughter.

There were enough men to circle the ship's exterior.

Where was Zavier? He was the marroweel killer. Was he still asleep?

Well, if he was in bed, he was on his own. I needed to get Jocelyn.

Only when I reached the mouth of the staircase, she was already climbing.

"Hurry." I waved her up, waiting as she hefted her own skirts higher. When she reached the top, I pushed her toward Brielle, letting her go first.

I was still on my feet when the ship jolted again. And then, all I could see were my own boots and blue sky as I flew backward, landing on my ass.

The marroweel. It must be trying to pound a hole into the hull with that bone on its skull.

"Starboard!" The Guardian pointed in the direction I was facing, and every man behind me ran forward, their spears poised above their shoulders, ready to throw.

I pushed up to my hands and knees, about to stand and sprint to a sobbing Brielle and a wide-eyed Jocelyn, when the monster attacked again.

Rather than strike the boat from below like it had before, its massive body came shooting out of the water, its scales dragging against the entire starboard side, launching us into the air.

The floor beneath me tilted skyward, my grip faltering as I fell to my stomach.

An ear-splitting screech ripped from the marroweel's mouth as it shot up as high as the sails. Its teeth gleamed white as it screamed.

The men held fast to the chains and ropes that were anchored along the boat's hull. Some managed to keep their footing enough to throw their spears. A few found purchase in the monster's hide, but not enough to bring it down. Another, the beast snapped into splinters with its massive jaws.

But I didn't have a rope or a chain. All I could do was slide, my hands frantically trying to get a grip on the smooth floor as I plummeted toward the port side of the ship.

Toward the water rushing my way.

My scream was lost in the noise and chaos. I twisted, looking over my shoulder just in time to see the railing come at my feet. It was only by Daria's luck that I managed to plant both boots on that railing and stop myself from flying overboard.

Water sloshed onto the deck, soaking my pants and shirt before the *Cutter* rocked violently in the other direction, returning to level as the marroweel's sleek body slithered into the depths, disappearing beneath the surface once more.

I was splayed on my stomach, wet and cold and terrified. But alive. I was still alive.

My heart was in my throat as I lifted to my knees.

Brielle was holding tight to a railing, tears streaming down her face as she mouthed prayers to the gods. Jocelyn had her arms around Brielle, either in comfort or as something to hold in case we rocked again.

The men with empty hands ran to replace their spears. Others unsheathed swords.

"Harpoon," the Guardian yelled from his perch, hand outstretched.

A large man threw the weapon in the air, as if to send it through the Guardian's chest.

But the Guardian caught it in his fist, spinning it into position at the exact moment the marroweel surged again.

Like before, the starboard side of the ship lifted into the air, catching me off-balance.

I should have been prepared. I should have expected the violent lurch of the ship. I should have listened to the Guardian when he told me to hold tight.

I should not even be on this godsforsaken ship.

And I wasn't, not anymore.

My boots lost purchase, and my spine slammed into the railing before I toppled into the water with a splash.

The cold was a shock, stealing the breath in my chest. Then came the tug from the currents of the waves and the ship, both pulling me away. Pulling me deep.

Swim. I kicked my legs, hard, reaching for the surface with my fingertips. Five hard strokes and I was free, sucking in a breath before a wave crashed over my head. When I gasped another breath, a screech rang out, and the marroweel dove into the water, abandoning the ship.

My heart stopped beating.

I was in the ocean with a marroweel. This was how I would die.

"Gods, save me."

"Swim!" The Guardian appeared at the railing, his focus on me as other men clustered around him, all armed for when the marroweel surfaced again.

I scanned the waves, searching for an iridescent fin or a flash of sapphire scales or razor teeth. But I was alone, and the ship was sailing away.

"Damn it, Cross." The Guardian slammed his fists on the railing. "Swim!"

Swim. Good idea.

I kicked with all my might, finding a rhythm with the waves. My legs had never pumped so hard, my arms pulling at the water with all their strength.

Faster. I had to go faster. Every muscle in my body began to burn, to ache in protest, but I pushed past the pain and did everything in my power to stay with the ship.

But it was getting smaller and smaller. I wasn't fast enough.

The sails began to crumple as the men let them down to slow the ship. Then they turned hard to the port side, banking like they were trying to come back and fetch me.

No matter how fast I swam, how quickly they changed course, it wouldn't be enough.

I'd never outswim a marroweel. And if they were stuck in the water, they'd be at the monster's mercy.

The strength, the speed, seeped from my muscles, the cold making it harder and harder to kick.

The Guardian stared at me, his focus unwavering, like he was willing me forward.

"Let's go!" He slammed another fist on the rail, and for a moment, I wanted to scream back that I was trying. Except he wasn't talking to me. He was yelling at the men.

A crewman appeared with a harpoon in one hand, its rope in the other.

The Guardian backed away until he was out of view. Then came the harpoon, flying through the air with the rope streaming behind it, a line of brown against the bright sky.

I gasped, certain it was going to sink into my flesh, when the pointed tip disappeared into the water beside my leg. The rope dragged along my arm, and I grabbed it with both hands, holding tight as it pulled me through the water.

My chest slammed into the waves, cresting their peaks, as the men on board hauled me faster and faster toward the *Cutter*.

I was going to make it. Twenty yards. Fifteen.

Something hard brushed against my leg. Something sharp.

"No." Wet warmth spread between my thighs as my bladder loosened.

Never in my life had I felt this kind of fear. It was down there, below my body. I couldn't see it, but it was coming. It would not let me reach that ship.

I was going to be eaten by the monsters I'd always found so fascinating. I'd never reach Turah. I'd never go home.

"Hold." The Guardian's command tore me from the dread. When I looked to the ship, his silver eyes were waiting. His harpoon was raised, his face eerily calm as he stared past the weapon's point.

There was a spraying noise behind me, the same sound a ship made as its hull cut through the sea.

But it wasn't a ship on my heels.

It was death.

If I was going to die, I didn't want my last sight to be rows of teeth, so I stayed locked on the Guardian.

He might be a jackass, but at least he was handsome. There were worse things to behold at the end of a life than a nice face.

My own was wet, my tears joining the salty water.

Ten yards. I was so close. So, so close.

And too far away.

"Now." On his command, the rope in my hands tugged hard, and I was yanked from the water so fast my stomach dropped. A scream tore from my throat.

But I wasn't the only being screaming.

The marroweel flew out of the water, mouth wide as it stretched to devour me whole. The screech coming from its throat was so loud it rippled across my skin.

I closed my eyes, my hands raw and throbbing as they began to slip from the rope. My grip loosened, the strength of my fingers faltering. But instead of falling into the monster's waiting jaws, I crashed on the *Cutter*'s deck.

My body crumpled as I toppled to the side.

"Don't let it drop," the Guardian shouted. "Haul it in."

Haul it in? I cracked my eyes open, lifting up on an elbow.

Blue scales. Inches from my feet.

"Ah!" I scrambled away, slipping and sliding along the deck as my gaze raked over the monster, following spine to neck to head.

A head skewered with a harpoon.

"Highness." Brielle and Jocelyn dropped to my side, both sobbing as they helped me to my knees.

Brielle wrapped her arms around my shoulders, crying into my soaked shirt. "I thought you were dead."

"So did I," I whispered, my breaths coming in ragged pants.

Beyond the men, beyond the dead monster at my feet, green sails appeared.

The *Cleaver* approached, gliding along the *Cutter* too fast to stop, but close enough that Zavier could leap from one ship to the other.

His face was hard, his expression unreadable as he took in the dead marroweel and the crew hauling its rear half from the water.

The Guardian had his hands on his hips, his chest rising and falling with labored breaths.

Zavier scanned the deck, finding me in the fray. His entire body sagged. Then he looked to the Guardian again and gave him a nod.

The Guardian nodded back.

"Zavier." One of his warriors waved him over to where a man was lying on his back, blood seeping onto the deck. A shard of wood from the ruined starboard side of the ship was lodged in his thigh.

Zavier. They didn't call him Prince or Highness.

The Guardian appeared, hauling me to my feet, and oh, he was pissed. "Leave us," he barked to Brielle and Jocelyn.

Both women scrambled away, seeming to realize for the first time there was a dead monster on the deck. Jocelyn yelped, then raced for the stairs to go below.

The silver in his eyes swirled to melting metal. He bent into my face, leaning in so close our noses nearly touched. "When I give you an order, you obey."

"I'm sorry."

My apology only seemed to make him angrier. That buzzing I'd felt in Roslo, the simmering rage, boiled to the surface. "If I tell you to run, you run. If I tell you to hide, you hide. If I tell you to hop on one foot and pat your hair, then you. Fucking. Hop. Do we have an understanding?"

"No."

The word surprised me as much as it did him. Maybe I'd ingested too much seawater? But I wasn't going to blindly agree. I'd spent twenty-three years taking orders from men who thought they could dictate my every move. And I was done.

I wouldn't—couldn't—cower for this man. I refused to give him that control.

Not when I'd already lost so much.

He blinked, clearly having expected a different answer. "What did you say?"

"No." I squared my shoulders, using my last shred of strength, and lifted my chin. "I will listen when it's a matter of safety for myself. For other people. I will do my best to 'stay the fuck out of the way.' But I will not bend to your every whim. I will not humiliate myself because you deem me insignificant. If you wanted me to stay quiet, then you should have let that marroweel kill me. I am not one of your warriors to lead. I am not your wife to command. So no, we do not have an understanding."

I didn't need him to agree or reply. I had nothing else to say and no energy to argue, so I turned on my heel, my feet squelching inside my boots as I made my way to the stairs.

But before I disappeared below, I paused, twisting to speak over my shoulder. "Thank you for saving my life."

Someday, if I had the chance, I'd repay that favor by taking his.

Twelve

The marroweel that had nearly eaten me yesterday hung from the *Cutter*'s mast on a thick chain. The monster's milky eyes greeted me as I stepped onto the deck along with the stench of rotting fish.

Maybe I should have stayed in bed. Maybe, if I had lain there long enough, I would have eventually fallen asleep.

I'd spent last night staring at the dark ceiling, listening to Brielle whimper through a nightmare while Jocelyn tossed and turned. Listening to hammers pounding on the hull as the crew repaired the damage to the ship.

Every time I'd closed my eyes, I'd been in the ocean again. I'd felt the monster's body touch my leg. Felt its breath on my feet and heard its scream in my ears.

A thousand years could pass, and I'd never forget that sound.

Brielle refused to leave our room until we reached Turah. Jocelyn would go to the galley, but she refused to step on deck. Maybe they had the right idea.

But fear wasn't going to keep me trapped below. It wasn't my life that had ended yesterday. If the *Cutter* had survived the attack, had kept sailing, then I would keep sailing, too.

So I set off across the deck, shoulders squared, and approached the beast.

The smell was overpowering. I gagged before breathing through my mouth instead of my nose.

Blood dripped from the marroweel's nostrils into a bucket. That bucket was nearly filled to the top, and the steady dribble meant someone had probably been emptying it often.

I gagged again.

The scent was a hundred times worse than the dye I'd worked into my hair this morning to replace what the ocean had washed away in yesterday's ordeal. With any luck, no one would remember that my hair had been more red than brown for those few minutes I'd been arguing with the Guardian. I didn't have the energy to defend my hair routine now or ever.

"Hungry?" An apple slice on a dagger's blade was thrust in my face.

"No." I pushed the Guardian's hand away, my stomach turning.

He popped that slice into his mouth, the fruit crunching as he chewed. His eyes were hazel today. Maybe that was their normal shade.

I preferred the vivid, bold colors. It made it easier to remember that he wasn't a normal man.

"Don't tell me you get sick at the sight of just a little blood?" he asked.

"I'd hardly consider a bucket's worth 'just a little blood.'"

He cut off another piece of the apple, then threw the core overboard. With it gone, he tucked his dagger into a scabbard strapped against his ribs. Then he swept the bucket from the floor, carrying it to the ship's edge to pour out.

I'd expected a stream of crimson, but the liquid wasn't red. It was a shade of the darkest green that reminded me of the Voster's eyes.

A shiver crept down my spine.

Uh... Shouldn't that blood be red? The marroweels on the docks had bled red. Why was this one different?

Fresh droplets fell from the monster's snout, splattering on the deck's boards, a few leaping out toward my slippers.

I jumped backward a step before those splatters stained the hem of my dress. After yesterday's swim, my boots, pants, and tunic needed a thorough wash. They'd been hung to dry, but they were all stiff with salt. So I was back to gray gowns and flat slippers for now. But not for long.

The Turan clothes had saved my life yesterday. Maybe that was giving a pair of pants and a tunic too much credit, but I'd spent enough time swimming in a gown to know that kicking was considerably harder with skirts around your ankles.

The Guardian set the empty bucket beneath the monster.

"That blood isn't red."

"Very observant, Cross."

I frowned. "The blood of the female marroweels Zavier killed and left in Roslo was red. Why does this one bleed green? Why are its eyes white, not black? Is it a male or something? A different type of monster?"

The Guardian stared at the monster, crossing his arms over his chest. "It is a male."

That explained why it was so much larger. It was nearly double the size of the females. The bone protruding from its skull was twice as tall. And its features weren't as sleek. Its face was angular, the nose broader.

The females were terrifying. The males? Bone-chilling.

There was no reason I should be alive today.

"It should have killed me," I said. "In the water, I felt something brush against my leg. It should have eaten me then and there. Why didn't it?"

"My guess? It was focused on the ship. With the commotion, it didn't even realize you were in the water until it touched you with its tail."

"I don't think I'm that lucky. Daria has never been a goddess on my side."

"Then be grateful she was yesterday."

Thank you, Daria. "You're a fast swimmer," I said.

"Are you going to keep stating the obvious today? Because I do have other obligations."

I rolled my eyes. *Smart-ass.* "Why didn't you jump into the water to rescue me? Wouldn't that have been faster?"

A night spent replaying every moment, and that was what seemed to bother me the most. Why he'd chosen to throw that harpoon, to stay on the ship, rather than swim to get me.

Either he wouldn't have risked his own life to save mine.

Or he'd been trying to accomplish multiple tasks at once. Save me. Kill the monster.

His eyebrows lifted. "Shall I consult with you first the next time you're nearly devoured by a marroweel to make sure the way in which you are spared from its jaws is acceptable?"

"I didn't mean—" I shook my head. I was too tired and too frazzled to articulate my thoughts, so I wasn't even going to try. "Sorry. I don't mean to sound ungrateful. Thank you, again, for saving my life."

He frowned but gave me a single nod.

"Why keep its body? Why not dump it overboard and save us all the stench?"

"Those scales are valuable. We'll dispose of it once they're harvested."

"Oh." I glanced toward the ocean. "Should I be worried about another marroweel attack?"

"It's unlikely. Though there are other beasts to fear on the Krisenth besides marroweels."

"Like you?" The retort came off my tongue automatically. A reflex.

It was one of those impulsive, snide remarks that would have enraged Father or Margot. It was one of those thoughts I'd normally keep to myself.

But where the Guardian was concerned, I couldn't seem to stifle the snippy comments. What popped into my head came out of my mouth.

He stared at the monster, and if my question had offended him, he didn't let it show. "Not all monsters are born from the gods, my queen. Some of us were made."

Us. Then he considered himself a monster, too. Who was his maker?

This was the time to ask. The time to prod for information to hoard for my father. But I didn't feel like prying for the Guardian's secrets today. So I glanced around the deck, searching for a different Turan.

My husband.

"Where is Zavier?"

"The *Cleaver.*"

"Is that where he stays?" It hadn't really occurred to me to ask before today. I'd assumed his quarters were somewhere on the *Cutter*, but considering that he hadn't been here yesterday during the attack, that our paths hadn't crossed often since we'd set sail, it made sense that he'd chosen to spend his time on a different boat.

Away from his wife.

"Curious about Zavier's whereabouts, Sparrow? Why don't you ask him where he sleeps?"

I'd walked right into that reply.

"Maybe I'm hoping he just shows me someday." I batted my eyelashes and gave him my sweetest smile.

A throat cleared from over my shoulder. The Guardian's smirk meant it could only be one person.

I turned and found Zavier waiting.

"My room shares a wall with yours," he said. "My rangers stay on the *Cleaver*. I was training with them yesterday when the marroweel attacked."

"Ah." I faced the monster again, hoping that if I stared straight ahead, neither man would see that my face was on fire.

The Guardian let out a quiet chuckle.

My lip curled. I'd never met anyone who seemed to thrive on humiliating me quite so much.

Zavier passed by, moving closer to the marroweel, inspecting its carcass.

The tail tapered to twin iridescent fins with ruffled edges. Like the females, the male had sapphire-blue scales tipped with turquoise. Even without the sleek features of the females, this monster was breathtaking in its beauty. And flawless except for a series of scales missing from its spine.

The U-shaped gap in its armor was gray and bubbled like a scar. Did marroweels fight with each other? Had another monster tried to take a bite out of this male? Maybe two of them had fought over territory in the Krisenth.

Did that mean there was another male lurking below, waiting to strike?

I shivered, wrapping my arms around my waist.

"Don't worry, my queen. We'll keep you safe," the Guardian said. "Especially if you stay. On. The. Fucking. Ship."

I believed him. I believed Zavier and his men would keep me safe. But what if I was tired of being kept? What if I didn't want to rely on a man to be my rescuer?

If I truly wanted to be in control of my destiny, then I couldn't wait for someone else to save me from danger. The only person who was always going to fight for me was me.

Too bad I didn't know how to fight.

"I want a sword," I blurted.

The Guardian, predictable as ever, let out a dry laugh. "Would you know what to do with a sword?"

Besides dream about burying it into his gut? No, not really.

"I've had training with our weapons master." It was nothing like the training Mae had received, probably because he'd given up on me years ago, but training was training. There had to be some lessons that had lingered, right?

"I don't want you to hurt yourself," Zavier said.

Ouch. What a vote of confidence from my husband. It might have stung less had I not heard the exact same excuse from the weapons master in Roslo.

It was the reason he'd ended my training. He'd told Father that he was worried I'd hurt myself or someone else—Mae. Really, he'd just wanted to dump me in favor of a better, easier student—again, Mae.

Well, I was done with excuses.

"I'll be fine." I planted my hands on my hips. "And I insist. You warned me Turah is dangerous. The least you can do is arm me against that danger."

Zavier's mouth pursed in a thin line.

There wasn't much I could do if he said no. Stomping my foot and pouting were more Mae's style than my own. But I held his green gaze, willing him to give me a chance. To believe in me more than most people had in the past.

Say yes. Please.

He stared at me, his expression unreadable.

Damn. He was definitely going to say no.

The hilt of a sword appeared in front of my face.

The Guardian held it by the blade, his fingers pinching on the smooth metal to avoid the sharpened edges. "Take it."

Wait. He was giving me his sword?

"Um, okay." The slice on my palm from the wedding fiasco was still wrapped, the scabs ripped open by the rope yesterday, so I gripped the sword's handle past my bandage. The indentations in the handle were too large for my hand, but I did my best to fit my fingers into the worn grooves.

The moment the Guardian let go of the blade, the weapon dropped, the tip sinking into the wooden deck. *Oops.*

"Lift it up," he ordered.

I fisted it with both hands and raised it into the air, making it as high as my waist.

"Heavy?" the Guardian asked.

"You know it is." I shot him a glare, using all of my strength to keep it from dropping again. "Now what?"

"Now, you hold it." He hooked a finger under the tip, lifting it until it was poised at his neck. "Right here."

Ah. So this was some sort of a test. "That's it?"

The corner of his mouth turned up. "For now."

I gritted my teeth, holding the sword as time slowed to a crawl. The sword was heavier, sturdier, than any weapon I'd ever seen or touched. Granted, I didn't spend a lot of time with swords. Was it supposed to be this massive? Wouldn't it be easier to use if it wasn't so heavy? Apparently not. The Guardian probably swung this thing like it was a feather.

He stared at me, those hazel eyes narrowed down the length of the blade.

His throat was right there. Right at the tip of the weapon. If I lunged, if I made one quick move, I could send it through his windpipe.

Was that the test? That I didn't try to kill him?

My heart was racing, the muscles in my arms beginning to burn. My palms were getting sweaty.

Hold it. Just hold it. I channeled all of my energy into this sword.

"Getting tired, Sparrow?" the Guardian asked.

"No," I lied.

"I'm hearing that word a lot from you lately."

"Get used to it." Sweat beaded at my temples. My arms started to shake.

"You can stop, Odessa," Zavier said.

I shook my head. "I can hold it."

"You'll drop it on your toe."

"I'm fine."

Gods. I was going to drop this sword on my toe.

Just a little longer. I could do this. Keep this sword at the Guardian's throat for ten more seconds.

Ten. Nine. Eight.

My arms were trembling so hard that the blade wobbled.

Seven. Six. Five.

I was going to drop it. Fuck. I was going to fail this ridiculous test.

Four. Three. Two.

The Guardian moved so fast I never saw him shift until it was too late. One moment, the sword was aimed at his throat. The next, he'd hit the blade, forcing it out of my hands and into the air, toppling end over end until the hilt crashed into his waiting grip.

Then the blade was aimed at another throat.

Mine.

I gulped as the cold metal touched the underside of my chin.

"Your former fiancé must not have a big sword." The Guardian's eyes flashed emerald green, the innuendo dripping from his tone.

I frowned and took a step backward, away from the blade. Then I faced Zavier. "Well?"

He looked to the Guardian so they could have another of their unspoken conversations.

Zavier sighed and nodded. "Fine. We'll get you a sword."

Hopefully it was one that I could actually swing.

"Thank you." I walked away before he could change his mind, hiding my smile as I crossed the deck.

Yes. My arms felt like limp seaweed, but I'd made my point. I'd passed that test and stood up for myself.

Maybe I should have done that a long, long time ago. Maybe Father would have trusted me if I'd shown more of a backbone. If I'd told him *no*.

That, or he would have made my life miserable.

I started down the stairs to go below, to tell Brielle and Jocelyn that I'd earned a sword today, but stopped three steps down.

There was nothing to do in my room. The reason I hadn't crossed paths with Zavier was because I'd been hiding.

Sure, it smelled like dead fish on deck, but if I stood at the bow, I'd have the marroweel at my back. So I turned and was climbing toward the door when a deep voice made me freeze.

"It's spreading." Zavier's voice was quiet.

"I know," the Guardian murmured.

What was spreading? The marroweels? Did that mean the Chain of Sevens wasn't going to keep them from the Krisenth? That Father's ships would still be in danger?

"Arming her is probably a bad idea." *Her.* Me.

"Probably," the Guardian said.

I inched back, sure they'd turn and find me eavesdropping. A good princess would have hastened below before she could get caught. But I wasn't a good princess.

"You realize she's going to try to kill you," Zavier told him.

My heart dropped, plunking down the staircase.

Did they know Father had asked me to kill him? Or was that just a guess? It didn't matter. Their suspicions were correct. Which meant the closest I'd likely ever get to killing the Guardian had been moments ago with his own sword at his throat.

"Do you really think arming her is smart?" Zavier asked.

The Guardian laughed. "I've had worse ideas."

As they walked up the stairs to the quarterdeck, moving to the stern, I slunk down the stairs.

And spent the rest of the day with Brielle and Jocelyn, hiding in our room.

Thirteen

The sound of seabirds woke me from a dead sleep. I burrowed beneath my covers, hoping Margot wouldn't berate me too much if I was late for breakfast.

Except my bed was swaying from side to side. The blankets over my body were not *my* blankets.

My eyes popped open as I lifted off the mattress and remembered that I was on a ship.

"Blarg." I face-planted and groaned into my pillow.

The birds outside were like those that used to swoop by my bedroom window. Their chirps and caws were so familiar that for a blissful moment, I'd been in the castle.

I'd been home.

Through the open window, voices from the deck mingled with the whoosh of waves and caws of gulls.

This was the first morning aboard the *Cutter* that I'd woken to birds.

I sat up again, so fast I got dizzy.

Birds. Birds meant land.

I whipped the covers off my body, shaking the sleep fog from my head as I leaped out of bed and rushed toward the glass. A white bird soared past, its wings outstretched as it circled and disappeared from view.

"There are birds outside," I said, hurrying to the closet for some clothes.

Brielle heaved a sigh as she pushed up from her bed. "It's early."

Jocelyn was still out cold.

"Get up. Get dressed." I yanked out a gray dress. "I think we're close to shore."

"What?" She swung her legs over the bed and, like I'd done, raced for the window. "Jocelyn."

Nothing. That woman slept like the dead.

I'd stripped out of my sleep shirt, about to pull the dress on over my underclothes, when something caught my attention from the corner of my eye.

A pile of clothes sitting beside the door.

The locked door.

"Did you put those there?" I pointed toward the folded stack, knowing that Brielle wouldn't have done it, but I asked anyway.

"No."

Would my room in Allesaria have a better lock? I walked over to collect the pile.

Another tunic, this one embroidered with green leaves along the sleeves. Another pair of leather pants, this time in dark brown. And a set of boots that hadn't taken a swim in the ocean, made from the same strange, scale-textured black leather.

Apparently, seeing me in my gray dress two days ago hadn't been to Zavier's liking.

Since his test with the sword, since I'd overheard Zavier warning the Guardian, I hadn't left this room, other than quick trips to the water closet down the hall. Neither had Brielle. Jocelyn had fetched our meals from the galley, bringing them to our table. While they'd napped or embroidered or vowed never to sail again, I'd sketched in my journal, drawing a picture of a marroweel. Another of this ship.

Gods, I was bored. My limbs were restless, so was my mind, and I was desperate for fresh air. To feel the sun shine on my face.

Maybe these clothes were an invitation for me to come out of hiding.

Maybe I'd accept.

So Zavier and the Guardian suspected I was going to try to kill him. Did it matter? No. Not really. Suspicion was not proof. And they would have been suspicious no matter what.

I'd still go to Allesaria and send word to my father about how to infiltrate the city. I'd still collect every tidbit about the Guardian's powers to pass along. I'd do everything else on Father's list.

But murder? I wasn't sure I had it in me to be an assassin. Though that wouldn't stop me from dreaming of ways to permanently wipe the smirk off the Guardian's face.

"You're not wearing those pants again, are you, Highness?" Brielle gave me a look of horror as I unfolded the tunic and pulled it over my head.

"If I had been in a gown the other day, I wouldn't have been able to swim as fast. Besides, I like them."

Her face soured. "You do? But they're so...male."

None of the men on the *Cutter* had embroidered tunics. Something she would have realized if she'd left this room. Not that I was going to force her out.

After days spent together, it was time we all had a break.

"I'm going to go above. Would you like to come?" I knew her answer before she gave it.

"Definitely not." She lay back down, curling into her pillow.

How she or Jocelyn could sleep so much was beyond me, but neither had truly gotten over their queasy stomachs. Brielle had hardly eaten since we'd been on the *Cutter*. Eight days and there was a hollowness to her cheekbones.

Hopefully, once we reached land, they'd both feel better.

"Need me to bring you anything?" I asked.

"I should be asking you that question." She closed her honey eyes and nodded off while I finished getting dressed.

With my hair braided in a thick, brown rope, I tugged on my boots on my way to the door, shutting it closed behind me. Then I climbed the stairs, a rush of nerves fluttering in my stomach when I reached the deck.

The dead marroweel was gone. Without its rotting corpse, the air smelled salty and fresh. The white gulls swept high overhead before diving into the water, some emerging with small silver fish in their beaks.

I walked toward a man standing a few paces away. He was older with brown skin and a white mustache that was curled at its ends. The rope he was coiling was as thick as my forearm. "Excuse me. How far away are we from Turah?"

He stared at me for a long moment, his gaze narrowing on mine. That assessment was so familiar that for a second, it was like being back on the docks in Roslo. Greeting a shop owner only to have them taken aback by the lack of amber starbursts in my irises.

Sometimes, people would ask about my eyes. But mostly, it unsettled others enough that they simply looked away.

This man didn't drop his gaze as his muscled arms still worked that rope. Finally, he jerked his chin toward the bow.

"Thank you?"

Would an actual, verbal answer have been too much? The only Turans on this boat who spoke to me were Zavier and the Guardian. Why was that? Had the crew been instructed to tell me nothing?

There was no point in asking this man, so I left him to his work, walking toward the bow.

Every member of the crew seemed to be on deck today, all preparing to reach shore.

I weaved past them, doing my best to stay out of the way. When I reached the front of the ship, I leaned my elbows against the railing and squinted into the distance.

Nothing. There was only water as far as I could see.

"You'll see land soon enough, Sparrow. We'll reach Turah before midday." The Guardian stood behind me, leaning against the ship's wall, ankles crossed.

He was like having a giant, burly shadow. Did this man have nothing else to do but pester me whenever I came up for air? Couldn't I have a moment of peace?

"I see you got my delivery."

"Stop breaking into my room."

"What's that word you like so much?" He tapped his chin, pretending to think it over. "No."

Midday. I only had to make it to midday. I wasn't sure what would happen when we reached shore, but at the very least, we wouldn't be trapped together on this damn ship.

He pushed off the wall and closed the distance between us, his strides deliberate, like a cat stalking a mouse. His emerald eyes were focused and sharp. His beard was thicker, reaching the point of unruly.

"You need a shave." It was an absurd comment. His facial hair was absolutely none of my business, but as always, where he was concerned, whatever thought crossed my mind came out of my mouth.

"Do I, my queen?" He reached for the dagger strapped against his ribs, taking it out of its sheath. He tossed it up, a quick flip in the air before catching it by the blade. Then he held it out, handle first, for me to take.

Were his hands made of stone? How did those blades never cut through his skin?

I gripped the weapon as he lifted his chin, exposing the long column of his neck. A strange shiver rolled over my shoulders as I stared at his skin.

It was just a throat. Every person had one. So why was my heart beating so fast? What was so appealing about his throat? The corded muscle. That bulge in its center that bobbed when he swallowed. The spicy, masculine scent that seemed to wrap around me like a satin ribbon.

"Here's your chance. Go ahead. Go for the throat."

I gulped. Was he really telling me to try to kill him? Was this another test?

"Are you going to give me a shave or not?" he asked.

I forced my eyes away from his neck as a flush crept into my face. "I'm not your valet. Do it yourself."

He dropped his chin, and our gazes clashed, his amused, mine annoyed. "We'll start with small weapons. There are no swords on board that you'll be able to wield, so we'll start your training with that dagger."

"Whoa." I lifted my free hand, palm out. "What do you mean, 'we'?"

"You asked to be armed in case of danger. We can give you a weapon, but it won't do much good if you don't know how to use it."

"Wait. *You* are training me?" No. Absolutely not.

"Someone has to."

Wasn't there an older, slower ranger who wanted the job? I really didn't need training from a renowned killer. Just a regular teacher would suffice.

"This was *your* idea," he quipped. "Unless you've changed your mind. Am I interrupting your napping schedule? Should we reschedule for another time?"

Like he'd said, I should have gone for his throat. "No." I plastered on my fakest smile. "Now would be lovely."

"Lovely," he mimicked. "First lesson, don't let me take that knife."

I nodded and gripped the handle tighter.

Don't let him take the knife. Okay. Easy enough.

Except the glint in his green eyes made my stomach drop. Wait. What was I missing?

He advanced a half step.

I backed away, checking over my shoulder to make sure I didn't get trapped in the ship's pointed bow. The railing was close, so I moved to the side, holding the knife higher. My ankle wobbled a bit, the edge of my boot catching on a floorboard as the boat rocked with a wave.

The Guardian stared at me like I'd sprouted bat wings.

"What?"

"Nothing."

"Something," I hissed. "Stop looking at me like that. You told me not to let you take the knife. This is me doing that."

"Maybe we should have started with something simpler. Like walking."

I fought the urge to stick out my tongue. "I'm not used to wearing shoes with thick soles."

"Should I send for your slippers?"

"No," I gritted out, backing away again as he advanced, this time a full step.

His eyes narrowed, his features hardening. And when he moved again, it was a blur.

The knife flew out of my hand before I even registered the sting in my wrist. Then I was falling, landing on my ass with a hard thump.

Ow. "You tripped me? Really?"

"All I did was take back my knife. You tripped yourself." The corners of his mouth quirked.

"If you laugh at me, I swear to Izzac I will find a way to stab you in the eye." I'd never prayed to the God of Death before, but there was always a first.

The Guardian dropped to a crouch, the knife dangling from his fingertips. "It is unwise to threaten me."

"Surprise, surprise. I'm not scared of you."

Even after hearing rumors of the Guardian, after listening to Banner's story about his brother, I wasn't scared. Why was that? I'd attempt to dissect why later. For now, I wanted that knife back.

I growled, forcing myself up off the deck. Then I held out my hand, waiting as he stood. "I want to try again."

"At this point, I think Zavier was right. Either you'll hurt yourself, or someone is going to kill you with your own blade."

It was entirely possible. But I snapped my fingers and opened my palm. "Again."

He shook his head but handed over the dagger. "Don't stand square to your opponent. Get into a fighting stance. Your weapons master must have at least taught you that."

It sounded vaguely familiar.

I shifted slightly to the side, mirroring his feet with my left ahead of my right. "Okay. I'm ready."

"Praise the gods," he muttered.

When he lunged, I really was ready. I shuffled backward, careful to pick up my feet so I didn't trip. "Ha!"

The gleam in his eyes made my stomach knot.

Shit. I was in so much trouble.

This time, he did trip me. One quick sweep of his front leg to mine, and my balance faltered. He took the knife straight from my grip as I dropped to my hands and knees.

Well, at least I hadn't fallen on my ass. This was slightly less embarrassing.

I pushed to my feet and held out my hand for the knife.

Except before he could pass it over again, one of the crew called his name. "Guardian."

He held up a finger. "That's enough for today."

"That's it? You're quitting already?"

"Walk around. Break in your boots."

So we really were starting my training at walking. *Wow*. How pathetic did that make me?

I wasn't going to think about the answer to that one.

"Fine. Guardian," I drawled. "Is that really what everyone calls you? You must have a name."

"I do."

I waited. And waited. And waited. "Well, what is it?"

He leaned in closer, his voice dropping low. "Maybe I'll tell you. If you earn it."

There was always a test when it came to this man. "Earn it, like your trust?"

His laugh was humorless. "You might earn my name one day. But make no mistake, Cross. I will never trust you."

Yeah, well, get in line.

He walked away without another word. Before he could see just how much his parting comment hurt.

Was it me? Was there something I did, I said, that made people inherently not trust me?

I didn't gossip. I couldn't remember the last time I'd shared someone else's secret. I did draw people sometimes without their knowledge. Maybe that was an invasion. Except very few saw my sketches.

After showing Father and Margot when I was younger and being met with scowls, I'd mostly kept my art to myself.

So what was so wrong with me that no one trusted me? Or was it really a lack of trust? Maybe the heart of the issue was faith.

No one believed *in* me. No one had trust that I was capable.

I couldn't fight. I had more than my fair share of clumsy moments. I wasn't cunning and sneaky like Mae. Had Father kept the whole truth about the crux and Allesaria from me because he feared I'd get caught and spill his secrets?

Well, he didn't need to worry. I'd never tell the Guardian the truth. My priority was my father's errand. To earn *his* trust. To prove to him I wasn't his worthless wallflower of a daughter. And in doing so, I hoped I'd help him find a way to save our people.

It might seem like an impossible task, but damn it, I wasn't giving up yet.

I looked at my boots, wiggling my toes. It was humiliating, walking laps around the deck, but I did it anyway, around and around.

Each time I made it to the stern, I paused to stare across the water. Somewhere in the distance was a golden city. My golden city.

Did Father worry about how I was faring on this journey? Did Margot stare at my empty seat at the breakfast table and wish I were there so she could scold me for running late? Had Mae already moved into my rooms? How was Arthy? He'd been learning his numbers when I left. How high could he count now? Was Banner still angry that his bride had been claimed by another?

A throat cleared behind me a moment before Zavier came to a stop at my side. His eyes were tired and his jaw covered in stubble. He needed a shave, too. And a long night's sleep. "We'll arrive in Turah soon."

"All right." I nodded. "Is the crew allowed to talk to me?"

"Yes." His eyebrows knitted together. "Why?"

"They don't."

"Ah."

Was that supposed to be an answer? Who cared if they ignored me? Why did that bother me so much? I'd likely never see this crew again.

Maybe the reason it bothered me was because they had good cause to be wary. Like Zavier had said, Turans were loyal to Turans.

No matter how I dressed, how I pretended, I was not a Turan.

But was I still a Quentin? Did anyone really claim me as theirs? Or was I like this boat, adrift between kingdoms?

"How did the training session go?" Zavier asked.

I shrugged. "Was it your idea for him to train me? Or his?"

"Mine. He is the best warrior in Turah."

I stared up at him, taking in the straight line of his nose and the band of silver above his brow. Did he always wear it? It seemed nearly set into his skin, like he'd grown into that crown.

"Are you all right?" he asked. "You seem...sad."

I shrugged. "Just homesick." It wasn't a lie. It wasn't the truth, either. "Zavier."

We both turned as the mustached man I'd spoken to earlier approached. "You're needed on the *Cannon*," he said.

Zavier nodded, glancing off the port side to see the other ship sailing closer. Then, without a word, he followed the mustached man off the quarterdeck while I took one last look at the sea that stretched toward Roslo.

If I wasn't homesick, did that mean everyone back home had moved on without me, too? Was Mae hugging Arthy like she'd promised? Did my brother even realize I was gone?

The answers would probably break my heart. So I abandoned the deck, leaving the men to make their final preparations while I went below to tell Brielle and Jocelyn it was time to pack.

Both girls came alive at the announcement.

Then, a few hours after midday, with anchors dropped and the crew preparing the rowboats that would ferry us to shore, I returned to the stern, staring across the open ocean one last time.

Did anyone miss me? Did I miss them?

Yes.

But not as much as I'd thought.

"Highness," Jocelyn called from the base of the quarterdeck's stairs. "It's time."

I turned my back to the life I'd once lived. I turned toward the future. Toward Turah.

Zavier's kingdom loomed beyond the ship, past shallow waters and sandy beaches.

I fell in line with Brielle and Jocelyn for the next rowboat, surveying the ship as we waited.

The Guardian stood at the bow of the *Cutter*, where we'd been earlier this morning. His arms were crossed and his jaw set. He seemed to be monitoring the rowboats, making sure they made it safely to shore.

Except his eyes didn't track the boats. He was staring at the land itself, his expression hard and unblinking.

Like Turah was an enemy.

Or a battlefield.

A chill crept down my spine like ice-cold water snaking along my skin.

For the first time since I'd set foot on the *Cutter*, I felt like I might be sick.

"Highness, would you like to go first?" Brielle asked, gesturing to where a crewman was waiting, his hand outstretched to help us down the ladder to the rowboat below.

"Go ahead," I told her.

She nodded, stepping past me. When she was safely below, I sent Jocelyn next.

Maybe I wasn't quite ready to leave the *Cutter* after all.

I was shuffling forward, nerves fluttering in my stomach, when I felt him at my side. "Any chance that this is where we'll part ways?"

"Not yet." The Guardian's smile was wolfish. Menacing. And not attractive, not in the slightest. "Welcome to Turah, my queen."

Fourteen

Jocelyn gripped my hand so hard my knuckles cracked. The bench seat on the rowboat was wide enough for three, but she was sitting so close she was practically on my lap. Brielle was seated on my other side, her back stiff as she watched the shoreline.

"If I never set foot on a boat again, I'll die a happy woman," Jocelyn said.

"Don't say that. You need to sail home."

Sadness filled her brown eyes.

"You'll go home," I said. "You promised your mother, remember?"

"Yeah." She looked behind us, past the *Cutter*, the *Cleaver*, and the *Cannon*, all anchored in the deeper waters along the shoreline.

Zavier sat in the front of our rowboat, his posture rigid and his shoulders tense.

He hadn't spoken a word as we loaded onto the rowboat to go to shore. He was back to the silent, brooding prince. Was that because my lady's maids were around to hear?

Probably. I hadn't told either of them that he could speak. I wasn't going to fail that test of his confidence.

If he stayed quiet, so would I.

The man rowing had gold hoops in both of his ears. A winding tattoo decorated the side of his neck. He wore leather cuffs around his wrists and a red scarf around his head. His arms flexed with every plunge and pull of the oars into the water.

I had a feeling that he'd return to the *Cutter* once we were on shore.

Where would the ships go from here? There had to be a port for ships their size. Why hadn't we gone to a city? Why drop us here, in the middle of nowhere?

The beach where we were headed was only a short stretch of smooth, gray sand. Rowboats from the *Cleaver* and the *Cannon* had already made land.

The four warriors who'd accompanied Zavier to our wedding were unloading, wading through the shallows to the beach. They had no trunks or cases. All they had were their clothes, weapons, and satchels strapped across their chests.

There were five trunks on shore. Mine. One for Brielle. Another for Jocelyn. Not even Zavier had much. Like his warriors, only a satchel.

Maybe they should have told us to pack light.

I scanned the beach, searching for the Guardian. After his ominous welcome to Turah, I'd lost him in my climb down to the rowboat. I'd expected him to follow, but when I'd looked up, he'd been gone.

Given his tendency to pop up like an itchy rash, I was certain he was lingering around somewhere.

"Do you think there's a city nearby?" Brielle asked, her voice low.

Our tattooed rower scowled, annoyed that she'd break the silence with a perfectly reasonable question.

"I don't know. I don't see anything."

If there was a town, it was camouflaged in the landscape. There was no sign of a road or trail through that forest.

Beyond the sand were reed grasses, their tips swaying in the breeze. And then came looming hills covered in dense pine trees and thick underbrush. A veil of mist cloaked the tallest peaks, and the air was cool, the wind sharp.

This beach looked lonely and out of place, like the gray rocks at both sides were slowly taking over, forcing it into the water to drown. It was so different from the Quentin beaches I wasn't even sure it could be called a beach. There weren't miles and miles of white, sun-kissed sand. It wasn't warm and welcoming.

Though it was beautiful. Rugged. Intimidating. But beautiful.

As we reached the shallow waters, Zavier stood and jumped over the boat's edge, his boots splashing with every step as he hauled us up on shore.

I didn't wait for his hand and stepped over the side, my booted heels digging into the sand. It wasn't soft and warm like the beaches in Quentis. It was stiff and unyielding, protesting against my heels with every step.

A stray tendril of hair caught the breeze and flew into my mouth, the taste of my dye bitter on my lips before I yanked it away.

Once Brielle and Jocelyn were on shore, Zavier motioned for us to follow him toward the grasses where the line of his stone-faced rangers waited.

"Our things?" I asked.

His gaze darted over my shoulder in silent answer.

Five men carried our trunks a few paces behind, following our tracks in the sand.

It was on that backward glance I spotted him.

The Guardian stood on the shore, just out of the ocean's reach. His clothes were wet, his hair dripping on his shoulders. And he wasn't alone.

He was speaking to the High Priest.

My breath caught in my throat.

I couldn't feel the Voster magic. Was he too far away? Was that why I hadn't felt him on the ships?

Oh, gods. Did this mean he'd be traveling with us to Allesaria? My insides knotted at the idea of his magic being constant and close. I wasn't sure I could deal with its sting day after day.

The High Priest and the Guardian kept their heads together as they spoke. There was a familiarity between them I hadn't noticed before. It was almost affectionate, like brothers.

Had the Voster given the Guardian his powers? Was that how he could swim so fast? Move so quickly?

It seemed too obvious. Too easy. But could it be that simple? Could they give their magic to humans?

The Voster were as secretive about their magic and their origins as they were about where they lived and how many priests made up the brotherhood. That book I'd read about them had been mostly speculation. Reports of witness accounts.

Father had asked me to discover the source of the Guardian's abilities. Maybe instead of asking me, he should have consulted Brother Dime.

The Guardian nodded at whatever the priest said, then took a step back and pressed both hands over his heart, giving a slight bow.

The High Priest made the same gesture. Then he put one hand on the Guardian's shoulder.

That touch would have sent me out of my skin, but the Guardian didn't so much as flinch.

There was a familiar black case strapped to the High Priest's back.

The Shield of Sparrows.

He kept that treaty with him. I'd never wondered where those documents were kept, but it made sense that the Voster would be responsible for their protection. What other treaties and accords did they control? Were there records of the Chain of Sevens stashed away for safekeeping?

What happened if those documents were lost?

Or destroyed?

Would the treaty be broken if there was nothing left? Was that Father's plan—to break the Shield of Sparrows? To hunt down the brotherhood's stores, then burn the treaties to nothing but ash?

The priest let the Guardian go, then walked down the sandy beach toward the rocks. He climbed them with deft ease in bare feet, his hand gripping the hem of his burgundy robes. Then he was swallowed up by the forest, disappearing from sight.

To where? Did the Voster live in Turah? Or was he on his way to Ozarth's border? Maybe the High Priest called Allesaria home.

Except he seemed to be going in the opposite direction. If he was traveling to Allesaria, too, it wasn't with us.

I faced forward, mind whirling with too many questions. The warriors ahead of Zavier broke from their line, each cutting a different path through the reed grass.

Brielle and Jocelyn stayed behind Zavier. And I came up behind them all, slowing only to take one final look at the place where the High Priest had vanished.

My problems had started the day I'd run into Brother Dime in the castle's gallery. The day the High Priest had floated into my father's throne room.

Dread pitted in my gut. This wasn't the last I'd see of the High Priest, was it? There was no way for me to be certain, but I knew, in my bones, he wasn't done ruining my life quite yet.

The Guardian began walking across the sand, dragging a hand through his wet hair and pushing it away from his face. His large hand pulled the water from his beard. His tunic, the same cream fabric as my own, was nearly transparent. It molded to the strength of his chest, to the contours of his rippled stomach.

A warmth spread through my belly, pooling lower. *Oh, gods, no.* I forced my eyes forward, clenching my fists and molars.

Yes, he was attractive, but I could not—would not—let a handsome face and body carved from stone distract me from my task. That man was a murderer. I refused to allow a spontaneous physical reaction to cloud my judgment.

I blocked out all thoughts of the Guardian, listening to the men behind me carrying our trunks.

"Thought Jack would be here," one man said.

Another man grunted. "He joined Ramsey's militia two months ago. Haven't seen him since."

Ramsey. As in King Ramsey Wolfe? Zavier's father?

He had a militia? Why? Wasn't his royal army enough?

Or was this militia an elite group of warriors, like Zavier's rangers? Maybe those training to lead safeguards and shelters during the migration?

I hung back, ears strained for more, but the men must have noticed me eavesdropping because they didn't speak another word.

The sound of a horse's whinny had me standing on my toes, peering past Brielle's head as we crested the slope. I paused at the top, taking in the horses and people crowded between us and the trees. There were five wagons, each hitched to a team. Two were brimming with chopped wood.

There were a few women milling around with the men, and their clothes were similar to mine. Leather pants and sturdy boots paired with loose tunics. Clothes that were plain yet practical. Most of the women had their hair braided, not entirely unlike mine.

Maybe I'd actually blend in with these people. There was no way for them to know I was the Sparrow, not having just arrived. There was a comfort in that invisibility. I'd spent most of my life avoiding notice. I'd never enjoyed an abundance of attention, and I certainly didn't need it in Turah.

Except even dressed the same, too many eyes tracked my way as we approached the group. Too many people openly stared. Men tending to horses paused and studied my profile. Women's gazes narrowed, not just on me, but on Brielle and Jocelyn, too. In their simple blue dresses, they stood apart.

We all stood apart.

Zavier's warriors, who'd already claimed saddled horses, must have made a quick announcement. News was spreading fast.

I was Zavier's princess bride. The Sparrow.

So much for invisibility.

Zavier walked to the wagon, and we all stood at its side while our trunks were loaded into the back.

A gorgeous woman with bronze skin approached. Her black hair was braided at her temples, three tight rows with the rest free to curl around her shoulders. She had a sword sheathed across her back. "Zavier."

He dipped his chin in acknowledgment, then motioned to me.

I guess that was as much introduction as he could give with Brielle and Jocelyn nearby.

The woman dropped into a small bow. "Princess Odessa Wolfe."

Was that how they were going to address me? Absolutely not. "Call me Odessa. Please. 'Princess' and 'Wolfe' are unnecessary."

She looked to Zavier, eyebrows raised. Her eyes were a rich, beautiful brown. With the Turan green starburst, they were the color of the forest beyond the beach.

Zavier nodded, giving her permission to drop the titles. And his name. Maybe he knew I'd just keep correcting her if she called me Princess Odessa Wolfe.

"Odessa," the woman said. "My name is Tillia. Welcome."

"Thank you."

She had three empty satchels looped over her shoulder. She slipped them off, extending one to me and the others to Brielle and Jocelyn. "If there is anything important that you want to retrieve from your trunks before we set off, I'd keep it in these."

"Wh-what?" Brielle stammered, taking hold of the brown leather strap. "Are our trunks not coming with us?"

"We'll be leaving soon, traveling together. But the supplies often don't keep pace. There's a chance we'll be separated. Best to keep what's most important with you."

"But—"

I put my hand on Brielle's arm, silencing her protest. "Thank you, Tillia."

"Odessa." Her brown eyes softened before she turned and walked away.

Brielle and Jocelyn shared a panicked look, then hurried to their trunks, flipping open the lids to stuff items into their satchels.

I closed the gap to Zavier, lowering my voice. "Tillia has a sword. It looks to be just my size."

The corner of his mouth twitched. Then his gaze shifted to my trunks, a silent command to pack.

"Does everyone here know you can speak?" I asked quietly.

He nodded.

"Does everyone in Turah know you can speak?"

He shook his head.

So much for Turans being loyal to Turans. Though I suspected it was more than some political strategy. Zavier seemed like a quiet soul. A man who didn't speak if there was nothing to say.

"So I shouldn't have told Brielle."

He bent, his voice barely a whisper as his mouth came to my ear. "You didn't."

"How do you know?"

"Because you're trying so hard to earn my trust."

My heart sank. It was the truth. The pitiful, real truth.

I was so far out of my depths it was almost comical. They'd read me like an open book days ago, hadn't they? They saw through every facade, every action.

What the hell was I doing here? I was no spy.

I turned, hiding a shaky breath under the guise of packing this satchel. The only thing I wanted from my trunks was my journal, but I packed a clean dress, too, just in case. Then I left the rest of my things, the books and slippers and jewels and jars, behind, following Zavier as he marched toward a pair of saddled horses.

His was a gorgeous bay stallion that stood tall and proud. It reminded me of Banner's horse. An animal fit for a commander. A general.

Beside it was a blue roan mare, her grayish coat a pretty contrast to her black hair. She sniffed at me as I approached, then went back to grazing.

Brielle and Jocelyn were taken to join a group of warriors. Apparently, we wouldn't be traveling together.

"Can you ride?" Zavier asked.

"Yes." Not well, but I wouldn't fall off. Probably. "I take it we're not camping here."

He handed me the roan's reins.

That meant no. So I took a deep breath, put my foot in a stirrup, then swung into the saddle, giving myself a moment to find my balance on the horse's back.

The clop of hooves was my only warning as the Guardian appeared at my side, riding a massive black stallion.

"Have you spent much time on a horse, Sparrow?" he asked.

"Can I ride? Yes. Do I often? No."

"Pity."

Meaning I'd be spending many, many hours on this horse.

What if I pushed him off his? Would he break his neck? Wouldn't that be nice.

"We're ready, Zavier," the Guardian said.

Zavier nodded, and without fanfare or announcement, we left the clearing, my horse keeping pace behind his. He rode to the trees, a cue for everyone to do the same.

A minute later, five warriors galloped past, the Guardian in the lead.

My heart hammered, louder than the hooves, as we descended into the forest.

When I looked back, the ocean, the ships, were gone.

I'd spent my whole life living by the sea. The crash of waves had been in the background my entire life. The rustling of tree leaves wasn't the same. It was too quiet, its rhythm too random.

It felt as if my heartbeat had changed. My ears were too empty.

The forest stretched before us like a different ocean, this one made of endless trunks and branches.

There was no trail, no path, but the warriors seemed to know the way.

I kept pace with Zavier, staying at his side, my gaze sweeping left to right and right to left.

Searching. For landmarks. For buildings. For anything to note in my journal. There might not be a clear path, but I was expected to find one anyway. And it was time to do what I'd vowed.

To earn my father's trust. To do this duty for my kingdom. To save my people.

To find the road to Allesaria.

Fifteen

How badly would it hurt if I jumped off this horse? More or less than the current pain radiating through my body?

Every second was agony. My back ached. My legs were cramped. My ass was numb. My skull was splitting.

At some point, we had to stop, right? We couldn't keep going forever. Or did they expect me to sleep on this horse?

Well, it hurt too much to sleep.

We'd ridden through the night, traversing through the forest. I'd never been in a place so dark. The towering trees and their heavy limbs had obscured all but a sliver of silver light from Calandra's twin moons.

Every other Turan had carried a torch, but the light had barely kept the shadows at bay. All they really did was allow a rider behind to see a rider ahead so that our caravan didn't get divided and people lost.

We'd stayed in a tight cluster, the horses kept close. The wagons trailed behind. My foot had rubbed against Zavier's on more than one occasion as we'd weaved through tree trunks and around areas where the underbrush was so thick not even the horses could trample it down.

The pace had slowed to a crawl at one point, and we'd shifted to ride single file so we could follow the trail.

A trail blazed by the Guardian.

He hadn't needed a torch.

Those ever-changing eyes must allow him to see in the dark.

It went on the mental list of powers I was noting for Father.

Considering I had nothing else of value to provide, it would have to be enough. Because I sure as hell couldn't explain where we were or how we'd gotten here. I was, well…lost.

Was that the point of this nighttime death march? To keep me in the dark? To shatter my internal compass? Not that it had ever been reliable, day or night. All I knew at this point was that the ocean was probably behind us. Maybe. It was a guess.

Later, when I had the chance to summarize our journey thus far, my only instruction would be *ride through the forest until your entire body screams in agony*. Oh, and *if you're not terrified, you're doing it wrong*.

Well, I'd been scared last night. Fear had kept me awake the whole night. Whenever there had been a gap in the treetops, I'd stared into the sky. Then, I'd prayed.

To Ama and Oda, the stars.

To the Six, their children, who made up the shades in between.

The trees had thinned near dawn, allowing us more and more space to travel. Then, a while ago, the trees had given way entirely to a sweeping plain. Behind us, the forest was a wall of green, growing smaller and smaller as we kept riding.

I had no idea how long it had been since we'd emerged from that dark forest. An hour. Two. Three. Ten.

This headache, this everywhere pain, made thinking nearly impossible. Even breathing hurt.

"Are you all right?" Zavier asked, his voice low.

"Fine." If fine meant I wanted to die, then yes, I was fine.

It was the first time he'd checked on me since we left the coast. It was the first voice I'd heard since then, too.

No one had spoken, not a single word. We'd all blindly followed the Guardian toward daybreak.

In the distance, a range of mountains cut a jagged line into the sky. Their sharp peaks were capped in white, glowing as the sun lifted higher. The land between us and those mountains stretched on and on. It would take us days and days to reach the foothills. If that was where we were even going.

How long would we continue? We had to stop eventually, right? If not for the people, at least the horses.

Brielle and Jocelyn were somewhere behind me, riding amidst the Turans. I wanted to turn, to find them in the crowd, but the last time I'd twisted in the saddle, not only were there too many people blocking the way, it had freaking hurt. So I stayed facing forward, glaring daggers into the back of our fearless leader.

The Guardian must have felt my stare. He shifted to look over his shoulder, checking to make sure all of his sheep were following, then urged his horse into a gallop.

"Oh, gods." I whimpered. Running? We were running now? Bouncing around in this saddle might kill me.

The thunder of hooves sounded before a group of Turans raced past us, hurrying to keep pace with the Guardian. But before I could urge my mare to do the same, Zavier held out his hand.

"They're going to set up camp. We don't need to rush."

My entire frame sagged in relief. "Thank the gods."

"The coastal forests are thick with grizzurs. Their nocturnal vision is poor, so it's safer to travel through those areas by night."

"Ah." Apparently, the monsters in Turah preferred to kill their prey during waking hours.

Another group of warriors passed, riding fast but not at the breakneck speed of the others. Behind them chased the two wagons overloaded with firewood. Their wheels left twin tracks in the tall grass.

The landscape had changed so quickly it was almost like being home in Quentis, taking an afternoon carriage ride through the countryside.

Except there were no farms or buildings or towns to be seen. In every direction, there were only these rugged plains of gold and green grasses, stretching to those mountains.

Was there a crossing somewhere out there to reach Allesaria?

I couldn't imagine attempting to go over those peaks. I'd never seen mountains like that before, so massive, so tall, they kissed the sky.

Turah was the largest of the five kingdoms, four times the size of Quentis, though it had less than half the number of people. I'd studied maps of Calandra. I had a general sense of the continent's geography. But those maps didn't do the difference justice. They'd never conveyed the magnitude of this landscape.

It was vast. Overwhelming. Magnificent. Frightening.

"I've never seen snow," I said, hoping some conversation with Zavier would distract me from the aches and pains. "It doesn't snow in Roslo. In our coldest months, all the worst days are gray and rainy."

He hummed. That was all I got.

Honestly, I should have known better. Zavier wasn't the type for small talk.

I shifted in the saddle, searching for a position that was less painful than the rest. I'd never, ever been so aware of my tailbone.

Despite the pain, the stiffness, I turned to look behind us. With the others having ridden ahead, I was able to see Brielle. She was slumped forward, asleep. Tillia rode at her side, ensuring she didn't topple to the ground.

When Tillia met my gaze, I mouthed, *Thank you.*

She nodded back.

The steady beat of hooves had nearly lulled me to sleep earlier. My eyelids had gotten heavy, drooping until I'd startled myself straight. The jolt of pain had been enough to deter me from letting myself drift off again.

I'd kept myself awake by memorizing anything that could be considered a landmark, from an outcropping of rocks to a cluster of trees. Anything to note in my journal that might help Father's troops find their way across these lands.

Go toward the mountains wasn't going to be enough detail with a range that stretched so wide I couldn't see either end.

A wagon came into view ahead, stopped atop a gentle rise. Beyond them were wisps of white, rising from the earth, and the scent of smoke in the air.

"Campfires?" I asked, sitting straighter.

Zavier nodded.

Was this how it would always be? Nods and short replies. He hadn't exactly been chatting on the *Cutter*, but since we'd reached Turah, he'd hardly spoken a word. At this rate, it might take me a decade to get to know my husband.

When I looked back to Brielle, she was awake, her pretty face etched in pain. Jocelyn had joined her, looking tired but not nearly as miserable.

It didn't take us long to reach the others. When we crested the rise, I spotted a cluster of tents surrounded by a circle of fires. At least twenty were being set ablaze, each growing larger as men added more wood from the wagons. Beyond them was a river that wound through the plains like a blue snake.

Zavier swung off his horse, his movements easy, like riding all night was nothing. He held out a hand to help me down.

My muscles were locked and tense, but somehow I freed my feet from the stirrups and slid out of the saddle, nearly crumpling when my boots touched the earth.

Would they let me walk the rest of the way to Allesaria? The idea of getting back on this horse made me want to scream.

"Zavier." Tillia joined us, hand outstretched. "I'll take care of your horses."

He passed her the reins, then took my elbow, urging me along at his side. Every step was stiff. Agonizing.

"I'm sorry," he murmured, his green eyes full of apology as he guided me toward a tent in the center of the campsite.

A man was hammering a stake into the ground, securing the canvas to the earth. "They're nearly finished inside."

Zavier gave him a single nod, then looked down at me like he wanted to say something.

"What?" I whispered.

"Highness." Jocelyn hurried to my side, clearly suffering through only a fraction of my pain. "Are you all right?"

"Tired." I forced a smile.

Zavier sighed. Whatever he wanted to say would have to wait.

Someday, maybe I'd learn to have those wordless conversations like he did with the Guardian. But we didn't know each other yet. So when he dipped his chin and walked away, I assumed he wanted me to stay put.

I couldn't have walked much farther anyway.

"Why do you think they're lighting so many fires?" Jocelyn asked, looping her arm through mine.

"I have no idea." I leaned into her side, using her strong frame to keep me on my feet. My very bones were weary. Even my hair hurt.

The scent of roasted meat mingled with the smoke, yet even as my stomach growled, I didn't have the energy to eat. I just wanted to lay down and close my eyes.

"You should eat something." Jocelyn slid her arm free. "I'll find Brielle. We'll bring you food."

"Sure." I didn't have the energy to argue, either.

As she slipped away, weaving past tents, I peeked into my own, finding a woman inside. She was setting up a small cot and—

Was that a bathtub? Or was I hallucinating?

Oof, my ass hurt. The feeling was slowly coming back, tingles and pinpricks shooting through my legs and backside. I was massaging the muscles through my pants, not caring how I looked, when a tug on my braid yanked my head back.

"Do you have no personal boundaries?" I swatted the Guardian's hand away.

His eyes were hazel again, a mix of the Turan colors that surrounded us, from brown to green to gold. He dragged his gaze down my tunic to where one of my hands still palmed my ass. "Sore, my queen? We'll have to add riding to your training regimen. That, or being ridden. I'll have a word with Zavier."

I hated the way my face flamed. I hated the way he could so easily grate on my nerves. Never in my life had I met someone so bold and unfiltered. He knew Zavier was as uninterested in me as I was in climbing atop that blue roan again, but he kept throwing it in my face.

Did I want to sleep with Zavier? Not yet. He was handsome and built, but he was a stranger. I'd never been the type for casual affairs.

"Don't you have anyone else to bother?" I seethed.

"Not today." The corner of his mouth turned up as the flap to my tent flew open and the woman inside stepped out.

"Princess." She waved me inside. "Your tent is ready."

"Thank you." I gave her a smile, then flicked the end of my braid, letting it smack the Guardian in the face.

His laugh followed me inside the tent.

It was more spacious than I'd expected. The cot was against one side, nothing more than a platform and two blankets, but the platform would keep me from sleeping in the dirt.

My trunks were still loaded onto the wagon, but there was a neat stack of fresh clothes on the foot of the cot. And against the other wall was a simple round tub that had been filled with steaming water. She must have brought it in through the flaps that opened on the back of the tent.

"Yes," I moaned at the thought of washing away the smell of horse and wind.

"Need help with your hair?" A rogue whisper caressed the shell of my ear.

I whirled on the Guardian, planting my hands on his chest as I shoved him out. Or tried to shove him out. The son of a bitch didn't so much as budge. "Do you mind?"

"Not at all." He smirked.

"If that water gets cold, I swear to Ama and Oda that I will kill you with my bare hands, here and now."

"Such rage, my queen. I am simply here to ensure you're comfortable."

"I'm comfortable. Happy?"

"Would you like a meal?"

"Not at the moment. Goodbye."

His grin widened. "You've got today and tomorrow to rest. We'll give the horses and weaker riders"—meaning me—"a break. The journey beyond the river will not be easy."

"Harder than last night? Actually." I lifted a finger. "I don't want to know."

"We'll train tomorrow."

That idea made me want to cry, but I wouldn't give him the satisfaction. "I'd love to. Anything else?"

"Don't wander past the fires. Not even for the river."

I opened my mouth to ask why but stopped myself. Why was it that the Guardian was always the man to deliver the messages? When would Zavier stop hiding from me? How were we ever going to get to know each other if he was always gone?

"Fine. Would you please tell Zavier I'd like to speak to him later? In private?"

The Guardian's eyes narrowed. "Why?"

"Because I'd like to speak to my husband in private. What we discuss is none of your concern."

"The crown prince is always my concern."

"If you're not going to send him here, I guess I'll have to find his tent myself."

"Feel free to wander into mine, Princess." He leaned in closer. "Zavier likes to share."

My breath caught as that statement drove straight through my chest like a blade. Had they shared women before? Would Zavier expect that from me?

I didn't want that. I didn't want the Guardian.

He studied me like he was reading every thought that passed through my mind. His eyes shifted from hazel to green. It wasn't a blink like I'd seen before, the colors changing instantly.

The green spread slowly, chasing away the other shades. It bloomed like the heat beneath my skin.

My heart beat faster, harder, climbing into my throat. It was dangerous, holding this man's gaze, yet I couldn't seem to stop. To blink. He snared me with that emerald green as if I were his prey, drawing me in closer and closer.

"No," I said. To him. To myself.

I took a step away, crossing my arms over my chest. I was not that woman. I was not that weak.

If this was another test, he could go fuck himself.

"Highness, are you—" Brielle's question was cut short with a gasp as she stepped into the tent and noticed I wasn't alone. "Oh. Uh…"

"The Guardian was just leaving."

He stared at me for another long moment. Then he was gone.

The air instantly felt thinner. Cooler. Easier to breathe.

"You should be careful around him," she said, checking over her shoulder, making sure we were alone. "He's dangerous."

"I'm aware."

He carried that danger in his body, like a permanent cloak of malice and rage. I'd noticed it before, but it had never been like this. Maybe because we'd always spoken in open spaces. But here, in this cramped tent?

Oh, yes, he was dangerous. In more ways than one.

I shivered, the movement sending ripples of pain through my limbs. "I'm sore."

"Me too." She shuffled to the bed, sitting at its end. "You should take a bath."

"Do you have a tent?"

"Jocelyn and I are sharing. It's not set up yet, but they're working on it. It's closer to the fires. They put you in the center of camp."

Where I'd be protected.

"Jocelyn went to find food."

"Okay." I walked toward the tub, every muscle in my arms and shoulders screaming as I stripped my tunic over my head. "That was…a strange night."

She closed her eyes. "I've never been in such a dark place."

"Neither have I."

"Tillia said it was safer to travel at night away from the coast because of the grizzur. Do you believe that?"

"I don't see why she'd lie to us." I kicked off my pants and underclothes, then climbed into the tub, sinking into the water with a low moan. "I've never hurt so much in my life."

"I used to ride all the time. At home on the farm," she said. "But nothing could have prepared me for this."

"You should lie down while you wait."

"It's your bed, Highness."

"I don't mind." I closed my eyes, leaning against the tub's edge. My braid draped over its lip. My knees were tucked close to my chest, but I was sitting in this water until it went cold.

"I think they made us ride all night so we couldn't tell where we were going," she said, curling up on her side, her hands tucked under her cheek. "They don't trust us."

And they shouldn't.

"I was sure we'd be attacked by a tarkin or bariwolf." She yawned. "Do you think the fires will keep them away from the camp?"

"I don't know."

At this point, I didn't know anything other than the aches in my body and the weariness in my soul. So I closed my eyes, savoring the warmth of the water.

I didn't get to sleep.

Before I could drift off, a roar ripped through the campsite.

A roar, vicious and feral, that sent a chill down my spine.

A roar that meant maybe Zavier had been telling me the truth.

That in Turah, it was safer at night.

Sixteen

Sleep was impossible. Not only was it too bright, but Brielle was passed out on my bed—and I kept waiting for another roar.

After I'd gotten out of the bath and dressed in fresh clothes, I'd squeezed in beside Brielle to rest. Except each time I shut my eyes, my ears would pick up on the slightest sounds—a fly buzzing, footsteps passing—and I'd crack an eyelid.

Something had roared, right? I hadn't made that up in the tub.

The noise had only come once, and at this point, I wasn't sure what was real. Was this delirium? Was I dreaming? Maybe I was still riding that horse, asleep and imagining baths and roars and tents.

"Miss you," Brielle murmured, snuggling closer. Her arm slid around my waist.

I shied away, checking that she was asleep. Yep. Dead to the realm.

Who did she miss? Her mother? A lover? Brielle had been my lady's maid for years, but I didn't really know her. We weren't friends.

I didn't have friends.

There'd always been so much activity at the castle, so many requirements between tutors and appearances and, as of late, wedding planning. When I had spare time, I preferred to spend it alone in the solitude of my room or reading a book in the library or hiking to my cliffside.

But it wasn't only a busy schedule that kept me secluded. It was also by choice.

I was a princess of Quentis. People expected me to know things. To be privy to Father's plans and aspirations.

When I was younger, I'd had a flock of friends, mostly daughters of wealthy noblemen in the city. The girls would come to the castle for tea, and we'd play with dolls. As we grew, we would attend balls and parties together.

And then they'd gossip about me behind my back.

They faked our friendships so they could glean information about my father to relay back to theirs. Or they faked our friendships because they thought it would improve their station.

I hated fake. I hated lies.

So I'd stopped making "friends."

Mae, on the other hand, loved to play the social game. She had a litany of friends, and she stole secrets from them all, collecting scandals the way she collected knives. She'd leverage her friends' mishaps and mistakes to keep them in line. To keep them loyal.

The papermen in Quentis would drool if they knew how many secrets she hoarded.

My sister didn't care that her friends would just as soon stab her in the back. She didn't seem to care that most of those girls called her a cunt and a whore.

But I wasn't Mae.

I cared.

So during parties, I'd stay long enough for Father and Margot to acknowledge my attendance, and then I'd slip away to my rooms alone. After Banner and I got engaged, I'd been expected to spend evenings at his side. My favorite time at parties was when the men would abandon the women to have hushed conversations and drink rye whiskey behind closed doors. The moment Banner's back was turned, I'd sneak away.

But here, in Turah, I didn't want to be alone. Maybe Jocelyn and Brielle could be my friends, at least before I sent them home. Station and status didn't seem to be as important here.

The tent's flap opened, and Jocelyn ducked inside, carrying a plate. She froze when she saw Brielle asleep.

I put a finger to my mouth and, careful not to shift the cot, slid out from beneath Brielle's arm and stood. Then I quietly pulled on my boots before following Jocelyn outside.

"Here you go, Highness." She thrust the plate into my hands. It was full of roasted meat and a chunk of bread with a hard crust. "I'll get Brielle. I'm sorry she fell asleep in your bed. She'll be mortified when—"

"Leave her," I said. "It's been a hard ride for all of us. And I can't sleep, not during the day."

"But—"

"I'm going to wander around the camp for a bit." I lifted the plate. "And I promise I'll eat."

"Highness." She dipped into a curtsy, then left me alone.

The bright sunlight made me squint, and I gave my eyes a moment to adjust, tilting my head to the heavens and letting the day's heat warm my face.

The sky was a blue haze, the smoke from all of the fires cloaking the air. The scents of charred wood and sweet meat filled my nose.

I took a bite, groaning as flavor burst on my tongue. My stomach growled, and my hunger returned with a force. It wasn't ladylike or refined, but I inhaled my food, setting the plate inside the tent once it was empty. Then I set off to wander.

While I'd been in my bath, the Turans had been busy. I walked through a sea of tan canvas tents stretching out in every direction. I picked a path that weaved toward the outer circle of the camp. Every Turan I passed ducked his chin, staring at the dirt. Most scowled.

The women seemed to have disappeared. Maybe they'd been given a chance to rest.

I followed my nose, the acrid sting of smoke getting sharper as I neared the camp's edge. Past the last row of tents was a wide swath of grass that extended to the fire and river beyond.

Sparks floated into the air, vanishing into flecks of ash. The crackle sounded in all directions, and though the smell of smoke was strong, I didn't mind the noise. It was almost a replacement for ocean waves.

"Highness." Tillia spoke from behind me, her hands clasped together.

"Odessa," I corrected. If Zavier wasn't called Highness in his own country, then I certainly didn't need the title.

"Is there anything I can do for you?"

"No, I was just wandering."

She didn't move, not until I took a step closer to the fire. Then she stepped, too.

Right. How dare I think I could walk around alone? "Zavier assigned you to shadow me, didn't he? I promise I'm no flight risk. I was only restless."

She nodded. "Of course."

But did she leave me alone? No.

As I walked through the grass, following the circle of fires, she stayed five paces behind me the entire way. I was used to guards constantly at my heels. I'd had them my entire life. Tillia's company shouldn't have bothered me.

But those days on the *Cutter* had given me the illusion of freedom.

There hadn't been a guard on the ship. There hadn't been a need. And stupid me, I'd thought maybe there wouldn't be a need in Turah.

That I could walk without a shadow. That I could have some space.

"Zavier said we'd be staying here for a few days," I said, turning to face her. "Will you be with me the whole time?"

"Yes. My tent is beside yours."

So she was my faithful babysitter. "Where will we go from here?"

"We'll travel to Ellder."

Ellder. The name was familiar from Father's hurried lesson on Turah the night of my wedding. It was a fortress, one of the largest, if I recalled the details correctly. But I had no idea how far it was from this camp. It could be a day's ride or seven and I wouldn't have a clue. "I'm afraid I'm a little disoriented. How far away is Ellder?"

"It's far. This is not an easy journey. There are some established encampments along the way. But in between, we'll set up temporary stations like this."

"Ah. And is Ellder where we'll pick up supplies before continuing on to Allesaria?"

The moment it was out of my mouth, I regretted the question. Because Tillia's brown eyes turned instantly wary and her expression hardened. "Perhaps."

That meant no.

Damn. I guess I couldn't count on Tillia to share details of the capital.

"Did I hear a roar earlier?" I asked, hoping a change in subject would soften her gaze.

She opened her mouth, but before she could answer, her attention shifted over my head.

There was no need to turn to see who stood at my back. I felt his presence. It was as noticeable as the waves of heat rolling off the fires.

Tillia ducked her chin, then disappeared into the cluster of tents.

Trading one babysitter for another.

"Am I not allowed to be alone?" I asked as I turned to face the Guardian.

"Your tent is safe." There was a taunt in that statement. No one, not even my husband, would venture inside.

"Have you no one else to pester?"

"Not today."

My mouth flattened into a thin line as I brushed past him. Whether he liked it or not, I was going to keep wandering.

I didn't stick to the ring of fires but ducked in and out of the tents. I passed men busy chopping wood or sharpening knives. With every turn I made, the Guardian followed, and when I risked chaste glances over my shoulder, his eyes were always waiting, always emerald green.

By the time I made it back to the other side of the camp, the exhaustion from earlier had returned. So had the aches the bath had momentarily soothed.

I only hoped I could find my tent. My pride had taken enough lashings from the Guardian today. I wasn't sure it would survive another if I had to ask him to return me to my bed.

The Guardian came to my side, his arms crossed, legs planted wide as I watched the flames from the closest fire tickling the air.

"About that roar I heard earlier," I said.

"What about it?"

Confirmation enough. At least I wasn't delirious. "What was it?"

"A monster."

I rolled my eyes. "That doesn't answer my question."

"Does it matter?"

"Yes." I looked up at his profile, waiting.

His silence gave me a moment to scrutinize his face, searching for flaws. There were none. In a way, he looked a bit like Zavier. The Guardian was larger, though. His features more pronounced. Bolder. But they had a few similarities. The straight nose. The slight hollows beneath cheekbones. The sharp jaw. How had I not noticed before?

Were they related? Cousins, maybe? Brothers?

"A grizzur," he said. "This is their territory."

Hence the fires. I shuddered.

Grizzurs were monsters I'd only read about in books. They were myths. Legends. In my world, they didn't exist beyond the page.

Except I wasn't in my world anymore, was I?

"Did you kill it?" I asked.

The look he gave me was the epitome of *What the fuck do you think?*

There were flecks and dots on his tunic. I hadn't noticed them on the walk because he'd been behind me. But the speckles had to be blood.

There was even a smear on his wrist. A drop on the column of his throat.

"Was anyone hurt?"

He scoffed.

Of course, the great and powerful Guardian would never let harm befall his people. Silly me.

"Can I see it?" I asked. "The grizzur?"

"Why?"

I shrugged. "I've only ever read about them in books."

"So curious, my queen."

Yes, I was. "I want to know what I'm up against."

With the monsters.

With him.

I wanted to see this beast he'd killed.

Without a word, he walked past me, his elbow grazing my own.

I followed as he marched along the camp, his strides so long that I had to run to keep up. My muscles screamed, but I was too curious—and too proud—to ask him to slow down.

By the time we reached the other side of the camp, I was out of breath. Sweat coated my brow. My heart pounded.

It came to a dead stop when I saw the grizzur.

Its bearlike frame lay prone on its belly. Its massive body was covered in coarse cinnamon fur. Along the spine, jutting through that thick, wiry hair, were spikes as long as my arm. They were as white as snow and as pointed as the Guardian's sword. They angled in all directions, some curving to the sides, others aiming straight.

Was that how they survived the crux migrations? There'd be no picking up a grizzur from above, not with those spikes.

Its feet, tipped in claws, were as wide as my shoulders. On all fours, it had to stand at least six feet tall. If it rose up on its hind legs, ten.

The grizzur's head was turned on its ear, enough to reveal the gash in its throat.

No, not a gash. A cut so deep that it left the monster's head barely connected to its body. It hung only by a sliver of that heavy hide.

I choked. "You cut its head off?"

The Guardian shrugged. "Almost."

"How?" Before he could answer, I held up a hand. "Actually. Never mind."

My imagination could fill in the gaps.

Predator to predator, the grizzur had met its match.

The monster's snout was longer than any bear's, double the size. Its black nose was shiny and wet. Its mouth was open, revealing teeth that didn't form neat rows. Instead, like the spikes on its back, they jutted at odd angles.

Could the grizzurs even close their mouths? Or did they just shred their victims and swallow jagged chunks?

There was a drag mark in the dirt that stretched from the body beyond the fires. Why would they bring it inside the camp? So its blood wouldn't attract others?

Its black, glassy eyes were open and lifeless. As we walked closer to the head, they seemed to track my steps, even though it was dead.

A rivulet of dark-red blood trickled from its nostril, puddling beneath its open maw.

Drip. Drip. Drip.

The sound made my insides twist.

Zavier had warned me on the *Cutter* that Turah wasn't gentle or kind. That his kingdom would not spare me mercy. This land, these monsters, would do their best to break me into pieces, wouldn't they?

To soak this earth with *my* blood.

"I want my sword."

The Guardian sighed like he'd heard that request a hundred times over a hundred years. Not twice in the past few days.

"You agreed."

"That I did." He rubbed a hand over his bearded jaw. "You look dead on your feet, Sparrow. Rest. Tomorrow, we'll train. Be ready at dawn."

What was it with the Turans and dawn? Something always seemed to be happening at dawn. "Fine."

"Don't go past the fires." He pointed a long finger at my nose.

Go into the wild where these monsters lived? "Not a chance."

"Can you find your way back to your tent?"

Probably. Though it might take me an hour. "Yes."

Then he was gone, leaving me alone with the grizzur.

Drip. Drip. Drip.

I stared at the monster for another long moment, marveling at its size. It shouldn't have been beautiful, not a beast so terrifying. Yet I couldn't seem to tear my gaze away.

Not until I heard the sound of horses, of hooves beating against the earth, carrying over the pop of the fires.

Zavier and three of his warriors raced away from the camp. A minute later, another rider broke past the fires, racing to catch up.

The Guardian. His coal stallion flew across the plain, its rider as graceful in the saddle as the animal itself.

Where were they going?

A decent spy would find a horse and follow. But me? Not a decent spy. So I slunk away from the grizzur, making a slow retreat to my tent. I only got lost twice.

Brielle was gone by the time I returned, presumably to her own bed, and I curled up on mine.

When the next roar came, when it seemed to shake heaven and earth, I pulled the pillow over my head.

Pretending to sleep until dawn.

Seventeen

The Guardian's sword cut through the space between us with a whoosh. That blade in his hand was a streak of silver, a bolt of lightning, wielded with only a roll of his wrist. "Ready?"

Was I ready to train with a man who could break my neck with a snap of his fingers or slice me in half with one flick of that sword?

No. Definitely not ready.

I want a sword.

What the fuck was I thinking? If I died in this makeshift training area today, it would be my own damn fault.

There was a circle in the grassy area between the fires and tents. A patch that had been trampled and flattened by boots. Probably from the warriors who'd trained in this ring yesterday.

But this morning, we were alone. It was a small mercy that no one was here to watch me trip over my own feet and fall on my ass. The only witness to my humiliation today would be the man delivering it.

The sun had broken above the indigo mountains just moments ago, tinting the plains beyond the camp's fires in a medley of green and gold. Storm clouds banked on the horizon, the winds blowing them toward camp. This landscape was as bold as any painting, as picturesque a scene as I'd ever seen.

The evil glint in the Guardian's hazel eyes said I wasn't going to have the chance to enjoy the view.

"What am I doing here?" I muttered under my breath.

"This was your idea, remember?"

Ten paces away, and still, he'd heard me. He could probably hear a cricket chirping on the opposite end of the encampment. Or he was simply plucking thoughts straight out of my head.

He used the tip of his sword to point at my feet. "Get in your fighting stance."

I adjusted my position, pivoting sideways with my left leg ahead of my right. Then I bent slightly at the knees, lifting the twin blades he'd handed me when I'd swept out of my tent earlier.

The weapons were longer than daggers, the blades about the length of my forearms, but shorter than the sword Tillia carried across her back. Why he thought it would be best to start with two knives instead of one sword was baffling, but after another sleepless night, I didn't have the will to challenge his decision.

It was going to take all my fortitude just to survive this training session. We'd save the verbal sparring for another day.

The Guardian had been waiting, casually eating an apple, with both of these knives tucked under an arm when I'd stepped out of my tent.

The weapons had been entirely unappealing. But that apple? Mouthwatering. Yesterday's meal hadn't been enough, and shades, I was hungry.

Maybe I'd track down some fruit of my own whenever I left this training ring. That was, if I could still walk.

The Guardian came to a stop in the center of the circle. "You have no chance at outrunning an opponent, either monster or man. You're too short and slow."

"Thanks," I deadpanned. "And I was certain I wouldn't earn any compliments today."

"Praise is for the bedroom, Cross. Not the training ring."

The image of him in a darkened room, shirtless, whispering praise into my ear, popped into my head before I could stop it.

No. *No, no, no.* I refused to let my thoughts wander in that direction. The only man who'd be in my bedroom was my husband.

Maybe. Someday. Gods, my marriage was weird.

Focus, Odessa. I gripped my knives tighter. "Noted. Next?"

He dragged his free hand through his hair, shoving the brown locks off his forehead. It was…not attractive. Not. At. All.

The Guardian moved closer, snaring me with his hard, intimidating gaze.

It took everything in my power not to gulp and shy away.

"Any opponent will likely move in close. To go for the kill. Your task will be to find your enemy's weak points. For most beasts, your only hope is to inflict a wound. Go for the throat. Slice a leg. Gouge an eye. Anything to slow it down so you can run and hide. If you're fighting a man, go for the kill." He used his free hand to take hold of the blade in my right, positioning the tip against his leather vest.

I was in yesterday's clothes, leather pants and a tunic without embroidery.

He was in the same attire I'd seen him in the day we'd met in the throne room. That vest, studded with silver and brass, molded over his torso and the off-white tunic beneath. I'd thought the Turan vests were simply for style, but they were part of their armor, weren't they?

My knives were sharp, but puncturing that leather would take all my might.

"Slide your knife past the ribs. Straight into the heart. Think you can do that?" he asked.

"Don't tempt me."

"It's not a joke. There's no point in you having these knives if you aren't going to use them. Could you kill a man, Cross?"

My eyes lifted to his. "If I must."

He leaned in closer, my knife pressing into that vest. The material resisted still, showing no weakness.

How hard would I have to push to reach his skin? What if I poured all my strength into one hard thrust? Would he stop me? Would I catch him off guard?

There was a dare in his eyes. He was baiting me to try.

Do it. Push.

My arm wouldn't move.

Could I kill a man? This man? No. I wasn't sure I could ever take a life, even his.

The corner of the Guardian's mouth twitched, like he read that realization on my face.

He stepped away. "Let's see how well you can block."

And with that, the training began.

Thunder boomed overhead. In the hours we'd been training, storm clouds had settled over the camp, and moments ago, they'd opened, releasing a deluge of rain upon our heads.

I'd hoped it would cut our session short. Nope.

The Guardian, apparently, trained rain or shine.

The droplets mingled with the sweat on my face, and every time one slipped into my mouth, I tasted salt and blood.

My chest heaved, my heart pounding so hard I feared it would sputter and quit.

I bent forward, bracing on my knees as I did my best not to vomit.

This was hell. Izzac had brought me to his shade to torture me for all those murderous thoughts I'd had toward the Guardian.

"Tired already?" The asshole wasn't even winded.

I squeezed my eyes shut, sucking in a breath through my nostrils, the oxygen making my lungs burn. Then I gritted my teeth and stood tall, letting the water cascade down my face as I resumed my fighting stance.

My pants were caked with mud. This tunic was slashed and ruined from the swipes of his sword, the fabric hanging in tatters along my sides. But I wasn't stopping, not yet. "Again."

His sword came down over my head as thunder cracked the sky.

I caught the blade this time, pinned it between my knives like he'd taught me to do earlier. Then, with my arms braced, wrists straining, legs burning, I fought to keep him from pushing his sword into my skull.

"Harder," he barked, adding more pressure.

A cry tore from my mouth along with a blob of spittle as I flung his sword to the side. It might have been impressive, except the ground was slick and I was unsteady. My boot slipped, and I crashed to a knee.

The Guardian didn't give me a chance to recover. He swiped for my neck, forcing me to my stomach to keep my head attached to my shoulders.

I rolled in the mud, frantically fumbling to get to my feet.

As soon as I was up, he swung at me again, this time aiming for my stomach, and I barely deflected the strike.

The metal of our weapons sang as they rebounded off one another.

"Faster," he barked. "Keep your feet."

I sucked in a breath before he came at me again, angling left, then right. My movements were sluggish, my hold on the knives faltering.

He knocked the blade from my left hand, sending it flying toward the edge of the training ring.

"Stop dropping your fucking knife," he bellowed.

"I'm trying," I screamed over the storm and my pounding pulse.

"Try harder," he sneered, then walked to pick up my knife, thrusting the handle into my palm. "Again."

I gritted my teeth, willing my body to stay strong, to endure this. Then

I anchored my heels to the slick earth.

"Don't fall," he ordered.

Don't fall, don't fall, don't fall.

He lunged, another overhead strike, and rather than stand tall, I shuffled backward, tripping over my own godsdamn feet.

I fell right on my ass. *Hell.* This was hell.

The Guardian glowered down at me, his frustration as palpable as the rain. He pointed the sword at my face, and for a moment, I wondered if this was it. If he'd tested me, deemed me unworthy, and would rid Turah of a weak princess.

The blade's tip was a whisper against my forehead as he used it to pick up a curl of my soaked hair.

The dye was washing out. I could practically feel the brown coating my cheeks. My shirt. It would mix with the mud, making me look as dirty as I felt.

"I said *don't* fall." He pulled back his sword, and the curl fell to stick to my face. "Ready to quit?"

I couldn't quit, no matter how much I wanted to say yes. "Never."

"Good." He waved me to the center of the ring. "Your first instinct is to retreat. You must stand your ground. Move to the side. Create an opening to strike. But do not go backward. You'll just land on your ass. Again."

"Move to the side. Got it." I pushed to my feet, taking one heartbeat to breathe. Then I pointed both knives toward his smug face. "Ready."

He swung so fast I didn't even realize the blade was close until I felt its wind against my cheek.

I shied away—backward, as always—rocking on my heels. But I didn't fall.

"Damn it, Cross. Attack!" he yelled, slicing at me again.

Except I couldn't attack, not when he was coming at me with murder in his eyes. My legs acted of their own accord, shuffling me away, away, away. Toward the edge of the ring. Toward the closest burning fire.

It blazed, despite the rain, the sparks reaching out to catch my clothes and hair.

"Move your feet," the Guardian shouted as he advanced again.

With the fire at my back, I had no choice but to sidestep his strike.

"She learns," he mocked. "Finally."

My nostrils flared as he continued to push me around, toyed with me like I was a plaything to amuse him on a stormy day.

I stabbed at him, aiming nowhere and everywhere, only to have my knife slide off the thick leather cuff he wore over his left forearm.

"You'll have to hit harder than that to pierce grizzur hide."

That made me pause. "That cuff is grizzur hide? Is that why you kept the monster you killed?"

Not to keep its blood from attracting other predators, but so that its hide could be used for cuffs and those vests.

The hide was incredibly strong. Tough. Durable. And probably more comfortable than breastplates of metal.

"Stop asking questions, Cross. Fight, damn it. Attack."

"I am fighting," I screamed, the sound tearing from my throat. "I'm trying."

"Not hard enough." He bent, getting into my face. His eyes shifted to swirling silver, and the rest of the realm melted away. "I don't know why I'm surprised. Quentins are usually better at running away than fighting."

"I'm not running away."

"Then stop backing away. You want to be queen of Turah? Then you must not be afraid."

"I don't want to be queen of Turah." The confession came so fast I flinched.

He scoffed. "So, you'd rather rot in a golden castle, withering away to nothing while your family forgets your existence? You were nothing to them. Your father gave you away without so much as a blink. Your sister put on a show of bidding you goodbye, but I'll wager she's already in your fiancé's bed. A man who also let you go without a fight. And don't you have a little brother? Did they even let you say goodbye?"

Not a single blow he'd landed today hit harder. It was every insecurity pulled from the deepest parts of my heart and plopped on the mud for him to stomp with his boot.

It was ruthless. Unforgivable.

The truth.

A wrath unlike anything I'd felt before burned beneath my skin. It was hot and vicious, and it vibrated through my entire being. My hands gripped my knives until my knuckles were white.

"Are you angry, Sparrow? Use that rage. Fucking. Fight."

I hate you.

If he could read my mind, I wanted that at the front. *I hate you.*

A slow grin stretched across his mouth. "There's my queen."

"Stop calling me that," I seethed.

"Make me." He stepped back, raising his arms as the rain poured over his shoulders, onto the soaked fabric that was molded around his roped muscles.

He dropped his sword, sending it splattering to the mud. Then he pointed to my blades and crooked a finger.

If he wanted to fight unarmed? Fine. I still didn't stand a chance, but I wanted his blood. I wanted his pain.

Before I could think about it too hard, I lunged, my knives aimed for his neck.

He'd told me to go after a monster's throat, and there was only one monster here today.

The Guardian twisted to the side, a quick sidestep that took him out of my path. It forced me to change directions, once again following his lead. Once again on his leash.

But I chased him anyway, never slowing my steps as I let my arms swing wildly through the air, hoping that I'd earn a bit of luck and find purchase. I didn't want much.

The shell of his ear. The tip of his nose. A finger or thumb.

Bloodlust surged through my veins like fire. My vision coated in red.

He dodged every strike, but I kept going, pouring out all of my anger at him, at Zavier, at my father for sending me to Turah.

I used that rage, infusing it into my arms and legs.

"Faster," he yelled as I stabbed at his ribs, missing completely. "Move!"

A raw scream ripped through my throat, the rain swallowing the noise.

My arms flailed, my movements getting sloppy, but I kept going, kept pushing, harder and faster.

The space around us faded to a blur. All that remained were those silver eyes.

I wanted to carve them from his skull.

But no matter how fast I ran, how quickly I brought down my blades, he was always out of reach.

It was effortless for him, wasn't it? I was about to collapse. The strength in my arms was waning. My legs were weak, my knees wobbling. I commanded them to push, but there was nothing left.

The Guardian had drained me to the core.

My vision was turning fuzzy, the rain getting into my eyes and stinging them with each blink. I collected the frayed ends of my control and made one final attack, whipping the knives in all directions in the hope I'd catch his flesh.

It was the quickest I'd ever moved. It wasn't even close to enough. The knife's tip whizzed past the Guardian's neck, only a smidgen away from slicing into his throat. But that smidgen might as well have been a continent.

A miss was a miss.

The knife was moving so fast it tore itself out of my grip, flying to the edge of the training circle, where it landed with a muffled thump.

I dropped to my knees.

"Get up," the Guardian commanded.

I closed my eyes, my shoulders sagging in defeat.

What was I doing here? In this training ring. In Turah. Why had Zavier married me?

A chill was soaking into my marrow, a cold that had nothing to do with the rain.

It was hopeless. *I* was hopeless. I was nothing but a toy. A doll. A trivial princess who had no business in this fray between kings. My father was likely making contingency plans for when I failed.

"Get. Up." The Guardian planted his hands on his hips. "Now."

"Enough." A new voice rang through the air.

Zavier collected my discarded knife, joining us in the circle. He crouched before me, handing over the weapon.

All I could do was look at it. My arm, limp and exhausted, hung at my side.

Whatever he saw on my face made him frown before he stood. Then he crossed his arms over his chest as he spoke to the Guardian. "Enough."

"She's not done," he said. "It's enough when I say—"

"When *I* say it's enough." For the first time, Zavier sounded like a prince.

The Guardian's nostrils flared. "Zavier."

There was malice in that tone. A challenge.

But Zavier stood his ground, eyes hard as he stared at the Guardian. When he spoke, it was with a calm like I'd never heard before, quiet and soothing. Like a man taming a beast. "She's had enough."

The Guardian clenched his jaw, then, without another word, collected his sword and walked past the fires.

Into the storm.

Zavier dragged a hand over his face, wiping away the drops, then held out a hand. "Are you hurt?"

"No." I shook my head, letting him help me to my feet. As much as I wanted to stand on my own, my legs were not going to cooperate.

"I came to tell you that I'm leaving. I have business to attend to in Perris."

The former capital. A port city quite capable of accepting three ships to harbor. Yet we'd landed on that tiny beach. Why? I tucked that question away for another day. "All right. I take it I'm not going along?"

"It's not safe." Well, that sounded like a lie. Nowhere around here was safe. "You'll travel with Tillia and the others."

To Ellder. The fortress. "Okay."

Abandoned by my husband to travel with a group of strange warriors through a foreign kingdom teeming with monsters that would love nothing more than to feast on my flesh. It could be worse, right? I wasn't sure how exactly, but it could probably be worse.

"The next few days will be...strenuous. Try to get some rest tonight. You'll leave—"

"Let me guess. At dawn?"

His eyes crinkled at the sides in an almost smile. "I'll see you soon, Odessa."

"Goodbye, Zavier." I waited until he was gone before I made my way through the tents.

Most people were huddled inside their own, sheltering out of the cold. I covered a yawn as I trudged through my tent's flaps.

A warm bath was waiting.

And an apple.

I didn't let myself think about who had likely arranged for them both.

Eighteen

"**D**o you remember what a real bed feels like?" Brielle whispered from her bedroll beside mine. "A bed that doesn't sway."

"A bed without rocks digging into your back." Jocelyn scowled as she tried to find a smoother place to rest.

"We'll have real beds again. Soon."

It was an empty promise. As far as I knew, there were no beds in Turah. We certainly hadn't seen one since we'd arrived.

Around us, men moved about the camp. Every few minutes, someone would shout.

As Zavier had promised, today had been strenuous.

When I'd awoken before dawn and stepped outside my tent, it had been the only structure left standing. All the others had been stowed in wagons. The fires were dwindling to embers, and the horses were being saddled.

Once my tent was packed away, we'd set off toward the mountains. Tillia, Jocelyn, and Brielle had ridden by my side. A group of warriors had lingered close, each at the ready to draw swords or bows at a hint of danger.

The ride had been punishing and fast. The entire party had pushed hard to get to this place.

We were sheltered against an outcropping of large rocks that jutted from the grassy plains. It wasn't as exposed as the previous campsite, but something about this place felt ominous.

Maybe because the best warriors, Zavier and six of his rangers, had left for Perris.

The Guardian was gone, too.

I stared up at Ama and Oda's stars and the shades of the Six in between. From white to gray to black, the night sky had never been so clear. So beautiful. Did it make the Turans closer to the gods, that they could see the stars and shades so openly?

I imagined lines between the stars, mentally invisible thrones for the gods. If they were watching, I prayed they'd get us through this night.

My entire body ached from the training session with the Guardian. Staying on my horse for the grueling ride had drained every bit of my strength.

It hurt to breathe. To think. My limbs were stiff, my muscles protesting even the slightest movement. I wasn't sure how I'd survive tomorrow after a night spent lying on the ground. There was a pointy rock digging into my left hip, but it hurt too much to move, so I didn't bother. Like Jocelyn, even if I shifted, I'd probably just find another rock.

Tillia had told us we wouldn't be bothering with tents. We weren't staying here for long. Instead, we had these bedrolls like everyone else. They were nothing more than scratchy blankets to wrap around our bodies.

The entire traveling party was clustered together, tucked beside the rock outcropping to protect our backs. And at the front, a half circle of fires was blazing into the night. Their spacing was more condensed, the flames from one licking another's. It was a fraction of the size of the previous camp. Less perimeter to defend, according to Tillia.

A series of clicks echoed through the dark, reverberating off the rocks.

Those clicks had been coming for hours and hours and hours.

At first, I hadn't realized what they meant. Now? I tensed, holding my breath for what would come next.

"On your left!" a man shouted.

Brielle took my hand.

Jocelyn signed the Eight.

"There's two," another man yelled through the night.

Then came the roars. The growls. The snarls.

A scream cut short.

More men shouted and yelled until the camp went quiet.

Eerily quiet.

No clicks. No shouting.

All I could hear was my own heartbeat and Brielle's muffled cries.

Had anyone died this time?

The warriors would fight all night. Once she'd ensured we were settled, Tillia had left to take her position at the fires. She hadn't even bothered laying out her bedroll.

"Report!" a man called.

"One."

"Two."

"Three."

Every warrior stationed at a post called out their respective number. When they reached thirty-six, the entire camp seemed to breathe.

Twelve fires. Three guards each.

Thirty-six guards, still alive.

A quiet settled over the camp, the only sounds the crackling of fires and popping of logs. All I wanted to do was sleep. To block out the noise and fear. I couldn't remember ever being this tired. But those clicks kept coming.

The monsters were everywhere.

Bariwolves.

Tillia said the packs used those clicks to communicate.

"I miss the sound of the ocean," Brielle whispered.

"So do I."

"I want to go home." She sobbed, the sound coming so fast she slapped a hand over her mouth.

Tillia had told us to stay quiet. But sometimes, there was no stopping the pain. The loneliness. The heartache.

Every part of my body screamed as I rolled to my side, keeping her hand in mine and clutching it tight. "I'm sorry, Brielle. I'm so sorry."

"It's not your fault."

"It is."

She used her free hand to wipe her face dry. "Was it your idea to get married?"

I sighed. *No.* "Okay, so maybe it's not my fault. But I'm still sorry."

"Me too." She gave me a sad smile. "I don't want to get eaten by a monster."

"Me neither," Jocelyn muttered.

Brielle let out a small laugh, then leaned in closer, her head resting on my shoulder. "Do you think they'll keep us safe?"

"Yes." I might not know why Zavier wanted me as his wife, but I did have faith that he wanted me alive. So did the Guardian. Otherwise, they would have let the marroweel swallow me whole.

We stayed together, holding hands, as the quiet lingered. No more clicks. No shouting. Eventually, my eyelids were too heavy to keep open, so I shut out the stars and drifted off.

A roar ripped me from sleep, my eyes popping open as I shoved up to a seat and stared toward the fires.

That roar wasn't from bariwolves. It was too loud, too deep, too terrifying.

A grizzur.

The fires tonight weren't as large as those we'd had at the other encampment. Were they big enough to keep a massive monster at bay? Or would that grizzur rip through the perimeter and tear us all to pieces, leaving only carrion come daylight?

Brielle curled into herself, drawing her knees to her chest and hugging them tight.

Others shifted to sit up, too. Some stayed down, staring at the stars.

Another roar blasted through the night, so loud the rocks behind us seemed to quake.

The warriors stationed at the fires drew back, inching away from the flames, their swords and knives raised.

"Steady," Tillia ordered. Her voice was strong. Calm.

It did nothing to stop the terror creeping through my veins.

A tremor shook the ground beneath my blanket. Then came another and another. They formed a rhythm like hooves. But bigger. So much bigger.

I stared unblinkingly past the fires and into the darkness.

Without moving my gaze, I felt around for my satchel. For the shoulder harness I'd tucked into the bag, and with it, my knives.

They'd be pointless against a grizzur. And I didn't really know how to use them yet. I might as well be defending myself with bare hands and the fingernails that I'd chewed short on today's ride so they wouldn't collect dirt.

Zavier had warned me that Turah was dangerous. Then he'd abandoned us. All of us.

So had the Guardian.

My heart raced as the pounding grew louder, stronger. So strong it was enough to bounce the tiny pebbles beside my bedroll.

Gods, save us.

Another roar rent the air. It was so close it seemed like a hot breath, a kiss of death, blowing through the camp.

"Praise Ama. Beloved Mother," Brielle murmured, "save us this night. Or bring us to your shores of starlight. Grant us quick deaths, Izzac. Let us rest upon Oda's golden rays and know peace, dear Carine."

A few of the men around us stood, abandoning their bedrolls. They were the men who drove the wagons. They backed away toward the rocks as if they'd climb out to freedom.

"Hold!" Tillia's command was unwavering.

None of the thirty-six moved.

And a secondary line formed at their backs. Not warriors, just men. But they went armed with swords and crossbows, bodies braced for whatever was coming through that fire.

Those earthquaking footsteps grew louder and louder as the beast raced for the camp. It had to be running full speed. Maybe it would simply leap over the fires and leverage the flames to light its midnight meal.

Brielle sprang to her feet, tugging on my hands as she tried to pull me up. "Highness, come. Hurry. We must run."

We'd never make it. So I stayed frozen to the ground, knives gripped in my palms, awaiting the death that thundered our way.

The roar that came next was savage. It was followed by a snarl that made Jocelyn yelp. The footsteps had stopped pounding, but the tremors beneath us continued, like the beast was moving, just not running. Another incensed snarl cut through the dark.

I lifted to my knees, squinting to see what was happening. Were the warriors firing at the grizzur with arrows? Had the fires scared the beast? What was happening?

The warriors all shifted, adjusting their stances. But they didn't move, either. They stared into the night, and all we could do was listen to the monster growl.

Something had to be attacking the grizzur. Something had interrupted its path.

The bariwolves? Except I hadn't heard their clicks. My ears and eyes strained, my heart in my throat.

The next roar was choked. Cut short.

It faded in a heartbeat, and then there was nothing.

The entire camp held its breath as the fires sparked and popped.

Then the Guardian stalked through the flames, covered in dark blood. It dripped from the ends of his hair and his chin. It trickled down his arms, down the length of his gleaming silver sword.

His eyes were the same color, swirling metal.

And locked on me.

The air rushed from my lungs.

He hadn't abandoned us after all.

"Izzac," Brielle gasped.

Maybe those rumors about the Guardian were true. Maybe he was the God of Death.

People began to cheer. Blades were thrust into the night as a chant erupted.

Guardian. Guardian. Guardian.

Brielle dropped to my side, her arms wrapping around my shoulders as she cried. "Oh, gods."

"We're okay." Jocelyn buried her face in her hands, her body shaking as she wept.

I tore my gaze from the Guardian and leaned into Brielle. "It's all right."

She clung to me, soaking the fabric of my tunic with her tears.

When I looked toward the fires, the Guardian was with Tillia, their heads bent in a private conversation.

He leaned in so close that their cheeks nearly touched. She rested a hand on his heart, shoulders falling away from her ears at whatever he said. Then her forehead dropped to his chest, resting beside her hand.

It was a private moment. Intimate. And I was intruding.

My gaze snapped to the ground.

Tillia and the Guardian? Were they together? It made sense. Both were warriors. Both were fearless. She was breathtaking, and he was…him.

A slimy sensation crawled beneath my skin, and I shoved it away, refusing to give it a name.

"I'm sorry." Brielle pulled away, wiping her cheeks dry as she sniffled. "You've had to console me since we left Roslo. Here, I'm the one supposed to help you."

"I don't mind." I gave her a soft smile, tucking a lock of her brown hair behind her ear.

Around us, the chants died out. The men who'd scattered to the rocks returned to their bedrolls, plopping down with relieved sighs.

"We should rest," I told Brielle. "Before tomorrow."

She huffed. "There's no chance I'll fall asleep."

But as she settled onto her side, as the terror receded and the camp quieted, her body relaxed, and before long, exhaustion won out.

I hung my head, still on my knees. Knives still in my hands. I couldn't seem to let them go. So I stared at their sharp edges, wishing I was made of steel, too.

A finger hooked under my chin.

I knew whose finger it was before I lifted my eyes.

The Guardian crouched before me, still covered in blood. He'd walked to me without a sound, his footsteps as light as feathers.

"Are you all right, my queen?" It was the gentlest I'd ever heard his voice. Low and smooth like silk.

"Was it a grizzur?"

"Yes."

"Is it dead?"

He arched an eyebrow. "Cross."

Right. Stupid question. Of course it was dead. It had bled all over him, too, leaving behind the stench of blood.

He let go of my chin and pointed to my bedroll. "Sleep. We leave—"

"At dawn. I know."

The corner of his mouth turned up. "Good night, my queen."

I should have thanked him before he walked away. For killing the monster. For checking on me. For putting my fears to rest with his presence alone. But I settled on my blanket and let him disappear into the dark.

He was probably with Tillia already, standing guard.

Together.

Well, at least they weren't cuddling on her bedroll.

By some miracle, I managed to sleep until sunrise. Then I climbed on my roan and joined the procession away from the dying fires.

Away from the body of a dead grizzur with milky white eyes. Foam at the corners of its mouth.

And the dark-green blood seeping from its slit throat.

Nineteen

W hen I was thirteen, a scullery maid poisoned me with fenek tusk powder.

She slipped it into my morning tea, and after she was caught, she admitted to being paid by a nobleman who'd fallen behind on his debt payments to Father.

The lord had been a habitual gambler who'd hoped a death in the Quentin royal family would buy him more time to win a fortune at the dice tables.

Instead, he and the maid were hanged in the Roslo public square.

As their bodies were left to rot for a week, baking under the sun and pecked at by birds, I spent a week on death's doorstep.

To my knowledge, the doctors still didn't know how I'd survived the poison. The powder was twice as toxic as the venom from any snake, but my body had fought the fever, and somehow, I'd lived.

It was the worst I'd ever felt.

Until now.

After three days of riding across the Turan landscape, I'd gladly welcome an unhealthy dose of fenek tusk powder.

Though fenek were rare in Calandra. According to my tutors, the foxlike monsters had been hunted nearly to extinction a hundred years ago. As far as monsters went, they were the smallest, and while equally as vicious as those larger, they were easier to kill than tarkin or bariwolves or grizzurs.

Calandra had nearly seen the last of the fenek. But then someone had discovered that grinding their tusks into a powder produced the finest poison on the continent.

Breeding fenek was illegal in all kingdoms, but that didn't mean much. For those with enough coin, the powder could be purchased on the black market.

Were there wild fenek in Turah?

I was too tired to ask Tillia. She rode at my side, her posture perfect and her expression relaxed. Clearly, her saddle didn't chafe her inner thighs like mine. She looked as comfortable on that horse as she would be lounging on a settee.

Meanwhile, I probably looked like Brielle and Jocelyn. Haggard. Frazzled. On the brink of a physical and emotional crack.

How much farther would we ride today? We'd reached the edge of the plains around midday and were riding through the mountain foothills. They rolled, up and down and up and down. We'd crossed a stream earlier, pausing only long enough to let the horses take a drink before we'd pressed on.

The scents of pine and dirt surrounded us, sharp yet sweet and refreshing. The trees and underbrush weren't as thick here as they'd been along the coast, giving us plenty of space between the thick, wide trunks for our party to weave through unencumbered.

It was no wonder that Turah provided lumber to the other four kingdoms. These trees seemed unbreakable. Unbending. Perfect for homes or ships. They were taller than any I'd ever seen, too. Their tops stretched toward the sky, their limbs providing shade from the punishing afternoon sun.

In Roslo, I'd always found a reason to leave the castle's walls and spend a few hours outside. Those short escapes were the best part of my day. I loved the fresh air and freedom.

Now all I wanted was a bedroom and a bath and to forget the outdoors forever.

This morning, not long after dawn, when the sky was still dim, I'd thought I'd seen the twinkle of lights from a town or city. I'd watched them fade as the sun rose, hoping we were near our destination. But we'd kept riding for these foothills, and whatever place we'd passed was now long gone.

Each night, we slept on the dirt after a meal of roasted meat. Each morning, we ate our breakfast on horseback. Dried, leathery strips of meat and hard bread. That apple I'd inhaled felt like a lifetime ago.

My horse, the roan I'd decided to call Freya, stepped over a fallen branch. The change in her gait sent me shifting in my saddle, and the pain in my ass spiked. I clutched the reins and gritted my teeth, holding back a groan.

"Are you all right?" Tillia asked.

No. "Yes."

"We're almost there. This is the last push."

"To Ellder?"

"Not yet," she said. "There's been a slight change in plan. We'll be stopping in Treow."

"Oh." Why the change in plans? She wouldn't tell me if I asked, so I didn't bother. "Is Treow a town?"

I didn't recognize the name, and it was embarrassing how little I knew of Turah. How much I had to ask. Here I was, the newest addition to the royal family, and I knew next to nothing about this kingdom.

"Yes and no," Tillia said. "You'll understand when we arrive."

I loathed vague nonanswers. And the Turans excelled at delivering them.

Whatever. I just wanted off this fucking horse.

Had Mae studied the Turan geography? Did she know all of their towns and cities by heart? Had she memorized maps? She wasn't even here, yet I was still lagging behind my sister. I was on the other side of the continent and still...less. Would that feeling ever go away?

Maybe. If I accomplished Father's mission.

My journal was tucked safely into my satchel. I'd added a few notes last night at our camp, and I'd planned to draw the mountains, except the moment Tillia had seen me sketching, she'd told me to put my journal away and not let anyone see me with it again.

I hadn't asked why. The severity of her tone had been enough for me to obey without question.

Besides, everything significant was locked in my head. Once we were somewhere safe, somewhere I could be alone, I'd start on a map.

"Would you like anything to eat?" Tillia asked.

"No, thank you."

"You haven't eaten much."

I waved it off. "I'm not hungry."

The food was tasty and nourishing, but my appetite was simply gone. My insides seemed to be in a permanent knot, with nothing else to do all day but ride and dwell.

So I dwelled.

On. Everything.

My own mind had become my worst enemy.

There wasn't a single safe topic. I dwelled on my family. I dwelled on

Brielle and Jocelyn and how they would undoubtedly hate me when this was over. I dwelled on Zavier and his disinterest. I dwelled on the gods and how they seemed to both love and hate humans. I dwelled on the stench of my breath and the stink of my body. I dwelled on the point of my chin and the taper of my nose.

And no matter how hard I tried to stop it, I dwelled on the Guardian.

He was a murderer. A legendary killer. Shouldn't he frighten me? So far, I'd only seen him fight monsters. Granted, I didn't expect to see him battle with his people, but the way they stared at him. It was in wonder. In devotion.

Not the way I would have expected people to act around a violent butcher. And no matter how hard I tried, I couldn't get the picture of Tillia and the Guardian leaning on each other out of my head.

I liked Tillia. She'd been nothing but kind and respectful since I'd arrived in Turah. If there was a person in this kingdom I wanted to trust, it was her. She cared for the Guardian. Maybe she was even in love with him.

She didn't seem like the type to love an evil man.

Maybe that was silly. We didn't know each other. But the reason Margot hated my sketches was because they were real. I drew what I saw. When I looked to Tillia, I saw a warrior. A leader.

A woman who was practically a stranger, but a woman I admired all the same.

But the Guardian had killed Banner's brother in a vicious, brutal way. Did Tillia know about that?

I lifted my hands to my temples, rubbing in angry circles. How did I shut off my mind? How did I make the thinking stop? Gods, I wanted off this fucking horse.

A noise rose up from the front of the group, a shout or a cheer. I couldn't tell from my position in the middle of the riders.

Tillia stiffened, lifting her arm to the sword strapped across her back.

"What's going on?" My knives were sheathed in their harness, the blades crisscrossed over my spine. Since that night with the grizzur, I hadn't taken them off, even to rest. The Guardian had left us again, and I was not going to be unarmed if we faced another monster.

Tillia's arm dropped to her heart as she exhaled. "Thank Arabella."

Why was she thanking the God of Love?

Unless...

The Guardian had returned.

The riders in front of us shifted, making room for a man galloping through the heart of our party, straight our way.

I recognized him from the throne room. He was one of Zavier's rangers, the man with long, black braids pulled into a knot at his nape who'd checked Father's chest of gold coin. And his eyes were locked on Tillia.

She brought her horse to a stop, waiting with her hand still pressed over her heart. The moment the ranger reached her side, he took her face in his large hands, cupping her jaw as he pulled her close to seal his mouth over hers.

My brain exploded.

Um, who was he? What about the Guardian? What was happening?

Their kiss was hungry, like they were starved for each other. Their mouths moved, their cheeks hollowed as their tongues twisted.

Like they'd done it a hundred times, he swept her off her horse, their mouths never breaking, and plopped her onto his lap. As he cradled her body, she slid her hands to his neck, her palms pressed against his pulse.

They kissed as if they were the only people in the realm. Like the rest of us weren't watching. I'd never seen anything like it before. And I'd never felt a kiss like that before. All-consuming. Desperate.

When they broke apart, Tillia laughed, tears streaming down her cheeks.

The ranger's face softened as he caught them with his thumbs. Then he dropped his forehead to hers, murmuring something I couldn't hear.

They were too locked on to each other to notice us staring.

"Come on," I told Brielle and Jocelyn, nodding toward where the others had continued onward. "Let's keep going."

They urged their horses forward as I did the same, stealing one last glance at Tillia and her warrior.

He dropped a soft kiss to her mouth. It was tender. Beautiful. He loved her. She was his universe. At her side, he was home.

Tillia curled into him, her arms snaking around his waist as he breathed her in.

My heart squeezed as I faced forward. Not in a hundred years would Banner have ever kissed me that way. Not in a thousand would I have cried if we were apart.

It wouldn't be any different with Zavier, would it? He would not adore me, worship me. I'd traded a loveless engagement for a loveless marriage.

I'd never had a man look at me that way. And I never would.

Why was this just occurring to me now? Why hadn't it bothered me before?

Maybe because I hadn't taken the time to dwell. The time to mourn the loss of a romance. Of passion. Of love.

It hit like a hammer to my chest. The envy I had for Tillia. The sorrow I felt because of that kiss.

"Highness," Brielle said. "Are you all right?"

I dabbed at the corner of my eye, stopping the tear I wouldn't let fall. "Fine."

"You haven't been eating enough."

I shrugged. "I'm not hungry."

"You need to rest."

"We all need to rest." Maybe we could once we got to Treow, wherever that was. I glanced behind us, searching for Tillia. She was still with her warrior, those trailing behind passing them with nods and smiles.

"Have you ever been in love, Brielle?" I asked.

"Yes." A sadness filled her eyes. "He broke my heart, but I still love him. I always will."

What? I gaped at her. When had that happened? Recently? I had no idea she'd had her heart broken. I'd never asked. "I'm so sorry. I didn't know."

"Why would you? You're a princess. I'm your lady's maid. My love life is hardly your concern."

But it would be if we were friends. "Titles and roles don't seem to matter as much in Turah."

"You're still a princess, Highness. No matter where we are, you're royalty. I am not."

What if I didn't want to be royalty? What if I just wanted the chance to be kissed the way Tillia had been kissed?

We rode for a while before Tillia returned to my side. A stunning smile lit up her face, and it was impossible not to smile back.

"That is my husband," she said. "Halston. He's been traveling with Zavier. The Guardian told me the other night that he was leaving Perris to join us, but I always worry when we're apart."

Her husband. Halston.

The Guardian had told her about her husband. That's why they'd been speaking so close. Not because they were together.

The relief was instant. The air rushed from my lungs. And with it, a guilt so toxic and ugly it might as well have been fenek poison.

I shouldn't be relieved. I shouldn't fucking care.

Tillia's husband raced through the group, galloping past the riders at the edge. He lifted a hand to her. She blew him a kiss.

With Halston in the lead, he set a new pace for our party, the slow march becoming a fast walk that jostled my bones.

Somehow, the trees seemed to get even taller. Wider. Stronger.

"Have you ever seen such tall trees?" I asked Brielle.

"No, Highness."

"You may call me Odessa."

"I—" She shook her head. "I'll try. But it will be a hard habit to break."

And from the sound of it, she wasn't really going to try. She'd keep our roles in place. Maybe that was the smartest choice.

Eventually, she'd leave. And I'd have something else to mourn.

"Listen," Tillia said. "Do you hear that?"

It took me a moment, ears straining, but then I heard the sound carry through the trees.

A whistle. Almost like a bird's but not quite.

"Come on." She urged her horse into a trot. "We're close."

I groaned at the idea of keeping up, but I nudged Freya to follow, hoping that whenever we reached Treow, there'd be a flat spot where I could collapse.

We weaved past the riders, making our way to the front of the group, where Halston rode side by side with two more of Zavier's rangers.

My husband? Nowhere in sight.

Should I be worried? If something had happened to the crown prince, surely someone would have told me, right?

"Ha," I scoffed to myself. Because I was so often the person in the know? I'd be the last to learn of his fate.

"What?" Jocelyn asked.

"Nothing." I shook it off. "Just reminding myself of my complete and utter insignificance."

She gave me a sideways glance.

"Kidding," I muttered. Not really.

Halston reached out to touch Tillia's hand as we passed by, and the rangers let us take the lead as we rode into a clearing. A perfect oval in the forest bordered by a simple wooden fence. A corral or paddock of sorts. At one end was a wooden building that looked to be stables. And then came another whistle.

I searched the paddock, trying to find the source, but there was no one around.

"There." Tillia pointed up and up and up.

To a watchtower built into a tree.

"Welcome to Treow." She stopped in the middle of the clearing and dismounted.

I did the same, practically leaping off Freya and landing hard on my heels. My legs were in agony. My back, misery. I grimaced as I rolled my stiff arms.

"You'll get a chance to rest now, Odessa." Tillia took Freya's reins, handing them to a boy who emerged from the trees.

Others followed behind him, each person wearing a smile as they raced to meet our group. They were all dressed in the same tunics and pants I'd been wearing for days, though they looked considerably less rumpled.

"Come," Tillia said.

"What about Brielle and Jocelyn?" Both had fallen behind a bit and had just reached the clearing.

"They'll be taken care of. Don't worry. They won't be far. Unless you need their assistance?"

"No."

There was nothing I couldn't do for myself. And with that came another wash of guilt.

I hadn't needed either of them since we left Quentis. They didn't need to be here with me. The sooner I could send them both home with the information for Father, the better.

Tillia led the way through the clearing to the tree line. We stepped out of the sun to the shade of branches and limbs.

To a place unlike anything I'd ever seen. It was like walking into a different realm.

When I'd asked her again earlier if Treow was a town, she'd said, "Yes and no."

Now I understood.

Treow wasn't a town with streets or roads or shops or squares. It was a town built into a forest.

Houses loomed above, secured to the massive evergreens. Some were connected by rope bridges. Others were unlinked, tethered to the earth by ladders.

Four little girls raced along a planked walkway above, leaning over the rail to giggle and stare down at us. Two of them were twins, each with olive skin and silky black hair.

Tillia brought two fingers to her lips and whistled up to them. It was sharp and loud, the same noise I'd heard before we'd arrived at Treow.

The girls all pressed their own fingers to their mouths, attempting to whistle back. It came out as mostly sputters and spit, which only made them laugh harder.

"We have lookouts at the perimeter," she explained. "We whistle so that no one gets shot in the heart with an arrow."

"Ah." I nodded. "I don't know how to whistle."

"You don't need to."

Because I wouldn't be staying? Or because I wouldn't be going past the perimeter?

Questions for Zavier, if my husband ever stopped avoiding me.

In the meantime, I'd teach myself to whistle, just in case.

"Why the treehouses?" I asked Tillia.

"It's safer this way. We're in tarkin territory now. There are the occasional packs of bariwolves that will venture close. Grizzurs typically prefer the coast and plains, though they are unpredictable. They've been known to wander this way. Most villages in Turah have had to develop ways to guard against monsters. This"—she waved a hand to the structures above us—"is ours."

"You live here?"

"Not permanently, but we spend a significant portion of the year in Treow." She turned to walk backward, pointing to a house overhead. "That's where Halston and I stay."

From down below, I couldn't tell one treehouse from the next. They all were just...floors.

"The one with the thatched roof and rope ladder," she said.

Was this a trick? "They all have rope ladders."

"But ours is the newest." She laughed and spun forward, continuing our walk.

How far were we going? I glanced back, hoping to see the clearing past trunks, but it was gone.

"Most of us spend our days down here," she said. "Cooking. Riding. Training. We take meals in the commons. I'll give you a tour of that tomorrow after you've had some sleep."

"How are the horses kept safe? Will my horse—" I stopped myself before finishing the question.

Freya wasn't my horse. Not really. I'd named her out of boredom, not ownership. But after these hard days together, I didn't want her to die.

"The horses are brought into the stables each night. Your horse is safe here, too."

"Thanks."

"You're welcome." She dipped her chin, then stopped at a rope ladder.

I looked up to find another treehouse. Maybe because I was standing directly below it, this one didn't seem as far off the ground as the others. And it seemed twice as large.

It also had no walkways or bridges. It was a house apart. Secluded. Private.

Was this Zavier's treehouse? Would he be joining me to finally...

I gulped.

Eventually, we'd have to suffer through a night of awkward sex. I just really, *really* hoped it wouldn't be today.

"After you." Tillia motioned me up. "Your trunks are waiting. The wagons rode ahead so everything would be ready for your arrival. They've also left you a meal. Please eat."

"Thank you."

"Do you need help?" Tillia asked.

To climb a ladder? Well, I'd never climbed a ladder before, wood or metal or rope. "Uh, no?"

I guess if I fell to my death, at least I'd get to skip that awkward sex.

With a fortifying breath, I started up the rungs, moving as fast as a sea turtle on sand. Sweat dripped down my spine and beaded at my temples by the time I finally reached the landing. There was probably a graceful way to get onto the treehouse's balcony, but I flopped on my stomach like a dead fish, rolling and flipping until I was finally able to push to my knees and stand.

I leaned over the railing and gave Tillia a thumbs-up. "Made it."

She looked like she was trying to hide a laugh. With a wave, she ran off in the direction of her own home, probably to hunt down her husband and find a bedroom.

Lucky woman.

I scanned the wide platform that ringed the structure, my hand skimming across the balcony's railing as I walked its edge. The wooden boards beneath my feet were clean and dry, the pine needles swept away. As I rounded the building, I found another treehouse tucked behind this one. They were only ten feet apart. Close enough that I could throw a pine cone from one door to the other.

Maybe a guard's quarters? Close enough to make a leap in an emergency?

I wasn't in the mood to greet a neighbor, so I steeled my spine and opened the door. If this was Zavier's treehouse, I couldn't avoid it forever.

The inside was a single room with a large bed at its center. The mattress was covered in plush, oatmeal-colored blankets and fluffy pillows.

"Yes," I breathed, my shoulders sagging. If enduring awkward sex meant I got to keep that bed, so be it.

There were soft, beige curtains on the ceiling, probably to drape around the bed for privacy. Or maybe to keep out bugs.

On one side of the room was a desk with a wooden chair. On the other was a carved wooden armoire. My trunks rested beside a floor-to-ceiling partition.

I went to peer around the partition's edge, and the moan that escaped my chest vibrated the treehouse.

A water closet, complete with a sink and copper tub.

The tub had been filled with warm, steaming water.

I reached for the hem of my tunic, about to strip it off my body when the sound of footsteps came from outside.

My stomach sank. *Damn.*

I smoothed down my shirt, making sure every inch of my stomach was covered. Then I moved to the center of the room, expecting Zavier to walk through the door.

Silly me and my expectations. When was I going to learn not to assume anything?

Of course it wasn't my husband who came inside.

It was the Guardian.

His beard was trimmed close to his jaw and his hair damp, like he'd just had a bath of his own. The collar of his tunic showed a triangle of taut, smooth skin above his heart. His pants molded to strong thighs and draped to scuffed boots. His eyes were that vivid emerald green.

He was the most beautiful man I'd ever seen.

I dropped my gaze to the floor. "You."

"Me."

"I thought you'd be Zavier."

He clicked his tongue. "Sorry to disappoint, my queen. He has been... detained."

"In Perris?"

"So curious." He took slow, deliberate steps into the room, wandering to the desk.

The plate on top was covered by a cloth. He plucked it free, revealing roasted meat and vegetables and a roll of dense, dark bread.

My stomach growled, hungry for the first time in days. "Why are you here?"

"I've never met a woman who asked so many questions."

"And received so few answers in return."

His low laugh filled the room. "How about I ask the questions for a change?"

"If I say yes, will you leave?" I wanted to climb into that bathtub before the water cooled.

He re-covered my dinner, shifting to lean against the wall, crossing his arms. "Where is your home?"

"What's the point to that question when you already know the answer?"

"Say it anyway."

"Ros. Lo." I articulated both syllables with my frustration. "Happy?"

"Quite. Was that so hard, Sparrow?"

"Is there a point to this?"

"Of course. Now I know what it's like to hear a truth roll off your tongue."

"Because you think I've been lying to you all this time?" I rolled my eyes. "We've already established that you'll never trust me. No matter what I say. Can we move this along? I'm hungry."

The corner of his mouth turned up. "How old are you?"

"Twenty-three. How old are you?"

He looked to be in his twenties, like me. Though maybe he was like the Voster and long-lived. Maybe he was a hundred years old and only looked like a man in his prime.

He tsked. "There she goes with the questions again. You really can't help yourself, can you?"

"No, I guess not."

"Your eyes. You don't have a starburst."

Neither did he. Did that make us similar somehow? Was he worried I was harboring gifts like his? The strength or speed? Our training sessions should have put those fears to rest. My eyes might be different, but I was nothing special.

"That wasn't a question. Anything else?"

"Are you a virgin?"

Did he actually care? No.

Was he asking to get a reaction? Yes.

Was it working? Unfortunately.

My cheeks flamed. My hands fisted at my sides. "Next question."

"Are you enjoying your time in Turah?"

"Not especially."

"Do you like the horse you were riding?"

"Yes."

"How sore is your ass right now?"

"Very," I answered through gritted teeth.

He shoved off the wall and stalked close, the tips of his boots nearly skimming mine. I could feel the heat from his chest. Smell the scent of his skin and soap. "Did your father send you here to spy?"

"No."

It was the best lie I'd ever delivered. Even *I* would believe me.

"You're a terrible liar, Cross." He touched a curl at my temple, the strand having fallen out of my braid.

I batted his hand away. "How long will I be staying here?"

He lifted a shoulder. "I'm not sure."

"When will I travel with Zavier to Allesaria?"

"Eager to see our pretty castle, my queen?"

My nostrils flared. "Ready to be away from you."

"You're assuming I don't live in Allesaria."

"Do you?" I couldn't picture him in a city. The Guardian seemed like a man more comfortable in the wilderness. A beast content to roam free.

A monster in his own right.

"You'll go to Allesaria when Zavier can trust you."

"And if he's like you and will never trust me? Then what? I live in this treehouse for the rest of my life?"

That made him smile. A menacing, evil, gorgeous smile.

"Go away," I snapped, turning to stare at the wall.

His laugh lingered, even after he walked out the door.

I waited a heartbeat, then followed, hoping to lock him out.

Only there wasn't a lock.

I expected to see him descending the rope ladder. Instead, he unhooked it from its fascinators and flung it to the ground. "Hey, what are you—"

He leaped over the railing, dropping to the earth.

I rushed to the edge, peering to the forest floor. Hoping to find his body bent and broken. Sure, this treehouse didn't seem to be as tall as the others, but the drop was still twenty feet.

The Guardian, completely unharmed, tucked his hands in his pockets and strolled away.

Certainly not worried that he'd just left me stranded.

"Jackass," I said, hoping he could hear me.

He kept walking but started whistling a happy little tune.

"Grr." I slammed my palms onto the railing, glaring at his back until he was out of sight.

This treehouse might not be as far from the ground as others, but it was definitely too far for me to jump. I'd break my damn neck.

And now I was trapped.

In a fucking treehouse.

Twenty

My rope ladder was back.

When I'd stepped outside a few minutes ago to wave down anyone who might get me out of this tree, I'd expected to find the ladder still pooled on the ground. But someone had reattached it to my balcony, either this morning or last night.

Last night, after my bath and dinner, I'd crawled into bed and passed out. I'd awoken to the sound of birds chirping beyond the treehouse windows. If not for my hunger pangs, I'd probably still be asleep. Strange how I felt even more tired today. My head was in a fog. My body sluggish.

I was going to hunt down breakfast, then crawl back in that bed for a week.

Testing the top rung of the ladder with a foot, making sure it was secure, I climbed down as clumsily as I'd climbed up yesterday.

How did they attach these ladders? Did someone scale the tree? Did they use rods and hooks to lift the ropes into place?

I made a mental note to ask Tillia about the mechanics as I hopped off the last rung to the ground, brushing my hands on the clean pair of charcoal pants I'd donned with my fresh tunic—this one the palest of blues and embroidered with navy and white stars.

I'd found all-new clothing in the armoire. There'd been another pair of boots, too. Whoever Zavier had tasked with keeping me clothed with Turan pieces was doing a fine job.

My drab gray dresses were still in my trunks. When I'd opened the lid to one last night, I'd also found my crown.

Zavier hadn't tossed it into the Krisenth. He'd given it back. I doubt I'd ever wear it again, but it was a piece of home.

The cut on my palm was healing, a scar beginning to form, but I'd wrapped it in a fresh bandage. My hair was shampooed, combed, and freshly dyed. My arms were too tired to bother with a braid, so I'd left the curls loose and wild. By midday, they'd be double the size, but hopefully by then, they'd be buried in my pillows.

Unlike the filthy corpse I'd been last night, this morning, I actually looked human. After a meal, I might actually feel that way, too.

"Odessa." Tillia walked through the trees, a smile on her beautiful face.

I waved. "Good morning."

"Afternoon."

Ah. "That explains why I'm so hungry."

She laughed. "We all deserved some extra rest. Come, I'll show you around, and we'll get you something to eat."

She led me along a different path than we'd taken yesterday. We wended through the trees, beneath more houses, to what I assumed was the heart of Treow. There were four sturdy log buildings positioned around an open square filled with tables and chairs.

"This is the commons." She pointed to the tallest of the four buildings. "That is the dining hall, where all the cooking is done and meals are served."

"Do we pay for them?" Like the vendors who'd sell bowls of rice and roasted vegetables and fish on the docks.

"Treow is run more like an encampment than a village. Most of the people who stay here are just passing through. Some stay longer than others, like Halston and me. But most are soldiers and their families traveling between fortresses. So, the king provides for our meals and such."

"Ah." Similar to the military outposts in Quentis.

Father made sure his soldiers had shelter and food in exchange for their service.

"This closest building is the mercantile," she said. "They keep limited quantities of the necessities on hand, but if there's anything you need, just ask the clerk. Ashmore is the closest town. We rode past it on the way here. They bring shipments over once or twice a week. If their merchants don't have what you need, they can request it from Perris or Ellder."

"Not Allesaria?"

Her smile dimmed as she shook her head. "No."

Just…no.

Okay. Why was it that every time I brought up Allesaria, the mood would change?

"Across from the mercantile is the laundry," she continued. "There are cleaning supplies inside, but your lady's maids will be attending to your treehouse every day. Just leave out whatever you'd like to be washed."

"All right." I nodded to the last of the buildings. "And that one?"

"The infirmary and library."

A library. This strange military outpost had a library? "I like libraries."

Especially when they came with history books and maps. Not that I was expecting to be handed a map, but it was worth a try. Maybe there was some bit of information to glean and tuck away in my journal.

Tillia took my elbow to steer me to the dining hall. "Food first. Then books."

The interior of the hall was clean and tidy. It smelled like sage and garlic and herbs. Tillia led me through a line to dish my plate with beans and squash and meat. Then she sat with me at a long, empty table while I shoveled food into my mouth, not caring at all that I wasn't eating like a princess.

Margot would have thrown a fit.

I smiled to myself and wiped my mouth with the back of my hand even though there was a napkin on my lap.

With my food finished and dishes sent to the kitchens to wash, we returned outside.

"Tillia." Halston's voice carried across the commons as he strode toward his wife.

"One moment." She gave me an easy smile, then walked over to meet him.

There was a group of kids in the square between buildings, chasing each other around in the grass.

"Got you!" A boy with a cloud of black hair laughed after tagging one of his friends, then racing in the opposite direction.

They were all smiles as they ran in sloppy circles, playing and giggling. Everyone except a young girl who stood apart from the others.

She was tucked against the back corner of the mercantile, watching me with her head tilted to the side, her eyebrows knitted together.

Her hair was silky brown and hung in loose, wispy waves over her shoulders. Her skin was as pale as starlight. And her doe eyes were gray with a starburst of cerulean blue, like the ocean I used to see outside my bedroom window.

The starburst of those born in Ozarth.

She was the most adorable child I'd ever seen. Even cuter than Arthy.

How was my brother today? I was already starting to forget what his giggle sounded like.

The children all seemed to realize I was standing close at the same moment. The laughter stopped. The smiles faded. One boy even gave me a sneer. Then they were gone, running away like I'd ruined their favorite playtime spot.

Wow. Okay, so I wouldn't expect a warm welcome from the kids.

"Sorry." Tillia returned, standing in front of me and blocking my view of the girl. "Ready to see the library?"

"Yes."

When she stepped out of the way, the girl had disappeared. There one moment. Gone the next. So fast, the hairs on the back of my neck stood on end.

I had the feeling I was still being watched, but she'd vanished.

Weird. I shook off the feeling, about to follow Tillia to the library, when the sound of hooves came from beyond the commons.

Tillia stilled, listening for a moment. "That's probably a pony rider. We'll go meet him in the clearing."

"Um, what's a pony rider?"

She grabbed my hand, pulling me in the opposite direction. "You'll see."

We changed directions, our pace quickening until we made it to the fence. The horses were grazing inside. I spotted my Freya, munching on grass and seemingly content not to be trekking across Turah.

"There were more horses than this yesterday," I said.

"Most of the traveling party set off to Ellder this morning."

Right. The change of plan had been for me. To stick me in that treehouse cage.

A lanky boy in his teens rushed out of the stables, and the lone rider came to a stop beside the building. The animal was out of breath, its coat foamy with sweat. The rider swung out of his saddle looking equally as winded, like they'd been sprinting across the plains.

The boy handed him a cup of water, and the rider drank it in a few hearty gulps, drops trickling off the sides of his chin. His face was tan and coated in sweat and dirt. His brown eyes were shielded by a hat with a wide brim. It was the same style of hat most of the farmers wore in Quentis. One large enough to block out both sun and rain.

The rider pulled off his hat, his dirty blond hair flattened from where it had been sitting, and wiped his brow with an arm. Then he donned the hat once more before unclasping a saddlebag and retrieving a bound stack of envelopes.

"Good ride?" Tillia asked as we approached.

He touched the brim of his hat as he dipped his chin. "It was fast. But no issues."

"Glad to hear it." She took the letters. "Will you stay and rest?"

"I've got to press on," he said.

The boy who'd brought him water nodded. "I'll get you a fresh pony and a quick meal."

"Appreciated." The rider smiled, then began to unfasten his saddle.

Tillia waved, then turned to walk away.

"That's it?" I asked.

She shrugged and held up the bundle of letters. "The pony riders don't linger. Once they've dropped off the post, they'll continue on to the next town and the next. They go as far and fast as they can during daylight hours."

So this network of riders basically controlled communication across the kingdom.

Quentis was small enough that we didn't have a need for such jobs. The post was carried on wagons that looped through the kingdom on regular routes, delivering every day or two. If I wrote a letter to a friend in Kolmberg, the city on the opposite end of Quentis from Roslo, it would arrive within two days' time.

At least that was my assumption. I didn't have a friend in Kolmberg to write.

"How many riders are there?"

"In Turah? Hundreds. It's a hard job but it pays well. Usually, it's young men who want to earn a living before settling down. But it's dangerous. They spend a considerable amount of time alone in the wilderness. It takes time to cross the country. These letters were probably written weeks ago."

"And they deliver the post across the entire country this way?"

Tillia nodded. "Every city. Every town. Every village. Even the encampments like Treow."

I hummed, a spark of hope lighting in my chest.

Would it be possible to get information on Allesaria from a pony rider? They had to know the way in and out of the city to deliver the post.

Except even as the thought crossed my mind, I turned to see the rider swapping his saddle from one horse to the next. If they didn't stay longer than a few minutes, it wasn't going to be easy to corner one for information. To earn that trust.

I'd have to keep watch for the next pony rider. Until then...

"To the library?" I asked Tillia.

"Sure."

We rounded the dining hall, about to cross to the library, but a large, annoying shadow fell over my shoulder.

I refused to change paths. I kept walking, eyes forward.

"Tillia." The Guardian walked so close that I caught a hint of his scent. Wind and leather and earth and masculine spice.

He'd left that scent in my treehouse last night. I wasn't letting myself think about how it had mingled so perfectly with the perfumes of my bathwater.

"You can deal with the post," he said. "Cross and I have business."

"What business?" My own damn curiosity won out, and I turned to glare up at his profile.

His smirk was waiting. "Training. Your idea, remember?"

"You certainly won't let me forget," I muttered.

I want a sword.

Never, ever would I regret a sentence more.

"You can quit," he said.

"I'm not quitting."

"Good for you," Tillia said.

She gave the Guardian a short nod, then left with the envelopes while I walked with him away from the commons. His strides were so long I had to jog every few of my own to keep up.

"Would you slow down?"

He ignored me.

"Jackass."

He walked faster.

By the time we reached the training area, I was out of breath.

"Your stamina is shit," he said.

My stamina was not shit. Swimming had always kept me in shape. But after traveling across the continent, eating too little, and being sleep deprived...

Today, my stamina was shit.

"Thank you." I mocked a curtsy. "You're too kind, sir. Really."

"Always with the sass. Let's see if that attitude holds over the next few hours."

My stomach dropped.

A few hours? I'd be dead in half that time if this session was anything like the last.

Like all things in Treow, the training area was situated beneath the trees. Their trunks served as boundaries for various stations. Two women were shooting crossbows at different targets. A couple of men were practicing with swords. A teenage boy with braids like Halston's was standing with a bow, arrow flying into a bale of hay.

The Guardian walked to the base of a tree where my knives were waiting.

"You could have asked me to get these. Not intrude on my private space," I said.

"And you should make your own bed every morning. Not leave it for your lady's maids. They'll be expected to contribute more in Treow than simply serving you, *Highness*."

He made me seem like a spoiled princess. Maybe I was. I hadn't made my bed because I'd planned to return to it. But I also didn't make my bed. For Brielle and Jocelyn's sake, I'd start.

"Fine." I held out my hands for the knives. "Anything else before we begin?"

"Try not to fall on your ass."

I tried. I gave it my all.

And failed miserably.

He'd trip me, I'd fall. He'd push me, I'd fall. He'd look at me sideways, I'd fall.

One night's rest hadn't been enough. I was still too tired, my movements too sluggish, and for nearly three hours, the Guardian showed me no mercy.

While others had come and gone, he'd kept pushing. And I'd kept falling.

My lungs were on fire. So were my legs and arms. My mouth tasted like blood, and it was a miracle I hadn't vomited up my lunch.

"Give up?" he asked.

"Has it been three hours?"

"Not quite."

Fuck. "Then no. I'm not giving up."

He came at me with a series of jabs and strikes. I managed to deflect his sword with my knives, but on the retreat backward, I tripped over my own heels, crashing into the ground on my hip.

I pushed up on my arms, drawing in my knees as I forced a few deep breaths. "Ouch."

He let out an exasperated sigh. "Take a breather, Cross. You're sloppy and slow."

"Aw, thanks." I feigned a smile.

He walked toward a tree and picked up two cups of water. I hadn't noticed them before. Someone must have brought them over while we'd been training.

The moment he handed me a drink, I guzzled it empty.

He quirked an eyebrow, his own cup raised to his lips.

"What?"

"Nothing." He took a sip. A polite, normal sip by a person who wasn't dying of thirst.

What kind of training did a man like the Guardian do each day? What strained the limits of his stamina? Killing monsters? Murdering foreigners?

"Is this the type of training all of your rangers go through?" I asked, hoping a few questions would buy me a longer break.

"Not just rangers. Most Turans know how to wield a weapon. Timbermen typically train with an ax. Others, swords and knives. Children learn basic skills either from their parents or in primary school."

"Ah." It wasn't entirely different in Quentis. People in the countryside all learned how to fight in case a wayward monster wandered onto their farm. Though I suspected the training in Turah was doubly as demanding and strenuous. "Did you learn as a child?"

He nodded. "I did."

"I bet you were the stoic, serious type as a boy, weren't you? The kid who always made sure everyone else was following the rules. Always came with an extra knife in case someone forgot theirs. The tutors' favorite student." Like Mae.

The Guardian scoffed. "Not exactly."

"Then what were you like?" I held my breath, hoping he'd answer just this one last question. Now that I had the image of a dark-haired boy in mind, I wanted to know if I'd pictured him right.

"I was a terror. My mother prayed to Ama daily that I wouldn't break my neck. I never walked when I could run. I never took the stairs if I could jump out a window. I snuck out of lessons to ride my horse. And the last thing I minded was the rules."

That mental image of him as a boy shifted and morphed. It wasn't what I'd originally expected, but this version fit, too. A wild, fearless boy with holes in the knees of his pants and a carefree smile.

What had changed him into this man before me? What or who had turned him into the Guardian?

His eyes stayed locked on mine as he took another drink. They were hazel today, a mix of moss and caramel and chocolate. But I noticed a few flecks of emerald green. A few striations of molten silver.

Was that how the color shift worked? It wasn't so much that they changed altogether, the colors were already there, chasing away the others depending on his mood.

My attention shifted to the leather cuff on his arm. There were carvings in the grizzur leather. Symbols and patterns. Notches and swirls. What did they mean? Were they significant?

Tillia wore cuffs on her forearms, too, but I hadn't noticed any carvings.

"What do those engravings mean?" I asked, pointing to the cuff.

He rotated his forearm as he stared at them. "They are for the lives I've taken. So I'll never forget."

That he was a monster? A murderer? Which mark was for Banner's brother?

"Does every warrior in Turah do that?"

"Some," he answered, tossing the remaining water from his cup.

"What other traditions do you have?" I asked, hoping to prolong this break. I wasn't ready to start again.

"That enough stalling, Cross?" A faint smile tugged at his mouth. "You'll learn our traditions. In time. You'll find that they are simple, my queen. But our loyalty to our country, to our people, runs to the bone."

His voice was smooth. Deep and rich. But there was no mistaking the threat.

If—*when*—I betrayed his people, that sword of his would find its way through my lying throat.

Maybe I wouldn't even blame him.

Twenty-One

I hated Treow.

Yesterday's training session had been child's play compared to the torture I'd endured since dawn.

I was going to die. This was it. This was the end of my life. I'd perish beneath these trees, and the Turans would leave my remains for the crows to scavenge.

Bent over at the middle, hands braced on my knees, I sucked in a breath, desperate to fill my lungs. The bastard had just knocked the wind out of me for the second time since he'd roused me from sleep.

To be fair, the first time hadn't exactly been his fault. I'd slipped on a rung of my rope ladder and fallen five feet to the forest floor, landing on my back. The son of a bitch could have caught me, but instead, he'd stood there to watch me fall.

This second time? Definitely his fault.

He'd elbowed me in the gut.

Or maybe I'd fallen into his elbow when I tripped? It didn't matter. It was his sharp fucking elbow and, therefore, his fault.

I hated him.

I hated him for stealing my rope ladder again last night, trapping me in my treehouse. I hated him for smacking me in the face with a pillow this morning. I hated him for his pointy elbows.

I hated him.

The end.

Would he die from a fall off my treehouse balcony? Obviously he had survived the jump. But what if it was him landing on his back? Would his spine shatter? Would his neck snap? If I just pushed him over the railing the next time he invaded my privacy, would he die?

A girl could dream.

With my eyes squeezed shut, I sucked in a breath through my nostrils, slowly exhaling through my open mouth. I repeated it, over and over, until

I was fairly certain I was going to live. Then I stood, expecting to find a smirking asshole staring back.

But the training area was empty.

He was gone.

"Hello?" I spun in a slow circle.

Empty. Nothing.

Where the hell did he go? Was this a trick? Was he staging a sneak attack as some sort of lesson?

He hadn't even brought his sword this morning. He'd fought me entirely unarmed—except for the elbows—while I'd sliced and stabbed with my knives.

"Hey," I called.

Silence. I groaned and cast my eyes to the sky, the dark slowly giving way to sunlight.

We'd been the only people in the training area so far. The other warriors were probably still in their beds.

"Guardian," I snapped. I hated calling him *Guardian*. That couldn't be his name. Who named their child Guardian?

Unless he didn't have parents. Unless he'd been birthed from Izzac's shade.

Each of the Six lived in a shade—a nether realm that served as their home. A place for souls to endure eternity. The purest of heart were given to Arabella, for the Goddess of Love's shade was light. The bright white of the twin moons.

Heaven.

From there, the shades became darker and darker until they reached Izzac, the God of Death.

Hell.

Souls sent to Izzac were punished by the dark, never to see light again, as they were tormented, endlessly, by his monsters.

Was the Guardian one of those terrors? A harbinger of death.

At this point, it certainly wouldn't shock me.

"Does this mean we're done for the day?" I asked no one.

I spun around again, searching through the forest. A chill snaked down my shoulders when I realized I was truly alone. He'd left me alone.

He wouldn't have done so if there were danger lurking, right? For his many, many faults, the Guardian didn't seem to want me dead. That, or Zavier didn't want me dead and the Guardian was following orders.

Well, if he wasn't going to stick around, I sure wouldn't.

"I'm leaving now."

A bird chirped.

"Since you were in such a godsdamn hurry this morning, I didn't get to make my bed." I really, *really* hoped he could hear me.

Careful not to slice off my hair, I put my knives in their sheaths, crisscrossing them over my spine. Then I started through the forest, trying to find the path to my treehouse. It was going to take me a while to figure out how to navigate Treow. The trails were thin and winding, and some were no more than a trodden patch of grass.

After two wrong turns and a backtrack, I found my treehouse waiting. I hurried up to my room, quickly changing into a pair of clean pants and a fresh tunic, then descended the ladder—apparently, it only disappeared at night—and made my way toward the commons.

Alone. All by myself.

Free.

What had happened to Tillia following me around? Did I no longer require an escort or guard? Why did my ladder disappear at night but remain available for me to come and go during the day?

Was the Guardian worried that I'd try to escape? That I'd sneak out in the dark?

Well, if he was worried, he shouldn't bother. Not only would I be going nowhere after sunset in a land crawling with monsters twice my size, but I was here to do my father's bidding.

Turah was home until further notice.

For me, at least.

I hadn't seen either Brielle or Jocelyn since we'd arrived in Treow. Yesterday, after training, I'd been too exhausted to seek them out. And I'd been too tired to return to the library. Tillia had brought dinner to my room, and after I'd inhaled the food, I'd crashed into a heap on my pillow until the Guardian had encroached on my privacy. Again.

I was on my way to the commons, hoping to find my lady's maids in the dining hall, when a woman with warm brown skin and graying hair twisted into a severe knot met me on the trail.

She came to an abrupt stop to bow as I passed by. "Princess Odessa Wolfe."

We were back to the formal name already?

"Good morning," I said. "You can call me Odessa. Please."

Her eyes narrowed as she frowned. Then, with a huff, she stomped away.

"O—kay," I drawled. What was that about? I scrunched up my nose and continued on toward the commons, glancing back a few times until the woman was out of sight.

Was it not okay that I went by my first name? Zavier went by his.

"Don't mind Mariette. She's stern but fair." A woman appeared at my side, emerging from the trees. She had a delicate, narrow nose with a few gentle lines at her eyes and mouth, like she laughed often. Her sleek white hair hung in panels over her shoulders, the ends nearly to her waist. "Mariette is the caretaker in Treow. And rather...traditional."

"Traditional meaning she'll want to use my formal name?"

"Or not drop your new *surname*."

"Ah." Asking her to call me Odessa was a slight against her royal family because I'd left off the Wolfe.

Well, tough. I didn't want to be a Wolfe. It wasn't my idea. In Treow, in Turah, until I was more comfortable on this land and with its people, I was simply Odessa.

"I'm Cathlin." The woman held out her hand, and when our palms touched, she clasped mine with both of hers. It was a hug for my hand.

I missed hugs. I missed forcing them on Mae. I missed sharing them with Arthy.

"Odessa," I said.

"Pleasure to meet you." Her chestnut brown eyes sparkled, the green starbursts bright, as she smiled, walking with me toward the dining hall.

Cathlin wore a simple tan dress with long sleeves. It wasn't all that different from the gray dresses still stowed in my trunks. I guess Brielle wouldn't be the only person in Treow in a dress, since she refused to try the pants.

The dining hall was quiet, a few tables occupied, but I didn't see either Jocelyn or Brielle.

"Aren't you eating?" she asked when I stopped inside the door.

"I was hoping to join my lady's maids. I haven't seen them since we arrived. Maybe I'll swing by the library while I wait."

"It doesn't open for another hour."

"Oh." *Drat.*

She reached a hand into one of her dress pockets to retrieve a set of keys. "Lucky for you, I happen to be the current librarian. Come on."

Lucky. Strange how I'd considered myself lucky more times since leaving Quentis than I had in, well, years. If Daria, the Goddess of Luck, was on my side for the time being, I wasn't going to question her reasons.

I would need her luck to find the road to Allesaria before winter. We'd left Quentis nearly three weeks ago. Time was not on my side. I picked up my pace.

"This library has been my passion project," Cathlin said, matching my stride. "It's not much, but it's taking shape. With each of my visits to Treow, I add more books to the collection."

So she didn't live here, either? Did anyone call Treow home? Maybe Mariette, the caretaker. Or was she a nomad, only ever passing through, too?

The library's door was at the end of the infirmary's building. Even from the outside, it was obvious the space was only the size of a closet. Maybe that's all it had been until Cathlin had commandeered it as her own.

"Where are you from originally?" I asked as she slid her key into the library's brass doorknob and flipped its lock.

"I've lived all over Turah. I was born in Perris. And I've spent many years in Allesaria." She pushed open the door, leading me inside.

My heart leaped so high I tripped over the threshold.

She was the only person, other than the Guardian, to have spoken the capital city's name since I'd arrived in Turah. Maybe she'd answer some of my questions.

"Oh dear." Cathlin grabbed my arm as I caught my balance. "Are you all right?"

"Fine. Sorry. I'm, er…clumsy."

Her laugh was gentle. Practiced. Easy. "I've been known to have those moments myself."

The scents of books and parchment and cloves filled my nose. I closed my eyes, breathing it in. The room was dim and without windows. Behind the first row of shelves, I couldn't make out anything in the shadows.

Cathlin walked to the center of the room and pulled on a long cord hanging from the ceiling.

There was a similar cord in the treehouse, latched on a hook beside the door.

As she tugged, a row of curtains on the ceiling collapsed on themselves, bunching to one side and revealing a row of windows in the roof.

The library flooded with daylight, filling every corner of the building.

Skylights. The cloths on the ceiling were covering skylights. The moment I was back at my treehouse, I was opening mine.

"There." Cathlin secured the cord out of the way, then clapped her hands together. "What can I help you find?"

A detailed map to Allesaria? "Oh, anything really. I love to read."

"So do I." She ran her fingers along the spines of a nearby shelf, her eyes softening as she touched the books. "Feel free to browse around, though I'll warn you, this collection has been tailored for children. Treow doesn't have a school, so I've tried to bring anything that might help parents who are teaching the little ones to read and write."

"There's no school." It was more of a statement than a question as I replayed my tour with Tillia yesterday. She hadn't mentioned a school.

"No." Cathlin sighed. "Not out here. Not in the wilds."

The wilds.

The wilds of Turah.

"It's too hard to get good teachers to live out here," she said. "It's understandable. They're less likely to be eaten by a bariwolf if they stick behind fortress or city walls. But that leaves parents with the burden of an education. Hence, my collection. But I do have a couple of rows for adults in the back."

"Do you mind if I poke around?"

"Not at all. Help yourself."

"Thank you." I smiled, then shuffled past the front bookcase. There was just enough room between it and the wall to reach the second and third rows. Cathlin had crammed everything in as tightly as possible.

I passed rows of readers for children, some of which I recognized from my own days with a tutor. When I made it to the rows of books for adults, I had to stand on my toes to read titles on the highest shelf.

Most of the books were related to Turah, and since that seemed like a good place to start, I plucked a handful out of the stacks, forming a pile on my arm as I perused. I added a book of monsters, complete with colored sketches. And when I spotted a dozen books about the other kingdoms in Calandra, my hand instantly reached for the book with *Quentis* stamped into its leather spine.

I set it on my stack and opened the cover, reading the introduction.

Traitors. Liars. Thieves. I spent a year in Quentis and can say with absolute certainty, they are a despicable people.

I harrumphed, double-checking to make sure I'd grabbed a book about my kingdom. That intro sounded more like a book about Genesis or Ozarth.

A YEAR IN QUENTIS BY SAMUEL HAY

It should have gone back on the shelf. I should have dismissed this author's opinions of my kingdom, my home, my people, immediately. Except before I could return it, I tucked it to the bottom of my stack, my curiosity winning out.

Was his opinion widely shared in Turah? If I wanted to keep my name, my heritage, would these people always scowl and sneer in my direction?

I kept searching for an atlas or a folded map, but there was nothing. My only hope was that the books I'd grabbed on Turan history might have a drawing in the interior. With my selections clutched to my chest, I returned to the front of the library, where Cathlin was waving a feather duster across a small desk.

"Finished?" she asked.

"I am. Would you mind if I took all these?"

"Not at all."

"Thank you." I returned her smile, then stepped outside, hurrying across the encampment for my treehouse to put these by my bed.

I was about halfway there when Brielle's voice carried through the trees.

"Highness."

"Brielle." I turned to find her rushing to catch up, a basket looped over one arm. I set my books on the ground and opened my arms for a short embrace. "Are you all right? Where are you staying? Are you with Jocelyn?"

"I'm fine," she said, out of breath. "Jocelyn is, too. They separated us, though. She's staying with one of the cooks who had a spare cot in her treehouse. I'm staying with the caretaker."

"Mariette?"

She nodded. "Yes. She's quiet. And I don't think she likes me much. I'm staying in her daughter's room, and I think I've become a constant reminder that her daughter is gone."

"I'll find you a new place."

"No, it's—"

"I insist. You'll need to be closer to me as my lady's maid anyway." If this was all I could do for the time being to make her stay in Turah more comfortable, then I'd find a way to make it easier.

"Thank you." Her shoulders sagged. "I've brought you breakfast. I waited for you in the dining hall, but when you didn't come, I had them prepare a plate."

"Oh." I'd forgotten about food. How long had I been in the library? "Would you come with me to my treehouse?"

"Of course. I'll help take this up. But then I'm expected in the laundry."

Right. She was taking orders from Mariette now. It was no different than her taking orders from the castle's seneschal. But here, it seemed like she should be under my authority.

Also something I'd be taking up with Zavier.

If Zavier ever showed his face in Treow.

In the meantime, I guess I'd have to ask Tillia. Or the Guardian as a last resort.

"Come." I bent and picked up my books, settling them on one arm. Then, with my free arm, I took hers, and we walked together to my treehouse.

She showed me the pulley and lift I'd overlooked along with the skylights—I really needed to pay more attention to the nuances of these homes—and we both climbed the rope ladder to haul up our belongings.

"Can I bring you anything else?" she asked. "They showed me how to haul up the water for baths, but it takes two of us. We'll be over later if you'd like."

"That would be—" *Wait.* "Have you had a bath?"

"Yes." She bent to sniff her armpit. "Why?"

"No reason." I waved it off. "I just wanted to make sure you have had a chance to rest, too."

"All rested." She forced a smile and pointed to the stack of books I'd set on the bed. "Can I assume you'll spend the rest of your day reading?"

"Yes." This wasn't the first time Brielle had found me with a stack of books. Granted, usually I was sneaking in a pile of sexy novels that I'd bought at the docks without Margot's knowledge.

"I'll bring you dinner." Brielle swept up the laundry from the dirty-clothes basket, then set off down the rope ladder, leaving me to my books.

I started with those on Turah. Then I dove into the book on monsters.

And I saved Samuel Hay's book on Quentis for last.

I should have burned it instead.

"Piece-of-shit filth," I muttered, tearing off my tunic.

Night had fallen outside the treehouse. Brielle and Jocelyn had brought me dinner hours ago and drawn me a bath. My food was as cold as the water.

But I stripped to nothing and sank into the tub anyway in an attempt to cool my boiling blood.

"Fuck you, Samuel Hay."

In his book, he called my country a land for thieves and traitors. He said Roslo was nothing more than a cesspool of immorality. And he speculated that my father was a murderer.

That the Gold King was behind more than one assassination attempt, including the death of the queen.

My. Mother.

Father wasn't perfect. He'd never claimed to be without flaws. But I knew, down to my bones, to the very threads of my soul, that he hadn't killed my mother.

It was no secret in Roslo that the day she died, he became a shell of his former self.

She'd been the love of his life.

Her ghost was Margot's biggest insecurity. Mother's memory was what drove Margot to demand perfection.

Yet we all knew, no matter how stoically Margot stood at his side, no matter how hard she tried, my father would always be in love with my mother.

The accusation that he'd killed her twisted so hard I wanted to scream. When my skin was covered in goose bumps, my arms shaking, and my teeth chattering from the cold water, I climbed out of the tub and dressed in a warm nightshirt. Then I burrowed beneath the covers, staring into the dark as that godsdamn book played on repeat in my mind.

If someone had told me at dawn there was a man in Turah I wanted to kill more than the Guardian, I would have called that person a liar.

But now?

I wanted to shove my knives through Samuel Hay's throat. I'd rip out his lying tongue. I'd break every finger he'd used to write those hateful, untrue words.

"Fuck you, Samuel Hay."

When I finally fell asleep, I dreamed of a grizzur. I watched as it tore the flesh from a faceless man's body. The monster devoured, tearing limbs from sockets. A scream ripped through the night. It kept shredding, clawing. But the face on its victim changed to Brielle.

She screamed and screamed. *Save me, Odessa. Save me.*

The monster became a crux, fur transforming to feathers. Not the auburn of the male crux, but the black feathers of females. It cut Brielle's body in two, swallowing entrails in a single gulp.

Then it fixed its beady eyes on me.

I woke in a sweat, my pulse pounding. I blinked and slapped a hand over my racing heart. "A nightmare." Only a nightmare.

I closed my eyes, wishing the vision out of my mind. Except I could still hear Brielle's scream. I could hear claws scratching against the earth. Against the trunk of my tree.

The noise came again, claws tearing into bark.

Not a sound from my head. A sound from outside.

I whipped the covers from my legs, the cold air instantly biting into my bare skin as I tiptoed to the door. On silent footsteps, I slipped outside and inched toward the balcony.

Aurinda and Aurrellia, the twin moons, were as bright as lanterns in the clear night sky. They lit up the forest, casting silver beams through branches.

I peered over the balcony's edge, my stomach pressing deep against the rail. My heart climbed into my throat as I lifted onto my toes and looked down.

At a lionwick sharpening its five-inch claws on the trunk of my tree.

I leaped away from the railing on a gasp.

My rope ladder was gone, and for the first time, I was glad to be trapped up here.

Lionwicks roamed the countryside in Quentis. They were nocturnal, and when the sun went down, they wreaked havoc on livestock, slaughtering herds of cattle or sheep or pigs.

They resembled mountain lions, but instead of sleek blond fur, they had smooth, leathery coats that shone like spun gold. Their hides were used to make the most expensive coats, gloves, and hats. Only the most elite and wealthy would wear lionwick to parties at the castle.

Their teeth and claws were as black as obsidian from the Evon Ravine. But the lionwick's spiked, barbed tail was its most noticeable feature. And deadliest weapon. Its tail was twice the length of its body and moved like a whip through the air.

They were wicked monsters, mean and vicious. They were fast and cunning. They'd hide in treetops and wait until—

My stomach dropped. *Oh, shit.*

Lionwicks were excellent climbers. I took another step away from the rail, my foot landing too loud.

"Shh."

I whirled toward the whisper. Toward the man standing outside the treehouse beside mine.

The Guardian.

He pressed a finger to his lips. In his other hand, he carried his sword.

I nodded, swallowing the fear clawing at my throat.

He peered over the edge of his own balcony as I inched closer to mine.

Another night, another place, I'd be shut inside, hidden beneath the bed. But with the Guardian here, with the slayer of monsters as my guard, I risked another look over my balcony.

The lionwick must have gotten bored with my tree. It prowled to the next, its muzzle against the ground as it sniffed.

I pointed to the monster, mouthing, *Kill it.*

The Guardian shook his head. "You kill it."

I gave him a flat look. *Yeah, right.*

He propped his sword against his door, then leaned forward, forearms to his own railing, seemingly content to watch that monster wander through Treow.

That's it? He was letting it go?

I planted one hand on my hip and jabbed a finger at the lionwick.

He picked up on my silent *are you going to do something about this or not?* without issue. "No."

I looked to the monster still prowling below. That tail flicked through the air in lazy, beautiful, deadly swirls.

"You're going to let it live?" I whispered.

"For the moment. I'm busy tonight."

I scoffed. "Doing what?"

He flashed me the smirk, then shoved off the rail, taking his sword as he disappeared inside his treehouse. With a click, he closed the door and shut me out.

I glared at the spot where he'd stood. Then I flicked the hair over my shoulder and turned for my own treehouse. I was almost inside when I heard his voice.

He was speaking to someone. He wasn't alone.

Unease crept through my veins like that monster through Treow.

Who? It wasn't my business who he spent his nights with. Who he invited into his bed. Especially considering I was *married*.

But the sinking feeling in my chest made it hard to breathe. It shouldn't bother me. I didn't care. Not. At. All.

If I practiced enough, someday, maybe I'd make a decent liar. I'd be like one of those Quentins in Samuel Hay's book.

I walked inside, latching the door to make sure it was secure. Then I tugged on the cord to pull back the curtains on my ceiling, welcoming the moonbeams inside. The skylights were strong enough to keep out a lionwick, right? Gods, I hoped so.

Collapsing on the bed, I stared up at the stars, doing everything in my power not to think about authors or monsters.

Or the man next door.

Twenty-Two

When I descended my rope ladder the next morning, it wasn't a lionwick or the Guardian waiting at the bottom—I'd worn my knives in case of either—it was Tillia.

"Good morning, Odessa."

"Good morning."

"The Guardian asked that we train together today. If you're up for it."

"And if I say I'm not up for it?"

"He told me to tell you that your next session with him would be twice as long and twice as hard."

My lip curled. "Jackass."

She fought a smile. "He said you'd say that, too."

"Then I guess he's got me all figured out." I sent a scowl to his quiet treehouse.

Was he up there? Sleeping late with whomever had shared his bed last night? Was he listening in on this very conversation?

"Well, I wouldn't want to disappoint the *Guardian*," I said, mocking his name and hoping he could hear. "Lead the way."

She set off down the path, her hands clasped together as we walked. She strolled, her pace easy as she tipped her face to the sky, her features relaxed as the sun kissed her cheeks good morning.

Shouldn't she be nervous? Hadn't the Guardian told her about the lionwick from last night? Maybe he'd gone ahead and killed it.

My fingers flexed at my sides, hands ready to pull my knives out in case of danger. But as we moved through Treow, every person we passed seemed calm. This was just another normal day.

"There was a lionwick here last night." Unless I'd dreamed it. Had I dreamed it?

"There was," Tillia said. "It's been dealt with. No need to fret."

"Oh." Had the Guardian killed it after all? "It's dead?"

"Not dead. We have snares. It was trapped and taken to the mountains this morning. They're not overly common in this area, but when they do visit, they love to poke around at night. We've got the snares in case. But not to worry. In all my years visiting Treow, I've never heard of one getting into a treehouse. Unless one is aggressive, we usually just relocate them elsewhere."

"Really?" I'd never heard of a monster being trapped before. Let loose. What if it came back and killed someone? Weren't they worried?

"They're a part of the chain. They keep the deer population in balance. Unless a beast is a threat, we avoid killing them if possible."

In Quentis, the only way monsters were dealt with was death. I hadn't considered how that impacted other species, other chains.

Like the Chain of Sevens.

"We're all connected," Tillia said. "Always seeking a balance."

Was that why the gods had created the crux? To balance the human population? To keep our numbers in check. To remind us that we were insignificant. To keep us at the gods' mercy.

Then what regulated the crux? Were there other monsters out there, bigger and larger? Or did they die from infection or disease?

"What if the lionwick comes back?" I asked.

She shrugged. "Then we'll trap it again."

"And if it won't stay away? If it comes again and hurts someone?"

"You're safe in your treehouse." She put her hand on my arm. "I promise."

I wanted to believe her. I really did. But so far, Turah had scared the hell out of me. It was going to take me a while to feel safe anywhere in this kingdom.

"What if a grizzur wanders into Treow? Would your traps hold?"

"No." She shook her head. "There are some monsters that are killed upon sight. Grizzurs. And bariwolves."

"What else?"

"Anything…feral."

Feral? "Aren't they all feral?"

These were monsters we were talking about, not household pets. Given the opportunity, that lionwick would have inhaled me skin and bones last night. They were uncontrollable, vicious, and deadly beasts with a taste for human flesh. Weren't they?

The answer to my question was either a *yes* or *no*. But she gave neither and continued on, and we made the rest of our walk in silence.

She'd been taking lessons from Zavier on ignoring my questions. *Blarg.*

"Let's start with your knives," Tillia said when we reached the training area.

"All right." I drew them and assumed my fighting stance. "Ready."

An hour later, with sweat running in rivulets down my back, I realized I'd been woefully mistaken in thinking it would be easier to fight Tillia. I'd take a thousand training sessions with the Guardian over one with her.

After one round with my knives, she'd decided I wasn't ready to train with weapons yet. Instead, we'd taken to sparring.

I'd read stories about torture that were kinder than this.

"One more," she said, fists raised. "Push yourself."

I wiped the spit and sweat from my lips, thirstier than I'd ever been in my life, and raised my hands.

She came at me with a quick jab to my nose and a punch to my chin that I managed to block with my left. When she went for my ribs, I lowered my elbow, just like she'd taught me, using it and my forearm to deflect the blow. When she swung again, I sidestepped to the right, keeping light on my toes with no weight on my heels.

"Faster," she ordered.

I gulped down a breath as she let her fists fly once more, another jab followed by a body punch. Each time I blocked, we'd pivot and start the routine again, the speed increasing.

Round six was when my form fell apart. When my aching, tired muscles began to lag. When I was simply too slow.

Her knuckles slammed into my side yet again, pain exploding through my torso.

"Oof," I hissed, dropping to a knee as I sucked in a breath.

This. Was. Awful. She was absolutely kicking my ass. And to add insult to injury, every training circle was full of other rangers. I could feel their stares. Hear them whisper when I let out a cry of pain.

"Better," Tillia said, not even out of breath.

"Really?" I scoffed. "I don't feel like I'm getting any better."

"Your footwork is no longer atrocious. Your balance isn't as weak. Your form is sloppy, but you're improving."

I wiped the sweat from my brow, forcing myself to my feet. "Thanks?"

Someone needed to teach these Turans how to give compliments. At this point, I'd settle for a pat on the back. Though I bet whoever was in the Guardian's bed last night had probably earned hours of praise.

Whatever. Not my business. Not my problem. And if I could just stop thinking about him, that would be fantastic.

Tillia waved over a boy who carried a bucket of water from circle to circle.

He produced two wooden cups, filling both. He held out a cup for me, but when his gaze met mine, he paused, his eyes blowing wide. He looked to Tillia, pulling the drink back toward his chest as he eased away.

She took it from him, then nodded to the men training beside us. "Off you go."

The boy didn't need to be told twice.

"Sorry." She handed over the cup. "We don't often get visitors from other kingdoms in Treow."

"It's all right." I shrugged, pretending the boy's fear didn't sting. "I know my eyes are…different."

It wasn't the first time the lack of a starburst in my irises would put a child on edge. It wouldn't be the last.

"Different." Tillia put her hand on my shoulder, giving me a soft smile. "But very beautiful."

"Thank you." I took another drink, then changed the subject. "Do you know if Zavier will be coming to Treow anytime soon?" It was time to focus my attention on my missing husband.

"I don't. I'm sorry. The last I heard, he was traveling from Perris to Ellder."

Traveling without a wife to slow him down. "Is he going to leave me here forever?"

She took a drink, draining her cup.

That meant yes.

I was the last of Zavier's priorities. He'd offloaded me onto his people, stuck me at this encampment, and forgotten about me entirely.

Why? Why had he wanted me in the first place?

Did Tillia know the reason? Had Halston told her about their visit to Roslo?

At this point, did it even matter? I'd been claimed. I'd fulfilled the treaty. Zavier was gone, as was the pressure to act like a dutiful wife. Maybe

I should simply be grateful that I was on my own. It wasn't anything new.

I'd always been on my own. The only person I could count on to take my side, to see me, was *me*.

"I think we've had enough for today," Tillia said as I finished the last of my water. "Get some rest. We'll meet again in the morning."

I stifled a groan. "I can't wait."

"You're an awful liar, Odessa."

"So I've been told." I collected my knives and walked away before she could change her mind. My tunic was glued to my skin, my hair soaked, and there was probably dye leaking down my temples.

With so much sweating, I was going through my dye too quickly, and soon, I'd need to ask the merchant if he could order a new jar. My plan had been to get more in Allesaria, but at this point, I doubted I'd be there before winter.

And I guess if I couldn't get more dye, Zavier would eventually learn that—*surprise!*—his wife had red hair.

I made my way toward the commons to get some breakfast and stop at the library. Maybe my next set of books wouldn't send me into a fit of rage and give me nightmares. Maybe a pony rider would come through today and I'd have a chance to ask a few questions.

Except before I could reach the dining hall, the thunder of hooves echoed through the forest.

The Guardian tore through the encampment, racing past me on his massive stallion without so much as a glance. His face was granite, and shades, he looked furious. His anger was so strong I could practically see it, like smoke trailing behind him as he rode away.

The hairs on my arms stood on end—that sinking feeling that something was wrong. I rushed toward the commons, seeing chaos through the trees. Mothers were collecting their children, grabbing hands or hefting them onto hips to carry away.

Every ranger in Turah was racing for the open square.

"Odessa, wait." Tillia ran up from behind, taking my elbow and pulling me to a stop.

"What's wrong?"

"Nothing."

Well, that was a lie.

"I need you to stay here." She urged me toward the closest tree, positioning me so I was mostly hidden from sight. "Please."

"Okay." Um, what the hell was going on? Panic surged as she walked away, her shoulders rigid and fists balled. I inched to the edge of the tree, pressing my body against the rough bark as I peered into the commons.

They came like a silent wave.

At least fifty armed men on horseback emerged from the forest, seeping into Treow like fog.

There'd been no warning whistles, yet the people in Treow had known to be scarce. How?

The men were soldiers, wearing metal arm and leg shields. Every man's hair was cut short, their blank faces clean-shaven. And they all had the same emblem stamped on their gleaming silver breastplates.

A wolf's head was set in the steel, its eyes bejeweled in green.

The soldiers all came to a stop at the commons, surrounding the Turan warriors and Tillia, who stood at its center.

A gap spread in their formation, making room for a man astride a stallion with a sleek gray coat. The animal was nearly as large as the Guardian's mount.

The man wore a circlet, thicker and more intricate than the one Zavier kept across his brow. The silver band was woven into his dark-brown hair.

King Ramsey of Turah.

My father-in-law.

Was he the reason Tillia had told me to stay out of sight? Why? Did I need Zavier here to present me or something?

I shifted closer to the edge of the tree to get a better look.

The Turan rangers were glaring at Ramsey's soldiers. The soldiers were glaring at the Turan rangers. Not a soul seemed to care what was happening outside of the commons. Not a gaze flickered in my direction.

Ramsey stopped beside Tillia, his horse lifting its tail to plop a pile of steaming shit in the same place where the kids had been playing minutes ago.

Tillia bowed her head, dropping to a knee.

"Rise." Ramsey's deep voice carried. It reminded me of my own father. Both were men who'd spent their lives infusing dominance into their every word.

She obeyed, taking his outstretched hand to kiss the signet ring on his middle finger.

I might not be able to see that ring, but I'd wager all of my father's gold it was that same silver wolf the soldiers wore.

"I take it my son is not here," Ramsey said. Even from thirty feet away, his voice was clear and crisp, laced with an undercurrent of superiority. He spoke above her head, projecting to the trees. Like maybe he thought Zavier was hiding, like me, behind a tree.

Tillia shook her head.

Was Zavier supposed to be here? Was he avoiding me *and* his father?

The king lived in Allesaria. If Zavier wouldn't take me to the capital, would the king? There was only one way to find out.

With my heart crawling into my throat, I pushed off the tree and squared my shoulders. I was about to step past the trunk when a hand touched my shoulder.

I jumped, slapping a hand over my mouth to muffle a yelp.

Cathlin stood behind me, shaking her head. She'd snuck up on me without so much as crunching on a branch or scuffling pine needles.

"Don't," she whispered.

I might have ignored her if not for the seriousness in the woman's chestnut eyes. So I nodded and slunk back against the tree.

She pressed into my side, both of us peering toward the soldiers.

The king was still talking to Tillia, quieter now so that only she could hear.

With every word, her shoulders seemed to curl deeper in on themselves.

"Go." With the king's command, the quiet vanished. Horses whinnied as their riders dismounted. Metal from armor and blades clanked as Ramsey's men fanned out, spreading like a fire to every building. Every treehouse.

"What are they—"

"Shh." Cathlin pressed a finger to her lips.

Questions later. *Got it.*

A crashing noise came from the commons. From the direction of the library.

Cathlin closed her eyes, like she couldn't bear to watch whatever was happening.

When I stole another glance, I realized why.

Soldiers were throwing books from the doorway into a heaping pile. Another man came from a nearby treehouse, a stack of children's books in one hand. They were tossed in the same heap before he turned on a heel, probably to search other treehouses for more.

"What are they doing?" I asked, voice low. "Why are they—" The sorrow in her gaze was all the explanation I needed. "They're going to destroy them."

Cathlin swallowed hard and nodded.

"Why?" They were just books.

Her jaw clenched as she said nothing.

A soldier produced a piece of flint rock and struck it against a knife, sending sparks to the pile. The fire was instant, and as it burned, the soldiers raiding treehouses kept adding their finds to the blaze, all while Ramsey watched on.

The bitter tang of smoke filled the air. When the flames were well and truly ablaze, when it was past the point of saving even one book, the king tugged on his stallion's reins, and as quickly as they'd appeared, the soldiers were gone.

The fire burned, sparks shooting into the air.

Not a soul moved in the commons. Every ranger stood at the fire, watching until the flames began to die, ensuring it didn't spread. Until all that remained of Cathlin's library was a smoking pile of white ash.

"I'm sorry," I whispered.

She squeezed my hand, brushing away a tear as it dripped down her cheek. Then she turned around and walked away.

I stepped out from behind the tree and headed toward the commons. Halston was with Tillia, his arm around her shoulders as they spoke, heads bent close.

Others emerged from the trees, wearing solemn faces.

Had those soldiers done anything but take books? Had anyone been hurt?

A few people stepped closer to the library's charred remains, inspecting the glowing red-orange coals. But most simply seemed relieved that the king was gone. They retreated to their homes, probably to right the messes the soldiers had made.

My appetite for breakfast was gone, so I made my way back to my treehouse, dread heavy in my gut as I climbed the rope ladder.

The door was ajar.

I'd closed it when I left this morning.

My heart sank as I pushed it open, taking in the disarray. Clothes were strewn across the room. The armoire was empty, its contents scattered with those from my trunks. My bed was off its frame, the blankets tossed with gray dresses. The stench of my hair dye clung to the air from the broken jar in the corner.

The crown I'd left on the bedside table was gone.

As were the books I'd borrowed from the library.

Some strange man had put his hands on my underclothes.

The violation made my stomach roil, my skin crawl.

Those books had been on the corner of my neatly made bed. The soldier could have just taken them without trashing my room in the process. He could have simply stolen the crown.

The walls inched closer. The air tasted sour. I spun, leaving the mess for the balcony. Then I walked around to the back of the treehouse. To the limb that hung low and close to the roof.

Carefully, I braced myself against the wall and railing, hoisting myself up toward that limb.

And the satchel I had hidden on a bushy, evergreen bow.

Flipping open the bag, I made sure my journal, my coin, and my necklace were all safely tucked inside.

After Tillia had warned me to keep my journal out of sight, I'd heeded her advice. And I'd learned a long, long time ago not to hide things under my mattress. Mae always looked there first when she was searching for my diaries.

A low chuckle startled me as I climbed down to the balcony. I whirled, finding the Guardian outside his own treehouse, a grin on his face.

"Clever, my queen."

Yes, it had been clever. A safe space for my secret things.

And now the bane of my existence knew I had something to hide.

Damn.

Twenty-Three

T he week that passed after King Ramsey's visit to Treow was uneventful. Peaceful, even.

I knew it wouldn't last. There was too much uncertainty, too many unanswered questions, particularly from my still-absent husband. But I let myself spend a week enjoying this semblance of routine.

Every morning, Tillia and I trained together for hours. She taught me how to fight as a woman, to use what we had to our advantage against larger and stronger opponents. She taught me how to strike a man's groin. How to gouge eyes. How to leverage the strength in our hips if we were ever pinned to the ground.

She pushed me harder and harder each day, almost like she was preparing me for a war.

Like she could feel a battle coming.

After my daily training with Tillia, I'd return to the treehouse, where Brielle or Jocelyn would stop by to visit and deliver breakfast. I'd spend a while sketching in my journal until midday. I'd taught myself how to whistle. Then, every afternoon, I'd go to the paddock to spend some time riding Freya. If I was going to be roaming the Turan landscape, I needed more practice on my horse. And after that daily ride, I set off to explore, wandering around the encampment and eavesdropping on its residents.

Mariette, I'd learned, was austere with everyone. Two of the cooks were sleeping with a boy who worked at the stables, and everyone but them knew he was playing them both. And the pony riders were as aloof to questions as the rest of the Turans.

I'd gone to meet yesterday's pony rider in the clearing. I'd casually asked if he ever visited Allesaria.

The man tossed the post at my feet and rode away.

Being a spy was hard.

In the evenings, I ate dinner with Brielle and Jocelyn. Neither loved their accommodations, but both insisted they were fine. I'd asked Tillia to move them closer to my treehouse, but apparently the only person in Calandra that Tillia feared was Mariette. So I was waiting for Zavier to show up.

The prince could overrule a caretaker, right?

After those evening meals with Brielle and Jocelyn, I'd return to my treehouse and go through the stretches Tillia had taught me, working the stiffness out of my muscles. Some nights, when I couldn't sleep right away, I'd lie in bed and stare through my skylights at the stars. I'd wonder if my mother was in Arabella's shade, watching me from her heaven.

Other nights, if the sky was too cloudy, I'd stare at my necklace, taking in the wing and metal.

And every night, I'd dwell. Any topic was open for overthinking.

Especially Zavier.

Was he going to come back? Was leaving me here his revenge against my father? Had it been his idea to take my rope ladder every single night?

I hadn't seen the Guardian in a week. He'd left the morning after King Ramsey's visit, and his treehouse remained dark and empty. But he'd clearly delegated the task of keeping me captive to another.

I'd go into my nightly bath with a ladder. Emerge soaking wet without. But by dawn, when Tillia was waiting, there it would be.

Just like this morning.

As I hopped off the last rung, she greeted me with a smile as we started for the training area. "Did you sleep well?"

"Yes. You?"

She shrugged. "I have a hard time when Halston is gone."

He'd left at the same time as the Guardian. As much as I wanted to know details, I refused to ask. Halston would come back. Eventually. Would the Guardian?

Part of me hoped he wouldn't. That he'd stay away from Treow, from me, for good. That was the part of me that wouldn't admit I hoped to see him again.

"We'll spar today," she said when we reached the training area.

"Can't wait," I deadpanned.

We both laughed.

Then we got to work. An hour into training, it was not going well. I couldn't seem to concentrate. The steps and moves she'd shown me yesterday flittered out of my mind like butterflies on the wind.

"You're distracted today," she said with a frown as we took a water break.

"No, I'm not."

I was definitely distracted.

Every training space was taken today, like it had been all week. The clang of striking blades and the whoosh of flying arrows mingled with shouts from the men and women who'd come to practice.

It had been this way since Ramsey's visit. Everyone in Treow seemed on edge. Why? What had he said to Tillia?

I hadn't worked up the courage to ask about their discussion. Yet. Maybe tomorrow. Or the next day.

"Odessa." Tillia snapped her fingers in front of my face.

"What? I'm listening."

"Really?" She fisted a hand on her hip. "And what did I say?"

"That I'm doing a great job today?"

She sighed. "I said that I want you to start running."

"Running." *Eww.* "Why?"

"Your stamina is shit."

It might have hurt my feelings if I hadn't heard that before. "You don't look like the Guardian, but you two sure sound alike."

A smile tugged at her mouth. "Thanks."

Of course she'd take that as flattery. "Where exactly do you want me running?"

"Make laps around Treow. Start with one. Increase to two, then three. Most of us run between five and ten a day."

My jaw dropped.

Treow was huge. One lap would be farther than I'd ever run in my life.

Now that I'd gotten to know the encampment, I'd learned about its borders and where the watchtowers were located. I'd also learned where they kept the lionwick snares so that I didn't accidentally spring one and find myself stuck in a net.

"Do I have to?" I asked.

Tillia arched an eyebrow. That meant yes.

"Fine."

My stamina, while improving, was still shit compared to the Turans. After each training session, my lungs were on fire and my muscles burned. I was coated in sweat, and though my body was adjusting to these new physical demands, there was still a long way to go.

"You can start running today," she said, setting her water cup aside and returning to the center of the ring. "After a few more minutes of sparring."

Gods, already? The water breaks she gave me seemed to be getting shorter and shorter. "How did you and Halston meet?"

"Stalling, Odessa?"

"Yes," I admitted.

Her smile said she was going to indulge me. "Halston and I have known each other since we were children. We grew up together in a small village along the border with Ozarth. Not far from Westor."

"Have you been together long?"

"Since we were young." The green starbursts in her gaze seemed to glow, like thinking of her husband lit her up from the inside out. "I had a dog when I was a child. Creed. He was big and loud and always by my side. He slept at the foot of my bed from the time I was just a baby. My mother called him my sentry. Creed died when I was thirteen."

"I'm so sorry."

She lifted a shoulder. "He was old. One day, he wandered off and never came back. It was his time to go to the shades. But it broke my heart. Halston found me crying one day after school. He walked me home and held my hand. We've been together ever since. I like to believe that Creed only left me because he knew Halston would be there to fill his place."

I pressed a hand to my heart, rubbing at the ache for a girl who'd lost her companion only to find another. Her soulmate.

Tillia blinked too fast, like she was fighting tears for her dog. Then she waved me forward. "All right. Let's get back to work."

I groaned, finishing my drink. Then I joined her with a heavy sigh, lifting my fists. Today, she was teaching me how to punch, which seemed ten times harder than blocking hers. "Okay. Ready."

"Try to hit me this time. Stop pulling your punches."

"It's rude to hit your friends."

Her expression flattened. "Odessa."

"I'm really better suited to defense." I dropped my hands. "I don't need to be a beautifully menacing warrior like you. I just want to keep myself alive the next time a marroweel tries to eat me."

"To accomplish that, all you really had to do was stay on the fucking ship."

I whirled at the rugged voice and found its source leaning against a tree.

The Guardian was dressed in his leather pants, but instead of a tunic, he wore a wool sweater. The beige fabric molded to his frame, making his shoulders look even broader than normal. The ends of his hair were past his shoulders now, windblown and messy like he'd been riding hard for hours. His beard was growing unruly again, like he hadn't bothered with a blade all week.

My heart leaped at the same time it sank. It was the strangest sensation, so odd that I choked.

"Good?" Tillia patted me on the back as I coughed.

"Fine." I nodded, rubbing at my sternum.

He smirked. "Miss me, Cross?"

"Never."

I was an awful liar.

"I'll take over." The Guardian pushed off the tree.

"Oh, hell." I grimaced.

I'd gotten comfortable with Tillia. Sure, she liked to torture me, but it was a relaxed torture. With her, my pulse didn't beat a little too fast. My lungs didn't struggle to breathe deep.

This man made me jittery.

It was his powers. That buzzing, raw energy put me on edge.

I really was an awful liar, even to myself.

Shades, this had to stop. Maybe now that he was in Treow again, I could stop wondering about his whereabouts and go back to loathing him instead. Go back to plotting his murder.

"Where did you go?" I asked as he stood in front of me, arms loose at his sides.

"Worried about me, my queen?"

I rolled my eyes. "Only that you'd die and I wouldn't get to spit on your grave."

His smirk widened. "Fear not. I'm still very much alive and back to be your keeper."

"My keeper?" Is that why Zavier had left me in Treow?

"Someone has to babysit."

Okay. *Ouch.* Was I really such a burden?

"Where is Zavier?"

"Longing for your beloved, Sparrow?"

My nostrils flared. "Do you know how annoying it is to ask a question and get one in return?"

"Do you?"

Days wondering where he had gone while I should have been praising Ama and Oda for keeping the son of a bitch away.

"Never mind." I flicked my wrist. "Are we training or not?"

He chuckled, reaching behind his head to fist his sweater and yank it off his torso, revealing the fitted sleeveless shirt beneath. His arms were corded in muscle, stronger than any man's I'd ever seen.

A shudder ran through my body, and I forced my eyes to the dirt.

He's a monster. *He's a monster, he's a monster, he's a monster.* A beautiful monster but a monster all the same. He'd killed Banner's brother. He was a murderer.

And I was married.

Married. Married. Married.

Shit, my face was hot.

The Guardian's finger hooked under my chin, forcing me to meet his gaze. "Need a moment?"

I swatted his hand away and took a step back, raising my fists. "No. Let's get on with it."

"Your wish." He mocked a bow, then slapped me in the face.

The strike was so fast I never saw it coming. I couldn't have blocked it if I'd tried.

My jaw dropped as I pressed my palm to the slight sting in my cheek. "You hit me."

Sort of.

If he'd actually wanted to hurt me, he would have closed his fist. Or added some strength to that slap. It had really been more of a tap. There was just enough of a smack that I'd learn a lesson.

"Only making sure you're awake." There was a glint in his eyes, the sadistic prick.

My teeth clicked as I closed my mouth, my molars grinding as I raised my hands again.

This time when his hand flew, I was ready. I let my shoulders twist at the same time my hands deflected the blow enough that only the tips of his fingers grazed my cheek.

"Ha." I pumped a fist as my smile bloomed. Was it stupid to celebrate? Yes. Was I going to do it anyway? Absolutely.

"You've been practicing. Not only with Tillia." Was that pride in his gaze? Probably not.

But I'd be proud enough for us both because I had absolutely been practicing. On the nights that were too quiet without the sound of ocean waves, I'd spend my midnight hours practicing. Dancing.

Tillia had told me to treat fighting like a dance. To find the rhythm with an opponent the way you would a partner.

My dance tutor in Roslo had been one of the few to tell me I wasn't entirely hopeless. I wasn't a great dancer, but I wasn't dreadful, either. So I danced and danced and danced until my mind was clear and my body drained. Then I'd fall into a hard sleep until dawn.

"Again," the Guardian said with a nod. Except as I lifted my hands, his gaze shifted over my shoulder. A slow smile stretched across his mouth.

Soft lips. Straight, white teeth. Sparkling eyes. That smile was breathtaking.

My heart fluttered for just a moment until I realized I wasn't the person who'd earned that smile. It wasn't for me.

And I shouldn't want it for my own.

Gods, what was wrong with me? What was it about him that stuck?

He needed to leave Treow again. For good.

"Spying, Evangeline?"

Evangeline. I turned, expecting to see a woman as beautiful as her name. But instead, there was a little girl standing nearby, wearing a frown with her arms crossed over her chest.

It was the little girl I'd seen in the commons. The girl with brown hair and big, gray eyes.

"She's not clumsy," Evangeline said.

I huffed, my attention whipping to the Guardian. "You called me clumsy?"

He shrugged.

"I hate you."

"Yes, you do. Don't forget." He walked by, his shoulder knocking into mine as he went to the girl.

She had to be four or five, a year or two older than Arthy.

The Guardian crouched in front of her, tsking his tongue. "You're supposed to be with Luella, doing your lessons."

Evangeline scrunched up her nose. "Lessons are boring. I only like the science ones."

Who was she to him? Was this his daughter? Oh, gods. Did he have a family? Was Luella his lover? His wife?

I was such an asshole. Not only was *I* married, but I kept gawking at a man who was taken. Guilt, sour and bitter and rotten, spread across my tongue. It crept beneath my skin, slimy and vile.

Enough. It was enough. It was time to get the Guardian out of my head. To focus my attention on another man.

Zavier.

"Evie," the Guardian said. "You promised to stay with Luella."

"But—"

"A promise is a promise."

Her sigh was so big it came from her whole chest. Then she kicked at a pine cone, sending it flying into the training area. "Oh-kay."

He turned her shoulders, aiming her in the direction of the commons, but before she could leave, the sound of hooves echoed in the distance. Then came a whistle, clear and shrill, announcing to whomever was riding this way that it was safe to enter Treow.

A pony rider?

Maybe this one would linger. Be more open to questions than the last.

Evangeline spun around, her face bright. "Is that him?"

The Guardian nodded.

A brilliant smile lit up her adorable face before she took off running in the wrong direction, toward the clearing where the horses were kept.

"Evie, wait," the Guardian yelled, but she was gone.

Arms and legs pumping. Chin tucked. Wild, loose hair swishing.

He chuckled, taking off after her in an easy jog.

"Does that mean we're done training for today?"

Yeah, I was talking to myself.

And standing alone.

Who was *him*? My curiosity was piqued, so I set off to follow them both.

It didn't take much to catch up. Evangeline was still running, pushing hard, while the Guardian lingered behind, his steps slow so she could stay in front.

They reached the clearing as a group of three rangers rode into Treow.

With them, my husband.

I wasn't sure how to feel at seeing his face. Glad. Relieved. Annoyed. Guilty. Angry.

It all came at once, making me dizzy.

Zavier sat proudly on his horse, his face unreadable. He looked exactly the same as when he'd left me at that first campsite. Stoic and serious.

His gaze surveyed the clearing, shifting from the Guardian's face to mine, lingering for just a moment, until a little girl captured his undivided attention.

He swung off his horse, leaving it free to roam as he dropped to a knee, arms held wide.

Evangeline crashed into his chest. "Papa!"

Um…

What?

Twenty-Four

The dining hall was full of laughter and conversation. All of Treow seemed to be crammed inside tonight, the room vibrating with excitement as Zavier's rangers were reunited with their families.

A man named Rafe sat on the table beside mine, his wife perched on one knee while their baby boy bounced on the other. His beard was just as bushy as it had been in the throne room weeks ago and still braided beneath his chin.

Marlowe, another of Zavier's rangers who hadn't been in Quentis, was sitting beside Mariette, her mother. The caretaker wore a smile for the first time since I'd arrived in Treow, overjoyed at her daughter's safe return.

And the third ranger, Hale, was holding hands with his husband. They were at a table in the center of the hall, but from the way they stared at each other, they might as well have been the only two people in all of Turah.

"This reminds me of home," Brielle said from her seat beside mine, sorrow dulling her eyes.

Jocelyn put a comforting hand on her shoulder. While Jocelyn had fallen into a routine, like me, settling into Treow life, Brielle had withdrawn. Each day, she seemed more melancholy and homesick. Watching these families reunite had pushed her to the verge of tears.

"I miss home so much it hurts," she said. "Don't you?"

"Yes."

No.

Maybe I should be sad. Lonely for my family.

Except I didn't miss Quentis. Not really. I missed the sound of the ocean. I missed the pastries the castle's chef would bake fresh each morning. I missed Arthy's laugh when I'd sneak a treat into the nursery.

But the rest? The castle. The city. My father and Margot.

They crossed my mind less and less each day. And when they did, all I could feel was the weight of responsibility on my shoulders.

Spy for Father. Kill for Father. Find Allesaria for Father.

How? I was stuck. Totally fucking stuck.

Maybe the reason I didn't miss home was because home meant Father. And when I thought of him, I pictured the disappointment on his face when I failed him completely.

"Highness." Jocelyn nudged my elbow with hers, jerking her chin toward the door.

A hush had fallen over the dining hall. A hush caused by a quiet man.

Zavier stood inside the doorway, arms clasped behind his back, posture rigid. He nodded to his people, then looked to me.

A summons.

I wasn't done eating my dinner, but I hadn't had much of an appetite today. Not since I'd watched Evangeline launch herself into Zavier's arms.

Her father's arms.

I'd spent less than a day in his company. He was as much of a stranger to me as most of the people in this room. Yet it hurt that he hadn't told me about his daughter.

"I'd better go," I told Brielle and Jocelyn, standing. "See you tomorrow."

Brielle forced a smile. "Good night, Highness."

"Odessa." It was a pointless correction but one I made anyway.

No one spoke as I weaved past tables to join Zavier. I'd give it to the Turans, they were discreet with their rumormongering. In Roslo, whispers and rumors would have been flying before I'd made it out of my chair.

Zavier nodded to the entire room, giving everyone permission to resume their conversation. Then he opened the door and escorted me into the muted evening light.

He didn't speak as we walked away from the commons. Just like we hadn't spoken in the clearing. He'd given his full attention to Evangeline, carrying her away with only a nod to me and the Guardian.

This reunion was inevitable. Still, I didn't want to talk. All those questions. All that dwelling. This was my chance for answers. Yet all I wanted was to put it off for another day or ten or twenty.

I had a sinking feeling that I wasn't ready for the truth.

"How are you, Odessa?" he asked as we started down the empty, narrow path that led to the training area. Away from the treehouses.

"Fine. You?"

"Fine."

I opened my mouth. Closed it. Tried again. Changed my mind.

Awkward wasn't strong enough a word for this. Even though we were walking, I started to squirm.

"So…" I said. "You have a daughter."

"Yes."

"That would have been good to know."

He ran a hand over his jaw. It was the hand he'd had bandaged at the wedding. Did he have a scar like mine, pink yet fading each day? "You and I haven't spent much time together."

"No, we haven't. Your choice, not mine."

I'd never asked him to stay away. I'd never asked for any of this. It was his doing. Since the throne room, this was all on Zavier.

And now, I wasn't only a wife, I was a stepmother.

When Father married Margot, she'd known he was a father. She'd known she'd be taking on the responsibility of his child.

Was that why Zavier had married me? Because he'd decided I'd be a better stepmother to Evangeline than Mae?

Well, he wasn't wrong. Mae wasn't the motherly type. But it was just another shock. Another secret. I was so, *so* tired of being the last person in the know.

"Evie is four," he said. "Very few people know she's my daughter."

"As in, don't tell anyone," I muttered. "If I hadn't followed her today, would you have told me?"

"No."

It was brutal. Honest. I tried to hide my flinch.

"I do not want her involved in court life," he said.

Fair. As a woman who'd been married off without her choice and forced to sign a magical treaty, I definitely couldn't recommend *princess*.

Was Turah next in line for the Shield of Sparrows? If the royal families in Calandra knew about Evangeline, would she be the next princess forced to marry to uphold the treaty?

It all depended on the next generation of royals. If she was the only princess, then Turah would give her up.

Zavier would give her up.

Unless no one knew she existed. Even the Voster.

"And her mother?" Was that Luella?

Oh, hell. Was this why he hadn't consummated our marriage? Was he in love with the mother of his child?

When it came to the Shield of Sparrows, love didn't matter. He was always going to be forced to wed. Maybe he'd thought I'd be more understanding of his situation than Mae.

"She died," he said. "In childbirth."

"I'm sorry." And more confused than ever.

"Evie has spent most of her life in Treow and Ellder. I'm with her as often as possible, but..."

But he was a prince with obligations. And if he spent too much time with her, people would become suspicious.

"How do you hide it?" I asked.

"She learned young to keep the secret."

"But she called you Papa today."

His mouth flattened. "And she was reminded that those kinds of slips cannot happen."

"Ah." *Oops.*

We walked for a few more paces, my mind still reeling. "I don't know what to do with this."

"There is nothing to do."

Would he hide her forever? Would she ever be able to claim him as her own?

I understood why he'd keep her hidden. Sort of. But my heart broke for her. And him.

"Do you mind if I get to know her?" I blurted. Maybe I was just missing my little brother, but I wanted to befriend this girl. This daughter. "I won't betray your secret. I'll understand if you say no, but I'd like—"

"Yes. You can get to know her."

"Thank you."

He stopped, staring at me for a long moment, his eyes searching mine. Then he brought his hands to his heart and gave me a slight bow.

That gesture was the same one the Guardian had given and received from the Voster High Priest. What did it mean?

Before I could ask, Zavier set off down the trail again. "How are you liking Treow?"

Was he asking because I'd be staying here for a long while? "It's been unexpected. But I like it."

It was the truth. I liked my treehouse. My time with Tillia. I liked that I had some freedoms.

"I'm glad."

"My lady's maids have been staying with others. Would it be possible to move them in together? One of them has been incredibly homesick. I think it might help if she had more time with a friend. Please."

"I'll see to it first thing tomorrow."

"Thank you."

Pleases. Thank-yous. If there was anything to say about our marriage, at least it was polite.

"Where have you been?" I asked.

"Traveling."

Did Evie get these vague nonanswers, too? Or were those just for me? "Will I ever go *traveling* with you? Or do I get to stick around here?"

Zavier stayed quiet.

"You just ignore the questions you don't want to answer, don't you?"

"Sometimes."

"It's rather annoying."

He smiled. "Evie says the same thing."

"Smart girl."

"That she is." He nodded. "It is safer for Evie here. As it is for you. But before long, we'll go to Ellder. As much as I love Treow, it's no place to be when the crux migration begins."

My heart, my hopes, sank to the dirt.

If he meant to keep me in Ellder, then we wouldn't be going to Allesaria before the migration.

There'd be no way for me to send Father information. Not while I was stuck in some fortress. And if Father was right, our people would die, as they had for generations, when the crux flew.

What did I do? How did I fix this? Was there any way to change his mind?

My head was spinning, whirling over the impossible, so that when we reached my treehouse, it took a moment for me to recognize my own rope ladder.

"Good night, Odessa."

I blinked, snapping out of my head. "Oh, um, good night, Zavier."

Fix this. Do something. Anything.

Before he could walk away, I rose up on my toes and pressed a kiss against his cheek. His jaw was smooth, and his skin smelled like cedar and soap.

He didn't jerk away, but his body stiffened. When I dropped to my heels, there was something like pity in his gaze.

"I don't know why I did that." I closed my eyes, shaking my head, wishing I could take it back. "Sorry."

"Don't be." His hand came to my cheek. His palm was calloused. Not typical for a prince. Though Zavier was nothing like any prince I'd ever met. He wasn't spoiled or cruel. Pompous or arrogant.

When he dropped his hand, I waited for the sound of his retreating footsteps. Then I cracked an eye, waiting until he was gone before I buried my face in my hands and groaned.

"Ugh." I stomped a clump of dirt before I started up my rope ladder. Once I reached the balcony, I trudged inside, about to kick off my boots, but froze when I found a visitor.

"Late night, my queen?" The Guardian lounged on my bed, his arms behind his head.

"Get your ass off my bed. Now." I raised my hands, fingers splayed and flexed, and envisioned them wrapped around his neck. How good it would feel to strangle him right now. "Go. Away."

He crossed his ankles like he was getting comfortable for a nap.

"Do you have any respect for a person's private space? Or is it just mine you insist on invading? Are you afraid to be alone? Is that why you're always here?"

"I think we both know something about being alone."

Was that vulnerability in his voice? Or was he taunting me?

His jaw was still clenched, irritation written all over his face. But something in his hazel eyes betrayed that expression. Something that said he'd come here to not be alone.

Or so that I wouldn't be, either.

Before I could make sense of it, the look was gone and his eyes were as hard and angry as ever. "Where is your home?"

"This again?" I tugged off a boot. If he was going to invade my bedroom, then he could deal with my smelly feet. "Roslo. Though at the moment, this charming treehouse is my home. Next question?"

The Guardian's eyes turned silver. "Careful."

"Or what?" I yanked off the other boot, tempted to throw it at him. "I'm not scared of you."

He was infuriating. But not a threat. The Guardian would never hurt me.

"Any more questions? Or can we call it a night?"

"How many men have you bedded? I know you're anxious to join

Zavier in his, but a word of caution—he's not fond of women who reek of desperation."

My jaw dropped. My nostrils flared, and my cheeks reddened. Of course he'd seen me make a fool of myself outside. This man was always lurking, ready to throw my humiliations in my face. "Get. Out."

He jackknifed off the bed, standing so fast to cross the room, I blinked and he was towering in front of me. He leaned in so close that his nose nearly touched mine. When he spoke, his breath caressed my cheek. "Did your father send you here to spy?"

"No." It was said too fast, too unsteady.

He scoffed and was out the door in another blink.

"Did I pass your test?" I called to his back.

He answered by unclasping my rope ladder and letting it fall to the ground. Then he stepped onto the railing of my balcony and leaped to his own.

"I guess not," I muttered.

He slammed his door.

"Evangeline." Zavier's fatherly tone was the perfect balance of gentle yet firm. "If you keep running away from Luella, she's going to think you don't like your lessons."

"I *don't* like 'em." She crossed her arms over her chest as she pouted. "Not even science?"

Her big, gray eyes turned pleading. "I wanna stay with you."

Zavier sighed, casting his eyes to the afternoon sky.

He was going to cave. When it came to that child, he had no spine. No one did, it seemed. She had all of Treow wrapped around her little finger.

"Fine," he said. "You may join us. But afterward, you'll go to your lessons."

Her smile was contagious. "'Kay."

It was warm today, the sun beating down through the tree branches. Almost too hot to enjoy the walk around Treow.

Almost.

For the past five days since Zavier's arrival at the encampment, each afternoon, he'd visit my treehouse and invite me on a walk.

We took the same path. We walked at the same leisurely pace. We talked about the same, safe topics. The weather. The previous night's dinner. My training regimen with Tillia. And when we exhausted those topics, we'd just walk, side by side, until we circled back to my treehouse.

Today was the first time Evangeline had been brave enough to follow. For ten minutes, she'd been sneaking behind us, running from tree to tree. Finally, Zavier had stopped and turned, catching her on a dash.

She took the space between us, holding his hand as she gave me a wary glance.

Evie had yet to speak to me. For a girl so bold, she seemed nervous where I was concerned.

Was that because she knew I was married to Zavier? Or because I was an outsider? Or because the Guardian had warned her not to trust me?

Turning a child against me seemed like his style.

I hadn't seen him in five days, not that I was counting. Apparently, he didn't need to *babysit* me with Zavier around.

Fine by me.

"Hi," I said, giving her my kindest smile. "I'm Odessa."

She leaned against Zavier's leg, sweet and shy and with the most precious face in the realm. "Hi."

Zavier winked, and a hundred butterflies fluttered in my belly.

Maybe this marriage wasn't entirely hopeless. Zavier as a father was different than the bored, indifferent man I'd met weeks ago. The protectiveness for his child was endearing.

"Pap—" Evangeline caught herself midslip. "Zavier?"

It broke my heart a little to hear her call him Zavier.

"Can I go with you when you leave?" she asked.

"You're leaving again?" I asked.

He opened his mouth to answer one of us, but his focus shifted into the forest. He held up a hand for us to stay quiet as a crease formed between his eyebrows.

I scanned the trees, searching for whatever it was he'd heard. But other than some birds chirping and squirrels chattering, the only noise was from the occasional falling pine cone.

He listened for another moment, features taut, until he exhaled and the worry vanished.

"What?" I asked.

Evie squinted into the distance, peering into the shadows. Then her face lit up as a man appeared, striding through the trees on near-silent feet.

The Guardian.

My babysitter had returned.

Damn my heart. It skipped.

Heartburn. It had to be heartburn. The cooks had added peppers to the eggs this morning. They'd been spicy, and now I had heartburn.

Zavier let go of Evie's hand as the Guardian approached. The men clasped forearms as Zavier asked, "How did it go?"

There was a seriousness to the Guardian today. A sharpness. He looked to Evangeline, his expression softening a bit, before jerking his chin for Zavier to follow away from our path.

He didn't so much as blink in my direction.

Also fine by me.

They stepped away, their backs turned to block us out. To block *me* out.

Evie crooked her finger, motioning me closer as she whispered. "He goes to fight the monsters. The bad ones."

Bad ones? "Like grizzurs and lionwicks?"

"No." She shook her head. "The sick ones."

Sick monsters. "What do you mean?"

"Evangeline!" A woman's voice echoed through the trees.

The girl's eyes blew wide. She turned, about to run away and hide behind a tree when the woman stopped her.

"I see you, Evie. Don't you dare run away from me."

Evie looked to the ground, chewing on her lower lip.

A woman swept down the path, marching our way. She was beautiful, with a slender, willowy figure. Her long, brown hair was braided much like mine, the thick plait draped over her shoulder. She walked with elegance and immediately reminded me of Margot. Straight spine, pinned shoulders, with a lifted chin.

It wasn't haughty or superior. This woman's posture was simply perfect.

She stopped in front of us, her green eyes narrowing. "Well?"

"Sorry, Luella," Evangeline mumbled.

Luella sighed, crouching in front of her charge. "It frightens me when you run off."

"But if I tell you where I'm going, you won't let me."

I pulled in my lips to hide a smile. At one point, I think I'd told my own tutors much the same.

Luella relaxed, the fear of losing Evangeline gone, and stood, facing me with a small smile. "You must be Odessa. I'm Luella. It's a pleasure to meet you."

"You as well." I gave her a slight bow.

I'd never bowed to my own tutors before, but it came automatically. As if Luella's grace demanded the respect.

"Odessa." I turned at Zavier's voice. "I'm sorry, but I'll have to cut our walk short. There's something that needs my attention."

"Of course."

He nodded, then bent to run his thumb around Evangeline's face. "Go with Luella."

Her tiny shoulders sagged. "Are you leaving?"

"Not yet." He pulled her into his leg, giving her a brief hug.

My gaze shifted to the Guardian.

His hazel eyes stared back.

There was no smirk today. There was no taunting or mischief in his expression.

Something was wrong. Something had happened.

A chill crept down my spine.

"Shall we?" Luella motioned to the path like she was to usher both me and Evangeline away.

I followed them to the commons before breaking away with a wave. Then I weaved through the trees, searching faces until I found the one I'd been looking for.

Brielle was hanging wet clothes on a line to dry. My clothes.

True to his word, Zavier had moved her and Jocelyn into a treehouse of their own. The privacy, the companionship with a friend, had done her wonders. She was less sullen, happier, than she'd been since arriving in Treow.

"Highness." She curtsied. "Is everything all right? Do you need anything?"

"No." I came to a stop at her side, standing close as I checked the space around us, ensuring we were alone. "Have you heard anything about sick monsters?"

Her forehead furrowed. "Sick monsters? No. What does that mean?"

"I'm not sure." What made a monster sick? "Just a rumor I heard today."

"I've heard nothing of monsters." She lowered her voice. "But I heard something last night at the bonfire, after you retired to your room. I was walking back and heard a couple of men talking. I, um, eavesdropped."

Since Zavier's arrival, there'd been a liveliness to Treow. Or maybe it was the doing of his warriors. Over the past five nights, there'd been a bonfire near the commons. People would gather and drink while they told stories. Jocelyn and Brielle had gone every night. They'd tell me all about it over breakfast.

But neither had invited me to attend. Nor had Tillia.

After a string of nights sulking that I'd been left out, I'd decided this was the Guardian's doing. The reason he took my rope ladder each night.

So I wouldn't make my way to the bonfire. I wouldn't overhear whatever it was that the Turans didn't want shared.

"What did you hear?" I asked.

"That a few men have gone missing from Treow."

"Missing? Like they left? Or were taken?"

"I don't know." She shook her head. "One of them saw me listening, and they stopped talking."

So they guarded their stories from Brielle, too.

Smart.

"Jocelyn said she heard someone talking about the king's militia. He's recruiting more men. I guess one of the pony riders quit to enlist. Maybe that's where these men went as well."

Why would Ramsey need to build his militia? The crux migration? Or for a war?

Father had told me he needed to get into Allesaria. But he'd never specifically said he'd be sending troops. I'd made that assumption. What if he'd never planned on invading? What if all of this was in reaction to something Ramsey was doing?

I hummed. When we were on the coast, the men hauling our trunks had mentioned the militia. Ramsey must be pulling people from across his kingdom.

Pulling them to Allesaria, maybe?

"Have you heard anything about Allesaria?"

"No." She frowned. "I asked Mariette about it once. She never spoke to me often before that point, but when I mentioned the city's name, she ignored me for days."

"It's been the same for me." Whenever I'd bring up Allesaria, conversation would either die or change direction.

It was almost as if the city was a myth. A legend.

What if Allesaria didn't exist?

Maybe the reason Father couldn't gain access to the Turan capital was because there wasn't a Turan capital. It had never been rebuilt. And if there was no capital, then there was nothing for Father to find that might help us against the crux.

No. Impossible. Children were taught the capitals of every kingdom. I'd known about Allesaria since I was old enough to read and write.

It existed. Somewhere.

Didn't it?

"We'll never learn anything if we stay here," I said.

Brielle bent to pick up a clean tunic and pin it to the line. "It seems, Highness, like that's the point."

They'd trapped us here.

For weeks, I'd accepted this place. I'd been biding my time, thinking eventually we'd go to Allesaria. But Zavier would take me to Ellder instead. I'd fail entirely. And my people would pay the price.

If I was going to find Allesaria, then something had to change.

Me. I had to change.

I could ask questions until I was blue in the face, and no one would answer. What exactly was a sick monster? Did it have anything to do with that green blood I'd seen from the marroweel and dead grizzur? Why was King Ramsey burning books and building a militia? What was happening in Turah, and how many secrets were these people keeping beyond the location of their capital?

It was time to stop waiting for the Turans to gift me information.

It was time to start acting like a spy.

It was time to figure my way out of Treow.

Brielle sat on the edge of my bed, frowning as she watched me comb out my wet hair. "This is the worst idea you've ever had."

She wasn't wrong.

"I have to try," I told her.

"What happens when we get caught?"

"They'll probably lock me in this treehouse and you in yours." My rope ladder would likely stop reappearing each morning, and I'd be trapped in this room forever.

But I wasn't letting the fear of getting caught stop me from my plan. I might not be a great spy or princess or warrior, but I had some practice at sneaking out.

Brielle was my unwilling accomplice. We'd decided to keep Jocelyn out of the fray so she could claim ignorance if—*when*—we got caught.

"What if you get eaten by a lionwick or bariwolf?" she asked.

"Then you get to go home."

"Highness." She flinched. "Don't talk like that. And don't do this. It's too risky."

I gave her a sad smile. "I have to. I have to try."

She hesitated for a moment. "Why?"

Because if I quit now, what kind of person did that make me?

My father might not be an affectionate man. He was hard and strict and unyielding. But he was fair, and above all else, he served his people. His crown. His kingdom.

Maybe I didn't know all of the details, but I had faith he'd given me this task for a good reason. I had faith that he wasn't a murderer or a conqueror. That if he did send his troops to Turah, it wouldn't be to viciously slaughter the innocent.

He hadn't said he was planning a war. He'd said he needed to find Allesaria. That he needed a way to enter the city. That he wanted to find a way to break the Shield of Sparrows and set me free.

If I were a better princess, a selfless princess, the notion of freedom wouldn't be so appealing.

What would I do if my life was my own? What would I do if I could break away from this marriage to Zavier? If the key to saving my people didn't rest on my shoulders?

Who would I become if I wasn't at the mercy of men?

An adventurer? A voyager? A writer? An artist who traveled the realm and never cared that her fingertips were stained with charcoal or paint?

Not once in my life had I let myself dream of those possibilities. Not once had I been given the luxury of dreams. If I could be anything in this realm, who would I become?

I wanted to find out.

So I'd leave Treow today. I'd find the road to Allesaria. I'd find out what was happening in Turah with these sick monsters and burning books.

And in doing so, maybe I'd set myself free.

No more bride prize, and no more Sparrows.

Would I fail? Probably. But maybe, just maybe, I'd find a way. For myself. And for the next princess who wanted a *choice*.

I was more capable than my family expected. I was more than I'd let myself believe. There was a girl inside me who'd once found the courage to jump off a cliffside. That girl had been stifled and smothered. Hidden except for those stolen moments of bravery.

It was time to let her stretch her wings and fly.

I tossed my comb on the bed beside Brielle. "They might not have said it, but my family expects me to fail. There's a reason my father chose Mae instead of me to be the Sparrow. And I think, in my heart, when I left Roslo, I expected to fail, too. I'm tired of being shoved to the wayside. I'm tired of being dismissed. I'd like to prove to them, to myself, that I am more than a token to be traded."

Brielle's eyes softened. "You want their love."

"I don't know if they're able to love." Probably not in the way that Brielle's family loved her. "I'd settle for their confidence and trust. Maybe a little faith that I'm not entirely useless."

That maybe I could be a queen.

"For what it's worth, I don't think you're useless or a failure," Brielle said. "And I trust you."

That was sweet. "Thank you. I trust you, too."

Enough that over the past four days, I'd told her about my plan to spy. How Father had tasked me with entering Allesaria. How he'd asked me to learn about the Guardian's powers. When I'd told her that he'd asked me to kill the Guardian, Brielle had been gracious enough not to laugh.

There were still secrets between us. I hadn't told her that Zavier could speak. I hadn't shared about Evie. But I'd confided everything else.

"Are you sure you don't want to wait?" she asked. "They might still take us to Allesaria."

I shook my head. "They won't. We'll be in Ellder for the migration. And the Guardian already suspects I'm spying for Father."

"Which you are."

"Which I am. The crux are coming. If we had years, I'd think of another plan. But I might not get this chance again."

I went to the small mirror mounted on the wall beside the bath, taking in my riot of curls. The red and orange spirals were bright beneath the skylights, the strands drying quickly from the warmth of the afternoon.

With the exception of Brielle and Jocelyn, everyone in Treow knew me with brown hair. And with the exception of Brielle and Jocelyn, everyone in Treow who knew me best was gone.

Zavier had left the encampment four days ago with Evangeline and Luella. Tillia and Halston had accompanied them to wherever it was they were going, acting as their guards.

The Guardian was gone, too.

Even Cathlin had left the encampment and its empty library. Brielle had been tasked with cleaning out her vacant treehouse.

They'd all left four days ago, after the Guardian had returned from hunting "sick" monsters.

Maybe they'd felt Evie would be safer elsewhere. Maybe Zavier had surprised his daughter with a getaway trip to Perris. Maybe they'd lassoed a crux and were riding it to the twin moons.

All I knew was that they'd left without so much as a wave goodbye.

It shouldn't have come as a surprise that I'd been left behind. To the Turans, I was no one important. I was an outsider. A second thought. A ward in need of watching.

A bug to be kept locked in a glass jar.

It was surprisingly similar to the life I'd lived in Quentis.

Well, I'd snuck out of Father's castle, crawling with guards, plenty of times. I could sneak out of this damn encampment, too.

"I'm praying to Daria her luck is on our side," Brielle said.

"So am I."

It hadn't taken long for me to hatch this plan—only one sleepless night. It was probably too simple, but I was giving it a shot nonetheless. Sometimes, all it took was a simple plan.

"What will you try to find?" she asked.

"Anything." Any hint of Allesaria. I wasn't holding my breath that I'd find a map, but there had to be one somewhere in this godsdamn kingdom.

Ashmore seemed as good a place as any to start my search.

I just had to get there.

Ashmore was the closest town to Treow. And the merchant who delivered supplies to the encampment's mercantile was my best chance at getting past the watchtowers.

I twisted my curls into a knot and pinned it to the base of my skull. Then I grabbed a gray satin scarf from the armoire, fitting it over my forehead and tying it around my hair. "Is it all covered?"

Brielle nodded, collecting my satchel from the bed and bringing it over. "Do you have plenty of coin?"

"Yes." Enough gold to rent a room at an inn for myself in Ashmore. Enough gold to bribe a traveler to smuggle me back into Treow in a few days' time. "You remember what to say if anyone asks where I am?"

"Yes. Your monthly cycle has arrived, and you're ill. You asked me to leave you to rest."

"Good." Whenever I'd mentioned my monthly cycle to men in Roslo, they'd run the other way. I was hoping that would be the case in Turah as well.

"I don't think the Guardian is going to believe you're sick," she said.

I shrugged. "Probably not."

But I'd deal with his wrath *if* he caught me.

For a man who swore he didn't trust me, leaving me alone was asking for trouble. He only had himself to blame for this.

Besides, there was a chance, a slim chance, that I'd return in two or three days with no one in Treow even realizing that I'd left.

"I can do this," I told her—and myself.

Brielle's smile was sweet and slightly disbelieving. Would she have doubted Mae? Probably not.

I looped the satchel across my chest, and then we left the treehouse for the commons.

The supply wagon was parked outside the mercantile, its cargo nearly unloaded.

The driver had arrived last night. Now that his goods were delivered, he wouldn't linger. He came at night. Unloaded in the morning. And left. Every time. With Ashmore being a full day's ride, he could make it back before nightfall.

"I wish you could take that horse you love so much," Brielle whispered. "Then you'd at least have a way back."

"Me too."

Freya had been a comfort since I'd arrived in Treow. She was by far my favorite Turan. But people here would likely notice her disappearance before mine. Horses, I'd learned, were essential to Turan life. Hell, they'd probably mount a search party to rescue Freya and leave me to rot.

So my plan was to ride in the supply wagon.

I'd be hiding in plain sight.

Brielle and I turned away from the commons, following the path of twin wheel tracks that marked the road the supply merchant would take to leave.

We made sure we were far enough from the treehouses and buildings that no one could see us from the commons. Then, standing in the shade beneath a towering tree, we waited until we heard the sound of wheels rattling.

I squared my shoulders, about to step out to the path, when Brielle seized my hand. "Maybe I should be the person to go instead."

"No." This was my idea. This was my task.

And I doubted they'd kill me if I was caught. Not when I was the Sparrow. Brielle? She was expendable.

"Besides, it's too late to change plans." I waved a hand at her clothes. "And you're already dressed."

She looked down at the pants and scowled, adjusting the waistband. "I don't know how you wear these. They're so tight."

"I've gotten used to them." It was amazing how quickly I'd adjusted to the Turan style. And how uncomfortable it was to don a dress again.

I pulled at the long, fitted sleeves of my gray gown, missing the loose, thin fabric of the tunics I'd been wearing lately.

Brielle was in a tunic instead, her brown hair plaited over a shoulder, similar to how I usually wore mine. Today, she was the princess.

"Here he comes." I tugged the scarf off my hair and pulled at the pins so the curls tumbled free.

Would a woman wearing a scarf draw attention from the watchtower guards? Possibly. But a woman with vivid, wild hair? Definitely. I'd draw notice. Without question.

But I was counting on their curiosity, not suspicion.

Today, I looked nothing like Princess Odessa Wolfe, the woman who'd made it a point to ride and run and walk past every watchtower in Treow since I'd arrived.

And since everyone had left me here alone, I'd started taking a crossbow on my daily walks.

If no one was going to train me on my knives, then I'd revert to the one weapon that seemed relatively straightforward. I'd pinched my fingers more times than I could count notching the bolt into the string, but I'd been using trees for target practice. Granted, trees didn't move like a monster or enemy, but I was missing less and less.

The guards were snickering less and less.

Today, I looked nothing like the princess who'd wave to the guards stationed above before attempting to shoot a helpless tree. The lady who fitted her fingers to her lips and practiced whistling until it finally worked.

Shades, this was a horrible plan, wasn't it? Brielle was certain I wouldn't make it out of the forest. She was probably right.

I should have taken the time to plot a more elaborate, believable scheme. But what if I didn't get this chance again? What if the Guardian, Tillia, or Zavier never left me alone again? What if they took me to Ellder and trapped me behind a fortress's walls?

This was it. This had to work.

"Ready?" I asked Brielle.

"Ready." She nodded, then steeled her spine and lifted her nose in the air as she stepped away from the tree's shade.

She'd spent years with royalty, observing our behaviors and mannerisms. She knew how to command attention like she was a queen herself.

At a raise of her hand, the man immediately slowed the two sorrel horses hitched to his wagon.

"Sir."

"Yes?" he asked.

She walked to his side, pulling a coin purse from the pocket of her pants. There was enough gold in that purse for this man to buy two other horses and a wagon three times this one's size. "My lady's maid is in need of a ride to Ashmore. There are items that I require within the week, but she's wary of making the journey alone. May she ride with you?"

He gave the purse a long, hard look before doing the same with me. "I won't be returning to Treow for another seven days."

Brielle waved her free hand. "She only requires passage to Ashmore.

She'll arrange for a ride back."

His eyes narrowed. "What is it you're needing? Why not request it from your shopkeeper?"

"That's my private business." There was an edge to Brielle's voice that sounded eerily like a threat from Mae. Clearly, she'd learned a few things from my sister.

The man frowned, and for a heartbeat, I was certain he'd drive on. But then he reached out, snatched the purse, and set it in his lap. "Get in."

No. Fucking. Way.

Six shades, it worked.

I darted to the wagon, nearly tripping on my skirts as I climbed onto the bench seat and settled in beside the man.

He frowned but urged on his horses, the wagon lurching as they moved.

My heart was pounding so hard it hurt when I risked a glance at Brielle. Either I'd see her in a few days. Or I'd see her in an hour when they hauled me back after catching me trying to escape.

The driver said nothing as he gave the horses more slack on the reins, the wagon lurching again as we gained more speed.

The clop of hooves drowned out the sound of my panicked, short breaths. Ahead, I picked out the boundary, finding the closest watchtower, then aimed my gaze forward.

Breathe.

My body began to tremble as we drew closer and closer.

A whistle rang through the air.

The whistle the guards made when someone was leaving, alerting the others of the departure. It was a short, shrill signal.

The moment I heard it sing through the trees, the air rushed from my lungs.

"Thank you, Daria," I whispered.

"What was that?" the man barked.

"Nothing," I murmured, pulling in my lips to hide a smile. The beaten path stretched before us out of the trees and onto the plains.

"There," the driver muttered, pointing into the distance. It was the one and only word he'd spoken since leaving Treow.

I squinted as a dark spot on the horizon slowly transformed into rooflines and wooden buildings.

Ashmore.

The trip had felt endless. The wagon's bench was uncomfortable, and the plethora of bumps in the road made my teeth shake in my skull. It had been unnerving to be out in the open again, to be unguarded. Exposed for any monster to attack.

Even with my knives strapped to my thighs beneath my skirts, I'd spent the entire ride sweeping the plains for predators.

The journey was terrifying and thrilling. It was a dive off a cliff. A leap of faith.

This was freedom.

And I was addicted.

The sun was dropping toward the horizon, and the last stretch of the trip seemed to take days, but the road finally widened as we came closer to town.

The driver pulled on the reins, slowing his team to a walk as we reached a row of wooden houses.

A little boy wearing a straw hat looked up from where he was playing in a yard of patchy grass. His mother stood in the doorway, arms crossed, expression neutral and assessing as we rolled by.

Either she didn't like the merchant.

Or she didn't like the looks of me.

I took out my scarf, quickly tying it over my hair.

More homes lined the road, and the closer we drew to the center of town, the closer together they were built. Most had small pens for goats and chickens. A dog leashed with a chain barked as we passed.

Tillia had told me that towns in Turah had developed different ways to protect against monsters. But Ashmore resembled the countryside towns that dotted the fields of Quentis. How did these people stay safe?

"What about monsters?" I asked the driver.

"What about them?"

"How do you keep them out of the town?"

His jaw clenched. "We don't. Not anymore."

Anymore? What did that mean?

Before I could ask, he tugged hard on the reins, bringing his team to a stop. Then he jerked his chin toward the road. "Out."

He'd earned his fare, and now it was time for me to leave.

My feet had barely hit the ground when he urged on his horses. The wagon's wheel nearly ran over my toes before I took a quick leap away.

"Thanks for the ride," I mumbled, scowling at his back.

I straightened, smoothing the skirt of my dress. I made sure the flap on my satchel was secured, then, with a hand on its strap, I started down the streets of Ashmore.

A man carrying a spear passed by, moving toward the road. Was he going to stand watch tonight? Shouldn't he have a better weapon? That spear looked more like a herding stick for sheep and goats, the blade only attached with twine. He had no knives or sword.

When he noticed my stare, he shot me a scowl that sent me on my way.

Ashmore wasn't a large town, and the houses quickly made way for stores and shops. The streets were narrow, the buildings separated by cramped alleyways. And beside every door on every structure was a brass bell. Did they use those instead of knocking?

The noise of people enveloped me like a soft blanket, the sounds reminding me of the days I'd wandered the docks in Roslo. Even on the nights when the dining hall in Treow was crammed full of people, it wasn't the same as the clamor of a town or city.

The streets were arranged in neat lines. I drew in a long breath, smelling food and horses and dirt and fires. Smoke drifted from a few chimneys, and my stomach growled, the nerves of my escape finally making way for hunger.

I'd made it. Thank the gods. I signed the Eight and pressed a hand to my heart to keep it from leaping out of my chest.

There was no way I should be here, but my silly plan had worked. My laugh was swallowed by the clatter of a different wagon coming down the street.

I walked in no hurry down the road, taking in the buildings, searching for a library or school. Ahead, in what looked to be the center of Ashmore, a hanging sign marked an inn.

I'd started crossing to the opposite side of the street, weaving past horses, wagons, and other people out walking, when a deep laugh caught my ear.

My legs locked, my feet stuck on the dry dirt. My stomach dropped.

I knew that laugh.

I knew it all too well.

Spinning in a slow circle, I braced for a blast of fury.

Of course it had been easy to get out of Treow. It had been one of the Guardian's tests. A trap. Had he followed us to Ashmore? Had he ridden ahead to wait while the driver shuttled me across the plains?

The laugh came again, echoing over all other noise.

The Guardian stood outside the tavern, arms crossed over his broad chest as he leaned against the open door's frame. A smile stretched his mouth, his eyes alight with humor.

But he wasn't laughing or smiling in my direction.

His attention was locked on a beautiful woman with straw-colored hair. Her voluptuous curves strained the seams of her purple tunic and its plunging neckline. She batted her eyelashes, giving him a coy smile as she stood on her toes to whisper into his ear, earning another of his rumbling chuckles.

His focus was so intent on the blonde that the rest of the realm might as well have been nonexistent.

Wait. He wasn't here for me, was he?

He was here for *her*?

I was standing in the middle of the street, and he hadn't so much as blinked in my direction. I was standing in the middle of the street and—

"Shit," I hissed, spinning around and ducking my chin. I pulled the longer ends of my curls over my shoulders, hoping that from behind, all he could see was this scarf.

A man riding a horse passed, and I rushed to catch up, moving to the other side of the animal in the hopes that it would shield me as I hurried to the inn.

What if the Guardian had no idea I was in Ashmore? What if this was a coincidence? Had he come to Ashmore to visit his lover, and I'd simply picked the wrong time to escape?

My mind was reeling, my heart trying to beat out of my chest again, this time in panic. I kept marching, face down until I glimpsed an alley out of the corner of my eye. I darted toward the space between buildings, slipping into the darkness and out of sight. Then I pressed my back against a wall, sucking in a breath.

I gave myself a few moments to calm down, then inched toward the edge of the alley, peering around the corner.

The Guardian was still at the tavern, still smiling and laughing with the blonde.

A mixture of relief and resentment surged, swirling so fast my stomach pitched. Or maybe that was from too much stress in a single day.

With his hand on the small of her back, the Guardian ushered the woman into the tavern, both of them disappearing from sight.

A sour taste spread across my tongue.

Not jealousy. Not for him.

No, this was annoyance. Pure annoyance. Annoyance so strong I couldn't see straight. Not jealousy.

"Not at all," I muttered, emerging from the alley.

But just because I wasn't jealous didn't mean I wanted to get caught. So I raced for the inn across the street, giving my best smile to the innkeeper at the desk. "Do you have any rooms available?"

Please say yes.

He looked me up and down, a severe frown wrinkling his face as he took in my dress and headscarf. "How many nights?"

"One." Tomorrow, no matter what, I'd be leaving Ashmore. The sooner the better. If the Guardian was this close, it was only a matter of time before he returned to Treow. There was no way I could linger, not now.

The clerk jotted down something in his notebook, then held up a finger. He ducked into a room behind the desk, taking his sweet time before he finally returned with a brass key.

"Room five. Second floor. Third door on the left."

"Thank you. Would it be possible to have dinner sent up?"

"Yes," he grumbled. "It's an added charge."

"No problem. Thank you." I traded coin for the key, then took to the stairs, climbing to the second floor without delay.

The sooner I was safe behind my room's door, the better.

The hallway was quiet, my boots sinking into the plush carpet. The hairs on the back of my neck prickled as I passed the other rooms, like the people inside were watching, so I quickened my steps to the third door on the left. My hand was shaking so badly it took a moment to get the key inserted into the lock.

I flung the door open, spinning inside and closing it quickly. Then I pressed my forehead to the wooden surface, exhaling as I closed my eyes. "This was a horrible idea."

"Agreed."

"Ah!" I yelped as I spun around.

The Guardian stood in the center of my room, his legs planted wide, arms crossed over his chest.

A breeze drifted in from the open window.

And he was livid.

"Hello, my queen."

Well, fuck.

Twenty-Seven

The Guardian's rage hung over the room like a thunderstorm. Any minute now, a lightning bolt would split the ceiling and strike me dead.

His gaze turned molten silver, and while I'd suspected that the colors shifted with his moods, I was damn sure of it now.

Silver was bad. Very, *very* bad.

I pressed myself against the door, palms flat on its surface, wishing I could dissolve through to the other side and escape.

"What the fuck were you thinking?" He paced the space between the bed and the wall, his fists tight. His entire frame vibrated like he was on the verge of an explosion.

How far could I get if I made a run for it? My hand slid across the door, wrapping around the knob.

He stopped pacing, leveling me with a glare. "Don't even think about leaving."

My hand dropped to my side.

Did I apologize? Beg for forgiveness? Make up some ridiculous excuse as to how I'd gotten lost on my way to the commons and ended up in Ashmore?

How had he found me? How was he in my room?

Unless my hunch earlier was right. This was all a trap. He'd set the snare, and I'd taken the bait without a second thought.

Then what was that show outside the tavern? Him pretending not to know I was on the street while he'd flirted with that blonde? Just an act to crush my soul?

Well, it had worked.

I hadn't escaped Treow.

The watchtower guards had let me leave.

They'd probably had a decent laugh at my pathetic attempt at a disguise.

"Fuck." The Guardian raked a hand through his hair, the lighter strands at the top catching the light. "Do you have any idea how reckless this was?"

I held up my hands in surrender. "I'm sorry."

Well, not really. But whenever Father was in a shit mood, an apology usually quelled his temper. Slightly.

"You're *sorry*?" He took a step backward, like he didn't trust himself to get too close. "Damn it, Cross. This is not Quentis. People die in Turah every day. Every. Fucking. Day. People who've spent their entire lives in this kingdom. People who are better equipped to deal with its dangers than a spoiled godsdamn princess."

He yelled so loudly that everyone in the inn, everyone in Ashmore, had probably heard him call me spoiled.

"Then why did they let me go?" I pushed off the door, my own voice rising.

His nostrils flared. "I'll find out when we return to Treow tomorrow."

"Um..." I blinked. "So the watchtower guards didn't know it was me?"

He scoffed. "Apparently not, if you're standing here."

Then my plan really had worked. I'd slipped away. I'd broken free. Pride swelled, and I dropped my chin to hide a smile.

"I leave you for four days, and you can't stay put. You are, without a doubt, the biggest pain in my ass I've ever met." His hand dove into his dark hair again, tugging at the roots. "Explain. What are you doing here?"

Spying.

I stayed quiet.

"Answer me," he ordered.

"Uh, exploring my new kingdom?"

He stopped pacing. "Exploring your new kingdom."

"Yes?"

They were supposed to be answers, but they came out with the lilt of a question.

He scoffed, dragging a hand over his face, then turned to the wall, staring at its paper.

Pink and plum roses threaded with green ivy. The seams were coming apart in a few places.

The silence that came next was tense and ugly and made me want to squirm. It went on and on and on, stretching so long that the light from outside began to fade, softening to an evening glow. He kept staring at that wallpaper, utterly unmoving other than the occasional blink.

It was torture, waiting for my punishment. Worse than his fury.

Finally, he faced me again. "We will leave tomorrow, and you will never do anything like this again, or the freedom you've been granted in Treow will vanish. Is that understood?"

Did he expect a *Yes, sir*?

In another life, that would have been my reply. It's exactly what I would have told my father.

"No." What the hell was I saying? This wasn't just bold—it was rebellious. But I wasn't taking it back. I stood tall, hiding my shaking hands behind my back, and said it again. "No, that is not understood."

His glare turned homicidal. "No?"

"No." I held that silver gaze, refusing to shrink.

Refusing to bend to his will.

"I didn't ask to be married to a stranger and shipped across the continent. I didn't ask to come to Turah. I didn't ask to be jailed in a wilderness treehouse. Those were decisions made *for* me by the whims of men. So you can threaten to take away my freedom all you want, but I will fight you. Every step of the way. Until my last breath. And I will not go quietly into a cage."

My chest heaved, my pulse pounding like I'd been running for hours.

I wanted to take it all back.

I wanted to say it all over again.

I wanted to swallow the words and forget them forever.

I wanted to scream it from the top of my lungs.

The Guardian only stared at me, his face unreadable.

That excruciating silence returned. It got so quiet I could hear footsteps in the hallway beyond the door, the murmur of voices.

It took everything I had to hold his metallic gaze. To stay upright and not sink to the floor as he stared and stared and stared.

"Why didn't you ask?"

"Wh-what?" I stammered.

His voice was calm. Collected. The silver in his eyes began to melt away, the hazel taking its place. "Haven't you been granted your every request? If you wanted to explore Ashmore, why didn't you ask?"

I stared at him, jaw slack and mind whirling.

"Did you ever stop to think that maybe the door to your cage has always been unlocked, Sparrow? And all you had to do was push it open?"

Was that really true? Could I have simply asked?

A knock came from the hall, and I spun to answer so fast that I whacked my forehead with the door as I yanked it open.

"Hello." I rubbed at the ache as I greeted a pretty young woman outside.

She carried a tray with both hands and peered past me to the brooding giant still occupying my room. "Your meal, miss."

"Thank you." I took the tray, trying to find a smile.

She was too busy staring at the Guardian to care. There was something like reverence and wonder on her face. The woman was clearly stunned to see a legend in the flesh.

I backed away, tray in hand, and kicked the door closed.

Carrying my meal to the small table in the corner, I set it down and pulled out the chair, uncovering a bowl of stew. Then I dropped the napkin on my lap as the scents of herbs, roasted meat, and potatoes filled my nose.

I wasn't hungry. Not anymore.

Did you ever stop to think that maybe the door to your cage has always been unlocked, Sparrow? And all you had to do was push it open?

Why did replaying that in my mind make me want to cry?

I wasn't used to testing doors.

I'd learned a long time ago that they were always locked.

Scooping a heaping bite of stew onto my spoon, I shoved it in my mouth. It was too hot and burned my tongue, but did I spit it out?

Absolutely not. I chewed and winced and chewed some more so that I wouldn't cry.

The Guardian grumbled something under his breath, but before I could make sense of it, he climbed out of the window, leaving me alone with my stew.

I yanked off my scarf, tossing it to the floor with my satchel.

There were still enough daylight hours left that I could wander around Ashmore. Now that I wasn't hiding from the Guardian, I could seek out their library.

But I stayed in my room, finishing my stew and setting the tray in the hall. Then I unpacked my satchel, changing into a long tunic that draped to the tops of my thighs. It would be comfortable enough to sleep in tonight and thoroughly rumpled to travel in tomorrow.

With my boots off and gray dress folded on the table, I washed my face and climbed into bed, staring up at the ceiling.

After the Guardian left, I hadn't bothered closing the window. Sounds from the street carried to my room. A man's hearty laugh. A woman's shout.

As tempting as it was to get dressed and join them, I stayed in my bed, hugging my pillow and feeling more alone than I had in years.

Why didn't you ask?

Fair question. Why hadn't I asked to leave Treow? Zavier had given me anything I'd requested without hesitation. Well, except for information. But anything material? He'd never denied my wishes. Though how would I have explained this trip? Certainly not with the truth.

Except this was my father's errand. The Guardian could claim I wasn't caged, but he wasn't the only one who'd put me behind bars.

What would happen to Brielle and Jocelyn if I sent them home without information? Would Father punish them for my failures? Was that why he'd sent them with me in the first place? Knowing I'd worry more about them than myself?

If only he'd given me more information. Something substantial. What was in Allesaria that could stop the crux? If the Turans had a weapon, wouldn't they have used it themselves?

Or what if Father hadn't told me the truth? What if he'd played on my sympathies? What if he'd leveraged my curiosity about the migrations, knowing I'd do anything for our people? What if I was doing all of this out of blind faith?

My insides twisted, my body restless. I flopped onto my other side, wishing I could fall asleep and wake up a different person in the morning. But I couldn't shut down my mind.

You must do this.

Father had pleaded with me to do this.

Treaties can be broken, Odessa. Remember that.

What if he was wrong? What if my actions caused a war between kingdoms?

I cupped my palms over my ears, wishing I could block out the noise in my head the same way I could muffle the sounds outside. I turned my face into my pillow, my eyes shut so tightly I saw black stars.

And then my pillow was gone, ripped out from under my face and off my bed.

I sat up in a flash, my jaw dropping as I watched the Guardian toss it onto the floor. "What do you think you're doing?"

He sat on the edge of my bed and pulled off his boots. "You can either have the bed without the pillow. Or the floor with it. Your choice, Cross."

I huffed. "You are not staying in my room. Get your own."

He smirked. "And leave my queen unguarded? Never."

Damn that smirk. Damn the way it made my heart trill.

The Guardian leaned closer, so close I could smell leather and wind and spice. "Unless, of course, you want me to sleep with you."

My breath caught.

The mental image that filled my mind was so vivid it was like an imprint. His weight, pinning me to the mattress. His skin hot against mine. His voice in my ear, his fingers threaded into my hair.

"Get. Out. Now." The image. The man. I kicked at him from beneath the covers.

He laughed as he dropped to the floor, lying on his back with my pillow beneath his head.

"I hate you," I seethed.

"Yes, you do. Don't forget."

"Never." I settled on my back, crossing my arms over my chest as I glared up at the ceiling. "How did you find me?"

"There's only one inn in Ashmore. And your hair isn't exactly subtle, Sparrow."

Blarg. My scarf must not have hidden the red. Except that would mean...

I pushed up on my elbows. "You know this is my real hair?"

"That dye you wear is as pungent as a dead fish. Did you really think I wouldn't notice?"

Yes. No one else seemed to care. Unless he was the only one who could smell it. The odor faded after the dye was applied. But his heightened senses must have been able to pick it up when others couldn't.

"Are you going to tell me why you came to Ashmore?" he asked.

Definitely not. I wasn't admitting my guilt. "I'll tell you that when you tell me your real name."

He hummed. "Then I guess we're at an impasse."

"I guess so." I sank onto the mattress, missing my pillow. "I hope my snoring keeps you awake all night."

He chuckled. "Good night, my queen."

The sound of his voice, haunting and beautiful, followed me into my dreams.

Twenty-Eight

My pillow was on the floor when I awoke, but the Guardian had disappeared, leaving behind only a note on the table.

I have business to finish before we leave. Don't wander far.

His handwriting was not at all what I'd expected. It was neat and clean. Practiced. Regal.

My own script was sloppier than his.

What business did he have to finish? Another rendezvous with his blonde?

It didn't matter. I didn't care.

His absence meant I had a morning to myself, and I wasn't going to squander the chance to explore. After yesterday, he could have locked me in this room. He could have dragged me back to Treow at dawn. Instead, he'd ordered me not to wander *far*, meaning he knew I was going to wander.

He was letting me test the open door to my cage.

So with my satchel strapped across my body, dressed in the tunic I'd slept in and the pants I'd brought along, I walked out of my room with the thrill of excitement bubbling in my veins. I'd left the shoulder harness for my knives in Treow, but they were in my bag, their handles sticking out slightly from one side. Even if I didn't know how to use them well, I felt better having them close.

The morning was crisp and fresh with a sweetness that I held in my lungs with every inhale as I left the inn for the bustling streets of Ashmore.

A woman with short, spiky gray hair sold sage sausage and potato buns from a cart outside the dark, empty tavern.

The man I'd passed yesterday, the man with the spear, trudged down the road, eyes tired. His makeshift weapon hung limply at his side. He glanced my way, but if he had the energy to shoot me another glare, it had vanished sometime in the night.

A man wearing a teal overcoat strolled down the center of the street, whistling as he walked. The color reminded me so much of Quentis, of our flags and uniforms, it gave me a twinge of homesickness.

I didn't ask for directions to the library. The sideways glances and wide berths the residents gave me were enough that I kept to myself. Besides, the town wasn't large enough to need instruction. I simply wandered up and down the streets, finishing my breakfast along the way.

It was on the third street that I found it.

There was no sign for the library. Nothing etched on the door.

There wasn't a door. There were no windows. There wasn't even a building.

What remained of the library was nothing but a charred pile of rubble.

Bookshelves burned and crumbling. A thick layer of fine ash from hundreds and hundreds of pages eaten by flame.

King Ramsey and his soldiers had paid a visit to Ashmore. Before or after his visit to Treow?

My heart ached as I stood in front of the wreckage.

The soldiers hadn't bothered removing books from this building. They'd just torched the entire structure. Would they have done the same in Treow had Cathlin's library not been attached to the infirmary? Had they raided homes in Ashmore, too?

My mood turned sour and sullen as I walked away from the rubble. "Why would a king want to burn books?"

"Fair question."

I gasped, doing a double take as a woman fell into step beside me. "Cathlin?"

"Hello, Odessa." She brushed her sleek white hair over her shoulder as she laughed. "Mind if I join you on your walk?"

"Not at all. I was heading back to the inn to meet the Guardian."

"Ah. I'm surprised he'd bring you here."

"He, um...didn't. I sort of came here on my own."

Her eyebrows lifted. "Did you now?"

"I was lectured, ad nauseam, about the recklessness of that decision."

"I'm sure you were." She tried—failed—to hide a laugh with a hand. "And where is he this morning?"

"I don't know." I shrugged. "He told me not to wander far."

"Ah. As irksome as he is, it's wise to listen. He *is* sworn to protect you."

"He is?" When had that happened?

Cathlin looped her arm through mine, her hand patting my wrist.

"Come, my dear. Let me show you around Ashmore."

We turned at the next corner, weaving through the streets until we came to a deep trench that cut us off from continuing. It was about five paces wide and stretched the length of three homes. The sides were sloped slightly, and there were footprints in the dirt where someone had crawled out.

"What's this?" I asked Cathlin.

"Migration tunnels." She pointed to the end of the trench where a hole opened beneath the ground. "This is the main access point for the community shelter. It'll be available for those who aren't digging their own private areas to stay during the migration. The tunnels will stretch beneath the town. Some of the larger buildings, like the inn, will have an entryway that connects."

"Did Ashmore not have this during the last migration?" I asked.

"They did." There was a melancholy to her voice. "But it wasn't deep enough. It wasn't reinforced enough. The crux were able to scent those hiding, even through the ground. They ripped through the earth and killed everyone."

I pressed a hand to my chest. "That's awful."

"Hopefully this will suffice." She turned from the tunnel. "Shall we continue?"

I fell into step beside her, taking a glance over my shoulder. In Roslo, we had tunnels and shelters built deep into the rock walls that surrounded the city. There was no way for the crux to find their way inside. But those in the countryside would dig shelters. Like the Turans, they'd already begun their preparations.

It had been easy to forget with all of the activity of the past weeks that the migration was coming. Now it rested heavy on my heart. How many people in Ashmore would survive? How many would rely upon those tunnels to keep them safe?

We walked in silence until we reached the same houses I'd passed yesterday on the way into town. The little boy who'd been playing in his yard was there again, chasing some pretend monster with a stick he wielded like it was a sword.

"What are you doing in Ashmore?" I asked Cathlin.

"Visiting an old lover. We reconnected recently, and I wanted to see if maybe there was something worth exploring."

"And?"

"She's lovely. But I don't think we've got a future."

"Oh. Sorry."

She sighed. "It's all well. I'd hoped that while I was here, I'd get to browse the library. Apparently, I was too late."

"I'm sorry for that, too."

Cathlin pursed her lips. "As am I."

"Why is King Ramsey destroying books and libraries?"

Her teeth clamped together so hard I heard the molars grind. "Because Ramsey has lost his godsdamn mind. I wish I had a better explanation."

Ramsey. Not King Ramsey or His Majesty. The casual way the Turans addressed their royal leadership still took me by surprise. Yet there were people who seemed insistent on calling me Princess Odessa Wolfe.

I was going to need a lesson on the nuances of Turan formalities.

"Why are you here?" she asked.

People were going to keep asking me that question. Since I couldn't tell the truth, it was time to come up with a believable lie.

"I also came for the library. I'm afraid I don't know much about Turah," I told her. "Not as much as I should. I wasn't really prepared to marry Zavier."

Her forehead furrowed. "But you're the Sparrow."

The Guardian called me Sparrow in jest. But there was respect in the way Cathlin spoke. To her, it wasn't only a nickname. It was a title to be regarded.

Like it or not, I was the Sparrow.

And these people had expectations of their future queen.

"The wedding was supposed to be at the equinox. I thought I had more time to learn about your kingdom." I hoped she'd believe these lies. I couldn't tell her why I'd come to Ashmore, and for some reason, I didn't feel like explaining Mae and the bride prize. "I'm trying, but..."

"It's difficult without books."

"Quite." I let her guide me on, taking me to the edge of town. "Can I ask you something? How do they keep the monsters out of Ashmore? The merchant who brought me here yesterday said they didn't." *Not anymore.*

Cathlin took another step forward, surveying the open plains beyond the road. "Most towns and cities in Turah are built against natural barriers. They're carved into our landscapes for protection. Ellder is tucked against the mountains. Perris has the ocean at its back. As you've seen, Treow is a shelter within the trees."

"But not Ashmore."

"No." She shook her head. "Our kingdom is vast, and as such, our cities spread apart. It's a long way from Perris to Ellder and anything beyond. Towns like Ashmore give travelers respite. People can find work here they might not elsewhere. A merchant can open a shop. A woman can run a tavern. And some are here simply because they prefer a quieter lifestyle. But living in the wilds is not without its risks."

"Monsters?"

"They're a more notable risk. So is the weather. Turan winters can be as vicious as any beast. In Quentis, your soil grows grains that would never survive here, especially with the drought of recent years. We raise livestock. We harvest lumber. That cannot be done within the confines of a city wall. Out here, these people are creating something. Those in the cities often take for granted where their food comes from. Where they get the wood for their homes. As does our king."

"What do you mean?"

"In the past, the towns where there are no rivers or mountains to aid in protection were given members of the army. Men and women tasked to keep any wayward monster from a village. Have you seen a soldier since you've arrived?"

"No." Not one.

"The villagers do their best to fill the gap. People stand watch. But they have their own lives and jobs to do."

The man I'd seen with the spear. He'd likely stood guard all night and was now going to work.

"Why would the king withdraw his protection?"

"You'll have to ask him." Her nostrils flared. "But I suspect it's because he wants people to move to the cities."

With the migration coming, if I was trying to keep my people safe, I'd want them behind city walls, too. They'd be safer than hand-dug tunnels. Father's staff was already preparing for the influx of people who'd seek shelter in Roslo when the crux flew.

Except if that was the case, why would King Ramsey leave them unprotected now? Even if the crux came earlier than predicted, there was still time for people to relocate. The migration wouldn't happen until spring.

Unless it had nothing to do with the migration.

"Does he want them to move to the cities to be safe? Or watched?"

Cathlin tapped her temple. "Smart girl."

Did this have anything to do with the militia? "Cathlin, what is—"

"Shh." She whirled, her hand gripping my arm as she scanned the street.

I turned, trying to figure out what had put her on alert.

The sound of clinking bells came from all directions. The bells by every door. They weren't to announce visitors. They were warning bells.

The little boy in the yard tossed his stick sword aside and sprinted for the door.

"Come with me." Cathlin pulled once on my arm, then let me go as she began to jog down the street.

People ran toward us, like we were swimming against the current in a stream. Each person ran to a house, shutting themselves inside.

"To the inn," she said. "Hurry."

I ran with her, holding my satchel so it wouldn't bounce. If an entire town had panicked, it could only mean one thing.

Monsters.

A series of clicks bounced from building to building, so loud I cupped my hands over my ears.

I knew those clicks. I'd heard them on a dark, terrifying night.

There were bariwolves in Ashmore.

Twenty-Nine

The clicks came in rapid succession, so fast they blended with one another as they ricocheted off buildings, doubling and tripling with every echo.

It was ten times louder than it had been that night on the plains. Ten times more terrifying.

"Get inside the inn," Cathlin shouted over the noise. "It's the safest building in Ashmore."

I didn't need her to tell me twice. As she tore off running, I was right behind her, letting panic push me faster than I'd ever run in my damn life.

A scream tore through the air. A woman's.

Then came another, this one a man's. It was cut short so abruptly, I nearly tripped over my own feet.

Roars mixed with snarls and more screams.

"Gods." I signed the Eight, praying the lost souls found a shade of light.

Cathlin ran faster, harder, and I stayed right on her heels.

We were close. Almost there. Five buildings away. Four. The door was shut, the windows dark, but I prayed the clerk would let us inside.

There were only three buildings left to pass when a woman ran into the street. It was the woman with short, spiky gray hair who'd sold me breakfast this morning.

She tripped as she ran, stumbling forward. When she stood, she hurried toward the inn as quickly as she could, but she gripped her leg and moved with a limp I hadn't noticed this morning.

Terror contorted her features as she glanced back.

Just as a bariwolf emerged onto the street.

I nearly crashed into Cathlin's body as we both came skidding to a stop, our boots kicking up dirt on the road.

She gripped my arm as I clung to hers.

My body began to tremble, fear stealing the air in my chest.

Like the other monsters in Calandra, bariwolves were depicted in drawings and paintings. But in person, it wasn't just frightening. That beast was a monster made for death.

Its face resembled that of a wolf. Its snout was sleek, its ears pointed and alert. Its fur was so black, so glossy, it shone blue when it caught the sunlight. But where the front half of the monster was hauntingly beautiful, its back half sent a shiver down my spine.

It was as large as the spotted pony Father gave Arthalayus for his third birthday. Smaller than a full-size horse but not by much. Its fur stopped halfway down the bariwolf's backbone, revealing scales that tapered to needlelike points. The white claws on all four feet were massive, each bigger than my whole hand. One swipe of its paw, and it could shred a person to ribbons.

The bariwolf growled, its lips curling to reveal a row of long, vicious teeth.

Teeth ready to kill.

It tipped its head to the sky, its throat working as it sent out a series of clicks. Then it swung its attention to the woman still hobbling toward the inn.

"She won't make it," I said.

"She's on her own. Go." Cathlin unfroze, nudging me toward the closest building. The tavern. Its front door was shut, the windows dark like all the other buildings.

We could escape inside. The bariwolf was too focused on easy prey.

Cathlin tore for the building, likely assuming I was at her side. But I couldn't just leave that other woman to die. I waited as Cathlin ran ahead. I waited until she was close to the tavern. To safety. Then I swallowed hard and lifted my fingers to my lips to blow a single, piercing whistle. The whistle I'd practiced and practiced from the safety of my treehouse walls.

It had never been so crisp and clear.

The bariwolf's attention snapped to me, and the growl that vibrated from its maw was so loud I whimpered.

The gray-haired woman had almost made it to the inn. The moment she was within reaching distance of the door, it flew open and the innkeeper yanked her inside.

Cathlin whirled, eyes panicked. "Run, Odessa!"

I was frozen, snared by the bariwolf as it snarled and crept closer, its feet sending up small puffs of dust with every step. A few pounces with those long, powerful legs, and we'd be dead. But it prowled forward as if it was waiting.

Hunting.

The hairs on the back of my neck stood on end as I turned to look over my shoulder.

Behind me, close enough that I could see the blood coating its tongue and teeth, was another bariwolf, inching my way with perfect stealth.

It only had one eye. And it seemed to smile when I met its cold, endless gaze.

This monster had decided I was to be its next meal.

Well, it would have to catch me first.

Moving faster than I'd ever moved in my life, I bolted for the tavern.

Both monsters roared and lunged. The one-eyed beast was so close I felt the heat from its rancid breath as it came at us, jaws open wide. But before it could catch me in its teeth, something plowed into its side.

The Guardian.

It happened so quickly, all I saw was a blur of black as the monster rolled and tumbled.

The other bariwolf changed course, leaping for the Guardian instead. I opened my mouth to scream, to warn him, but then I saw the flash of metal, the glint of a sword as it sliced through the air, cutting the bariwolf's snout off at the bridge.

Half the monster's face, gone. Its muzzle landed with a sickening plop before the monster staggered away, blinking twice before it collapsed.

"Run, Cross," he bellowed. "Go."

"Odessa." Cathlin ran to my side, pulling my arm so hard it jolted in the socket.

The one-eyed monster had backed away, out of reach of the Guardian's sword. It tipped its head to the sky as more clicks came from its throat.

Oh, gods. Was it calling for help?

They faced each other, prowling in a semicircle, searching for a weak spot to strike.

The Guardian moved like the wind, launching himself toward the monster. His sword flashed and sliced at the bariwolf's throat.

But the monster was fast, moving before the weapon could slice through its neck. It answered the Guardian's strike with a snap of its teeth that he twisted to avoid, but only just.

Cathlin and I stumbled up the tavern's porch stairs, clinging to each other, as we watched the battle on the street unfold. She pounded on the door, testing the locked handle. "Open the door."

While she kept pounding, yelling for help, I watched the Guardian, unblinking, as he danced with that monster.

He countered every lunge with a swipe of his sword. He spun and whirled, his blade skimming off those scales and spikes. But no matter how fast he moved, he couldn't seem to find a weakness, a moment to strike.

The monster swiped at him with those claws, cutting a gash in the Guardian's arm.

"No!" I gasped, taking a step away.

And that's when I saw the others.

Dark shadows emerged from behind buildings. Seven bariwolves prowled into the street.

Monsters answering a call.

"Shit." Cathlin pulled me against her side, dragging us both against the tavern's wall as the pack stepped into view.

A bariwolf emerged from beside the corner of the tavern.

All it had to do was turn, and it would see us pressed against the locked door.

It was five feet away, the fur on the back of its neck raised. It was either the largest in the pack or it was just the closest, because the godsdamn creature was enormous.

My breath lodged in my throat. I refused to blink. I stared at it while its focus was solely locked on the Guardian, still fighting. Only now he had more monsters to slay.

How? He couldn't fight nine monsters alone.

The door at our back swung open, swallowing Cathlin and me whole as we both fell backward, her keeping her balance as I landed hard on my ass.

The curvy blonde I'd seen yesterday dragged me away enough to slam the door, then barricade it with a board.

I crawled on my hands and knees to the nearest window, pressing my face to the glass in time to see the bariwolf that had been standing beside us leap onto the tavern's porch. My elbows knocked hard as I threw myself on the floor.

The woman slid down the door, tears coating her cheeks as she curled herself into a ball.

Cathlin crouched beside her, meeting my gaze as she pressed one finger to her lips.

On the street, the monsters roared. There were more screams from beyond the tavern's walls. And the thud of enormous feet vibrated from the bariwolf just outside.

Was it waiting us out? Were these monsters smart enough to know we couldn't hide in here forever? How long until it broke through the window's glass?

We were all hiding.

And one man was out there fighting.

He was going to die, wasn't he? He couldn't fight that many monsters, not alone.

My heart lurched. He was too stubborn, too much of a monster himself, to die. He hadn't pestered me enough to die. Not today.

I shifted my satchel, opening the flap. Then I took out my knives, clutching them in my shaking hands.

I couldn't hide. Not while he was out there.

A snap of fingers drew my attention to Cathlin. The blonde was curled at her side, head in her lap. She shook her head, gaze flickering to my knives. Then she pointed to the far wall.

To the crossbow mounted above a shelf of bottles.

I set my knives and satchel aside and began crawling, creeping past table legs until I was behind the bar. Then I stood and lifted the weapon off the wall. The bolts were loose beside a jar of pickled eggs.

With them in my fist, I risked a look at the glass.

The bariwolf stared back.

Its hot breath fogged a circle on the window.

There was murder and hunger in its soulless eyes as I loaded a bolt, gritting my teeth as I locked it into the taut string. Then I lifted the weapon, which was heavier than the one I'd been practicing with in Treow. But I summoned all my strength and aimed for the monster's face.

How many times had my weapons master in Roslo bemoaned my poor aim? I was going to miss. Without a doubt, I was going to miss.

But what if I didn't? What if all that shooting at trees meant I wasn't going to be bariwolf food?

I adjusted my grip, drawing in a breath as the monster backed away from the glass. Any moment now, it would come forward. Any second, it would dive inside.

Except it never came. I waited and waited and waited, until my arms began to tremble from the weight of the crossbow.

Cathlin shifted, standing tall. She gave me a wary look as she shuffled toward the window, standing at its edge to peer outside.

And that's when the crash sounded.

Not from the window beside Cathlin. From the one on the other side, closest to the blonde.

The giant bariwolf flew inside, shards of glass spraying across the tavern.

The blonde's scream was drowned out by the bariwolf's roar as it pivoted, sinking its teeth into her back, picking her up with its jaws and flinging her body across the room.

I pulled the trigger and sent the bolt flying, the force of the recoil sending me crashing backward into the bottles of liquor. They broke around me as the bariwolf snarled.

The bolt jutted from the monster's chest. Wounded but certainly not dead.

Shit.

"Run!" Cathlin screamed, racing for the hallway that extended past the bar.

I flew through the narrow space, following her down the length of the building.

The bariwolf thrashed as it knocked into tables and walls and chairs. As it slipped on the shards of broken glass before it could leap into the hall.

Cathlin shouldered a door at the back of the building, sending us outside and into the blinding sunlight.

"Upstairs." She shoved me to a staircase that led up the building's backside.

As we climbed, I loaded another bolt into the crossbow, heart racing.

There was a vibration in the building, like the bariwolf was ramming its head against the door that had been flung closed.

We reached the landing and Cathlin yanked open the door, then slammed it behind us and slid the locking bar into place.

An apartment. Probably the blond woman's home.

There was a moment of stillness, my pulse a thunder in my ears as I stared at the door. Waiting for the horror to follow. Beyond the apartment, roars and screams came from every direction. Muffled. Petrifying.

"The woman. Downstairs." My voice cracked. "Is she dead?" She was probably dead.

Cathlin swallowed hard. "I don't know."

We'd left her. We'd left her down there with that monster.

We'd left the Guardian alone on the street.

I spun and raced through the apartment, heart drumming as I darted through a simple room with a vase of freshly picked wildflowers beside the bed.

Had he brought her those flowers this morning?

My insides twisted, my stomach churning so hard my breakfast threatened to come up as I went to her bedroom's window and peered onto the street.

There were five black monsters lying on the ground. Dead.

And the Guardian was battling three.

Blood ran down his face and arm. He fought with his sword in one hand while the other stayed clutched to his side, pressed to a wound that gushed around his fingers.

How much longer could he fight? How much more could he withstand?

Despite what he wanted everyone in Turah to believe, he wasn't immortal. His movements were slower, sluggish. And the bariwolves attacked in unison, moving more like one monster than three.

He was going to die.

While I stood and watched.

I set the crossbow on the bed and forced the window open. Then, with the weapon in one arm, I climbed out to the narrow balcony that ran the face of the tavern. It groaned and creaked beneath my weight as I shuffled toward the wobbling rail.

"No." Cathlin reached for my arm, but I was too far gone.

"I can do this."

I can do this.

Her eyes flooded with worry as she looked past me to the Guardian.

And as she watched him continue to fight alone, I saw her do the same calculation I'd done a moment ago.

He was losing this fight.

I took another step, and the balcony shifted, dropping an inch as it groaned beneath my weight. "Shit."

"Odessa," Cathlin gasped, her eyes wide as I froze.

I held my breath, staring at the boards beneath my feet. Just a few more moments. It only had to hold for a few more moments.

Mack, guide this bolt.

It was the first time I'd prayed to the God of War.

"Careful," she hissed, the vibration from the bariwolf inside still shaking the walls.

I positioned the crossbow, taking a fortifying breath as I aimed for the fray.

Don't miss, don't miss, don't miss.

I squeezed the trigger, hearing a yelp as it struck a monster, causing its hind leg to buckle.

The Guardian took advantage, his sword slicing through the bariwolf's neck until its head dropped to the dirt with a thud. Then his eyes found mine, just long enough for him to send up a warning glare.

I was supposed to be hiding.

I loaded another bolt instead.

The bariwolves were relentless, their jaws snapping at him in rapid succession. But he managed to dodge their teeth, deflecting them with that sword as he gripped the hilt with both hands.

Blood poured from his side.

I aimed the crossbow, taking another steadying inhale. Then I pulled the trigger, missing entirely as it flew into the dirt. "Damn it."

The Guardian let out a roar of his own as he jumped, his back rolling over a bariwolf's as he came down on its opposite side, putting both wolves on his right. Forcing them to reposition if they wanted him to be surrounded.

The one-eyed monster let out a snarl that filled the street. It took a step back, letting the other bariwolf face off with the Guardian while it stayed out of reach.

I loaded another bolt and took aim at that one-eyed terror. It was in my sights, its heart my target. I exhaled. I blinked.

And it was gone.

It fucking ran away.

I shifted my aim for the last remaining monster, but before I could shoot, the Guardian pivoted, stepping into my line of fire. Blocking my shot.

The bariwolf bared its teeth, sinking onto its haunches like it was about to leap.

The Guardian didn't give it a chance to attack. With that unnatural speed and grace, he dropped to a knee and rolled, bringing his sword across the monster's knees, cutting off its front legs. Then he plunged the sword through the bariwolf's chest.

Through its vicious heart.

"By the mother." I sagged, letting the crossbow drop. My knees began to shake, my arms trembling. Tears filled my eyes as I stared at the carnage below.

The Guardian jerked his sword free from the monster's body and turned, chest heaving.

I shifted my weight, ready to get off this rickety balcony, but as I took a backward step, the entire thing collapsed, disappearing from beneath my feet.

"Ah!" My scream was cut short as I managed to grab the balcony's railing. Half of the platform stayed attached to the building while the other fell past me, dropping onto the porch below.

My feet dangled in the air, the crossbow still tight in my hand.

"Odessa!" Cathlin yelled.

I eyed the drop, my grip already beginning to falter. There'd be no water to break this fall. No, this was going to hurt. But I couldn't hold on. Not for much longer.

So I held tight to the crossbow and counted to three.

One. Two.

Three was a quick drop and a jolt through my legs that was so hard I careened sideways, my temple smacking against the porch's post. White spots exploded behind my eyes as I fell to my side, and wood splinters rained down from above.

"Ouch." I pushed up on an arm, pain radiating from my head to my toes. But I climbed to my feet, not wanting to stay if the rest of the balcony decided to crumble.

"Cross!"

I blinked, clearing the haze from my vision as I looked out across the street, finding the Guardian's silver eyes.

They were wide. Panicked.

And he was running.

Why was he running?

Then I felt the porch shift, the planks shudder beneath my boots. I whirled, knowing what I'd find.

The bariwolf that had hunted us inside, that had killed that beautiful blond woman, was barreling toward me through the tavern, toward the window it had shattered.

I lifted the crossbow, my fingers fumbling for the trigger as silver streaked past my face.

The Guardian's sword lodged itself into the bariwolf's skull.

The monster crashed into me, sending me flying off the porch and into the dirt as its head was split in two.

It dropped with a sickening thump in the exact spot where I'd been standing.

My face was sticky and hot. I raised a hand, touching my cheek, and my fingertips came away coated in putrid green.

Blood.

The same green blood of the marroweel that had tried to kill me in the Krisenth. The same green I'd seen from a grizzur weeks ago.

My fingers began to tremble as I stared at the blood, realizing just how close I'd been to death. Again.

He'd saved my life. Again.

He's sworn to protect you.

The Guardian.

The slayer of legends.

His hand clamped around my arm, hauling me to my feet.

I found my balance, about to thank him for saving my life—again—but his expression blanked my mind. So did the blood and gore and dust and sweat that covered his face and caked his beard.

There were cuts on his face. A gash on his arm. Every injury of his was coated in that horrid green.

Fury quaked through his body, his grip on my arm punishingly tight. The silver in his eyes swirled so fast, so dark, they were like storm clouds streaked with lightning.

I was still holding the crossbow. As he leaned in closer, the weapon became trapped between us. The tip of the bolt dug into his vest.

My finger was still on the trigger.

All I had to do was squeeze.

"Do it." His voice was a terrible whisper. A challenge. A dare.

His fingers dug into my flesh. His eyes bored into mine.

Do it.

This was the chance I'd never have again. This was how I proved to my family I was more than they believed.

I closed my eyes. I blocked out those silver eyes.

Pull the trigger. Kill him.

My finger wouldn't move.

His hold on my arm tightened. "Look at me," he growled.

My eyes flew open.

And what I saw made my knees buckle.

This wasn't the same man I'd been verbally sparring with for weeks. This wasn't the same man who'd taunted me relentlessly.

This man was a monster.

"Odessa!" Cathlin burst through the tavern's door, nearly tripping over the dead bariwolf. She jumped over its body and leaped off the porch.

By the time she reached my side, the Guardian was already gone.

Thirty

My room at the inn was as quiet as a tomb. Light from the twin moons streamed through the window. There were no clouds in the sky, nothing to obscure the beams. It was as if Ama and Oda knew that Ashmore needed a bright night.

My hair was still damp from the bath I took after the attack. I'd been so filthy that the maid had asked to hose me down outside before letting me climb in the bath. My clothes were disgusting, my tunic not even worth washing. She'd taken it to burn and lent me a too-large tunic to wear to bed.

Seventeen people were dead, including the blond woman who'd owned the tavern.

Sariah. Her name was Sariah.

She'd inherited the tavern from her parents, who'd died six months ago on a trip to Perris. They'd gone for supplies and never arrived, their bodies never found. Whatever monster had eaten them had consumed them entirely, skin and bones.

Now their daughter was buried in a fresh grave that I'd helped dig. There was no room left in Ashmore's cemetery, so she'd been laid to rest beneath a nearby tree.

The infirmary was overflowing with injured survivors. The air reeked from the fires that burned the bariwolf corpses.

My body was clean. My face scrubbed. But I could still smell the stink of that rotten, green blood. I could still feel it coating my cheeks. And every time I closed my eyes, I saw a monster's face.

So I stared at the ceiling, idly toying with my necklace, its weight and warmth a familiar comfort as I waited for dawn.

I assumed that would be when the Guardian would come to collect me. Unless he'd left Ashmore already. I hadn't seen him since the tavern. Since he'd dared me to shoot him.

Where did we go from here? What happened next?

I'd been in Turah for over a month. There were moments when it felt like no time at all had passed since I'd met Zavier and the Guardian in the throne room. Then there were times like this, when it felt like a lifetime had passed since I'd sailed away from Quentis's shores.

What now? What did fate have in store for me next?

I guessed I'd wait for someone to give me orders. I had no illusions that I'd be granted any semblance of freedom after this foolish, ridiculous trip.

My journey to Ashmore had been an epic mistake. If not for me, Sariah wouldn't have opened the tavern door. She wouldn't have risked her hiding spot.

Maybe the sixteen others might not have survived, but she would have lived. Her death wasn't my fault, but I felt the responsibility for it anyway. I would for the rest of my life.

"I'm sorry, Sariah." The guilt was so stifling I could barely breathe. The regret sat so heavily on my chest it pinned me to this bed. My entire body hurt from the fall off that balcony. Bruises would appear in a few days, on my ribs and hips and legs.

My arm.

But nothing hurt worse than my heart.

The door flew open.

I gasped as it slammed against the wall.

And then the Guardian staggered inside, swaying with every step. "Talking to the dead?"

His words were slurred, his movements listless.

"Are you drunk?"

He lifted a shoulder. Not a yes. Not a no.

His clothes were clean. His hair was wet. There was no sign of the injuries he'd had earlier. The gash on his arm had vanished. The cuts and scratches on his face were gone. He wasn't clutching his side like he had been during the fight.

Was that another of his powers? The ability to heal an injury that would have laid low any mortal man?

He shuffled forward a few steps before dropping to the floor, landing hard with a grunt. "I didn't think I'd find you here."

"Where would I be?"

"On your way to Quentissssss." He hissed the *s*, letting it stretch too long. "Scampering back to your precious kingdom."

"You are drunk." I flopped onto my back, crossing my arms over my chest. Except as my head sank into the pillow, the guilt returned.

He'd known Sariah. As far as I knew, he'd cared for her. I'd cost him someone special, and the guilt kept on building.

"Here." I lifted off my pillow and tossed it to the floor.

"So generous, my queen."

He shouldn't call me that. I was not a queen.

Queens didn't sneak out of encampments. Queens didn't put others at risk. Queens helped people. They did not hurt them.

I was never supposed to be here. I was not the right person to be the Sparrow. I wasn't brave enough, strong enough, for Turah. This was a place for a woman like Mae. Someone bold and fierce. Someone unbreakable.

"I'm sorry about Sariah. It's my fault."

The Guardian scoffed. "Did you shred her spine with your teeth? I didn't realize you had such a vicious bite. I'll have to be more careful."

"You know what I mean. If I hadn't gone into the tavern, she'd still be alive."

He sat up, punched the pillow into a ball, then stuffed it beneath his head. "Every person in Ashmore knows the risks of staying. It's their choice. It was Sariah's. Don't play the martyr, Cross. She would have hated that."

"I'm still sorry."

"So am I." His breathing evened out, and when I lifted off the mattress to peer at the floor, his eyes were closed. But he wasn't asleep, not yet. He crossed and uncrossed his legs, probably trying to get comfortable.

"Stop staring at me, Sparrow. Go to sleep."

I curled onto my side, still too raw and ragged to risk closing my eyes. So I stared at the pretty wallpaper, my hands clasped together beneath my cheek. "Why do you call me Sparrow?"

Why didn't he use my first name?

"Because you're a bird."

"What?" Meaning I was trying to fly away? Or that I was small?

I was certain that in his fuzzy brain, that answer made sense. Maybe I needed to stick with simpler questions tonight.

"Will we go to Allesaria before the migration?"

"No."

It was what I'd expected. Just not what I wanted.

"There was something wrong with those bariwolves, wasn't there? It's the green blood."

Those beasts had been sick.

"Yes."

My insides knotted. "What's wrong with them?"

He was quiet for a long moment. Then he whispered, "Lyssa."

"What is Lyssa? I've never heard of it before."

Silence.

When I twisted to peer over the edge of my bed again, the Guardian was asleep.

Thirty-One

The déjà vu of waking to only a pillow on the room's floor and a note on the table was so strong I almost hoped yesterday had been a dream. That I'd leave the Ashmore inn and find Sariah at her tavern.

But when I slid out of bed, I was still wearing the borrowed tunic, and when I pulled on my boots, they were speckled with putrid green blood.

I slipped out of the room, my satchel strapped across my chest, more than ready to leave Ashmore. The Guardian wouldn't need to worry that I'd dare more escape attempts from Treow. At least for now, I wanted nothing more than to hide away in my treehouse and nurse my wounded heart.

And body.

Shades, I hurt. Every step was agony as I descended the staircase to the inn's lobby. My muscles were sore and tender. Bruises were blooming across my skin.

I was alive to suffer today. I'd swallow these pains. Seventeen people could not say the same.

"Odessa." Cathlin stopped me as I passed the inn's small parlor.

"Good morning." I gave her a sad smile as she pulled me in for a hug.

It was nice to be hugged.

"Are you all right?" she asked, letting me go.

I shrugged. "You?"

She shrugged, too. "You're leaving today."

A statement, not a question.

She walked to the chair where she'd been sitting, retrieved a book, and handed it over. "I brought you this. It's a book on Turan customs. I'll bring more when I see you again."

"When will that be?"

"Soon. I'll be leaving Ashmore within the week. I have a goodbye to say first. Though I don't want to rush it."

"To the woman you came to visit."

Cathlin nodded. "Yes."

"I'm sorry I didn't ask about her yesterday." I'd been preoccupied with digging graves. "Is she...all right?"

"She's fine. Devastated like most. But Turah is full of survivors. She'll endure, like you. She's strong, like you."

"I don't feel strong," I said on a breath.

"Yet you are." Cathlin's eyes softened as she brushed an errant curl off my forehead. Then she took a step backward and pressed both hands over her heart, giving me a slight bow.

"What does that mean? That gesture?"

"It means I wish you a safe journey, Princess Odessa Wolfe."

Normally, I would have balked at the formal name, but there was something in her voice that gave me pause. Something serious that said I needed to get used to that title.

To embrace it.

Who was this woman? We'd survived the unthinkable yesterday, and I didn't even know her last name. Maybe it didn't matter.

I put my hands over my heart and bowed.

Boots thudded across the floor. Purposeful, long strides that I was beginning to recognize.

The Guardian stopped at my side, his attention on Cathlin. "You're leaving."

Another statement.

"Yes."

I waited for his hands to cover his heart, but instead, he pulled her in for a hug.

Wait, he hugged? That seemed so...sweet. Very un-Guardian-like. When he let her go, he jerked his chin for me to follow. No sweet for me.

"Goodbye, Cathlin," I said.

"Farewell, Odessa."

I hoped I'd see her again soon. Life felt fragile at the moment. Fleeting.

With my book tucked into my satchel, I rushed to catch up to the Guardian.

He and his horse waited outside. The stallion's black coat was glossy beneath the morning sun.

The Guardian stroked the animal's cheek, murmuring something low. The horse leaned into his touch.

It was a lovely day, clear skies and a crisp sweetness in the air. It seemed like a waste. No one here would enjoy it, certainly not me. People walked with their heads bowed as they hurried down the streets.

All happiness had been slaughtered.

"They should have had a warning. Protection," I said.

The Guardian's jaw clenched as he fastened his sword and its scabbard to the saddle.

I hadn't meant it as an insult, but as I replayed my words, I heard it from his side of the horse. I'd just implied he'd failed these people. "I didn't mean from you."

"And who else would protect them?"

"The king. The crown. Can't Zavier step in? Send some of his rangers to these towns to help?"

The Guardian's eyes, hazel and angry, met mine. The glare was all I needed to realize I'd crossed a line.

A reminder that this princess, this future queen, this Sparrow, was to be seen and not heard.

"I'm only asking. I think I have that right."

"Really?" He arched an eyebrow. "Who gave you that right?"

"My blood. The moment I signed my name on that treaty. The day Zavier claimed his bride prize. I'm here. I'm in Turah. I have the right just like any other person in this kingdom. This cannot stand. This cannot continue."

"And what do you suggest, my queen? What should we do about this? What solution do you propose that Zavier, myself, and all of our rangers have not already considered?"

A flood of embarrassment made me draw my shoulders up to my ears, wishing I could be like a turtle and duck my head inside a shell.

I didn't have a solution. I didn't know anything about Turan politics.

So I kept my mouth shut.

"That's what I thought," he muttered, turning to adjust the stirrup.

"I want to make a difference," I said. "I want to do what's right. I want to help."

The Guardian stilled but didn't turn. "Get on the horse, Cross."

I shifted closer to the stallion, hiking up my skirts in an attempt to put my foot in the stirrup. But the animal was too tall, and I was too short. I couldn't reach.

The Guardian let out a frustrated growl, picked me up by the waist, and plopped me onto the saddle.

"Thanks?" I adjusted my skirts, wishing I had another pair of pants. "What about you?"

"What about me?"

"What horse will you ride?"

"Mine."

Oh, hell.

He flicked the hems of my skirts. "Move these out of my way."

I balled them up as best I could, the fabric bunching on my lap. Then he swung into the saddle behind me, his thighs hugging my own. His chest pressed against my back as he took up the reins, his arms locking me in place.

Without delay, the horse started down the street.

The movement forced me deeper into the Guardian's hold. The heat from his body, the scents of leather and spice and wind, were inescapable. Damn how I wished I hated that smell.

This ride would be agony. Absolute torture.

Maybe that was the idea.

"Relax," he ordered.

Relaxing meant I'd have to lean against him. Sink into that broad chest. Melt against his frame. Not. A. Chance.

"I am relaxed."

"Sure you are." His voice was too close to my ear.

A shiver rolled down my spine.

And without a doubt, he felt it.

Another day, he probably would have teased me for the reaction. Another day, he would have reveled in the way I squirmed. But today was not a day for jokes. Not as we passed the burial grounds outside of town.

I took a long look at the tree where we'd laid Sariah to rest, then cast my gaze to the sky, to the twin moons' faint outline. Even battling the sun, they shone white.

The color of Arabella's shade.

I hoped that Sariah's soul, that all those from Ashmore, had come to rest with the Goddess of Love.

There were those in Calandra who didn't worship the gods. They didn't believe in the Six or their shades. They believed our bodies returned to the earth as dust. That we simply ceased.

Then there were those who believed our souls were reborn, that for every life lost, another was created. That somewhere in this realm, Sariah's soul was breathing anew.

"Do you believe in the gods?" I asked the Guardian.

"Why do you ask?"

"No man should have survived that fight yesterday. You have powers unlike anything I've ever seen. I guess I wanted to know if you believe the gods gave them to you as gifts."

His laugh was low. Menacing. A rumble from his body that vibrated against mine. "What you call gifts, I call a curse. Yes, I believe in the gods. I believe they watch us from their precious shades. And I believe they're vindictive, manipulative bastards intent on tormenting us from their thrones."

Never in my life had I heard a person speak of the gods with such hate. Such malice. I wasn't sure what to say to that. It felt like we were inviting trouble, taunting them so.

"Any other questions this morning, Sparrow?"

I shook my head.

We passed the edge of town and set out on the road that would lead us to Treow. A day. That was all I had to endure. Just one day.

Except with a tug of the reins, he steered the horse off the road. He turned us away from the forest and toward a range of mountains, its peaks jagged and capped in white. Beneath them looked to be a river valley.

"We're not going to Treow, are we?"

"No."

"Where are we going?"

"Ellder."

"Why?" What about my things? What about Brielle and Jocelyn?

"Will you always ask so many questions, Cross?"

"Yes."

He sighed. "Zavier."

My stomach twisted. My husband was in Ellder. And I was being returned to my keeper.

"All right." I sat tall and rigid, attempting to maintain a fraction of space between our bodies. I didn't let the sinking feeling in my chest weigh me down.

This was for the best. I should be with Zavier. We needed more quiet walks, time to be alone. I wasn't certain, but I had the feeling that the Guardian wouldn't stay at the fortress. Not once I'd been locked behind its walls, no longer needing his protection. Which meant after this ride, he'd likely disappear.

Good. I needed him to disappear. To go away for weeks, months, and give me time to put my head, my heart, back into place. To banish him from my mind.

We argued constantly. He was a thorn in my side. The sooner he was gone, the better.

The horse's hooves were the only sound as we rode across the landscape. We flowed up and down the hills that surrounded Ashmore, until the town itself was nothing but a memory. My restless night caught up to me by midday, and every few minutes, I covered a yawn.

"You should rest." It was the first thing the Guardian had spoken in hours.

"I'm fine," I lied, righting my shoulders from where they'd slumped.

"Sure you are."

I concentrated on the foothills in the distance, forcing my eyes open as the trees slowly grew taller and taller against their mountain backdrop. Every few moments, I'd look left, then right, searching for any monsters that might come out of hiding and attack.

"The pack from yesterday. Is that the normal size?" I asked.

"No. It was larger. Usually bariwolves travel in packs of three or four."

Gods. That pack had been more than double. Was it their number that had made them fearless enough to strike a town?

Those people in Ashmore were lucky to have had the Guardian around. To rid this area of that pack. But I had a feeling if I told him that, he'd only scoff.

I might blame myself for Sariah, but he blamed himself for all seventeen deaths.

The hours dragged on, and the heaviness in my eyelids became impossible to fight. Until the battle was futile.

Until somewhere in Turah, curled against the wrong man, I drifted off to sleep.

Thirty-Two

*O*dessa.

The sound of my father's voice startled me from a nightmare.

I'd been in the throne room, on my knees. Mae's knife at my neck.

He'd ordered her to kill me. My punishment for returning to Roslo with no information about Allesaria. Beside me on the marble floor, blood seeping from their open throats, were Brielle and Jocelyn.

I shook the mental image away, blinking clear the fog of sleep as I took in my surroundings.

The early light of dawn colored the sky. I'd slept all night against the Guardian's chest.

He'd stopped us atop a steep rise. He sat motionless behind me, his horse unmoving beneath.

There was a cliff beside us, its jagged rocks dropping to a raging river. The water crashed as it traveled, and for a moment, I closed my eyes and just let myself listen. I pretended that noise was ocean waves and I was on my cliffside in Roslo.

Something stirred in my chest as I took in the view. A sense of wonder. Peace.

It might not be *my* special place, but there was so much beauty here it was hard to comprehend it all.

On the other side of the river was an endless forest, thick and green. It filled the space between us and the looming indigo mountains with their pristine, snowcapped peaks. The colors were so vibrant, it was like stepping into a dream.

"When I was a boy, my mother brought me here for the first time. She made me sit beside her for an hour, even though all I wanted to do was chase around and hunt for berries. At the time, it felt like a punishment. Now, I see what she was trying to do. It was one of those lessons I couldn't appreciate until I got older."

He'd only mentioned his mother once before. What about his father? Did he have siblings?

It was an odd feeling to know this man yet know nothing about him.

I knew his expressions. I knew the way he moved. I knew how the air charged when he was angry and the realm blurred when he was close.

He was fiercely loyal to his people. He loved his kingdom. He was strong and unbreakable, but gentleness could emerge from that hard exterior. In the way he hugged Cathlin. How he acted with Evangeline. Even the affection he showed his horse.

But I didn't know if his mother was alive. I didn't know about his family or his education or his childhood home. I didn't know if he'd been born with these powers, these gifts. Or if he'd been cursed by a spiteful god.

It bothered me, more than it should, that at best, I could only consider him an acquaintance.

The Guardian stared into the distance, his eyes a different shade of green. This was a new color. Not the vivid emerald I'd seen countless times when he was in a mood to tease me mercilessly. No, this was a deep shade of hunter.

The color of Turan forests.

"It's beautiful." The forest. Those eyes.

He dropped his gaze, meeting mine.

I was still cradled against him, having shifted in my sleep toward the arm he'd curled around my shoulders. I should move. Sit straight. Get off this horse and put some distance between us.

But the truth I was terrified to admit, even to myself, was that I didn't want to move.

Unless he tossed me out of this saddle, I was going nowhere.

His expression was open and unguarded. Utterly consuming. More magnificent than even this Turan scene. He searched my eyes the way I searched his. For answers. Salvation. Mercy.

There was a tether between us.

Gods save us when it snapped.

Why couldn't I feel this way for the man who'd claimed me?

Our mouths were too close. All it would take was a shift and we'd collide. We'd crash into each other, and the shock waves would destroy us both.

I needed him to say something mean. To strike a nerve. To bruise my heart. I needed him to hurt me so thoroughly, I'd never forgive him.

"I hate you."

It should have broken the moment. It should have pissed him off. But he stared at me like I was something to behold. Something to cherish.

Something to protect.

"Yes, you do," he said. "Don't forget."

"Never."

There was no such thing as forgetting a man like the Guardian. Not for me.

Still, once we reached Ellder, I would try.

"We must go."

I nodded, sitting tall. Then I took one last look beyond the cliff. "Thank you for bringing me here."

"You're welcome, my queen."

We didn't speak for the rest of the long journey, not even as we ate dried fruit and nuts and meat, sharing water from a canteen.

The trail through the forest was thick. Rain from a recent storm clung to the branches, and whenever a limb skimmed my dress, water would soak into the material. Night was falling, and beneath the trees, it was becoming difficult to see the narrow path ahead. A howl rang out from somewhere in the woods, making me tense.

The Guardian didn't so much as flinch.

By the time we reached the fortress, I was wet and cold. Part of me was glad to be here. To get off this horse. The other part wasn't ready for this ride to be over.

Torches mounted on the fortress's walls burned bright against the dark. The walls stood as tall as the surrounding trees, rising so high that no monster could scale their face. There were hundreds and hundreds of logs, each stripped of their bark to form a smooth barricade. It stretched so far I couldn't see where either side ended in the darkness.

The Guardian stopped his horse outside the gates and fitted two fingers to his lips, letting out a piercing whistle, different from those I'd heard in Treow.

"Open the gates!" a man shouted from the ramparts above.

The hinges groaned as the men hauled the heavy wood open, swinging like double doors for us to ride inside. As soon as we were beyond the threshold, the soldiers closed us in.

The courtyard was alight with fires, burning hot in small basins.

Men dressed in grizzur leather, similar to the Guardian, all nodded and dipped their heads as we came to a stop. Whispers filled the air as he dismounted.

That's the Guardian.

He's here.

The Guardian. The Guardian. The Guardian.

Did he not come to Ellder often? The wide eyes and open stares answered my question.

A young boy ran up to him, taking the horse's reins.

"See that he gets plenty of water and food," the Guardian said. "He doesn't like sharing a stall with other horses."

"I'll put him in his own, sir."

"Good." He clapped the boy on the shoulder, then came to my side, holding out a hand to help me down.

I tried to slide out of the saddle gracefully, but after yesterday's fall and a day spent riding, my legs didn't cooperate. I crashed into his chest as I tipped off the side.

He caught me at the waist and set me down, holding on for a moment until I was steady. Then, while he unlatched his saddlebags, I smoothed down my skirts and adjusted the strap on my satchel, busying my hands as the people around us continued to stare and whisper.

Who is she?

Do you know her?

Who's that riding with the Guardian?

He flung his saddlebags over a shoulder, then clamped a hand over my wrist, pulling me along as he walked out of the courtyard and toward a road that seemed to split the town inside the walls in half.

Streets were organized much like Ashmore, in straight lines and orderly rows. Except there were holes down the center of every lane, holes as wide as my waist that looked to be as deep as I was tall.

"What are those?" I asked.

"For the migration. We put wooden spikes in each, crowding the streets so it's difficult for a crux to land. Once they're dug, workers will start on the spikes. They'll be buried as deep as they are tall, just like the exterior walls."

"Ah." Another deterrent for the monsters. Another way the Turans protected themselves.

The buildings all had wooden roofs, but there were some with metal spikes that stuck up at all angles, likely other measures to protect against the crux. Golden light spilled from windows, but we moved so quickly I didn't have a chance to see inside.

"You can explore tomorrow," he said. "Think you can manage to stay within the fortress's wall?"

I couldn't make that promise. I didn't want to lie.

So I stole Zavier's tactic and stayed quiet.

The Guardian grumbled under his breath.

We passed three side streets before we finally turned off the main road.

He didn't let go of my wrist as he marched us to a wide house with a square front. It was a simple building, and like the others we'd passed, its exterior was covered with rich, russet boards. Every window was dark, the house either empty or asleep. A walkway ran the length of the second floor.

The homes in Turah seemed to be built for function, not flash. The only thing extravagant about this one was the front door.

Inlaid into its wooden face was a carving of a wolf. The Turan emblem. This was Zavier's house.

The Guardian let go of my wrist as he led me to a staircase that curved around the building's corner, leading up to the walkway.

I kept my hand on the railing as we climbed, my heart inching into my throat with every stair. Was Zavier up here? Were these his quarters? Was I being delivered to my husband's bedroom?

The Guardian's boots thudded along the walkway's boards, the rhythm matching the beat of my pounding heart as he walked to the single door and turned the knob.

I stayed outside, hand still clutched to the railing as he went inside and lit a lantern, then another. Well, if Zavier was in there, the Guardian wouldn't have simply barged in. So I pried my hand off the railing and walked through the door.

It looked to be a private suite. The sitting room had two brown leather chairs bracketing a fireplace. They sat atop a rug woven with bold colors, burgundy, chocolate, and pine green.

The Guardian was crouched beside the hearth, striking a flint box to get a fire going.

Beyond the sitting area, through an open doorway, a large bed sat covered in a thick, taupe quilt and plush pillows. And against the wall, lined in neat rows with the lids propped open, were my trunks. Most held my dresses. One had a glass jar of my hair dye on top.

When had he sent for those?

"I'm not going back to Treow, am I?"

"No." The fire crackled to life, and he stood, brushing his palms clean.

My heart sank, missing that little treehouse already. "What about Brielle and Jocelyn?"

"They'll stay at the encampment for now."

Was that my punishment for Ashmore? That we'd be separated, like children who'd been caught causing trouble?

"Get some rest," he said, walking past me for the door.

"Guardian." I grabbed his wrist, my grip firm on the leather cuff that molded to his forearm.

His hand fisted, but he didn't pull away. "What?"

"I…" *I don't know.*

I wasn't ready to be alone.

I wasn't ready for him to leave.

Once he stepped out that door, I was going to have to let him go.

And I wasn't ready.

His free hand touched my arm in the exact place where he'd grabbed me yesterday outside the tavern, and I winced. "I'm sorry."

"You didn't hurt me." Yes, it was tender today. My entire body was sore. But there were no marks. No bruises from his grip.

"Maybe not." The sadness in his green eyes cracked my heart. "But I could have."

Was that why he'd gotten drunk last night? Because he'd lost control? Because I could have been a victim of his rage?

His gaze shifted to my nose like he was counting the freckles dusted across its bridge. His hand lifted to a curl at my temple, tracing the spiral with a fingertip. "You don't have to hide who you are, Cross. Not here."

Not in Turah.

Not with him.

The Guardian opened his mouth like he was about to say something. But then he must have changed his mind. He eased out of my grip and, before I could blink, disappeared into the night.

I gave myself a few moments to breathe, to close my eyes and savor the scent of him lingering in the air. It would be gone by morning.

And if I had to guess, so would he.

It was for the best. It was better this way. I repeated those lies over and over and over as I unpacked my trunks. As I settled into this new home.

As I emptied my jar of hair dye out the bedroom window.

Thirty-Three

The knocking on my front door wasn't really a knock but a constant stream of taps.

"I'm coming!" I laughed as I walked out of my bedroom.

The knocking continued.

And with it, my day would begin. Just as it had every morning for the past week since I'd arrived in Ellder.

The moment I opened the door, my visitor streaked inside, racing into the sitting room to launch herself into a chair.

"Good morning, Evie."

She giggled as she pushed her dark hair out of her face. "Want to play hide-and-seek?"

"After yesterday? Not even a little bit," I said, closing the door.

The rules we'd established for the game should have been easy to follow. She was allowed to hide anywhere in my suite or her house while I counted to fifty. Except she'd changed the rules during our third game and snuck out to the gardens to play with a litter of baby kittens. I'd spent nearly an hour searching for her, turning this place inside out. Then I'd had a panic attack because I'd lost Zavier's child.

When I'd frantically told Luella that I'd lost Evangeline, she'd frowned and helped me search. We'd found her ten minutes later, sitting between the rows of carrots with five balls of white-and-gray fur.

I was never playing hide-and-seek again.

"Then what are we going to do?" She kicked her legs, her boots smacking against the chair's side.

"What if we explored?"

She sat up straighter. "Explore where?"

"I don't know." I shrugged. "Ellder. Maybe you could show me around."

I'd spent a week hiding from the world, either in this suite or Zavier's rooms on the first floor. Hiding.

And punishing myself.

For Ashmore. For abandoning Brielle and Jocelyn. For the Guardian.

Each morning, Evie would come to visit. The first day, Luella had joined her to say hello. After Evie had invited herself inside the suite, she'd also invited me to become her newest playtime companion.

Luella didn't seem to mind having a few hours to herself each morning, and I'd needed Evie's knocking like I'd needed Arthy's hugs when I lived in Roslo. She was filling the hole in my heart, the place where I'd always kept family.

This girl's smile had become the best part of my day.

Returning her to Luella for lunch and afternoon lessons was the worst.

With nothing else to do, I'd slink upstairs to the suite. I'd read Cathlin's book, practice with my knives, and sketch my version of a Turan map in my journal. When I was finished, I'd stare at the ceiling and dwell on my mistakes.

The pity party was over. I wasn't quite sure where I fit in yet at the fortress. It was time to find out—I had a feeling I'd be in Ellder for a while.

"Let's go." Evie jumped off the chair and ran for the door, snagging my hand as she passed. Then she pulled me outside to the walkway, leading me to the staircase.

It had been too dark the night the Guardian brought me here to appreciate the size of Zavier's house. It took up nearly an entire block. Most of the home was allocated to Evangeline and Luella. But it also included kitchens, laundry, and quarters for Evie's nanny and the other staff.

My suite upstairs was more room than I needed. I had the sitting room and a dining area. There was my bedroom, plus a spare. There was even a washroom, complete with a pitcher pump to fill the tub. The water wasn't hot, but I'd add a few boiling kettles and it was divine.

But my favorite part of this suite was the private balcony. From my perch on the second floor, I could see to the main road that split Ellder down the middle, and I'd watch people come and go.

There was a bakery across the street, and the owner brought his wife fresh flowers from the center market every morning. A teenage girl worked at a corner café, and so far, she seemed to be the only person who noticed me watching. If she saw me sitting outside, she'd give me a tiny wave—I'd wave back.

Every other afternoon, a young man carried a stack of papers from building to building. Ellder did have a paperman. He printed only fortress news, but when the paper arrived at my doorstep, I devoured every word.

Soldiers wandered up and down the streets, nodding and greeting those they passed on their way to and from the courtyard. From what I could tell, their shifts at the wall changed three times a day.

Each day, more wooden spikes were installed along the streets, their tips pointed and sharp.

Ellder was home to merchants and traders. Teachers and nurses. Families with children of all ages. And that massive wall and its soldiers kept them all safe.

It kept Evie safe.

From everything but trouble of her own making.

Five days ago, she'd escaped Luella's watchful eyes and snuck to the house kitchen, where she'd stolen a handful of tarts to eat instead of her regular lunch. She'd gotten sick all over her bed.

The day after that, she'd "accidentally" painted flowers on her armoire. The day after that, she'd "borrowed" a tin of rouge from Luella's vanity and smudged it all over her cheeks.

I'd never fallen in love with a person so fast.

It made the sting of being dumped here hurt a little less.

She'd been dumped here, too.

Zavier had left Ellder not long after relocating his daughter here from Treow. And the Guardian had left the same night he'd delivered me to my suite.

"Should we tell Luella that we're going to explore?" I waved to the carved front door.

"She's not in there. She made me promise to stay with you until she was done in the dungeons."

"Uh...Ellder has dungeons?" Why would Luella be visiting dungeons?

In Quentis, criminals were kept in a camp close to the Evon Ravine, though there were cells at the barracks where Banner's soldiers could keep them before they were transported to the camp.

I guess in Turah, criminals were kept in fortress dungeons.

"Yes, and they're creepy." Evie's face lit up. "Let's go there."

"Absolutely not."

"Why not?" Her smile morphed into a pout. It was adorable. Too adorable. She wielded that pout like a sword. "There's all these books and scrolls and weird stuff. Luella calls them trinkets."

"Wait. There are books in the dungeons?"

"Yep." She nodded, pulling me closer so she could whisper in my ear. "She doesn't know that I know about it, but I do."

Luella must be hiding them so that Ramsey's soldiers couldn't burn her books.

"Show me."

"Yes!" Evie pumped an arm in the air, then tore off down the street.

"Hey, wait up." I laughed, jogging to keep up as she ran for the main road.

Evangeline checked over her shoulder every now and again, making sure I was still behind her. Each time, her smile would widen, her bright eyes sparkling, the blue starbursts as bold as the sky above. Blue, the eye color from Ozarth's land.

Why would Zavier, a crown prince, not ensure his child was born on Turan soil so she'd have green starbursts? Maybe her mother had insisted she be born in Ozarth.

If—when—Zavier and I had children someday, how would Evie fit into the mix? Zavier didn't want her to be a part of royal life. But at some point, we'd be expected to produce an heir. Was he going to hide all of his children?

Or just his daughters?

It felt like there was a set of scales in my mind, on one side questions, the other answers. The question side was so heavy that they were spilling over. The answer side was all but empty.

And I had a hunch I wasn't going to learn much locked away in this fortress.

As Cathlin had promised, Ellder was built against the mountains. Cliffs rose up before us in sheets of smooth, gray rock. It reminded me of the second campsite, where we'd slept on the dirt and nearly been attacked by a grizzur.

It might be possible to scale the cliffs, to climb out of Ellder, but I certainly had no desire to try. A fall from those rocks would mean a quick death.

I hadn't tried to leave through the front gate. I doubted the guards would let me.

Maybe these dungeons would prove useful.

Evie slowed to a walk, waiting until I caught up. Then she took my hand, holding it as we walked down the center of the main road, taking in buildings and homes and the trees and small gardens planted in between.

The barracks started in the heart of Ellder, about halfway from the mountains to the fortress's wall. The units were simple cabins arranged in neat, uniform rows. If they were anything like the barracks for Banner's soldiers in Quentis, they wouldn't be more than a bedroom and bath. Meals were likely served in a communal hall for the soldiers.

Evie led me all the way to the mountain, then turned and walked along the cliffs, her other hand constantly reaching out to tickle the rocks.

Ahead, the timber wall met stone. The logs seemed to have been carved and molded to fit the surface, not leaving so much as a gap to squeeze through, making the only way in and out of Ellder the monitored gates.

Evie slowed, and for a moment, I thought maybe she'd gotten lost. But then an opening in the rock appeared, its angle such that unless you were standing right in front of it, you'd never know it was here.

"The dungeons are a cave?" I asked her.

"Yes. I told you it was creepy." She ducked inside without any hesitation, so I followed her into the darkness, giving my eyes a moment to adjust. "Come on, Dess."

She slipped her hand in mine, holding tight.

A few nights ago, Luella had invited me to eat dinner with them in the main house, and Evie had talked through the entire meal, only eating when Luella would remind her that her flatbread and chicken were getting cold.

She'd asked if I had a nickname, and so I'd given her the name Father used sparingly. Evie hadn't called me anything but Dess since.

We walked along the slanting floor, descending deeper through the tunnel. The rocks were smooth, the occasional step dropping us lower. The ceiling was taller than I'd imagined, farther up than I could reach, even on the tips of my toes. The light from outside was fading too fast.

"Evie, maybe we should turn back before it's too dark."

"No, keep going."

No sooner than she'd insisted, an orange glow flickered ahead. It grew and grew until we passed a lantern hung from a hook in the wall. Beside it was an empty cell. Its iron bars were secured in the rock but the door was open and unlocked.

Dungeons without prisoners.

"The bad guys go to the jail by the side gate," she said, reading my thoughts. "I can't go there."

"No, you cannot."

"This is Luella's secret spot now." She lowered her voice, like she was afraid of being caught by her governess. "It's where she hides her special books."

My heart leaped. And what, exactly, was in those special books? Hopefully more than just readers and lesson books for Evie.

The tunnels were damp, trickling water tinkling in the distance. Not exactly where I'd choose to keep books, but it was the last place I'd think to *look* for any if I were a soldier charged with burning books on the king's order.

We kept walking, moving from one lantern's glow to the next, until Evie pressed a finger to her lips and began to tiptoe. At the next cell we came to, she slowed, pointing past the bars.

There were no shelves inside, just stacks of books with objects piled on top. There were carved figurines of the gods. Medallions with various emblems. Trinkets, as Evie had promised.

Her hand clasped around my thumb as she pulled me forward to the next cell. Like the last, there were no shelves, but an empty cot was pushed against the back wall, and on its surface were piles of rolled scrolls.

Please let one of those be a map.

I'd need a day to go through them all. I'd have to come back without Evie. When Luella wasn't here. But for the first time in a week, a spark of hope burned to life.

Maybe there was a chance at finding information after all, even if I was trapped behind Ellder's walls.

Evie kept pulling, and I kept following past three more cells, these all empty. There were puddles of water on the floor formed from the weeping rock.

The tunnel continued on, cell after cell, except before we could continue, a throat cleared.

Evie and I both gasped as we spun around, finding a woman at our backs.

"What are you doing here, Evangeline?" Luella asked. "You said you were playing hide-and-seek with Odessa."

"It's my fault," I said. "I wanted to explore Ellder a bit today. I'm sorry."

"And you chose the dungeons?" Luella could give Margot a run for her money on withering looks.

Evie's frame slumped. "Sorry."

Luella shook her head but let out an exasperated laugh. "How long have you known about the dungeons?"

Evie shrugged. "I dunno."

"I suppose I should have expected you to follow me here eventually."

"Does that mean I'm in trouble?" Evie asked. "Or not in trouble?"

"Not in trouble." Luella crouched in front of her, tucking a lock of dark hair behind the girl's ear. "But I don't want you coming here without an adult. Understood?"

"Understood." Evie gave her a sure nod. "Can we keep exploring?"

"Oh, I love exploring." The woman's voice that came from behind Luella was familiar.

"Cathlin." I smiled as she walked our way, her chestnut eyes dancing in the lantern's light.

"Hello, my dear." She hugged me tight, then bent to drop a kiss on Evie's hair. "My darling. Have you been tormenting Luella today?"

"No more than usual." Luella stood, giving Cathlin a once-over, head to toe. Relief softened her gaze when she saw the librarian was unscathed.

"I have a few additions to your collection." Cathlin opened the satchel hung over her shoulder, pulling out three leather-bound books. She handed them to Luella, then gave her a quick hug. "Hello, my friend."

"Hello," Luella said. "I'm glad you're here and safe. I heard about Ashmore. Besides the attack, how did it go?"

She must mean with Cathlin's lover?

"I'll tell you about it later." Cathlin put her hand on my shoulder. "Did you read that book I gave you?"

"I did. Thank you. It was incredibly helpful."

Some of the Turan customs the book described, I'd learned about in my time here. The various leathers taken from monsters to use in crafting armor or clothing. The way encampments and towns were built into natural barriers for protection. The pony riders who delivered the post.

But otherwise, the book had been a wealth of knowledge. I'd known that the Turan economy depended on lumber production, but I hadn't realized that their blacksmiths and forges were some of the best across Calandra. The raw metal they imported across the border they shared with Ozarth wasn't only used for weapons, but for tools like axes and saw blades. They were excellent horsemen, learning to ride at an early age. Young adults often went on hunts when they came of age, killing a bariwolf or tarkin as a rite of passage. And the women were trained, like the men, to fight and use weapons, too.

"If you've finished that book, let's find you others." Cathlin waved me into a nearby cell, bending at the waist as she ran her fingers over spines.

By the time we left that cell and the next, I had a stack of five books to read. She'd picked a few on Calandran history. Another on the animals and monsters in Turah. And a book on the crux and what we knew about their migrations.

It was the thinnest of the five.

"One more," Cathlin said, plucking a red book from the shelf with a matching leather strap wrapped around its cover. "This one is full of old myths and legends. And it has my favorite myth of all."

"What's that?" I asked.

"It's about a woman named Sora who sailed across the horizon. She was gone for a hundred years, but when she returned to Calandra, she brought with her creatures and animals our realm had never seen. Some believe that is where our monsters came from. Not the new gods, but a god we've never known. A god more powerful than any other. It always made me wonder. What other stories are out there? What if some are true? What if we've burned too many books?"

I had the overwhelming urge to sign the Eight.

It was just a story, but a twang of fear pinched at my ribs, like this was not a topic we should be discussing. Like we were courting disfavor with the gods.

Part of me wanted to leave this book behind, to skip it altogether. The other wondered what else it might contain.

Was there a story in this book about the Chain of Sevens? Was that how the Turans had known they could claim a bride prize? Had Zavier read this book?

"You'll love it. It's a favorite." Cathlin looked at the stack she'd pulled for me and gave an exaggerated frown. "I might have gotten carried away. The king hasn't discovered this hideaway yet. I'm certain when he does, all of these will go. It feels urgent, in a way, to absorb it all while we have the chance."

"Why is he burning books?" I asked.

"Odessa?" Luella appeared at my side, her hand resting softly on my wrist. "Would you mind escorting Evie to the house? She's loaded her pockets with trinkets to put in her room. I'm afraid if she stays any longer, we won't be able to cart it all back. I'll blow out the lanterns and be right behind you."

So much for getting a straight answer on why King Ramsey was burning books.

"Of course." I smiled at both women, then retreated down the tunnel in search of Evangeline, finding her in the cell with the scrolls.

The pockets of her simple dress were stuffed. She stood at the bars, a finger to her lips as she pointed down the hall at Luella.

This girl. She was a better spy than I'd ever be.

I slipped into the stall, pressing my back against the wall beside her. Then I listened to the whispering voices that carried farther than their owners must have realized.

"What do you think you're doing?" Luella hissed.

"What do you mean?"

"Don't play coy with me, Cathlin. I've known you my entire life. You're up to something."

"They're books, Lu. I'm giving that poor girl something to read. That's all."

"That's all? She's the last person who should be here," Luella snarled. "I should have known Evie would follow me. That girl."

"She's too much like her mother," Cathlin said.

Luella sighed. "If he finds out, there will be hell to pay. And I've paid enough."

He. Did she mean Ramsey? Or Zavier? Would Luella be punished if Zavier learned his daughter had been down here?

Their voices dropped too low to make out the rest of their conversation.

Evie must have realized our eavesdropping was over, too, because she grabbed my free hand and led me out of the cell.

We walked out of the tunnels and into daylight, but I might as well have stayed in the dark. That's where I seemed to be stuck these days.

Constantly questioning. Constantly guessing. About the king and these books. About Zavier and the Guardian. About Lyssa and the "sick" monsters.

At the cave's entrance, Evie peered past the rock outcropping, making sure we were alone. Then she darted to the nearest row of barracks, settling into an easy pace like we were just out for a morning stroll.

Yep, she was a tiny spy.

"Want to play with the kittens?" she asked when we'd made our way back to my suite to drop off the books.

"What about your lessons?"

She stuck out her tongue.

Well, Luella wasn't here, so why not? "Kittens it is."

"Okay," she said brightly.

The girl was only four, and she could read and write. Zavier might not want her to be a princess, but he was preparing her for it nonetheless. Mae and I'd had the same rigid structure with lessons when we were her age.

When we made it to the garden, Evie went straight to the pen where the kittens were napping. She gave them each a snuggle, then plopped on the ground and started taking trinkets from her pockets.

"This is Ferious." The golden figurine of the God of Mischief's head glinted in the sun. "He's my favorite god."

"Why does that not surprise me?" I muttered. "You're not supposed to have a favorite god."

She shrugged and kissed the figurine's bald head. "That's what Papa says."

"And maybe someday, you'll listen to me." The baritone voice startled us both.

"Papa?" Evie's attention flew to the doorway where Zavier stood, a smile on his lips. "Papa!"

She nearly tripped as she ran for him, but he caught her before she could crash, sweeping her into a hug as she wrapped herself around his body.

"I've missed you." He kissed her hair, cradling her to his chest. "Hello, Odessa."

"Hello, Zavier."

I should have been glad to see my husband, to know he was here and safe, except there was a sinking feeling in my stomach. A wave of self-loathing. I wished I was excited to see Zavier. But I wasn't.

No, I was longing to see another man.

And I hated myself for missing the Guardian.

I joined them at the door, ready to see myself out. "I'll leave you alone."

But Zavier stopped me with a sideways glance. "Your hair is different."

"Oh, um…"

"It's red." Evie declared the obvious, and before I could explain, she did it for me. "She had to dye it. All the time, too, because Margot—that's her stepmother—said the brown was better suited for her coloring, but I think Margot is wrong and the red is a lot prettier. Especially with her eyes. Aren't they bright? You can't even see her starbursts."

I didn't have a starburst, but when Evie had assumed mine was simply disguised, I hadn't made the correction. I didn't want to explain that I was different. I wouldn't have answers for her inevitable questions.

Zavier smiled at his daughter. "I think the red is prettier, too. Sounds like you both have been getting to know each other?"

"We have." I winked at Evie. "You have a very curious, very lovely daughter."

"Yes, I do." He kissed her forehead, then studied her face. "You've changed since I've been away. You've grown three more freckles."

"Five," she corrected.

He hummed. "I suppose I'll need to do a thorough count."

Evie beamed, running her hands over his face, like she wanted to make sure he was really here. "Want to see the kittens?"

"I would love nothing more." Zavier touched my arm before I could leave. "Join us for dinner tonight?"

"Of course." I waved to Evie, then weaved through the house, making my way out the front door and upstairs.

Those books wouldn't read themselves.

Except when I reached the walkway on the second floor, my feet stopped.

The Guardian stood outside my door, casually leaning against the wall.

His eyes were emerald green. His hair was damp at the ends and in need of a trim. His clothes were clean, and if he'd found any trouble, he'd washed it away. Along with his beard. His face was clean-shaven, and I'd never seen such a chiseled jaw, the corners as sharp as my knives.

Gods, he looked gorgeous. With or without the beard, I didn't care. He was here, and he was safe. He might be the Guardian, but that didn't stop me from worrying.

"Hi." My voice, damn it, was too breathy.

He pushed off the building, walking closer as he tossed a sheathed sword my way.

I went to catch it, but it slipped out of my fingers and clattered at my feet. "Oops."

He cast his eyes skyward. "Oda, save me."

"Well, I didn't know you were going to throw it at me." I picked it up, letting my hair cover the blush of my cheeks. "What is this for?"

"My queen demanded a sword."

So he'd brought me one. He hadn't forgotten.

He walked past me, his arm brushing mine. "Let's go."

"Where?" I asked, even as I spun to follow him down the stairs.

"Someone has to train you to use it."

The idea of training shouldn't have given me butterflies.

But they fluttered in my belly regardless, even when they shouldn't.

Thirty-Four

The sword he'd given me was elegant yet simple. Exactly what I would have chosen for myself. The weapons that Mae collected were embellished with fancy flourishes and inlaid with jewels. I didn't want or need an extravagant sword.

The steel blade was so smooth and clean I could see my own reflection in its edge. The pommel and cross guard were gold. The grip was black and narrow to fit the size of my hand.

I spent a week learning how to wield it. A week scrambling around Ellder's training center, dodging blows and falling on my ass. A week earning the Guardian's frowns and scowls and grumbled critiques.

It was the best week I'd had in a long time.

Every muscle in my body ached. As soon as one bruise faded, another bloomed. Even my hair hurt from where he'd yanked too hard on my braid yesterday to teach me a lesson—cut it or keep it out of the way.

I was not cutting my hair.

So today for training, I'd pinned the braid in a twist at my nape. We'd been at it for nearly two hours, and not a single pin had stayed in place.

I flicked the sloppy braid over my shoulder as I faced the Guardian and readied for his next attack.

"For the love of Mack, would you fucking relax, Cross? Breathe before you pass out." He mentioned the God of War often. Not really a surprise. I bet they were good friends.

I tightened the grip on my sword's hilt. "I am relaxed. And breathing."

"Then tell your shoulders to climb down from your ears."

My shoulders dropped. "Happy now?"

"I'll be happy if you keep me from drawing blood." He lifted his sword, eyebrows raised. "Ready?"

No. Was anyone ever *ready* to fight the Guardian? "Yes."

He came at me with a strike to my ribs. I deflected, barely, and took a quick side step to my left. Then the blows came one after another, pushing me around the ring until we'd moved through the whole circle.

I managed to block each of his strikes, which meant the last would be so fast I wouldn't even see it coming.

A silver streak.

It flashed in my periphery, and I moved too late.

His sword stopped at my throat, the blade only a hair's width from my skin.

My heart thundered, and my chest heaved with every breath. But I kept my neck taut, not wanting to feel that razor-sharp tip dig into my flesh.

The Guardian's hazel eyes were hard as he stared down the length of his sword. Those eyes were always hazel when we trained. But as his gaze dropped to my mouth, the color shifted, slowly, like clouds overtaking a clear sky.

The gold and chocolate speckles became smaller and smaller as brilliant, bold green filled his irises. His tongue darted out, licking his bottom lip, and the dip in my belly was instant. Heat blossomed in my core, desire pooling between my thighs.

The blade was still at my throat, but it was that stare, it was the way I couldn't look away from his own soft lips that was the real danger here.

I took five shallow breaths. Six. It was easier to pretend I didn't want him when he wasn't staring at my mouth. When I didn't let myself consider that he might want me, too.

The moment ended in a blink, the green in his eyes flashing back to hazel as his sword fell away. "That's all for today."

I exhaled, dropping my arms to my sides. Brushing off the moment and willing that dull throb in my center to stop.

"Your stamina—"

"Is shit." I sighed. "I know."

"It's better."

I feigned shock. "Was that... Did you just say I was improving?"

"Don't let it go to your head."

"Never." A smile toyed on my mouth.

His face had a light sheen of sweat. Every day, he'd arrived clean-shaven. Except today. His jaw was covered in a dusting of day-old stubble, and after one look, I'd decided instantly it was my favorite version. Then I'd tripped over my own feet.

He, of course, had laughed.

"I noticed the soldiers work their horses out by riding the perimeter of the fence," I said. "If there's a horse available, I was wondering if I could resume riding again."

"So that when you sneak out of Ellder, this time you do it on your own and not in a merchant's wagon?"

"Exactly." I lifted my chin, meeting his gaze.

Emerald green.

My belly fluttered. I dropped my head and stared at the dirt.

Every evening, I told myself to skip training the next day. To stay locked in my suite until he left Ellder. And every morning, I met the Guardian at dawn.

He'd told me on that horseback ride from Ashmore that the gods were vindictive, manipulative bastards. Maybe he was right.

By this cruel twist of fate, I was married to Zavier while this man haunted my dreams.

This was all we'd ever have together. Morning training sessions with veiled compliments and unfiltered mockery. It wasn't a friendship. But when I thought about my days in Turah, the best had been with the Guardian.

Maybe that was why I couldn't seem to let him go.

"What did Zavier say when you asked him to ride?" he asked.

"I didn't ask him. I'm asking you."

It was my turn to give him a test. Was it really Zavier granting me my wishes? Or was it the Guardian?

"I'll mention it to Zavier." He dipped his head, and then he was gone, stalking across the training center, passing other warriors and soldiers—all of whom paused to gape as the legend walked by. He disappeared around the corner of a building.

Yet those emerald green eyes would linger in my mind for hours.

Emerald meant he was amused. Intrigued. I wasn't sure if I'd ever seen him actually happy, but green was the color of his gaze when he wasn't pissed off. They changed to varying shades of hazel when he was serious or focused or annoyed. And then there was the silver of his rage.

I shouldn't be able to read his eyes. I should have been concentrating on Zavier's instead. Yet my husband had made himself scarce, spending most of his time with Evie.

So I'd memorized details about the wrong man's eyes.

When my heart was crushed, I'd only have myself to blame.

With my sword sheathed, I left the training center, nodding to those I passed along the way. The area was more formal than the areas of dirt in Treow. Here, there were racks of weapons to borrow. For every sparring space, a girl or boy was stationed with a bucket of drinking water. A row of targets was lined up along a wooden fence for use in archery and crossbow practice.

Once I was out of the training area, I wound along the streets of Ellder, in no rush to return to my lonely suite.

Most people in the fortress didn't pay much attention to this princess. No one seemed to realize I was the Sparrow, and I doubted the majority of Turans even knew Zavier had gotten married. Most probably expected him to wed at the autumnal equinox.

It meant that I was just another person in Ellder. From time to time, I'd get a lingering glance, but I credited those to my hair and golden eyes.

Not a soul had called me Highness since I'd arrived at the fortress, and the reprieve made me realize just how much I'd needed this place. This chance to breathe and flourish without the titles. To escape the pomp and pageantry of royal life. To observe the Turans and make my own opinions about this new kingdom of mine.

I liked how they didn't shy away from hard work. How even when they had sweat running down their backs, there were smiles on their faces. I admired their devotion to family. I envied it, too. They were kind to their neighbors. They'd been kind to me.

What if Father had lied? What if he wasn't after something in Allesaria but did plan on starting a war after he broke the treaty? How many Turans would die if he invaded? How many Quentins?

The people here would not go down without a fight. They were as loyal as they were brave. If Father brought his army to Turah, blood from both countries would be on my hands.

The notion of disappointing Father made my skull ache. But the idea of betraying the Turans made my stomach churn.

I was stuck. And considering I had nothing to give Father, I'd stay stuck.

The books Cathlin had given me were entertaining, but they hadn't solved the problem of Allesaria. And when I'd gone to the dungeons five days ago, hoping to sneak a look at Luella's scrolls, every cell had been emptied.

She'd taken everything and hidden it away.

As it had been in Treow, no one in Ellder spoke of Allesaria. A few days ago, I'd asked a housemaid if she'd ever been to the city. After a quick no, she'd curtsied and hurried away. Yesterday, I'd visited the bakery for the first time, and there'd been a soldier in line, waiting to buy a fruit tart. We'd idly chatted as we'd waited, and I'd asked if his only station was Ellder or if he'd also been to the capital. He'd made up an excuse about being late for his shift on the wall and left without a tart.

What if Allesaria didn't exist?

That thought had crossed my mind more than once. I'd dismissed it initially, certain that no kingdom could pull off the ruse of a fake city.

But what if Allesaria was a lie?

We'd landed on that nowhere beach. Perris, the former capital, was a port city. Zavier had gone to Perris and left me behind. What if it was still the capital?

Or what if there was no capital at all? No castle? What if after the migration three generations ago, the Turans had decided to fool us all. To lead us on a chase to a place that did not exist?

If anyone mentioned Allesaria, the Turans would know that person was likely up to no good.

If the city didn't exist, there was nothing I could share with Father. I couldn't fail a task that was doomed from the start. So in a way, it wasn't my fault for letting him down this time.

Well, there was no way to know. For now, I was erasing Allesaria from my vocabulary. The encounter with the soldier had scared me enough that I wouldn't bring it up again. I was enjoying my own invisibility too much and didn't want to court unnecessary attention.

The only people who knew I was married to Zavier were Zavier, the Guardian, Luella, Cathlin, and me.

Not even Evie seemed to know I was married to her father. Yesterday, she'd asked me my last name. She had no idea I was a princess from Quentis. She had no idea I was Zavier's wife.

Thank the gods, I hadn't slipped and told her the secret. Was it a secret?

I'd planned to ask Zavier about it last night, but he'd missed dinner. Maybe today I'd find out. Or maybe I'd just let my identity remain a mystery.

Maybe it was easier for all of us if I was just Odessa.

Dess.

I was about to turn off the main road for the house when a scream rent the air. I spun toward the noise, finding the Guardian stalking my way with a kicking, frantic Evie slung over his shoulder.

"I'm going with him." She pounded her fists on his back.

"Evie. Stop."

She kicked harder, wiggling to be put down.

His nostrils flared. The hazel was back.

"Let me go." Evie screamed again, so loud I winced.

"No." The Guardian marched on, ignoring the curious and pointed stares.

"I can fight!" Evie thrashed so violently that she worked a leg free. She twisted fast, forcing him to set her down. She lunged to the side, about to bolt away, but he caught her around the belly, hoisting her up again, her feet kicking like she was trying to run through the air.

"Evangeline." He roared her name, and all her flailing stopped. If he had yelled my name like that, I would have frozen, too.

She folded in half, draped over his arm like a sack of potatoes.

He closed his eyes, heaved a sigh, and stopped, setting Evie on her feet as he crouched in front of her.

Her shoulders began to shake before she collapsed into his chest and sobbed.

"I'm sorry." He wrapped her in his arms.

"He always leaves me," she cried.

Zavier.

My hand came to my aching heart. This poor girl. She loved her father, and he was gone more often than not.

"I can fight. I can go hunting with him. Please," she pleaded as the sobs continued.

"It's not safe." The Guardian spoke in a voice so gentle I didn't recognize it. Probably because that voice was only for her.

"But I'm strong and brave."

He eased her away, wiping the tears off her cheeks with his thumbs. "Sometimes being strong and brave means staying behind and out of the fight."

She shook her head. "No, it doesn't."

"What if we did something special?"

Evie sniffled and wiped her nose with the back of her hand. "Like what?"

"I was going to ride to Treow tomorrow. To get a horse."

My horse. Freya.

He was going to go get my horse.

The Guardian's eyes flicked my way, acknowledging for the first time that I was standing there.

"Can I go with you?" Evie asked him.

"Only if you promise to behave."

She signed the Eight. "I swear it by the gods."

"What about you?" He stared at her but spoke to me. "Are you coming with us, Cross?"

Evie whirled, finding me standing behind her. She clasped her hands together and nodded. "You have to come. Please, Dess. Please."

"Hmm." I tapped my chin, pretending to think it over. "I'm very busy, but I guess I could make time for a trip to Treow."

Thirty-Five

"**N**ow are we more or less than halfway?" Evie asked for the third time in as many minutes.

She was riding with the Guardian, sitting in front of him on the saddle, while her attention floated in all different directions like dandelion wisps on the wind.

"More," he said.

"Finally." She stared up at the sky and sighed.

We'd been riding all day, following the scouting party that had left Ellder ahead of us this morning, ensuring the journey to Treow was safe. The Guardian had, as expected, roused us at dawn so that we'd make it to the encampment by evening. We'd kept to the trees to avoid the scorching summer sun, and though the pace hadn't been grueling, we hadn't dawdled, either.

Given Evie's restlessness, she was more than ready to get out of the saddle.

She exhaled, leaning over the side of the horse, inspecting his legs and tail. "Can I give him a name?"

"Who says I haven't named him already?"

"Did you?" She twisted to stare up at the Guardian, poking a finger in his cheek. "What is it?"

"He's not one for sharing names," I said from my spot beside them atop a brown gelding.

"Maybe I just don't share names with you." He smirked, then cupped a hand over Evie's ear, whispering something that made her gray eyes pop.

"Aurinda? That's a girl's name." She dissolved into a fit of laughter and would have fallen to the ground if not for the arm he kept banded around her waist.

He chuckled, tapping her nose. The tenderness he had with her might be my undoing.

"Aurinda," I said. "After one of the twin moons?"

Aurinda and Aurrellia. They were nearly identical, except for the massive gray crater that marred Aurinda's surface.

He nodded to his stallion. "He was a twin, born prematurely on the winter solstice. His sister did not survive. No one expected him to, either, but against all odds, he thrived. A Voster priest said it was because she gave her spirit to him, like the way Aurinda gave part of herself to keep Aurrellia."

I'd just read the legend of the twin moons in one of the books Cathlin had given me. Though I'd known the story ever since I was a child.

According to legend, Ama and Oda had crafted the sky for a single moon. Two would be too heavy and pull at the Six's shades.

But as with all of their creations, everything born from Ama and Oda was a twin.

Not wanting to lose her sister, Aurinda cut away her own flesh, a crater in her heart. She sent the crater away from the stars and shades. Not so far that it vanished, but far enough that Aurrellia could remain at her side for all eternity.

The crater was Calandra.

We were born of Aurinda's heart.

And the Guardian had given his horse her name.

It wasn't a name I ever would have guessed, but now that I knew the story, it was exactly what I would have chosen, too.

"Have you ever seen a Voster priest, Dess?" Evie asked.

The topics on today's ride had ranged from horse names to favorite colors to guesses at how far she could throw a pine cone. For as quiet as Zavier was, Evangeline was the opposite. As with most four-year-olds, lulls in conversation made her squirm.

"Yes," I said. "The brotherhood often sent an emissary to my home in Quentis."

"What's an emzery?"

"Em-is-sar-y. It means a contact or representative. The Voster assigned a priest to aid my father."

"Oh." Evie cocked her head to the side. "Why?"

"My father is an important man."

The Guardian scoffed.

I rolled my eyes. He might not like my father, but a king was a king, and even the great and powerful Guardian had to admit Father was important.

"Who is he?" Evie asked.

"He's the Gold King of Quentis."

If Zavier didn't want me sharing my heritage with his daughter, he should have left behind instructions. But I wasn't going to hide who I was, not from her. I'd let him go through the details of our marriage, but I was proud to be a Quentin.

"What?" Her mouth fell open. "He's a king? Does that mean you're a princess?"

"Yes."

She blinked, letting that sink in. Then her forehead furrowed. "Is that why you don't live in Quentis anymore? Because you got sent away? I get sent away a lot, too, because I'm a princess—"

She gasped, realizing her mistake. Her panicked gaze lifted to the Guardian's. "I didn't mean to."

"It's all right." He tucked a lock of hair behind her ear. "You can tell her. But no one else, okay?"

Evie nodded, her shoulders sagging. "I'm not supposed to tell anyone that," she mumbled.

My heart lurched.

She was so young but older than her years. She'd learned lessons she shouldn't have had to yet. To hide. To pretend. To lie. Those were lessons for adults, not children.

"Your secret is safe with me." I gave her a soft smile. "And someday, I'll tell you all about why I left Quentis."

About the Shield of Sparrows. About the Chain of Sevens. About anything she wanted to know. I hated how so many of my own questions went unanswered. I didn't want that for Evie.

"Papa says that, too. That he'll tell me someday. Someday, I'm gonna know lots."

The Guardian chuckled and bent to kiss her hair. "You'll be the smartest princess in all of Calandra."

Evie smiled up at him, then rested her head on his chest as she yawned. "What's your necklace?"

The pendant had come loose from my tunic. I picked it up, letting the red metal catch the light before I ran my thumb over the silver wing. "I don't know."

"Why not?"

"I found it a long time ago. I'm not sure what it means. But I wear it because it's pretty." Because of foolish hope. Because it may or may not have belonged to my mother.

"Oh." She yawned again.

"You can take a nap." The Guardian shifted his hold so she could rest against his arm while he kept Aurinda's reins in his other hand. "Luella said you didn't get a very good night's rest."

Probably because she'd been too excited to sleep.

Evie shook her head and yawned again. "I'm not tired."

Ten minutes later, she was asleep.

Which meant it was time for me to ask the questions.

"How do you know where to go?" There was no road or trail through the forest, but I was certain he knew the path. "The trees all look identical. Is there a map or something you've memorized?"

"Once you know the way, it's not hard to find."

So no, there wasn't a map. *Drat.*

"Why didn't Luella come with us?" Or Evie's nanny. Maybe there was someone already in Treow who'd care for her?

"No need. I'll watch Evie."

Was he sworn to protect her, too? Was he her Guardian as well as mine? Well, she'd have two. I'd made no vow to protect that girl, but I would with my life.

"Where is Zavier?"

"Hunting."

"Monsters?"

He nodded. "Yes."

"Is that because of Lyssa?"

His gaze shot to mine. "Who told you that?"

"Uh, you did. In Ashmore. When you were drunk. Right before you passed out on my floor with my pillow."

"Oh." He scowled.

Apparently, Evie wasn't the only one who slipped from time to time. "So are you going to tell me about it, or am I going to have to guess?"

Lyssa had to be linked to that putrid green blood and the monster attacks, but confirmation would be nice.

He stayed quiet, facing forward.

"Please don't leave me in the dark. I have been pushed to the side, dismissed, and overlooked my entire life."

This time when he glanced at me, it was with pity.

I didn't want his pity, but if I had to strip myself bare to get answers, then I'd tell him my entire life's story. I'd explain just how useless I'd been as a princess in Quentis.

"It's an infection," he said, the words hoarse, like he'd never had to explain it before.

"That's why Evie thinks they're sick."

"That's what she said?" He shook his head. "She picks up on more than we realize."

"Yes, she does."

He held her closer, like he was trying to shield her from the terrors in this realm. From this conversation. "We don't know much about Lyssa. We don't know how it started. We're just trying to stop it from spreading."

"Is it the reason Zavier is gone so often?"

"He's leading one of the hunting parties. There are three. Halston, Tillia's husband, commands the second. The captain of the *Cutter* commands the third. He patrols the Krisenth and the shoreline."

It seemed strange to send the crown prince on a hunting party, but he had killed seven marroweels to claim me as his bride. So maybe he was needed. Maybe he'd rather risk himself and leave the Guardian behind to watch over his daughter.

And his wife.

"What does it do? This infection?"

"A monster is deadly without the infection. They kill for nourishment. To protect their young. To defend a territory. But at their core, a monster is no different than a bear or lion or other predator. The Six simply made their beasts better killing machines."

What would this realm be like if there were no monsters? If the only beasts that roamed the five kingdoms were animals created by Ama and Oda? Was Lyssa just another curse from the Six?

"When a monster gets Lyssa, they're even more savage and vicious, aren't they?" I asked, though I already knew the answer.

"Yes. They kill because they can, slaughtering everything in their wake."

"Like the bariwolves in Ashmore."

"Yes. It's not unheard of for a pack to attack a town, especially after a long, hard winter. But Ashmore wasn't about food."

It had been bloodlust. It was exactly what I'd heard about the migration. "Like the crux."

"Yes."

My head began to spin. The migration was horrific enough. Older generations, those who'd survived the last, were terrified of the monsters. But at least we had a reprieve. Years to rebuild, to plan for another attack.

What happened when that was gone? How could we survive monsters who never let us find peace because they carried some magical infection?

"Do you think that the crux brought it with them?" I asked.

He shook his head. "It's unlikely. The last migration was nearly thirty years ago. We've only learned about Lyssa within the past four. I doubt it's been spreading for an entire generation. We would have seen signs long ago."

The steady clop of our horses' hooves filled the silence as my mind raced. "But you don't know when or how it started. It could have existed before then. Maybe it was lying dormant."

"It's possible. But the Voster have spent years learning everything they can about the infection. They've ruled out the crux."

Of course the Voster were in the middle of this. And he'd taken them at their word.

Did my father know? Or had the brotherhood kept this Lyssa a secret?

What happened when it crossed borders? What happened when more innocent people were slaughtered because the Voster and Turans had decided to keep this infection to themselves?

"How does it spread? Is it from the green blood?" Because I was fairly certain a few drops from that bariwolf in Ashmore had come damn close to getting into my mouth.

"By bite."

"Not blood?"

He shook his head. "Only by bite."

There'd been a bite on the tail of that marroweel.

"Does it infect other animals? Like dogs or cats?"

"I don't know. As far as we can tell, no animal that's been bitten by an infected monster has survived."

"And people? What happens to people if they're bitten?"

I asked the question but realized as the words tumbled off my tongue that I already had the answer.

The Guardian.

There was a vulnerability in his green eyes when he looked at me again.

"You have Lyssa," I whispered.

Keeping Evie tucked against his chest, he worked free the cuff on his forearm. The cuff that he'd engraved and carved to mark the lives he'd taken so he wouldn't forget.

The cuff that concealed a scar.

His skin was perfect save a crescent-shaped series of white dots. A row of jagged teeth.

"What bit you?"

"Bariwolf." He refastened the cuff, hiding that scar. "Four years ago. I was wearing a similar cuff. If not, it would have taken my arm off."

A knot formed in my stomach. "Has anyone else been bitten?"

"Not that I know of. Anyone bitten was likely also slaughtered. Few survive an attack when the monster isn't infected."

"You're really the only one?"

"As far as I know."

I rubbed my temples, my mind swirling. This was so much more than I'd expected. More than I could immediately comprehend. "What do we do?"

"We?"

"Yes." I was part of this now. This country.

I glanced at Evie. This family.

Whether they wanted me or not.

"We kill the monsters. We kill them all. Every last one."

Him. He meant to kill the monsters.

Then himself.

He smirked, his arrogant mask falling into place. "Just think of how happy your father will be when I'm dead. You can even tell him you killed me, just like he asked. My queen the assassin."

Thirty-Six

"W h-what do you mean?"

The Guardian gave me a flat look. "Cross."

Okay, so I wasn't great at playing dumb. And he was always five steps ahead.

I wasn't sure how he knew that Father had ordered me to kill him, but clearly, he knew. Either because he had a spy in Roslo or he'd guessed.

If I were a better liar, I might have been able to salvage this mess. Except, as he'd pointed out, I was a shit liar.

"What did it do to you? Lyssa? Is it the reason you move the way you do?" Was it the reason his eyes changed colors? Had it altered the magic in Calandra's very soil that gave people their starbursts at birth? Had Lyssa ripped away that connection, forging something new?

"It heightens natural abilities," he said.

"Does it make you more, um..." How did I say this? Violent? Aggressive?

"Monstrous?" he quipped. "Yes."

Monster versus monster. That's why he'd been able to kill those beasts. "On the road to Treow, the night we were camped against that rock cliff. Was the grizzur you killed that night infected with Lyssa? Was that why it didn't fear the fires?"

"Yes."

"And the bariwolves that night?"

"Cunning enough to know they were outmatched by the grizzur. I don't know for certain, but it might have been the same pack that attacked Ashmore." He stared, unfocused, into the trees. "I should have tracked them down."

The guilt he carried for Ashmore went so much deeper than I'd realized. What other lives lost did he hold on his conscience? How many others did he believe he'd failed?

"Did you know about Lyssa before you were bitten?"

He shook his head. "No. I think because I was bitten, because I... changed, we started to ask more questions."

"We?"

"The Voster. Zavier."

"And that was four years ago?" I didn't expect him to answer. At any moment, his indulgence in my questions would end. But until he told me to shut up, I was going to keep trying.

"Yes. Not long after I was bitten, I got a fever. I was delirious for a week. When it finally broke, everything was normal. The rest came on over the course of a few months. A cut that should have taken days to heal was gone in hours. I could see clearer. Hear better. I had always been good in a fight. I had always been fast. Now, I'm faster. Stronger."

"That doesn't sound so monstrous."

He barked a dry laugh. "These gifts, as you once called them, come with a price. Monsters aren't the only ones who thrive on bloodlust."

That day in Ashmore, when I'd stared at him and seen the monster inside looking back. The days when silver swirled in his irises.

"I lose a part of myself. I lose all but a shred of my control." When he faced me, there was a warning in his eyes. "It's not easy to break free. It's getting harder and harder."

There could come a time when he couldn't stop. When the monster erased the man entirely.

And when that time came, I shouldn't be anywhere near.

"Where do you think Lyssa came from, if not the crux?"

"No one knows."

"Not even the Voster?"

"No." He shook his head. "But they can feel it. Sense its wrongness. Maybe the Six felt humans were becoming too strong. That their monsters weren't enough to keep us in check, so they cursed Calandra with Lyssa to torture us with more death and blood."

I'd had the same thought myself.

"The High Priest believes it could be a mutation," he said. "A sickness that has morphed over time, becoming stronger and stronger."

"And what do you believe?"

He sighed, adjusting Evie slightly in his hold. "That our priority must be to stop it from spreading."

By killing every beast infected.

That was Zavier's mission.

"Why only three hunting parties? Why not more?"

"We need warriors to guard villages and towns. There are only so many men Zavier can spare. His rangers are the best, so we've relied upon their strengths, sacrificing numbers for skill."

"What about the king? His army?" Or this militia I'd heard about?

He ground his teeth together so hard I heard them grate. "Not an option."

"Why not?"

"It's not an option." His tone brooked no argument.

So King Ramsey was out. "Does he know about Lyssa? The king?"

"Yes."

My eyes widened. "But he's not helping?"

The Guardian arched an eyebrow.

That meant no.

"What about a cure?" Instead of eliminating Lyssa from Turah, cure it instead?

"The Voster have tried. There is no cure."

"But what if—"

"There is no cure," he repeated. "All we can do is purge Lyssa from Turah. It's already spread to the Krisenth. It can't go farther. We're running out of time."

"Time?" My forehead furrowed. "For what?"

"You've heard the stories of the crux. They're deadlier than any monster in Calandra. Can you imagine how it might be if they were infected with Lyssa? Not only would the death toll be insurmountable, but they could carry it across the continent in a week."

"Oh, gods." My insides twisted.

It would change Calandra forever.

Maybe it already had. "How do you know it hasn't gone past the Krisenth? To other kingdoms?"

"We don't. Not with certainty."

"What is the farthest place where it's been seen?"

"Perris."

"The coast?"

He nodded. "It's why the captain of the *Cutter* commands a hunting party. It's spread, somehow, to the marroweels."

"How?"

"The grizzur often wade into the ocean for fish. They're excellent swimmers. It's likely a marroweel was too close to shore. The grizzur attacked, but the marroweel managed to swim away." He shrugged. "But that's just a theory. No one knows for sure."

"If the Krisenth is infected, Lyssa could find its way to Quentis. My father should know about this. You must tell him. You must send a warning."

The Guardian's eyes narrowed. "What makes you think he doesn't already know?"

"Does he?" Was this the reason he'd insisted I spy?

"Every king in Calandra knows of Lyssa. They have simply decided it is Turah's problem to solve."

My jaw dropped. "They don't care?"

"The Shield of Sparrows prevents war, my queen. It does not require allegiance."

So Turah was left to suffer. Its people to die.

Was that because they'd isolated themselves over the years? Or the reason they'd withdrawn from diplomatic affairs?

"What about your people? Do the Turans know about Lyssa?" If so, why hadn't anyone mentioned it to me before?

"Not many know."

"You've kept it a secret from your people. Why?"

His nostrils flared, my question striking a nerve. "The king decided it would cause too much panic. He doesn't believe the infected monsters are any more vicious than a monster without Lyssa."

"What? How can he think that? Whether he believes it or not doesn't matter. People should know what is happening if they're at a greater risk. After what happened in Ashmore, this can't remain a secret."

"It is not my decision to make. Or overrule. All I can do at the moment is try to stop it from spreading."

"How far do you think it's spread?" I asked.

"I believe it's mostly in this region. On the other side of Turah, there are no signs. The hunting party on the *Cutter* hadn't seen an infected marroweel in months before the one that attacked our ship. We've gone town to town, asking if there have been any attacks. Any monsters with blood that runs green, not red. Along the coast, the reports are few and far between. But as you move toward the mountains, there are more and more."

So it had likely originated somewhere around here. "If it spreads across the border to Ozarth, I expect kings will change their minds."

"By that point, it could be too late to stop," he said.

I pushed a curl from my temple, closing my eyes as I let it all sink in. My father knew about this. And he'd done nothing. If Lyssa spread to Quentis and people died, it would be his fault. "Do the other kings know you have Lyssa? Does my father?"

"No. Very few people know the truth."

"But you told me. Why?" Was this another test? A way of securing my silence? I couldn't tell Father the Guardian's secret without condemning myself at the same time.

He swallowed hard, glancing at Evie, still asleep against his chest. When he looked to me, his eyes were changing, shifting from green to hazel. He opened his mouth, closed it. Opened it again. He almost looked nervous.

My stomach knotted.

That was not a face about to deliver good news.

"What?" I gulped. "Tell me."

Except before he could explain, a scream echoed in the distance. Even faint, there was no mistaking the fear in that sound.

My knives were strapped across my back. As much as I'd wanted to bring my sword, the knives were smaller, and I'd had more practice using them. Shades, I didn't want to use them today.

The Guardian's eyes narrowed at the trees ahead, seeing something I couldn't. Then came the dull thud of hooves, growing louder and louder until two soldiers from the scouting party barreled through the forest.

"What is it?" he demanded, his voice hard and loud enough to rouse Evie.

She startled awake, blinking the sleep from her eyes as she straightened.

"Tarkin," a soldier said, eyes panicked. "It attacked us ahead."

"Fuck." The Guardian dragged a hand over his face. "Deaths?"

"Five. Maybe more. The party broke apart. Some of us rode ahead, to Treow. We turned back to you. I can't be sure, but I think it followed on to Treow."

"Damn." The Guardian urged his stallion beside mine, lifting Evie onto my saddle. He looked around, nostrils flaring. "You can't stay out here. Not if it doubles back."

"We can ride," I told him.

He leveled the soldiers with a glare that drained the color from their already ashen faces. "You'll ride with us. You've got the outer positions. No matter what happens, nothing gets past you to her horse. Understood?"

"Yes, Guardian."

My arms cinched around Evie, holding her between them as I gripped the reins. "Hold tight, little star."

She nodded, grasping the saddle's horn with both hands.

"Stay behind me. No matter what happens," the Guardian said, eyes dropping to the girl.

"I've got her," I promised.

"I fucking hate this." His eyes swirled, silver chasing away hazel.

He might have hated this, but staying together was our best option. It was safer by his side, even if that meant riding toward danger.

The soldiers were just boys, probably only nineteen or twenty. Too young and inexperienced to face a monster. Especially if it had Lyssa.

"To your treehouse." He pointed ahead, and I followed his finger, marking the invisible path. Then he took off without a word, hooves thundering.

My gelding, not wanting to be left behind, only needed the slightest nudge before he chased off after the Guardian. Evie and I both jostled in the saddle as we hung on for dear life, but we managed to stay seated as we streaked past trees and bushes.

Something wet hit my hand that gripped the reins.

A tear. Evie's tear.

"It's okay," I said. "It's going to be okay."

The soldiers flanked us as we approached the nearest watchtower, obeying the Guardian's orders to stay at our sides.

I glanced up, expecting to see a warrior stationed above like I had on all of my rides and runs around Treow, but it was empty. Everyone had probably abandoned their posts to fight the tarkin.

Even over the noise of the hooves and my pounding heart, I heard the shouts and screams from the encampment.

The Guardian's stallion reared up as he came to a quick stop beside my treehouse, the rope ladder hanging to the ground.

We stopped so fast I nearly tipped out of the saddle, barely managing to swing my leg over and jump down. Then, arms outstretched, I pulled Evie to me.

"Climb," the Guardian ordered.

"The horse—"

"Damn it, Cross. Climb." He wasn't going to leave until we were safe above.

"You first, Evie."

She hurried to the ladder, taking the rungs quickly like she'd done it a thousand times. Probably because she had. I'd only had weeks in Treow. She'd had months, possibly years.

I followed her up, glancing over my shoulder as I climbed.

The Guardian drew his sword, rolling his wrist, the blade a swoosh in the air. Impatient.

The moment my knees were on the platform, he was gone, riding toward the commons and the shouts.

The two soldiers shared a look, like they weren't sure where to go. Then they took off after him, leaving my brown gelding alone.

A woman's scream made the hair on my arms stand on end.

"Dess." Evie's voice was small and scared.

"It'll be okay." I hugged her, staring into the trees, wishing we weren't so removed from the others so I could see.

Wishing we were farther away so Evie wouldn't have to hear the screams.

"I want Papa." Evie burrowed into my neck.

My hand ran up and down her back as a snarl came from below. It was too loud, too close, to have come from the commotion in the commons.

"Shh," I whispered, picking her up and carrying her inside.

She didn't stay on the bed when I set her down. She leaped over its edge and slid underneath, gray eyes peering out from the floor.

I pressed a finger to my mouth, then inched to the door, closing it behind me before I crept to the balcony's rail.

Beneath my treehouse, walking on silent paws, was a tarkin.

My heart stopped. Moving slowly, silently, I took my knives from their sheaths, tensing as the metal scraped against the leather.

From this vantage point, I had the perfect view of the red-and-orange armor that covered its back. The scales were as large as my hand, as thick as iron. They shifted, moving in unison, as smooth as running water, as the monster prowled.

Tarkin were similar to the tigercats that roamed the lush riverlands in Ozarth. The fur of a tarkin was as red as rubies, striped with pink. The only way to kill the monster was with a blade through its gullet or heart. Those scales along its back were impenetrable. Its fangs and claws, as white as snow, could tear through a human's flesh as if it were wet parchment.

Of all the monsters that roamed Calandra, the tarkin were the most beautiful. If a hunter managed to kill the beast and harvest its scales, they were sold on the black market for as much as fenek tusk powder. Their hides, that rich, smooth red coat, were twice as valuable as lionwick hides.

The monster below paid me no mind as it stalked past my treehouse, tail flicking as it weaved through the forest.

Was that the monster that had attacked the commons? It seemed so docile. Unperturbed. Why the hell was it still alive?

Where was the Guardian, and why hadn't he killed this monster?

Unless there'd been more than one. Unless this attack was like the bariwolves in Ashmore, and while the other monster was keeping the Guardian busy, this creature was on the hunt, searching for easy prey.

It must not have found any. It continued on through the forest until I lost sight of it behind a tree.

My exhale felt like a gust of wind. I was turning for the door, relaxing my hold on my knives, ready to rescue Evie from beneath my bed, when I heard a voice.

"Hurry, Marco."

My head whipped around so fast a jolt of white-hot pain shot through my neck.

A girl with flawless brown skin and spiral curls held a young boy's hand, guiding him toward my rope ladder.

What the hell were they doing out here alone? Where was their parent?

I ran to the other side of the treehouse, searching for the tarkin, but it was gone. "Thank you, Ama."

Moving to the ladder, I set my knives aside and dropped to my knees, waving the children up. "Hurry. Come up here."

The girl's face lifted, her cheeks tearstained, eyes wide as she pulled the boy with her.

They'd almost made it when I felt the breeze. The shift in air that blew our scents in the wrong direction.

The girl stepped on a stick, snapping it in two.

The noise wasn't loud. In any other situation, I wouldn't have paid it another mind. But that crack combined with the wind might as well have been a thunderclap.

The Guardian was going to be so, so mad at me.

Without thinking, I spun and started down the ladder, moving as fast as I could to the bottom. I reached the ground at the same time a low, throaty growl carried from the distance.

Fuck.

A sob came from the girl, but she slapped a hand over her mouth, muffling the cries that came next.

"Climb. Go." Now I sounded like the Guardian. But she listened, moving as quickly as Evie had up the ladder.

The boy shook his head, eyes wide with fear now that the girl was halfway up.

"Come on." I picked him up, propped him on a hip, and started up, my progress slow and awkward with a child in my arms.

We made it five rungs before the hairs on my neck stood on end. One moment, the forest was empty. The next, the tarkin bounded from the trees, teeth and fangs bared, its claws digging into the earth.

"Shit. Shit. Shit." I kept climbing, checking on the girl above.

She'd made it to the balcony.

And Evie, my brave little star, had left the safety of the bedroom to help the other girl up.

"Marco!" the girl cried, hands outstretched.

The tarkin's roar vibrated against my skin. It was running so fast it was a blur of red and orange. That massive, muscular body was honed for speed. For death.

It was going to leap for us. Rip us off this ladder and send us tumbling to the ground.

I climbed faster, shifting the boy as he began to wail and reach for the girl.

"Dess!" Evie yelled.

The tarkin leaped, claws outstretched, jaw wide.

I wrapped my arm around the rope, holding to it and the boy with every bit of my strength.

The monster slammed into the ladder, sending us spinning. Pain burst through my leg as its scales collided with my calf.

My leg slipped, and I dropped a rung, the rope skinning and burning my palm and arm. But I managed to hold on and get both feet back on the ladder.

"Look out," Evie screamed just as the tarkin jumped again, swiping at me from the base of the ladder.

The boy wailed so loudly in my ear that I couldn't hear anything else.

I tightened my arm around his waist and kept climbing.

Not yet, Izzac. I wasn't ready to submit myself to the God of Death. Not yet.

But the strength in my arms and legs was beginning to wane. With my teeth gritted, I managed one more rung. Then another. Then another.

All while the tarkin clawed at the ladder, spinning and pulling it so wildly that we twirled around, forcing me to stop climbing every few moments to simply hold tight.

"Help!" Evie's shout was loud and clear. "Help us! Please!"

I shifted the boy closer to the ladder, hoping that if I fell, he could at least stay here. "Hold on. Grab the rope."

His entire body shook as he cried.

"Please. Hold on."

The boy, Marco, was frozen in fear.

I tried for another rung, getting my foot onto the next spot as the ladder whirled again. Then I forced myself up, exhaling when both boots were locked on the rope.

We weren't even halfway up yet. We weren't going to make it to the top. But if we could just hang on, hold fast, help would come. The Guardian would save us.

"Help!" Evie kept screaming, hands cupped around her mouth.

The ladder swung sideways, so hard my stomach pitched. I braced for another shake, another spin, but it never came. The ladder began to settle and calm.

I risked a glance below.

The tarkin was backing away to make another running jump, lips curled to reveal those pristine fangs.

My heart dropped.

It had missed me before. It would not miss again.

Hell, this was going to hurt.

It took three bounding strides and flew into the air, hitting the ladder so hard its body tangled into the rope.

I heard the snap before I felt it. The left side of the ladder broke from its hook on the balcony, collapsing the rope into a single strand. Then we were falling, sliding down what remained of the ladder, my legs wrapped around it in a desperate attempt to slow us down.

It wasn't a free fall, but it was close. The impact with the ground was so jarring that my knees buckled and I flew backward, the air stolen from my lungs as I slammed into the dirt.

My vision blurred, and for a moment, I was sure I heard Izzac's voice. The God of Death welcoming me to hell.

Odessa.

My name had never sounded sweeter.

Except the fuzzy edges sharpened, the spots clearing from my eyes. And it all came back to me in a blink.

The boy was flopped on my chest. My body had broken his fall, but it still had to hurt. He whimpered as I pushed up on my elbow.

Beyond my ruined ladder, I met a pair of violet eyes.

The tarkin had taken a tumble after that leap, and bark from one of the trees dusted its scales. But it found its footing.

And its next kill.

My stomach bottomed out. There was nowhere to go. No escape.

So I rolled myself on top of the boy, shielding him with my body curved around his. Then I closed my eyes, hoping that by the time the monster had finished with my flesh, help would have come to save Marco.

The tarkin's growl was all I could hear beyond the blood rushing in my ears. I held my breath, waiting. Except claws and teeth never sank into my flesh. All that came was a snarl and a kiss of wind on my hair.

Then nothing.

Peaceful nothing.

Carine, Goddess of Peace, had welcomed me to her shade.

Though I doubted Carine wore boots.

A pair, scuffed and splattered, appeared at my side. Then I was lifted up off the ground, the boy still clutched in my arms, and set on my knees. The Guardian's hands and eyes roamed over my body, searching for injury as he knelt beside me.

"Where are you hurt?" His voice was frantic.

"I'm okay." We were alive. I sighed, hugging the boy.

Later, I was sure my arms and legs would hurt like never before. But for now, we were alive. Thanks to the Guardian.

He took my face in his hands, dropping his forehead to mine. His thumb traced my cheek, and tingles exploded on my skin. "You're okay."

Was he reassuring me? Or himself?

"I'm okay."

He leaned away, my face still in his hands. Thumb still tracing. I never wanted it to stop, but as shouts rang through the trees, he let me go.

I twisted, looking over my shoulder. And found a lifeless tarkin's eyes staring back.

The violet color was already beginning to fade to milky white.

The Guardian sat back on his heels. "Fuck, you are reckless, woman. Does your life mean nothing to you?"

"Not when the lives of innocent children are at risk."

He dragged a hand over his face.

We both knew he would have done the same.

"Marco." A woman rushed over, stealing the boy from my arms and crushing him to her chest.

The girl in the treehouse cried, "Mama."

"Thank you," the woman sobbed. "Thank you."

I wasn't sure if she was talking to me or the Guardian, so I offered a wobbly smile, then shifted to stand.

The Guardian rose first, his hand on my elbow as I stood on shaking legs, not sure if I wanted to cry or scream or laugh.

The tarkin lay in a ruby red heap five feet away, the Guardian's sword lodged through its ribs. Blood seeped around the blade.

Putrid, dark green.

Except before I could move in for a closer look, a prickle crept over my skin, the sensation of spiders crawling up my arms.

I shivered and looked toward the commons.

And met the fathomless gaze of the Voster High Priest. He always seemed to pop up at the worst moments. Coming out of hiding from wherever he called home to make a shitty day even worse.

I tilted my head to the sky, closing my eyes.

I was surrounded by monsters.

Thirty-Seven

The fear from the tarkin's attack was withering, and my body was beginning to shut down. My legs felt weak, my steps unsure. My arms were tingling and my head spinning. And the addition of Voster magic was not helping.

The High Priest was standing beside the Guardian as they inspected the dead tarkin. The Voster's magic had whittled away the last of my strength.

How could the Guardian stand it? It took the last shred of my energy not to squirm.

Tillia strode through the trees, coming from the direction of the commons. She gave the Guardian and High Priest a quick glance as she came to my side, her hand resting on my shoulder. "Odessa, I heard what you did. Are you all right?"

"Yes," I lied. "I'm fine."

If fine meant seconds from screaming or crying or both.

All I wanted was to crawl into bed. The Guardian had sent a soldier to fetch a new rope ladder and the poles they used to attach them to treehouse balconies, but it was taking forever. So for now, I was stuck, wishing I was with Evie instead of standing down here with a tarkin corpse.

The Guardian had climbed his own ladder after the attack, then leaped across the space between our balconies to take care of the girls. Marco's sister had been brought down and reunited with her mother. Evie had been taken to his treehouse and left with three guards to watch her until he was finished with the Voster.

How much longer did they need to poke and prod at the monster? It was dead. Couldn't they burn the body and be done with it?

The Voster said something that only the Guardian could hear. Then they both walked away, and finally, I could breathe. It felt like steam escaping a bathhouse when the windows were opened. As the sting of magic was swept away, my body swayed.

"I'm taking you to the infirmary." Tillia's arm looped through mine, and as she pulled me along at her side, I was helpless to resist.

"But Evie—"

"Is fine. She's got three guards with her. They won't let her out of that treehouse until the Guardian comes to relieve them himself."

"I don't want to go to the infirmary." No sooner were the words out of my mouth than a fresh wave of dizziness hit me so hard I swayed. "Okay. Maybe I should go to the infirmary."

Tillia scoffed. "You think?"

Tillia was at my bedside when I awoke, still foggy but not as weary.

"How long was I asleep?" I asked, pushing myself up to a seat.

"Not long."

Sunshine streamed through the infirmary's windows, bright like it was still midday.

"Better?" she asked.

"Much."

"After a scare like that, I would have passed out, too. What you did for those children was—"

"Reckless." I stole the Guardian's word.

She patted my arm. "I was going to say brave."

No one had ever called me brave before. "What were those kids doing out alone in the middle of an attack?"

"All of the children were playing in the commons when the alert sounded. Their mother was working with Mariette. There were two tarkin, a male and female. The male cut off her path so she couldn't get back. Then they were separated from the others and ran to hide. None of us knew there was a female. We were all too busy attempting to corner the male."

"How many people died?" I asked but didn't really want the answer.

"Five soldiers from Ellder. Three people in Treow."

I swallowed hard. "Any children?"

"A boy, seventeen, who worked in the stables. One of the cooks is dead. And a maid."

"Not Brielle or Jocelyn?"

Tillia shook her head. "They're fine. Both were here while you were asleep. They promised to be back soon."

I wanted to curl up on the cot and go back to sleep, to pretend this was all a bad dream. "How did this happen? Why weren't they killed at the watchtowers?"

"The tarkin came at Treow at full speed, intent to kill. With their armor plating, it's almost impossible to take them down with an arrow from above. The three dead were killed within moments of the male reaching the commons. Once we were alerted, we came running, but…"

But that monster had been intent on killing.

"The Guardian was able to bring it down. Then we heard Evie scream." Tillia swallowed hard. "I've never seen him move so fast."

Lyssa was to thank for that speed. Though I suspected it was the infection that had brought the monster to Treow in the first place.

"Did the male have Lyssa?"

Tillia's eyes flared. "He told you about Lyssa?"

"I don't think he meant to, if that makes any difference."

She glanced around, making sure the healers were not within range to overhear our conversation. "Yes, it did. So did the female. Normally, tarkin are solitary creatures, especially the males. They'll find a female to mate with, but otherwise, they aren't like bariwolf packs. But these two? I'm convinced they came together, one drawing attention as the other hunted."

A chill skated down my spine. "It's not safe in Treow, is it?"

"This morning, I would have promised you it was secure. Now? I'm not so sure." She gave me a sad smile, then stood. "I've got monster carcasses to burn. Will you be all right?"

"Yes. Thank you."

She dipped her chin. "My queen."

"Ugh." I groaned. "You've been spending too much time with him."

Tillia's smile was pretty, albeit a bit evil. "I'll see you soon."

I waited until she was gone before I swung my legs off the side of the bed, giving myself a few moments for my head to stop swimming before I stood. Then I shuffled down the hall to leave.

My bed was calling. If I could convince the guards to move Evie to my treehouse instead of the Guardian's, maybe she and I could cuddle.

I could use a cuddle and a hug. Especially since my skin was still irritated from the Voster encounter.

Except the closer I came to the exit at the end of the hall, the more that irritation intensified. With every step, the crawling sensation on my arms and legs got worse. Then I heard a low, familiar voice, and I knew exactly who I'd find in the infirmary room on my left.

The Guardian sat on the edge of a high table, facing the wall, not the cracked door. His shirt was pooled on his lap, as was the cuff that covered his bite scar.

Standing beside the Guardian was the High Priest. His green fingernails had grown even longer since my wedding ceremony and resembled tiny snakes. He had a palm hovering over the Guardian's naked chest. The other loomed above that crescent-shaped scar.

"Whenever you're ready, brother." The Guardian gritted his teeth, chiseled jaw clenched.

Then the Voster touched the Guardian's skin, murmuring something low and smooth.

The Guardian's frame tightened, every roped muscle flexing. His hands balled into fists on his knees as the cords in his neck popped, his body beginning to vibrate.

I took a step closer, eyes wide as the priest kept speaking. What spell was this? What was he doing?

The light in the infirmary seemed to shine through the priest's skin, making it appear even more translucent. It was so pale, I could make out green veins beneath his bald head that seemed to pulse, like his magic was flowing through him to his hands.

And the Guardian continued to tremble in pain, tipping his face to the ceiling as tears dripped from the corners of his eyes.

I gasped, moving for the door.

But the Voster flung out a hand, sending a wave of wind blasting my direction.

The door slammed shut in my face.

I stood dumbfounded, mouth flapping open.

What was going on in that room? It was as if the priest had sent all of his wicked magic into the Guardian's body. Why?

I took a step away, a new ache flowering in my skull.

The Guardian's faith in the Voster was unwavering. But what if the High Priest was wrong? What if Lyssa wasn't some sort of mutation or disease? What if they'd been the cause?

The Voster's eyes were the same dark-green shade as blood from the infected monsters. That couldn't be a coincidence.

I walked out the infirmary's exit, not sure what to think anymore, and nearly collided with a woman.

"Highness." Brielle hauled me into her arms, holding tight. "You're alive. Thank the gods. I've been so worried."

"Brielle." I hugged her hard, then relaxed and took her in, from the tunic she wore to her pants hugging her generous curves. "No dress?"

She shrugged. "When in Turah."

I laughed, something I didn't think would be possible today, and hugged her again. "How are you? Tell me everything. I've missed you."

"Oh, no you don't. You were supposed to be back in a few days. It's been weeks. You're the one with a lot of explaining to do."

And so I explained. For an hour, we sat in the dining hall while I told her about Ashmore. About the bariwolves. How the Guardian had taken me to Ellder, where I'd been for weeks. And how we'd returned to Treow just in time to face the tarkin.

I told her almost everything, except about Evie. And Lyssa.

"Have you found anything about Allesaria?" she asked, voice low, when I was finished.

"Nothing. At this point, I'm starting to wonder if it even exists," I told her. "Maybe it's only a myth."

It was said mostly in jest, but Brielle hummed, her eyebrows knitting together. "Interesting. It would certainly prove elusive to foreign kings. Draw their curiosity like it has your father's."

"Maybe," I murmured. It still seemed like a stretch.

If Allesaria was a myth, the people in Turah had been putting up that ruse for a long, long, long time.

What if we all believed in a city that didn't exist?

My headache spiked, and while it was an interesting theory to entertain, I was too tired. "I think I'll head to the treehouse now. I could use some rest."

"Of course." Brielle stood and walked with me through the commons. "Jocelyn and I will bring you dinner and water for a bath. I'm not sure where she went. But she's anxious to see you, too."

"Thank you." I hugged her again, then left for my treehouse.

A ranger fell into step behind me, following me as I left the commons. Either Tillia's or the Guardian's doing, no doubt. But I was glad for the company when I approached the treehouse.

The rope ladder had been replaced. The tarkin's body was gone, and the dirt had been raked to hide any trace of its blood.

I put my first foot on the lowest rung and froze. My heart began to race. My limbs felt too heavy. When I closed my eyes, I heard that growl. I saw claws and teeth.

"Are you all right?" the ranger asked.

"Yes." I forced my eyes open, put my hands on the ladder.

And climbed.

Evie's three guards were waiting on the balcony when I reached the top. I guess I wasn't the only one who wanted to cuddle. She must have convinced them to let her move.

One guard held out his hand, helping me up. Then I slipped into the room, finding Evie asleep on my bed, beneath the pillows.

I pulled them away and shifted her to the side, then lay beside her, our bodies curling together. We cuddled until Brielle and Jocelyn brought us a dinner that we shared.

Evie was quiet through the meal, picking at her food.

"Scared?" I asked.

She shrugged.

"Me too."

"Were those monsters sick?"

"Yes."

She thought about it for a moment. "When I grow up, I'm going to have a pet monster. And then if a sick monster comes after me, it will protect me. And then I'm going to become a monster hunter, like Papa."

Not a chance her father or the Guardian or Luella would let her have a pet monster. Or become a monster hunter. "What will you name it? This pet of yours?"

"I dunno." She poked at a carrot, then looked to me with pleading gray eyes. Those blue starbursts in her irises always seemed to shine brighter when she wanted something. "Dess? Can I sleep with you tonight?"

"Does anyone say no to you?"

She shook her head.

"You can sleep with me if you eat your dinner, little star."

Her forehead furrowed at the nickname. "What's that mean?"

"That you're bright and beautiful. That you're brave, even in the night."

Her face pinked as she gave me a shy smile. Then she dove into her meal, taking bites so large they bulged her cheeks.

Margot would have scolded her for unladylike behavior.

I shoved a huge bite into my own mouth instead.

We played games and told stories. When Brielle and Jocelyn returned with water for a bath, I let Evie use it instead. And once she was clean and in a fresh sleep shirt, I combed and braided her hair. Then we lay on my pillows, her yawns keeping me company as night fell over Treow, until eventually, she drifted to sleep.

The stars were shining when I snuck through the door to the balcony.

The Guardian was waiting on his own. He looked…miserable. His skin was sallow. There were dark circles beneath his eyes. And even though hazel wasn't my favorite color of his eyes, I'd take it over the flat, muted gray of his irises tonight.

"Are you okay?" I asked.

He dipped his chin. "How's Evie?"

"Asleep."

"She usually steals my bed when she's in Treow and Zavier is gone. I have a cot brought in for her, but I'm the one who ends up using it."

Was that who he'd been talking to all those nights ago? Not a woman sharing his bed. A girl who'd stolen it.

It was more of a relief than it should have been, but I was still raw from the attack. Tonight, I didn't have it in me to fight my own damn feelings.

"I should have come to see her earlier." He blew out a long breath. "I was tied up."

"With the High Priest? I, um, saw you. In the infirmary earlier."

"Ah." He dropped his forearms to the rail, staring into the forest. "He was siphoning Lyssa from my blood."

"What?" Not what I had expected to hear. He could do that? "Why? Does he think he can cure it?"

"There is no cure, Sparrow. Get that notion out of your head."

Why did it seem like he'd given up? His voice sounded hollow. It was different than when we were in Ashmore. This wasn't just sadness and guilt. This was emptiness. Hopelessness.

"He's been studying the infection," he said. "Trying to find out where it came from. How it started."

"And?"

He stared into the night, jaw flexing.

"The High Priest found something," I guessed. And whatever it was did not make the Guardian happy.

He nodded. "He thought at first that it had come from another animal. That a disease had morphed over time, rotting its host. Possibly a fenek.

He said Lyssa felt the same as the blood of someone poisoned with fenek tusk powder. But it was different enough that he's kept searching. When we were on the Krisenth, he siphoned more from my blood and took it to Laine, hoping to speak to their healers and alchemists."

They were known to be the best in Calandra. Mostly because they had unlimited access to the kingdom's array of spice fields. Their alchemists had the luxury of experimentation, while those in other kingdoms had to pay handsomely for raw ingredients to make medicines.

"Did they know anything?" I asked.

"No." He stared, unblinking, toward the forest floor. "Only that it had a strong reaction to korakin. Lyssa and korakin seem to adhere. That they were alike."

"Korakin. As in, kaverine dung?"

The Guardian nodded.

Kaverine were some of the smaller monsters in Calandra. They were twice as vicious as their cousins, the wolverines. Kaverine lived in the Laine deserts, burrowing into the sand dunes and hunting for prey at night.

Why an alchemist would ever decide to experiment with kaverine dung was beyond me, but long before I was born, someone had discovered its use and named it korakin.

When korakin was boiled to mush, then reduced to a paste, all a person needed was a taste and they'd hallucinate for hours. They'd feel no pain. They'd forget their own name.

The infirmary in Roslo used it for patients who needed amputations or surgeries. It left some with a horrible addiction, and since korakin was nearly as expensive as fenek tusk powder, most who craved it ran their lives into ruin in search of more.

Why would an infection have similarities to fenek tusk powder and korakin?

That sounded like alchemy, not magic.

The Guardian stayed quiet. He gave me time to come to the realization on my own. And when it dawned, my knees nearly gave out.

"When you told me about it, I assumed Lyssa was magic. Is it? Or do you think someone created it?"

The Guardian sighed. "I don't know."

"Only the Voster have magic in Calandra."

"That we know of," he said.

My heart began to race. "What are you saying? There are other magical beings?"

"Possibly. I'm not sure. But I intend to find out. And if someone did create it, then I'll string the fucker from his entrails and watch him rot while the crows pick the meat from his bones."

I grimaced. Gross. Though whoever had done this deserved to be punished. "Well, I'm going to help. Not with the entrails. But finding the source."

The Guardian barked a dry laugh. "You're not, actually."

"I am." I raised my chin. "I insist."

"You insist." He pushed off the railing, mocking a bow. "Forgive me, Highness, for not giving a fuck. You're not involved in this."

"Then you shouldn't have told me about it in the first place. That's on you."

He frowned, more to himself than to me.

"Please don't ask me to sit idly by and do nothing. Not while people are dying."

"It's too dangerous."

"Even if I'm with the great and powerful Guardian?"

His nostrils flared. "Don't ever call me that again."

"Tell me your real name, and I won't."

He crossed his arms over his chest.

"Listen, I know you don't trust me."

"I do not."

That pinched, but at least he was honest. "Margot always said I had a penchant for finding trouble. Well, if there is a person who created Lyssa, that person is certainly trouble. Think of me like a magnet."

"Cross," he warned.

"Please." I clasped my hands together. Tonight, I was not above begging. "Let me help. Eight people died today. Seventeen in Ashmore. How many more before this is over? I can't just wait and hope. I promise to behave. When we were on the *Cutter*, you said, 'If I tell you to run, you run. If I tell you to hide, you hide.'"

"And you told me 'No.'"

"I did. Can I amend my reply? I promise to listen. And I know now that when you give me an order, it's so I stay safe. Please let me try to help. Don't shut me out. I'm so tired of being the last to know what everyone already does. I'm not a warrior. I'm not a scholar or healer or even a decent princess. But I'm capable. I taught myself how to whistle. How to shoot a crossbow with marginal accuracy. I haven't cut myself with my own knife or sword. I can help. I want to help. Please?"

The Guardian closed his eyes, rubbing a hand over his stubbled jaw. He looked exhausted. He looked like the weight of this kingdom rested on his shoulders.

Well, here I was, offering to share the load.

"Fine."

My jaw dropped. Really? Had that actually worked? I clapped my hands together and fought a smile. "Thank you."

"I'm going to regret this."

"Probably." I backed away for the door, about to duck inside before he could change his mind.

"Odessa, wait."

It wasn't his order that made me stop.

It was my name.

I was always *Cross* or *Sparrow* or *my queen*. But rarely Odessa.

I'd never loved my name more.

"Thank you. For saving those children." He put both hands over his heart and bowed. Then he slipped into his treehouse, closing the door.

And my rope ladder? It stayed attached. All night long.

Thirty-Eight

Tillia's fist slammed into my stomach.

"Oof." I doubled over, my knives dropping from my hand to the ground as I struggled to fill my lungs.

"That's what happens when you don't pay attention." She tsked, then patted my shoulder before going to get a drink of water. "I've missed training with you."

"You mean you've missed kicking my ass."

Her smile was vicious. "Exactly."

It hurt to laugh, but I did it anyway. "I've missed training with you, too."

The Guardian had taught me a lot since those days on the *Cutter*, but there was something different about working with Tillia. She didn't hold back because I was a woman. She came at me like she would any opponent, knowing that a real enemy wouldn't lessen the strength of a blow or stop a punch when I wasn't paying attention.

I'd earned that hit to the gut. My focus had been split between her attack and the man I'd just watch disappear through the trees.

"Are we finished?" I asked. *Please say yes.*

"Yes. Well done. Other than the last minute, you fought hard today."

"Thank you." I picked up my knives and stood tall. "Tomorrow?"

"I'll be waiting in the commons."

With a wave, I headed into the trees, hoping that the Guardian wasn't in a hurry, because if he was, I'd never catch up. But a sliver of white popped ahead, the sleeve of his shirt, so I kept my steps light as I jogged to get closer.

He walked alone, his sword strapped across his shoulders, as he made his way toward the edge of the encampment.

Where was Evie? She'd woken me at dawn with a swift kick to the ribs as she turned sideways in her sleep. I'd finished reading a book on legends and monsters while she'd flopped around, and when she'd finally woken up, we'd gone to the commons for breakfast.

Tillia had claimed me for training, and the Guardian had taken Evie to the stables for riding practice. Maybe she was playing with some of the other children? I wasn't sure I liked the idea of her being left behind.

He could simply be going to check Treow's perimeter, but there was something in his stride, a purpose and intent, that made me think he was not staying in the encampment.

The Guardian slowed, and before he could turn and spot me, I jumped behind a nearby tree trunk.

"Shit," I mouthed to myself. Then I counted to five and peeked past the bark.

He was still walking forward.

Phew. I slipped from tree to tree, zigzagging through the forest while keeping my distance.

We were almost to the first watchtower, and my heart was beating so loudly I was sure he could hear it.

A whistle cut through the forest, a signal from above that he was crossing that invisible boundary.

I leaped behind another tree. What were the chances I could get through without being noticed?

Another whistle sounded.

Apparently none.

"I know you're there, Cross. You're about as stealthy as a trumpet brigade."

"Grr." I jabbed my elbow into the bark. "Ouch."

Rubbing at the pain, I walked out from behind the tree, then plodded to where he was waiting, arms crossed over his chest.

"Want to tell me what you're doing following me around?" he asked.

"Want to tell me where you're going?"

"No." His mouth flattened, but there was a glint in his green eyes. At least I was amusing everyone today.

"Where's Evie?"

"With the other children in the commons. Surrounded by a wall of parents and rangers who are unlikely to let anyone under the age of sixteen out of their sight for the foreseeable future."

"Good."

He nodded. "What are you doing out here? Honing your spy skills?"

"No." I kicked a clump of dirt. There were no skills to hone. I was Calandra's worst spy. "You said I could help find the source of Lyssa."

"Okay," he drawled.

"So wherever you're going, I want to go, too." Did that sound desperate? *Yes*. At this point, I was desperate.

"What makes you think where I'm going has anything to do with Lyssa?"

I shrugged. "A hunch."

"And do you have those often? Hunches?"

"Not real— Actually, yes. I do."

In Roslo, there were always goings-on in the castle that piqued my interest, that gave me pause. That made me curious about the people coming and going. About the real reasons for hushed whispers and chaste meetings. But I'd never acted upon those hunches. I'd never dared follow Margot or Mae or Father around to find out what it was they were doing.

Satisfying my curiosity hadn't been worth the risk of being caught.

But here I was, standing before arguably the most dangerous man in Calandra, a known murderer, and I should be terrified.

Except he wouldn't hurt me. Without a shadow of a doubt, I knew the Guardian wouldn't hurt me. Yes, he'd tease and scold and ridicule me until I wanted to strangle him to death. But he wouldn't hurt me.

"Maybe I'm wrong," I said. "But yes, my hunch is you're going somewhere because of Lyssa."

His eyes narrowed. "I said you could help. And you promised to listen to me. If I asked you to go back, would you turn around?"

"Yes." Would I throw an absolute tantrum first? Definitely. But I'd go. "Please don't make me turn around."

He rubbed a hand over his jaw. "You're a pain in my ass, Cross."

That meant yes. My smile was instant. "Where are we going?"

"So ready to leap into danger."

"Um, is it dangerous?"

He arched his eyebrows.

"Right. We're in Turah, where everything is dangerous. How dangerous, exactly?"

"Guess you'll find out." He spun around and resumed his trek through the forest with me at his side, jogging every few steps to keep up.

When he noticed, his eyebrows came together, a frown pulling at his gorgeous mouth. Then he slowed his pace to match mine.

"We sent scouting parties out to make sure there were no other tarkin in the area. They found a den. We're going to check it out."

I tripped over my own feet and would have landed face-first in a clump of pine needles, except a strong arm wrapped around my waist, keeping me from falling.

The Guardian's scent filled my nose, wind and leather and moss, mingling with pine and earth. The heat from his body spread against mine as my back pressed into his chest.

A tingle spread through my entire body, and the forest around us faded to a blur of brown and green.

"All right?" His voice was a low murmur in my ear.

I nodded. "Just…clumsy."

"You're graceful in your own right."

Damn, that voice. Rugged and low, a murmur in my ear that made my insides liquefy.

This was when I should be squirming to be set free. To put at least five feet between us. Except I couldn't move. I didn't want to lose that arm banding tighter or the feel of his chest rising and falling with every breath.

Not my husband. Not my husband. Not my husband.

I closed my eyes and pictured Zavier's face. Then I wiggled out of the Guardian's hold, taking a few long strides away. My face was on fire, lust turning to embarrassment.

Was this part of Zavier's plan? To leave me with the Guardian, hoping I'd fall for that gravelly voice and handsome face? To catch me in a mistake so that he could hold infidelity against me whenever he needed to keep his wife in line?

Or maybe to throw an affair in my father's face.

That notion was sobering.

I swallowed hard and straightened my spine, willing the color from my cheeks. "Please don't touch me like that again."

"Odessa, I—"

"I've never seen a tarkin den. Let's go."

The green of his eyes changed to hazel in a blink. His jaw clenched. Then he stormed past me, stalking into the forest with me hustling to keep up.

Part of me wanted to turn around. To forget this entire ordeal and hide in my treehouse. But just like I'd asked for a sword, I'd asked to be included. I was too stubborn to give up.

The truth was, I couldn't trust him. I couldn't trust Zavier. Hell, maybe I couldn't trust my father, either. The only person I could rely on at the moment was myself.

There was only one way for me to break free.

Knowledge.

Every secret I exposed would lead me to freedom. The freedom of choice. So I could decide where I wanted to go. Where I wanted to live. Who I could become.

Sweat beaded at my temples by the time we reached a formation of tall, gray rocks that seemed to have pushed through the earth, carving away the forest.

The Guardian stopped before we reached the stone, crouching to the dirt. He flicked a leaf aside, revealing the perfect imprint of a tarkin's paw.

The area was rife with footprints. "How many lived here?"

"Just the one. The female. She had teats, and it appears that she gave birth not long ago."

"We're here to find the pups."

He nodded and stood, eyes raking over the area. "She'll have put them in the den."

"Do you think they have it? Lyssa?"

"It's possible."

And that was why we were here. "How will you be able to tell?"

He didn't answer.

He didn't need to.

"Their blood. It will be green." Like his. Like the blood I'd seen gushing from his wounds in Ashmore. The blood I'd assumed belonged to the bariwolves.

"And then what?" I asked. "You'll kill them?"

"If I must."

"I should have stayed in Treow," I whispered. I didn't want to be on this hunt. Not to slaughter babies.

He moved to walk away but stopped. "For what it's worth, I don't think they'll have it."

"Why?"

"Because I doubt they were bitten."

"But they would have come in contact with her saliva. If she licked them clean."

"It doesn't seem to transfer that way."

"How do you know?" Had this happened before? Had he killed a mother and hunted down her cubs?

He raked a hand through his hair, a sign that my questions were growing old, but I was just going to keep asking. We both knew that.

"After I was bitten, after the fever, I felt different. But like I said, the changes came on over time. I didn't realize there was anything wrong with me for months. I felt different but assumed it was just lasting effects from the fever. I was at a tavern. I met a woman."

"Oh." *Gods.* Me and my fucking mouth.

The jealousy was instant. A punch to the gut stronger than Tillia's this morning. I wanted to take back my question, take them all back, so that the image of him with another woman would forever be gone from my brain.

Was it Sariah from Ashmore? Was that who he'd taken to bed? Who he'd kissed?

This was not a story I wanted to know. Not even a bit.

"She didn't get Lyssa," he said.

"Good." My voice was too bright. "That's great. I'm sure your future wife will be glad that you can, uh…" This just kept getting worse. "You know what I'm saying."

"That my future wife will be glad I can kiss and fuck her."

"Yes. Great news." My insides twisted as mortification crawled beneath my skin. If there was a stray tarkin nearby, I wouldn't even try to stop it from killing me right now. "I guess you'll just have to be careful not to bite her."

What in the six shades was wrong with me? Why couldn't I shut the fuck up?

"I'm not much for biting women."

Why were we still talking about this?

"We'd better find those pups." I set off for the rocks, feeling his gaze on my shoulders.

"Cross."

I stopped. Groaned. Turned. "Yes?"

"You wanted to know about Lyssa."

So this topic of conversation was my fault? *Obviously.* I could not have regretted it more. "I did. Thanks for sharing."

His eyes flashed from hazel to green.

Did that mean I was amusing him again? At the moment, I think I'd prefer his fury.

"No need to be shy, my queen."

I gave him a flat look. "Just incredibly uninterested in your sex life."

"Noted." He smirked.

It had been a while since I'd gotten the smirk.

I wished that I still hated it. I wished that it didn't make him more attractive. I wished that I wasn't wondering how many women had gotten that smirk before he'd whisked them away to a bedroom.

"The pups?" I hooked a thumb over my shoulder toward the rocks.

The smirk widened to a grin as he walked past me, his arm brushing mine, to start up the rocks. Most were too sheer to climb, but the closest had a more gradual slope that rose to a ledge. It was steep enough that I had to use my hands to crawl my way up.

So did the Guardian. He went first, and when I looked up, I had the perfect view of his perfect ass. Hell, he had a great body. Strong and muscled in all of the right places. Firm and—

"Gah." What was wrong with me?

His wasn't the first good behind I'd ever ogled. It wouldn't be the last. Why couldn't I stop thinking of him that way?

"What's wrong?" he asked.

"Scratched my palm," I lied.

He cast a disbelieving look in my direction and continued the climb toward the ledge. When he reached the top, he brushed his hands on his pants, then reached out to help me to my feet.

An animal's yowl came from a darkened corner, the sound similar to a kitten's meow.

The Guardian took a knife from the scabbard on his hip, then slowly moved toward the noise.

I stayed close, looking past his arm as a cluster of figures appeared.

Three tiny tarkin bodies were on their sides, ribs stretching fur. Lifeless eyes open to nothing.

My chest pinched. "They starved to death."

The Guardian exhaled, crouched beside them. "She must have gone a couple of days ago. They're young. Maybe a week old. They'd never survive long without milk."

"But the noise—" I spun, searching for the source. And there it was, across the ledge on its own. A tarkin whose eyes weren't dead.

Yet.

I rushed over, about to pick it up, but the Guardian's hand closed around my elbow, holding me back.

His knife was firm in his other hand. "Turn around. Don't watch."

"Wait." I stared up at him, searching those green eyes. "Don't kill it."

"It's dying. My blade will be a mercy compared to starvation."

"Why does it have to starve?" I tugged my arm free of his grip and bent, fitting my palms beneath the small creature as I picked it up and laid it in the crook of my arm.

"What are you doing?" the Guardian asked. "That's a monster."

"Does it have to be?"

Evie's words from last night rang in my head.

When I grow up, I'm going to have a pet monster.

People kept dogs and cats as pets all the time. We'd named the tarkin monsters. After yesterday's attack, it seemed accurate. But what if they didn't have to be feared? What if there was more to these creatures?

Something thrummed in my chest. Something strange and unfamiliar. Something that I couldn't explain. I just knew, like I knew the Guardian wouldn't hurt me, like I knew my name was Odessa, like I knew my eyes were gold and my hair was red, that we couldn't kill this monster today.

"I want to keep it."

"No." He reached for it, but I shied away. "It could have Lyssa."

"It might. You can test it when it's stronger."

"And if it bites you in the meantime?"

I rolled my eyes. "It can't lift its head. I think I'm safe for today."

"Cross," he warned.

"Death isn't the only mercy." I ran my finger along the tarkin's forehead. "When it's old enough to survive on its own, I'll set it free."

"No."

I looked up and met his glare with my own. "Yes."

"And if it's infected?"

"I'll kill it myself."

"I'm not taking a chance." He pulled out a knife and pressed it against the tarkin's thigh.

"Fine." I inched closer, and as he nicked the baby's leg, I squeezed my eyes shut.

Please be red. Please be red.

I cracked my eyes open.

And found gleaming red blood on his blade.

Phew.

The Guardian's gaze shifted, not to the hazel I'd expected but to that rich forest green. "Would you really have killed it?"

"Yes." It would have taken a piece of my soul, but I would have done it.

"Would you kill me if necessary?"

The question startled me into silence.

So we stared at each other, a dying monster in my arms, and I realized that he was asking for the same mercy. That if he became a monster, if he lost control, he'd want a quick death.

"Yes," I whispered. "If I must."

"Swear it." There was an intensity, an edge, to his voice that made it difficult to breathe.

"I swear it."

"I will hold you to that vow." He dropped his gaze to the tarkin. "Odessa."

He used my first name so rarely, whenever he did, I paid attention.

"You asked for my name," he said.

"You told me I had to earn it."

He nodded. "Ransom. My name is Ransom."

Thirty-Nine

My tarkin let out a *rawr* from its crate.

"Let me sleep." I buried my face in a pillow.

Rawr.

"You just ate."

Rawr.

"Ugh." I folded the pillow up over my ears for a blissful moment of silence. But the guilt might as well have been another *rawr*.

I flung the covers from my body and crawled out of bed, padding to the crate to pick up my tiny monster. As soon as he was tucked into the crook of my arm, his violet eyes closed.

"You're spoiled." I stroked the scales along his spine.

There was only a narrow strip of scales, four rows total. It wasn't the full armor plating he would have as an adult. And his were hard yet flexible, like fingernails. The baby's fur was as fluffy and soft as feathers. The color wasn't the rich ruby red of his mother, but the lighter shade of pink that would someday become his stripes. His belly was so pale it was nearly white.

I shuffled to the bed, plopping on its edge. Then I lay down, propped against my pillows, positioning the tarkin on my chest as I closed my eyes. He curled into a ball and promptly fell asleep, his heartbeat a steady flutter against my chest.

In the past four days, this little beast had thrived. All he'd needed was goat's milk, water, and constant attention. He was still too thin, but his ribs weren't as prevalent beneath his fur. His violet eyes weren't as cloudy.

"So much for the crate." Ransom's voice came from the doorway.

For as long as I'd known him, thought of him as the Guardian, it had taken no effort to adopt his name in my mind. It was like there'd always been this empty space, a hole, and I'd been waiting all this time to fill it with a name.

Ransom.

I couldn't imagine it being anything else.

"I'll teach Faze to stay in the crate later." I yawned and didn't move.

"After it's big enough to jump over the side? Or after it can shred through the slats with its claws?"

"After I've slept for more than two hours at a time."

"Tired, my queen?"

Exhausted. I hadn't been this worn out since our trek from the coast across the plains. But I refused to admit that I was tired. That this monster was zapping my energy. "I'm not tired. I'm moping. I miss Evie."

He'd taken her back to Ellder and Luella two days ago. I'd missed her immediately. I think Faze missed her, too.

She'd been my helper with this tarkin. She'd given him the name Faze.

I had no idea what it meant or where it came from, but Evie had started calling him Faze, and now that was his name.

When we'd returned from the den, I'd worried that Evie might be scared of the monster, especially so soon after his mother's attack. So I'd kept Faze to myself, staying in the treehouse as I fed him milk from a makeshift bottle.

Ransom had told Evie to stay out of my treehouse. He might as well have carried her up my rope ladder himself. My little star wasn't one to be told no.

She'd taken a single look at the pup and squealed for joy.

In that moment, Faze was *her* pet monster.

The fit she'd thrown when Ransom had come to take her back to Ellder, to separate her from her baby, was a tantrum that had rivaled one of Mae's. But the fortress was a better place for her to stay, where she was safe behind its walls and under Luella's watchful gaze.

I was certain I'd join her soon. Whenever Ransom was tired of babysitting me, too. I'd be dropped at the fortress, and he'd go about his monster hunting.

Maybe that was why he was here this morning.

Well, when I returned to Ellder, at least I'd have this little beast to keep me company. He was mine, for now. Until it was time to set him free.

"How long will this moping continue?" Ransom asked.

"I don't know. A day or two." Or until I had a nap.

"That's unfortunate."

I cracked one eye and lifted my head off my pillow. "Why?"

He leaned against my door, chiseled arms crossed over a broad chest. Green eyes. Dark green.

My favorite color.

"A lionwick was killed in a nearby village."

I sat up entirely, catching Faze before he plopped onto my lap. "Lyssa?"

He nodded.

"You're going?"

Another nod. "It's a hard ride. Over a day and a half."

"Can I come?"

"The only stop will be to sleep and not for long."

"Is that a yes?"

"Your choice, Sparrow."

"I'm coming." I flew off the bed, setting Faze in his crate and ignoring his whine. "Give me a minute to get dressed and pack."

Rushing to the bath, hiding behind the partition, I traded my long sleep shirt for pants and a ruby tunic that would probably clash with my hair but was such a bold color I didn't care.

With my hair secured with a leather strand at my nape, I rushed to grab an extra set of clothes, stuffing them into my satchel beside my journal. After pulling on my boots, I strapped the carrier I'd fashioned for Faze across my chest.

When Arthy was a baby, his nursemaid had used a carrier like this. So I'd made one of my own from an old gray dress.

Faze fit in the pouch it formed, and after he was settled, squirming to get comfortable, I secured my shoulder harness for my knives so they were crisscrossed over my spine. Then I grabbed my sword and his bottle. "Ready."

"We're not going to war, Cross."

"Says the man who's always dressed for battle." I flung a hand toward the sword hilt peeking out over his shoulder. "Where are we going, exactly?"

"Ravalli."

Never heard of it. "Great. What will we be doing in Ravalli?"

"Research. We'll ask some questions. See if there have been other instances that we haven't heard of before."

"Okay. Let's go." I crossed the room, but he shifted, filling the doorframe with that huge body. "What?"

"Leave the beast."

"I can't."

"Why not?"

"Because someone told me to keep his existence a secret." He'd been worried that others might try to kill Faze and, in doing so, break Evie's heart. "And there's no one to watch him. You took Brielle and Jocelyn to Ellder, too, remember?"

Not that either would have welcomed him in their treehouse. They were both terrified of the tiny monster.

The first night Faze had been here, the night I'd rescued him, Jocelyn had come to visit. One look, and she'd screamed. Brielle had signed the Eight and asked if I had a death wish.

Both of my lady's maids had seemed more than happy to get out of Treow. Hopefully they'd find life in Ellder a bit easier. Maybe it would remind them of Roslo, and they could settle into a new home. At least until I could send them home.

Ransom scowled at Faze. "No."

"Yes. You already invited me along. There's no taking it back now."

He turned and grumbled something under his breath. It sounded a lot like *pain in my ass*. Then he walked out the door and jumped off my balcony to the ground, where his Aurinda and my Freya were both saddled and waiting.

"What if I had said no to this trip?" I called down to him. "You would have gotten Freya ready for no reason."

We both knew I wouldn't have said no.

He sighed, looking skyward as I climbed down the ladder. "How many questions can I expect on this ride?"

"It's anyone's guess." I smiled as I stepped off the last rung and made my way to Freya.

We set off into the forest, a watchtower guard's whistle our farewell as we crossed the encampment's boundary. Five minutes into the ride, I was already lost in the trees, but I stayed beside Ransom, my frame rigid and alert as my gaze swept our surroundings.

He seemed perfectly at ease in the forest. I didn't relax until we'd descended a switchback hillside and entered a river valley lush with grass.

At least in the open, we could see a monster coming.

The landscape was stunning and green. Indigo mountains cut a jagged line into the horizon. White and yellow wildflowers sprang up through the grasses. The river sparkled blue as it wound through the valley. And far, far in the distance was a waterfall that hung like a curtain over the mountain's side.

"Ready for my first question?" I asked, breaking the silence.

"If I said no, would you ask it anyway?"

"Yes."

"Then by all means." He rolled a hand for me to continue. "Please. Ask."

"You made me swear to kill you. Who else has sworn that vow?"

"What makes you sure there are others? A hunch?"

"No. It's what I would do if I was in your position." If there was a chance I could hurt the people I loved, then I would have made those people promise to take my life.

He dragged a hand through his hair, the silky brown locks separating between his fingers.

"You need a haircut," I said.

"I need a haircut." He faced me, green eyes swallowing me whole. "Tillia. Halston. All of the rangers in his hunting party. They've all sworn to do what is necessary should I lose control."

"And Zavier?"

"He was the first to promise. And when the time comes for my death, I'd prefer it be his blade."

When the time comes. Not if. When. He was so certain that this ended with one possible outcome.

"What if there's a cure?"

"There isn't. I'll be out of your pretty hair before you know it."

I couldn't fathom the idea of Turah without the Guardian.

I'd been in this kingdom for nearly two months, and somehow, he'd become the center of this new life. The axis I seemed to orbit.

He saw me in a way that no one else had ever tried. He didn't stifle my sarcasm or snide remarks. He teased me about the questions, but lately, he'd indulged my curiosity the way he did Evie's. He gave me the freedom to be myself. To stop hiding.

He was a man who'd follow me off the cliff, who'd jump at my side, not pull me away from its edge.

He couldn't die. I refused to believe that was his only fate. Ransom might have ruled out a cure. But I hadn't. Not yet.

"So we're going to Ravalli for research. What are you hoping to find?" I asked.

"Hear, actually. You grew up in a castle. You know how valuable gossip can be. If there really is a person who created Lyssa, then there's a chance they told someone. Up until this point, we've been mostly concerned with tracking monsters. It's time to start listening to other rumors, too."

And maybe, in those rumors, find a thread of truth. "Why Ravalli?"

"With the recent lionwick attack, I assume there will be more chatter than normal."

"Ah." I nodded. "Whoever created Lyssa won't be easy to find."

Not if Ransom had been hunting monsters for years and had yet to hear whispers of a source. Not if they had some sort of unique magic.

"No, they won't," he said. "But creating something like this, it's unlikely they acted alone. To trap a monster. To give it this infection. All I can do is hope that we find one decent lead. I doubt we will today. But this is a start."

"There's a chance that people will stay quiet if I'm along." I was an outsider. Someone to fear, not trust.

"Possibly. Or they'll leap at the opportunity to have their future queen's ear."

I scoffed. "People don't seem to know I'm married to Zavier. He hasn't even told Evie. Also, I'm no queen."

"Yet here you are, helping to save our people."

I shrugged. "It's the right thing to do. For all of Calandra."

He reached out and flicked the end of a curl. "Spoken like a queen."

"Stop." I bristled, swatting him away. "I don't want to be a queen."

"Tough shit."

I scrunched up my nose. "Moving on. Have you spoken to any pony riders? They blaze across the kingdom. They probably spread as much news as they deliver. Maybe they'll have heard a rumor or something."

Ransom's eyebrows came together, his mouth turning down.

"What?"

"That's a good idea."

"And you're annoyed you didn't think of it yourself."

"Yes," he admitted.

I beamed, sitting taller in my saddle.

"There's an outpost for the pony riders past Ravalli," he said. "We'll go when we're done in the village."

Faze squirmed, awake from his morning nap, and let out a whimper.

I fished his bottle from my satchel and held it for him to drink.

"You're really keeping the cat?" Ransom asked.

"Did you think I'd change my mind?"

"Honestly? Yes."

I smiled at Faze. "I guess I have a soft spot for monsters."

Maybe they were all more than they seemed.

Or maybe this little tarkin would kill me in my sleep.

Forty

Ravalli was as different from Ashmore and Treow and Ellder as they were from each other. So far, each Turan town I'd visited was unique.

It wasn't this way in Quentis. Roslo was the largest city, and the only feature that made it stand apart from the other cities along the coastline was the castle. The villages and towns inland were all similar, dotted with the same style of buildings. White or gray plaster walls with gray thatched roofs. Most homes incorporated a splash of teal to represent the royal color.

The buildings in Ravalli were all constructed from rough-hewn logs, reminding me more of Ellder's fortress walls than a family's home. They were wooden, top to bottom, with small windows. And all of them were sunken into the ground so that to enter through a door, you had to descend four or five steps first. The roofs were nearly at eye level, and each was spiked with metal spears, like the roofs in Ellder. Spikes to deter the crux. Sunken homes in place of underground shelters.

Nothing had been built to align with the dirt roads. Instead, each road flowed around whoever put their house in its path. The village was a series of brown log boxes that sat at odd angles. Shops were scattered from one end of town to the other, mingled in between homes.

By the time we weaved through the village and found the inn, I was utterly lost. If not for the mountains and hills beyond the town, I'd have no reference as to which direction we'd come from.

Ransom dismounted Aurinda and took Freya's reins as I swung off my saddle to the ground.

"We'll leave the horses here." He tied both to a hitching post. "I'll have a stable boy come and get them."

"All right." I followed him through the inn's front door, watching as he ducked through its frame.

After spending last night sleeping on a thin blanket with a rock digging into my back, I was hoping to crash in an actual bed tonight.

The inside of the inn was dark. The bottom floor was a tavern lit by a chandelier of elk antlers and the small fire burning in the hearth. Summer was fading, and the cool mornings proclaimed that autumn was on its way. But the afternoons were still hot, and that fire made the space sticky.

Ransom cut a path through the tables toward the long bar at the far side of the room.

A man with a red scarf tied around his neck nodded as Ransom stopped beside a row of wooden stools.

Not a single person was here besides the barkeep, but the smell of people lingered, sweat and smoke and stale beer. There wasn't a single window. Not one. And the door was as thick as the walls.

Even the largest of grizzurs wouldn't be able to claw its way into this tavern.

Ransom set a stack of coins on the bar, then shook the barkeep's hand. When he returned to my side, he had two brass room keys.

"Not sleeping on my floor tonight?" I asked as he gave me one.

"Don't make me regret giving you your own space."

"Please." I huffed. "I would never cause trouble."

"That you actually believe yourself is the most terrifying part of that statement."

I threw up a hand. "Hey, trouble finds me. I don't go looking for it."

He nodded to Faze. "Says the woman with a tarkin strapped to her chest."

"Fair point," I muttered. "Now what?"

"Would you like to sit down? Get something to eat or drink?"

In this hot, stuffy room? "No."

"Then let's go." Ransom led the way out the door, taking us back outside.

I filled my lungs with the sweet afternoon air laced with the scents of grass and water from the river nearby. "What will we do first?"

"I'd like to find whoever killed the lionwick. The local blacksmith should know. We'll start there."

"Lead the way."

We fell into step, side by side, winding through the roads and alleys until the sound of hammers pounding on metal brought us to the forge. Like I did at the tavern, I hung back while Ransom greeted the smith.

The older man had tufts of white hair above his ears, but otherwise, his head was bald. His gaze floated in my direction once and only once before he turned and addressed Ransom alone.

"Good day, Guardian."

Damn. This was what I'd been afraid of. Maybe I shouldn't have come.

These people weren't going to lay out their truths with a golden-eyed stranger in their midst. Despite what Ransom believed, they didn't trust me. Hell, *he* didn't trust me.

"And to you, smith."

"Who is your companion?" the smith asked, his voice low but not low enough.

"Princess Odessa Wolfe."

"Wolfe?" The smith choked on his own spit, coughing to clear his throat.

"Wolfe. She is the Sparrow."

The smith turned, eyes wide, and dropped into a bow.

Ransom smirked.

So that was his plan. He hadn't been worried about these people distrusting a stranger. This was the first stop on my introductory tour of Turah. And he was going to use my novelty as the Sparrow to lure information out of these people. Not that I was really necessary.

The Guardian was a novelty all on his own. But this might draw a bit more fanfare. Bring people in from the outskirts.

Smart. Damm it.

"It's a pleasure to meet you," I told the smith. "You have a lovely forge."

I didn't know much about forges, but I'd been reading up on Turan customs and specialties, metal forging being toward the top of the list. I was probably going to sound like an ass, but I pointed to the tools he'd organized on shelves and hung on hooks.

"I don't know if I've ever seen such an impressive collection of chisels and dies and cone mandrels before."

The man stood tall, smiling, his cheeks flushing red. "Thank you, Highness. It's taken me a lifetime to acquire it all."

"A lifetime well spent." I smiled.

"We were traveling by and heard a rumor that you've had an unfortunate encounter with a lionwick." Ransom walked to a row of hooks hung from a beam. He took one out, weighing the metal in his hand. "Was anyone killed?"

"No. Thankfully. But it took six men to bring it down. Something wasn't right with that monster."

Like the fact that it had green blood. People might not know it was called Lyssa, but green blood was hard to ignore. How many Turans had started to suspect that something was wrong?

"The paperman, he's new in town, got a nasty slice on his arm," the smith said.

"Paperman?" I asked, instantly perking up. Papermen meant information, hopefully more than was shared in the paper in Ellder.

"He's from your kingdom, Highness," the smith said. "Left Quentis after his wife was taken to the shades. He's been in Ravalli six months. Nice fellow. Keeps to himself. Though I'm afraid there's not much happening around these parts that isn't shared first at the tavern. By the time he prints his paper, it's usually old news."

A Quentin paperman. Did I know him? Had I read his work before?

The smith shuffled closer, checking behind me to make sure no one was eavesdropping. "If he was smart, he'd stop printing facts and start telling stories. We don't have many storytellers in town. He'd make far more coin spinning tales. I even suggested it to him once. But he's stuck on these suspicions about the king's militia."

Ransom shot me a look that said *don't you dare*.

I ignored it and inched closer to the smith. "Forgive me. I'm new to your kingdom. The king's militia?"

"Yes, Highness. King Ramsey is recruiting for his militia. There hasn't been one in an age. I think it's in preparation for the migration."

"Ah. What exactly is suspicious about that?"

The smith shrugged. "Not sure. They haven't made the paper yet."

"I see." Our next stop would be the paperman's office.

"I think he's leading some of the more gullible folks on," the smith said. "Speculating about something amiss. Making sure those of us who subscribed to the paper when he moved to town don't drop him. A salesman if I ever saw one."

"I'd have to agree. I'm certainly intrigued." I gave him a kind smile. "Thank you for your time. It was lovely visiting with you."

"And you, Highness." He bowed again.

Was this how it would be from now on? Bows and formal titles? How long until news of the Sparrow spread across Turah? The secrecy had to end at some point. But I still wasn't ready.

"Shall we, my queen?" Ransom extended a hand toward the road.

I waved goodbye to the smith.

He dipped his chin, and for the first time he seemed to notice that I was carrying something across my chest. But before he could peek inside the wrap, I turned, keeping Faze hidden from sight.

Then I waited until we were out of earshot before I asked Ransom, "Is the militia for the migration? Or something else?"

Like an invasion.

Or to defend against one.

"I have bigger problems than Ramsey." Ransom flicked his wrist. Topic over.

I'd never seen a king dismissed so quickly.

"You told the smith who I was. That's your plan, isn't it? That's why you brought me along? I'm here to get attention."

Ransom looked down, green gaze finding mine as another smirk toyed on his mouth. "Worked like a charm."

I rolled my eyes. "You could have told me."

"It was more fun this way."

"For you," I muttered. "We should talk to the paperman."

Ransom stopped walking.

"What? Don't you think he'd be an important person to question?"

He raised his eyebrows. And waited for me to realize we were standing in front of a building with a small placard on the front door.

Ravalli Paper.

"Oh."

"After you." He took the steps down to the door, then opened it and waved me inside.

It was brighter than the inn, thanks to the small windows cut into the logs, but not by much. If we kept going in and out of buildings today, I was going to get a headache as my eyes adjusted to different lights.

A long, sturdy table acted as a partition in the entryway. Beyond it were other tables, all crowded with papers and ink. And against the far wall, a press spanned the entirety of the space.

Ransom rapped his knuckles on the wooden table, and a moment later, the paperman appeared from the hallway.

He wore a smile and thin, wire-framed glasses. His amber starbursts over brown eyes and his mop of blond hair reminded me of home. His left arm was in a sling, and a bandage poked out from the sleeve of his tunic. "Hello. How can I help you?"

Before Ransom could answer, a boy flew in from the hallway. He had his father's features but with lanky limbs and the kind of uncontrolled movements that happened when children grew too fast.

The boy panted, out of breath, as he clutched his father's uninjured arm. "Papa. The Guardian. He's in Ravalli! Do you think we can meet him?"

One corner of Ransom's mouth twitched, and he cleared his throat. "There's a good chance."

The boy did a double take. Then he swayed to the side, barely keeping his balance.

"Jonas." The paperman steadied his son and shook his head. "Take a breath."

The boy stared, jaw on the floor, at Ransom.

I pulled in my lips to hide a smile.

"We're honored by your visit," the paperman said. "Welcome. How can I help?"

"I'd like to ask you about that." Ransom pointed to the bandage.

The man sighed. "I'm a better writer than I am a warrior. I probably should have just stayed out of the way. But that monster was vicious, and I wouldn't have been able to live with myself if someone had died."

"What happened?" Ransom asked.

"Papa saw it first," Jonas blurted, then pointed to the window beside the front door. "He was in here working and saw it walk down the street. He took his crossbow and went after it. Shot it clean in the gut, and it didn't stop. Took six men shooting at it to bring it down. The monster looked like a pincushion by the time it was dead."

Ransom looked to the paperman, waiting for confirmation of the boy's story.

"It's as Jonas says." He nodded. "I've never seen anything like it."

"How'd you get hurt?" I asked.

"It came for me after that initial shot. I yelled for help. By that point, others had come out armed. I was reloading my crossbow but wasn't fast enough. I fired a second bolt, sent it right into the monster's neck, enough to slow it down, but its tail whipped out. Caught me in the arm and cut it to the bone."

I winced.

"The healers were able to sew me up. I'll be right as rain in no time." He put his free arm around the boy's shoulders.

The color had drained from his son's face, like he was reliving the incident and seeing his father hurt.

"Was there anything else you noticed about the monster?" Ransom asked.

The man glanced at his son like he didn't want to keep talking about the attack, but for the Guardian, he did it anyway. "Its eyes were cloudy. And its blood wasn't red, but green. It's got a lot of people scared and talking. And the stink of that monster." He shuddered. "I'll never forget that horrid smell. It was like being in the middle of an Ozarth cave ginger bog."

"Cave ginger? The candy?" It smelled sweet and spicy. One of my personal favorites.

"Only after it's been harvested and crystalized. They grow it in alligask bogs that give off the most vile, rancid smell. If you love the candy, never see where it's farmed. You'll never eat it again."

"Noted."

The alligask lived in swamps and bogs. Their bodies were covered in lime-green scutes, and their tails were twice the length of their bodies. They could walk on land, though their legs were so short their bellies scraped along the dirt. The monsters could unhinge their massive jaws to swallow prey whole.

"You're well traveled, if you've been to the bogs in Ozarth," Ransom said.

The paperman shrugged, his eyes growing distant as he kept his arm around his son's bony shoulders. "My wife was the traveler. We were simply her willing companions."

"Mother died two winters past," the boy said, his throat bobbing as he swallowed. "She was killed by a cutpurse."

My hand came to my heart. "I'm so sorry."

"We came to Turah to start over." The man and son shared a smile. "Just the two of us."

"Why Ravalli?" I asked. There had to be larger towns where they could sell more papers.

"It's about as far from Quentis as we could get."

Ouch.

Ransom held out his arm. "I didn't ask your name."

"Samuel Hay."

My mouth fell open. "Samuel Hay? As in the author of *A Year in Quentis*?"

"Um, yes." He let out a small laugh. "Not many people around here know I wrote that book."

The book of lies? Heat flared in my veins as my blood began to boil. Red coated my vision.

This was the asshole who'd accused my father of murdering my mother?

"It's a pleasure to meet you," Ransom said. "This is Odessa Wol—"

"Cross," I said. "Odessa Cross."

Samuel's smile fell flat. His eyes bulged.

"From Quentis," I added, crossing my arms over my chest.

"Princess." Samuel dropped into a bow, hauling his son along. "I, uh…"

The moment was awkward and tense. He looked like he wanted to crawl beneath this table and hide.

Good.

The tension must have stirred Faze, because he chose that moment to awaken from his nap with a whining growl.

The boy, Jonas, shot upright and pointed to my carrier. "What's that?"

"Oh, um." *Shit.* This kid had just watched his father get sliced by a lionwick. He probably didn't need to see a baby tarkin. "We should probably go."

Except Faze squirmed enough that the covering slipped, revealing his face and violet eyes.

"Is that a tarkin?" The boy's face lit up, and he planted both hands on the table, leaping over the surface. "Is it yours? How long have you had it? What does it eat? What's its name?"

"Jonas," Samuel hissed.

The boy's hands flew into his blond hair, pulling at the strands as his body vibrated with excitement. "Where did you get it? How old is it? Can I see it?"

This kid was so much like Evie that all I could do was laugh. "His name is Faze."

With a hand under his belly, I fished him out of his carrier and set him on the floor.

Jonas dropped to his knees, smiling at the monster as he held out a hand. His face was alight with wonder as he watched Faze stretch and flick his tail in the air. "Wow."

"You can pick him up."

Jonas didn't hesitate as he hauled Faze into his lap, stroking along the row of scales down the tarkin's spine. "You're a princess. *And* a legend tamer."

A flush spread across my cheeks. When I glanced to Ransom, his emerald eyes and a smirk were waiting.

"Legend tamer."

The last thing I needed was another nickname. But maybe, someday, if I ever saw Mae again, I'd tell her that once upon a time, a boy called me a legend tamer.

She probably wouldn't believe me.

"Thank you for your time," Ransom told Samuel. "We'll be on our way."

"You're leaving?" Jonas clutched Faze to his chest. "Already?"

"Why don't I stay a while longer?" I offered. "So Jonas can play with Faze?"

In truth, I wanted to find out about this militia and Samuel's suspicions. And I wouldn't mind setting the record straight about Quentis.

Especially that libel he'd printed about Father killing my mother.

Ransom's eyes narrowed. No doubt he knew I had my reasons. "Don't wander off. I'll be back."

I nodded, waiting for him to leave. Then I plastered on a sugary smile and faced the author.

"So…let's talk about your book."

Samuel had the decency to cringe.

Forty-One

Samuel's parents were Quentin traders. They were some of the very few who braved the Evon Ravine to deliver goods to Genesis by wagon.

His beloved wife, Emsley, had been the daughter of their family's biggest rival.

Samuel and Emsley met as children. Fell in love as teenagers. And when they left Quentis together, her pregnant with Jonas, it caused quite the uproar between their families, as both had been expected to take over as merchants.

Instead, they'd spent years exploring Calandra. Her dream had been to see every corner of the continent, so he'd traveled at her side, selling stories to papermen for coin to fund their journey.

Jonas was eleven when they returned to Quentis to care for Emsley's ailing mother. A year later, Emsley had been murdered in Roslo. And another hard, miserable year after that had inspired Samuel to write his book.

About my people.

His, too.

After Ransom left, Samuel had invited me in to sit for tea. Both of our cups had grown cold as he'd told me the story of his wife. Of how they met.

Of how she died.

And of why he'd written that book after her death.

"I regret it," he told me. "If I could go back, I'd toss that book into the Marixmore and forget it ever existed."

"Why did you write it?"

"I was angry. Lost in grief. Bitter at how hard life was in the city. Foolish enough to think that coin would solve our problems."

"You called us traitors and thieves. You accused my father of murdering my mother."

His gaze slammed to the floor. "I'm sorry. I exploited a rumor from a drunk nobleman without proof. I embellished because I knew it would sell."

"Did it?"

"Enough to buy us passage across the Krisenth. To bring Jonas here, where the children at school don't taunt him for his father's mistakes. Enough to build this house. To buy a used Turan press. To give me the chance to be a better man."

A part of me wanted to know more about that rumor from a drunken nobleman. To find out exactly why someone thought my father capable of killing my mother. The other part of me knew I wasn't ready for that story, so I changed the subject.

"The blacksmith said you've been writing about the king's militia."

Samuel straightened, shock that we were on to a different topic flashing across his face for a moment. "Y-yes."

"You're suspicious?"

"Quite." He took a sip of his cold tea, cradling the cup in his hand. "From what I've heard visiting with families, not a single soldier who's gone to join this militia has written home. They enlist and all but disappear. Don't you find that strange?"

I shrugged. "I guess. But maybe the training regimen is different for Turan soldiers than it is in Quentis."

For soldiers in Quentis, living in barracks was optional. Most stayed with their families unless they had no home to begin with.

"I thought the same, but I've spent months talking to men who served the king in their youth. They all find it strange how letters go unanswered and visits home are never made."

I hummed. "It is odd. Do these men all go to Allesaria?"

"Possibly. I'm not sure."

"Have you been to the capital?" I picked up my own tea, hoping to mask the hint of desperation in my voice.

"No."

Damn it.

Samuel exhaled a long breath, sinking deeper into his chair. "You know, I thought that maybe the mystery surrounding Allesaria was all an exaggeration. That once I arrived here, I'd learn it wasn't Calandra's best-kept secret."

"It's no exaggeration, is it?"

He shook his head. "No. The paperman in me wants to dig and find the truth. To expose the reason for why the Turans would keep the location of their capital a secret. But the father in me has decided to let it go. I won't risk Jonas. I'm all he's got. We're safe here, despite the incident with the lionwick. My son is happy. That's really all that matters."

"Understandable." I gave him a small smile. "I can't quite wrap my head around the mystery of Allesaria, either. Part of me isn't even sure the city exists."

Samuel barked a laugh. "I actually wondered that myself. But there is a woman in Ravalli who has been there. According to her, the road is treacherous. It is guarded by a stone wall, and the only way to be granted entrance through the gates is by blood oath."

I blinked. "A blood oath to enter a city?"

"To keep its location a secret."

Okay, now I was even more interested. That was beyond extreme. What the hell was happening in Allesaria to keep it so secret?

"Now my curiosity is piqued," I told him.

"Be careful of that curiosity." He lowered his voice, like even within his walls we were risking this conversation. "It has not been easy to find my place in Ravalli. The Turans are incredibly distrustful of outsiders. Even as the Sparrow, they won't welcome you with open arms."

A few people had made me feel welcome. Tillia. Evie. Luella and Cathlin. But I understood what he was saying. For the most part, the people of Turah avoided me.

"I wasn't even supposed to be the Sparrow."

"It was to be your sister, right?"

"Mae." I nodded. "This was very unexpected. And sudden. I don't know much about Turah. I've never even seen a map."

Samuel set his cup aside and leaned in closer. "Maps are forbidden. If you're found with one, it is punishable by death."

"Death? Over a map?" Well, fuck. No wonder I'd had such a hard time finding a map. A map likely didn't exist.

"Like I said, Princess. Be careful."

A shiver rolled down my spine. "I just don't understand. A capital is home to a kingdom's leaders. The place for diplomacy. To establish governance. A center for trade and commerce. A place to celebrate culture and preserve history. Why keep Allesaria a secret? What happened three generations ago that made the Turan rulers withdraw so severely?"

"That, I do not know," he said. "For all intents and purposes, Perris serves as the capital. It is the Turan center for trade and commerce. The king makes his decrees there, and they are disseminated across the kingdom."

"By pony riders?"

Samuel nodded. "In part. Also by the Turan army. Each town has its own governance system, but it all rolls up to the king. The soldiers stationed in Ravalli ensure peace and compliance. Any resistance is met with a heavy hand. At least that's how it was before the soldiers left."

They'd been pulled away. Just like they had been in Ashmore. The king had left these people to fend for themselves against monsters. Against Lyssa.

"From what I have gathered, the wealth of this kingdom's knowledge lives behind Allesaria's walls. And they do not share. It's not like healers in Laine who make discoveries and force other kingdoms to pay for their knowledge and resources."

"The Turans keep it to themselves," I guessed.

"They keep it in Allesaria. I've heard more than a few bitter comments in the tavern about how those who live in the wilds are treated as less than the Turans in the city. That their scholars and alchemists and healers look down upon those who choose to mill lumber. Ironically, the industry that actually funds this kingdom."

Scholars. Alchemists. Those with the knowledge and skill to create a deadly infection.

Allesaria, apparently, did exist. I could toss out the idea that the capital city was a myth. A ruse. And the only way I'd see that city was with a guide and another blood oath.

Would Ransom take me there if I told him I suspected that Lyssa had been created within the city's walls? That it might have been crafted beneath Ramsey's nose?

Hell, maybe Ramsey had sanctioned its creation himself. Maybe that was why he'd refused to tell people about the infection.

That thought made my heart climb into my throat. Was that what Father wanted in Allesaria? Was Lyssa the secret to saving our people from the crux? Was Ramsey going to use it to save the Turans? But if he'd found a way to protect his people during the migration, wouldn't Turah have more Guardians already?

The front door opened, and Ransom walked inside. His ears must have been burning. He spotted Jonas still on the floor with Faze. And me sitting beside Samuel.

"Thank you for the tea." I set my cup aside, then stood, making my way toward the front of the room. I stole Faze from Jonas's arms and tucked him back into his carrier.

With a farewell to them both, I followed Ransom outside and along the roads to the inn. "The lionwick?"

"Lyssa."

"Did you learn anything else?"

"There was an attack in the mountains weeks ago by a grizzur. Two hunters. Both dead. A pack of bariwolves killed a merchant and his daughter. There's no way of knowing if any of the monsters were infected or not. But there have been more attacks in these parts. It's set everyone on edge."

"It means you might be getting closer to the source. What if…" I trailed off, knowing as soon as I finished that sentence, he was going to close up. I could already feel it. But I had to get it out there. I had to ask. "Samuel mentioned that most of Turah's alchemists and scholars live in Allesaria. What if someone in the capital is the source?"

He scoffed, shaking his head. "No one in Allesaria created Lyssa."

"How do you know?"

"I just do."

"But—"

"You know nothing about the city, Cross." The bite in his voice was a sting. "Don't bring it up again."

Gods, these Turans were stubborn. This Turan in particular.

The rest of the walk to the inn was in silence. The common room that had been empty earlier was now teeming with patrons, some drinking ale, others inhaling plates of food.

As Ransom walked through the room with me trailing behind, conversation and laughter dimmed to murmurs and whispers. About him. About me.

Word of my identity had already spread like wildfire. Was that why it was so crowded here tonight? Why the barkeep was smiling wide?

Our visit meant every table in his establishment was full.

We didn't linger around the others, instead moving down a narrow hallway with six doors in total. My key fit the last door on the right, Ransom's across the hall on the left.

"We'll leave for the outpost tomorrow. Be ready by dawn. The barkeep knows to bring you dinner."

"All right."

Ransom paused, one hand on his door. "Ramsey is rumored to be on his way here tomorrow."

"Oh." I blinked. Was that the reason for his sour mood? Or was it because I'd brought up Allesaria? Or both?

"We will not be here when he arrives," Ransom said.

"All right. Do you have a problem with Ramsey?"

"Something like that." He glanced over his shoulder, eyes meeting mine.

I expected him to disappear into his room, but he paused, staring at me like there was something important on his mind. Something he needed to say.

"What?" I whispered. *Tell me. Just tell me.*

He shook his head. "Nothing. Good night, my queen."

Blarg. "Good night, Ransom."

His eyes went from green to hazel in a blink. He walked into his room and slammed the door. The lock flipped.

Did he regret telling me his name?

Well, too bad. I liked saying it.

The twin moons still lightened the sky when I walked outside the inn the next morning. Dawn had yet to arrive.

Faze was curled in his carrier, asleep after the bottle of milk I'd fed him earlier. My satchel hung over a shoulder, my hair tight in a braid except for the errant curls at my temples.

The road outside the inn was empty, all of Ravalli still asleep in their beds.

Except for the man walking down the street, leading two horses to the inn.

"How early do I need to wake up to beat you to one of these dawn rendezvous?" I asked Ransom.

"Get ready. We need to leave."

So much for my attempt to lighten the mood and move past the awkwardness from last night. I snatched the reins from his grip and moved to Freya's side. Except before I could put a foot in the stirrup, a horse nickered in the distance.

Aurinda danced at the sound, his hooves clomping on the dirt.

"Fuck," Ransom hissed.

"What?"

He looked both ways like he was searching for an escape.

I followed his gaze, seeing nothing but boxy buildings and lonely roads. But then the ground beneath my feet began to vibrate, like a ripple spreading across calm water.

They swept into Ravalli like a storm. In a blink, the deserted streets were flooded with riders. Some of the men were dressed in clothes like mine. Others were soldiers in uniform. Their clothing and armor bore the crest of King Ramsey Wolfe.

We were too late. Ramsey had arrived in Ravalli before we could leave.

Who were the men dressed in regular clothes? Recruits for this militia?

Whoever they were, they'd certainly drawn attention. Doors opened, people still dressed in nightclothes filling thresholds to see what the commotion was about.

The king's soldiers converged on the inn like flies to honey. Like they knew exactly where to find Ransom. They came from all angles, blocking us in. No weapons were drawn. No threats were made. No one spoke a word. They simply stared at us, waiting.

Ransom scowled at a few in the front row—the men smart enough to shy away. Then he went about tightening Aurinda's cinch and securing his saddlebags. "Get on your horse, Cross."

Did he actually think these men were going to let us leave?

"Cross," he growled.

"Right." There were too many eyes on me as I climbed into Freya's saddle.

Would he fight his way through this throng? Or would they move to let us pass?

Ransom swung onto his stallion, and the atmosphere shifted. A charge rippled through the men.

Were they going to lock arms and form a blockade? Two men, both in uniform, shared a look as Ransom cleared his throat. Then they parted, guiding their horses to the side to make a path.

"Are they really going to let us leave?" I whispered.

"Of course not." Ransom lifted his chin, his face hardening to stone as his eyes turned to liquid metal. Molten silver.

Well, that wasn't good.

"Say nothing," he said. "Not a single word."

I gulped and mouthed, *Okay.*

Ramsey rode through the gap, sitting taller than any of his men. His horse was the same sleek gray mount he'd ridden into Treow, the animal nearly as large as Aurinda. And the king himself had an imposing figure, as tall and broad as Ransom. He wore a circlet, like Zavier, the silver glinting above his brow.

He had been too far away when he came to Treow for me to get a good look, but he had strong features, from his wide nose and stoic brow line to his square jaw and the dimple in the center of his chin. Ramsey's eyes were a steely gray that might as well have been ice. He stopped in front of Ransom, and their glares clashed.

It lasted an eternity, their silent standoff. They stared at each other, locked in a soundless war, while I did my best not to breathe.

Shouldn't Ransom have bowed? Should I have? My nerves spiked as Faze shifted in his carrier, letting out a snort.

It might as well have been a clanging bell.

All eyes shifted in my direction, including Ramsey's.

His gaze narrowed as he studied my face, my hair. "You're the bride prize. The Sparrow."

I have a name.

Ransom's face whipped to me, his nostrils flaring.

Oops. Sorry, I mouthed.

Apparently, in times of stress, the thoughts that were supposed to stay in my head came out of my mouth.

But Ramsey wasn't interested in learning my name. His focus returned to Ransom. "She should be in Allesaria."

My heart thumped. A good thump? A bad? I wasn't sure. Yes, I wanted to go to Allesaria. But not with Ramsey. He wouldn't take me away, would he? Like some sort of kidnapping?

Was that why Ransom looked about ready to commit murder? Was he going to fight off the king, this mob of men, so I wouldn't be dragged to the capital city?

"Not until she can be trusted," Ransom said.

It hurt more than it should have. He'd promised never to trust me. And silly me, I'd thought maybe he'd changed his mind.

If I had a map to Allesaria right now, would I find a way to get it to my father? Could I betray these people? Could I betray Ransom?

Everything I'd been raised to believe seemed fragile. My father had asked me to trust him. I had trusted him. I did trust him.

But...

Could I betray the Turans?

No. No, I couldn't.

Even with the uncertainty about the coming migration. Even facing Ramsey. I couldn't betray Tillia or Luella or Cathlin or Zavier.

I couldn't betray Ransom.

He might not trust me. But somewhere along the way, he'd earned my loyalty.

Gods, it was like my father all over again. But I didn't care if the trust only went one direction. I wasn't sure what my father was so determined to get from Allesaria, but I wasn't going to let him harm these people.

"We have somewhere to be," Ransom said. "Was there anything else,

Majesty?"

Oof. Not in all my years had I ever heard a person use that title with such disdain.

If the insult bothered Ramsey, he didn't let it show. A slow grin stretched his mouth, a challenge in his pale eyes aimed at Ransom before he glanced once more to me. "Such pretty hair. It's no wonder you caught my son's eye, Princess."

Except when I met Zavier, I had brown hair. I gave Ramsey a practiced, cloying smile. "Thank you, Majesty."

Ransom urged Aurinda forward, his stallion snorting at the king's like the beasts were engaged in this standoff, too.

Ramsey shifted to the side, waving a hand toward the opening in his line of soldiers. He made a show of granting us permission to leave.

Ransom's molars clenched so loudly I could hear them crack, but he started down the line, with me following close behind.

I wanted out of this town. Immediately.

It shouldn't have surprised me that the gods had other ideas.

The shout came at the same time I spotted a cloud of thick smoke lifting above the rooflines.

"Ransom," I gasped.

But he was already moving, guiding Aurinda through the men, sending them scattering as he drew the sword from its sheath.

They parted like curtains over a window, making room for us to tear past homes toward the smoke. Toward Samuel Hay's home. It was surrounded by men with burning torches.

"No," I cried, heart seizing.

Jonas stood outside his home, watching as flames licked the walls, spreading up the wooden logs. His eyes were wild as he cupped his hands to his mouth and screamed, "Papa!"

People ran toward the commotion, carrying buckets of water. But before they could get close enough to douse the flames, the soldiers blocked their path, pushing them away.

"Papa!" Jonas's voice cracked as he screamed again.

"Samuel." I looked to Ransom, but he was already off his horse, racing past soldiers before they thought to stop him. He moved like the wind down the stairs and into the house, the fire blowing back as if the flames were terrified to touch his skin.

My heart climbed into my throat as I leaped down from Freya, rushing to Jonas's side and clutching the boy tight before he dared go inside, too.

Tears streamed down his cheeks. "Papa."

"It's okay," I said, signing the Eight. "He'll be okay."

Ama, save him.

I didn't pray for Ransom. My heart knew he was alive. That a fire would not claim his body. So I prayed for this boy's last remaining parent as I stared, unblinking, at the door.

The fire raged, higher and hotter, singeing my face. But as I tried to pull Jonas away, he fought me, taking a step forward instead.

"We must move back."

"No." He sobbed. "Please."

Samuel must have heard his child's plea. He ran out the door, arms laden with books and clothes and anything else he could carry up those steps.

"Papa." Jonas jumped to his feet, colliding with his father as the two embraced, their belongings sinking to the dirt along with them as they dropped to their knees.

The soldiers converged on them, trying to rip the books from his hold.

"Touch them and you die." Ransom, covered in soot and ash and sweat, walked through the door with a haul like Samuel's.

The soldiers, smart men, backed away.

Ransom set everything in his arms beside Samuel, then stood tall, his lip curled as a growl tore from his throat.

This wasn't Ransom.

This was the Guardian.

The monster.

Brutal. Menacing. Lethal and fearless.

Power pulsed off his body, as hot as the fire. His frame vibrated, his hands fisted. His control was leashed. But barely.

"We ride. Now." Ramsey's order cut through the roar of the fire. It carried over Jonas's cries and the whimpers from others watching on.

The Ravalli people were out in force, most carrying buckets of water to keep the flames from spreading.

The soldiers backed away from the Guardian, from the house they'd set on fire, needing no second order from their king.

Bastard.

This was his doing, just like the libraries. On Ramsey's order, Samuel's life was going up in a blaze. A single fire could have destroyed this entire town.

I whirled, finding Ramsey on his horse, watching the fiasco with a glint of approval in his eyes. "Coward."

His eyebrows arched. "What did you call me, Princess?"

"I called you a coward." The gasps at my back only fueled my rage.

"Watch yourself, girl. Your ignorance is showing."

"As is your true nature," I spat. "Only fools and liars burn books and people's homes."

Ramsey leaned forward in his saddle.

If he thought it would intimidate me, he was sorely mistaken. I squared my shoulders and let the two words in my mind bleed all over my face.

Fuck. You.

He straightened in the saddle. "I was told the Gold King's eldest daughter was weak. I see my spies have been mistaken."

It was a slice to the heart, and I smothered a flinch, refusing to let it show.

"There are many things happening in my kingdom, Princess Odessa Wolfe." His gaze left mine, flames dancing in his eyes as he took in the building at my back. "What Turah needs are a few fires."

"Leave." Ransom's voice was low and close, the command mere inches from my ear. He stood at my back, his body blocking the heat from the fire. But not the heat from his own fury.

"You have one month," Ramsey told him. "Do not make me come and find you again."

A month? What happened in a month?

Ramsey turned his stallion and sauntered off, his men falling into ranks at his flank.

Chaos erupted as the last soldier rode away from Samuel Hay's home. People frantically worked to extinguish the fire, to keep it from spreading to the neighboring houses.

"What did he mean, you have a month? A month for what?" I asked Ransom. But when I turned, he was already gone.

Forty-Three

The sun was setting on the longest day I could remember. Yesterday's fire seemed a lifetime ago.

Ransom and I had stayed in Ravalli after the king left with his men. We'd watched as Samuel Hay's house burned into a pile of charred rubble.

The coals had been too hot to wade through the ashes to search for anything salvageable. The only things that had survived, beyond the Hays themselves, were the armfuls Samuel and Ransom had carried out the door. Those meager belongings were now loaded into the rickety wagon that tumbled along the trodden path toward Ellder.

Ahead, Ransom led the way back to the fortress, his pace slow for the wagon. At my side, Samuel and Jonas were leaving one home in search of another.

We all smelled like smoke. It clung to my clothes and hair. My eyes were scratchy and dry.

Our small caravan had ridden into the night until we'd made a somber camp. Then, at first light this morning, we'd continued the slow journey to Ellder.

Many people in Ravalli had begged the Hays to stay. To rebuild. But Samuel was heartbroken. It was etched into every line of his face. He needed time to recuperate. To let his arm heal from the lionwick's attack. To get over the hacking cough that came from breathing in too much smoke.

I had a feeling that once he recovered, the Hays wouldn't stay in Turah for long.

His neighbors in Ravalli hadn't let them leave empty-handed. They'd offered extra food, clothing, and supplies. The wagon hitched to their gray mare was loaded to the brim. Jonas sat atop a crate behind his father, who held the reins.

The ride through the river valley had been eerily quiet. We'd seen no other travelers. No animals. Not even the birds seemed to chirp as they soared overhead. A cloud hung above us like a poisonous fog, chasing joy away.

Every time I thought about Ramsey, my rage would return. My teeth hurt from grinding them too hard.

Faze squirmed in his carrier, more than ready to roam free. He'd have the chance as soon as we reached Ellder.

We wouldn't be making a stop at the pony rider outpost.

"Not yet," I said, scratching his head.

"I could hold him," Jonas said. "If you want."

"Sure." I nodded, inching Freya closer to the edge of the wagon. Then, with both hands, I handed Jonas my tiny monster, hoping it would do them both some good. "Here's his bottle."

The boy took it after I fished it from my satchel, and because I had nothing else to do, because if I kept replaying that encounter with Ramsey I'd scream, I took out my journal.

Freya didn't need me to guide the way. She'd follow Ransom.

As I opened the journal's flap, I was careful to keep the loose pages tucked inside. Last night, in the solitude of my room, I'd taken them out and spread them across the floor until they'd formed my map.

For weeks, I'd been creating a map.

Now that I knew it was forbidden, that I was risking execution, I praised Ferious for his inspiration on this particular project. It must have been the God of Mischief's guidance that had made me disguise my map.

Rather than draw it on a single page, I'd used the edges and corners of many. They overlapped, fitting together like a puzzle.

If anyone did find my journal, they'd find drawings of monsters and treehouses and mountains and towns, each bordered with a few embellishments that looked like nothing on their own. But put together, lined up and overlapped just right, it was Turah.

Last night, I'd added a star for Ravalli. A winding line for this trail. And a single tick mark for a lionwick with Lyssa.

I had no way to know if my map was accurate. No way to plot Allesaria on these pages. That mission seemed bleak today. Pointless. So I turned to a fresh page and began a drawing of Faze.

"What are you working on?" Samuel asked.

"Oh, just a sketch." I held it up so he could see the rough outline of Faze's face.

"That's quite a likeness. You have a talent."

Had anyone ever called me talented? Not a mentor or teacher. Not Father. Not Margot. My drawings annoyed them. Another day, I would have beamed. Today, any show of pride was stifled by our solemn mood.

"Thank you." I gave him a smile, then tucked the journal away. Not even sketching could take my mind off that fire. "I'm sorry, Samuel."

It wasn't my fault, my apology to make, but I'd said those words a dozen times today.

"So am I." He glanced over his shoulder to his son playing with Faze. "All that matters is that Jonas is safe."

"And so are you."

"Because of him." His eyes flooded with tears as he pointed to Ransom. "I sent Jonas out while I tried to grab everything I could carry. Some of his clothes. What we kept of Emsley's. Her diaries. A portrait and her wedding ring. Her favorite shawl. The booties she knitted for Jonas when he was a baby. I was leaving my bedroom when the fire spread across the hallway floor. The smoke was so thick. So dark."

A cough ripped from his mouth, and he doubled forward, hacking until it passed.

"Papa?" Jonas held Faze tight as he stared at his father.

"I'm all right, son." Samuel forced a smile as he sipped from a canteen—a gift from the Ravalli blacksmith. Then he breathed for a few minutes until the fit passed. "The Guardian walked through the fire. And I swear to you, Princess, those flames shied away. He picked me up, smashing everything in my arms between us, and carried us through the house until we reached the door. I dropped half my pile when he set me on my feet, and I left it behind. Decided it wasn't worth the risk. But he collected it all, every piece, and saved it. Saved me."

Could Ransom withstand flames? Was that Lyssa? Or was he simply unafraid? Was he willing to burn to save a father's life?

"I've heard the rumors. The tales," Samuel said, his voice low. "Jonas believed the legends, but I was always skeptical. They were true. He isn't a normal man. He really is a Guardian."

"Yes, he is."

"You're lucky to have him at your side."

"That I am."

Samuel looked like he had more to say, but instead, he dissolved into another fit of coughs.

Not wanting him to strain his voice, I urged Freya forward until we were at Ransom's side.

"How is he?"

I shrugged. "Sad, as expected."

Ransom exhaled. "As expected."

"But grateful. For you."

He shifted in his seat like the praise made him uncomfortable.

"I'm going to ask you questions now," I said.

"You wouldn't be you if you didn't come armed with questions. Honestly, I'm starting to feel like the weapons are unnecessary."

This. This was what I needed to chase away some of the fog. Bickering with Ransom.

"How did you get your nickname?" I'd heard stories in Quentis of how he'd slain monsters across Calandra. Of how he'd killed a band of Laine warriors who'd raided Turan border towns. Of how he'd rescued an orphanage from an avalanche.

It was probably all true. But I wanted to hear it from Ransom.

I wanted to know how the man who'd murdered Banner's brother over a woman could have been proclaimed the protector of Turah.

There was more to what had happened with Banner's brother, wasn't there? A piece of the story I was missing.

Ransom wasn't a murderer. I'd only ever seen him raise his weapons to monsters. To defend his people.

So what had really happened with Banner's brother? I had a hunch it had everything to do with his nickname.

"I was in Westor, on the coast," he said. "A port on the Krisenth. It was the year I was bitten. Lyssa didn't even have a name at that point. Only the Voster knew what had happened, how I'd changed. The High Priest was still trying to understand the infection. And I'd been following rumors of vicious monsters with green blood. Hunting for the bariwolf that bit me."

"Did you ever find it?"

"Yes." He paused. "In Ashmore."

"What?" I gaped. "How do you know?"

"Because I took its eye the day it bit me."

A one-eyed bariwolf.

The monster that had escaped.

"Oh, gods." I signed the Eight.

That monster was still out there, hunting. Killing. Infecting others.

Was that why its pack was so large? I didn't know enough about bariwolves. Were they that intelligent?

Ransom waved it off. "There was a girl in Westor, maybe thirteen or fourteen. Her mother was a widow, and she let out the spare room in their home to travelers. Not exactly the safest choice, inviting strange men into their home, but it was better than the alternative."

Inviting strange men into her body.

"The girl went to the market the day after I arrived and never came home. Her mother was sick with worry. By nightfall, she was certain her child was dead. I went and found her."

"Alive?"

He nodded. "She'd caught the attention of the wrong group of men. The kind that have no qualms about luring young girls to their ships."

My insides twisted, and I wasn't sure I wanted the rest of this story.

"The man who'd taken her had taken three others."

"He was kidnapping and selling them, wasn't he?"

"Probably. I didn't give him a chance to explain before I crushed his throat."

Gruesome. But deserved. "Good. And that's how you became the Guardian?"

He dragged a hand through his hair. "The girl's mother called me a guardian. Others heard. It all but carried on the wind."

"And floated all the way to Quentis."

"I'm not surprised. There are countless warriors and soldiers in Calandra, but the names of the best are widely known. Especially in royal circles."

"Who is the best in Quentis?"

"Banner." No hesitation. "His skill with throwing knives is unmatched."

It had been a while since I'd heard that name. In another lifetime, I'd stood on my cliffside, begging Banner not to seek revenge against the Guardian.

I'd believed Banner's story. Why wouldn't I? Except now that I knew Ransom, I couldn't imagine him killing so violently, crushing another man's windpipe, over a lover's quarrel. Banner must have been mistaken.

Gods, I hoped he'd been wrong.

"What happened with his brother?" I asked.

"I killed him."

That, I already knew. "Why?"

"Because he was the man who took those girls in Westor."

My hand pressed against my heart as it sank to my toes. Maybe it was naive, but I had to believe that Banner had no idea about his brother. I wanted to believe the man my father trusted hadn't known the full truth.

Not that it really mattered. I doubted I'd ever see Banner again.

"What did you do before you were the Guardian? Before you were bitten?" I couldn't picture him as anything other than Ransom, but he must have had an occupation.

"I was just another man at the king's disposal." His eyes turned distant, like it was so long ago he could barely see the man he'd been.

"What did Ramsey mean, you have a month?"

"He expects me to join him in Allesaria on the autumnal equinox."

The date when Mae was supposed to marry Zavier. "Why?"

"Because he's a fucking piece of filth."

"I won't argue with that," I said. "But that still doesn't answer my question."

"He has requested my presence in Allesaria to act as his general."

"Oh. Will you go?"

"No." He answered without hesitation.

"Will he force you?"

Ransom let out a dry chuckle.

"I'll take that as a no."

"Well, he'll certainly try." He tossed me a smirk. "But he won't succeed."

I tucked a curl behind my ear, knowing it wouldn't stay put. That felt like a theme at the moment. Fighting the inevitable, but fighting nonetheless. "If he knows about Lyssa, why won't he do anything to stop it?"

"I don't know."

Instead, Ramsey was more concerned with burning books and papermen than saving his people. My shoulders sagged, the weight of today heavy. "I hate him."

The corner of his mouth turned up. "I told you to stay quiet today."

"I couldn't help myself. He made me mad."

"Gods save the men who make you mad." He shook his head, and then a chuckle came from his throat. It preceded a smile.

A real smile, wide and white.

My heart skipped.

It was a smile to chase away that sullen fog. A smile to brighten a miserable day.

A smile, just for me.

It lasted for only a heartbeat. Smiles faded too fast these days. "Now what?" I asked.

"Nothing has changed, Cross. The goal is the same. Kill the monsters. Find the source."

"And a cure."

He sighed. "There is no cure."

I didn't have the energy for a debate today. "Is it working? These hunts?"

"I believe it is."

"How do you know?"

"To borrow your word…a hunch." He looked at his cuff like he could see through the leather, through the carvings, to the scar from his bite.

I'd seen that cuff countless times, but I hadn't really studied its markings. Some of the lines and indents weren't as prominent as others. They'd been flattened over time. Others were lighter, fresher cuts. His recent additions. One looked so new it could have been added today.

He'd told me those markings were for the lives he'd taken. Had he gone on a recent killing spree that I didn't know about?

There was a small diamond-shaped fleck above a square. A dashed line connected that square to another and another. And that square was surrounded with nine more diamond-shaped flecks. They were so small they must have been nicked into the leather with the tip of a knife.

Nine cuts.

For nine bariwolves at Ashmore?

Was the fresh mark from Ravalli?

What. The. Fuck.

Was that a map? Had Ransom defied the rules against charting Turah and made marks on that cuff for his kingdom?

What if all this time, what I'd been searching for was right there? Etched into that leather.

A map of Turah.

Was Allesaria on that leather?

"The reports are coming less and less," he said, bringing me back to the conversation. "I haven't spoken to Zavier since we left for Treow, but he'll be in Ellder. I'll talk to him about the source. We'll need to start searching for the fucker who created this."

"Zavier is in Ellder?"

"Yes."

Dread pooled in my gut. Not the feeling a wife should have at the prospect of seeing her husband again. "That's wonderful."

Ransom stared at my profile, his gaze burning into my cheek. "Is it?"

"Of course." We both knew I was a horrible liar. "I'd better check on Faze."

I pulled on Freya's reins, slowing her until I was beside the wagon. Then I made myself stay there for the rest of the journey, staring at Ransom's back.

It was dark by the time we arrived at the fortress, and goose bumps covered my arms from the night's chill.

Soldiers greeted us in the courtyard, others closing the gates at our backs. Stable boys rushed to secure our horses. And then a warrior appeared, a man I recognized from Treow, his forehead furrowed with concern.

"We didn't expect you tonight," he told Ransom, looking to Samuel and Jonas. The pair was standing together beside their wagon, taking it all in. "What happened?"

"Ramsey," Ransom growled, then waved Samuel closer. "That is Samuel Hay. He'll be staying in Ellder for the time being. Give him anything he requires."

"I'll see it done." The warrior couldn't have known about the hardships they'd faced today. About the hardships ahead. But when he faced the Hays, it was with a kind smile and warm welcome. "Come with me. I'll show you to a place you can stay."

"Good night," I told Samuel. Then I took Faze from Jonas's hold, the boy reluctant to set him free. "I'll bring him for a visit tomorrow."

Jonas's chin quivered, like the boy was on the verge of more tears.

Samuel wrapped an arm around his son's shoulders, and together, they followed the warrior down the main road, a stable boy leading their horse and wagon behind.

"Are you all right?" Ransom asked me.

"Fine." I wrapped my arms around my waist. "Tired."

"Are you hungry?"

"Not especially. But I'd like to say hello to Brielle and Jocelyn. Where are they staying?"

"The servants' quarters at Zavier's. Do you know where it is?"

"Evie showed me." She'd given me a thorough tour of the house, showing me every room, including those that were not hers to share.

"Cross, I—" Ransom snatched my hand, stopping me before I could leave. The touch sent a spark through my veins. The calluses on his palms felt like a dream on my skin. I didn't want them on just my hand.

He stared at me, hazel eyes reflecting the torchlight, and there it was again. The look of a man who was trying to figure out what to say.

I waited. And waited. And waited. "What?"

"Nothing." He dropped my hand, dragging his own over his face. "Good night, my queen."

My shoulders sagged. "Good night, Ransom."

I felt his gaze on my shoulders as I walked away, my footsteps heavy as I took the familiar path to the house.

Faze squirmed in my hold, but I kept him on my arm as we headed toward Zavier's and the servants' quarters on the main floor. Each room had its own door, giving the staff their own privacy to come and go as they pleased.

I rounded the corner of the house but came to an abrupt stop when I saw a man in the open doorway of the first apartment.

He wasn't alone.

A woman was in his arms, her lips on his as they kissed. She was as lost in him as he was in her.

His arms were banded around her tight, hiking up the hem of her tunic to reveal her bare legs and the curve of her naked ass. He was tall and dark and handsome. When he let her go, he pushed the blond hair away from her pretty face. Then he glanced over her head, shuffling himself and Jocelyn out of the doorway.

For their other companion to step outside.

He was in the middle of pulling a shirt over his head. Strange that this was the moment I saw my husband's bare chest for the first time. We'd been married for nearly two months. And now I knew the reason he didn't visit my bed.

He'd been in Jocelyn's instead.

A distant conversation, from a tent in the Turan wilds, clawed its way to the forefront of my mind.

Zavier likes to share.

He'd been sharing Jocelyn.

Faze let out a *rawr*.

Three faces whipped in my direction.

The color drained from Zavier's face.

"Highness." Jocelyn covered a gasp with her hand. "You're—"

Done.

I was very, very done with this fucking day.

Forty-Four

"**O**dessa, wait. Please." Zavier's boots pounded on the steps behind me as he followed me to the second floor.

I ignored him, taking the stairs two at a time until I reached the walkway. Then I marched toward my door, more than ready to disappear inside and block out the realm.

Except I wasn't going to get that wish. Not yet.

There was a scowling warrior blocking my path.

Ransom shoved off the wall where he'd been leaning. "What's wrong?"

"Nothing. You're in my way."

Did he move? No. He filled the walkway with his massive frame, forcing me to stop. His hazel eyes flickered over my head to Zavier. And then the hazel gave way to molten silver.

Was that anger on my behalf? Did he recognize the signs of a man who'd just fucked my lady's maid—the rumpled clothing, flushed cheeks, and finger-combed hair?

Zavier wasn't wearing his crown tonight. Maybe he'd forgotten it on Jocelyn's bedside table.

"I'm sorry, Ranse," Zavier said.

Why was he apologizing to Ransom? How about a godsdamn apology for me, the wife?

At this point, I didn't even want to hear it. I shoved past Ransom, my shoulder knocking into his arm as I clutched Faze to my chest. And when I reached my suite, I threw the door open and slammed it closed, dropping Faze to the floor as my hands dove into my hair, tugging and pulling at the braid that was already coming loose. "Damn it."

There were tears in my eyes.

Why? Why was I crying over this?

How could I be angry at Zavier? It wasn't like there was a smidgen of attraction between us. He'd never once expressed a romantic interest, and I couldn't even consider us friends.

It hadn't even bothered me to know that Banner, my fiancé, had kept a lover in Roslo. Yet this was bringing me to tears? Affairs were commonplace in my father's court. Of course there'd be affairs from Turan royals, too.

But why did he have to pick Jocelyn? Why, of all the women in Turah, did he have to choose my lady's maid as a lover?

I couldn't even blame him.

Jocelyn was beautiful and smart. Witty and strong. Most men gave her a second glance.

The only thing that earned me a second look was the crown some Turan soldier had stolen from my treehouse in Treow.

It wasn't that he'd chosen Jocelyn.

It was that he hadn't chosen me.

Why was I never the first choice? Why was I always the consolation prize? With Father. With Margot. With my tutors. And now with Zavier.

What was wrong with me that I wasn't enough?

Hot tears spilled down my cheeks, and I swiped them away, breathing through the sting in my nose.

It wasn't the first time I'd been overlooked. It wouldn't be the last. So when would it stop hurting? When would I stop expecting anything different?

"Damn it." I wiped the next batch of tears, then pulled the last tangles of my braid free, letting my curls spill around my shoulders.

Where did we go from here? Was I supposed to pretend it hadn't happened? Did they expect me to turn a blind eye?

If Zavier thought I'd invite him into my bed after this, he was fucking dreaming.

The door opened at my back. It was one of two men, and at the moment, I didn't want to see either.

"Go away."

"No." Ransom shut the door with a click.

Of course it was him.

It had always been him.

Maybe that was the real problem. Maybe that was why I couldn't stop the tears. Because all this time, all this guilt, and for what? Loyalty to a prince, a husband, who would never be loyal to me?

"Did you know?" I asked. It was a foolish question, but at this point, I simply wanted to understand how deep this betrayal cut.

"No. Zavier just told me."

Well, that was something.

"Will you look at me?"

I didn't turn. "Please, Ransom. Just go. I want to be alone."

"You're really that upset."

"Yes. No." I shook my head, my hands diving into my hair. "I don't know. It's wrong. It's all wrong. I shouldn't feel…"

The air shifted as he moved closer. The warmth and scents that were Ransom might as well have been strong arms wrapping around my shoulders. Moss and cedar. Wind and rain. It was heaven and hell.

"Feel what?" His voice was a low murmur.

"Relieved."

It was relief.

These tears might have started because of Zavier and Jocelyn and my wounded pride. But they kept coming from relief.

I didn't want Zavier to want me. And if he'd found a connection with someone else, that meant I could stop feeling guilty. I could stop loathing myself for falling for Ransom.

I'd spent weeks and weeks smothering the truth. Stifling the guilt. And now I didn't have to anymore. Because Zavier had fucked up first.

Shades, what a mess.

"A wife shouldn't feel relieved that her husband is sleeping with her lady's maid."

He touched the end of a curl, and a tingle shot down my spine. "Is that why you won't look at me? Because you're relieved?"

"No." If I looked at him, everything I'd been keeping inside would come tumbling out. And once I said it, there was no taking it back.

"Look at me, Odessa."

No one would ever say my name like Ransom. These feelings I'd had for ages wouldn't stop, no matter how hard I tried to forget. And in the end, it didn't matter that Zavier was with Jocelyn. It wouldn't matter how many lovers he had in his bed.

He was a crown prince. A king.

And I was a silly princess who was expected to give him heirs and stand at his side.

The rules were different for women. I doubted Zavier would be willing to let me shatter my vows, even for the Guardian.

Ransom wasn't mine. He wouldn't be mine.

"I have to let go."

"Of what?"

"You," I whispered. "You are not mine to keep."

He breathed, shifting so close his chest brushed against my back. "What if I was yours?"

"How? I signed my name in blood, remember?"

His exhale was so deep that it seemed to come all the way from his toes. A breath he'd been holding for months. "I saw you in Roslo. On the cliffside."

My heart quit pumping. My lungs seized. Was this what he'd been trying to tell me all this time? Was this another secret I'd have to suffer?

He'd seen me that day, my wedding day, months ago. And he was only telling me now. Why?

"You went into the water with brown hair and emerged with red. And as you hurried into the castle, dripping wet, I couldn't tear my eyes away. Then you were there, in the throne room, your hair dyed again. And I saw in you what I see in myself."

My hands trembled. My pulse raced so fast I was getting dizzy. Hope and dread began to battle in my chest. Hope for what he might say. Dread for the same. If it had taken him months to tell me this truth, I wasn't sure I wanted to hear it.

"I know a thing or two about pretending," he said. "About leading a dual life and wearing a disguise."

"Ransom." My voice wobbled. "Don't tell me something that will make me hate you."

"You already hate me, remember?" His hands, warm and strong, settled on my shoulders. "I came to Quentis to sniff out the Gold King. Figure out why he'd hired my warriors to kill a handful of marroweels when I know for damn sure his own soldiers could have done the job. I came to set eyes on the daughter who'd become the Turan queen. But then I saw you, and everything changed."

"What did you do?"

"I decided to set you free."

I whirled, his hands falling off my shoulders as I stared up at him. "Free? You think I'm free? Married to Zavier? You think that claiming me as a bride prize rescued me? I'm wearing twice the shackles I was before. You didn't set me free. You chained me to two kingdoms instead of one. To a man more interested in his wife's lady's maid than. His. Wife."

His jaw clenched. "You are not chained to Zavier."

"There's a treaty somewhere on this continent that proves otherwise."

Ransom growled. "Who did you exchange vows with, Odessa?"

"Zavier." He'd stood at my side. He'd signed his name in blood. He'd vowed.

Except he hadn't uttered a word. Not once.

The Guardian, Ransom, had volunteered to speak for his prince.

Oh, gods. The color drained from my face.

Zavier hadn't spoken a word, not until we were aboard the *Cutter*. It hadn't been his voice in the sanctuary, it had been Ransom's.

"The blood. The vial." Zavier had kept it tucked into his palm, obscuring the edges. Had he held it to the light, it wouldn't have shone red.

It would have been the darkest of greens.

"But he signed the treaty," I said, shaking my head.

He took my hand, opening my palm.

The scar from Father's knife was nothing more than a pale pink line in my flesh. In the darkness, it wasn't even visible.

He splayed my fingers, spreading my hand wide. Then he held out his own to show a cut healed long ago. All that remained was a faint white line.

Twin scars.

The scars of a Sparrow.

And her king.

"With my blood," he said. "With my oath spoken."

My knees began to wobble and weaken. I yanked my hand free of his hold. "You tricked us. It was a lie. It was all a lie. What about the Voster?"

"The High Priest knew I had my reasons."

So he'd allowed Ransom to deceive us. All of us. "And what, exactly, are these reasons? That treaty has been in place for generations. It binds countries through royal marriages. You are not a prin—"

A prince.

"It's you." I swayed, my balance faltering as the truth crashed, shattering everything I'd known for months into pieces of jagged glass. "You are the crown prince. It was all a ruse."

"Not all of it." His eyes darkened, shifting to that forest green as he took my arms, keeping me on my feet. Pulling me close and into his chest. "You have always been my queen."

My queen. How many times had he called me that? How many times had he referred to me as the Sparrow? Countless.

He was the crown prince. Ramsey's son. There was a reason Tillia didn't bow to Zavier. Didn't call him by a title.

It wasn't Zavier's to claim.

And neither was I.

"Why?" My voice cracked.

"I told you."

"To set me free?" I jerked myself out of his hold. "You forced me into a *marriage*. That's not setting me free."

The softness in his expression made my heart pinch. "I am not long for this realm, Odessa. And when I'm gone, you will be free. Your tie to me will be broken. Your life can be of your choosing."

He was going to set me free with his death.

My heart split, a crack down the center that would be impossible to repair. Tears flooded my eyes, making his handsome face blurry. My chin quivered. "You lied to me."

"Yes."

"I hate you." The lie came off my tongue, past my teeth, and for once, it sounded convincing.

"Yes, you do." Ransom tucked a curl behind my ear. Then left me alone.

Forty-Five

When the knock came the next morning, I glared at the door, hoping it would make its way through the wood to whoever stood on the other side.

The only person I wanted to see was Evie, but it was too early for her to be awake. Besides, she didn't know how to knock only once.

If it was Ransom, he could fuck off.

If it was Zavier, he could rot for participating in Ransom's charade.

And if it was Jocelyn, well…

I hadn't figured out what to say to her yet. Did she know Zavier's real identity? Did she know he wasn't my husband? Or did she believe we were married?

Either he'd confessed a truth to her he hadn't trusted with me.

Or she'd fucked my husband.

They'd made me a fool. All of them. It was going to take more than one sleepless night for my wounded pride to heal.

I'd spent last night in this chair, staring into the darkness of my sitting room. Replaying every moment from the past two months. Running through a gauntlet of emotions. Anger. Humiliation. Sorrow. Relief. So much of that infuriating relief.

I'd expected—hoped—to greet dawn feeling numb and exhausted. To crawl into bed and sleep for the foreseeable future. Instead, I was nursing a festering rage. Shades, I was mad. Really. Fucking. Mad.

The knock came again, twice as loud as the last. "Highness?"

Jocelyn.

Part of me wanted to ignore her. To let them all suffer in my silence. But the other part knew there'd be no avoiding her forever. I'd have to face them all eventually. And I might as well start with her. So I climbed out of my chair, my legs stiff, and crossed the room.

Her hand was raised for another knock when I pulled the door open. Her cheeks were splotchy, her eyes red-rimmed.

I shifted to the side and waved her in.

"I'm sorry, Highness." Jocelyn's hands were clasped behind her back. Her head was bowed. "I don't have an excuse. I'm sorry. Whatever punishment you deem fit, I will deserve."

A punishment? Jocelyn was too used to Mae's tantrums. Unless a nasty scowl counted, a punishment hadn't even crossed my mind.

"I'm not going to punish you." I returned to my chair, sweeping a hand toward the other in the sitting room. "Sit down."

The order came out with a bite. A Margot-style bite.

Yes, I was angry. I would be for a while. She'd lied to me. They'd all lied. Every time I thought about how I'd been duped, I squirmed. But I refused to let this give me my stepmother's jagged edges.

She walked over, sitting stiff as a board, eyes still downcast.

"I'm mad," I told her. "I'm hurt. I'm embarrassed."

"I'm sor—"

"Sorry." I held up a hand. "Let's move past the apologies. Starting with the truth. How long has this been going on?"

"A while." She kept her gaze on the floor, her hands clasped in her lap. "I met Vander in Treow. We started first, whenever he was in the encampment. He asked if Zavier could, um…join us."

Did Zavier speak to her? Had he revealed that part of himself to her?

"I'm sorry." Jocelyn shook her head, eyes flooding with tears. "He is your husband."

Well, at the very least, it was nice to know I wasn't the only person who'd been tricked by this sham. "Do you have feelings for him? Them?"

"It's not like that." She sniffled. "It's only sex. It's an escape. A way to feel something other than sad."

My heart pinched.

I hadn't realized she was sad. Brielle was the one who seemed most homesick and lonely. Brielle was the one who seemed to be slipping further and further from the person she'd been in Quentis.

Jocelyn had been so stoic, steady, since we'd arrived, but maybe that was just a mask. A brave face.

We'd been here for months, and for the majority of that time, Jocelyn and I had been apart. While I'd been exploring, consumed with Turah and Lyssa and Ransom, she'd been alone, missing her life.

"What do you want, Jocelyn?"

"To serve you, Highness. To earn your forgiveness."

I scoffed. "That's the most practiced line I've heard in weeks. Try again."

She chewed on her lower lip. "I want to go home."

Home. I envied that she knew exactly where home was. "All right. I'll see what I can do."

Her face lifted, her eyes swimming. "Really?"

"No promises. If there was an excuse to send you away, this is it." Everyone could think I was devastated by her affair with Zavier and Vander. They could see this as her punishment. "But I'll need you to do something for me. I need you to deliver a message to my father."

"Of course. I'll take whatever you need."

There would be nothing for her to take. This was a message she'd have to deliver in person. "My father asked me for information on Turah. Has Brielle told you anything about that?"

"No." She shook her head. "What information?"

"He was hoping I could discover the way into Allesaria."

She glanced to the door, checking that we were alone. "And have you?"

"No. And it's unlikely that I will. It's forbidden for people to include it on any maps. And Zavier has no intention of taking me there. Certainly not before the migration." I swallowed hard. "You must tell my father that I've failed. The Turans suspect he's trying to find their city. And the last person they'll ever trust with that information is me. Please tell him I'm sorry."

I wasn't sorry. Not even a bit. But even I thought this message sounded believable.

Jocelyn would report to Father that I'd failed. She'd likely tell him about her liaison with Zavier. Shades, maybe he'd put her up to it from the beginning. He'd be angry. He'd be irked that I'd sent her home with nothing useful. But would he be surprised? Not in the least.

I was always going to fail him.

But this failure was my choice.

Jocelyn didn't need to know about Lyssa. She didn't need to know that Zavier's identity was a ploy. She didn't need to know that the road to Allesaria was likely etched into a leather cuff around Ransom's arm.

The message she delivered would be of my choosing.

"I believe the Turans are more cunning a foe than we've ever considered," I said. "Tell my father to be cautious. They're amassing a militia. Probably to defend against the migration, but he must consider this in whatever he is planning. I don't know where King Ramsey is training these soldiers, but the barracks in Ellder are full. And it seems that both

Zavier and the Guardian consider this their home."

Lies and truths, woven together, in the hopes Jocelyn wouldn't just believe my story, but that she'd sell it to Father, too.

"All right." She nodded. "Should I tell him about Treow? About the day the king came and his soldiers burned those books?"

"You can tell him anything he desires. I have no secrets from my father." The lie slipped off my tongue without a hitch. I almost patted myself on the back.

"Highness, do you think I should stay? In case you learn more? So that I can tell your father something. Anything is better than nothing."

Was she really worried for me? Or was she scared to be the messenger?

"By the time you return to Roslo, we'll be close to the autumnal equinox. Winter won't be long to follow. I'd rather send this message than none at all. Besides"—I gave her a pointed stare—"you're my husband's lover. I cannot allow you to stay."

She gulped.

"Go home, Jocelyn. Hug your mother."

Her eyes drifted to the floor again as she stood. "I'm sorry. I have let you down."

I'd hoped that maybe Jocelyn and Brielle would become my friends. But then she'd fucked Zavier.

We weren't friends.

"Goodbye, Jocelyn."

She curtsied and made her way to the door, slipping outside and leaving me alone.

I steepled my fingers at my chin, staring at her empty chair.

Would Father believe her message? Did it matter?

I was here to uncover Turah's secrets. That hadn't changed. But instead of acting for my father, I was doing this for myself. For my freedom.

And what better person to help me in that endeavor.

Than my husband.

Forty-Six

My knives were sheathed in their harness, crossed over my spine, as I made my way through Ellder to the training arena. While I loved the sword Ransom had given me, I'd still spent more time with the knives, and today, I needed as much confidence as I could muster.

Nearly every square in the training center was taken by sparring soldiers. The sounds of steel clashing and warriors grunting echoed from all directions as I started toward Ransom's favorite space—the largest, central square.

All this time, I'd assumed he was given preferential treatment because he was the legendary Guardian. Was that the case? Or did these soldiers know that Ransom was their crown prince? That despite the metal band Zavier wore across his brow, he was not the heir to the throne?

A cluster of sweaty warriors stopped fighting as I passed their square. They were warriors who traveled with Zavier on his hunts, and with them stood the man from last night.

Vander.

He was even more beautiful in the daylight than he'd been outside Jocelyn's room. His black hair was done in intricate braids, similar to Halston's. He dipped his chin as I passed. "Princess."

The title made me falter a step.

The people in Treow knew I was the Sparrow. Brielle and Jocelyn referred to me as Highness, and now that they were in Ellder, others would overhear. If the warriors all called me Princess, too, it wouldn't take long for news to spread. Soon, everyone in this fortress would know that I was Princess Odessa Wolfe.

My anonymity was all but gone. I'd mourn it later.

There were two men standing in the middle of Ransom's square. Exactly the two men I'd come to find.

Zavier's back was to me, but when Ransom's hazel eyes flicked over his shoulder, he turned, bending at the waist. "Odessa."

"Zav—" I stopped myself as yet another realization struck. It was like being pricked in the finger with a needle. His name couldn't be Zavier. All of Calandra knew the crown prince's name was Zavier. So who was he? "What's your real name?"

He glanced around, making sure no one was close enough to overhear. Then he lowered his voice to a whisper. "Dray. Though no one has called me that in over a decade."

"A decade?" Was that how long this charade had been going?

Zavier nodded, taking a step back, effectively removing himself from the middle. *Smart man.*

Ransom stared at me, his arms crossed over his chest, legs planted wide. There was a scowl on his face.

Probably because there was a scowl on mine.

"How much does Jocelyn know?"

"Nothing. She believes I'm the prince. That I cannot speak." Zavier— Dray, whatever the hell his name was—turned to Ransom. "I'm sorry, my prince."

"It was time for the truth." Ransom spoke to Zavier, but his gaze never left mine. "Leave us."

"Before you go." I crossed my arms over my chest. "Jocelyn is to be sent back to Quentis. Immediately."

Zavier glanced to Ransom, waiting for approval.

My *husband* gave it with a single nod.

"I'll see to it now." Zavier walked away, disappearing past the racks.

The noises in the training area quieted, like all of the soldiers and warriors had been ordered to leave. I didn't bother looking around to see if we had company, instead keeping my gaze locked on Ransom.

We stared at each other, and with every passing second, that simmering rage I'd stoked all morning blazed hotter. There were a hundred questions to ask. Countless answers to demand. My nostrils flared, and my teeth clenched so tightly I could have ground rock to dust.

Apparently, my anger amused my lying husband.

The smirk I'd seen countless times stretched across his perfect mouth.

That fucking smirk.

My blades sang as I ripped them from their sheaths, and before I even knew what I was doing, I brought them down toward Ransom's neck.

He bent backward, his smirk widening as he dodged the strike.

I slashed at him again, forcing him back a step. "Does everyone know?

Does everyone in Turah think I'm the fool who believed your lies?"

"Very few know the truth. And none think you're a fool, Odessa."

I readjusted my stance, readying for another attack. "Let's talk about names, shall we? What the fuck is yours, *Guardian*?"

"Ransom." He leaned left, then right as I came at him again, avoiding each of my swipes. "Zavier Ransom Wolfe. I've always gone by Ransom. Not everything has been a lie."

"Not everything, just the important pieces." I scoffed and stabbed at his stomach, forcing him to shift to the side. "How long has Zavier been pretending to be you?"

"Eleven years."

"Why?" My blades whooshed in the air as I sliced them toward his throat.

He moved away, holding up his hands in surrender. "Every prince and princess of Turah has a double until they come of age. A hundred years ago, the king's son was murdered when he was fifteen. Since then, it's become practice within the royal family. It is an honor to be chosen to represent a royal. Zavier has been with me since I was thirteen. He is my cousin."

Hence their resemblance. If it was such an honor to be chosen, then their families had probably all been overjoyed for Dray to leave his own name behind and take on Zavier.

"Is that why he pretended not to speak in Quentis?" I asked.

"Yes and no. I'm sure he told you, but silence is usually the best way for someone else to stumble and share. It's something we started long ago. When we were younger, if Dray was acting as my double and didn't know what to say, he'd just stay quiet."

"Well, you're well past being of age for this charade. Why continue the facade?" I struck for him again, but it was sloppy and slow.

"There are reasons," he said, jaw clenching.

"Reasons you won't tell me, right?" I was so godsdamn tired of his omissions and lies. This entire kingdom was built on a mountain of secrets, from Allesaria to their crown prince.

Did these people come out of the womb suspicious? Did they teach toddlers how to keep secrets? Were children instructed to give outsiders hostile glares and sneers?

Another surge of anger flowed through my veins, and I went after him with abandon, swinging without control or aim. I tripped over an uneven spot in the dirt, pitching forward, but I managed to catch myself before I fell on my own damn knife.

"Enough." Ransom cut a hand through the air. "You'll hurt yourself."

"Fuck you and your concern." I straightened, filling my lungs as I readjusted the hold on my blades. Then I raised them in the air. "Are you going to fight me? Or keep running away like the coward you are? Like father, like son?"

"Cross," he warned. "I said *enough*."

"Draw your sword." The hilt glinted over his shoulder.

"No."

I swung low with my left and across with my right, advancing in a move Tillia had taught me weeks ago. "Fight me."

"No."

I went after him again, pushing him toward a corner. "Does your father know of all this? The lies? The pretending?"

"Yes."

Ramsey's visit to Treow when he'd asked for his son. He'd been looking for Ransom. Their encounter in Ravalli and Ramsey's demand that Ransom go to Allesaria. He'd been calling home his heir.

"Was it his idea? The bride prize?" I spat, then lunged and struck for his thigh. The blade's tip grazed the leather of his pants.

"Damn it, Odessa," he hissed. "Stop this."

"Answer me," I yelled, advancing again.

But Ransom kept moving out of my reach, forcing me to chase him around the square.

"For once, tell me the fucking truth. Was this your father's idea?"

"No," he shouted. "It was mine. Your father plans to invade Turah. He's desperate to find Allesaria. And I was always going to have to satisfy the Shield of Sparrows with a union to his daughter. We've known for years that he's been training your sister as a spy. She's almost as good with throwing knives as Banner. I needed a way to choose a different Sparrow."

"The weaker daughter." Just like Ramsey had said, their spies had told them I was the lesser daughter. The throwaway princess.

Gods, it hurt. My chest felt like it was being cleaved in two.

"You're not weak," Ransom said. "I knew that the moment you jumped off that cliff."

But he'd turned my life upside down anyway.

"I hate you," I sneered, swiping my blades left, then right. Hoping to draw blood. "You said this was for my freedom, but you don't give a damn about my life. I'm just a pawn in your sick, twisted game. You used me to manipulate my father. And yours."

His eyes flashed silver, his own rage bubbling to the surface. *Good.* Maybe now he'd actually fight. "You are not a pawn, Odessa. Not to me. You are the Sparrow. You are my wife. You are the future queen of Turah."

"A queen people think is married to another man." My arms were growing tired, but I didn't stop attacking, pushing him around the square, moving us from one side to the other. "Who do your people believe is the prince?"

"It depends. Outside of Allesaria, very few people recognize me as the prince. They assume, if Zavier's wearing the crown, that it's him. We look enough alike, people believe the act."

"So you lie to everyone. At least I'm not the only one."

"What would you have me tell them?" He stood before me in a blink, eyes silver and expression hard. He grabbed my wrists, holding them at my sides.

Trapping me so I couldn't fight.

I tried anyway, squirming and pulling and kicking him in the shin.

He didn't move.

"The truth!" I shouted into his face. "You should have told them, you should have told me, the truth."

"That the Turan prince, the heir to the throne, is dying? That he has the same infection as the monsters hunting them in their very towns? Is that what I should tell them? Send them into a panic less than a year before the migration?"

"At least it would be honest." I stood on my toes, leaning closer. "You're a coward *and* a liar."

"Careful," he growled.

"Or what?"

I dropped my blades, hands splaying wide, and let them fall to the dirt. They landed with a clang. Then I rolled my wrists, yanking my hands free from his grip. "You're a fucking asshole."

"Yes, I am a fucking asshole. And this asshole is as good as dead to these people. They need a leader, not a corpse. Zavier will become the crown prince."

"Then why even tell me? Why not let me continue believing your lies like everyone else? Why tell me the truth?" I took a step away, my hands diving into my hair before they flopped at my sides.

My fury had deflated. My anger withering to dust. All that remained was the heartache.

Ransom was my husband. There was no need to keep fighting my own feelings. I no longer needed to convince myself that he hadn't stolen my heart.

But if Zavier was to be the prince, if Ransom was so sure he was dying, what was the point? To have him and lose him? To break my heart into a thousand pieces when I had to go back to pretending?

Why give me hope only to rip it away?

If Ransom died, I'd never be free. I would be left to mourn his ghost for the rest of my days.

My eyes filled with tears as I stared at him. At the man who I'd believed, down to my bones, wouldn't hurt me. I guess I was a fool.

"Why would you make me suffer losing you?" I swiped at the tears that tumbled down my cheeks. "Why not let me stay believing I was Zavier's wife?"

Ransom closed the gap between us in a single stride, his hands framing my face, fingertips diving into my hair. His eyes changed as they searched mine.

Not silver. Not hazel. Not even emerald green.

They turned gold.

The same gold I saw each morning in my mirror.

"You are mine, Odessa." It was a growl, more animal than human. And the shiver that cascaded down my spine might as well have been my own blades, cleaving me in two.

Mine.

It was everything I'd wanted to hear for weeks. It was the lie that shattered my heart.

I planted my hands flat on his chest and shoved with all my might.

A roar came from my throat, raw and ravaged.

I'd trusted him. I'd believed in him. I'd begged and pleaded and bared myself to the core for him.

"You should have told me." I pushed him again and again and again, enough that he let go of my face. Enough that we made it back to where I'd dropped my blades.

I swept them from the ground and sliced them through the air, holding nothing back as I tried to sink them into his flesh. But every time the blades came close to contact, I felt the resistance in my own grip. In my will.

It wasn't Ransom or his skill or his speed that kept me from cutting him to the bone.

It was me.

It was the blood that I'd signed onto that treaty.

A King cannot kill his Sparrow, and a Sparrow cannot kill her King,

either directly or indirectly, without death befalling them both.

Had that been his plan, too? Either he knew or he'd guessed that Father had asked that I try to kill him. So he'd trapped me with Voster magic.

I released my knives, sending them flying to both sides of the training square. Then I launched myself at Ransom, fists pounding into a chest that might as well have been made of stone.

He lifted his arms, opening himself wide, and took every blow.

"You're a coward." *Punch.* "You're a fake." *Punch.* "And I hate you."

"Now who's the liar?"

I shoved at his chest, but he caught me in his arms, hauling me close.

No matter how hard I fought, how hard I squirmed, he held me close as angry tears and sad tears and embarrassed tears dropped down my face and into the dirt.

Why was I fighting? It was pointless. He was too strong, and I'd never win. And if I didn't get out of his arms right this instant, I might never let him go.

"Release me."

"No." He dropped his forehead to my hair.

"I hate you." There wasn't even a bit of truth to those words. So I pushed at him one last time, knowing it was futile. And when his arms only banded tighter, I gave up the struggle to sag against his chest. "Why me?"

"I told you. You are mine."

He sighed, loosening his arms.

It was my chance to get away, but my legs didn't want to move.

Ransom cupped my jaw, his thumb catching the last tear. "I'm sorry, my queen."

"We shouldn't have to fight this hard, Ransom," I whispered. Love shouldn't come with this many lies.

"Why not? Isn't this what we should be fighting for?" His thumb drifted to my mouth, tracing my lower lip.

My breath hitched.

Gone were the golden eyes. He stared at me with irises of the richest green. Of moss and earth and Ransom.

Irises that haunted my dreams.

I wasn't sure who moved first. One moment, my heels were on the ground. The next, a hundred butterflies took flight in my belly, lifting me off my toes, reaching for him as he crushed his mouth to mine.

The world around us began to spin, fading into streaks of light and dark, until the colors blended together in a swirl of gray and white and black. Until the only color that remained was green.

It was like that first breath after jumping off a cliff, plunging into the ocean, and breaking free from the surface to fill my lungs.

It was like being remade.

Ransom's lips moved over mine in a slow kiss. Teasing. Testing. Then another raw growl ripped from his throat, the vibration shooting to my core. His tongue licked the seam of my lips, asking, pleading, for me to drop my guard. To let him inside.

Another princess might have mustered one last fight. A decent princess would have stood her ground.

But I wasn't a good princess.

I parted for him, gasping as he slanted his mouth over mine, stealing his way past my lips.

Reality vanished. Gods, how I'd wanted this. For weeks and weeks, I'd refused to let myself want this. To crave Ransom. I'd refused to believe this was ever a possibility.

What if this kiss was just another lie?

It was like having a bucket of cold water dumped on my head. I tore my mouth away, the realm slamming back into sharp focus.

The morning was too bright, too cheery, for the torment in my soul.

I stepped out of Ransom's reach, glancing around the training center. Empty.

Ransom dragged his thumb over his wet mouth. "Odessa."

It hadn't taken him long to master my name.

I left before he could wield it like that sword he carried.

Forty-Seven

E vie poked her finger into my arm. "Are you listening to me, Dess?"

"I'm sorry." I shook myself out of my thoughts. "What did you say?"

"I asked if there was something wrong with your lips. You keep touching them."

My hand dropped away from my mouth like it was a hot stone. "Oh. I'm, uh…thirsty."

She cast a sideways glance to the canteen of water on the grass at my side.

I picked it up, twisting off the lid for a drink as she returned her attention to feeding Faze.

Shades, I was a mess, and it was all Ransom's fault.

A week had passed since he kissed me in the training square, and no matter how hard I tried, I couldn't stop thinking about it. About him.

It was the best kiss of my life. I could still feel the heat of his lips, taste him on my tongue.

Damn him. He'd ruined me. Entirely. I hoped that wherever he was at the moment, he was miserable, too.

"Dess?" Evie asked as she stroked one of Faze's ears.

"Evie?"

"Will we really have to let him go?"

"Yes, little star." I ran a hand over her dark hair. "Someday."

Our tarkin was curled in her lap, drinking a bottle of milk as we sat in the center of the yard at Zavier's. Or Ransom's. Who actually owned this house? The prince? Or the pretender?

Who actually had the claim to Evie? Was she Zavier's daughter? Or was that a lie, too?

A week was a long time to go without answers to important questions. Every day, I added more and more to my ever-growing list.

Maybe that was why Ransom had left. To avoid my questions.

That, or he'd known I needed time and space.

He'd left Ellder with Zavier and a band of rangers the same day I sent Jocelyn home.

That very afternoon, she'd been given a seat on a wagon bound for Perris. She should be sailing over the Krisenth Crossing by now. In another week, she'd likely be in Roslo.

Would Father believe her report? He'd probably corroborate it with whatever other spies he'd sent to Turah over the years. Were there any in Ellder? Had I passed one of Father's men in the streets without even knowing?

"Evangeline," Luella called from the doorway of the house. "Time for lunch."

Evie scrunched up her nose. "Lunch, then lessons."

"It's important you know how to read," I said, stealing Faze from her lap.

He yawned, white fangs flashing, as I settled him into the curve of my arm. He was getting heavier and heavier, already the size of a fat house cat. Soon, I wouldn't be able to carry him around. Soon, we'd have to set him free. Soon, it would be just another goodbye.

Evie pushed to her feet, brushing off the seat of her pants as she gave Luella a dramatic pout.

The older woman pulled in her lips to hide a smile.

"I'll see you at dinner," I told Evie as I stood. Then, with a gentle nudge, I sent her toward her tutor.

After a quick stop in my suite to leave Faze napping on a chair, I collected my satchel and made my way into the streets of Ellder.

Men stopped walking to bow as I passed. A cluster of women ceased talking, each dropping to a curtsy. A boy and a girl chasing each other outside the bakery both froze, eyes wide as they whispered, "The princess."

As I'd feared, I would never again be just another face in the crowd behind the fortress's walls. The attention meant I'd stayed in my suite more often than not this past week. But today, it was time to pay a friend a visit.

The house where Ransom had taken Samuel and Jonas Hay was in a row of identical narrow homes. The buildings had two levels and were stacked side by side. In a way, they reminded me of the falconry mews in Roslo, where the falconers would cram as many bird cages into a space as possible. The homes were fitted with metal spears on their roofs, a defense for the migration.

Samuel's neighbor had a pot of mums with burgundy blooms beside their front door. The rich color complemented the leaves from nearby trees. Autumn was sweeping across Turah, and greens were giving way to golds and russet reds. I needed a blanket on my lap for breakfasts on my balcony. When I returned from my early morning jogs around the fortress or after riding for an hour with Freya, I'd have cool cheeks and pink ears.

I knocked on Samuel's door, straightening the hem of my sweater as I waited.

He answered with a scowl that shifted to a smile when he saw my face. "Odessa. Welcome. Please, come in."

"How are you?" I asked as I stepped inside.

He shrugged. "Lonely. Bored."

"Ah. Jonas started school today?"

"I taught him at home when we were in Ravalli. I know it's best that he make friends, but…I miss him."

"Have you given any thought as to what you'll do?" I asked, following him past the front room to the galley kitchen, then taking a chair at his small dining table.

"Wait, I think." He sank into the chair across from mine, drumming his fingers on the table's wooden surface. "Wait until the spring. Then we'll go home to Quentis."

"To the land of traitors and liars?" I teased.

"You'll hold that against me forever, won't you?"

"That's my plan."

He laughed, relaxing into his seat. "To what do I owe the pleasure of your visit?"

"Well, I mostly wanted to see how you were doing. But I also have a task, if you're interested."

Samuel sat up straighter. "What task?"

A task that, by rights, I should keep to myself. But a task I wouldn't be able to finish on my own. At least not with any accuracy.

So I took a deep breath, swallowing the doubts, and opened my satchel. "I'm making a map of Turah."

His eyes widened. "Princess."

"I know." I chewed on my lower lip. "Remember when you told me the paperman in you wanted to dig into Allesaria? I have that same inkling. And I can't let it go. If I'm to be the queen, then I need to know what's going on in this kingdom."

I wasn't doing this for Father. I was doing this for *me*.

"Odessa." Samuel lowered his voice. "If you are caught…"

"I have no intention of getting caught." I pulled the map from my bag, unfolding it until it was spread across the table. "I know that I'm asking you to put yourself at risk. Please know that if there was anyone else I could ask for help, I would. But you're a Quentin. None of the Turans trust me."

Not even their crown prince.

"I'll understand if you refuse. I will not hold it against you. But I'm no mapmaker, and I've only been here for a short time. I'm certain there are many errors and many omissions. I'd like your help filling in the blanks."

I'd spent the past week drafting this version from my journal's drawings. It was only temporary. When it was finished, I'd make the adjustments to my journal and burn this copy.

Samuel studied it intently, warily, his eyes following the roads I'd drawn to the towns I'd sketched.

My journal's pages included markings for monsters with Lyssa. This copy did not. But even though they were missing, I could see them on the paper like invisible blinking lights.

"What is this road?" Samuel's finger traced a winding line that snaked into the mountains at the top of the map.

It was a guess. All I could do was guess. But somewhere in the mountains was a hidden city.

And that line, an unknown road to Allesaria, that would likely get me killed or exiled.

I stayed quiet, watching as Samuel put that together for himself.

He looked up from the map. "What are you doing, Princess?"

"Finding the truth."

"And what will you do with this truth?"

"Set myself free." I was at the mercy of secrets. Until I discovered the truth, I'd always be trapped. By Father. By Ransom.

I was tired of being a Sparrow in a cage.

"It is forbidden," Samuel warned.

"I know. There is something going on in Allesaria. Something that isn't right. You suspect it, too." I was counting on Samuel's hatred of Ramsey to buy me his allegiance. His silence.

"Ramsey's militia," he murmured.

Among other things.

I had no proof that Lyssa had originated in Allesaria. But I wanted to investigate. I wanted the means to find out if my hunch was true. The way to do that was to get into Allesaria. Even if that meant taking another blood oath.

The source had to be the priority. Ransom and Zavier could kill all the monsters in the realm, but if they didn't stop the infection at its source, it would never end.

Samuel stared at the paper, a crease forming between his eyebrows. "I have never been to Allesaria. I cannot help with that portion of the map."

"That's all right." If he could help me plot the bulk of Turah, that was at least a start. And if I could find a chance to study Ransom's cuff, if it was indeed a map, then maybe it would complete the puzzle. "I'll take anything you can give me."

He sighed, turning to stare at the wall for a few agonizing heartbeats.

I wouldn't blame him if he refused. Not in the slightest. But it would sting.

If I couldn't find loyalty with my own countrymen, then what was left? I truly would be on my own.

"I'll see what I can do," he said, refolding the map. When it was in a neat square, he took it to a cupboard and put it on the top shelf. Out of Jonas's reach.

"Thank you." My exhale was audible as I stood from the chair, then pushed it into the table.

He escorted me to the door, waving goodbye as I left.

I was on my way back to my suite when a commotion in the courtyard lured me in the opposite direction. A cheer filled the air, followed by the sound of male laughter.

Others rushed past me, anxious to see what the excitement was about.

I quickened my steps, falling into the rush. Except the moment I stepped into the courtyard, I came to a quick stop as a prickling sensation raked over my skin.

The High Priest stood before a group of smiling children. Their faces were lit with awe and wonder as they watched him spin a string of leaves into the air, sending it swirling higher and higher.

The children clapped and giggled as he collected more and more. Enough to separate the spiral into tiny wreaths, enough to fit on each of their heads.

Parents smiled on as their children laughed.

A young girl with black ringlets ran past me into the fray, pushing her way to the front, where she tugged on the priest's robe and pointed to her head, wanting her own wreath. How could anyone stand to be that close? To touch him? Did his magic not affect children the same way?

The creeping, crawling sensation worsened as his magic swelled, more leaves flying.

The priest looked up from the children, fathomless eyes finding mine, as if he'd known the exact moment when I'd stepped into the courtyard.

I spun around to leave, only to smack face-first into a wall.

No, not a wall. A man who smelled of spice and earth. Leather and wind.

Ransom.

"Easy." Strong arms closed around me, keeping me from falling on my ass.

I shimmied out of his hold, not trusting myself to be so close, considering what had happened the last time I'd been in those arms.

His hair was damp, and his clothes were clean. His beard had returned, but his sword was missing. There was a gray pallor to his skin, a dullness in his hazel eyes. He looked tired and sick, ready to collapse and sleep for days.

"You're back," I said.

"Miss me, my queen?"

Yes. "Not in the slightest. What is he doing here?" I hooked a thumb over my shoulder at the Voster.

"Entertaining the children. And keeping me alive. For now."

"He siphoned Lyssa from your blood today, didn't he?"

"That he did." Ransom nodded. "I'm a bit tired. So, if it's all the same to you, let's save the sparring for another time."

"Of course." I moved to the side, about to walk away when his hand caught mine.

Rough calluses caressed my palm. He laced our fingers together, threading them so quickly it was as if he'd done it a thousand times before. "Walk with me? It helps afterward. To clear the fog."

"All right." He didn't fight me as I pulled my fingers loose, clasping both hands in front of me as we set off away from the courtyard.

"Ready when you are."

"Ready for what?"

"Whatever questions are shaking around in that beautiful head of yours."

I almost laughed. Almost. "Where do you stay when you're in Ellder?"

"The rooms beneath yours."

And now I wouldn't sleep a wink. I'd be too consumed thinking about him beneath my floor. "Are you sure you don't want to rest?"

"I'm certain."

We fell into step beside each other, our pace as gentle and easy as the fall breeze.

"Have you spoken to any healers about Lyssa?" I asked.

"I saw a healer after I was bitten. He told me I was lucky to be alive and that I should praise the gods. When I started noticing changes, I went to him again. He told me it would pass. He didn't want to admit he had no idea what was happening to me. He was the best healer in Turah. If he didn't know what to do, then none of them would. I went to the High Priest after that."

"And that's when he started pulling it from your blood?"

"Not immediately. It took him nearly a year to attune his magic to the infection."

"Attune?"

"That's his word, not mine. He told me that when the Voster are young, their magic must learn. He can command wind and water because he's taught his magic how to manipulate fluids. He's learned to use blood in bonds. It took a year for his magic to learn Lyssa. Since, he uses what he takes to try to identify its elements. And enough so that it won't consume me whole. He's prolonging the inevitable."

"Why can't he just take it all?"

"It's bound to me. It has become a part of my very being. To take it all would be the end."

"Bound to you. Like blood magic."

"Yes."

When he'd told me the Voster had identified elements to Lyssa, the fenek tusk and korakin, I'd thought maybe it was mundane. That an alchemist had created this infection.

And if that was the case, then there'd be a cure.

But Lyssa wasn't like other diseases. Other infections didn't alter men's speed or stealth or strength. That was magic. If the High Priest couldn't rid it from Ransom's body, maybe there really wasn't a cure.

Unless the High Priest was deceiving us all.

My father was certain he could break ancient treaties bound by blood magic. There had to be a way to break a magical infection, too.

Ransom interrupted my thoughts as he snatched my hand. This time when I tried to wiggle free, he didn't let me go.

No matter how hard I tugged, his grip was iron, and I was very aware of the eyes on us as we passed people on the street. Their gazes took us in and instantly dropped to our linked hands.

"Ransom."

He smirked. "Odessa."

"I don't like holding hands."

"How do you know? You've never held mine."

I frowned and gave another last, futile pull. "You're not going to let me go."

"No, I am not."

"People will see." And then they'd think their princess was having an affair with the Guardian.

He swung his free hand into the air, toward the empty street. "What people?"

No one. We were entirely alone. He'd led us to Ellder's quietest streets. Past vacant homes. Community gardens. Livestock pens. A loop that meant there'd be few prying eyes to see as he laced our fingers together.

So I let loose a sigh and let him hold my hand, because damn it, I liked it. "You're a pain in my ass."

"So eloquent, my queen. Also, that's my line."

I shot him a pathetic glare that only made him grin. "If Lyssa is magical, then it must have been created by the Voster. They're the only magical beings in Calandra."

"It wasn't the Voster."

"How do you know?"

"I know," he said. "I have faith in the Voster."

Well, I did not. And I didn't trust magic.

Ransom might not want to consider the Voster, but I'd suffered through enough of their magic to know it wasn't a blessing but a curse.

"Where were you?" I asked, trading topics. We'd debate the Voster when he was feeling better.

"Hunting. Outside of Frezan. It's a town similar to Ravalli in the mountains."

A town I didn't have on my map but would ask Samuel about when we spoke next. "And?"

"A grizzur killed a man who was trying to defend his cattle from being slaughtered."

I winced. "Lyssa?"

"No. Just a monster," he said. "The hunts are working. I have to believe they're working. We're getting fewer reports all the time. Less evidence of the infection. And I took your advice and stopped at a pony rider outpost."

My pulse quickened. "Did they tell you anything?"

He nodded. "They've heard some news of attacks. But nothing we didn't know about already."

I hummed, and when I opened my mouth to say something, I wasn't even sure where to start. Countless questions had crossed my mind in the past week, and yet at the moment, they seemed to flutter away like dragonflies.

It was his hand. His warm, strong hand with long, calloused fingers. A warrior's hand, not one that belonged to a prince. A hand that had no business fitting around mine as well as it did.

"You're quiet," he said.

"I don't know what to say."

"Still angry with me?"

"You lied to me."

"I did." His fingers flexed. "I should have told you a long time ago."

All those times he'd stared at me as if he wanted to say something. "Why didn't you?"

"Because I knew you'd look at me differently."

"Like you were my husband?" I quipped.

"Like I was another person to wrap you in chains. Like the way you looked at Zavier."

How did I look at Zavier? Like my jailer? An enemy? How should I have looked at the man who'd tipped my life upside down?

It wasn't until Ransom pulled on my hand that I realized I'd stopped walking.

"Come along, Cross. I'm too tired to carry you back."

I unstuck my feet, following him around a corner. We'd reached the wall, slowly following the logs around the fortress's perimeter. If we kept going, we'd reach a side gate manned by soldiers. I passed it and the guards stationed beside it every morning when I ran a lap around Ellder. Guards who should not see our hands linked.

Ransom slowed his pace to a near crawl.

"You asked me about my father," he said. "If he knew about this. He knows Zavier is still acting as my stand-in. He knows I'm the Guardian. He knows about Lyssa. But if he's tied it all together, I'm not sure."

"Ramsey doesn't know that you have Lyssa?"

"He might. We haven't discussed it. Until that day in Ravalli, I hadn't spoken to my father in four years."

"Wh-what? Why?"

"Evie."

My stomach dropped. "Is she your daughter?"

What was I going to do if that answer was yes? It wouldn't change my feelings toward her. I loved Evie no matter who her father was. But it would change how I looked at Ransom.

It would be yet another lie, and at some point, there'd be no coming back. Like swimming through the ocean too far from shore. Too many lies, and they'd drown us all.

"She's not my daughter, Odessa," Ransom said, and the breath I'd been holding rushed past my lips. "She's my sister."

It was a surprise but not the shock it should have been. I hadn't really thought about it until now, but the way he was with Evangeline was the way I saw myself with Arthy. Even Mae.

"My father has no idea that she exists, and we'd like to keep it that way."

"Okay," I drawled. "You should be able to guess my next question."

Why?

"Because he tried to kill my mother."

Ramsey had tried to kill Ransom's mother. Evie's mother.

So who was Evie's father? Ramsey? Or Zavier? Had Zavier and Ransom's mother had an affair?

"I have questions," I said.

"Of course you do." Ransom chuckled, leading us down a different street, taking a path that would extend this walk and, hopefully, give him time to explain. "My mother is the daughter of a Turan nobleman from Perris. He amassed an incredible wealth from shipping lumber across Calandra. My grandfather, my father's father and the king, needed coin. My mother's father wanted his daughter to be queen. So, he bought my mother a crown she didn't want to wear. And the first time my parents met was on their wedding day."

"Sounds familiar," I muttered.

"She never loved my father," he said. "But she did her duty, ensuring Turah had an heir to the throne. And my father…"

"Resented her?"

"No." Ransom slowed, pressing his free hand over his chest. "He loved her. He used to tell me that she was his life. He tried, for so many years, to make her love him, too. He hung on her every word. He indulged her every wish. If she wanted to sail to Laine for the summer, he'd send her with his best rangers and enough coin to fill a ship of its own with herbs and spices and oils."

Ramsey wasn't a person I wanted to pity, but I felt for the king. For a love unrequited.

"Mother didn't loathe my father. She knew he had feelings for her that she didn't return, and she was always gentle with him. She let him have those feelings, not encouraging them, but not smothering them, either. She simply accepted them. But my father is a king. He wanted her love, and as the years passed, as he realized he would never earn it, it changed him. He sharpened and hardened."

Was that why Margot was so rigid and bitter? Because she loved my father and Father loved my mother's ghost?

"He used to laugh and smile. He was my idol," Ransom said. "Exactly the man I wanted to become. But it's been so long now, I can't remember what his laugh sounds like."

"I'm sorry."

"Don't be. He made his choices." A ripple of anger rolled off his frame as we continued down the quiet street. "To my knowledge, my father never strayed from my mother. He was wholly devoted to his wife. But I cannot say the same about her."

Ouch. "She had a lover."

"Yes," he said. "My mother's parents and her brother were killed during the last migration. They took shelter as soon as the first scout was seen. They had a room built with supplies stocked beneath their home in Perris. But at some point, they took ill during confinement. Likely from mold and poor air supply. Maybe if they'd waited another few weeks after the scout, they might have survived. We'll never know."

Every migration began with the scouts. Solitary crux that warned the migration was on its way. According to records, once a scout was spotted, the horde of crux usually came within a month or two.

Margot had told me we wouldn't shelter until the horde. That we'd spend as little time as possible beneath the castle.

Burrowing into the ground or finding shelter in caves was said to be the best way to survive the crux. Some risked their homes, would stay indoors and simply pray to the gods for mercy. Sheltering wasn't without its own risks. Many who hadn't planned accordingly would starve. And others would succumb to sickness.

Humans weren't meant to live without the sun and moons and clean air to breathe.

"Had Mother not just wed Father, not been in Allesaria, she might have been in that shelter, too. As it was, she became the sole owner of her father's empire. Someone had to take over the shipping business. And since she couldn't run it herself, she chose her father's replacement. Mikhail was a young captain from Ozarth. Her brother's best friend. And her lover. I'm not sure how long their affair lasted. Maybe years. Maybe the reason she didn't love my father was because her heart had already been claimed when she was young."

"You didn't ask her?"

"I love my mother." Ransom frowned. "But I empathize, in a way, with my father. He wasn't the only one who was hurt by her affair."

"Is Mikhail Evie's father?" If he'd been from Ozarth, maybe Ransom's mother had gone there to have the baby. It explained the blue starbursts in Evie's eyes. Except Evie looked like Zavier. The chocolate brown hair. The shape of their faces. Their smiles.

She looked like Ransom.

Granted, I wasn't sure what their mother looked like, but Ransom resembled Ramsey.

"No, she is not," he said.

So Evie was Ramsey's daughter. A princess of Turah.

"It wasn't something she'd planned or expected. She hadn't told Father yet when all hell broke loose. I think, had Father known, I wouldn't have had to stop him from killing her."

"*You* stopped him?"

"He was strangling her." Ransom's hand clamped tighter on mine, hard enough that I flexed my fingers to remind him that we were interlocked. He jerked away, his hand flying open, fingers splayed wide. "Did I hurt you?"

"I'm not made of glass."

"No, you're not." He dragged a hand through his hair as we continued to walk. He made no move to touch me again.

I'd never been so aware of my hand hanging at my side before. I'd never worked so hard not to reach for someone. But it was for the best that we kept our space. Besides, I didn't even like holding hands.

"Mikhail was in Allesaria under the guise of a meeting with Mother to discuss the shipping enterprise."

Ransom's throat bobbed as he swallowed hard. "Father caught them in bed together. I'll never forget her screams. They echoed through the castle. I wasn't even supposed to be there. I'd gone out for training, but the master blacksmith had stopped me on my way to the training arena. He'd forged a dagger for my birthday. I came inside to put it away."

He slowed, coming to a stop. Then he tilted his head to the sky above, his eyes closing. Like he was trying to forget the unforgettable memories.

"The guards stood outside her chambers and did nothing. I ran past them into an ocean of blood. It was everywhere. The walls. The floors. The bedsheets. Mikhail's body was by the door, like he'd tried to escape. His face was...pulp. Nothing but pummeled flesh and bloody pools."

I swallowed the bile that surged up my throat.

"Father had pinned Mother to the floor and wouldn't let her go. He kept screaming, 'You killed him. You fucking killed him.' No matter how hard I tried to haul him away, he just kept his hands wrapped around her throat. He just kept screaming. Until I took the hilt of that new knife and knocked him on the skull so hard he collapsed."

Ransom scrubbed his hands over his face, taking a minute to shake off the memory. When he looked at me, the color bled from his cheeks. "I'm sorry. That was too much. It was gruesome, and I shouldn't have—"

"I'm not made of glass," I repeated. A violent story wasn't going to turn me away.

His frame sagged with an exhale. "I guess I'm just used to guarding the harsh truths."

"You don't need to. Not from me." I scanned the street, grateful that we were alone today. Grateful that the High Priest had drawn such a crowd to the courtyard.

Gods. What a mess.

Would Evie ever know the truth? Would they keep telling her lies for the rest of her life? Maybe I didn't blame them.

"What happened with your mother?"

"I took her somewhere safe, hiding her away while she recovered. It took weeks for the blood to drain from her eyes. For the bruises to fade."

"Did she ever go back to Allesaria?"

"No."

Where was she hiding now? In Ellder? In Treow? Was she hiding in plain sight? "Have I met her before?"

Ransom looked at me but said nothing. It was yet another secret he'd keep from his wife.

I couldn't even hold it against him. If I didn't know the truth, I couldn't be made to reveal her hiding place.

"That was over four years ago. When Mother told me she was pregnant, I took her to Ozarth. I thought she'd stay there. Start over. But after Evie was born, she asked me to bring her back. She didn't want to live apart."

"From you." Her son.

"From me." He nodded. "I went to Allesaria when Evie was a baby. Father begged me to bring Mother to the city. When I asked why, he told me that he needed to finish the task I'd interrupted. I left that day and never went back."

"What? He still wants her dead?"

"He'll never forgive her betrayal. It was more than a husband scorned. He's a king with a disloyal queen. His pride won't let her live."

"And Evie?"

"He will take her. And ruin her."

I shook my head, giving myself a moment for this to all sink in. "So you decided to keep Evie a secret. And let Zavier pretend to be her father."

"Make no mistake, Zavier is her father. He loves her with every beat of his heart, whether she shares his blood or not. Zavier has sacrificed more for me, for this kingdom, than is fair."

Which meant Ransom would never punish Zavier for stealing slivers of happiness like the one I'd witnessed with Jocelyn and Vander.

"We hadn't planned on Zavier continuing the facade as my double. But not long after I left Allesaria, I was bitten. And everything changed."

He'd become the Guardian.

And let his childhood double wear his crown.

"Zavier is my cousin. He is the son of my aunt, my father's sister. He was next in line, after me. Until Evie was born."

"But she's a girl."

"Succession in Turah does not work the way it does in Quentis. The crown passes to the eldest child of the king and queen, regardless of gender. Evie is Father's daughter, and when I am gone, she will have a claim to the throne."

Then Evie would become a princess, and Ramsey would rip her from the only life she's known.

"When she's older, if she wants a life in court and I'm still alive, I won't stand in her way. But I want it to be her choice."

He was giving his sister the choice he had not been given. The choice I hadn't been given.

If I hadn't already fallen for this man, that might have pushed me over the edge.

"She's only four," he said. "She's had enough encounters with monsters already. She doesn't need to be taken to Allesaria. As far as I'm concerned, she'll never set foot in the castle until my father is in his grave. By that point, I'll be in mine, too."

"Stop saying shit like that," I snapped. "Please."

Ransom exhaled, and the weariness on his face made me want to scream.

He wasn't dying. I refused to accept that fate. Not without exhausting everything in my power for a cure. For some way to stop the infection, magical or not.

"Hey." Ransom shifted to stand in front of me. "I'm not dead yet."

"No, you're not." I crossed my arms over my chest, giving him my best scowl.

A bit of color returned to his cheeks with a hint of his smile.

Better.

I stepped past him, waiting until he fell into step at my side before I asked my next question. "Does your father know about Evie? That she's Zavier's daughter?"

"I'm not sure. It's no secret that Zavier has a ward."

"Why not have him claim her as a daughter? Why make her call him Zavier, not Papa?"

Ransom sighed. "For her protection. When she was born, it seemed like the best option. If people believe she's of a royal bloodline, then she'll always be a target. We have done our best to make them think she was born to a woman in Ozarth who died in childbirth. That Zavier has decided to raise her as his own."

"Why not find someone else to fill the role as her parent? Someone far away from the crown."

"Zavier was with us when I brought Mother back from Ozarth. He took one look at that child, and she was his. It didn't matter then. I was the prince. He was Dray, a ranger and my cousin."

But then Ransom was bitten, and everything changed.

"Maybe we should have made other arrangements, but you will take Evie from Zavier over his cold, dead body."

"Even if she'd be safer with someone else?"

"I don't disagree. But I also won't force him to give her up. Despite what you may think, I am not that cruel."

I'd never thought of him as cruel. Unrelenting. Stubborn. Arrogant. A massive thorn in my side. But never cruel. "So she stays with Zavier. And your mother? Is she all right with this arrangement?"

"Yes and no. It's been years, but she's still coming to terms with the man my father has become. So am I. As a boy, I never once questioned his decisions. I believed his every word."

"And now?"

"He is doing what he believes is right. I won't stand against him. Instead,

I'll do what I can from this position."

"You mean as the Guardian? You have the entire realm fooled. They all think Zavier is the prince."

"I am Zavier."

I rolled my eyes. "You know what I mean."

"I am loyal to my people. Does it matter who they believe I am? A prince or a guardian? I strive to keep them safe. From the monsters with claws. And the monsters with crowns."

"Like your father," I muttered.

"And yours."

I scoffed and came to a stop. "My father is not a monster."

He might not be the kind of father who doted on his daughters, but he loved his kingdom. He put Quentis above all else. Was that really so monstrous?

Ransom kept walking, forcing me to hurry and catch up. "There is a storm on the horizon, Odessa."

"Yes, it's called the crux migration."

"That's not what I mean."

"Then what do you mean?" I threw up my hands, stopping again. He wasn't the only one exhausted today. "I'm tired of asking questions, Ransom. I can assure you, when it comes to my father's plans, I'm none the wiser. He trusts me as much as you trust me. Meaning not at all."

Ransom turned and faced me, staring down at me with hard hazel eyes. When had they changed? I'd been so lost in his story, I hadn't noticed the shift from green. "I believe your father has found a way to break the Shield of Sparrows."

Father had hinted as much. It would cause chaos across Calandra. It would mean kings were free to attack other kings, and the fragile peace would shatter forever. It was an impossible feat. Or should have been.

"How?" If Father wouldn't tell me, maybe my husband would.

"By killing the Voster. End the brotherhood, and you end their magic bonds."

Forty-Nine

"You cannot kill the Voster." Right? I was fairly certain it would be impossible to kill beings with magical powers.

"He will try," Ransom said.

Why? Since my father wasn't here to ask, Ransom was going to get my questions. "What would that accomplish? If the treaties are dissolved, it would mean war. Quentis is strong but not that strong."

Quentin soldiers did not fight the way the Turans fought. Father's legion would be slaughtered.

"You have a geographic advantage," Ransom said. "You share only a single border with Genesis on the Evon Ravine. And your father has enough gold to secure a navy the likes of which Calandra has never seen. He doesn't need to stage a war. He only needs to be the last king standing. To wait out the migration. To let other kings war with one another. Then sweep in and claim the spoils."

"For what? Gold?" He was rich beyond measure.

"Power."

"Except wouldn't my father be more powerful if the Voster were on his side? They have *magic*."

"Magic that comes with strings. The brotherhood will never answer to a mortal king. But they will stand behind those of their choosing."

So that was the issue. Not only had the Voster wound their magic into countless treaties and legends, like the Chain of Sevens, but they were a threat. If Father wanted to expand his rule, there was a good chance they'd stand in his way. Even if the Shield of Sparrows didn't exist.

And the Voster, if I had to guess, would stand behind the Turans.

Behind Ransom.

"Well, even if he could figure out a way to kill them, no one even knows where they live," I said.

Ransom hummed.

Not a yes. Not a no.

"Husband." I narrowed my gaze. "You know where the Voster live, don't you?"

Ransom held my eyes. And didn't speak a word.

He didn't have to. His silence was answer enough.

Allesaria.

Was that why the Turans had moved their capital? Had they sought refuge with the Voster after the migration three generations ago? Or had the city been constructed to protect the brotherhood? What had happened three migrations ago to send this kingdom into spiraling secrecy?

The man with answers stared at me, mouth shut.

We'd get nowhere with this topic, so I found a new one. "What if my father comes after the Voster?"

"Then my father will defend them."

But what if Ramsey wanted their hold over him to vanish, too? Would he forge a new alliance with my father? "Are you certain of his loyalties?"

"Without doubt."

There was magic involved, wasn't there? Had the Turans been sworn to protect the Voster? Somewhere in Allesaria, was there a treaty signed in blood that the other kings knew nothing about?

"Ramsey will have to take a break from his book burning." No sooner had the words left my lips than realization crashed into me, knocking the wind from my lungs.

The books. The Voster.

Ransom had mentioned Father's spies in an offhand remark a while ago. He knew of Father's plans, or at least a hint.

Ramsey wasn't burning books to take information from his people. He wasn't punishing the Turans. He was destroying information that might bring invaders to his door.

"He's burning them to keep information out of Father's hands."

"Maybe." Ransom ran a hand over his jaw. "I honestly don't know. Nothing makes much sense where my father is concerned these days, and aside from going to Allesaria to find out, he is all but lost to me at the moment. He is not the king or man I knew. He might be trying to hide information. To keep Lyssa a secret and not send our people into pandemonium. Or he's burning books to provoke and punish my mother. After I took her from Allesaria, he set her library ablaze. Nearly took out an entire wing of the castle. It was her favorite place, and he knows she's hiding somewhere. I think he hopes that she'll try to stop him one of these days."

The day Ramsey had come to Treow to destroy the library, I'd watched from behind a tree. I'd stayed hidden. With Cathlin.

Was she Ransom and Evie's mother? I doubted Ransom would tell me if I asked.

Burning books seemed like petty vengeance, but who knew how far he'd go. People changed when they were heartbroken.

Years ago, at a party in the castle, Margot had guzzled too much wine. She'd made a random comment about how much Father had changed after my mother's death.

Love had its way of building us up.

And bringing us down.

"Let's say that Ramsey does know about my father's intentions," I said. "That he will protect the Voster. Is that why he's creating this militia?"

"Doubtful. It's customary for kings to bolster their military before the crux migrations. From what I've been told, every king in the five kingdoms is currently training and recruiting more soldiers. Your father included. Mine has been constructing catapults for every major city for nearly a year."

"While leaving towns like Ashmore undefended from monsters. And foreign invaders."

Ransom's jaw worked as he nodded. Then he set off again down the street, turning us around a corner. "I don't agree with it, Odessa. But I see his reasoning. My grandfather encouraged people to take shelter in the cities, but most stayed in their homes. My father saw the destruction the crux left behind. People were slaughtered, entire villages destroyed. Even the strongest houses, like those in Ravalli, cannot withstand a monster that can rip its roof off. He is trying to send them to a place where he stands a chance at keeping them safe."

"The migration is projected for spring. If it's later than that, as it has been in the past, it could be up to a year from now. Can you blame them for wanting to stay in their homes for as long as possible? He knows about Lyssa. Abandoning them means he's left them to die. What difference does it make, which monster does the killing?"

Ransom turned, holding out his arms. "What do you want me to say? I do not control his army."

"I know, I just…" My hands balled into fists. "This cannot be the way."

"What about your people? Those who live on the land and do not have the luxury of hiding beneath a castle? Where do they go during the migration?"

"Most come to the cities."

"And those who don't?"

Died.

Some farmers spent years building shelters and digging tunnels beneath the earth, like the people in Ashmore. Sometimes those hideouts kept them alive. Other times, they did not.

The crux were ruthless in their pursuit of prey.

Even when people came to the city, it did not mean they were safe. Thousands had been killed in Roslo during the last migration. It had lasted nearly two months, and for all the strength of our walls, our keeps, there was only so much they could withstand. There were only so many people we could shelter.

It was the same across all of Calandra.

The weight of countless lives rested on my father's shoulders. He knew there was only so much he could do. Maybe Ramsey felt the same. Not that I wanted to have any sort of empathy for the man, but in his position, I wasn't sure what I'd do, either.

"I wish there was a way to stop the migrations. To effectively fight the crux," I said.

Ransom gave me a sad smile. "Me too."

Not that we didn't try.

The alchemists in Laine had invented flamethrowers to torch the monsters from the skies. Roslo had plenty of catapults, too. Father's smiths were already forging bolts for the large crossbows mounted on the castle towers and walls. Ellder had similar versions of the weapons on their ramparts.

Yet while we had the means to kill a crux, there were simply too many monsters to fully combat during the migration. For every one slain, ten took its place.

We could fight and die.

Or hide and live.

Ransom and I walked to the house together, but each of us was lost in our own thoughts. We'd set out on this walk so he could clear the fog from his mind. Now I felt it clinging to mine. By the time we returned to the house and he'd escorted me to the suite's front door, I was reeling.

"Why did you tell me all of this?" Was he trying to make up for the lies?

Maybe I should have doubted his every word, worried that this was another elaborate scheme. But it didn't sound like a lie. Granted, I'd believed everything he'd told me since the beginning, so what the hell did I know?

Yet this felt like the truth. Like he'd let down his walls to share the ugly truths about his family.

Ransom had never referred to Zavier as my husband. Over the past week, I'd replayed every moment I could recall. I'd picked apart my memory. And I couldn't remember a single time when he'd called Zavier my husband.

He'd teased me. Made crude comments. It had been implied but never stated plainly.

Lies of omission were still lies.

But they were easier to forgive.

"I cannot trust you with all of my truths, Odessa." He stepped closer, his hand lifting to the hair at my temple. To a wild red curl that he twisted around a finger. "But I will give you as many as possible."

He pulled the curl straight before letting it spring free. Then both of his hands were in my hair, pushing it away as he took my face in his palms. "Forgive me, my queen. Please."

Ransom didn't give me the chance to respond before his mouth brushed across mine. He kissed the tip of my nose. He nipped at my bottom lip. Then he sealed his mouth over mine, his tongue darting out for a taste.

This kiss was different than the last. It was gentle. Soft. Sweet. It liquefied my insides, melting away my frustration. Peeling away the hurt until all that was left was the spark. The pull to this man that I'd never been good at resisting.

The secrets and lies faded away, for just a moment, until a scream tore us apart.

Ransom's entire body went tight as he whirled toward the noise.

A symphony of shouts and screams filled the air, all coming from the direction of the gates. Of the courtyard.

Where a monster had been entertaining children with flying leaves.

"Stay here." Ransom gripped the railing of my balcony and launched himself over its edge, leaping to the ground. Then he was gone, a blur of dark hair and a clean white tunic as he ran toward the commotion.

I flung my door open, racing inside to grab the knives I'd left beside the door. If Ransom really expected me to hide away while there were children at risk, he didn't know me at all. I flew down the walkway and stairs, reaching the ground as the front door to Zavier's opened.

Luella filled its frame, one hand holding Evie back.

"What is it?" she asked.

"I don't know."

"You should stay here where it's safe."

Not happening. I pointed the tip of a blade at Evie. "Watch over Faze?"

"I got him." She nodded and pushed past Luella's hold, running by me for the stairs.

Luella frowned, following her charge toward my suite as I sprinted for the courtyard.

People came chasing toward me, fleeing in the opposite direction, terror and tears on their faces.

It was the High Priest. He'd done something. He'd hurt someone.

I gripped my knives tighter as I made it to the mouth of the main road. To the courtyard. Whatever I'd expected to find, this was worse.

There were bariwolves in Ellder.

Their coats gleamed black. Their fangs flashed white.

It was chaos. Soldiers were trying to evacuate the people while others were racing into the fray, drawing blades to fight back the beasts. Mothers and fathers were carrying away their children. And in the center of it all was Ransom.

He was fighting. Somewhere, he'd borrowed a sword. But it was like watching him swing a blade through water. He moved like a normal man, sluggish compared to his usual speed.

The High Priest had weakened him today with whatever *treatment* he'd performed.

Had that been the plan? To draw innocents into the courtyard, knowing that their famed Guardian was not at his best?

The thought crossed my mind at the same time I spotted the Voster.

The High Priest did not wield a weapon. He carried no shield. But he fought the bariwolves, taking on two of the monsters with shards of ice he formed from the air.

His hands were raised, those gnarled green nails splayed wide, and with a sweep of his arms, he sent an icicle the size of a grown adult into a bariwolf's open mouth.

It sliced the beast in two, blood and entrails flinging wide, falling on those still trying to flee.

Green blood. Dark, putrid green.

"Oh, gods." I breathed, swallowing down the bile rising in my throat.

The bariwolves were everywhere, crashing through the open gates as the soldiers tried to get them closed.

"Close the gates!" Ransom roared as he brought a sword down on the head of a bariwolf.

Except it wasn't his sword. It was too small. Too fragile. It wasn't strong enough to cleave a monster's head at the neck. The blade snapped.

Ransom drove it into the bariwolf's eye instead, pushing it deeper and deeper until the monster collapsed dead.

"The gates!" Zavier came running from behind a building, three of his rangers, including Vander, trailing behind.

A bariwolf leaped at him, teeth bared, but Zavier dodged its jaws, sinking his sword into the monster's heart. Then he kept running, arms pumping, as he sprinted toward the gates.

There were too many of them. Fifteen. Twenty. Thirty. I'd never seen so many monsters at once.

Ransom grabbed a sword from a fallen soldier's body and kept fighting.

They all kept fighting.

Move, Odessa.

I ran to the first person I saw who wasn't trying to flee.

A teenage girl was hiding behind a spike in the middle of the road, clinging to it with all her might. That spike might keep her from a crux's talons, but not a bariwolf's jaws.

With my hand on her arm, I hauled her up. "Run. Go! Get inside."

She screamed, tears streaking down her face.

It took a solid shove for her to move. Then she disappeared behind me while I ran to a soldier curled in on himself, clutching a gaping wound in his leg. "We have to get you inside."

He shrieked in agony, lost to the pain.

"Come. On." I pulled on his arm, dragging him through the dirt and away from the fighting. It took all my might to get him to the nearest building, the livery.

The horses inside were stomping and whining, as frightened as the rest of us.

I dragged the soldier to the closest stall, propping him against the wall. Then I tore off a piece of cloth from his shirt, tightening it around his leg and above the wound. "I'll send help."

"Don't go, Princess." He clutched my arm, eyes wide.

I shook off his hold, closing the stall door. Outside, a little boy was on his knees, a leaf from the Voster's magical crown still in his brown hair. A woman lay on the ground beside him. Her eyes were as open as her gut.

"Mama!" The boy shook her arm like he could bring her back to life.

The snarls. The growls. The shouts. They faded until all I could hear was that boy's cry.

He would die. If he stayed there, he would be next.

"Cross!" Ransom's voice boomed. "No!"

I ignored him.

It was the fastest I'd ever run in my life. I was halfway to him when I felt the shift. When I felt the attention of a monster.

A bariwolf, jaws clamped around a man's neck, shook the body so hard it was like a dog shaking a snake. It dropped its kill and turned its attention to me. Blood dripped from its maw as it tracked my destination with a single eye.

My heart stopped.

The one-eyed bariwolf.

The monster that had infected Ransom.

It should have been a mindless, bloodthirsty beast. But it knew exactly where I was running. And in that moment, it seemed to smile.

"No!" I screamed, still running, as it lunged for the boy.

Three massive strides. And it ripped that child's head from his body, tossing it to the side.

Then it locked on me.

My boots skidded to a stop as it sent out a series of clicks. That noise was a promise of death. A vow that I wouldn't survive this day.

The sound might as well have turned on a flashing light over my head. Every bariwolf in the courtyard looked in my direction, where I stood, frozen, with only my knives.

Shit.

"Run!" Ransom bellowed. "Odessa, run!"

I spun on my heels, tripping as my feet moved faster than the rest of my body. But I caught myself, knuckles scratching on dirt, as I barreled toward the livery. The snarls were deafening. The pounding of paws seemed to shake the ground beneath my feet.

A swarm of black raced my way. Every monster in Ellder was hunting me down, getting closer and closer.

The livery was too far. I wouldn't make it. Even if I did, they'd crash inside and claw me to pieces if the horses didn't trample me to death first.

A wind slammed into my chest as I faced forward, blinking through the cloud of dust that blew past my body.

When it cleared, I saw burgundy robes and endless eyes.

The High Priest had changed positions, standing in front of me and blocking my path.

Trapping me between him and the bariwolves.

A cold blast of icy wind blew the hair from my face as the priest lifted his arms. And with a flick of his wrist, an ice shard launched from above his head and over mine, crashing into the monster on my tail.

The bariwolf slammed into the ground, dead. It had both eyes.

No, that one-eyed murderous fucker was running in the other direction, toward the gates that Zavier and his warriors were still fighting to close. Running toward another escape with a handful of bariwolves chasing behind.

It had commanded the rest of its pack to come after me while it fled.

Another icicle flew by. Then another.

The agony of the High Priest's magic drove into my skin, a thousand needles stabbing straight to the bone, but as much as it hurt, I ran toward the Voster, letting him fend off the monsters giving chase.

I darted past his towering frame, catching the side of his flowing robes with my boot. This time when I tripped, there was no keeping my balance.

With an *oof*, my shoulder hit the ground, sending a spray of dirt blasting into my face.

I groaned at the pain, forced myself up to a seat, and blinked away the grit in my eyes as seven more ice shards whipped from the High Priest and straight through the bodies of the seven bariwolves surging our way.

It rained blood, green and sticky. And as the last droplet floated into the ether, the courtyard stilled.

The gates closed.

Ransom stood ten paces away, his face coated in both shades of blood. It dripped from his hair, the tip of his nose.

The lips I'd kissed only minutes ago.

"Thank you." His chest heaved as he spoke to the priest.

The Voster nodded, then turned, hand extended to help me up.

But I'd already pushed to my feet and was racing for Ransom. "The bariwolf. Did you see it? It had—"

"One eye. I know." Ransom's hands roamed my shoulders and arms, his silver gaze searching for any injury. "You're all right?"

I nodded as tears burst from my eyes. "That little boy. He—"

Oh, gods. It was a nightmare. A scene I'd play out for the rest of my life, wondering if it was real. "Ransom."

"I know." He hauled me into his arms, crushing me against his chest.

I clung to his tunic, balling it into my fists as I breathed in his scent. Despite the blood, it was there. Wind and leather. Earth and moss. Cedar and Ransom.

"Ranse." Zavier appeared at our side, breathless and also covered in green blood.

Ransom growled but let me go, taking one last scan of my body to search for injury. "I have to go."

I nodded and released his shirt.

He stalked through the courtyard, picking up a fallen soldier's sword.

And with it in his hand, the Guardian ordered the gates reopened.

To kill a monster.

Evie was on my bed, wrestling with Faze, when a knock came from the door.

"I got it." She jumped to the floor and tore through my suite, our tarkin leaping down to follow as she weaved past furniture in the sitting room.

I hurried after them, as anxious as Evangeline to see who was at the door.

Please be Ransom.

It had been a week since the bariwolf attack. Since Ransom, Zavier, the High Priest, and a score of rangers had gone to hunt the pack that had killed thirty-one people in Ellder.

We'd had no word since they left, and every day that passed, I felt more and more on edge. If something happened to Ransom…

I shoved those fears from my mind as Evie yanked the door open.

The hope on her face died a swift death when Samuel Hay greeted us with a bow.

"Good morning, Miss Evangeline. Princess Odessa."

Evie leaned past the doorway, searching for someone else.

Zavier's absence had hit her harder than usual. Probably because she knew where he'd gone was dangerous. Despite Luella's and my best efforts to keep news of the attack out of this house, she'd overheard her nanny talking about the people who'd died. And while it wasn't always easy answering her questions, I couldn't pile more lies on her tiny shoulders.

So we'd told her about the attack. She knew something had happened that day. And while she didn't often play with the other kids in Ellder, she'd been heartbroken to learn that five children were now dead.

She'd cried on my shoulder and on Luella's, but the person she needed, her father, was gone. Her worry for Zavier was more than any four-year-old child should have to suffer.

"Were you expecting someone else?" Samuel asked, following Evie's gaze down the walkway. "I don't want to interrupt."

"You're not." I waved him inside. "Please. Come in."

He followed me into the sitting room as Evie stayed in the open doorway.

"You'd better run back down for your lessons," I told her. "I'm sure Luella is waiting."

"Okay," she muttered, then trudged out, closing the door behind her.

"Still no word from Prince Zavier?" Samuel asked.

"No."

To my knowledge, Samuel, like everyone else in Ellder, knew that Evie was Zavier's ward, but not that she called him Papa behind closed doors. Maybe they suspected she was his daughter.

Adopted daughter. A detail that didn't matter. The only person the whole truth would hurt was Evie. She was Zavier's, as he was hers.

"Hopefully, they'll return soon." He gave me a sad smile. "Unharmed."

"I hope so, too."

It had taken nearly the entire week for the dust to settle after the attack. Men, women, and children had been buried. The fortress had mourned. And its people had talked.

Some believed the bariwolf pack had numbered twenty. Others claimed there'd been over thirty of the monsters. It was the largest pack to have ever been seen in Turah.

Maybe they'd come together because they'd all been infected with Lyssa. Maybe the monster with a single eye had bitten each of the others in its pack and that had created some sort of alpha bond. Regardless of their number, they had brought death to Ellder.

And now there were whispers through the fortress about monsters with green blood.

They might not know its name, but the rumors and speculation about Lyssa were spreading as quickly as the infection.

Maybe once that happened, Ramsey could no longer feign ignorance. He'd have to send help. And the other kings in Calandra would start to take it seriously. Maybe then we could get some fucking help to kill these monsters.

The bariwolves had struck the walls at different points, drawing the focus of the soldiers stationed on the ramparts. I'd ventured out yesterday afternoon to see the claw marks. Some cut three inches deep.

Mindless, crazed monsters shouldn't have had the intelligence to coordinate such an attack. Maybe it hadn't been orchestrated and we were simply reading too much into it. But whatever their intent, they'd managed to distract the guards and cause a ruckus.

While the bariwolves outside the fortress had clawed and scratched, some trying to scale the walls, the others had raced for the gates before they could be closed, breaking into the courtyard.

The soldiers stationed atop the tower who'd survived were all distraught, carrying the blame for the thirty-one souls now resting in the shades.

The gates were typically left open during the day for people to come and go. They'd closed behind Ransom and Zavier a week ago and hadn't reopened until yesterday. Even then, they were open for only minutes — enough time for those who'd decided to leave Ellder behind to drive their wagons out of the fortress. Enough time for me to see the claw marks, then retreat inside.

It shouldn't have happened. Had the monsters not been infected, the barrage of arrows that had rained down on them from the ramparts would have deterred them. But they'd been driven by bloodlust.

And it had been satisfied.

The slain monsters had been burned, and I wished there was solace in their deaths. I wished I could feel a sliver of relief that at least they couldn't harm another person. But for a week, all I'd felt was hopeless.

There were too many monsters.

Was this what we could expect from the crux? It was no wonder the older generations were terrified of the migration.

No matter how much time passed, how many years I lived, I would never forget this attack. I would never forget the sight of that boy dying.

"Are you all right, Princess?" Samuel asked.

I shook myself out of the memory and forced a smile. "Of course. How are you? How is Jonas?"

"Back in school today. With the other kids." The survivors. "It was difficult to send him out the door this morning."

Most of the children who'd gathered in the courtyard had been at school that day. Two of the teachers had been killed. Jonas and some of the older boys had hung back from the little ones. When the attack started, they'd raced to the nearest building and barricaded themselves inside.

"I suppose, if anything, this was a reminder of what's to come during the crux migration."

"I suppose." I nodded for Samuel to follow me to the chairs in the sitting room.

"I didn't think Turah would be like this." Samuel took a seat, swallowing hard. "When Emsley was alive, we visited Turah. We stayed along the coast. Spent a month in Perris. She wanted to go deeper into the kingdom, to explore the mountains. But we tried for weeks to hire a guide. No one would take us, so we tabled that journey for another time. Part of why I chose Ravalli was because she wanted to see it herself. I think I'm glad she didn't."

Zavier had warned me months ago, on the deck of the *Cutter*, that this kingdom was dangerous, but nothing he could have said would have prepared me for this reality. Turah was perilous. Majestic. Horrifying. Stirring. It was every emotion, good and bad, woven into a landscape that had stolen my heart.

Like its guardian.

"Anyway." Samuel shifted in his seat, checking over his shoulder to the closed door. Then he opened the satchel he'd brought along. "I was able to finish your map."

"Oh. You didn't need to worry about that."

"It was a welcome distraction on sleepless nights." He stretched to hand it over.

I unfolded the paper, scanning new lines mingled with old.

He'd adjusted the path of a few roads and towns. He'd added many that I hadn't known about. He'd expanded the mountain ranges and detailed rivers beyond my initial sketch. He'd infused the parchment with detail and depth.

"This is beautiful." Not something I'd ever said about a map. "Thank you."

He nodded. "I've done my best. But I'm afraid it is lacking. The area you'd hoped to add, I cannot. And I don't think you should, either."

When I dropped this off, I'd added a line, a guess, to Allesaria.

That line had been erased.

I couldn't blame him for being nervous.

"I appreciate this," I said. "I know it was a risk. I swear no one will ever know this exists."

It would be a shame to toss this work of art into my fireplace once I'd transferred the details to my journal's loose pages.

Samuel smacked his hands to his knees before standing. "I will take my leave, Princess."

"Odessa."

"Princess Odessa." He bowed, smiling as I rolled my eyes. "Good day."

"Thank you again." I escorted him to the door and sent him on his way with a wave. Then I went to my room, retrieving a charcoal stylus from my vanity.

And the journal I kept hidden beneath my chest of drawers.

After fitting the pieces together, aligning some edges and overlapping others until the puzzle was complete, I went about transferring Samuel's additions and corrections.

I hadn't touched these pages since Ravalli. So far, I'd been noting monsters with Lyssa with tick marks, but there'd been so many bariwolves in Ellder, I simply added an *X*.

With it complete, I stood, surveying the pages, letting the lines and marks blend together.

Lyssa had started somewhere. Some place. An epicenter. But as I squinted my eyes, hoping a pattern would leap off the parchment, all I saw were fuzzy splotches of gray and white.

There was no cluster of monsters. No convergence on a certain point.

"Damn," I breathed.

Was this a waste of my time? Maybe the source, the person who'd created Lyssa, traveled too widely to pinpoint. Maybe the monsters themselves were too nomadic and because they wandered so freely, by the time they attacked, it was impossible to know where they'd been infected.

It was Allesaria.

It had to be Allesaria. And it had something to do with the Voster.

There wasn't a single reference to other magical creatures in all the books I'd read since coming to Turah. Certainly nothing I'd read at home in Quentis.

Regardless of what Ransom believed, if Lyssa was magical, the Voster were involved. The brotherhood had to be the reason my father was so determined to find Allesaria. It had to be the Voster stronghold, somewhere deep within the Turan mountains.

Samuel had embellished the landscape, and according to his map, the range north of Ellder seemed to be the largest.

There weren't any markings in that area.

So either my assumption was entirely wrong and Allesaria wasn't anywhere near that range. Or Allesaria wasn't the source, the Voster were innocent, and Ransom was right about everything.

I was stuck. Again. Did all spies have these moments when nothing came together? Or was that just me?

I needed Ransom's cuff. To see if it did mark the capital. But he wasn't here, and even if he were, I doubted he'd hand it over for me to trace.

My frustration cloaked the room, stuffy and hot, so I collected the pieces of my map, tucking them back into the journal. Then, with it hidden beneath my chest, I went to the hearth and burned Samuel's map.

Faze was on the sitting room's windowsill, asleep. He didn't even crack a violet eye when I scratched behind his ear. The scales along his spine were beginning to harden. His canines were getting longer. Sharper.

He nipped at Evie's fingers every now and then. Each time I caught it, I bopped him on the nose, hoping I could teach him not to bite. But the first time he broke her skin...

Well, that would be the end. There'd be no more days of them playing together. No more nights of him sleeping on my extra pillow.

The longer we kept him, the harder it would be to set him free. But he wasn't big enough to hunt yet. To provide for himself. To stay clear of the other predators in the wild.

I stroked along the fur of his nose, the same light pink as on his belly, then touched the tip of a fuzzy, ruby red ear before I left him to nap and went outside.

I set off for no destination in particular, simply needing the fresh air to clear my head. The streets in Ellder were quiet today. They'd been quiet all week. People walked with their heads down, their bodies tense and alert. No one left the safety of their homes unless it was necessary.

Had it not been so quiet, I probably wouldn't have heard the thunder of hooves echoing from the gates. I'd been waiting for that sound all week.

I changed paths, jogging toward the courtyard. It hadn't been easy to come back here this week, but the day after the attack, I'd forced myself to return. To stand, with tears streaming down my face, in the place where that boy's blood had stained the dirt.

His name was Witt.

Witt. Sariah.

I would remember their names. For the rest of my life.

My heart was in my throat as I made it to the end of the main road just in time to see a band of warriors ride through the gates, dust puffing from beneath their horses' hooves as they came to a stop. There was a wagon in their midst.

Tillia stayed in her saddle, the brown skin around her eyes looking tired and her expression hard. It only softened as Halston rode up beside her.

I scanned faces, searching for Ransom, but this was Halston's hunting party, not Zavier's. These rangers hadn't been in Ellder when the bariwolves had attacked. Tillia had been in Treow.

Stable boys and men from the livery came forward to collect the animals, taking them away to water. The horses looked as exhausted and dusty as their riders.

Tillia and Halston dismounted and stood together, his arm around her shoulders, as the other warriors all scattered, probably to find a place to crash.

Halston murmured something into his wife's ear as his hand moved to her belly, splaying across the slight swell.

My jaw dropped, my hand coming to my heart.

Tillia looked up and caught me staring. She smiled, her hand covering her husband's.

Halston followed her gaze and gave me a slight bow before he kissed her temple, then collected her bags, carrying them to wherever they stayed while in Ellder as Tillia came my way.

"Hi." She pulled me into a hug. "I missed you."

"I missed you, too." I let her go, eyes dropping to her stomach. "What is this? You're pregnant?"

A brilliant smile lit up her face and pretty brown eyes. "The healers cautioned us that much can happen early on. We kept it to ourselves for a while. But there's no hiding it now."

"I'm happy for you."

"Me too." She looped her arm with mine, pulling me along as we left the courtyard. Like she knew I wasn't ready to linger for long. "Halston and his rangers have been with Zavier and the Guardian."

The air rushed from my lungs. "Are they—"

"On their way here. They split off to scout the area. We've come from Treow. Halston wants me in Ellder until the baby is born. Apparently, now that I'm carrying his child, I can no longer climb a rope ladder."

"Aww. It's sweet that he's protective. And maybe, right now, it's smart to be cautious." Though after last week's attack, I wasn't sure anywhere was safe.

Her smile faded. "I heard what happened."

"Did they find the pack?"

Tillia shook her head.

My insides knotted as dread pooled. Everyone here was waiting for news that the pack was dead. That the threat was eliminated. That vengeance was ours.

But this news would break hearts.

"The Guardian won't give up." Tillia patted my arm. "He won't stop hunting."

"When—?"

A call from the ramparts rang out. "Open the gates!"

We both turned, unlinking our arms as we stood in the courtyard, watching as Zavier and his rangers rode inside. Two of them had been with him in the throne room. Another three I didn't recognize. Vander rode beside my fake husband.

And behind them all, hanging back with Aurinda, came Ransom.

His face was streaked with dirt and dark smudges, likely blood. There was a sword strapped across his back. His clothes were filthy, and his hair was in disarray. He was a mess. And so beautiful that my throat burned with the threat of tears.

The anxiety I'd been battling for a week vanished, and for the first time in days, I could take a full breath.

His gaze cut through the others, landing on me like he could sense me in the crowd. Like he was as linked to me as I was to him. His expression didn't change. Didn't relax. But his eyes shifted from hazel to green.

Zavier came to a stop, blocking my view of Ransom as he swung off his horse. His left arm was in a sling, and he limped. There was a sheen of sweat on his face, but he wasn't as dirty as the others.

"His shoulder was dislocated," Tillia said. "He was thrown from his horse when it was scared by a lionwick. He's been in Treow for a couple of days with the healers while the others were hunting."

Hence why he was clean and the others were not.

Except Zavier hadn't bothered to shave while he was recovering. With his short beard, he looked more like Ransom than ever before.

"You can see now why it works," Tillia said. "That he can pretend to be the prince."

Of course she knew. Maybe I should have been upset that she knew, but Tillia's loyalty to Zavier, to Ransom, was part of why I admired her.

"I'm sorry, Odessa. For the lies."

"You were following orders. I understand." I shrugged. "How many others know the truth?"

"Halston. Vander. It is different in Allesaria. Those around court recognize Ransom. But here, in the wilds, only those in their closest circle know the truth of their identities. They see Zavier as the prince and Ransom as the Guardian."

There was comfort in knowing I'd been brought into Ransom's closest circle. Tillia's, too.

"Who are they?" I pointed to the wagon that had come in with Halston and Tillia.

There were two men being carried on stretchers from the back and taken to the infirmary.

"They wandered into Treow three days past. Both took ill the day they arrived. We haven't been able to wake them since."

"Lyssa?"

"The healers checked them extensively for bites. Nothing. It could be that they were out hunting and got lost. Both are dehydrated and undernourished. All we can do is pray to Ama that they'll both survive so we can find out where they came from."

After all I'd seen last week, I wasn't sure Ama was listening to prayers from Turah.

The men and horses seemed to part for Ransom, who led Aurinda our way. He paused beside Zavier, saying something no one else could hear. A stable boy came to take his stallion's reins. Then he walked to me with long, purposeful strides.

My belly fluttered. Shades, I'd missed him.

"I'm going to go find Halston." Tillia touched my arm, then walked away as my husband snared me with that emerald gaze.

He stopped in front of me, crossing his arms over his chest. "Cross."

"Wolfe."

The corner of his mouth turned up. "Miss me?"

"Never."

"Has anyone ever told you that you're a horrible liar?"

"Has anyone ever told you that you stink?" I scrunched up my nose, not caring that he reeked of blood and horse and sweat. Beneath it all was that wind and earth and the spice that was wholly Ransom. "Are you all right?"

"Yes, my queen." He bowed. "Are you?"

I am now.

The relief lasted but a single heartbeat. On the next, I felt the telltale prickle of magic. The sting of the Voster.

A shiver raced down my spine as the High Priest appeared over Ransom's shoulder, walking through Ellder's gates just as the soldiers began to push them closed. With him was Brother Dime, Father's emissary.

It was like being snatched back in time, to the day in the throne room and sanctuary. The magic of one was uncomfortable. But two of the priests? I fought to fill my lungs, to tamp down the pain.

I scratched at my forearms.

"What is it?" Ransom asked.

"Nothing."

He frowned. "What did I just say about lying?"

"You're one to talk."

Ransom's jaw clenched. It was faint, barely a tick to his jaw, but it was enough to know the sharpness in my voice had grated on a nerve.

I blamed it on the Voster. On the way they set me on edge.

The High Priest came to Ransom, levitating instead of walking, with Brother Dime at his side.

Ransom turned, bowing to the priests.

Brother Dime returned the gesture.

But the High Priest kept coming, floating on that phantom wind until he was close enough that the barbs from his magic rocked me on my heels.

Without a word, he snatched my hand before I could shy away.

Pain, as sharp as knives and as hot as fire, lanced through my arm like it had been cleaved in pieces. My legs buckled as a cry tore from my throat.

"Stop." I jerked my arm, trying to pry myself free, but the High Priest's grip only tightened, keeping me from collapsing on my knees.

Ransom's sword was a blur of silver steel, stopping a whisper from the High Priest's throat. "Let her go. Now."

The High Priest released me, and I dropped, knees cracking on the ground.

Ransom was between us in a flash, sword still raised as he held out a hand to help me to my feet.

I swallowed hard and stood, gulping down a breath. The pain faded instantly, leaving only the prickle in its wake.

"What the fuck are you doing?" Ransom roared.

The High Priest only sank to the soles of his feet, seemingly unconcerned with Ransom's blade, and turned to Brother Dime. "Did you know?"

"I thought she was simply frightened. Like so many."

The High Priest cocked his head to the side, dark eyes locked on my face and hair. "Who is your mother, child?"

"M-my mother?" Why was he asking about my mother?

But before I could ask, a shout carried across the courtyard.

"Zavier!" We all turned to see Luella racing our way, her dark hair unbound and the color drained from her face.

Ransom lowered his sword but didn't drop it completely. With his other hand, he kept me behind him, shielding me from the priests as he looked to Luella.

Zavier abandoned his warriors and horses, rushing toward us as quickly as he could with the limp.

But Luella raced for Ransom, clutching his arm.

"What is it?" he asked.

"Evie." She gulped. "She's gone."

Fifty-One

Zavier and the rangers clustered around us, all eyes on Luella.

"When did you see her last?" Ransom asked.

"She went to Odessa's suite after her morning lessons to play with Faze."

"And I sent her downstairs over an hour ago."

Luella shook her head, eyes wide and panicked. "She never came. When she was late, I checked your suite, but it was empty. I've been looking, thinking she was hiding again, but she always comes out when she knows I'm getting scared. She's not in the house. And her satchel and bow are missing."

"Fuck." Zavier gulped, then took a step away from the group, cupping his good hand over his mouth. "Evangeline!"

"Find her," Ransom ordered.

Every ranger burst into action, fanning out to search.

My gaze turned toward the gates, which were slowly being closed but still open.

"She wants to be a warrior. She wants to hunt monsters." I locked eyes with Zavier. "Like you."

Except if she'd come to the courtyard, she would have seen that he'd returned. And she wouldn't have been able to get past the gates unless...

"The side gate?"

"The guard would never let her out."

"The escape tunnel," Luella whispered. "From the migration cellar. I didn't think she'd know about it, but..."

But Evie knew about the dungeons. I doubted there was much they'd ever been able to hide from her.

Ransom spun for the main gates, holding up a hand to keep them from being shut. "Stop."

Then he was gone, running so fast none of us stood a chance at keeping up as we all hurried beyond the fortress walls.

"Evangeline!" Ransom's roar bounced off trees, filling the forest.

"Gods," Luella sobbed. "Where is she?"

"Evie," I shouted, eyes sweeping everywhere, looking for the girl. She'd been in a pink shirt today with flowers at the neck. Yellow and blue and purple flowers.

"Evie." Zavier's voice cracked as he yelled and yelled her name, his eyes wide with panic.

I cupped my hands over my mouth, about to shout again when Ransom held up a hand, silencing us all.

A whistle, distant yet clear, rang out from our left. A whistle from someone who'd spent long enough in Treow to know the sound for safety.

Zavier blew past us, not stopping as he ran along the wall, his limp slowing him down but not by much.

I was out of breath, my heart a frantic drumbeat in my chest. "Where?"

Luella moved to Ransom, gripping his arm. "Do you see her?"

"There." He pointed toward the trees, but it took a few more agonizing moments for me to see what he could.

A swish of white hair. A woman wearing a simple tan dress with long sleeves. And a girl in pink with a quiver of arrows on her back and a bow in her hand.

Zavier reached them first, sweeping Evie into an embrace with only one arm.

She wrapped her arms around his neck, legs around his waist, clinging to him as we chased their way.

"I found her on the road," Cathlin said. "Not far from the tunnel hatch."

"Evangeline," Zavier clipped.

Tears swam in Evie's eyes. "I'm sorry, Papa."

"You cannot leave the fortress. Is that understood?"

She nodded.

He was livid, his anger fueled by fear, but he closed his eyes, let some of it go, and exhaled. Then he kissed Evie's cheek, holding her close. "Let's go home."

She buried her face in his neck, and though he could only carry her with one arm, he set off along the wall, his limp more noticeable than it had been, and carried his daughter toward the gates.

Ransom put his hand on Cathlin's shoulder. "Thank you."

"That child was born to fly." Cathlin stared at Evie with love brimming in her gaze. A mother's love? "You will all need to be mindful not to clip her wings."

"It's more important to keep her safe," Ransom said.

"You must find a way to accomplish both. Or you will lose her to the wind."

Luella wiped her face dry and pulled Cathlin into an embrace. "Thank you."

Cathlin hugged her back—the hug of women who'd been friends for decades. Maybe Luella had been Cathlin's lady's maid in Allesaria? Maybe the lover Cathlin had gone to visit was a woman she'd met at court?

Luella pulled away. "Come and find me later? So we can catch up?"

Why did that sound like something more serious than a friendly chat over tea?

Cathlin studied Luella for a moment before giving her a nod.

Then Luella rushed to catch up to Zavier and Evie.

Ransom's hand came to the small of my back, urging me toward the gates. "I'm going to make sure the side gate is secure."

Once we reached the courtyard, once the gates were closed and locked, he stormed off in the direction of the side gate.

"That girl will be the death of Luella. But she loves Evie with her whole heart." Cathlin's attention was fixed on Luella's retreating figure. "Luella has been my best friend since we were children. Did I tell you that?"

"No." But if I were Cathlin and had a secret daughter, I'd choose my oldest friend to watch over my child.

"She wanted to become an alchemist and a healer and a traveler. She did not want to limit herself to only one thing, but to try them all. To be around her was to feel inspired. Energized. She believed anything was possible. I wasn't sure how I'd been lucky enough to fall into her orbit. I was simply glad to be there."

The Luella I knew was stoic and stalwart. She rarely smiled or laughed. I couldn't imagine her as an inspiration. A free spirit. Only something horrific could have caused such a change. "What happened?"

"The crux." Cathlin wrapped her arms around her waist, like even speaking their name was difficult. "Her family was killed. So was mine."

"I'm so sorry."

"The migration changes us all. You'll see."

A shiver of dread chased down my spine.

"I didn't realize that Ellder had migration tunnels, too."

"It's not like those in Ashmore that lead to shelters. There's only one, and not many know where it is. It serves as more of an emergency escape."

"Or as an Evie escape," I muttered. Had Ransom really gone to check on the side gate? Or was he barricading the entrance to these tunnels?

"That as well." Cathlin straightened, forcing a smile that didn't reach her eyes. And without another word, she walked away. Maybe to a hiding place? A secret apartment in Ellder where she'd be close to her daughter yet always kept apart.

I was walking through the courtyard, wanting to check on Evie, when the people in front of me parted like a curtain being drawn. They moved out of the way for the Guardian.

Ransom's expression was murderous, his eyes silver.

"Will you show me the tunnel?" I asked when he stopped in front of me.

"You've already found it. The farthest cell in the dungeon. There's a false wall. It will take you into the forest. But don't—"

"Use it? Fear not, I have no reason to leave Ellder. But thank you for telling me." It wasn't a declaration of trust, but it was something. "Is Cathlin your mother?"

His eyebrows lifted. "No."

"Oh." That one-word answer was all he was going to give me. Well, then I guess I'd find out his mother's identity through a process of elimination.

"What happened with the Voster?" he asked.

I grimaced, having forgotten about the ordeal earlier. Probably because the sting of their magic was gone. Spinning around, I searched the area for the brothers. "Where are they?"

How was it that the one and only time I actually wanted to have a conversation with the High Priest, he had vanished with Brother Dime?

"I don't know." Ransom's tone was razor-sharp. "We'll find them in a moment. First, tell me what happened."

I shrugged. "I've never touched a priest before. I didn't realize it would hurt so much."

"It doesn't hurt."

"I beg to differ." I rubbed my arm where I'd been touched. "It was like feeling their magic but a thousand times worse. Like it went straight into my bones."

His eyes narrowed. "What do you mean, feeling their magic?"

"You know, the stinging, prickling sensation like spiders are crawling on your skin." The blankness of his expression made my stomach sink. "You can't feel their magic? But I saw you that day in Treow's infirmary. The

High Priest touched you, and it looked like you were in pain."

"It is painful when he siphons Lyssa. But not to touch him. And I've never felt his magic otherwise."

My pulse began to race, my insides knotting. The Voster had been rare in Quentis. When Brother Dime came to visit, he spent time with Father, conducted whatever business necessary, then left. I'd always avoided him.

Since I'd come to Turah, encounters with the Voster seemed inescapable.

Why could I feel their magic? Why didn't others? Children didn't rush toward beings that made their skin crawl. "Can anyone feel it? Or is it just me?"

Ransom stared over my shoulder, his jaw clenched. "I don't know. I've never heard anyone say they could feel it before."

Then what was wrong with me? And why had the High Priest asked about my mother?

It would have been nice to ask. To get answers from the brotherhood.

Except after an hour of searching, of asking where they'd gone, we learned from a guard that they'd left through the gates while we were searching for Evie.

The Voster were gone.

Fifty-Two

Night was falling over Ellder, and like I did every evening, I curled into a chair on my suite's balcony to watch as Ama and Oda's stars blinked into sight.

Faze wound his way around my ankles, flicking his tail against my calves.

I bent and picked him up, stroking behind his ears as I settled him in my lap.

"Weird day, huh?"

Faze purred and ran his wet nose against my forearm.

As they had been all week, the streets below were quiet. Too quiet. I missed the noise from before the bariwolf attack. I missed distant laughter and conversation. I missed sitting here alone but not feeling alone.

Evie wouldn't make her pre-bedtime visit, not with Zavier home. And as Faze's eyes fluttered closed, I knew he wouldn't keep me company, either. So I stood and carried him inside, putting him on a chair in the sitting room as a knock came from outside.

Was it Ransom? I hadn't seen him since we left the courtyard earlier. He'd gone to do whatever it was the Guardian did while he was in Ellder. And I'd come here to ponder my encounter with the Voster.

My heart began to gallop as I crossed the room, and when I opened the door, there he was.

It was actually unfair for this man to be so handsome. One look at his perfect face, and my breath caught. "Hi."

He'd cleaned off the dust and dirt and blood from his week away. His hair was shorter, his face shaved, and without the beard, the corners of his jaw were as sharp as granite.

Ransom wore fresh clothes, his tunic open at the throat, revealing a sliver of smooth skin. He was breathtaking. His eyelashes framed moss-green irises, my favorite color. He smelled of soap and masculine spice, my favorite scents.

"My queen." He held up a dagger in a plain scabbard, extending it over the threshold. "A gift."

I took it from him, pulling out the blade. The hilt was smooth and simple. No jewels or gold. Just a smooth wooden handle that might as well have been made for my hand.

"It was mine," he said. "When I was a boy. It's not a fancy weapon, but it's sharp. If anyone ever touches you against your will again, it will leave a mark."

"Thank you." I returned the blade to its cover, then set it inside, on the small table beside the door. "Tell me about the hunt."

He stepped back against the railing, keeping the width of the walkway between us as he crossed his arms over his chest. The fabric of his shirt strained and molded to the muscles of his arms. "It didn't go as planned."

"How so?"

"I don't know." He frowned. "We followed their trail for three days. Then it was gone."

Gone where? Had they returned to Ellder to wait for an opening for another attack? Or had the pack gone elsewhere to wreak devastation on other innocent souls?

"There was something wrong with that bariwolf in the courtyard," I said. "Something different. It looked at me like it was after *me*. And I know this sounds like a stretch, but I swear to the gods, it ordered the others to go after me." I loosed a dry laugh. "I can't even believe I'm saying this out loud. It's a monster. Mindless and ruled by bloodlust. But I can't stop seeing its eye. Hearing those clicks. What if…"

There was a sinking feeling in my stomach. The feeling that I was about to admit something I'd been pondering for hours. And if I was being honest with myself, something I'd feared for longer.

"What if it's me?"

Ransom's eyes dropped to the boards beneath his boots. He did that at times, looked to the ground when he was hiding something. If I had noticed that small tell weeks ago, it probably would have saved my heart a mountain of strife.

"You think so, too, don't you?"

His silence was answer enough.

"Be honest with me. Please."

"How is your tiny monster?"

"Changing the subject. Really? Maybe that works with the women you keep in your Turan courts. But I won't let this go, Ransom."

"Of course you won't," he muttered.

I raised my eyebrows, waiting.

"It's only a theory. Do you remember the night at the camp when I killed a grizzur? The night it charged the fires?"

Not a night I'd ever forget. "Yes."

"I've never seen a monster, with or without Lyssa, attack fires before. Then there was Ashmore. Then the tarkin in Treow. Even Faze. He plays with Evie, but he is drawn to you."

It was more than me being *his* guardian. Even if I was the person who fed the little beast.

Ransom's eyes softened as he held up his hands. "Just a theory."

A theory in which he believed monsters were drawn to me. A theory I'd been dwelling on myself.

Monsters with or without Lyssa. Monsters who'd slaughtered those people in Ashmore. The people in Ellder. That boy, Witt, who'd clung to his mother's lifeless body.

"Oh, gods." My insides knotted. Those lives lost, their blood, was because of me. "Why? How?"

He dragged a hand through his hair. "I don't fucking know. It was just a thought."

"How long have you been having that thought?"

"A few hours. After what happened with the Voster, I started thinking."

I'd been thinking, too.

That bariwolf had seemed intent on me during the attack on the fortress. The same had happened in Ashmore. And the tarkin in Treow had turned back to come after me.

Maybe it was all a coincidence. Maybe I'd just been in the wrong place at the wrong time.

But what if there was more to these attacks? What if something about my being was drawing them close? I wrapped my arms around my waist as a tremble started in my fingers.

"Hey." Ransom pushed off the rail, coming into my space to take my face in his hands. "Breathe."

I shook my head, feeling the color drain from my cheeks. "It could all be my fault."

"No. Never." He bent so our gazes locked. "Not your fault."

"But if they came because of me. Whatever is wrong with me has—"

"Nothing is wrong with you, Odessa. Nothing. Understood?"

"But, Ransom... Oh, gods." My heart climbed into my throat, the sting in my nose so sharp I couldn't breathe.

Sariah. Witt. Names I'd vowed to remember. Names of people who would still be alive today if I'd stayed far, far away from Turah.

"I should leave."

"No."

"Rans—"

"No." He didn't shout or scream, but there was an undercurrent of rage in that word, of finality. His eyes shifted to silver for only a blink before they settled again on green.

I was not leaving Turah.

I was not leaving him.

"It's an idea." He let me go to pace the walkway in front of my door. "Not even a good one. My other theory is that it's me. That I'm drawing them in. Or maybe Lyssa has changed over time. I'm just...trying to make sense of what's happening and grasping for answers."

I wanted answers, too. "We have to test it. If it is me, we need to know."

He scoffed. "Absolutely not."

"I cannot put these people at risk."

"No."

"But—"

"It's not your choice, Odessa."

"My choice?" My jaw dropped, my anger igniting in a snap. "You stole most of my choices the day you set foot in my father's throne room, *husband.* But we're talking about putting innocent people at risk. Whether you like it or not, this is my choice."

"I'm trying to keep you safe."

"While giving me my freedom, right? Isn't that what you told me? You were setting me free? This"—I waved a hand between us—"this doesn't feel like freedom. This feels like being locked away where I'll suffocate."

"Suffocate?" Ransom moved into my space with a single step. "You were suffocating in Quentis. You were fucking wasting away in that golden castle. I'm not trying to trap you here, Odessa. But I need you to live. I won't..." He dragged a hand over his face. "I have never been more scared than when I saw you run for that boy."

"Witt," I whispered past the lump in my throat. "His name was Witt. And I couldn't save him."

"Neither could I." He cupped my cheek, his thumb touching the freckles across my nose. "I don't know what to do. I'm failing you. Do you really want to go back to Quentis? If you do, then say it. Tell me you want to leave, and I'll take you back to Roslo myself."

He was giving me the choice.

All I had to do was say yes.

"No," I whispered.

His eyes drifted closed, his forehead dropping to mine. "Good. I have no desire to live in Quentis."

"Wh-what?" I leaned away.

"You are mine." His hands dove into my hair, fingers threading through my curls. "Even if we are kingdoms apart, you are mine. But I'd rather not be a kingdom apart."

My breath hitched. Would he really follow me across Calandra? Leave his homeland, his people, behind? "You can't leave Turah."

"When I am nothing but dust and ash, Turah will endure. I do not need a crown. And I have made peace with my destiny. But before I step into my grave, my choice is you." He dropped a kiss to my temple, his fingers tracing along my jaw as his hand fell from my face. Then he stepped away, about to disappear into the night. "Sleep well, my queen."

My choice is you.

I was his choice. Above all else.

"Ransom." My hand grabbed his wrist, stopping him before he could leave.

Maybe I should have given myself time to think about everything he'd said. But gods, I was tired of thinking and overthinking and doubting and dwelling.

He'd lied to me, and it hurt. He'd tricked me, and it hurt. He'd embarrassed me, and it hurt.

But as we stared at each other, as the space between us crackled, all that hurt faded away.

Ransom was mine. Every flaw. Every perfection.

"This is my choice." I slid my palm into his.

Scar to scar.

I pulled him close, holding those green eyes as I lifted onto my toes and let my whisper caress his lips. "You. You are my choice."

A growl tore from his throat before he crushed his mouth against mine. He stole the air from my lungs, a beat from my heart, as he carried me inside and kicked the door closed behind us. With a spin, he pressed me against the wood as he licked the seam of my lips.

A whimper escaped my throat, and his tongue swept inside my mouth, swirling against mine. A pulse bloomed in my core, a heat spreading through my veins.

My hands dove into his hair. My arms clung to his shoulders, holding him close. Gods, I wanted him. More than I'd wanted anything in my life.

Ransom's hands slid along my ribs to my arms, lifting them above my head and pinning them to the door at my wrists. And then he plundered my mouth, kissing me until I was delirious.

I wrapped my legs around his hips, rocking my center against his growing arousal. Every part of him was hard, and I wanted it. Every inch.

He tore his lips away, his chest heaving as his forehead dropped to mine. "What have you done to me?"

I leaned in, smiling against his mouth. "Stop asking questions, Ransom, and kiss your wife."

"Yes, my queen." He grinned, then sealed his mouth over mine.

If the last kiss had ignited the spark, this kiss set me aflame.

He nipped and sucked and licked, devouring me whole. That throb became an ache as I rocked against him, desperate for friction.

"More," I murmured, locking my heels at his lower back.

He hauled me off the door and carried me across the suite to my room, his mouth never breaking from mine until he set me on my feet.

I dove my hands beneath the hem of his shirt, desperate to feel the warmth of his skin against my palms. My fingers skimmed the ridges of his stomach, trailing to his chest, his tunic bunching as it lifted.

His hands sunk into my hair, threading through the curls. He tugged at the roots, pulling until I arched my neck, revealing my throat, and he bent and latched onto my pulse, sucking hard enough to leave a mark before peppering a wet trail of kisses along my jaw. "This hair. I love this godsdamn hair."

"Off," I panted, tugging at his shirt. "Take this off."

He broke away, reaching for his nape to fist the fabric and yank it over his head.

Ransom was nothing but hard muscle beneath taut skin. My mouth watered, a throb pulsing from my core, spreading through my body. He was magnificent. A sculpture depicting a god.

I wanted to memorize every line. Every peak. Every valley. The strong plane of his chest. The cut *V* at his hips. The ripples of his abs and the cords of his arms.

Dark veins spread from his sternum, faint beneath his skin. But there was no hiding them, not with the moonlight streaming through the windows, silver beams caressing his skin.

The moment I reached for those dark striations, Ransom's hands came to my shoulders and spun me around to face the bed.

He lifted my hair off my shoulder, pushing it to the side as his mouth came to my ear, licking the shell. His hands cupped my breasts, and through my clothes, he pulled and twisted at my nipples until I moaned.

I reached back, dragging my palm over his hardness.

Ransom hissed, pressing against my hand as he ripped the shirt from my torso. There was a slight sound of tearing seams before it plopped on the floor.

I'd liked that shirt. But not enough to keep it on.

The rest of our clothes, our boots, came off without fanfare, scattered across the room as we crashed onto the bed in tangled limbs and fused mouths.

He swept me into his arms, his body covering mine as he kissed me until I was breathless. His elbows bracketed my face, his eyes a color I'd never seen before. A color without a name. They encompassed every shade of green from emerald to jade.

"I—" His throat bobbed.

I lifted a hand to his hair, pushing the dark locks away from his temple. Then I leaned up, taking his mouth as he settled into the cradle of my hips, positioned the crown of his cock at my entrance, and drove inside.

"Gods." My fingernails dug into his back, holding tight as my body stretched around his length, hard and thick and so fucking perfect.

"Odessa," Ransom groaned, and it was my favorite sound.

He buried his face in my hair, sucking in a sharp inhale as he took a moment, his entire body vibrating like he was testing the limits of his control. When he finally moved, I melted.

Stroke after stroke, he brought us together, our bodies moving like old lovers. Like a husband who had loved his wife for an eternity.

Dreaming. I was dreaming.

"It's real," he murmured, slowing his pace as our gazes locked.

It was real.

And we'd never be the same again.

He fucked like he moved, with a grace and fluidity that wasn't natural, but gods, I wasn't complaining. He took me higher and higher, driving me to the edge of a cliff. The fall would break me apart, and though the fragments would stitch together again, the woman I'd been once would be gone.

I was his. Not bound together by blood or vows or the treaties of men and magic.

Bound by this night.

"Fuck, you feel good." He pushed an errant curl away from my forehead, then captured my mouth, our tongues twining as he drove deep, hitting that spot inside that made my toes curl.

I whimpered against his lips, holding tight as he rocked us together and an inferno blazed beneath my skin. It was too much, too intense. I writhed beneath him, my movements no longer my own, until I detonated on a cry of his name, clenching and pulsing around him as the release ripped through my body. I shattered into a thousand pieces, white stars breaking behind my eyes as I cried out.

Ransom held me, kept me tethered to this realm, moving inside me as I floated to the stars.

The orgasm quaked through every muscle, every fiber, until I was boneless. Until finally it ebbed, leaving me with tears at the corners of my eyes while the aftershocks faded.

"Ransom," I panted, my legs wrapping around his hips, sending him deeper.

He groaned, thrusting faster, harder, chasing his own orgasm as my heart continued to thunder. He gritted his teeth, his body trembling, his jaw clenched as he fought to keep control.

I leaned up and took his bottom lip between my teeth.

Ransom's control snapped. He came on a roar, pouring inside me as the sound of his release filled my room. And when he was wrung out and spent, he collapsed on top of me.

His arms banded around me, hauling me close as he rolled to his back, propping me on his chest. "You've ruined me."

A smile toyed on my mouth as I shoved up on an elbow. "And here I was thinking you had stamina."

He flipped us so fast I gasped, my eyes wide as he stretched out beside me, his fingers trailing invisible patterns around my nipples. Then he bent, sucking one into his hot mouth.

"Gods." I clung to the silky strands of his hair as a coil of desire wound through my core.

When he leaned away, he wore that smirk.

That fucking sexy smirk. It stayed on his face when he rose to his knees, and before I knew what was happening, he flipped me onto my belly.

"Ransom," I gasped.

"Hands and knees, Cross." There was something dark, something dangerous, in the tone of his voice. A promise that if I obeyed, I'd get everything I wanted and more.

So I lifted to my hands, letting him haul me to my knees by my hips.

"I fucking love this hair." He collected the curls, wrapping them around his fist. Then he tugged, just enough that I arched for him, his hard cock fitting between the cheeks of my ass as he bent to kiss my bare spine. "We're just getting started. Wife."

Fifty-Three

"Hiding from me, Cross?"

I looked up from the book I'd been reading. Ransom stood in the balcony's open doorway, wearing only a pair of low-slung pants.

His hair was mussed thanks to my hands last night. His expression was softer, sleep lingering on his features. He was more stunning than any sunrise.

And he was mine.

"You were hogging the bed." I closed my book, setting it beside Faze on my lap. "Has anyone ever told you that you sleep like a starfish?"

He chuckled, walking to the back of my chair and taking my face in his hands as he brushed a kiss to my forehead. "Thought you might have had second thoughts."

"No." I reached for his cheek.

Relief washed over his expression as he kissed me again, then plopped into the chair beside mine. His abs bunched, his arms flexing as he moved.

Gods, he was perfect. Desire pooled between my thighs. Even after a night exploring that body, I only craved more. It might take me an entire lifetime to satiate my need for Ransom. It sounded like a good way to spend a life.

"At least I know where my shirt went." He arched his eyebrow at my tunic. His tunic. I'd dragged it on this morning, wearing nothing beneath when I'd slipped out of the bedroom to let him rest.

Faze lifted his head off my bare thigh, giving Ransom an appraising look. He didn't quite trust my husband. Or maybe he was just pissed that Ransom had commandeered his pillow.

"What are you reading?" He pointed to my book.

Cathlin must have brought it early this morning. There was a note under the door and a fresh stack of books waiting outside. They were a welcome sight, since I'd already read the others she'd given me—twice.

I flipped the cover closed for him to see. "It's a book about Calandran folklore. I was hoping to find something about the Chain of Sevens."

He smirked. "Searching for a loophole, wife?"

"Always," I teased. "I'm just curious. But there's nothing written about it. At least in what I've read. This book is about tales from migrations past."

Ransom hummed, sinking deeper into his chair. "Tell me one."

I opened the book, flipping to the story I'd found earlier to read aloud. "'There was once a man from Laine who wandered the desert for ninety days beneath a sky darkened with crux wings. Without shelter, without weapons or magic, he should have been easy prey for the monsters. But Mack, the God of War, took pity on the man. For he had once been a great champion and gladiator, winning every battle in the Laine arenas, pitted against man and beast alike. His name was Sonnet. And he survived by speaking to the crux. By whispering the words Mack planted in his mind. They flew over his head, leaving him untouched and unharmed, as he whispered stories graced by a god. A new tale for each day he wandered. Those stories have lived on for hundreds and hundreds of years, surviving long after Sonnet died an old man in his bed.'"

"Sonnets Ninety."

"You've heard this story before."

"I've read them. His stories. They were mostly of magic and monsters. Of battles fought and lost. They're bound in a book in the library at Allesaria." Ransom frowned. "At least, they were. I don't know if that book survived my father's fire."

"I hope it did. I'd like to read it." If he ever took me to Allesaria.

Would he someday? Or would he always have a reason to keep me away? Would he ever trust me enough to take me to the capital?

He rested his head against the back of the chair as he held my gaze. "Go ahead. Ask whatever questions you're thinking."

It was both endearing and perplexing that he seemed to know me so well already. Because I desperately wanted to know him, inside and out.

"You can't tell me about Allesaria, can you?"

He shook his head.

"Are you bound by a blood oath?"

He didn't answer. And like his other silent moments, it was answer enough.

"I think that's where it started. The source of Lyssa came from Allesaria. Someone there created it."

"I realize the mystery around Allesaria makes it suspicious. But if it had originated there, the Voster would have felt it."

"But what if they didn't?" What if the High Priest's magic hadn't *attuned* itself to Lyssa yet?

He sat up straight, leaning his elbows on his knees. "They are not the enemy."

His faith in them was as frustrating as his lack of trust in me. "Can you understand, after yesterday, why I don't feel the same?"

Ransom hung his head but nodded.

"Maybe Lyssa didn't start in Allesaria. But maybe that's where it can end. Maybe your healers and alchemists and even the Voster can find a cure."

He looked up, eyes sad. "There is no cure."

"Yet. There was no Lyssa until these recent years. Why can't there be a cure? Why are you giving up?"

"The priests have spent years trying to find the cure. If they tell me it cannot be cured, then it cannot be cured." He stood from his chair, dropping to a knee in front of me. "I don't want that hope, Odessa. I'd rather live expecting the end than wait for a cure that will never come."

I fitted my hand to the stubbled line of his jaw. "Then I'll keep that hope for myself."

"I don't want that for you, either." He leaned into my touch. "We'll keep hunting. Despite the attack, it's working."

Was it? He was so sure he'd be able to eradicate Lyssa from this realm. But what if the hunts weren't enough?

Maybe Ransom was only saying that to give me hope. Maybe it was him holding on to that hope himself. Today, I wasn't going to steal it from either of us.

"Come on." Ransom stood, holding out a hand.

I shifted Faze off my lap to the floor, then stood, letting him wrap me in his arms and breathe in my hair as I buried my nose in his bare chest. Holding his scent in my lungs until I'd never forget his smell.

"We have training to do," he said, voice low.

I groaned. "Fine. Let me get dressed. I doubt anyone in the training area will appreciate a princess not wearing pants."

"Who said anything about the training area?" He leaned away, hooking his finger beneath my chin. Then his lips were against mine, a deviant smile stretching across his mouth. "The training I have in mind does not require pants."

My breath hitched as he nipped at my lower lip. As he lifted the hem of his tunic, his fingers trailing along the curve of my ass, my nipples pebbled against the fabric.

Ransom swept me into his arms, cradling me against his chest as he stalked through the suite for my bedroom, but before we could lock ourselves inside, a knock came at the door.

"Don't answer it," I whispered.

He growled, and for a moment, I thought he'd ignore our visitor. But then the knock came again, more insistent than the last and loud enough I knew it wasn't Evie.

Ransom set me on my feet and walked to the door, opening it to Zavier. Ransom shifted aside, waving our guest in.

"I'm sorry to interrupt." Zavier gave Ransom a slight bow, then did the same to me. "Odessa."

"Good morning."

"A pony rider just arrived. He said he spotted a pack of bariwolves on the way here. He rode hard to avoid them, but it was less than an hour ago. I don't know if it's the same pack."

"Fuck." Ransom dragged a hand through his hair.

Were they on their way back here? Had I drawn the monsters closer? "Ransom, we could test—"

"Please do not ask that of me."

I sighed. "Fine."

This wasn't something I'd forget, but after last night, I wouldn't push for him to test it out.

"Give me a minute," Ransom told Zavier, then followed me into my room.

As the door clicked shut, I slipped off his tunic, laid it on the unmade bed, and picked up my own clothes from the floor, dressing quickly as he did the same.

"Be careful," I said.

"I will." He kissed my forehead before we returned to the sitting room.

"Wait here," he told Zavier. "I need my sword."

Zavier nodded, stepping out on the walkway as Ransom vaulted over the railing.

I went outside, my feet bare, and stood beside Zavier. "I hate when you all go on these hunts. Are they working?"

He scoffed. "No."

Not what I wanted to hear before they headed into the wilderness.

"No matter how many monsters with Lyssa we kill, there are always more. I want to believe it's working. But…" He was leaving again on another hunt, leaving his daughter behind. Zavier dipped his chin, moving away, but before he could reach the staircase, he paused. "He's a good man. It did not sit well with him to lie to you for so long. But you should know, it wasn't done to hurt you."

I gave him a sad smile. "I know."

He jogged down the stairs, joining Ransom as he came out of the house, fastening the clasps on his vest, his sword strapped across his back. He glanced up to find me, pressed a hand over his heart, and then they were gone.

Off on another hunt.

They had to be working. At least slowing the infection. I couldn't fathom the other option. That everything they'd done had been for nothing. That Lyssa would continue to spread, out of control, until it blanketed the continent. It would only make the migration worse. And if the crux got infected…

Gods. What horrors would we face?

No, the hunts had to be working. Ransom, for all his talk about not holding on to hope, wouldn't have exaggerated about that.

The Turan warriors would kill until the infection was gone. And we'd find the source, the person who was responsible for this blight on Calandra, and scorch their life from existence.

A restlessness crept into my limbs, and while I hadn't slept for long last night thanks to Ransom's delicious torments, I couldn't stay inside. So I hurried to pull on my boots and pack my satchel, adding my new dagger to the pouch.

Then I went outside in search of breakfast.

Brielle usually brought it upstairs before she tackled her duties around the house, but this morning, I needed to move.

"Good day," I greeted the baker and his wife as I went into their shop, the scents of flour and salt filling my nose. With a fresh scone, I set out for a walk, breathing in the clean air.

Despite everything happening, the worries and fears and uncertainty, there was a lightness in my steps. A shy smile on my lips. My muscles felt languid today, my movements flowing like I was floating underwater.

Ransom as a lover was a dream. Never in my life had I felt the way he'd made me feel last night. I hadn't known sex could be so centered around my pleasure instead of a man's. But gods, Ransom had been generous. Orgasm after orgasm, all night long, until finally I'd collapsed on his chest and slept like the dead.

I wanted a thousand nights to sleep with the beat of his heart in my ear.

He might not want me to hope, but I was going to do it anyway. If we could find a cure, then this charade would end. Ransom could assume his role as prince.

How was I supposed to pretend to be Zavier's wife? How was I supposed to look at Ransom in public but not touch?

Everything hinged on a cure. Then there'd be no more hiding. No more pretending. No more talk of his death.

I refused to lose him to Lyssa.

If the Voster couldn't find a cure, then we'd have to enlist others. Healers. Chemists. Scholars. He'd hate the idea of asking other kingdoms for help, but to save his life, I would do anything.

A door flung open at my side, bouncing off its hinges and startling me from my thoughts. I whirled at the noise.

A man dressed in an infirmary gown stumbled onto the street, his arm wrapped from wrist to shoulder in gauze. He looked moments from collapse, his steps swaying as he staggered my way.

He was one of the men who'd been unloaded from that wagon yesterday. One of the men Tillia had said they'd found outside Treow.

"Sir, are you all right?" I reached out to catch him before he could fall, gripping his good arm. The moment I touched his skin, I gasped, pulling away. It was so hot it nearly burned. "Shades. You need to get inside. You need a healer. Let me help—"

His hand flew to my throat, and before I could comprehend what was happening, he squeezed.

My eyes bulged, my breakfast dropping to the dirt. My mouth opened, gulping for air as I pulled and twisted and fought to get loose.

His choke hold only tightened.

"Stop," I wheezed, slamming my fists into his forearm, trying to break free from his grip.

"I'm burning." He stared at me, unblinking. The green starbursts in his eyes were dull and pale. "It's melting me inside. I swore to serve my king and burn burn burn."

Help, I mouthed, but gods, he was strong. More than was natural. Even with only one arm, I couldn't break free.

With every passing moment, my strength faded, my head dizzying.

The street was empty this early. People were still in their homes. There'd be others in the courtyard, but I had no way to scream. No way to call for help.

I struck at the man's forearm again, but the hit was too sluggish, too soft. The edges of my vision began to blacken, like smoke was creeping into my consciousness.

A shout rang out in the distance. "Stop!"

"Kill her. Kill her. Kill her." The man shook me with every word, like I was nothing more than a doll.

Ama, save me.

I wasn't ready to die. Not today. Not after last night with Ransom.

With fumbling fingers, I reached inside my satchel, feeling around the bottom. The dark spots in my vision were doubling, tripling. Tears streamed down my face.

"Make it stop. Make the burning stop." He lifted his injured arm, his hand joining the other in a death grip.

The pressure around my neck was excruciating, my lungs on fire as I fought to suck in a sliver of air.

"Hey!" Another shout.

Would they make it in time to save me? Or would they be the person to tell Ransom I was dead?

The strength flowed from my body like water spilling from a cup.

My knees buckled. As I sank toward the ground, the man's hold faltered, but it wasn't enough to draw an inhale.

My fist closed around the hilt of my dagger. I slid it out, using my last shard of strength to take it from the sheath and slice it across his throat.

Blood sprayed, coating my hand. My chest. My face.

And then I dropped, crashing to my knees as I gasped for breath. My throat was on fire, and the inhale only made me cough and hack as I fell forward to my hands.

"Princess!" A soldier skidded to my side while the man fell to the dirt.

Blood poured from his throat, forming a puddle on the street. He didn't press his hands to the wound. He didn't try to stanch the flow. He smiled, and a white foam formed at the corner of his mouth. The angle of his lips was the same as the slice I'd drawn with that dagger along his neck.

And as the life drained from his body, the color vanished from his eyes, leaving nothing but milky white. For a moment, it seemed as if his body was steaming.

I coughed, still gasping for air as I curled into a ball, fighting to breathe.

"Healer!" The soldier held my arm. "Oh, gods. Breathe. Try to breathe."

More people appeared at my side, but they all faded to nothing as I stared at the lifeless man on the ground.

I'd killed that man. I'd taken his life.

And his dark-green blood soaked the earth.

Fifty-Four

I pushed up from my bed, about to refill my cup of water. Except before I could swing my feet to the floor, Tillia shoved me back onto the pillows.

"Don't get up." She snatched the empty cup from my hand.

"I—"

"Don't talk." The glare she sent me was enough to have me lay back down and wait for her to return with my water.

"Tillia—"

"What did I say about talking?"

I scowled and took a drink, hoping it would sooth the ache in my throat and clear the rasp from my voice.

She sat beside me, frowning as she took in my face and neck. "You're already getting bruises."

Damn. Ransom was going to lose his mind.

"Ransom is not going to handle this well."

I wanted to joke that she was reading my thoughts, but she'd just bark at me again, so I stayed quiet.

"It's my fault." She took my hand, squeezing tight. "I'm so sorry."

I pinched the hell out of her index finger.

"Ouch." She snatched her hand free.

I cut a hand across my throat and mouthed, *Stop.*

She slumped. "It was my idea to bring those men here. They could have stayed in Treow."

"How could you have known?" I whispered. My voice wasn't as hoarse when I spoke quietly. "Not your fault."

"You shouldn't talk."

"I'm fine," I lied.

My neck was throbbing, and even after hours in the infirmary with the healers applying poultices, cold compresses, and herbs, it was going to ache for a while. But at least I was alive.

The man? He couldn't say the same.

I'd killed a person today. I'd taken a life.

All this time I'd spent training, I'd only ever envisioned fighting monsters. Sure, I'd had delusions in the beginning about strangling Ransom, but even without blood magic forbidding me from murdering my husband, I wouldn't have had it in me to kill.

A chill breeze wafted in through the open window, making me shudder. Or maybe the goose bumps on my arms weren't from the weather, but the image of that man's lifeless eyes, forever frozen in my mind.

A lump formed in my swollen throat. I swallowed it down, wincing at the burn.

I was cracking apart. Splintering into pieces. But it hurt too much to cry, so I drank another gulp of water and savored a deep inhale.

Faze was curled against my hip with a gaping space on his other side. Ransom's side.

Strange how Ransom had only spent a single night in this bed but that space was now his.

Where was he? After the attack, Tillia had sent a band of warriors to track him down, but I had no idea how long it would take for them to find him in the forest.

I knew he was busy, hunting that deadly pack. But I wanted him here. I wanted to curl into his arms and feel his warmth. I needed to tell someone about the man's ramblings, and I wanted that someone to be Ransom.

Make it stop. Make the burning stop.

I swore to serve my king and burn burn burn.

Kill her. Kill her. Kill her.

Me? Why would Ramsey want to kill me? Or had that man only been talking nonsense? Had Lyssa addled his brain to the point where nothing he said was believable?

The soreness in my throat expanded to a painful drumbeat behind my temples.

"Would you like the tea the healers sent?"

The tea was intended to ease the pain and put me to sleep. I'd hoped to avoid it, wanting to be awake when Ransom returned. Well, I guess if I was asleep, Tillia could explain everything.

Yes, I mouthed, rubbing at my skull. But before Tillia could leave for the kettle, I caught her wrist. "I need two teas."

Her eyebrows knitted together, but as my gaze dropped to her belly, she realized what other tea I'd need to take before the day was over. "Do you have any?"

I pointed to the vanity.

She went to the drawer, found the contraceptive tea Margot had sent with me from Quentis, and took it with her as she left the room.

I relaxed against the headboard, closing my eyes as a fresh wave of exhaustion crashed hard.

My healer—Geezala—had helped Tillia bring me to the suite so I could rest.

After another round of poultice and a compress, Geezala had returned to the infirmary, leaving me behind with the tea and Tillia's watchful gaze.

Gentle footsteps beyond my door made me open my eyes, expecting Tillia. Instead, Luella swept into the room, her skirts swishing as she came to my side.

"Oh, Odessa." She sank to the side of my bed, concern etched on her face as she pulled me into a firm hug. "You're all right."

Not a question. Reassurance.

I was all right. I would endure this. I would recover stronger than before.

I'd never hugged Luella before, but she had a warm embrace. A mother's embrace. Her shoulders were strong. The type of shoulders children cried upon.

I didn't miss Margot. But right now, I kind of missed Margot. She wasn't the warm, loving type, but she was the only mother I'd ever known. Today, I needed a mother's hug. So I stole one from Luella instead, clinging to her as that threat of tears came again, stronger than before.

The cracks kept expanding. Fracturing. It wouldn't be long now until they broke apart.

"Breathe," she murmured.

I sucked in a breath through my nose, the air burning as it filled my lungs. Then I exhaled as she ran a hand up and down my spine.

"Again. And again. Keep breathing to remember that you can."

It was exactly what I needed to be told. So I breathed, holding on to Luella as Tillia brought in two cups of tea, then closed the door behind her as she left us alone.

"Better?" Luella let me go, pushing the hair away from my face.

I nodded. "Thank you."

"Try not to speak unless necessary." Her eyes softened. Eyes a familiar, rich forest green.

She raised a hand to my neck, her touch soft as she ran her fingers over my throat. A frown pulled at her mouth. "You'll have bruises for a week or two. Your eyes will be black. But the blood in them will fade. And your body will heal. It only takes time. Unfortunately, there is no quick recovery from this."

As she prodded my neck, I let my gaze sweep over her face. The silky chocolate hair. Those familiar green eyes. When I first met Luella, her regal, poised composure had reminded me so much of Margot.

Of a queen.

Ransom might look like Ramsey.

But his mother had given him a few features of her own.

"You're his mother," I whispered.

Her eyes lifted to mine, her hands going still.

"You're Evie's mother."

Luella's fingers flew away, fear widening her gaze. "He told you."

The betrayal, the terrified tremble in her voice, made a shitty day worse.

"No. He didn't. I guessed—I'm sorry." Even though it hurt to speak, I wasn't going to stay quiet. "Please know I will keep your secret. And Evie's. I wouldn't want you to feel as if you had to take her away."

She swallowed hard, her gaze dropping to her lap. "Ellder is the farthest fortress from Allesaria."

I tucked that tidbit away for my map as she continued.

"The first time I came here, I was pregnant with Ransom. The second, he was only a baby. It was always such an ordeal to visit. The journey was miserable, so I told Ramsey never to bring me back. He assumed I thought it was too primitive for a queen. That I needed the finery of the city and hated it here. Mostly, it was easier to breathe when we weren't trapped in a carriage for days on end with nothing but his undying affection."

Luella turned to the open window, staring out to the soft evening light beyond. "I realize how that sounds. Most women would do anything for the undying love of a king. And I loved Ramsey, in my own way. He was my friend. My companion. The father of my children. But there are only so many pieces of a heart. And I gave mine away long before I met Ramsey. To…"

"Mikhail," I whispered as she trailed off.

"My father adored Mikhail. But given that Mikhail was from Ozarth, he considered our affection inappropriate. Not suitable for marriage. And for a long time, too long, my father's opinion was all that mattered."

So she'd let Mikhail go and married Ramsey.

"I am no longer the person I once was," Luella said. "All that matters now are my children. I will do whatever I can to protect them. Ramsey will find me eventually." Her tone was hollow. An empty resolution that she could not avoid him forever. Maybe she was right. "But until then, I want as many days with Evie as I can manage. She loves the forest. She loves the rugged, untamed land. She's like Ransom in that way. She is fearless. Maybe, if I'm lucky, I'll have the chance to take her sailing one day. To let her feel the salt breeze on her face as she sets off into the unknown. To give her the freedom I didn't fight for myself."

"Why not take her away?"

"She is not my only child."

Luella would not leave Ransom behind. I'd suspected as much, but it made me respect her more. That even though he was an adult, she was still his mother.

"Drink your tea." She handed me a cup, and with it, I knew our conversation was over.

The liquid had grown cool, but it was still a balm to my scratchy throat. I'd just finished both cups when a loud crash sounded from the sitting room.

"That would be my son." Luella stood, smoothing her skirts. Then she collected my empty cups, looking entirely unsurprised as he burst through my bedroom door.

His hair was windswept like he'd ridden hard for hours. His face was stone, his eyes liquid metal. The rage he kept so under control was unleashed, radiating off his frame.

"Calm down, Ransom," Luella said.

"She was almost killed today."

She was sitting right here, alive and not exactly well but…alive.

But before I could say as much, Luella's eyebrows arched. That expression was Ransom's through and through. "Zavier Ransom Wolfe. Calm down. Now. Or you will leave this suite."

Wow, I really had been oblivious. If I hadn't noticed their similarities before, that look and chiding tone would have done it.

His nostrils flared, but he heeded her warning—a queen's command, a mother's. He shook his fists loose. His chest rose and fell with a deep breath. And the silver bled from his eyes, making way for hazel.

"Better." Luella gave him a sidelong glance as she moved toward me, bending to drop a kiss to my forehead. "Rest. We will see you tomorrow."

"I don't want Evie to see me like this."

"You shouldn't be talking," Luella said at the same time Ransom barked, "Don't talk."

Despite the day, despite the horrors, I smiled.

And that smile made Ransom's eyes shift to green.

He moved to the bed as Luella slipped from the room. He smelled like horses and wind and sweat. Like a crazed, hard ride.

I curled into that scent, pressing my nose into his chest as he wrapped me in his arms.

One hand splayed over my lower back. The other dove into my hair as he breathed me in. "I should have been here."

"I'm okay," I murmured.

Now that he was here, I was okay.

His arms tightened, hauling me so close that Faze squirmed between us, letting out a grunt as we closed around him.

Ransom picked him up by the belly, lifting him over my hip. But rather than scoot him to the floor like I'd expected, he set my tiny monster on my pillow.

I wouldn't be needing it tonight. I'd sleep on Ransom's chest instead.

If I could manage sleep.

Every time I closed my eyes, I saw green blood and milky-white irises.

"I killed a man today."

He exhaled, pressing a kiss to my head. "I'm sorry."

Even with him here, the cracks kept growing and growing and growing. "Do you remember the first person you killed?"

"Yes. I was sixteen," Ransom said. "He was Zavier's stepfather."

I leaned away so I could see his face. "Really?"

He nodded.

"Will you tell me about it?"

"You should rest."

"Please?" I was desperate for a distraction. To know that I wasn't alone in this feeling.

Ransom frowned but relented. "Zavier's real father died when he was three. After my aunt's mourning period, my grandfather arranged a marriage to a nobleman's son. Horace. He was a beast of a man. Taught both Zavier and me how to fight. He was the one who advocated for Zavier to be my stand-in when we were just boys. Father agreed. And Horace loved that his stepson was paraded around as a prince. So much so that he wanted it to be real."

"He tried to kill you," I guessed.

"Shh," he murmured, pressing a finger to my lips. "I know you start to squirm if you go more than ten minutes without asking a question, but I promise to tell you the whole story."

I rolled my eyes but listened.

"The day I killed him, Horace had taken us to the woods to hunt deer. He sent Zavier one way, me another. Then he came after me and tried to push me off a cliff. He nearly succeeded. But he wasn't the only person who'd trained me to fight. I caught him with a dagger I kept in my boot. Drove it through his skull, from beneath his chin. There are still nights when I see his face. When I wonder if there had been another way. You'll never forget. All you can do is keep on living."

I wanted to forget. I wanted to push that man's face from my mind.

I wanted to know who he'd been before Lyssa.

Was he a husband? A father? Was there a family somewhere in Turah who would mourn his death? What was his name?

The lump in my throat returned, the sting of tears. And this time, there was no stopping the cracks from splitting.

The first cry escaped, so raw, so full of heartache, I almost screamed. Then the tears came as a flood, cascading down my face as sobs ripped through my chest.

"I've got you," Ransom murmured. "I won't let go."

He didn't.

Everything would be different now. I was forever changed. I had sliced away something from myself with that knife. I might have washed away the blood staining my hands, but I would feel it until the end of my days.

By choice or force, I was a killer.

Ransom held me as if he was absorbing the pain from my body into his. He held me as I mourned the life I'd ended. As I mourned the woman I'd been before today. He held me until the tears finally stopped, until the fire in my throat burned so hot it became numb.

He held me until I fell asleep.

Until we reached the dawn of a new day.

Until the cracks I feared would never join slowly began to fuse.

Fifty-Five

"Ransom," I whispered, tracing the strong line of his nose. There was a slight bump at the bridge that rippled beneath my fingertip.

It was one of many features I'd discovered about my husband's face over the past two weeks. His eyelashes were the purest of black and as soft as feathers. The apple of his throat fit perfectly beneath my lips. He liked to sleep with a window open, letting in the cool night air, and the only reason I didn't freeze was because he kept me tucked close, wrapped in his warmth from dusk to dawn.

"Ransom."

He hummed, eyes closed.

I kissed the underside of his jaw, his dark stubble rough against my mouth.

His hands skimmed up my naked back, finding the tendrils of my hair and twisting them between his fingers.

The dusting of hair across his chest tickled my nipples as he hauled me closer, pressing our bodies together, erasing any space.

Our legs were tangled beneath the sheets. I splayed one hand over his heart, and the other molded to the hard curve of his ass.

We'd spent countless hours entwined in my bed over the past two weeks. Most of those hours had been for me to rest. To heal. Ransom hadn't strayed far, hardly leaving my side as we'd hidden from the world in my suite.

It had taken nearly the entire two weeks to convince him I wasn't made of glass. That I needed to be kissed. Fucked. When I'd told him last night that I needed to be treated like I wasn't broken, he'd finally relented, worshiping my body with his fingers and tongue and cock.

It was the first night since the incident that I'd slept without a nightmare.

My body ached in all the right places, and I craved more.

Ransom groaned as I kissed the corded column of his neck. His arousal was hard between us, my core throbbing as he rocked it against my clit.

With a quick spin, I was on my back and pinned beneath him.

My legs wrapped around his hips as he fitted himself to my entrance and slid home. So deep I gasped.

"Gods." My body melted and shaped to his, stretching around his length.

We moved together without hurry or haste. He thrust in and out, his lips and tongue and hands leaving no inch of my body untouched.

"Odessa," he murmured in my ear, reaching between us to feel where we were connected.

I fluttered around him, my pulse quickening as he circled a finger around that bundle of nerves. My nails dug into his taut shoulders. "Ransom. More."

He grazed my earlobe with his teeth. "Mine."

"Yours," I breathed, my limbs beginning to tremble.

Last night, we'd fucked hard. He'd push my body to new heights, taking me to the edge only to haul me back, dragging it out for hours until I begged him to come. Last night was all about pleasure. About a release.

But this lazy morning felt different. Important. It was about the feel of us joined together. The words neither of us were ready to say.

He drove inside, hitting the spot that made me gasp. It was as if the power from his body swept into mine, the strength, the resilience. He rolled his hips, bringing us together in long, languid strokes until I shattered.

He muffled my moans with his hand covering my mouth, burying his own in the thickness of my hair.

Beyond these walls, beyond that open window, the Turans thought I was married to Zavier.

Within them, I was Ransom's.

We came together, clinging to each other until we were boneless, panting for breath.

He lifted to his elbows, taking most of his weight, and stared down at me with eyes that shone every shade of green.

Like every morning, the green didn't last. His gaze drifted to my throat, and his eyes seemed to take on the mottled yellow of my neck, transforming to hazel.

A frown tugged down the corners of his mouth.

Even after the bruises faded, I doubted he'd ever look at my neck without a ghost of a frown on his lips.

I ran my hand through his hair, pushing hard at the strands until he met my gaze. "Not your fault."

He gave me a sad smile before dipping to kiss my throat. "My fault."

His sigh tickled my neck, and then Ransom rolled out of bed and walked naked to the window to close it.

I propped up on an elbow, taking a moment to study the perfect silhouette of his body as he crossed to the washroom and closed its door. Then I hauled myself out of bed, wrapping myself in a robe from the armoire before I took a seat at the vanity, pulling at the collar to expose my skin.

The bruises were fading fast. Thanks to the herb poultices, teas, and compresses from Healer Geezala, the coloring of my neck had shifted from black to purple to green and now yellow. Some marks were gone entirely. My eyes were no longer bloodshot, and the dark circles were gone.

The horrors of that day were fading with the bruises, but the weight of it all would linger. For years and years.

Ransom emerged, fastening a pair of pants around his waist. He came to the vanity, hands settling on my shoulders. A faraway look settled over his expression, like he wasn't staring at me but into the past.

At his mother. At the bruises she'd worn after Ramsey's attack.

"Ransom." I put a hand over his. "Talk to me."

He blinked, then slipped his hand free. "Do you want me to fill the tub?"

"Later." I waited until he left the bedroom before I sighed and stood, going about my morning routine.

Once my hair was combed and braided, I dressed in a tunic and pants, then wrapped a scarf around my neck. When I walked out to the sitting room, Ransom was opening the front door to Zavier.

He came every morning to check on my recovery. To play the role of doting husband. To have hushed conversations with Ransom on the balcony while I attempted to eavesdrop.

Zavier strode inside, circlet shining across his brow. Only when the door was closed did he bow. "My prince. Princess."

He'd become more and more formal over the past two weeks. The bows. The titles. Something was shifting, but every time I brought it up to Ransom, he'd wave it off. He'd distract me with a kiss or carry me to bed.

Maybe I should have insisted we talk, but the truth was, I'd craved the distraction, too.

For two weeks, all I'd wanted was Ransom. Some time to stop pretending and be together. Even if it meant hiding in this suite.

Even if it meant that Zavier was trapped in Ellder, sending Halston to lead the warriors on hunts in his stead, so that when Brielle came each morning to tidy my suite, she'd think he was the man who'd slept in my bed.

This was the game. The show we were all a part of now. The characters we were playing.

Maybe someday, we'd all stop pretending.

"Where's Evie this morning?" I asked. She usually came with Zavier to play with Faze before her lessons.

"With Cathlin. They're practicing her letters, so, as you can imagine, she's grumpy. But Tillia promised to take her to the training area later today so she can practice with her bow."

Evie would likely be the best shot in Ellder by the time she was ten. The bow and quiver of arrows Zavier had given her were her prized possessions.

"And Luella?" I asked.

Zavier shook his head, sharing a look with Ransom.

The morning after my attack, Luella had left Ellder. Without a word to Ransom or Zavier. But she'd left a note for Evie, promising to return soon.

I had no idea where she'd gone, and if Ransom knew, he wasn't sharing. With me, at least. He seemed as interested in discussing his mother as he was in the man I'd killed or the fact that he'd had Lyssa.

Ransom jerked his chin for Zavier to follow him to the balcony, and before I could protest, they were gone.

"Damn." I plopped on a seat, picking up the book that Cathlin had brought over yesterday.

She'd taken up tutoring Evie, and she'd made sure that while I was healing, I had plenty to read.

I opened to the first page, but as I stared at the words, they blurred together. Concentration was futile with the questions beginning to stir, demanding attention. I'd spent two weeks ignoring the realm. Letting myself grieve. Postponing conversations overdue.

Two weeks was long enough.

Faze wandered over from the sitting room's window, where he'd been napping. He let out a tiny *rawr* as he rubbed against my calf, then leaped to the chair's arm, claws sinking into the already ruined fabric, before he settled onto my lap.

"Time to stop hiding, isn't it?"

He nudged my hand with his head.

I'd take that as a yes.

On the balcony, Ransom and Zavier's voices were low as they spoke, and whatever Zavier had come to report, it only made Ransom's jaw clench.

I focused on the book, waiting for them to finish. It would be easier to get answers from Ransom after Zavier left.

The book was an encyclopedia of sorts. Its pages were filled with summaries and drawings of different leaves and roots. But unlike most of the books Cathlin had brought me, this seemed more akin to a journal than a printed book. The pages were handwritten, the drawings sketched and hand colored.

I flipped to the front, finding no author or artist listed, and the last twenty or so pages were all blank. They hadn't been filled yet.

It was a record log. A diary, not unlike my own, but instead of drawings of monsters, this was about plants.

I skimmed through the pages, scanning drawings and notes. But I stopped in the center of the book.

Cave Ginger

I lifted it closer, eyes narrowed to read the inscription.

Native to Ozarth. Harvested in bogs. Outer skin gives off a rancid smell, but when peeled, pulp can be shaved and dried with sugar crystals (commonly sold as candy). Peel is typically discarded. When boiled and fermented, pulp can be used as pigment. When ingested, suggested good for healing. Alligasks shed their hides in bogs. Possibly absorbed into peel?

Testing: Limited Extensive

The drawing was of the outer shell, the plant more like a berry and a green so dark it was black.

My stomach knotted. I knew that color.

The drawing on the opposite page was of a bog. The snarky note below seemed like one I might have written.

Not a cave in sight. Who came up with this plant's name?

Who wrote this book? I closed it, inspecting the front and back again. There wasn't a name. Maybe I didn't need one.

Instead, I found myself back in the dungeon from weeks ago. Eavesdropping on a different conversation.

They're books, Lu. I'm giving that poor girl something to read. That's all.

Luella had warned Cathlin that day. And the next time I'd gone to the dungeon, it had been empty.

But Cathlin had continued bringing me books. She'd kept feeding me from wherever she hid her stash. If I had to guess, I'd say without Luella's knowledge.

Why?

Why? Why? Why?

I'd had a two-week break from asking why. The reprieve was over.

Closing the book, I set it aside and stroked Faze's spine. The largest scales were now bigger than my thumbnail. They were stronger, too, growing harder and thicker every day. His fur was changing slowly, faint stripes appearing along his ribs.

How was I going to let him go? What if he was killed by another predator after we set him free? What if he got bitten and infected with Lyssa?

We had to find a cure. There had to be a source. Someone had created this atrocity. Who?

There was a niggling in the back of my mind. The beginning of a hunch. But I couldn't make sense of it yet. It was a jumbled mess of pieces, and I wasn't sure how to shuffle them into the correct order.

Was it right in front of me? Was it staring me in the face, and I'd been too preoccupied with Ransom and Turah and Father's demands to find Allesaria to see what was obvious?

Every book I'd read, every story, every tale, seemed to wind together in my mind. I started pulling on strands, like errant curls, arranging them into rows. Weaving them into a braid.

Allesaria. Ozarth. Laine. Cave ginger. Alligasks. Korakin. Fenek. Magic.

Damn it, what was I missing? I squeezed my eyes shut, rubbing at my temples.

Ransom's hand on my shoulder jolted me out of my thoughts. "Hey. Are you all right?"

No. No, I wasn't all right. Not even a bit.

"Odessa." He knelt in front of my chair, worry lines marring his forehead. "What is it?"

"We have to talk about the man I killed," I said. I wasn't sure why it seemed important, but it was another piece. Another fragment that was connected, somehow.

"No. I don't want you reliving—"

"I'm not asking, Ransom."

He frowned, twin lines forming between his eyebrows.

I lifted my finger and rubbed them away. "His skin was so hot it hurt to touch. His body was *steaming*. His blood wasn't red, and there was foam on his lips. His eyes went white, and he looked relieved to finally die."

Was that what Ransom had in store? Was that the torment the Voster High Priest was keeping away with his visits to see Ransom and siphon out the infection?

"He had Lyssa. I killed that man, and I deserve to know why he tried to kill me."

Ransom's jaw worked as he stayed quiet.

He wasn't going to answer me, was he? He was going to keep me here, trapped away where he thought I'd be safe, and not tell me a fucking thing.

I opened my mouth, about to unleash a fury only known in Izzac's shade of hell, when Ransom looked to Zavier.

"Tell her," Ransom said.

Zavier frowned but did as commanded. "Yes, he had Lyssa. And no, we've never noticed an infected monster's body being hot like that before. We've seen the milky eyes and foam but not the heat. We think it affects humans differently than it does beasts. In the end."

In the end. Meaning before they die. "Why would he come after me?"

"I don't know." Zavier rubbed a hand over his jaw. "There's not much to learn. I'm sorry."

Right. I'd killed him, and there were only so many answers they could glean from his corpse.

"What kind of monster infected him? Could you tell from his bite scar?"

Zavier hesitated. "He had no bite scar."

"But he had Lyssa. How is that possible?" The answer was another piece, wasn't it? Another thread to untangle and pull and weave with the others. Another part of the big picture I was missing.

"There were fresh injection marks on his arm." Zavier extended his own, pointing to the soft skin on the inside of his elbow. "Here."

Healers used the hollow bones from small birds to create needles to inject their medicines.

Or poisons.

"So whoever created Lyssa isn't only infecting monsters." Not anymore.

Ransom could kill every monster in Turah. Every monster across the continent. But it would make no difference until the person responsible for this was gone.

"Why would—"

I couldn't finish my question. I didn't need to. The answer was kneeling before me.

Why would someone infect humans with Lyssa?

Because of the Guardian.

Because here was a person who was nearly impossible to kill, by man or monster. "Whoever gave that man Lyssa knows you have it. They're trying to give it to others. To recreate you."

Ransom nodded.

"When did you figure this out?"

"Not until after your attack," he said. He'd known and kept it from me for two weeks.

"You should have told me."

His eyes softened and dropped to my throat. "Can you understand why I didn't?"

"Yes." I exhaled. Because I'd needed two weeks to heal. "The man I killed. Where was he from?"

Ransom's nostrils flared. "Allesaria."

Damn. It all came back to that hidden city. To a city that held the wealth of Turan knowledge. To a city barred to outsiders. To a city bound by blood oaths and magic.

To the city of the Voster.

Allesaria. Ozarth. Laine. Cave ginger. Alligasks. Korakin. Fenek.

Magic.

The threads were untangling. The pieces were coming together, forming a fuzzy picture. An idea.

"I need…" More. I needed more pieces. So I shoved to my feet, Faze growling as he fell toward the floor, twisting to land on his paws.

"What?" Ransom stood at my side, his hand on my elbow.

I was already moving to the door, flinging it open.

Ransom and Zavier's boots pounded on the walkway and stairs behind me, both following me to the first floor. To the room where Evie had her daily lessons.

"Odessa?" Cathlin's eyes went wide when she saw me race inside.

"I need to talk to you."

Evie looked between all of us, sensing the tension and gripping the edge of the table. "Papa?"

Zavier walked past me, picking up his daughter. "Let's go for a walk."

She wrapped herself around him as he carried her away.

Ransom's hand came to the small of my back. "Odessa, what is going—"

"I have a hunch," I told Cathlin. "And I think you're the reason I have that hunch."

She gulped as she rose to her feet. "I don't know what you mean."

"Cathlin." My eyes were pleading. "How long have you known the king is giving his soldiers Lyssa?"

Ransom's entire body went rigid, his hand on my back fisting my tunic. But he stayed quiet, giving Cathlin a moment as she closed her eyes, her shoulders sagging.

Part of me knew he'd suspected this. But the other part knew he didn't want to believe that of his father. That he was so sure there was nothing to fear in Allesaria. That the High Priest wouldn't keep something like this from him.

But this suspicion, this hunch, meant giving up that last bit of faith he'd held in his father.

And the mountain of trust he'd given the Voster.

"This is his militia," I said. "The reason soldiers leave home and are never heard from again. He's trying to replicate the Guardian. To create men with powers that might stand a chance against the crux. But it's not working. Lyssa is killing them instead."

The silence that followed was so heavy it crushed the air from my lungs.

"Cathlin," Ransom growled. "Say something."

My heart raced. Why wasn't Cathlin agreeing with me or telling me I was dead wrong? Why point me in the right direction but not say anything—

My eyes widened, another piece of the puzzle falling into place.

"She can't. She took a blood oath." I reached for his hand, linking our fingers. "So she's been feeding me information instead. Books and journals. Ideas and tales. So that I might put it together and be the one to tell you the truth, since she's sworn to secrecy."

Cathlin looked to the floor as she nodded, her shoulders dropping so low that when she crossed her arms, it was like she had to rest them on her lap or they'd fall to the floor.

"Who?" Ransom demanded. "Who forced you to keep this secret?"

The heavy silence made my skin itch. Why wasn't Cathlin telling us? Who had made her take this oath of secrecy? It couldn't be King Ramsey. She wouldn't be working with him. Then who?

But before I could ask, there was a scratching at the door, and then the heavy wood swung open.

All eyes turned as one to stare as Luella walked inside.

She wore a scarf over her dark hair and around her neck. A coat, thick and lined with fur, covered her body. When she saw us, she froze, eyes blowing wide. Her cheeks were flushed, a sheen of sweat across her forehead, like she'd rushed here from wherever she'd been hiding.

And in her hand, a jar packed full of berries.

Berries with a shell of green. A green so dark it was black. The same color as Lyssa.

Cave ginger.

I had no proof it was an ingredient in this horrid infection. Nothing but the scent and color and a hunch. But at some point, a coincidence is not a coincidence. And a hunch might be the truth.

Why would Luella have a jar of cave ginger? Unless...

The clues weren't meant to lead me to Ramsey. He wasn't the person with the answers.

My gaze swung to Cathlin's, but she wasn't looking at me. She was staring at Luella, her cheeks flushed with guilt.

The pieces, the seeds Cathlin had planted, the threads she'd woven, pulled taut. The feminine handwriting in the book upstairs about extensive testing of cave ginger. The only lesson that Evie loved being science with Luella.

"It's you," I whispered, my stomach twisting as I turned to face Luella again.

She knew the "how" about Lyssa. How it had started.

I slid my hand into Ransom's, holding fast as those twin lines knitted between his eyebrows again.

"What do you mean?" he asked, looking to me, then Luella. "You're working with Father?"

No, she wouldn't partner with Ramsey. Not after everything he'd done. But she was a part of this, somehow. I felt it in my bones.

Luella was a mother, first and foremost. She could be living on the other side of the continent, apart with Evie. But she hadn't wanted to leave Ransom. She'd do anything for him, to keep him safe.

Gods. My head was spinning. I reached out to hold on to Ransom with both hands. "I think the person with a story to tell is your mother."

Fifty-Six

Luella whirled for the door, but before she could flee, Ransom stopped her with a single word.

"Mother."

She turned slowly, hands clutching the jar of cave ginger. It took her a moment to meet his stare. When she did, the tears were already flowing. "It was never meant to go this far."

"What have you done?" he asked, hand tightening over mine.

I needed her answer more than my next breath.

And it was the last thing in the realm I wanted to hear.

"Lu," Cathlin whispered. "It's over."

Luella shook her head, dark hair swishing over her shoulders. "I need more time. I will find a way to undo this."

Cathlin sank into her chair like she'd heard that a hundred times before. Argued the opposite a thousand times before. "Come inside. Tell them the truth."

The color leached from Luella's face, but she closed the door and crossed the room, taking the seat beside Cathlin.

Ransom stood rigid, unmoving, until I pulled on his hand, urging him to the table.

The scrape of chairs on the floor was booming in the silence. The wood creaked beneath our weight.

Luella had a satchel strapped across her body. She set the cave ginger on the table and hauled the pouch into her lap, hugging it close. "We stand no chance against the crux. We will die trying to fight them. And I will not lose my children to the shades in some underground shelter where they're left to rot for weeks and weeks."

The way her family had died. This had all started from a good place, hadn't it? From a mother's love.

Luella dabbed the corners of her eyes, clearing her throat as she sat straighter. "We must be stronger to survive a migration."

"Mother." Ransom's fists landed on the table, slamming so hard the jar of cave ginger nearly toppled over. "What have you done?"

She met his eyes, defiant and bold. "I can't lose you. I can't lose Evie. I won't. I did what I thought was best to keep you safe and alive."

"Alive? You created Lyssa. And now it's killing me." Ransom shot out of his chair, the backs of his knees sending it skidding across the floor. His arms opened wide before he pounded a hand over his heart. Over the place where dark veins snaked across his chest.

The veins I slept on each night. The veins I prayed would disappear each morning. He planted both hands on the table, leaning forward until he was inches from her face. "I can feel it sucking the life from this body with every swing of my sword, every beat of my heart."

"I'm sorry. I didn't mean for this to happen. If I'd known…" Her chin quivered. "I can undo this. I'll find a cure."

Ransom sneered. "There is no cure."

"But what if there was?" I put my hand on his arm. "Please. Sit down. Let's hear her out."

There was more to this story. Maybe if Luella filled in some of the gaps, the missing pieces, we'd see a path to the cure. I wasn't giving up hope we could stop Lyssa from killing Ransom. I refused to lose him to this infection.

Ransom's body vibrated with rage, with hurt, his eyes silver. The monster was trying to break free from its leash.

"Please," I pleaded, my heart in my throat.

He gritted his teeth but backed away. Not for his chair, but to stand on the other side of the room against a wall, arms crossed as he listened.

"Did you create Lyssa?" I asked Luella.

She swallowed hard. "Lyssa is magical. And I am not. But Calandra has magic. Just look at the different eyes in this room."

What if magic went beyond the soil? Beyond eye color and Voster magic?

"I believe that the monsters of Calandra are a part of that magic," Luella said. "And I've spent years learning how to extract it from them."

Extracting a monster's power? "How?"

Luella reached for the jar, tracing the rim with a finger. "Science is a magic of its own."

"Speak plainly," Ransom demanded.

She drew in a deep breath. "A monster's very *being* has magic. They are extraordinary. Stronger. Faster. Better in all ways. I think they leave traces of that magic in this realm." Her voice was a whisper, as if she was afraid to even speak it aloud. "So we strove to harness those traces to make everyone's bodies less susceptible to illness. To give us all strength to heal."

"'We'? You mean you worked with the Voster." I knew it. I fucking knew it. They were behind this from the beginning.

"No." She shook her head. "My alchemists."

"Oh." Well, damn. "But the Voster are the only creatures who have magic."

"Are they?" she mused. "What are the Voster but other beings? Some might look at them as monsters in their own right."

Me. I'd considered them monstrous myself.

"The Voster simply know how to use their powers. Monsters do not. But that doesn't mean it doesn't flow through their veins. Through their skin and bone and blood and saliva."

"Mother," Ransom barked, his patience hanging on by a thread. "I want to hear how you created Lyssa. Why do this?"

"Lu." Cathlin stretched an arm across the table, close but not quite touching her beloved. "Start at the beginning."

Luella nodded, straightening, hands flat on the table. "I spent my youth traveling Calandra. One of my favorite places to visit was Laine. I got ill on a trip and was taken to their healers. My father had business matters to attend to in Genesis, so he left me behind to heal for a month. My time spent there sparked a curiosity about alchemy. It became a hobby."

And likely the start of a journal cataloging various plants.

"I tinkered for years," she said. "I built a small workshop where I could make teas from different herbs and spices to see how they made me feel. Then I met your father, and my hobby was put on hold for a time."

When she moved to Allesaria. When she took on the role of queen. When the crux flew and her family died what must have been agonizing deaths.

"I started getting to know the healers in Allesaria while I was pregnant," she said. "After you were born, after you were no longer a baby, I had more time on my hands. The healers introduced me to the city's best alchemist. He owned a small apothecary and invited me to visit whenever I wanted."

"So you rekindled your hobby," I said.

"Yes." Luella's fingers resumed their ministrations on the jar. "In those days, I spent most of my time in the library. Collecting books. Reading stories and myths about monsters. I started that library as a way to escape. Alchemy was another escape."

"From Father?" Ransom asked.

"From my life," she corrected. "In those books, I found the adventures I'd been denied. And then I stumbled upon one book that changed everything. It was full of stories that sparked an idea. I don't know where the book came from, but I found it hidden away at the apothecary's shop and took it for my own."

Luella opened the flap of her satchel and took out a book. It was bound in black leather with a clasp keeping it shut.

"It's written in the old language," Cathlin said. "They're stories, almost like a person's dreams. Like Sonnets Ninety."

Luella stroked the book's spine. "There is one story that tells the tale of a monster's claw given to a man as a gift for saving the beast's life. When the claw was worn around his neck, the man never again felt pain or sickness. The day he took it off and gave it to his son was the day he died."

That did sound like a dream. Like a child's bedtime tale.

"It made me start to wonder," she said. "What if we could be stronger? What if we could fight infections? What if we could hide away for months at a time and emerge no different than the day we went underground?"

"So, you were looking for a way to stop an infection but created one instead." Ransom sneered. "Brilliant."

"No." She shook her head. "We did not create Lyssa. Not how you think. We made an elixir that would enhance a human's natural abilities. We created potions and tonics from ingredients linked to monsters."

"Like korakin?" A kaverine's dung.

"The kaverine can see almost perfectly at night," Luella said.

Like Ransom.

"And the cave ginger?" I pointed to the jar.

"The bogs where it's grown are home to the alligasks. When they shed their skin, the particles are absorbed by the ginger peels. An alligask has incredible healing abilities. They're almost impossible to mortally wound. To kill them, you must cut off their heads."

"So you used pieces of different monsters for this elixir. But the elixir isn't Lyssa?" My head was beginning to spin. What was I missing?

"Correct." Luella nodded. "We created potions and tonics, testing them on ourselves. Most made us sick. Some did nothing. And others seemed to make us less prone to illness. It took years to formulate something we were confident in using outside of the small team I had amassed. When we got to that point, we asked a healer to try it on a dying patient. It was a man who'd had his leg taken by a grizzur, and the flesh around the wound had begun to rot. He shouldn't have survived with the advanced state of the wound. But he lives to this day."

So Luella and her alchemists created a concoction of the ordinary. Biproducts of monsters to strengthen normal bodies, to help fight infections and sickness. The reason the Voster had never felt Lyssa's magical signature in Allesaria was because the magical signature didn't exist. At least not yet. All she'd done was create a medicine.

"So how the hell does this elixir tie into Lyssa?" There had to be some connection, right?

Luella's gaze shifted to Ransom. "Your father knew I was spending time with the alchemists, but it was not a hobby he particularly cared for. He never denied me my interests, but he didn't fully support them, either. I knew if I asked to give you the elixir, he'd tell me no. And I needed you stronger before the migration."

"So, you did it anyway." Ransom's voice sent a chill down my spine. "When?"

Luella had the sense to look ashamed. "Not long before your father found me with Mikhail. It was that day you were training and got sliced along the leg. It was a terrible gash. I was worried you'd lost too much blood. You were unconscious, so when my healers sewed the gash…"

"You had them give me the elixir, this nightmare that you created, without my knowledge." Ransom's body vibrated, his eyes a brighter silver than I'd ever seen before. "Why did it work on me and no one else?"

"It didn't work on you."

He tugged down the collar of his tunic, revealing those dark veins. "I beg to differ. You did this. And instead of telling me the truth, you let me believe for four years that I got Lyssa from that bariwolf bite."

"You did." Luella rose from her chair. "I think."

"You think?" His voice bounced off the walls.

"I'm still trying to figure it out. I can't explain it. Yet. But that bite transformed you. There are ten of us who took the elixir, and not a single one has gotten Lyssa. I think the elixir we gave you was the fundamental magic for Lyssa and the bariwolf's saliva was the missing piece. When it bit you, a bond formed. A bond between man and monster and magic. That day, you both created Lyssa, and it has since morphed in your bodies. The bariwolf continued to spread it as it bit other monsters. Then as they bit others, and so on and so on. In you, it has given you powers beyond that of a normal man."

"Gods." I stood, unable to stay seated. Then I slapped a hand over my mouth as the realization hit so hard I nearly got sick.

Even from across the room, I felt Ransom's heart break.

Lyssa was born from two beings.

A bariwolf. A one-eyed monster.

And Ransom.

"That bariwolf was never the beginning." His voice cracked. "It was me. I started Lyssa."

Fifty-Seven

"What have you done?" Ransom's throat bobbed.

It was the third time he'd asked her that question.

It was the only time it sounded like an accusation.

"I will find a way to cure it." Her chin quivered. "I swear to you. I will undo this magic."

He shook his head, eyes dazed. "All the people who have died. The lives we could not save."

Sariah. Witt.

Ransom kept a list of his own, didn't he? And now he would bear the weight of every soul lost because of this infection. He would carry this blame.

I'd seen so many versions of Ransom since we met. The warrior. The prince. The lover.

But this version? He was lost. Unrecognizable. I hated the ruin on his face. The pain he couldn't hide.

"It's not your fault." Tears spilled down Luella's cheeks. "I'm sorry, Ransom. I'm so sorry. I didn't know."

He dropped to a crouch, hands diving into his hair as our world seemed to tip on its axis, up swapping with down.

"What is Father's involvement?" he asked.

Luella closed her eyes, but not before guilt flitted across her features. Another secret.

Was this woman's body fueled by lies?

"One of my alchemists betrayed my trust. He went to your father."

Ransom's eyes lifted. Narrowed. He stood. "When?"

Luella's hand drifted to her throat. "The day he tried to kill me."

Ransom went so still that even the dust motes stopped floating, afraid of what was coming next. "Did he try to kill you because of your affair? Or because he found out you gave me this elixir?"

"I don't know," she whispered. "He came to my bedroom in a rage. It escalated when he saw Mikhail."

My hands came to my face, pressing against my cheeks to keep my jaw from dropping. Again.

Had Ramsey found out that Luella had injected her creation into Ransom? Was that why he'd been furious? Because she could have killed his son?

Well, something must have changed. Because now he was trying to replicate it with his militia.

"He can't reproduce it," I said. "Can he? The Lyssa or elixir, whatever you want to call it?"

"No," Luella said. "But he's trying. And in the process, killing them."

Those soldiers were burning alive from whatever he was putting in their veins.

"They don't have the missing piece." Luella sank into her chair. "Ramsey hasn't made the connection that Ransom was given the elixir and then bitten. That the combination is what I believe created the infection. But Ramsey's team has been experimenting. If I had to wager a guess, they're taking blood from an infected monster and injecting it into his men."

"Except it doesn't work that way, does it?" I guessed. "The bite was the missing piece. The magic."

"Yes," Luella whispered.

The irony was stifling.

Ramsey had set out to create an army strong enough to fight the crux. Instead, he'd stolen able-bodied men from their villages and towns. Men who could have fought the monsters already in Calandra. And by the time the migration came, they'd likely all be dead.

"There must be something to undo the magic. I just need time." Luella's eyes were pleading. "I can fix this."

Ransom scoffed. "Let's pretend for a moment you manage that feat. What if Father isn't interested in a cure? What if he realizes that all he needs to do is inject your elixir in his men and have them bitten? Then what? He won't care that those men will die, not if it saves the kingdom from the crux."

Ramsey would be unstoppable with an army of men who could move and fight and heal like Ransom.

Maybe he did want to defend against the crux.

Or maybe, like my father, he was tired of the ancient treaties. The borders. The kingdoms.

Maybe he wanted to take Calandra for his own.

Well, he'd have to stop his soldiers from dying first.

"He must not find out. No one can know," Luella said. "We cannot sacrifice our sons."

The pain etched in that last statement, the way Luella's eyes pleaded with Ransom for forgiveness, made my chest squeeze tight. And I still had more questions. "Why is he burning books?"

Cathlin's lip curled. "Because he's a menace."

Luella pulled her books closer. "When we were formulating the elixir, we spent a lot of time in the library. Some chose to leave their notes in books and journals there. It's where I kept mine."

Notes and knowledge that other kings might want for their own. To give to their own alchemists and healers in an attempt to create their own versions of a Guardian.

Was that what my father wanted in Allesaria? Was that how he thought he'd stop the crux? By creating Lyssa for himself and making an army of Guardians?

Father could have just gone after the other alchemists rather than send me to find the city. Though if the alchemists feared Ramsey might consign them into his service—injecting healthy men with a potion of death—those people would likely be in hiding, like Luella.

No, Father was running short on time before the next migration. His most viable option was to pluck Ramsey's secret from the capital. To steal Lyssa for himself.

All he needed was a key to unlock the Turans' castle door.

Mae. She'd been trained to be that key.

And now it was me.

Ransom thought the other kingdoms didn't realize he had the infection, but my father must have suspected as much. The Guardian and Lyssa. It was all connected.

Father's desire to get into Allesaria had to be tied to his need to understand the Guardian's powers.

Before I could voice my suspicions, Ransom strode to the table and ripped the book away from his mother. "Maybe we should burn this."

Luella shot to her feet, trying to snatch it back, but he kept it out of her reach. "Don't. That book, like all the others I've collected, is part of my research to find a cure."

"There is no cure," he seethed. "You've had years. It's too late. If the Voster cannot stop it, no one can."

"Ransom—"

"Damn you, Mother." He threw the book on the table, sending it sliding across the surface. "Damn you."

Without another word, he marched from the house. The door flung open too hard and slammed shut with enough force to rattle the walls.

Luella slumped in her seat, burying her face in her hands as she cried. Cathlin put an arm around her shoulders, murmuring reassurances in her ear.

I needed to go after Ransom. To chase him down and make sure he was all right.

Except I was frozen in place, eyes glued to that book on the table.

It had flipped over when Ransom had tossed it, showing the other side.

There was an intricate etching on the cover. A winged emblem.

The same emblem on the pendant I wore around my neck.

Fifty-Eight

"**H**ave you seen Ran—the Guardian?" I asked a soldier stationed at the front gates.

He bowed as he spoke, bending at the waist. "No, Princess Odessa Wolfe."

I pushed the curls out of my face, turning to scan the courtyard. *Shit.* "Did he leave?"

"Not through these gates, Highness."

I kicked a rock with my boot. "Then where the hell did he go?"

"I'm sorry. I don't know. I can help you find him if you'd like."

"No. Thank you." I walked away, following the wall along the outer edge of the fortress.

This was my third lap around Ellder.

In the hours since I left Luella and Cathlin, I'd gone up and down every street. I'd peered through windows and stopped in shops. I'd gone to the dungeon twice, venturing to the false wall that opened to the migration tunnel—when I'd called for him, only my echo had answered. I'd even searched the barracks, startling more than one soldier as I'd peeked through open doorways.

Wherever Ransom was hiding, he didn't want anyone to know.

I didn't want to give up my search. I didn't want to quit. But it was pointless if my husband did not want to be found, so I retreated to my suite, my footsteps heavy and slow.

If not for that godsdamn emblem on Luella's book, I would have followed him from the house when he stormed out. I wouldn't have lost him in the first place.

What did all of this mean? What was that winged symbol? Was my necklace just a trinket? Or something more?

I couldn't worry about it right now. Maybe, after we sorted out Lyssa and Ramsey and monsters and a migration, I'd pull Cathlin aside and ask if she'd ever seen the emblem before. Until then, I needed to find Ransom.

Gods, I was livid with Luella. How could she do this? What was she thinking? What she'd done to Ransom was beyond comprehension.

Ransom blamed himself for the deaths caused by the infection.

Well, I blamed her.

And damn it, she had better find a cure. If she'd created this mess, then she could fucking unwind it.

I wandered to the house, fists clenching and unclenching at my sides, my eyes downcast as I walked, only looking up when I reached the base of the staircase. And there he was, sitting on the top step, elbows to knees, hands clasped. "Hi."

Ransom stared down at me with enough heartache that it felt like a war hammer had slammed into my chest. "Hi."

"I've been looking for you."

"I know."

"Have you been here the whole time?"

He twisted, reaching behind him for something. When he faced forward, he had Faze draped over his forearm. "He's a demon. I went inside the suite and found him sharpening his claws on the sitting room chair."

"Sounds about right."

"He darted outside before I could shut the door. I guess he didn't want to get left behind, so he's been keeping me company out here."

It should have been me keeping him company, but in my absence, I was glad that he'd had my tiny monster.

"I'm sorry, Ransom."

"So am I." He scratched behind Faze's ear, then stood, carrying the tarkin to the suite's door and leaving him inside. Then he descended the stairs, meeting me at the bottom. "Take a walk with me."

We fell into step beside each other, weaving through Ellder to the side gate.

It was located toward the back of the fortress, close to the barracks and stables, where the horses were kept in a paddock large enough for them to roam. I searched for Freya, finding her against a fence, nibbling a tuft of tall grass. Aurinda wasn't far from her side, standing taller than any other horse.

A stable boy walked through the animals, a halter rope in his hand. When he spotted Ransom, his eyes blew wide and his feet stopped.

Sheer awe. That's how people looked when they saw the Guardian. No matter how many days he spent in Ellder, he would always be a legend. A savior. A hero.

But he would have been a hero with or without his powers. The greatness didn't come from Lyssa. It was simply Ransom.

He approached the six armed guards stationed at the gate. They parted, expressions neutral, as one man turned the lock.

The gate was only tall enough for a horse without a rider, but even then, I suspected a stallion like Aurinda would have to duck. The iron hinges groaned as the door swung open wide enough for Ransom and me to step beyond the fortress and into the forest.

We walked for what felt like an age, weaving past trees and thickets of underbrush. When we passed a bush with bright-orange leaves, Ransom plucked one from a branch, twirling it by the stem between his fingers.

When he let it go to flutter to the ground, he reached for my hand, lacing our fingers together. We were well beyond the walls now. Beyond the sight of any soldiers on the ramparts who might see.

"I wish…" He trailed off, shaking his head.

"What?"

He lifted my hand to kiss my knuckles. "I wish we didn't have to pretend."

"Me too."

But it was just a wish. He wouldn't drop this facade with Zavier while Lyssa coursed through his veins. Better his cousin take the throne than risk his sister's life. Better the Guardian die than a crown prince.

Neither had to happen if Luella found a way to untangle this disaster.

I was no alchemist or healer or scholar, but if I had to steal those books, if I had to take them to the best alchemists in Quentis or Laine, I would find a way to break this magic.

"I'm a fool," he murmured. "I should have figured this out on my own."

"There's no way you could have known."

Beyond that, his faith in those he loved was part of what made him so special. He believed in his mother. He even believed in his father. To think them both capable of such horrors would have crushed his spirit.

"It's too late to stop what my mother has done," he said. "But I must stop my father."

"How?"

He slowed, his broad shoulders curling as he hung his head. "I have to leave you, Odessa."

"What? No."

He turned to me, taking my face in his hands. "I will not take you to Allesaria."

Will not. He didn't say cannot. Will not.

"You still don't trust me." It made sense. In his position, I'd probably do the same. But that didn't mean it hurt less.

The worst of it was, I didn't blame him. People he had known his entire life, his own mother, had betrayed him. I wouldn't trust anyone, either.

Certainly not his wife.

"If the men in my father's army are like the man who tried to kill you here, Allesaria is the last place in Calandra you should go." He dropped his forehead to mine. "And there's only one way to stop this."

"Kill the monsters," I whispered.

"Kill them all."

Except *monster* had taken on new meaning. He wasn't talking about four-legged beasts with claws and fangs. Unless his father stopped this madness, stopped killing men in some impossible quest to replicate Ransom's gifts, then the monster the Guardian would slay next was his king.

He would end this forever.

"Okay." I burrowed into his chest, breathing him in. Wind and earth. Leather and spice.

Maybe a better princess would insist there was another option. Maybe a better princess would find a way to stay at her prince's side.

But I'd never been a good princess.

So I unwound my arms from his waist and stepped away.

Maybe the only way I could truly help was by giving him my truths.

"My father sent me here to find the passage into Allesaria. I was to spy and send word back to Quentis with Brielle or Jocelyn as soon as possible. He didn't tell me what he was looking for, but he said it could save us from the crux. Given your father's penchant for book burning, it must be Lyssa. If Father doesn't know you have the infection, I think he might suspect. Because he also told me to find out about your powers and, if I had the chance, to kill you."

The confession came out in a flood, and as it settled between us, a weight I'd been carrying for months eased.

Ransom scowled. "Cross."

"Sorry?" I gave him an exaggerated frown. "I'm guessing you already knew all of that, but I wanted to say it out loud anyway."

He sighed, shaking his head before he let out a laugh. "You are a horrible spy."

"True."

He tipped his face to the sky. "Fuck, we're in a mess."

Pretty much. "Now what?"

"This is bigger than Turah. Lyssa, in man or monster, is nothing but death. It must be stopped. If the crux get the infection…" He sighed. "We'll never survive. We should be using the king's army to hunt down every infected monster before the migration."

"What if it's too late? What if it's already gone too far?"

"It started with me. And I will end it, too, even with my last breath. I have to try."

Of course he did. Ransom wouldn't be Ransom if he gave any other answer. "How?"

"I don't know. Somehow convince my father he's wrong. Ask him for soldiers. At the very least, stop him from killing innocent men by giving them whatever version of Lyssa he's concocted." He raked a hand through his hair. "But Allesaria is…changed."

He winced, his hand pressing against his heart, like even saying that much about the capital caused him pain.

"What can you tell me?"

"Very little."

"Fucking blood oaths." If he couldn't answer, then I'd do what I did best. Ask questions.

"Can you go to Allesaria?"

He nodded. "Yes, I can go."

"What about Zavier? The rangers?"

"They need to remain in the wilds, making sure the infection doesn't continue to spread."

"What about the soldiers in Ellder?"

"The soldiers loyal to the crown?" He tapped his brow. "I don't wear a crown."

"You know what I mean." I tossed up my hands. "Would they fight your father and his army if necessary?"

He exhaled. "I cannot ask that of them."

"Why not?" If it meant saving other people from a horrible, burning death, I had to think there were men here who would gladly volunteer.

"I *cannot*," he said with another flinch.

It took a moment, but then I understood what he couldn't tell me. He could not order anyone against his king. A precaution taken by a ruler paranoid that his heir would try to assassinate him for the crown.

Maybe it was a Turan tradition. Or maybe Ramsey was a real jackass.

"It's a shock you even have blood in your veins for all the godsdamn blood oaths you've sworn. Let me guess. You can't share the details?"

He shook his head.

"So you'll go to Allesaria to convince your father to stop his foolishness. And if he doesn't listen, then what? You'll kill all the infected men in your father's army yourself? A thousand men against one? You are the Guardian, but there are limits, Ransom."

"What difference does it make if I die because of the infection in my veins or at my father's sword?"

I flinched, then scowled. "Don't say that."

He shifted closer, brushing the curls away from my temple. "It was always going to end with my death."

No. "Stop it." I refused to think his life was ending.

How could he just accept this fate? Why was he so set on climbing into his fucking grave? I wanted to scream. I wanted to wrap my hands around his throat and strangle some sense into him. But the burn in my throat was choking. The tears in my eyes made him a blurry mess.

"You are not fucking dying, Ransom Wolfe."

"Hey." He hauled me into his arms, holding me close as I fisted the back of his shirt.

"Please don't leave me," I whispered.

He kissed my hair, arms banding tight.

"There has to be another way."

"I don't have an army for this fight, Odessa."

No, he didn't.

But *my* father did.

Fifty-Nine

Ransom gave me three days.

Three blissful days in which we didn't leave my suite. Three days to pretend like the horrors beyond the walls were only a dream. Three days to spend endless hours woven together.

And though we hadn't spoken the words, three days to say our goodbyes. Then it was over.

I'd woken up alone this morning. Ransom hadn't left Ellder yet, but today he was making preparations. And tomorrow, at dawn, he'd ride for Allesaria.

Alone.

He'd warned me last night that he was meeting Zavier in the training area early—I hadn't been invited. Probably because their conversation would only make me cry or scream or both.

Ransom hadn't told me specifics, but if I had to guess, they were strategizing. About the monsters. About Ramsey's army. About what to do if—when—this all turned to shit and Ransom died.

Gods, my heart hurt. So much that it was hard to breathe.

How did I watch him go?

Sunshine streamed through the open window in my bedroom. Part of me wanted to curl up with a pillow and cry for a month. The other part knew no good would come from my tears, so I got dressed for…something.

It was time to do something, even if it was drastic. Like travel across the continent and bargain with my father.

Ramsey wasn't going to give up on Lyssa. I knew it in my bones. He was intent on weaponizing the infection. And I suspected my father wanted to do the same.

But if I told Father that Lyssa was killing innocent men, that the bigger threat was a crux carrying the infection, maybe he'd change his mind. Maybe he'd see the reason that Ramsey would not.

Father had lived through a migration. He'd kept those paintings and murals in the crux art gallery for a reason. A reminder.

The crux were nothing but death and destruction. We had to stop Lyssa before it turned the horrors of a migration into the end of Calandra.

Whether Ransom wanted to admit it or not, he needed help. He needed an army. If Ramsey wouldn't give him one, then maybe my father would.

But before I gave Father the location of the capital, he was going to give me open access to his vaults. I'd use every gold coin in his coffers. I'd hire every healer across the realm.

To make a cure to save Ransom's life.

Luella had her chance. Now it was mine.

While I was making demands of my father, I also wanted information about my mother. Why the Voster had asked about my heritage.

I'd never demanded anything of my father before.

But I was not the same daughter he'd sent away on the *Cutter*.

It was time to leave Turah, to find my way back to Quentis. Soon. Once Ransom was gone.

I opened the door to leave the suite, to get some fresh air and walk off my nerves, and found a visitor on the walkway.

Evie stood outside, hand poised to knock. The tunic she wore was yellow, embroidered with red and pink flowers at the collar. It was getting too small, and she'd ripped a hole in the elbow. It was time for a new shirt, but this was her favorite, one I saw more than any other. And based on her pout, she'd worn it today to feel a little less sad.

Zavier must have told her he was leaving tomorrow.

While Ransom was going to deal with Ramsey in Allesaria, Zavier, Halston, and their rangers would continue their hunts. There was a pack of bariwolves that needed slaying. A one-eyed beast that had to die.

My exit planning could wait. If everyone, including me, was leaving her behind, another day together first wouldn't hurt.

"Good morning, little star." I crouched down, tucking a lock of silky brown hair behind her ear. "How are you today?"

She shrugged.

"I'm kind of sad."

"Because Papa is leaving?"

"Yeah."

Evie, like nearly every other person in Calandra, believed I was married to Zavier. I hoped that someday I could tell her the truth. That Ransom and I could be free to be ourselves with his sister. But not yet.

"Want to play with Faze?" I asked her.

She shrugged again. "Or we could play a game. Luella is still gone, and Cathlin said I don't have to do my lessons today."

"Lucky girl."

After Luella's confession to Ransom, she'd left Ellder again, leaving Evie under Zavier's, Cathlin's, and the nanny's care.

Faze wandered over, nudging his nose against Evie's hand for a pet.

I swept him into my arms and put a palm over my eyes. "Hide-and-seek? *Readysetgo.*"

Evie's giggle was enough to chase away a few of the storm clouds over my heart. Her boots thudded on the walkway, growing distant as she raced down the stairs.

I cracked my fingers, stealing a peek, then kissed Faze's brow. "Go find her for me."

He took off with a pounce, tail swishing as he ran for the stairs.

These monsters…

We didn't understand them, did we? They were more than animals. More than beasts. They truly had magic. Faze was only a baby, but I was constantly surprised by how much he understood. Not just commands but moods. There were times he'd look at me and it was like he knew exactly what I was feeling.

Joy. Anger. Heartache.

Like he wanted to say something, but whatever it was, we didn't speak the same language.

I took off after him, finding him waiting at the door that Evie must have gone through on the main floor.

When I bumped into Evie's nanny during my search, I promised to take over for the day, and she was more than happy to be excused. As she left for her own quarters, I followed Faze as he weaved through the house, snaking through empty rooms, sniffing and lingering in a few places Evie must have deemed unworthy of a hiding spot.

He nudged open a half-closed door, walking into a room I hadn't seen before. It was a suite, similar to mine upstairs, with a sitting room and dining table. Through another door was the washroom and bedroom, decorated like the rest of this house. Planked wooden floors. Thick woven rugs in rich hues of maroon, olive, and chocolate. Quilts and blankets in the same shades.

My rooms in Quentis were white and cream and beige and gray. Clean and crisp. But I much preferred this life in bold color.

Faze scampered beneath the bed, and when he found her, she let out another musical peal of laughter.

I dropped to my hands and knees. "Gotcha."

"You cheated!" She wiggled out from beneath the bed's frame, popping up to fist her hands on her hips. "This time, Faze comes with me."

"Deal." I put a hand on her shoulder before she could run off. "Hold on. Whose room is this?"

"Luella's."

"Ah. And are you supposed to be in here?"

"No." She smiled, crooking her finger so I'd give her my ear. "Wanna see something?"

"Always."

She snatched my hand, pulling until I was off my feet and following her toward the wall behind the bed. She let me go to push and pull a bedside table, inching it out of our way. Then she splayed her hands on the wall and used all her might to push, grunting as she dug in her heels.

"Evie, what are you—"

The wall cracked.

"Whoa."

Evie smirked, something she'd clearly learned from Ransom, and shoved the door open wider. She put a finger to her lips and stepped through the doorway. "This is a secret place."

"Is it?" I picked up the lantern on the bedside table and ignited the flame. Then, with it held against the dark, I followed Evie down a staircase.

The air was dry, the temperature dropping with every step. After ten, I began to count. Fifteen. Twenty. We went farther and farther, the scents of earth and dust tickling my nose, until we reached the bottom. My light flickered over the room's wooden walls.

The space was a large rectangle with four cots along one wall and shelves along the other. Shelves for supplies. Shelves for food.

A migration cellar.

There were rooms like this in Quentis, too. Rooms where people would shelter for as long as possible. And like in Quentis, oftentimes, the entrances were hidden.

In cellars like this, stockpiled supplies would be rationed. Allocated for exactly the number of people intended to use this room. But the migration didn't just bring death from the crux.

People would kill for these rooms. For the food and safety they afforded.

I hadn't checked when we started down the stairs, but there was likely a lock on that secret door. Not to keep people in. To keep people out.

Evie went to the shelves, dragging her fingers across the spines of the books arranged in careless rows and stacks. On the bottom row, below the books, were trinkets and scrolls piled in disarray.

"These are from the dungeon," I said.

Luella had cleared out the dungeon and brought everything here instead.

"Yep." Evie's gaze tracked over my shoulder, like she was checking to make sure no one was listening. "She doesn't know I saw her bring them down here, but one night when I was supposed to be asleep, I heard some noises so I came to see what she was doing."

I shook my head, fighting a laugh. "You shouldn't be spying on people."

"Why not?"

"It's rude."

She cocked her head to the side. "But isn't it rude to keep secrets?"

"It's rude to— You know what? Never mind."

Luella was her mother. She could address the spying at some point.

I walked to the shelves, bending to take in the book's spines. A few familiar titles jumped out at me but nothing I cared to read.

"Want to see something else?" Evie asked.

At this point, why not? "Sure."

She skipped past me for the stairs, bending to the lowest step. Her fingers felt along the side, pulling and tugging until the front of the step folded open, revealing a hidden compartment.

"How did you find that?" I went to her side, bending low and setting the lantern on the cold stone floor.

"I came down here yesterday when Cathlin thought I was upstairs playing with Faze."

"Evangeline," I scolded, but there wasn't much heat behind it.

Because inside that compartment were three books. One of which was black leather with the emblem of my necklace.

Luella must have been planning to come back. Otherwise, she would have taken these with her wherever she'd gone. That, or where she'd gone wasn't safe. I wasn't sure what the other two books contained, but her tucking them under the stair meant they had to be important.

"We should go." I urged Evie's hands aside so I could refit the compartment and close it shut. Then I grabbed the lantern, standing and holding out a hand to lead her up the stairs. "No more sneaking down here, all right? I don't want something to happen with the door and you be stuck."

"Fine," she grumbled as we reached the bedroom.

I closed the door, making sure the compartment was hidden again, that the seams in the wood paneling blended together. Then, as Evie hoisted Faze into her arms for another round of hide-and-seek, I began to count.

"One. Two. Three." They were gone by the time I made it to five. And by twenty, I forced myself out of Luella's rooms before I could give in to temptation and steal those books.

Later. Now that I knew where they were hidden, I'd get them later. They were certainly coming with me to Quentis.

Without Faze's help, it took me a while to find Evie—tucked inside a kitchen cupboard with a stack of wooden bowls. We played a few more rounds before we ventured outside to wander Ellder's streets. We went to the small toy shop, buying her a fuzzy rabbit with floppy ears to cuddle when she was lonely—she named it Merry.

We ate sweets from the bakery for lunch. We took carrots and apples to the horse paddock, spoiling Freya, Aurinda, and their friends. And when it was time for dinner, we ate together in my suite as Faze, worn out from all the activity, slept on my lap.

Evie was a balm to my heart, as I hoped I was for her. But as nightfall settled over the fortress, Zavier came to collect his daughter, carrying her off to bed.

The suite was too quiet alone, and I was too restless to stay still, so I went outside, hoping that if I killed another hour, when I returned, Ransom would be waiting.

The courtyard was alight with the fires they burned in barrels each night. Windows glowed gold from the lights within. Laughter and music drifted from the tavern three streets from the house. It was all too cheery, too warm. So I made my way toward the gates and a staircase that led to the wall's ramparts.

The guards stationed at the wall did a double take as I approached, but neither stopped me as I started up the stairs. When I reached the top, a soldier with a broadsword across his shoulders met me with a scowl.

"You can't be up— Princess Odessa Wolfe." He bowed. "Apologies, Highness."

"I was hoping for a few quiet moments alone. If you don't mind."

He bowed deeper, backing away as I settled against the wall, my elbows resting on the rough surface of a log as wide as my shoulders.

Torches lit the ramparts, but they were only enough to chase away the shadows. Most of the light came from the twin moons.

These walls stood taller than any treehouse in Treow, giving me a different glimpse of the forest and silhouette of the trees. The sky was a beautiful swirl of gray and blue and twinkling white. It was different than my cliffside in Quentis, but it was a sanctuary of its own.

A breeze blew against my face as I drew the cold night into my lungs, holding the breath until it burned. On my exhale, I felt him. As I felt the wind. As I felt my own heartbeat.

Ransom's arms wrapped around me, pulling me against his chest.

The only person who might see us together was that soldier, and even if he noticed in the dark, I didn't care. Not tonight.

I rested my head against Ransom's shoulder, holding to his arms with my hands. "All ready to go?"

"More or less."

I swallowed the lump in my throat. "Say you'll find me again."

He rested his chin on my head but didn't speak a word.

"Say it."

"You deserve your freedom, Odessa. I won't make you fight for it."

"Freedom?" I whirled, breaking out of his arms to poke a finger into his chest. "You're an idiot."

He chuckled. "Tell me how you really feel."

"I'm serious, Ransom. You keep talking about my freedom. There is no freedom. I'm not talking about an ancient treaty or blood oath. I'm talking about you and me. I'm talking about this." I pressed my hand over his heart. "If I died, would you be free?"

Ransom's hand fitted over mine, holding my palm to his chest. "No."

"Then you have to come back to me. Or I'll hate you forever."

"You already hate me."

"Yes, I do." I'd never hated him. Not even in the beginning. Not really. But hate was the safer word to use. Even if we both knew it meant something else.

He leaned in close, his mouth brushing across my forehead. "Don't forget."

"Never." My chin wobbled, tears filling my eyes.

Ransom caught them with his thumbs. "I don't regret it. Not a moment."

"Neither do I."

"I have no right to ask, but I must. I need you to watch over Evie. I'm taking my mother to Allesaria."

"Wh-what?" Was he really so furious that he'd take her to Ramsey?

"It was her idea," he said. "She wants to undo what she's done. And she might be the only person who can convince him that all he's doing is dooming Turah to death."

My insides knotted. "But what if your father tries to kill her again?"

"I'll do what I can to protect her. She knows it's dangerous, but it's her choice. She's had enough stripped from her. I won't deny her the chance to atone. She just left Cathlin's place after saying her goodbyes. She went to sleep beside Evie."

"She can't leave her behind." That little girl might lose a mother and a brother before she had the chance to know they were hers.

Ransom took my hands in his, looking down. "Will you take care—"

"Yes." He didn't need to finish his question. It would change my plan to leave Ellder, but that was tomorrow's problem. Tonight, my husband was asking me to watch over someone he loved.

I wasn't going to say no.

"I'll look after her," I promised.

"If something happens to us, to Zavier, get her out of Turah. Take her to Quentis."

I nodded, heart climbing into my throat. That was not an outcome I wanted to consider. Not a situation I could even fathom at the moment. "I will."

"Thank you." He tucked a lock of hair behind my ear. "Tillia will be here for anything you need. Zavier and Halston will return as soon as they can. Just…be careful. Promise me you won't do anything reckless."

"Promise," I lied.

His eyes changed to a color I hadn't seen before. They swirled orange and red and yellow. They were both bright and dark at the same time. A color for sadness. A color for goodbye.

If my eyes could change, they'd be the same.

They kept changing, the colors flashing like flames.

Ransom looked over my head, the softness in his expression fading. Those twin lines formed between his eyebrows as he shifted me out of the way so he could stand against the wall.

"What is it?"

He narrowed his gaze, and as I stared at his profile, his eyes were green, shifting slowly to hazel.

It wasn't a new color I'd seen. It was a reflection.

The sound of hooves echoed through the trees. Then came the clink of metal as the fiery glow of torches gleamed off breastplates and helms. It took a moment to comprehend what I was seeing. When I did, the night swallowed my gasp.

An army marched through the forest, descending upon Ellder.

"Oh, gods," I whispered at the same time Ransom turned and roared, "Do not open the gates!"

Sixty

The soldiers manning the gates obeyed Ransom's command, but not a single one didn't stare up at the ramparts with bewilderment. Their confused expressions matched those of the soldiers stationed on the ramparts.

They stared at the army beyond the walls, probably wondering why we'd bar entrance to soldiers wearing the Turan crest and the king—their king.

I stared into the trees, watching as the torchlights doubled, then doubled again. The army approaching stretched along the length of the wall, stacked rows and rows deep.

"Mack, be with us," I whispered, signing the Eight. If this came to a fight, the God of War would stand with a side tonight. I prayed it was ours.

Ramsey hadn't just brought the band of soldiers he'd traveled with in Ravalli or Treow. He'd brought an entire legion. Was this his militia? How many of those men had Lyssa coursing in their veins?

Shouting rang out below as other soldiers came into the courtyard from the barracks.

"Open those gates," a man yelled, pointing to the heavy wooden plank that barred the gates.

"Do. Not." Ransom's order boomed through the courtyard, and the man who'd said otherwise quickly dropped his attention to his boots. "Find Zavier. Now."

"What's going on, Guardian?" A soldier came to stand at his side. "That's the king."

Another night, I might have rolled my eyes at the obvious statement. Tonight? I wanted to know what the hell was going on, too.

"I'm not sure," Ransom said. "Until Zavier or I give the order, that gate stays closed. Understood?"

"Yes, sir." The man nodded.

"Come with me." Ransom took my arm, pulling me away from the wall and down the stairs. When we reached the bottom step, he leveled the gate guards with a glare so sharp it could cut through bone. "Barred. Until I say otherwise."

"Yes, sir."

They might not understand, but they trusted their Guardian enough not to question the order, even if it was Ramsey waiting outside.

"What's going on?" I asked, voice low.

"He warned me." Ransom's nostrils flared. "In Ravalli. He warned me I had a month. I should have left for Allesaria sooner. My father does not make idle threats."

"All this to collect you?" I flung an arm toward the wall. "That's extreme. You are the Guardian, but there's no need for that army."

His jaw clenched. "Something is wrong. I don't want him inside Ellder, but I don't know if I have any other choice. We can't fight. And I cannot order these men against their king."

"Your oath."

He nodded, dragging a hand over his face. "Fuck."

Zavier's footsteps pounded on the ground as he jogged toward us. His tunic was open at the throat, and one leg of his pants was lifted, stuck in the shaft of his boot. He righted the circlet that was crooked on his head. "What's happening?"

"My father. He's brought a legion."

Even in the dark, I saw the color drain from Zavier's face as his gaze flew to the gate. "Your mother?"

"It's possible," Ransom said. "Where is she?"

"With Evie." Zavier inched closer. "We cannot fight them."

"No, we can't." Ransom sighed. "I won't ask that of the soldiers in Ellder. And the longer he waits beyond the gate, the longer he will wonder what we're hiding."

Likely the reason for this surprise visit anyway. Ramsey had forced Ransom's hand. If he was here for Luella, there'd be no time to get her out of the fortress.

Ransom and Zavier shared a look, a silent conversation like so many I'd seen before. Then Zavier raised an arm, giving a signal to the soldiers at the gate to bring in their king.

"Stay behind me," Ransom said.

"What about Evie?"

"Mother will hide her," he murmured. "With Daria's luck, he'll order me to accompany them to Allesaria immediately."

Where he'd been planning to go at dawn regardless.

But what if Ramsey wanted to camp here tonight? What if he wanted to stay in Ransom's house?

My entire body began to tremble as I clutched his arm, holding tight as the gates creaked open.

The thunder of hooves was instant as the lead riders barreled through the opening, single file at first until the gates spread wider, allowing for two, then three, then four to ride in, side by side.

They parted when they reached the courtyard, just as they had in Ravalli, forming an aisle for their king.

Ramsey entered in no hurry, his horse's stride haughty and deliberate, like he'd been taught to saunter.

The prickle of my skin was instant as Brother Dime came through the gates.

Why was he with King Ramsey? Wasn't he Father's emissary?

Maybe now that he was back, he'd stick around long enough for me to ask. Maybe he'd explain how it was that I could feel his magic. Find out why the High Priest had asked about my mother. But if those answers had to wait simply so that Ramsey and this traveling army would leave sooner than later, so be it.

The Voster was enough of a distraction that it took me a moment to notice the man riding in behind him.

A man I'd mostly forgotten. A man wearing not the emblem of the Turan wolf but instead a symbol I'd seen my entire life.

A crossbow woven with leaves and stalks of wheat.

The symbol on every flag in Quentis.

Banner.

My gasp was only loud enough for Ransom to hear. *What the hell?*

"What. The. Fuck," Ransom said through clenched teeth.

Why was Banner here? Were there more men from Quentis?

When we were up on the walls, I hadn't really given the legion a thorough inspection. Were they all Ramsey's soldiers? Or had my father sent his troops to Turah?

It wouldn't be considered an invasion—not if he'd been invited.

Gods, what was happening?

More and more soldiers filtered through the gates, both men and women, each in Turan uniform. Had Banner come alone, then?

Every soldier was armed, their swords and knives and shields catching the firelight from burning barrels and torches. As the legion filled the courtyard, the people of Ellder began to flow out of their homes and buildings behind us, curious about why their king would visit. Most wore sleep clothes beneath cardigans and coats, the soft textures a sharp contrast to the metal decorating Ramsey's legion.

Tillia and Halston pushed through the crowd, coming to stand behind Zavier. Vander and Zavier's other warriors were not far behind.

When Ramsey stopped his procession, I expected him to stay in his saddle, to stare down at us with that circlet resting boldly above his brow. But he swung out of his seat and came to stand before us.

Every person around me dropped to a bow. Everyone.

Except Ransom.

And me.

Ransom stared at his father with utter hatred and contempt. His eyes swirled silver. In the commotion, I hadn't noticed that he'd drawn his sword. His knuckles were white as he gripped the hilt, the blade at his side.

"Majesty," Zavier said, rising to address the king. "Welcome to Ellder."

Ramsey scoffed, speaking to Zavier but keeping his gaze on Ransom. "Let's not pretend I'm welcome here."

The sounds of metal clanging, boots stomping, echoed behind us, and the only reason I could see Ramsey's soldiers coming up the streets was because everyone was still bent in a bow. But as they realized we'd just been surrounded, blocked in at all sides, most stood tall, fear rising and cloaking the air like smoke.

Those soldiers must have come through the side gate. The guards stationed there wouldn't have heard Ransom's command and known to keep them out. There was no reason to bar entrance to those in the same uniform.

Other soldiers dismounted their horses, including Banner, who came to stand beside Brother Dime.

He looked the same as the day he watched me sail away on the *Cutter*. He wore his teal coat, gold buttons shining in the courtyard's light. And there was rage in his eyes, those amber starbursts flaring bright, as he glared at Ransom.

Was he here on Father's command? Was he here to take me home? Or was he here for another reason entirely?

I'd always praised Banner for his loyalty to my father, but maybe that loyalty had been tested while I'd been in Turah. Maybe Banner was here for what my father had not given him.

Revenge against the Guardian.

Ramsey wouldn't let Banner kill his own son, would he? Not that Banner stood a chance against Ransom. My head was starting to hurt with all of the questions, and the Voster's magic was setting me on edge.

Zavier and Ransom stood shoulder to shoulder, both waiting for Ramsey to speak.

Ramsey didn't make them wait long. "A crux scout was spotted along the western front two days ago."

"No." I rocked on my heels, my heart dropping as a tidal wave of terror washed over the crowd.

A woman cried out. People began to whisper, to pass the news backward to those who hadn't been able to hear. A man nearby clutched the arm of the boy at his side, turning and pulling him past bodies, retreating home.

It was too soon for the crux. The migration wasn't supposed to happen until next year at the earliest. It always came in the spring. Always. We still had winter to prepare.

It was too soon. We weren't ready.

"Any troops not necessary to run this fortress are needed in Allesaria," Ramsey said. "Those people not wanting to stay in Ellder are welcome in the city. We leave tonight."

So that was why there were so many. He'd been collecting soldiers to take to the capital.

"You will ride with us," Ramsey told Ransom. "That is an order."

Ransom ignored it, lifting his sword to point the tip at Banner. "What is he doing here?"

"I've made a bargain with the Gold King and General Banner." Ramsey crossed his arms over his chest. "He'll be taking his fiancée back to Quentis."

"No." Ransom's fingers opened and closed on his sword as he adjusted his grip. He wouldn't be able to use it against Ramsey, but the warning was clear. Blood oath or not, he'd sure as hell try. "She stays."

"I'm not leaving." I spoke in unison with Ransom.

Part of me was overjoyed that Father had kept his promise to bring me home. But he was too late.

I was home.

Banner gave a choked laugh. "I am not here for you."

Wait. "What?"

Then who? I was his fiancée. Or I had been once. If he wasn't here for me…

Banner's focus shifted over my head.

Enough people had slipped out of the courtyard, retreating home to spread word of the crux scout sighting, that no one blocked my view as a group of soldiers stalked our way.

A group that had come through the side gate led by a woman who'd lived here not that long ago. A woman with a pretty face and large brown eyes. Her blond hair was braided away from her face in warrior braids.

"Jocelyn?"

For a heartbeat, I was relieved to see her again. To know that she'd made it home to hug her mother. Had she and Banner gotten engaged since I sent her back to Roslo?

She was carrying a sword. It was smaller than any belonging to a man, but she seemed comfortable with it in her grip. Practiced and sure, the way Tillia carried her sword. Too practiced for a lady's maid.

The joy of seeing her faded fast as dread pooled in my gut.

Jocelyn wasn't simply a maid, was she? Was she a spy of Banner's?

Or Father's?

There was a reason she'd come on this journey, and it had never been to draw my baths.

All this time, as I'd built confidence in myself, I'd forgotten just how little faith Father had in me. Seeing Jocelyn was a brutal reminder, like being dragged backward in time. It was old wounds being reopened.

I was not the same princess who left Roslo. Had she told them how much I'd changed? Had they even asked about me? Or had it always been for Allesaria? For his plans?

She'd played me for a fool, hadn't she? Jocelyn had gathered whatever information she'd been ordered to glean, then given me the perfect excuse to send her home. She'd even conjured tears.

Jocelyn twisted, waving someone forward.

Brielle appeared at her side, and when she spotted us all, a strangled cry came from her throat. "Banner?"

Relief washed over his face as he opened his arms. "Brielle."

She blew past the soldiers and Jocelyn, running for him, hair streaming at her back, legs and arms pumping until she crashed into his chest. "You came for me."

"I promised I'd find a way." He leaned back, taking her face in his hands as tears streamed down her cheeks. Then he kissed her like they were alone in a dark bedroom, not standing amidst a crowd of people.

That kiss knocked the wind from my lungs.

Banner and Brielle.

She was his fiancée? And this was the bargain Banner had made? Jocelyn's information for Brielle.

Shades. I wasn't sure I could take any more surprises tonight. But as the shock wore off, the truth made sense. I could see it now.

Banner had stayed on that cliffside the day we sailed away, not to watch me leave, but for her. The woman he'd had in the city, the lover I'd heard about in castle rumors. It was Brielle.

When I'd asked her if she'd ever been in love, she'd said yes but that he'd broken her heart.

Banner had broken her heart when he'd agreed to marry me.

And she'd loved him anyway, despite the pain.

They broke apart, foreheads resting together, like all was right in the realm.

Brielle wasn't the only person Jocelyn had taken from the house.

The soldiers behind Jocelyn dragged Luella into the fray, her arms clasped in their unrelenting grips.

Ransom turned and lifted his sword as he stepped away from my side. "Let her go."

Luella's dark hair was loose, her robe open to reveal the sleeping-gown beneath. They hadn't let her put on slippers, so her feet were bare on the dirt.

Ramsey wasn't only here to claim his son. He'd come for his wife.

I wasn't sure how he'd found her, but I had a hunch it was also because of Jocelyn. Maybe my former lady's maid had been able to match the queen's description to the woman who was often seen at the Guardian's side.

If my hunch was right, then Jocelyn had betrayed us all.

Bitch.

Zavier shifted, peering past the soldiers, searching.

For Evie. Oh, gods, where was Evie? Please let her be safe.

Given Zavier's audible exhale, she was likely hidden away.

My exhale was loud, too.

"Stop!" A streak of white flashed through the crowd as Cathlin pushed her way to the front, trying to get to the guards. When she spotted Ransom already blocking their path, she slowed, breathing heavily as she changed course, coming to stand behind Zavier.

Fury rolled off Ransom's frame as he blocked the guards' path, standing before his mother. "Release her."

They had sense enough to listen.

He might not be able to strike down the king, but a guard? Their heads would roll before they could blink.

"Turn around," he told Luella. "Walk away."

She gave him a sad smile, lifting her hand to his cheek. "Whether this happened in Allesaria or Ellder, it was always going to happen. It's time for me to face him again. To end this."

No. Ramsey was going to kill her. She wouldn't be speaking that way if she thought they could work this out. Would he do it right here in front of everyone? Would Ramsey kill her in front of Ransom?

There was a menacing, victorious smile on the king's face when I turned to take him in. After over four years of searching for Luella, he'd found her. Whatever information Jocelyn had given him had led him to this fortress.

She should have left.

We all should have left.

Luella stepped around Ransom, walking with her chin held high to stand in front of her husband. "Ramsey."

"Lu." His voice was cold. "I was certain, after all this time, I'd have to travel to the opposite end of the realm to find you. Imagine my surprise when I learned from a Quentin spy about a woman who was never far from the Guardian's side. A woman who bears a remarkable resemblance to descriptions of the queen. A tutor for a four-year-old girl."

My hunch. It was correct.

My jaw clenched, anger coursing hot through my veins. I was going to kill Jocelyn if Ramsey found Evie.

"Who is this girl?" Ramsey asked. "Or should I kill you first, then find out?"

"You've lost your mind, Ramsey," Cathlin spat. "You've become a fool, blinded by jealousy and vengeance."

He ignored her, steely eyes locked on his wife. His queen.

"Ramsey." Luella's voice was gentle. "This has gone too far."

"Not far enough." He lifted a hand to her face, fingertips caressing her cheek.

She flinched, and it turned his arrogant smile into a sneer.

He fisted a handful of her hair, pulling hard enough that she yelped.

We all surged forward, unsure of what to do other than move closer.

The soldiers around us closed in, too, all reaching for their weapons. This would turn into a bloodbath if we weren't careful. Every person was waiting for a command. To flee. Or to fight.

"Enough." Ransom's sword was shaking but stayed at his side. *He* was shaking, like he was fighting his own blood trying to raise that weapon.

Except he wouldn't be able to stop this.

I moved without thinking, stealing the sword from his grip. Its weight settled into my hands like a brick of iron. I'd forgotten just how heavy it was. But I was stronger than I'd been on the *Cutter*. When I raised the blade into the air, I knew I wouldn't be able to hold it for long, even with both hands.

I only needed to hold it long enough. "Let her go."

Ramsey did a double take, like he couldn't believe there was a blade at his throat.

The soldiers stepped forward again, but Zavier and Tillia and Halston, Ransom's warriors, even Cathlin, formed a blockade, keeping them out. For now. More weapons were drawn, and the tension was so thick it was becoming difficult to breathe.

My heart hammered, and I willed my hands to remain steady. I'd never be able to truly wield this weapon, but Ramsey didn't need to know that. "I have sworn no oath to you, but I swear this now, I will not let you kill her."

Ramsey's eyes blazed, his expression turning to stone. He was a king who was not used to being challenged.

If he expected me to cower, he'd be disappointed.

"Your wife is a nuisance," he spat, pushing Luella aside so hard she tripped. She would have fallen if not for Halston reaching out to catch her.

Ramsey moved faster than any man I'd seen, save Ransom. He yanked my arm, sending me off-balance, the sword clanging on the ground as it fell from my hands.

"No." Ransom leaped forward, but the soldiers behind him managed to seize him by the arms, four men holding him back while another four came to stand in front.

Eight men wasn't enough. He should shake loose. But then what? That godsforsaken blood oath to his king meant there was only so much he could do.

Tillia and Halston, Zavier and his rangers, were all still bracing against the hundreds of soldiers around us, warriors ready to strike us dead if given the order.

There was no one to stop Ramsey as he gripped me by the arms, holding tight as he shook my entire body so hard my teeth rattled. "Who do you think you are, Sparrow?"

"The future queen of Turah," I hissed through gritted teeth. "Let. Me. Go. Now."

He didn't listen.

So I used a move Tillia had taught me in one of our many training sessions.

I drove my knee into the king's groin, hard enough that his hands dropped and he bent forward with an *oof*.

Jackass. My elation was instant. And short-lived. Like he'd done with Luella, he fisted my hair, twisting tight as pain exploded from my scalp. I cried out, unable to keep it inside.

A growl came from Ransom's throat before he was free, casting those soldiers aside like they were nothing. Then his heat was at my back, a snarl in his voice as his father's grip only tightened. "I will kill you. I swear it."

Ramsey's nostrils flared. "I see the way you look at her."

"She is my life," Ransom said.

"She will be your death. As your mother will be mine."

"Father. Please." Ransom put a hand on Ramsey's arm. "Let her go."

"Father?" Banner asked. "The Guardian… He is your son?"

Ramsey didn't answer. He looked to his son again, eyes still blazing, and when he finally let me go, it was with a shove to Brother Dime. "You wanted her. You deal with her."

I flailed, falling forward into the priest's burgundy robes.

The moment his hand touched mine, fire exploded through my skin, agony ripping through my bones. A scream tore from my throat, and my knees cracked as I dropped to the dirt. Even after the priest took his hand away, the screaming continued.

The pain wouldn't stop, and that shrill sound split the air, getting louder and louder.

Except I wasn't screaming, not anymore.

Brother Dime backed away, endless eyes turning to the night sky.

Ransom hauled me to my feet, holding me tight as he shuffled me backward, out of reach from both the priest and his father.

Someone was still screaming. I pressed my hands to my ears.

"What is…" I trailed off as the entire courtyard stilled, everyone going quiet.

What came next wasn't another scream.

It was the unmistakable beating of wings.

Crux.

Sixty-One

"**C**rux!" The warning wasn't enough. It came too late.

The crux dropped to the courtyard, landing in front of the open gates. The soldiers who'd been posted there, those of Ramsey's who'd stopped just inside Ellder's entrance, died the moment the monster crushed them beneath her claws.

She was enormous, bigger than I ever could have fathomed, even after years studying those paintings in the gallery in Roslo. When she stood upright, her head was three times the height of a man. All the other monsters we'd faced in Turah. The terrors I'd witnessed. Nothing compared to the crux.

I gaped, unable to breathe or think or move. All I could do was stare at the female, at the eyes and feathers blacker than ink.

Her talons clawed into the earth, gouging and scoring the dirt. The slashes were so deep they could be used for graves. Her beak curved to a point as sharp as any sword.

The males were always drawn with horns, but this female had spikes of her own on the front of her wings. With every swipe through the people in the courtyard, she ripped through flesh and bone.

The courtyard was pandemonium.

Ramsey's soldiers fled, most running toward the heart of Ellder while others near the walls urged their horses behind the monster, trying to escape her wrath. A few people managed to get free.

Jocelyn tried to slink to the wall, but the crux pecked at every human, like a chicken eating bugs. My former lady's maid was gouged in two.

"Ama, save us."

Arrows flew from the ramparts, most bouncing off the monster's body. Some seemed to find purchase, but the beast barely flinched, like they were mere pinpricks.

"Take shelter!" Ransom yelled, bending to retrieve the sword I'd taken from his grip, holding it in defense as he pushed me backward. "The spikes. Go."

I was still frozen, watching the horror unfold.

"Cross," he barked, snapping me out of it. "Run."

I whirled, about to make my way to the main road, but people rammed into my side, tripping over one another in their hurry to leave.

An arrow zinged past my shoulder, and I crouched, pushing forward with Ransom at my back.

Screams mingled with the screech of the monster, the noise so loud my ears hurt as I weaved through people.

"Watch out." Ransom's arm wrapped around my middle, and he swept me to the side.

A soldier's body flew past my face. His chest had a hole in it.

A hole the size of a monster's talon.

"Hurry." Ransom set me on my feet, urging me on, his hand on my back the entire time.

He should have been fighting that monster, not running with me, but he wouldn't leave my side. Not until I was out of this courtyard.

So I pushed my legs faster, leaping over a body in my path, sidestepping anyone in my way until I was at the nearest spike in the road, my boots skidding to a stop as I ducked behind the wooden pillar.

I looked to the courtyard in time to see the crux slam a wing into the gates, nearly knocking them off their hinges. The vibration of that hit made the soldiers on the rampart above lose their footing, giving the monster a momentary break from the barrage of arrows.

"Ransom. Go." I pushed at his shoulder. "Your mother."

Luella was still in the fray, helping an injured man to his feet. She looped his arm around her shoulders and began inching him toward the wall.

"Evie," he said.

"I've got her."

He nodded, pressing a hard kiss to my forehead before he was gone.

I needed to move. To get to the house. Except I couldn't stop staring at the carnage. There were so many people. Where were Tillia and Halston? Where was Zavier? Cathlin?

Someone had knocked over a burning barrel, and the fire had caught in the stables. The boy inside was shooing out the horses, their frightened whinnies mingling with the shouts and death.

My nails dug into the spike as I searched frantically for familiar faces.

When I spotted Tillia, my body sagged against the post.

She was running toward the wall, away from the monster. Her face was coated in blood. But beyond her, Halston and two other rangers ran toward the crux.

They ran to slay a monster.

The crux saw them coming and stretched out an enormous wing, the full span so wide I gasped. Then she swept that spiked wing forward like she was clearing a path. Catching those trying to escape.

"Tillia!" Halston screamed.

She was in that path.

Tillia bent forward, dropping into a tucked roll on the ground as the crux's wing swept over her spine, missing her by a hair.

Halston's body sagged when she stood upright. But he'd been too focused on his wife. He'd taken his eyes off the crux.

And the monster's talon took off his leg, tearing through flesh and bone.

He fell to his side, eyes wide, blood spurting from the wound as his limb landed on the dirt.

Tillia's mouth was open in a scream as she changed direction, dodging another wing sweep to get to her husband. She slid on her knees when she reached his side, whipping off her belt to tighten around his thigh.

Ransom had run for his mother, to help her with that wounded soldier, but Luella pushed him away, shaking her head.

He kissed her forehead, too, then left to battle the beast.

He charged the crux, a streak of flashing silver as he did his own tucked roll, slicing at the monster's neck while he flew beneath her body.

She reared back, a deafening screech filling the air. Then she snapped and snapped at Ransom, trying to catch him in her beak, but he evaded her, a blur of movement, faster than I'd ever seen him move, cutting into her wings and belly and neck, over and over and over again.

What the fuck did it take to kill that monster? Were her feathers made of iron?

Ransom aimed for her legs, but before he could strike, the crux stood tall and backed away. Her wings stretched wide, and with a single beat, she lifted off the ground.

The wind sent a cloud of dirt and air into my face, grit scratching my eyes. The blast was enough to knock Ransom to the side.

"Luella!" It was Ramsey's shout that carried above the chaos.

She was still with that injured soldier—one of his soldiers—and their progress was slow. Too slow.

"Run!" He screamed for her, pushing off the wall where he'd taken shelter.

She looked up, looked over her shoulder.

But it was too late.

With that single beat of her wings, the crux leaped from one side of the courtyard to the other. And with a snap of her beak, she cleaved Luella's body in two.

The monster flung her torso to the side. Her hips and legs collapsed.

I dropped to my knees, mouth open, unable to breathe as tears flooded my eyes.

Horror consumed Ransom's face. "Mother!"

My pulse was so loud it drowned out all else.

This couldn't be real. This wasn't real. This wasn't happening. The migration wasn't until months from now. Until next spring. This was only a nightmare. I'd wake up safe in bed, in Ransom's arms, and Luella would be alive.

She'd be downstairs, drinking her morning tea, waiting for Evie to wake. She'd be making notes for lessons, preparing to teach her daughter about arithmetic and science.

The crux turned to Ramsey, but then a roar stole her attention. Her head whirled at the sound as Ransom leaped onto the monster's back, his sword raised to drive through the crux's skull.

Except before he could drop the blade, she took to the air, tossing him to the ground.

Zavier and three of his warriors had raced up the wall, taking up bows and arrows.

There were huge crossbows mounted to the ramparts. Remnants of migrations past. Except Ellder had only begun preparations. The blacksmiths had been focused on weapons for other monsters, the bariwolves and grizzur. They hadn't started forging the large crux bolts yet.

Zavier and his rangers fired at the beast in rapid succession, hoping one arrow would find its target true, maybe an eye to blind the crux.

But all it seemed to do was piss her off. With another screech, she flew higher and higher, taking a few soldiers from the walls with her into the skies.

I didn't wait to see where she'd land. I pushed off the spike and raced for the house.

For a girl who had no idea she'd just lost her mother.

"Evie!" I burst through the door, running for her room.

Her bed was rumpled and empty. So was Luella's.

"Evie," I called again, my voice cracking.

Where was she? Where had Luella told her to hide? She wouldn't have gone into the streets, would she? To fight monsters?

Faze. She'd be with our tarkin.

I grabbed a pair of her boots and pants from her bedroom, then took the stairs to my suite two at a time, my footfalls loud as I flew through the door. I ran straight for my room, dropping to my hands and knees to find Evie under my bed, her new stuffed rabbit, Merry, clutched to her chest beside Faze.

Thank the gods.

"Come on, little star." I waved her out.

She shimmied across the floor, and as soon as she was free, I hauled her into my arms, her legs winding around my hips, her arms around my neck.

I held her for only a moment before I set her on the bed to collect my things. "Put your pants and boots on for me."

She nodded, obeying as I moved without thinking, collecting my journal from beneath my chest of drawers and stuffing it in my satchel. I grabbed the dagger Ransom had given me, refusing to think of the last time it had been in my hand. And then I donned my weapons, strapping on my shoulder harness for my knives and adding my sword to its sheath across my spine. I slung Faze's carrier across my chest, and then I collected Evie from the bed, where she sat with Faze in her arms.

"He's scared." Tears glistened in her eyes.

"I'm scared, too. But it's going to be okay." I took him from her, tucking him in his pouch. Then I clutched Evie's hand and led her outside.

In the streets, people ran in all directions, shouting and crying.

"Dess?" Evie whimpered.

"Hurry." I pulled her behind me to the main level and into the house, moving through the living space to Luella's suite. When we reached the bedroom, I let go of Evie's hand to shift the bedside table out of the way and opened the migration cellar's door.

"Careful on each step." I took the same lantern I'd used earlier, lighting it on the top stair, not worrying about closing the door before we descended into the cellar, taking the stairs slowly until we reached the bottom.

"Hold this." I gave Evie the lantern as I dropped to my knees and popped open the hollow beneath the last step.

The books barely fit in my satchel, but I forced them inside, closing the flap before taking the lantern.

Evie's sniffles filled the room.

"Be brave for a bit longer." I smoothed the hair from her face, kissing her cheek. Then I took her hand in mine once more and jerked my chin to the stairs. "Up you go."

"We're not staying here?"

"No." There were no spikes on the roof, not yet. Without them, there was nothing to keep a crux from smashing this building to splinters. Now that I saw just how big they were, I wasn't taking that chance. The last place I wanted Evie was trapped beneath a house, but I wasn't leaving these books behind.

"We'll go to the dungeons," I told her as we climbed. "It's going to be frightening outside. Just hold my hand. Don't let go, no matter what. Can you do that for me?"

"Y-yes."

"That's my brave girl." We climbed upstairs and moved through the house, my heart beating so hard it hurt as we made it to the back door. I checked left and right and above for the crux, and seeing it was clear, I stepped into the night.

But we were not alone.

Banner emerged from the shadows, from Brielle's doorway in the servants' quarters. Even in the dark, I could make out the wildness in his eyes that I'd seen in the courtyard when he learned that Ransom was Ramsey's son.

He walked toward me with an eerie stride, measured steps. The hairs on my neck stood on end. I might not have thought much of it except for the sword in his right hand.

"Banner. Where's Brielle?" I tucked Evie behind me, searching past him.

"Hiding." He took another step forward, his eyes sweeping me head to toe, noting my own weapons.

"What do you want?"

"You should send that child inside, Princess."

My stomach dropped. I'd spent enough time around monsters lately to know the look of a predator hunting prey. I reached over my shoulder, pulling a knife from its sheath. "What are you doing, Banner?"

"They've made fools of us with their lies. Of me."

I pushed Evie away from the door, angling my body in front of hers. "You're not a fool. You're a general with a fiancée who is probably scared and wondering where you've gone. Go to Brielle. Take her home to Quentis."

"I made a vow. I promised to avenge him." He swallowed hard, staring at me for a long moment. Almost like he wanted to let this go, but the ghosts of his brother, his mother, and his pride would not let him quit.

He might have come to Turah for Brielle. But he'd stay for vengeance.

By killing me.

The person the Guardian loved most.

Sixty-Two

Banner lifted his sword, taking another step forward.

Godsdamn it, I was carrying too much stuff. I backed away, sloughing the carrier and satchel while Banner continued to advance. Faze ran into Evie's waiting arms.

I reached for my other knife, raising both as I took up my fighting stance. "Stay back."

"Do you know what you're doing with those weapons?"

"Come closer and you'll find out." My grip tightened on the handles as I swallowed a gush of terror. I wanted my sword. I'd been practicing with it more. It would allow me to keep more space from him than the knives. But I didn't trust him not to lunge if I made a change to swap out weapons.

All I could hope was that the months of training, the countless hours with Tillia and Ransom, would be enough.

"Put them down, Odessa. And I vow to make this painless."

"Fuck you."

The words were barely past my lips when he advanced and swung, fast and deadly. His sword crashed into my knives, tossing my arms to the side. He was fast—but I'd trained with faster and managed to stay on my feet.

"Dess!" Evie cried as I backed away into the middle of the street.

Ransom would criticize me for retreating. Not my greatest reaction to an attack, but Banner had taken me by surprise. I wouldn't let it happen again.

I sucked in a breath and took one heartbeat to reset. To breathe and bend my knees and find my center. I could do this.

I can do this.

I had no other choice.

"Do you really think fighting will change the outcome?" he asked, circling me with a hunter's gaze.

"Do you really think I'll just let you kill me?" I tuned out the chaos in the streets. I put myself in a training arena with Ransom, and today, I would not fall.

There was pure murder in Banner's gaze as he came at me again, swinging hard. His movements were that of a loyal and lethal general. Swift and smooth. He was tall. Strong. Fast.

But he wasn't as good as Ransom. And all those days I'd cursed the Guardian for the training meant I kept my balance.

Every strike, I blocked. Every slice, I evaded. Sweat beaded at my temples, and my pulse was a hammer in my ears, but all those miles I'd run meant my muscles were warm, not tired. Not yet.

"Godsdamn you." Banner bared his teeth as he swung for me again, his gaze flickering toward Evie still against the house, Faze clutched in her arms.

Would he go after a child to get his revenge? Would he use her against me?

I shifted in front of her, blocking her from his view.

The chaos beyond us grew louder and dimmer at the same time, like my ears were absorbing it all yet dismissing anything that wasn't Banner, shutting out anything but this fight.

"It doesn't need to be like this," I told him. "Get Brielle out of here before it's too late."

"I'll never get this chance again."

No, he would not. If my father learned he'd tried to kill me, Banner's life would be forfeit. The same was true with Ransom.

Banner was already dead. He was simply prolonging the inevitable.

"You are not killing me today," I told him.

This was the reason I'd asked Ransom and Zavier for a sword. This was what I'd spent months and months training for. Not for someone else to come to my rescue.

To rescue myself.

So far, I'd been evading his moves. Time to attack.

I feinted to the left, then struck to the right. The edge of my knife sliced through his thigh, through pants not made of grizzur hide.

He bellowed at the cut, touching it with his hand and coming away with blood. He stared at it, then me, like he'd never seen me before. He wiped the blood clean and came for me with movements uncontrolled yet lethal.

I blocked his strikes, left and right and above and left again. Over and over and over again until the vibration in my palms made my hands ache. Until the sweat threatened to loosen my grip.

But I wasn't giving up. I managed another cut on his bicep, the blood seeping through his teal coat.

He sliced for my gut, and when I leaped back, he took his chance to go for the kill. He drew one of those knives he was so famous for throwing from his belt, flipping it in his hand until he held it by the blade.

My stomach dropped. I didn't know how to stop a throwing knife. Ransom hadn't taught me that yet.

"Evie!" Zavier's shout filled the street as he rounded the corner of the house, racing for his daughter.

"Papa!" Tears streaked her face.

Except Zavier changed course, not going to his child but running toward Banner instead.

"No!"

It all happened at once.

Banner whirled, gaze wild. His hand moved like a bolt of lightning, flicking that knife, sending the blade tumbling end over end.

It buried deep into Zavier's gut.

At the same time, I drove my knives through Banner's.

Then the realm went quiet. The last thing I heard was Evie's scream.

It was as if my mind had reached its limit. There were too many sounds, too many horrors to comprehend. Something had to give.

It was the noise.

It faded to a dull hum, and all I could do was watch the nightmare.

Evie's mouth was open in a wail. Her lips were moving.

Papa. Papa.

He stared down at the knife, his eyes unblinking. His sword fell to the ground. Blood seeped from the dagger's hilt, coating his tunic. He wasn't wearing his grizzur vest. He'd left the house in a rush and forgotten his armor.

A bubble of red came from his lips, dribbling down his chin as he dropped to his knees.

Evie ran to him, pressing her hands to the knife, her fingers instantly coated in blood as she tried to stop the flow.

A scream penetrated the nothingness, chasing away the silence.

My own scream.

The noise was an explosion, so loud my ears had to be bleeding.

"Papa!" Evie stared at his stomach, eyes wide and panicked.

Then Zavier fell to the side, coughing as his shoulder hit dirt. The blood from his mouth splattered on Evie's face.

I left my knives in Banner's body and ran for Zavier, my hands covering Evie's, holding the blood like I could keep it in his body. "It's okay. It's okay, it's okay."

This wasn't okay.

There was too much blood.

"Papa!" Evie's voice cracked, and with it, another piece of my heart.

His eyes filled with tears of his own as he reached for her with garbled, bloody words on his lips. "I love you."

I pressed my hands harder into the knife. "Help."

Gods, I needed help. A healer or magic or anything to stanch this bleeding.

"Help!" I screamed, hoping anyone would hear.

"Go." His panicked green eyes searched mine. "Run."

"Help me!" My voice cracked. Where the fuck were the healers? Didn't they know people were dying?

Zavier shook his head, gasping for a few last breaths. And when he spoke next, it was barely a whisper. "Evie."

She couldn't stay out here. Not like this. And so he would bleed out on this street. Alone.

"I'm sorry," I sobbed, my tears falling onto his blood-soaked shirt.

Zavier's eyes fluttered closed as I pulled my hands away.

Lifting my fingers to my mouth, I closed my eyes, tasting his blood on my lips, and blew the loudest whistle I could muster. A whistle from Treow, hoping someone, anyone would recognize the signal.

The signal that things were not okay.

I swallowed back a sob as I pushed to my feet, my balance faltering as I started down the road, past Banner's lifeless body.

The fastest way to the dungeons was down the center of Ellder, but I wouldn't risk being that exposed. So we'd stick to alleyways and gaps between buildings along the main road, slinking our way through the fortress until we reached the barracks. Hopefully we could slip by to the wall, unnoticed by the terrors in the sky.

I hurried to my satchel, pulling it on again along with Faze's carrier. I put Evie's rabbit inside and collected Faze. He was trembling by Evie's side. With him in the pouch, I sucked in a fortifying breath and lifted Evie into my arms. "Come with me, little star."

"No!" She kicked and screamed, fighting me as I took her from Zavier. "Papa!"

"I'm sorry. We have to go. We can't stay here." I held her tighter, turning her away.

"Papa!" She reached over my shoulders, hands stretched for her father.

I marched on, arms banded around her until we'd left Zavier behind.

She slumped against my shoulder when we turned a corner and she lost sight of him.

"I'm sorry." I kissed her temple as we stopped beside the toy shop where we'd bought Merry the plush rabbit.

Today. That had just been today.

A window of the shop was broken. A lantern lay shattered on the floor, flames licking the shelves of toys.

The world was on fire.

Where was the crux? I searched the skies, trying to see past roofs. The steady beat of wings, blasts of wind, filled the streets.

She was flying, swooping down to pick at her prey. Out of reach from Ransom's sword.

Where was he? Helping people escape?

There were people in nearly every shadow, people trying to make their escape from Ellder, either to the courtyard or the side gate.

Down the road, the baker, a man who brought his wife flowers each morning, was risking a crossing of his own. His wife was clutched at his side. They were fleeing their business, likely trying to find a shelter.

Like she could sense their desperation to survive, the crux swept down from the night and, with a slice of her talon, separated the man's head from his shoulders.

My hand slapped over my mouth to stifle a scream. I used my other to keep Evie's face buried in my shoulder so she wouldn't see.

The wife dropped to her knees.

And tried to put her husband's head back on his body.

The crux circled around, this time targeting a building. She sank both feet into a house, lifting off a section of roof, carrying it for a moment before letting it go. Sticks and beams exploded from the heap as it smashed to the ground, blocking the path I'd planned to take. Forcing us closer to the main road.

I adjusted my hold on Evie, waited until the crux flew the opposite way, then ran across the road, not stopping until I was through another alley and ducked beneath an overhang. I slid along the wall, moving toward the corner so I could look down the main road, hoping to catch a glimpse of Ransom.

There was a woman walking along the row of spikes. She had two knives—my knives—in her bloody hands.

"Brielle," I gasped. She was dead out there. She had to run. To hide. "Run!"

She stopped instead. She dropped the knives. And lifted her face to the stars.

"No." My body seized.

A shriek ripped through the air, so loud Evie cupped her hands over her ears. Then came the pulse of flapping wings.

The monster dove from the sky, another shriek piercing the night.

Brielle didn't make a sound as she lifted her off the ground. As she carried her into the shades.

I hoped it was Arabella's heaven.

My knees wobbled, the weight of this death too heavy to bear.

"Can you walk?" I asked Evie.

She nodded, so I set her on her feet.

"We're going to run, okay? All the way to the dungeons."

She closed her eyes, fat tears clinging to her sooty lashes.

I kissed her forehead, took her hand, and then we ran across one street, then the next.

The beat of wings made me stop and huddle beside a wall as the crux swept down again. This section of the street was without spikes, so it had room to land.

Firelight caught the monster's wings, making the black feathers glow red and orange.

I ducked back, breath lodged in my throat. *Fly away. Leave.*

Faze let out a squeak, his tiny claws digging into the fabric of his carrier, like he knew the real monsters had arrived in Calandra.

The ground beneath my boots quaked as the crux pushed into the air, flying toward the courtyard.

My body sagged against the wall. "Okay. Let's go again. On three. One. Two. Three."

I pulled Evie with me, my grip on her hand fierce, until we finally made it to the last building. Across from us were the barracks. If we could just make it to those rows of small homes, we might be able to get to the wall. But there was a large expanse that separated the town's buildings and homes from the soldiers' quarters.

The gap hadn't seemed that wide before. Now, it might as well be the Krisenth. And it was littered with bodies and blood. Soldiers who'd come out of the barracks to fight. To die.

"Last push." I swept her into my arms, waiting until she wrapped her legs around my waist.

I filled my lungs, willing strength into my legs. Then I tore off, leaping over bodies, over entrails and gore.

I reached the barrack rows but didn't stop. I set my gaze on that dark stone at the back of the fortress and kept pushing, never more grateful for the laps and laps I'd run around Ellder and Treow.

My stamina wasn't shit, not anymore.

But I was no match for a massive flying monster. She screeched as a wind pushed hair into my face. A wind so powerful it pushed me forward.

"Down!" Ransom's shout came from my side.

I dropped to my knees, my body curling around Evie's as I craned my neck to the sky.

The monster came like an arrow, shot straight and true. Her talons were extended, ready to sink into our bodies, to steal us off the ground.

All I could do was hope she would take me and not Evie.

I loosened my hold, putting an inch of space between my body and hers as I braced for the impact.

But it came from the side, not above, as Ransom barreled into us both, hurling us out of the crux's path.

Pain exploded through my shoulder as we rolled. Ransom's body slammed into mine, but he made sure Evie was cushioned against his chest. He landed beside me, his sister clutched in his arms and his eyes on the sky.

I looked up in time to see the crux choose another target, a horse that was galloping away, trying to run free.

"Odessa." Ransom's silver eyes were wild as he scooped up Evie and helped me to my feet, pulling me to the closest barrack house. He set her down, his hands roaming her body, then mine, searching for injury.

"I'm okay. But Zavier. He's…" I couldn't say it. Wouldn't say it.

His silver eyes flashed with disbelief. Then anguish. He dropped his forehead to mine.

The crux shrieked from the skies. A war cry. A death promise.

He leaned back, eyes searching mine as he threaded his fingers, slick with blood, into my hair. "It's not safe for you here."

He wasn't talking about the fortress. He wasn't talking about Ellder.

It wasn't safe for me in Turah. Not if his theory was correct and these monsters were drawn to me.

Not if the migration was starting already.

He'd said it himself, months ago. Quentis was always better at hiding than fighting. And for the migration, all we could do was run.

And hide.

I shook my head, desperate for another way. "What about you?"

He pressed his lips to my forehead. "Go."

"Ransom—"

"Please." He untangled his hands from my hair. Then, with a hopelessness the depths of which I'd never seen before, he unclasped the cuff on his forearm. And fastened it around mine. "You know what this is?"

The road to Allesaria.

"Yes."

"I don't know where my father went. If he's still in the fortress, then you cannot be. Neither can Evie."

"Does he know about the dungeon and the tunnel?"

"Probably."

Shit. "Then Treow. I'll find my way to the encampment and wait there." I remembered most of the path. Granted, that had been in the light, but I'd find it by sheer will alone.

"Walk toward Aurinda," he said, pointing to the moon above. "She will lead you to Treow."

"All right." I gulped.

"If I don't arrive by the day after tomorrow, you must go. Take Evie from Turah. Do what needs to be done."

Give *my* father what he'd been after all this time. Even if it meant Turah—Calandra—would be changed forever.

"Are you certain?"

This could mean the death of the Voster. The end of Allesaria. The spread of Lyssa. I had no idea what my father was planning.

He hadn't trusted me with his truths.

"I trust you." Ransom tucked a curl away from my face as the beat of wings grew louder and louder. Then his mouth crushed mine in a hard kiss that ended too soon.

I wouldn't get a long goodbye, not with that monster in the skies.

"I love you, Evie. Stay with Odessa." He bent to kiss her hair, then took a step away, looking up to the night. His jaw clenched, his grip on his sword tightening. "Run. Now, Cross."

Hot tears dripped to the dirt at my boots. "I love you."

"Yes, you do. Don't forget."

"Never."

"Neither will I." His throat bobbed as he swallowed. "I will find you. Here, or in the shades."

The crux landed at his back, the ground shaking as she dropped. And Ransom, my Guardian, turned to fight.

To show that bitch who the real monster in Calandra was.

To give us time to run.

He kept the crux away long enough for me to pick up Evie and sprint through the remainder of the barracks. I risked a backward glance at the last row.

The crux flew into the air, high above the fortress's towering walls. Beating black wings. A screech ripping from her throat.

And Ransom in her talons.

My heart cleaved in two.

"He'll be okay," I told Evie, forcing one foot in front of the other until we reached the dungeon. "He'll kill the crux."

He'd kill the monsters. He'd kill them all.

And then he'd find me. There was no other outcome that I'd accept.

"We'll see him in Treow. Come on." I pulled Evie along the dark walls of the dungeons, letting my eyes adjust and using my feet to feel for the lantern that had been here last time.

It clanged as I kicked it over, but I bent and picked it up, using a match from its tray to light the wick.

Squinting against the sudden brightness, I held it high with one hand, taking Evie's in my other as we made our way to the hidden tunnel entrance.

Her footsteps were getting sluggish, like her body was shutting down from the stress of this night.

"We'll rest in a minute," I promised.

First, I wanted to be behind that tunnel's door.

It opened with a hard push of my shoulder, the air inside stale and dank. The tunnel was tall and wide, the darkness eating the lantern's light. We walked ten paces to the first corner, and when I rounded the smooth stone edge, I flinched at another light.

Then I felt the crawling sensation of spiders on my skin.

We weren't alone.

"Do not run." Brother Dime appeared from the shadows, and if not for the horse at his back, I would have turned around. He held Freya's reins, my darling horse alert but not scared.

"What do you want?" I pushed Evie behind me.

"You must come with me now, child."

It wasn't a suggestion.

Ramsey had said Brother Dime wanted me. And he'd found me. Why? "Does this have anything to do with my mother?"

He didn't answer. He simply turned Freya around and led us through the tunnel to the hatch that opened beyond the walls, into the forest.

Brother Dime was careful not to touch me as he handed me the reins. That caution was the only reason I didn't climb onto Freya's back and ride across the continent.

I didn't trust the Voster. But Ransom did.

That was enough for tonight.

"Up you go," I told Evie, putting her in the saddle first and handing her the lantern before I settled in behind her.

She sagged into my arms, her nose pressing against my chest. Her hand slipped into Faze's carrier, taking his paw.

I kissed her cheek, feeling tears on my lips. "Hold tight, little star. You're safe."

It was a lie. But I said it anyway.

Brother Dime lifted his bony hand, holding up a single finger, and sent a whoosh of air to the lantern, extinguishing the flame.

And then he led us into the night.

Sixty-Three

RANSOM

My boot squelched in a puddle of blood.

There were too many to avoid. They soaked the ground as if they'd come from a heavy rain.

The stench of gore and death clung to the air. I walked through the rows and rows and rows of bodies in the courtyard, counting each as I passed. The number would never be accurate. Men, women, children. So many had met gruesome fates that it would be impossible to fit pieces together.

To make wholes from halves.

Cathlin stood at the end of the last row, staring at the body stretched on the ground awaiting a grave.

My mother's body.

A sheet covered most of her form, but I knew the skirts of her dress. The heels of her boots. They'd been my gift to her last year at the equinox.

Pain and grief swelled so fast they choked, but I swallowed the emotions down, pushing them deep where they could fester and grow. Where they would live to fuel my rage.

The fires that had broken out during the attack had finally stopped burning. A few buildings were nothing but cinders and ash. After the crux had died, the survivors in Ellder had managed to snuff out the flames.

The walls were still standing, but the gates leaned on each other like two pieces of straw, ready to collapse at the first strong breeze.

At some point while I'd been knocked out, my father and his surviving soldiers had left through those gates. The bastard. I'd deal with him later.

Cathlin wiped at her cheeks, at the endless tears. Her hair hung limp around her shoulders, and the hem of her dress was soaked red.

I stopped at her side and took her hand, staring down at my mother's boots.

There was a good chance that another body would join these rows. Maybe two.

Halston was fighting for his life in the infirmary.

So was Zavier.

A healer, Geezala, had found Zavier's body last night. She'd heard a whistle she'd learned from her time as a healer in Treow. She'd warned me to prepare for the worst. That no man could likely survive such a wound.

When Tillia had overheard, she'd told Geezala to fuck off and save Zavier's life.

By sheer, stubborn will, Tillia would see that Halston survived his injury. And she'd see to it that Zavier lived to witness another dawn.

The circlet that normally kissed his brow was tucked away in my vest.

He'd sacrificed enough for Turah. For me.

If Zavier—Dray—lived, then it was time for his life to be his own.

No more pretending.

I pressed a kiss to Cathlin's temple, squeezing her hand, then stepped past my mother's body and walked to the one corpse that rested alone.

In the center of the courtyard, a woman's naked body rested in a pool of blood.

I crouched beside the figure, surveying it from head to toe for the tenth time.

Was this real? Or were my eyes playing a trick on me? Had the crash addled my mind and memory?

After Odessa had fled to the dungeon with Evie, the crux had plucked me off the ground and carried me into the sky. Probably to drop me from some unfathomable height. But the bitch hadn't counted on my rage.

I'd driven my sword into her chest, straight into her heart. And then we'd fallen from the shades.

The monster had taken the brunt of the impact, but I'd been thrown hard enough that when I woke, the faint rays of morning were kissing the horizon.

There should have been a monster's lifeless body in the courtyard. There should have been a winged beast with my sword in its chest.

Instead, I'd pulled my sword from this woman's body.

A woman with red hair, the spiraling curls a mix of orange and strawberry and copper.

Odessa's hair.

I unsheathed a knife from my belt and sheared off a lock. Then I tucked it into my vest beside Zavier's circlet.

My circlet.

I stood, taking one last look at the woman. The crux.

"Have you seen or heard of this before?" I asked Cathlin as she appeared at my side.

"No," she said. "Any crux killed was just a monster. What do you think this means?"

"I don't know." But I intended to fucking find out.

I stepped over the woman's body, looking to the soldier standing guard. "Burn it."

"Yes, sir." He nodded as I strode past him for the gates.

"Where are you going?" Cathlin called.

I kept walking.

"To find my wife."

Acknowledgments

Thank you for reading *Shield of Sparrows*! Writing this book was a journey that filled my soul. I've wanted to delve into romantic fantasy for years, and I'm so very grateful to Liz Pelletier for giving me this opportunity to stretch my wings.

Thank you, Liz, for all the time, energy, and love you've put into Odessa and Ransom's story. And to the entire team at Red Tower Books, thank you for your awesomeness!

Thanks to Georgana Grinstead for believing in me and fighting for my dreams. You are my ray of sunshine and hope. I am beyond thankful for all you do.

To Elizabeth Nover, thank you for your willingness to always be the first brave soul to dive into my first drafts. Your advice and input are invaluable.

Thank you to Logan Chisholm for all the work you do behind the scenes each and every day. Because of you, I can get lost in these imaginary worlds, knowing you're there to steer the ship. Thank you for a thousand voice texts, for being there to listen, and for always having my back.

Thank you to Nicole Resciniti for being such a champion of this book and of me. For always being there to talk through a hiccup.

To Samantha Brentmoor and Jason Clarke for making time in your schedules to fit in a not-so-small project. Thank you! I adore you both.

To Kaitlyn for being the best friend I could ask for and always being there to brainstorm. To Monica, Marni, Valentine, and Karla for being the best cheerleaders. To the basketball moms who always bring an extra Diet Coke because you know I probably need one. Thank you!

I wouldn't be able to do this job without the undying support of my incredible family. Bill, Will, and Nash, you'll never see this, but know that you are my whole heart.

And lastly, thank you, again, for reading. With all the books in the world, I'm honored you chose to read mine. I cannot wait to take you on the next part of this adventure.

THE GODS LOVE TO PLAY WITH US MERE MORTALS.
AND EVERY HUNDRED YEARS, WE LET THEM...

I have never been favored by the gods. Far from it, thanks to Zeus.

Living as a cursed office clerk for the Order of Thieves, I just keep my head down and hope the capricious beings who rule from Olympus won't notice me. Not an easy feat, given San Francisco is Zeus' patron city, but I make do. I survive. Until the night I tangle with a *different* god.

The *worst* god. Hades.

For the first time ever, the ruthless, mercurial King of the Underworld has entered the Crucible—the deadly contest the gods hold to determine a new ruler to sit on the throne of Olympus. But instead of fighting their own battles, the gods name *mortals* to compete in their stead.

So why in the Underworld did Hades choose me—a sarcastic nobody with a curse on her shoulders—as his champion? And why does my heart trip every time he says I'm *his*?

I don't know if I'm a pawn, bait, or something else entirely to this dangerously tempting god. How can I, when he has more secrets than stars in the sky?

Because Hades is playing by his own rules...and Death will win at any cost.

AVAILABLE NOW WHEREVER BOOKS ARE SOLD

CONNECT WITH US ONLINE

📷 @redtowerbooks

f @redtowerbooks

♪ @redtowerbooks

RED TOWER
BOOKS™